The Thing About Balloons

Baylea A. Osborn

This is a work of fiction. Names, characters, businesses, places, events and incidents are either the products of the author's imagination or used in a fictitious manner. Any resemblance to actual persons, living or dead, or actual events is purely coincidental.

Printed in the United States of America

First Printing, 2016

ISBN-13: 978-1519499394
ISBN-10: 1519499396

Dedicated to my best friend.

Acknowledgments

To **Faith**, the one who first coaxed this story out of me and told me that Alyson's story should be shared. I wouldn't have made it without you. Thank you for always being my Danielle. To **Boze**, the one who loves fixing my commas and allows me to pester him with questions about anything. Thank you for reminding me that I was capable of making this book great. To **Anndrea**, who set aside hours of her time to research, read, ask questions, share information, hate pronouns and give it to me straight. To **Benny** for helping me gain my second wind and always being willing to help in any way. To **my dad**, for reading the first draft and still finding things to like about it. To **my mom**, for helping me through Chapter 19 and making it some of my best work. To **Demetrius** for letting this be the first book to make him cry since *Where The Red Fern Grows*. To **Tim, Anna B.** and **Cathi** for their grammatical genius and keen eyes to spot the little mistakes. To **Asa, Janessa, Jana, Sarah,** and **Serena** for reading it all the way through in its various stages and showing me how to make the story better. To **Sasha, Abigail, Kalina, Amy, Katie S.,** and **Tisha,** for reading this book from cover to cover, loving my characters and allowing Alyson's journey change the way you see the world. To **Jessica** for helping me get Garret's story right. To **Rebecca** and **Kaylee** for sharing your artistic talents with me. To **Phillip Ortiz** for a cover that is better than I could have imagined. To **Talia, Suzy, Anna J.,** and **Theresa** for being some of the first fans of this book. To **Annalise** for spending an evening looking at every novel in Barnes & Noble. To **Katie L.** for being such a sweet, encouraging friend. To my **Bethel family** for being supportive in every way. Special shout out to my few but faithful **Twitter followers** for coming with me on the journey from start to finish, to **family** and **friends** who have shared about this book in any way, and to **Zoe** and **Alfie** for making the research process so much more enjoyable. And most importantly, to **The One** who redeems and makes every broken, hurting heart new and beautiful. To You be the glory.

This story is for the girls who have to hold their heads high while people send judgmental glances in their directions.

This story is for the men who would rather run away from their pasts than fix what they have broken.

This story is for the couples who have to decide whether or not they are going to choose love and forgiveness.

This story is for the friend who opens up their heart to be a safe place in the midst of chaos.

This story is for the men who decide to become a better person for those they love.

This story is for the person who was given a fresh start from a dark past and is reaching out to help others.

This story is for the ones who are learning to let go.

"There's a little bit of Alyson in all of us, because every single one of us fights to come to terms with our own messiness and heartache." -Anna B.

Chapter one "Anything. Everything." 7

Chapter two "Tonight is so screwed up." 25

Chapter three "Okay. Breathe." 44

Chapter four "You can't just fix this with an apology!" 57

Chapter five "You've been staring at him for hours." 79

Chapter six "I told my mom that you cry a lot." 98

Chapter seven "Bambi." 122

Chapter eight "It's cold, sweetheart." 147

Chapter nine "Just don't ever forget how much I love you." 170

Chapter ten "Sweet Dream Baby" 192

Chapter eleven "Life sucks, apparently." 210

Chapter twelve "Be kind. Forgive. Love others, even when they hurt you." 232

Chapter thirteen "It's not your fault, baby. I promise." 253

Chapter fourteen "The ache never really leaves." 275

Chapter fifteen "If you knew, you wouldn't touch me!" 298

Chapter sixteen "I've never seen you look at anyone like that." 315

Chapter seventeen "Do you think we'll make it?" 332

Chapter eighteen "Sorry I've been gone. But I'm here now." 356

Chapter nineteen "I'll remember. I'll never forget." 384

Chapter twenty "The thing about balloons is that..." 413

Chapter twenty-one "You can't give up on this!" 427

Chapter twenty-two "I don't want to feel like this anymore." 449

Chapter twenty-three "Look. Balloons." 469

Epilogue "I'm trying to quit." 482

Chapter one
"Anything. Everything."

July 31st

Alyson Abidi woke with a start and sat bolt upright. She trembled as she slowly roused her senses and took in her surroundings. She found herself on a thickly carpeted floor in a dark, strange room with a pounding headache.

For a moment the girl sat frozen while her mind scrambled wildly to place where she was and what had happened. Loud, unfamiliar sounds whooshed and whirred somewhere on the other side of the wall, but those gave her no indication as to where she was. The only light was a faint glow from the horizon that could be seen through a large window that was on the other side of the room. The night was almost over.

A queasy stomach told her she had done something, but her memory had yet to tell her what. Alyson wasn't the kind of girl who woke up not knowing what she had done the night before, and it was scary. She bit the insides of her cheeks, eyes squeezed shut.

Why can't I remember? What have I done? The girl struggled to recall something. Anything.

Wisps of a conversation from the evening before floated through the fog in her mind, and Alyson suddenly remembered. Not everything, but enough to make her wish she could forget all over again. No wonder her stomach hurt. And her heart.

The ceiling was high above Alyson as she lay on her back. She wrapped her arms around herself tightly. Minutes ticked by, and the sky grew lighter. It cast an ethereal glow over the room, which was a welcome change to the palpable pre-dawn darkness. The night had been hot, but she was cold now without a shirt on. Alyson stopped. Why was her shirt off?

Something moved beside her, and the girl stared with wide-eyed horror. It was a person; still asleep yet visible in the gray light. Alyson tried to stifle a panicked cry with a hand over her mouth, but when the stranger's arm flopped over and brushed against her leg, she shrieked and scrambled away.

She tripped and stumbled, desperate to distance herself from the stranger who had been lying next to her. One bare foot caught on an item of clothing in her attempt to escape, and she caught herself against the wall with a loud thud. The sound startled the young man from his slumber.

He swore as he sat up slowly. His hands reached for his head and he swore again, more loudly this time.

The girl stood huddled against the edge of the room, the man's British accent prodding at her memory. All of a sudden clarity sliced through the haze in her mind, and Alyson rushed at him. She lunged into his solid torso and nearly bowled him over as he sat there.

"You!" she screamed as she pummeled her fists against his shoulder.

"What in the world are you doing?" The man stopped the fists that flailed at him with one hand as he squinted at Alyson's face. "Who are you?"

"Who *am* I? What have you done to me?!" Alyson's whole body shook as she realized that the young man was only in boxers. "What did you do?!"

"I haven't done anything! Stop shouting!" The man groaned and gripped his forehead. "Ugh, my head!"

"You made me drink something! I know you did! Y-you did something to me!" Alyson yanked her hands away from his grip and sat back on her heels. She hugged herself and cried quietly.

"Oh, for pete's sake, what are you on about?" He was annoyed. "I would never!"

Alyson looked around the room in horror. There was her tank top. There was his shoe. Socks. Pants. Everything scattered about them, and the door locked behind them. What had they done? What had she done? There were whispers of voices and flashes of faces from earlier in the evening, and Alyson swallowed hard.

"Listen." The man's voice showed he had calmed. "Do you remember how we got here?"

"N-not really..." Alyson clenched her teeth. "There was... something... I... I can't put the pieces together."

The man sighed heavily and rubbed his hands through his hair.

"Wait! Aren't you that girl Jamie met in Minnesota a few weeks back? A-... Amy? Aly? Aly. You're Aly!"

"Yeah." Alyson nodded, and bit her lip so hard it almost broke skin. "That's me."

"We were dancing! I-I was... Jamie wasn't with you, so I was keeping an eye on you."

Alyson didn't respond.

"Why weren't you with Jamie?"

"Jamie doesn't want me." Alyson's voice cracked. "Not anymore."

The young man leaned back against the wall and shook his head. They were silent. An awkward tension sat between them. Alyson sniffled and wiped at the tears on her chin. Everything ached on the inside. She wanted to disappear; to sink through the floor and be forgotten forever. That would be preferable to the knowledge that someone else knew what she had done. She was slender, five inches over the five-foot mark, but in that moment, the girl couldn't get small enough.

"Do you..." The man licked his lips nervously. "Do you think we... slept together?"

"We're practically naked," said Alyson bitterly. "Who knows what we did. This is all your fault."

"My fault?" The man pointed at his bare chest before he pushed himself to his feet.

"Yes, you!" Alyson backed up to put more space between them. "You're the one who told me to have that stupid drink!"

"I didn't know you couldn't handle a little alcohol!"

Alyson snatched her shirt up off the floor and put it on. Being fully covered changed nothing about how she felt on the inside. "Who knows what we did, and who knows if we'll ever know."

"But I... I can't just... I have to know!" he shouted.

"And I don't?"

What Alyson had done that night was more than just go against her own moral code; she had gone against everything her family stood for. They were the Abidi family from Islamabad, Pakistan, one of the most honored families in the community. Anything that went against the good name of Alyson's grandfather was forbidden. Alyson had felt the pressure to be perfect since she was little. But... now what?

"I'm sorry, I didn't mean it like that, it's just that... I have a lot of people, you know, counting on me to not, you know... mess up," said the man.

"Yeah." Alyson looked toward the window. "I know."

"Are you going to tell anyone about this?"

"Not interested in hearing what people think about me waking up next to a naked man."

"This is serious. You have to tell me. Straight out."

"I will never, ever, ever tell anyone about this."

She would never tell anyone about anything that happened that night. No one would ever know. She couldn't let them.

"What happens now?" His question hung in the air without an answer for several minutes.

"I guess I get on an airplane and fly back home." Alyson picked up her purse from the floor and looked around. It felt like there was something she had missed, but she didn't know what it was. Her dignity? Her virginity? Her common sense? Whatever it was, she knew she would never find it, so she turned to leave. The young man lifted his hand in farewell as she glanced at him.

"I'm sorry."

Alyson didn't respond, just opened the door and walked out.

8 Weeks Earlier...

The first thing Alyson did when school let out for the summer was travel up to Minnesota to visit her best friend, Danielle Ledger. They had been best friends since the start of high school when they were teenagers in Nebraska. At age twenty-two they were seeing their high school dreams fulfilled. They were both responsible adults with jobs that paid their bills and five-year plans to ensure that they would reach their life goals. Danielle had just finished her third year in undergrad for chemical engineering, and Alyson already had a job as a teacher in Des Moines, Iowa. It had been a long, hard school year, and they wanted to use the summer to pretend they were young again. The highlight of the trip would be a concert for a musical group called *Jupiter Waits*. The band consisted of a main singer and two musicians and the girls had been fans since high school.

On the night of the concert, the girls lucked out and gained entrance to the club where the band had gone when their show finished. Alyson had been unsure about whether or not she wanted to go in, but Danielle made the choice for them. She pulled her friend along behind her excitedly.

"Look! Balloons!" Danielle grabbed at a bunch of balloons that were floating right inside the entrance. "How could you possibly feel guilty about going into a place where they have balloons?"

"Elle!" Alyson groaned and shook her head. "Let them go."

"Do you want one?" Danielle held onto one string stubbornly.

"No! What would I do with a balloon? Now let go of it!"

"There are so many things, Aly!" Danielle finally left the bobbing spheres and continued on. "That's the best thing about balloons; you can do so many things with them!"

"You'll have to tell me all about it someday," joked Alyson wryly as they left the balloons behind and continued into the club.

They entered a large room and stopped. It was dark and extremely crowded. The smell of a hundred different perfumes on sweaty bodies mixed together, and Alyson felt nauseated.

"Do you see them?" Danielle shouted to Alyson. Her voice sounded far away. The music blared so loudly that it vibrated in their bones.

"No. They're probably hiding somewhere." Alyson shrugged. "Now what?"

"Hey! Look!" Danielle turned Alyson by her shoulders until she was pointed in the same direction as Danielle. "It's Adam!"

Happy to see their friend, they pushed their way over to where the nicely dressed young man was surrounded by a group of girls. Danielle had met Adam when she bumped into him at the on-campus library late one evening. They had been studying two very different subjects, but chatted for a few minutes and decided to study together anyway. Over the course of the evening, it came out that Adam's family was from Pakistan. Danielle and Adam became fast friends, and the next time Alyson visited Minnesota, Danielle introduced them.

Even though ethnically they were the same, Adam and Alyson were actually very different. Alyson's family was strict, Adam's was not. Alyson had been very careful to maintain her family's honor, and Adam had been left to do mostly as he pleased. Alyson was a girl, and Adam was a boy. Because of that, Alyson knew that Adam's parents would have no problem knowing he was in a club with a scotch in hand.

"Adam!" Danielle shouted as they approached him.

"Elle! Aly! What a surprise! Join us!" The young man stood and welcomed his friends into the circle with a big smile. "Do your parents know you are here, little Miss Goody Two Shoes?"

The teasing jab in Alyson's direction produced red cheeks and a smile, while a hint of guilt appeared in the back of Alyson's expression.

"Shush! Do you know how much I had to convince her that she could come in and not drink? Don't ruin it!" Danielle punched Adam in the shoulder.

"You've got a wild side!" Adam lifted his eyebrows as he studied Alyson's face. His smile deepened. "I like it."

"I'm not wild, Adam…" she said with little conviction. Adam's smile made her feel uncomfortable, as if he was about to tell on her.

"Why are there so many people here tonight? Was there a concert?"

"Yeah! That's where we came from!" Danielle took the drink Adam offered her. "It was *Jupiter Waits*."

"Oh! That new, acoustic-sounding, British group? I think I've heard of them."

"Jamie Donald's not new! He's been around for years!" Alyson stood close to Danielle. The foreign ambience of the club was intimidating, and she felt the need to be connected to something familiar. "You should have gone to the show!"

"Nah!" Adam smiled widely and poked a finger in Alyson's direction. "I'm not a fan of bands that play songs I can't dance to. You like it 'cause there's a cute guy playing guitar, but if I can't dance, what's the point?"

Alyson shrugged again. She didn't mind Adam, he was an entertaining person to be around, but he was too much for her sometimes. It baffled her how easily he could go through life without a single worry about what his family would think.

A girl from Adam's preexisting entourage put a hand on his arm to distract him from Alyson. The others stood and sipped on their drinks, trying to talk over the music while Alyson looked around the room and shifted uncomfortably. She couldn't really hear what the others were saying, and she was the only one without a drink. A few minutes passed before she decided she was tired of standing on the sidelines and being a Debbie Downer. She had gone into the club; she might as well enjoy the music.

"I want to dance!" Alyson grinned at Danielle and Adam. "Come on!"

"What?" Adam turned in her direction and saw her smile.

"Dance! I want to dance!"

"Ha! Yes!" Adam set his drink down and followed her eagerly. A couple of Adam's female admirers tagged along eyeing Alyson jealously as she continued to hold Adam's attention.

The song ended shortly after they reached the floor, and Alyson frowned.

"The night is young, Aly! Don't be sad!" Adam laughed at Alyson's expression. "This DJ is awesome, he'll play something good!"

A song with a more Middle Eastern feel to the rhythm began to pulse through the speakers, and Adam's face lit up. Alyson had never heard the song before, but the rhythm was familiar. Adam grabbed her hand and pulled her into him so she could hear what he was saying.

"Let's show them how to really dance!"

Alyson's laugh could barely be heard above the music as she left Danielle's side. Her body remembered the way she had danced in Pakistan with her cousins when she was younger. The little voice in the back of her head told her to stop since there were people watching, but she ignored it. Nothing was going to happen. People danced at clubs all the time. She knew Adam was impressed when he gave her a nod and a crooked grin.

"I didn't think she could dance like that!" One of Adam's friends watched in amazement.

The others on the dance floor backed up to form a little circle around the two of them. There were whistles and claps as the pair went all out. They breathed heavily and ignored the sweat that dripped down their faces. The feeling was electric. It seemed as if the entire club was watching them. The applause thundered from the onlookers when Alyson and Adam bowed to their audience and stepped out of the middle of the circle.

"I have never seen you dance like that before!" Danielle told her friend as the song faded out.

"I don't think I've danced like that since the last time I was with Sumaya!" Alyson laughed and placed a hand over her racing heart. "Wow, that was incredible!"

Another song started, and Danielle cheered.

"My favorite song!"

By that time, the two girls had almost forgotten about Jamie Donald and *Jupiter Waits* as they remained on the dance floor. The point of the evening had been to be together, and as long as that happened, they were satisfied.

Halfway through the song, Alyson felt unfamiliar hands on her waist that pulled her away from Danielle. The hands spun her around, holding onto her tightly. Alyson's stomach flip-flopped as her mind registered the intimate gesture, and she looked up to find the smirking face of Jamie Donald, the newly single heartthrob and singer she had just seen in concert. Her jaw dropped.

"I liked the way you were dancing!" Jamie shouted by her ear so the girl could hear him. His British accent seemed even thicker on the dance floor than it had been on stage earlier that night. His scruff brushed against her cheek and tickled her skin. His high cheekbones caught the dancing shadows, drawing her attention to all the beautiful details of his face. His dark brown hair fell across his forehead and drops of sweat were beginning to form on the long, straight line of his nose.

"Thank you!" Alyson finally found her voice. "Y-you're so handsome!"

Jamie laughed again before taking Alyson's hand and making her spin around. He kept her dancing until the song was over, then pulled her along behind him towards the VIP area. Alyson grabbed Danielle's arm, making sure her friend didn't get left behind. Adam had gone back to the sidelines with his other friends and didn't even notice the girls leaving. Fans were screaming at Jamie for autographs and pictures as he hurried past, the two girls in tow.

"Sorry, another time," he shouted back before disappearing behind a door that led them into a quieter and more private section of the club.

"Ah, Jamie. There you are." A young man that the girls recognized as someone Jamie brought with him on tour spotted their entrance and moved towards them. "I see you brought company."

"Yes!" Jamie buzzed with a contagious excitement and energy which made Alyson giggle. She loosened her grip to see if he would let go of her hand, but his fingers held on tightly. "I'd love to introduce them, but I don't even know their names. We were much too busy dancing!"

"This is Aly," Alyson's best friend offered first.

Alyson was thankful her friend had spoken for her. She couldn't remember how to breathe, let alone how to say her name. Jamie's gaze caught her attention out of the corner of her eye, and she glanced up at him shyly. He gave her a lopsided grin and pushed a hand through his shaggy hair before looking away.

"Garret. Pleased to meet you." Garret smiled at them and nodded, then eyed Jamie warily. He had been worried about Jamie since his breakup and hoped that any type of fling he planned on having wouldn't be complicated or messy. The girl attached to Jamie's hand seemed sweet and nice, but he had been in the music industry long enough to know people can be very different than they first seem.

"Girls, this is Serenity, the angel that graces us with her presence because she's in love with this thick-headed guy for some reason." Jamie gestured towards the beautiful young woman that followed behind Garret and now stood at his side.

"Hello!" A sweet smile appeared on Serenity's face and Alyson suddenly felt very self-conscious about her appearance. The young woman from London held out her hand to Danielle and spoke again; "I don't think you told us your name yet?"

"I'm Danielle."

"Danielle!" Jamie pointed his finger at the girl with short, dark hair and brown eyes. "Garret had a girlfriend named Danielle once."

"Jamie!" scolded Garret.

"It's true! Sorry, Serenity, but you are not the first love of Garret's life."

"Jamie, you're being proper obnoxious tonight! Are you drunk already?" Garret shook his head and looked apologetically at the two strangers and his own girlfriend. "I apologize for Jamie's behavior at the moment."

With a dismissive laugh that said she was used to such behavior, Serenity Fitz smiled and grabbed Garret's hand. Her long, dark hair swished down her back, contrasting and accenting her short, cream-colored dress. Alyson tried not to stare, but Serenity was the most beautiful human she had ever seen. It wasn't just physical beauty; there was something welcoming and gracious in her eyes. They were big and brown and gazed up at Garret softly.

Alyson took the opportunity of everyone looking at Garret and Serenity to survey the room. It was much more laid-back and chill than where they had just come from. No one even gave them a second glance as they walked past. There were plenty of other people there, enjoying their drinks and their conversations, but Alyson felt like her world was suddenly just her and the man holding her hand. She turned her attention back to Jamie and found him staring at her. He studied her eyes, her nose, her mouth, her hand as she reached up to smooth her dark hair... She looked down at the floor. His fingers tightened around her hand, and her cheeks flamed into a scarlet color.

"Hello! New friends, Jamie?" A young man with a mop of sandy blond curls held back with a bandana approached the group with an unhurried gait.

Alyson looked up just in time to see her best friend begin to dance with excitement.

"Eddie! Mate! This is Danielle, and Aly." Jamie gestured towards the bass player of his band. "Girls, this is Eddie..."

"We know Eddie Mallory." Danielle had a huge grin on her face as she shook his hand. "You're kind of my favorite."

"Well in that case." Eddie's dimples were showing as he held out his arms for a hug.

"Ah, we've an Eddie fan in our midst!" Jamie let out a little laugh as Danielle melted into Eddie's arms.

"And clearly, a Jamie fan." Eddie jerked his chin towards Alyson who was standing silently at Jamie's side, her fingers still intertwined with his. "Aly, was it?"

"Yes." Alyson smiled brightly and gave the young man a side hug with her free arm once her friend finished her embrace.

"Very nice to meet you both." Eddie looked back over at Danielle and chuckled at the shining look in her eyes. "Would you girls like a drink?"

"Yes!" Danielle jumped at the chance, then gave her friend a questioning glance. "Aly?"

"Uh, no." Alyson wasn't sure what she was supposed to say. She had been chosen out of a club full of people by British singer and celebrity Jamie Donald, and she didn't want to leave him. She didn't drink anyway, so she stayed.

"You sure?" Garret asked as he and Serenity stepped away to follow Eddie and Danielle to the bar. Garret had his hand on the small of Serenity's back, and she leaned into him with a fondness in her eyes.

"Yeah, I'm fine." Alyson beamed and shifted her weight from one foot to the other.

"Was good to meet you, Aly!" Serenity waved as Garret led her away, smiling down at her affectionately.

"You, too!" Alyson returned the wave and watched the couple slip into a world that was just the two of them. She smiled at the sight.

"They are so in love it's almost sickening." Jamie nodded at his friends as he watched them sit down at the bar. "Serenity goes back home in a couple days, though, so I won't have to watch them be all lovey anymore."

After Jamie spoke, he and Alyson found themselves standing alone in the middle of the room, their hands still joined together. Alyson had never felt so shy before in her life. It took all of her strength to simply look up at the young man when he started talking to her.

"I guess we never officially met." Jamie's voice was suddenly very low and gentle. The sound made Alyson's stomach feel a rush. He turned to look into the girl's face with a sweet smirk. It was strange to see the twenty-six year old celebrity appear bashful. "I'm Jamie. It's nice to meet you."

Alyson found her tongue and managed to say words that were intelligible. "I loved your show tonight."

Jamie chuckled and played off the comment. "I loved your dancing. I hope I wasn't too forward in the way I met you. I figured that would get your attention."

The girl smiled timidly, her cheeks red as she looked at her feet for a moment, just long enough to take a deep breath. Jamie grinned when their eyes met, and he pulled on the hand he was still holding onto.

"Tell me about yourself, Aly."

"What about myself?" she asked.

"Anything," Jamie encouraged. "Everything."

It was strange to be the one who talked the most when the conversation was with someone who had been plastered in magazines, but Alyson found Jamie a surprisingly good listener. His blue eyes lit up as she grew more comfortable and allowed herself to laugh and talk more freely. He led her over to an empty table and finally slipped his hand from hers as they sat across from each other. Alyson recounted stories from her past, and forgot that she was sitting with a man she had paid money to see perform earlier that day. Her witty jokes and comebacks spiced up their conversation as he gazed, enraptured. A random story about a horrible haircut in high school amused him, and he roared with laughter.

"I don't know why I told you that." Alyson chuckled at herself and felt her cheeks go hot.

"No, I love it!" Jamie could sense that she was embarrassed and hurried to assure her that he thoroughly enjoyed their conversation. "You're ace at telling stories."

It wasn't long before Alyson and Jamie were joined by the others. Hours passed before they decided it was time to call it a night. They all shook hands and said how much they had enjoyed their time together. The girls were given autographs, and they laughed as they remembered how starstruck they had been at the beginning of the evening.

While the others were distracted, Jamie gave Alyson a tight hug. His arms wrapped around her slight frame and he pulled her as close to himself as he could, her arms holding onto his waist. He felt her heart pound against him; it matched the way his own heart slammed against his ribcage. Alyson stood on her tiptoes and rested her chin on Jamie's shoulder. It made him smile. Before Alyson left the club, she had Jamie's number in her phone.

"So, was that crazy or what?! Ah! I'm not going to be able to sleep for days! I just spent the evening with Eddie Mallory and Jamie Donald!" Danielle was in the front seat as Alyson drove them home with the windows open. "Can you believe that happened to us?!"

"It's crazy!" Alyson didn't know how to get rid of the butterflies. One hand pressed against her tingling stomach as she remembered how tender his voice had been when he spoke to just her. His persona on stage was loud and engaging, but with her he had been so gentle. She could still imagine what his hand felt like when it was resting on her knee.

"What was it like to be Jamie's girlfriend for the night?" Danielle asked with a laugh.

"You were Eddie's girlfriend for the night," Alyson deflected. "I'm so happy you got to meet him! This is your sixteen-year-old fangirl dream come true!"

"He's so amazing. I can't believe that happened. Ah! Aly! We hung out with famous people!" Danielle squealed.

"Did you see how beautiful Serenity Fitz was? Wow! I could not believe it. And she is seriously the nicest person I have ever met."

"Oh my gosh, I didn't tell you!" Danielle reached over with a hand to grab Alyson's arm as she spoke, startling her friend.

"You're going to make me crash! What?!"

"You remember how Serenity and I had to use the bathroom?"

"Yes?"

"The line in the club was so long!"

"That explains why you guys were gone for forever."

"No! Wait! That's not what happened!" Danielle was trying to keep a straight face. "So, there was a really long line, right? And we both had to go really bad, so..."

"Why... why are you laughing?"

"Shh! Just listen! Listen! Okay, so we decided to leave the club and find a bathroom somewhere else. We found this really sketchy drugstore a block away and the guy said, he said we could use it..." Danielle paused to compose herself. "But the doorknob was completely broken and didn't lock."

"You went to a sketchy drugstore and used a bathroom that didn't lock? Sounds super safe. Your mom must sleep so well at night."

"Shush! We guarded the door for the other one! But!"

"I knew there was going to be a plot twist..."

"Serenity tried to get out, and the handle literally fell off in her hand!"

"What!"

"The guy had to get a drill and take the entire knob off before we could get her out."

"No. No! That is terrifying!"

"Oh, and then there was a cockroach. It fell off the ceiling into the toilet while Serenity was locked in."

"I now officially hate this story."

Danielle laughed at Alyson's obvious disgust.

"Anyway, we were so traumatized we went to the convenience store that was across the street and bought ice cream bars."

"And you didn't bring me one?"

"Sorry, Aly, but Serenity and I are best friends now."

"Oh, perfect. I'm so happy for you both." Alyson turned to see Danielle grin mockingly. "How does it feel to have your relationship with your new best friend based on a cockroach?"

"We're very happy together."

"What happens to me?" Alyson's melodramatic response was coupled with wild gestures.

"You can keep Garret. Serenity and I discussed it." Danielle giggled despite her attempt to keep a straight face.

"Great, just what I always wanted!" Alyson raised one eyebrow.

"Hey! He's an important guy! He's the tour manager! Serenity told me that he is the one that keeps the whole band together and knows everything about everything."

"And he is also Jamie's best friend," said Alyson. "So thanks, but no thanks."

Danielle laughed and reached over to give Alyson's arm a squeeze. Alyson smiled back. It was impossible to put into words how surreal it felt.

"We swapped phone numbers so we can keep in touch."

"You and Serenity?" Alyson smiled at Danielle. "That's really cool. She seemed sweet."

"She is sweet."

"I wonder where Tommy was tonight," said Alyson.

"Tommy?"

"You know, the drummer. He wasn't at the club tonight after the show." Alyson saw the blank look in Danielle's eye. "He's blond like Eddie, and he talks funny sometimes because his parents are from France, but he grew up in London."

"Oh yeah! I forgot about him."

"That's because all you care about is Eddie." Alyson rolled her eyes again. "And now Serenity as well."

"You want to know what I can't get over?" Danielle hardly waited for Alyson to finish before she spoke. "I still can't believe Jamie just grabbed you on the dance floor! The club was packed, yet he chose *you*..."

Alyson blushed at the compliment. "It's not that big of a deal."

"Oh please!" Danielle could tell that her friend wanted to burst from all the attention she had received that night. "Aly, I know he's a hot celebrity and everything, but just remember, we don't know anything about him really. It's cool that he was flirting with you and stuff tonight, but don't... don't think he's safe just because he's famous."

"I know." Alyson gripped the steering wheel tightly. "I'm not expecting him to do any sort of follow-up from this."

"It was just one night." Danielle looked at her friend and smiled. "And it is a night we will never forget."

"Never," Alyson promised.

The day after Alyson returned home from Danielle's, she went out with a few of her friends. The night didn't end until well after midnight, and Alyson realized too late she had left her phone at home for the evening. It didn't seem that important as there were very few people who ever contacted her, and all of them knew about her evening out.

She was exhausted as she tiptoed quietly back into her apartment, ready to go straight to bed. It didn't take too long to strip off her fancy dinner clothes and get into a pair of comfortable pajamas. A faint buzzing sound reached her ears right before she could pull back the covers.

"Oh, shoot." Alyson remembered her phone. "Where are you...?"

It was a struggle to keep her eyes open as she patted around her dresser and on the floor for her phone. It buzzed again, and she spotted a glow that appeared on the bookshelf in the corner.

"Thirteen messages and four missed calls? Who in the world is spamming my phone? No one ever texts me..." Alyson yawned as she walked back over to her bed. She stopped and smiled when she saw text after text from the handsome singer she had met in Minnesota a few days earlier. He was asking her if she was free to talk, if she was okay, if there was anything he could do for her...

"What in the world!" Alyson's face went pink, and she giggled as she twirled around, her phone clutched against her chest. "He just texted me one minute ago! Oh my word, is this real life?"

Alyson's first thought was to text Danielle and tell her that Jamie had reached out to her, but she stopped. This should be her secret, at least for now. She didn't want anyone to ruin this magical moment.

"Why is he awake?" Alyson glanced at the time. "I suppose it's only midnight in San Diego."

She typed back a quick message saying that she had forgotten her phone at home and would be more than happy to talk to him the next day when he was free. She anxiously watched the screen for thirty seconds before she pushed the button to lock her phone.

"Breathe, Aly. Geez, stop being a spazz over a boy! Who are you even right now?" She pretended to slap herself as she shook her head.

Maybe it was because of her parent's strict rules, or because no one had ever seemed so sure about how they felt toward her before, but Alyson had never been very interested in guys. There had been the occasional crush; otherwise, she had been content to stay to herself and keep her heart hidden. It was safer that way, and she knew for sure that no one would ever break her heart or make her parents angry. But now...

"Why do I even feel like this?" Alyson mumbled under her breath as she finally crawled into bed. "I've never been crazy over a guy before. This Jamie, though... Man alive, does he make me feel something different on the inside."

The phone in her hand started ringing just as she closed her eyes. It was Jamie. She screamed silently into the pillow before answering. Her hand shook as she put the phone to her ear.

"Hi!" Aly tried to mask the quivering of her voice by sounding extra cheerful.

"Are you safe?" He sounded worried.

"What?"

"Safe. Are you safe?"

"Yes, I'm safe!" Alyson laughed a bit self-consciously. "What do you mean?"

"I've just read your text. You were out so late, and you didn't have your phone with you! Something could have happened!"

Alyson felt a rush in her stomach as she realized Jamie was being serious. He had genuinely been worried about her. Her. Alyson Abidi from a small town in Nebraska. She had been on his mind, not some other girl with designer clothes and expensive haircut. Just plain, old Aly. Her face ached as her smile stretched across it.

"No, yeah, I'm, I'm good. I'm fine. I was just out with some friends." She wanted to kick herself for stuttering.

"Good, good! You know, I was thinking of all the reasons why you wouldn't be answering me back and then I thought maybe something horrible happened to you. I could be texting you for weeks and never know."

"Or I might have been ignoring you." Alyson hoped Jamie would know it was a joke.

"That's what Garret said," Jamie chuckled. "Told me to give it up."

"Why didn't you?"

"I wanted to give you at least twenty-four hours before I gave up on you. You were worth at least that."

Alyson pulled on her bottom lip with her teeth, her thoughts whirling.

"I'm happy that wasn't the case, though."

"Me, too." The whisper was all Alyson could manage to say.

"As soon as I got your text I told Garret I had to leave straight away so I could call you. I'm actually on my way back to the hotel for the night."

"Oh, Jamie, you didn't have to..."

"It's fine. Serenity is back in London for a couple weeks so Gar has been stuck to my side all day whinging like a baby. He'll be fine without me for a bit."

"You and Garret are close, huh."

"Yeah. He's my best mate."

Alyson could hear the smile in Jamie's words as he spoke about his friend. The young man with broad shoulders and happy smile was often overlooked in the spotlight as he was the tour manager and not one of the lads on the stage, but when Alyson had met him in Minnesota, he fit right in with the others. It was obvious they all enjoyed each other's company and were like family.

"Then I'm sure he's wonderful." Alyson smiled up at the ceiling.

"He's the best, Aly, he truly is. Big nutter sometimes, and loves to laugh way too much, but he's always been there for me. A more honest, brave man I have never met in my life."

"Are you like him?"

Jamie gave a low laugh.

"No, I'm serious. How do your friends describe you?"

"Stubborn. Impulsive. Cheeky."

"Ha! Fine then, be that way."

"I-I don't know! I'm not used to talking about myself to people like you."

"People like me?"

"Yeah. A girl like you is way too good for me."

"Pshh..." Aly began to discount his words, but he stopped her.

"No, I'm serious. You're out there loving people and finding exciting things to do in the middle of ordinary life, making others feel important and taken care of. I'm just a man who gets to sing and play guitar for people."

"How do you see all of that in me?" Alyson put a hand over her cheek. It felt hot against her fingers.

"It's not that hard to see, love."

Love? Did he just call me love? Alyson couldn't breathe.

"I've been thinking about you a lot since I met you the other night."

"This seems... so unreal. Just meeting you was a big deal, but for you to actually want to, to, to talk to me and... I don't know! I haven't had a guy notice me in so long, and now I'm talking to *you*, of all people, at two in the morning!"

"Oh, Aly! Two in the morning? Why didn't you tell me! You must be exhausted!"

"I'll be okay, tomorrow is a slow day." Alyson tried to sound convincing, but ended with a yawn.

"No, no, no! I just wanted to check and make sure you were safe. You need sleep. Can we talk more tomorrow?"

"I would really like that."

"I would very much like that, as well." Jamie's voice was gentle.

Alyson could only grin. Her heart pounded as Jamie said one last goodbye and hung up. She was certain that she smiled in her sleep all night long.

At first Alyson was excited to hear from Jamie. It was sweet and felt safe, but the third time, fourth time, fifth time...

She attempted to make excuses as to why she couldn't talk, but they would still end up having two-hour conversations. She would ignore his texts for as long as she could, only to end up having extensive discussions that lasted for days at a time. For two weeks she played hot and cold before she finally gave in and let herself appreciate his attention.

Alyson had a summer job working with a local church doing summer camps with kids from the community. When she wasn't busy working, she was talking to Jamie. When Jamie wasn't busy doing interviews or shows, he was talking to Alyson.

Their video chats consisted of crazy dancing and corny jokes, sharing their dreams and telling stories about their lives. The later they stayed up, the more personal the stories became. Jamie remembered details from previous conversations, and surprised Alyson with the way he paid attention to her. He made the things that were important to her, important to him, including her heritage and beliefs.

"Tell me how you became a Christian," said Jamie.

"Well, there's not really anything to tell. I used to go to church with Danielle's family when I was in high school. It was one of the only things I was really allowed to do outside of the house without my parents freaking out." Alyson gave a tiny laugh. "They assumed if I was going to a church that I couldn't get into trouble, and my mom's parents go to church so my mom was fine with it. Over the years, I became a different person because of that, and I felt like I was finally free from all the rules and pressure to be perpetually good and perfect. I felt like I was good enough for Someone without having to pretend. So, I decided to say yes."

"Are you the only one in your family?"

"Yeah. I can choose to be a Christian if I want." Alyson didn't mention how she kept her beliefs to herself.

They didn't get into many details about her family, just enough for Jamie to know that Alyson was even more interesting than he originally thought. She mentioned they were strict, but she loved her parents and extended family. It was a topic that Alyson seemed happy to avoid, so Jamie kept his questions to himself. There were plenty of other things to focus on.

There was gold and green in her irises, the soft sprinkle of freckles on her nose and wrinkles that appeared around her eyes when she laughed. He loved the sound of her excitement, the way she always moved her hands when she spoke, and her ability to read a person's mood and match it with her own. This whatever-it-was he shared with her was not what Jamie had planned. When he had seen the girl dancing in the club, he wanted an evening of fun and flirting. But their conversation had been so comfortable and interesting that Jamie took a chance and decided to see where the passing fancy would take him. Every day it became more obvious how much this was not just a passing fancy.

"You're gorgeous,"

"Thank you." Her blush drove Jamie mad. "And I really must get to bed now."

"Ah, unlucky," said Jamie with a grin. "I get to stay up past eight o'clock now that I'm a big boy."

"It's a quarter to eleven where I am and I have a job to go to in the morning, so unlucky nothing."

"But if you go to sleep I'll have no one to talk to."

"Unlucky." Alyson smirked. "Good night, Jamie."

"Go ahead and lie down, love. I'll hang up when you're all tucked in."

"You just want to get the last word in." Alyson moved her laptop and pulled back her sheets.

"So what if I do!"

"Jay, having the last word in a conversation literally means nothing!" Alyson laughed as she set the computer back down and slipped under the sheets beside it.

"That's what you think."

"You're seriously so strange."

"Well, thanks then, for that," Jamie huffed as Alyson chuckled. "You don't even want to know what I think before calling me names! I see how it is!"

"Okay, fine! Tell me, Jamie, what do *you* think?"

"I'm not going to tell you."

Alyson rolled her eyes and turned on her side to watch his face on the screen. She had never enjoyed talking to someone who wasn't Danielle as much as she enjoyed Jamie. There was a confusing mix of emotions wrapped up around him; he was a person to whom she felt like she could tell the story about setting the microwave on fire, yet a person whom she knew was out of her reach.

"Well, I guess I'll just have to continue thinking it means nothing." Alyson shifted the pillow under her head and stifled a yawn.

"I guess so." Jamie's voice had gone soft.

Jamie didn't say anything for a few minutes as he watched Alyson's eyelids droop down. Minutes ticked by, and her breathing slowed.

"Good night, Aly. Sweet dreams," he whispered.

"Good night," she mumbled in her almost-asleep consciousness.

"Sleep well."

"Mmm. K."

"Shh." Jamie smiled even though Alyson's eyes were closed. "Good night."

This time Alyson kept her mouth shut and let Jamie have the last word. It didn't mean anything, but it was beginning to mean everything.

Alyson was barely home from work on the third Friday of July when her phone rang in her hand. She glanced at the time before answering Jamie's call and guessed that their conversation would have to be short; sound check for that night's concert would start any minute.

"Hi!" Alyson's voice was cheerful.

"What if I told you that you could stop missing me for one night?"

"Wait, what?" Alyson froze. The smile left her face.

"I can fly you out to see me!" Jamie exclaimed excitedly.

"Wait, *what?*"

"We're going to have a huge show in L.A. the thirty-first of July. Please, Aly. Come see me."

"I-I... I can't!" Alyson was flustered. To have a relationship over the phone was one thing, but to see him in person and hold his hand? To let him hug her and stare into her eyes with nothing between them? Alyson knew that seeing him in person would only tie her heart to him even more than it already was. She couldn't expect him to keep her around longer than his time in the States lasted. "I have a job, and, and, and I'm starting to get ready for the next school year! I can't just leave."

"Come on! One day!" he begged. "Soon you'll be too busy with teaching, and I really want to see you again while we're still in the States. We're leaving to go back to London as soon as the tour ends."

"I know." That was what worried her.

"I don't understand why you don't want to go for this. We like each other. We miss each other! I can fly you to be with me so we can spend time together. That's what people who like each other do. We don't have to say we're dating if that makes you feel better. "

"No, it's not... it's not that." Alyson's cheeks were red.

"Are you done with me? Is that what this is about? Just, bam, finished?"

"No, Jay. I'm not done with you."

"Then I really don't know why you're acting this way." Jamie sighed. "Please explain yourself."

"I just don't think it's a good idea."

"Aly..."

Alyson bit her lip, and said nothing. She turned to look out the window of her apartment and saw the curtains. She didn't like curtains.

"Well, if you change your mind at all, the offer still stands." Alyson could hear the disappointment in Jamie's voice.

"I'll let you know," Alyson conceded.

Chapter two
"Tonight is so screwed up."

July 31st

Jamie reached for Alyson's hand and let their fingers intertwine. They walked close. Close enough that their arms brushed and the scent of their skin mixed. He leaned over and felt her hair against his face as he whispered in her ear. She smiled, tightening her grip on his hand. His eyes lit up and he brushed his lips against hers in a kiss. The chemistry between them was electric.

A crowded room became the perfect place for Jamie to hold her close to make sure they weren't separated. A strand of hair across her face was a chance for Jamie to tuck it away behind her ear and stroke her cheek as he pulled back his hand. Walking through a crowded club allowed Alyson to hold onto Jamie's arm and stand much closer to him than normal.

"You comfy, love?" he had asked before he left her to go on stage and perform. "Watch me wink for you in the show. See you at the end!"

The couple was joined after the concert by Tommy, the drummer with thick blond hair and ice-blue eyes. His eyes sparkled when he laughed, which was often. Alyson hadn't met Tommy in Minnesota, but she quickly learned that he was the life of the party and treated everyone as a friend. They reached the club where everyone was meeting up and were immediately surrounded by a crowd of people ready to have a good time.

"I'll be right back, love!" Jamie shouted to Alyson half an hour after they arrived.

"Where are you going?" Alyson tried to hold onto his arm, but he pulled it away. She licked her lips nervously.

"I have to find something! Stay with Tom!" He gave her hand a reassuring squeeze and turned away.

Alyson watched Jamie push through the crowd and disappear down a dark hallway. She looked back towards Tommy and peered cautiously up into his face. Alyson had always considered Jamie the most attractive, but seeing Tommy in real life and not hidden behind a drum set, she realized he was also handsome with his square jaw and the slight indentation in the middle of his chin.

"Where did Jamie go?" Tommy leaned close to the girl to hear her response.

"Said he had to find something."

"Right now?" asked Tommy with a laugh. "You know, he hasn't stopped going on about you since Minnesota."

The words surprised Alyson, but she tried to keep her cool. She had to duck her head to hide her elated expression and pink cheeks. Tommy's stare caught her attention from the corner of her eye. His Adam's apple bobbed when she looked back up at him.

"He's a pretty great guy." Alyson's voice broke through the din of the crowd.

"Jamie's one of the best." Tommy put a hand on her arm to talk by her ear. He was surprised by how soft her skin was. He purposefully left his hand on her. "I'm glad he flew you out for our show."

"I am, too! Tonight's show was the best concert I have ever seen you guys do!"

Tommy nodded and gave her a thumbs-up. They stood for a moment, unsure of what to do with the person beside them. Alyson hoped that Jamie would return soon.

"You want to dance?" asked Tommy abruptly.

Alyson nodded with a smile.

Tommy jerked his head towards the middle of the room and pulled her along behind him until they were lost in the midst of couples and friends enjoying the songs the DJ was playing. Jamie found them there. He grabbed Alyson by the waist from behind and pulled her into his arms.

"Did you miss me?" he teased, his mouth near Alyson's ear so she could hear him. His only answer was a smile and a flush of color on her face.

"She's great, Jamie," Tommy yelled to his friend. "I'm going to go find Eddie. Nice dancing with you, Alyson!"

It wasn't too long before Alyson found herself following Jamie down crowded hallways, a nervous knot in the pit of her stomach. Her palm sweated against Jamie's, and the sound of her heartbeat rushed through her ears. She was amazed at his ability to get through the masses of people as he led her further away from the dance floor. He stopped at a room that was empty with the exception of a few boxes and a couch.

Alyson tripped over the edge of a rug as she walked in and felt him catch her by the elbow. Her whole body shook as they began to undress, her fingers barely able to undo the button on her pants. Jamie looked over when he heard her tiny gasp of frustration. He gave her a charming smile and pulled her into his arms.

"It's okay, love. I promise you." His hands were gentle on her arms as he calmed her racing heart. His fingers slipped under the short sleeves of her t-shirt and felt her skin. "You okay? You ready?"

She purposefully ignored the doubts that screamed at her as she looked up at him with big, trusting eyes and nodded. She bit her bottom lip and let Jamie lead the way. Everything was fine. She was fine. The thrill of intimacy was louder than the wildly protesting voice of reason, and Alyson felt herself melting under Jamie's touch. Why had she been so afraid of seeing him? Why had she been so afraid of letting him love her the way he wanted to? What was so wrong with...

But something was wrong. Something changed. Alyson could feel it in her bones as he paused to lean back and look at her face. She couldn't see the same light, the same adoration that had been there just moments before. Alyson didn't dare move as she waited for him to explain himself.

He left the couch, leaving her skin cold and clammy as his heat disappeared from her side. She pushed herself up onto her elbows and watched as he hurried to cover himself with his clothes.

In a second he'll turn around and tell me what's going on. Alyson swallowed hard as he covered his chest and shoulders with his t-shirt. *He's not... He's not leaving me. He wouldn't. He cares about me. He'll tell me in a second why he's getting dressed. He'll tell me.*

A quick kiss on her cheek startled her from her thoughts just in time to watch Jamie leave the room without a word. She lay alone in the small room, half-naked. The sound of the door latching shut behind Jamie echoed around Alyson's head to the rhythm of her pounding heart. That was the first moment the regret hit. But it was too late; the deed had already been done, and she couldn't take it back.

A row of alcoholic beverages were lined against the wall in glass bottles, all different shapes and sizes. Alyson jumped up from the couch and grabbed one without a glance at the label to see what it was called. She unscrewed the top and took as big of a gulp as her mouth could hold. The liquid burned, and Alyson spat it out onto the floor. She swallowed the next mouthful, and the next and the next until the bottle was empty.

Alyson was curled into a ball on the couch when another person walked into the room. Her shirt was still laying on the floor where it had landed when Jamie pulled it over her head. She wished her eyesight wasn't so clouded so she could see if Jamie had come back for her. When she heard the gasp, though, she knew it wasn't him.

"Aly! What happened? Are you okay? Where's Jamie?" Eddie knelt down beside the couch, suddenly aware of Alyson's lack of clothing. "Let me go get Jamie!"

"No!" Alyson held onto Eddie's wrist. "H-he's g-..."

It took a long time for Eddie to piece together what Alyson was struggling to say. She had loved him. She had given him everything. He had left her. Eddie said nothing as he stroked her hair back from her tear-streaked face and rocked her gently. Alyson's head ached, and she wanted to throw up.

The tears ended, and she reached for her shirt. Eddie helped her pull it over her head as she swayed on the edge of the couch. His hand on her arm kept her from losing her balance.

"I want to go home," she whispered. She kept her eyes on the floor, too embarrassed and ashamed to look at Eddie's face. He had been in there with her for over an hour. She could only imagine what he thought of her right then.

"We'll get you home, Aly. Don't worry."

Alyson nodded.

"You okay?"

"Can we please leave here?" Alyson sniffed and wiped at some tears on her cheek. "I want to go somewhere else."

Eddie held her hand with a steady grip as they left the room. His body acted as a shield to protect her from the hundreds of staring eyes that greeted them. She followed behind him on shaky legs, hyper-aware of the glances and whispers that seemed to be directed at her. The crushing weight of guilt and regret came to rest on her like a cloak of shame.

As soon as Eddie had Alyson seated in the quietest spot he could find, he ran off in search of Tommy. A moment later, someone grabbed his arm.

"Where've you been, mate? I thought you were going to play pool with us!" Tommy noted the disheveled look of Eddie's curls and the way Eddie's gaze shifted around the room. "Wait, are you okay?"

Eddie pulled Tommy to the bar and hurriedly told him what had just happened.

"She wouldn't stop crying over him, Tommy. She was absolutely falling to bits." Eddie scratched at his head. "Have you seen Jamie? Is he still around?"

"No, he's left." Tommy put a hand on Eddie's shoulder to calm him. "I think he went back to his."

"She wept for almost an hour. She's absolutely gutted that he walked out on her."

"Did she give you a reason why...?"

"He slept with her." Eddie exhaled sharply and shook his head. "I'm pretty sure he was her first time."

Tommy's eyes widened, but he said nothing.

"Things with Aly just went too far too fast. You know he's not over Beth yet."

"But you saw them together today..."

"I know! He finally looked happy. Like, proper happy. *She* looked happy. And now..."

"If Jamie left her, you know he's never going to look back. He never does. When he's done with a girl, he's done with a girl." Tommy could still see the fretful look in Eddie's eyes. "What Jamie's done is not your fault. You've helped her..."

"She's a mess, Tom. She's not crying now, but she's here until her plane leaves in the morning. I can't imagine..."

"Where is she?" Tommy scanned the crowd for the girl.

"I sat her over there. I tried to find someplace where she was a bit out of the way. I'm going to keep an eye on her until she leaves."

"No, you stay here. I'll go and keep an eye on her for a bit." Tommy nodded at his friend.

Eddie let his bandmate attend to the girl in the corner while he slammed back a drink and tried to not think about Jamie and how he had treated Alyson. There was no sign of Jamie anywhere. Through the bobbing sea of heads on the dance floor, Eddie noticed Garret having the time of his life with a few of their local friends. Normally he would be with Jamie, but he had spent the day with other people, allowing Jamie to have time with Alyson.

"Hey, you remember me?" Tommy shouted through the noise.

"Tommy. Yeah." Alyson forced a smile and nodded while avoiding eye contact.

"Let's go out where I can hear you better." Tommy put his hand out to help Alyson up from her chair. She grabbed onto it tightly, showing more confidence in her grip than in her gaze. The touch made Tommy's nerves tingle. He held Alyson's hand firmly as they made their way through the crowds towards the exit. The hot summer air hit their faces, and the music grew dim as they stepped out and the door shut behind them. Tommy watched the girl pull her hand away from his and place it on her forehead. She looked like she was about to be sick. "You okay?"

"I've never... I've never drank before." Alyson leaned back against the wall and put her other hand on her stomach. "I feel terrible."

"There's a shop right up on the corner. Let's get you some Tylenol and a bottle of water." Tommy was eager to help. He walked slowly beside Alyson as they made their way down the sidewalk towards the convenience store at the end of the street. The silence felt awkward, but he didn't know how to fill it.

"Tonight is so screwed up." She looked straight ahead to hide the glassy film of tears covering her eyes as she hugged herself.

"Well, if it drove you to drinking for the first time, I can imagine." Tommy tried to sound understanding.

Alyson didn't say anything else as they walked. Tommy glanced over and noted the hunched shoulders and red-rimmed eyes. Jamie had gushed about her for almost two months, but that was all he knew about the girl.

"I'm sorry for what happened..." Tommy's mouth twitched nervously as he spoke. "I hope you're, you know, okay."

Alyson gave a short, bitter laugh and glanced at him briefly. He saw the heartbreak in her eyes before they flitted away. He thought back to the first time someone broke his heart and remembered how deep that pain went. That was what Alyson was feeling as she walked next to him; she was an exposed and bleeding heart.

"I can't imagine how hard this must be for you." The words came out with more compassion than the first set of words had.

"Two hours." Alyson's lips trembled. "It has been two hours since Jamie left me. How can this be so painful? We were together for two months! Not even! Two stupid months!"

Tommy didn't know what to say, so he remained quiet.

"But he made me feel so much." The lines in Alyson's forehead deepened as the lump in her throat grew. "I never felt so much for someone before. I really thought... I really thought he felt those things, too. But I was wrong."

"No! He's crazy about you!" Tommy protested. "He really likes you."

"You don't treat people that you like the way Jamie treated me," Alyson whispered, as she stopped in her tracks. She clenched her fists by her sides and felt her nails dig into the flesh on the heels of her hand. "I may not know a lot about love, but you can't just... You don't walk away from someone like that... It was all just a game to him."

"I know Jamie... It was real." The words sounded lame.

"No... Not anymore." Alyson looked away to hide the tears in her eyes. A gentle hand on her shoulder turned her back to face her companion. She felt him step closer until he was looking down directly into her face. Alyson couldn't breathe.

"You're worth more than that," he whispered before leaning down to kiss her.

The kiss took Alyson off-guard, but she quickly let herself melt into his arms. She didn't care that they were in the middle of the sidewalk. Her head ached and her thoughts were jumbled, but the kiss made her feel something other than the miserable self-hatred that was growing inside of her. It was her escape from the awful reality she had created for herself. Tommy tried to pull back, but Alyson pressed in.

"Wait! Wait, now." Tommy put his hands on Alyson's shoulders to push her away. "You were just with Jamie!"

A flash of pain went through the girl's eyes at his words; they were a cold reminder of the actions she wasn't ready to take responsibility for. Alyson let out a deep breath and rubbed her hands over her face. Her lungs spasmed as she filled her cheeks with air to stop from melting into a sobbing mess.

"I'm sorry. I'm, I'm, I'm... I don't even know who I am right now. This isn't me... I'm sorry."

"Don't. Don't be sorry," Tommy murmured with an awkward reach for her shoulder to comfort her.

"I am, though. I'll probably be sorry for the rest of my life." Alyson walked away from the young man as she spoke.

"Alyson." Tommy spoke her name gently. She stopped, but didn't turn around. "Alyson, it's okay."

Okay.

It's okay.

She began to shake her head and laugh hopelessly through her tears. She turned around slowly. Tommy's eyes looked so blue in the light of the street lamp. She flung her arms wide, as if she was challenging him to prove it.

"How am I ever going to be okay again? You don't know my l-life, and what this means f-for me... what this means for my future!" Tears poured down hot and fast, and Alyson didn't even care that she was stuttering. "I'm going to fly back home in the morning without my virginity, without my s-stupid boyfriend, without my dignity... I'm going to have to look people in the eye and pretend I did n-nothing while I carry this huge mountain of regret for the rest of my life. Alone. I'm going to have to deal with this alone!"

"Shh." Tommy walked up to her and pressed a finger to her lips. "I'm here right now. Let me help you tonight."

Alyson didn't know how he thought he could help, but she didn't have any more words left to argue against him. So she let him keep her close. She let him use his cool hands to soothe her feverish face, and his steady arms held her upright when things began to spin again.

Getting a room at the nearby hotel didn't seem like a bad idea at the time. Alyson was exhausted and nauseous and wanted to lie down on something comfortable to rest her aching head. Tommy drew the curtains shut while she sat on the edge of the bed, her shoes off and bare toes pushing against the thin carpet. Alyson bit her lip and cringed at the sound of the metal rings scraping across the rod that held them up. She didn't like curtains.

"You want the light on?" Tommy asked. He watched Alyson shake her head no.

And so the room had remained dark. She was still buzzing from the alcohol she had consumed, and she didn't mind Tommy lying next to her. They talked quietly. Tommy's hand found Alyson's, and she grabbed onto it. One touch had led to one kiss, and that kiss had led to a passion Alyson had not been expecting. The next thing Alyson knew, she found herself sleeping with another man.

The regret felt different with Tommy than it had with Jamie, but it was there. Tommy had tried to get up, but Alyson knew that when he left she would be alone. She would have her conscience, aching heart and bruised body to deal with, and she wasn't prepared for that yet.

"Please stay," she whispered through the tears.

"Course." Tommy didn't tell Alyson he needed the assurance of human comfort as much as she did in that moment. "I'm right here."

How could I have given him everything, just like that? Alyson stared at the curtains and bit her lip. *With Jamie I thought I was in love, so I said yes. I don't even hardly know Tommy, but now...*

A numbness began to creep over the girl, and she focused on breathing.

"I'm ready."

Tommy's cheeks were red as they returned to the club. He quickly located his friends and walked over to them, Alyson in tow. Insistent that she didn't need any special treatment, she hit the dance floor, determined to just dance until it was time to catch her flight. She ignored Tommy and Eddie as they snuck off to the side of the room to talk. They gestured at her from time to time while they looked around nervously. When Alyson glanced back later they were gone.

Arrangements with the driver who would take her to the airport in the morning had been made before Jamie's show; all she had to do was hold herself together until then. All she had to do was pretend that she was fine. Garret spotted her dancing alone and quickly made himself her dance partner. He gave her big smiles when the troubled look tried to sneak back into her eyes. He had no idea what had happened between her and Jamie. She wasn't going to be the one to tell him.

"Hey! Do you need a drink?" Garret asked as one song ended.

"Yeah, I'm thirsty." Alyson followed Garret to the bar. She ordered a water, and Garret eyed her drink of choice with surprise.

"Don't you want a real drink?"

"No. My family doesn't drink because of... well, it's an honor thing..." Alyson tried to explain, but Garret gave her a blank look. "We don't drink."

The choice to not drink after all she had done that night already seemed like a useless reach for propriety. Alyson grimaced at the bitter irony of the situation. There was a man at the end of the bar that stared at her, and she turned her back on him.

"Let me buy you something!" Garret ordered a drink and handed it to Alyson. He watched her make a sour face and struggle to swallow. "Do you like it?"

"It's so strong!"

"Here, let me buy you a different kind."

After sampling two other drinks, Alyson and Garret were given shots from the staring man. They gave him a nod and swallowed. Alyson hated the sensation of burning in her throat and told Garret she was done. Alyson felt very unsteady on her legs as they went back out to the dance floor.

"Hey, do you feel hot? It's so hot in here!" Garret slurred his words into Alyson's ear.

Alyson didn't remember what she said. She didn't remember what they did. All she could remember was that she woke up in a dark room with most of her clothing on the floor. What had they done? Alyson was almost angrier at what she didn't know than what she did know. Going back to life after that night was the hardest thing Alyson had ever done.

August 20th

Red numbers on the clock by her bed greeted Alyson's blurry vision as she opened her eyes. They slowly came into focus and told her it was still early in the morning. She sat up in her bed and sighed. She wouldn't have to get up for work for another few hours. The words from her dream echoed around her head as she lay in the dark.

It's okay, love. I promise you.

I promise you.

I promise...

Was it a dream? No, it was a nightmare. A nightmare that refused to stop haunting her. It didn't matter how many times the scene replayed in her mind, the past could not be changed. Her hands were unsteady as they reached for the cup of water beside the bed, and she sat up to take a drink. She wished more than anything that she could wash away the memories like the liquid washed down her throat.

She couldn't close her eyes without the memories crashing down on her. She didn't remember what it felt like to live without the burden of her secrets. How wonderful it must have been to have lived with carefree abandon, unafraid to say what she felt! Alyson wasn't that girl any more. It had been three weeks, yet she still felt tormented by her actions.

She went over the night again for the millionth time as she lay on her back and stared at the ceiling, tangled up in her sheets. The harder she tried to remember and figure it out, the less it all made sense. She had messed up more in those few short hours than she had ever messed up in her life, and she had to live with that. Over and over she prayed, repenting of her actions and begging for relief from the inner turmoil, but none came.

Alyson's eyelids drooped down. They grew heavier until she couldn't keep them open any longer. It only seemed like moments before her alarm blared in her ear to wake her from the brief moments of peaceful sleep she had finally found in the end. She looked in the mirror and cringed. People had already been asking her about the dark circles under her eyes, but that morning she looked like a victim of abuse. Little did those around her know just how much more bruised her heart felt than her body looked. Alyson crumpled in a ball on her bed and let herself cry.

"Alyson! You're going to be late!" Alyson's roommate called through the door. "You have school this morning, right?"

"Y-yes! Thank you." Alyson quickly stood back up to her feet and wiped the tears off her face. She had made her choices; now she had to live with the consequences.

For the rest of the day, Alyson held herself together, lying to everyone who asked her how she was doing. She loved her job, her co-workers and her students, but she did not love herself. Every day she would rush home from work and get in the shower, scrubbing her skin raw in an attempt to feel clean. No one knew what had happened, or just how much Alyson was struggling to make it through.

"Are you working out again?" The Roommate asked as she came home from work. "Didn't you work out yesterday?"

"I work out every day." Alyson was panting from the exertion of the physical activity. "It helps me focus and stop thinking."

"You're gonna be skinnier than you already are." She rolled her eyes and left for the kitchen.

Truth was, Alyson felt so out of control of her life, the only thing she could control was her workout routine and the bottle of birth control in the bathroom. She blasted music that didn't remind her of *Jupiter Waits* and pushed her body harder than she ever had in her life. Papers didn't get graded. Lessons were never made. Field trips didn't get organized. Alyson was struggling.

"Why don't you go home early and get some rest?" Alyson's boss suggested one day after school when they were supposed to work on some things. "You can hardly keep your eyes open."

"I'll be fine!" Alyson was horrified. She had wanted this job so badly and now she was ruining it. "I'm sorry, I've been having a hard time keeping up with stuff, but I'm working on it. I promise."

I promise.

"I know. I understand." Alyson knew that her boss meant what she said, but Alyson didn't believe her. "We'll meet another day."

With a sigh that was both one of frustration and of relief, Alyson gathered her things and left the school. She cried as she drove. She wished she knew how to get her life back together again, but in one night, in one choice and in one moment, her whole life was changed and she could never turn back time and fix it.

Another week passed, and Alyson started to feel nauseous when she woke up in the morning. She passed it off as the virus that was going around her classroom. A few days went by with no other signs of having the flu besides the upset stomach in the morning. Alyson tried to ignore it.

"It's like the Virgin Aly has morning sickness," her roommate joked once after she noticed the daily habit.

Virgin.

That was the word that had set Jamie off and started everything. Her stomach churned as she thought about it.

"You're a virgin?" His voice sounded surprised from the other end of the phone.

"Yes? So?" Alyson always said she was going to save herself for marriage and had stayed true to her word. She had never regretted her decision. Her off-handed comment to Jamie had meant nothing to her.

"You're, like, old, though."

"So?" Alyson shrugged it off.

It seemed like such an insignificant piece of information, but it sparked a fire. That fire had burned her, engulfed her and threatened to suck her life away. Those burns were all she could think about as she drove home. The tears ran down her face.

She had given away something she could never get back, and there was only silence from Jamie. All the attention and empty promises were gone, and Alyson felt used. He was never coming back for her

"I gave you so much of me. Whatever you asked for, I gave you." Alyson sat in the parking lot in her car for a long time after she reached her apartment complex. "I thought I meant something to you, that what we shared would mean something to you... I thought you would stay."

Alyson trusted the pills that she swallowed each morning to ensure she wouldn't get pregnant, but there was a thought that started to nag at the back of her mind that maybe they didn't work. She refused to look up symptoms for morning sickness and choked back tears every time she had to run to the bathroom. The mask she wore at school in front of the others was so thin she was sure it was see through. Still, no one seemed to be too worried about her. Finally, Alyson knew what she needed to do.

"Hi, Aly!" Danielle called out with a cheery voice when their Skype call connected.

"Danielle, I did something very stupid and I regret it very, very much." Alyson tried to keep her voice steady as she spoke. She saw her best friend drop what she was doing and push her homework off her lap so she could hold her laptop. Aly took a deep breath and started again; "You know how you told me to be flattered by Jamie's attention but to not take it seriously or go along with it because he's a famous rock star and was just using me as a rebound?"

Alyson saw the color leave Danielle's face.

"Aly, what happened?"

"I, uh..." Tears crept up in Alyson's eyes. She tried to laugh them away, but she couldn't. Faster and faster they fell, a testament to the pain she had bottled up inside of her. Danielle sat and tugged on her hair as she waited for her friend to finish her sentence. "He flew me out to L.A. and, uh, I spent a day with him."

"What? When?" Danielle was shocked. "Why didn't you tell me? What did he do to you? Are you okay? Why are you crying? Why did you go see him again?"

Jamie's gestures toward Alyson the night in Minnesota had appeared to be sincere, but wasn't that how he treated every girl he picked out to spend the evening with? Danielle didn't know him beyond what the tabloids said, and all those told her was that the rock star was seen out with a different girl almost daily since his break up. At least that's what it seemed like. She hadn't really paid them much attention. Their one night at the club with Jamie, Garret and Eddie had been fun, but it was supposed to have been just that; one night.

"It happened in July. We had been talking every day, and he was just super sweet. W-we liked each other." Alyson continued to cry.

"Why didn't you tell me about this earlier?" Danielle knew there was something else. There was something Aly wasn't saying.

Instead of answering her friend's question, Alyson held her face in her hands and wept. For over a month she had held the burning secret and tried to keep it hidden. Now, the words she had been desperate to say were stuck inside, and she couldn't make them come out. Flashes from that night went through her mind; lyrics to the songs she had danced to, the hands she had held in the crowd, the eyes that had watched her with jealousy as she clung to the arm of the handsome celebrity. Later, those same eyes seemed to see right through her and read her mind to know what she had done.

"I'm buying a plane ticket to come see you next week," was all Alyson managed to get out.

"Okay, great. Whatever you need, Aly." Danielle bit her tongue to stop herself before she demanded that Alyson answer her question immediately.

"And..." Alyson let the word become drawn out as she struggled to say what she wanted to say next. She grabbed a tissue out of the Kleenex box that was next to her. "I'm going to, uh, be bringing a, um, a pregnancy test with me, just in case the throwing up isn't just from... I don't know."

Danielle didn't say a word. She saw the dark circles under Alyson's bloodshot eyes, the frown lines around her mouth and the hollows in her cheeks. She had been Alyson's best friend for close to nine years and she knew Alyson had never once contemplated sleeping with anyone before marriage. It wasn't just something forced on her by strict parents or fear, she genuinely wanted to wait. Jamie had barely been a blip on the radar for Danielle; she never imagined Alyson would actually go along with it.

"Aly, did he rape..." The question was too horrible to say.

"No." Aly quickly shook her head no and looked down in shame. "I'll explain when I get there."

Neither girl said anything else for a long while. Alyson only felt a fraction of the relief she wanted to feel after disclosing her secrets.

"Have you told anyone else?"

"No. I can't. Can you imagine me going into work as a teacher at a private, Christian school and telling people I chose to sleep with someone before marriage because I got caught up in the moment?" Aly had never hated herself this much before. "I-I can't imagine the type of shame I would bring on the family through this. If my grandfather found out I would be punished for sure. I don't want to think about what he would do. I'll never be able to tell my parents."

"Then don't tell them." The friend sounded honest and tender at the same time. "Come see me and we'll talk. I'll take care of you."

"Thanks, Elle." Alyson choked up again. "I just bought the tickets. We only have half a week of school next week so I'll be there Wednesday night."

"I'll be waiting with fluffy pillows and ice cream." Danielle pushed up the corners of her mouth sadly at her friend.

"Love you." With one last smile clouded with regret, Alyson turned off the webcam and hung up.

She breathed deeply, using an old piece of advice her mother had told her years before about how to lower stress. She had been deep breathing a lot in the last few weeks and hadn't seen much of a difference, but it gave her something to concentrate on outside of her thoughts.

She stood up from her bed and grabbed the cup of water from the bedside table. She drank it slowly as she paced back and forth in her room. She knew Danielle would always love her, but her actions would forever change how her friend saw her. How long was this recovery process from one night of stupidity going to take?

There was a perpetual ache in her head, and sometimes the pain flared up into a headache that made it hard to think straight. She hoped and prayed time would go by quickly as she set her heart to just make it for one more week; all she had to do was make it to Danielle's.

Someone came up behind her as she was eating her lunch at school the next day. She quickly hid all traces of pain and smiled brightly as her boss joined her.

"You seem to be really enjoying yourself today!" Alyson's boss smiled at her when she saw the fake grin on Alyson's face. "Have you been sleeping better since I gave you that afternoon off?"

"Yes!" Alyson lied. "Thank you so much! You've been so good and patient with me!"

"You're one of our best teachers; we love having you at our school." The words hit Aly like a ton of bricks. She had already told herself that if she was pregnant, which she was too afraid to think about, she was going to have to quit. "You represent our school so well!"

After their conversation, Alyson went into the bathroom and did her deep breathing. All she could do was hope that her body was simply stressed and would soon go back to normal. Alyson stayed in the bathroom for as long as she could before she returned to her classroom.

"Miss Alyson, I picked you flowers again!" A little girl ran towards her with a handful of pretty blossoms that grew next to their school building.

"I love them! Thank you!" Aly took the purple and yellow flowers and held them in her hand. Their green stems were broken and warm from being in the rough grasp of the child. Her own heart felt like the stems at times; battered and clinging to the last bit of life that was left. The child hadn't meant to hurt the flowers as she yanked them from their source of life, but they had been hurt just the same. Alyson knew the flowers wouldn't even make it an hour before they wilted completely.

Her thoughts were interrupted by another child who ran up in a state of frustration. She listened to the little voice go on and on about how so-and-so had done such-and-such and now they weren't friends. Alyson worked as a peacemaker and listened to both sides of the story before she reminded the children they really did love each other. The smiles that lit up the faces of the youngsters as they ran back out to play brought a twinge of bittersweet emotions to the teacher.

Those kids had become her life over the last year, and she knew so much about them and cared about their lives and wellbeing. They were her kids. To love and teach them was her dream job, even on the days when she wanted to give up on life. The kids had no idea how much they had helped her. Her desk was stuffed with letters and pictures her students had made for her in the past few weeks. Any type of recovery that had happened was because of them. Yet if there was a baby, she would have to leave them...

She leaned on the doorframe of her classroom and looked out at the sea of small bodies that were constantly in motion on the playground. Each student had a special spot in her heart, especially the ones she had had to fight for to earn their trust and respect. What would they think of her if she left them? She pressed her quivering lips together and turned away from the sight. She would do everything she could to stay.

A tear trickled down Alyson's face as she sat by her window seat on the airplane and thought about Jamie. They had become so attached in those two short months.

Thoughts of what her dad's family would do and say if they found out what she had done haunted her. She always thought of her extended family fondly and loved them very much, but she began to remember incidences from the past when the family's honor had to be restored. Her cousins had scars, and there was always a flicker of fear that hid in their eyes whenever they were in the same room as their grandfather and uncles. Not every family was like that, but Alyson's was. Her relationship with her grandfather was relatively good, but then again, she had always been good. "The good one," someone had spat out jealously the last time she visited them.

"What happened?" Alyson remembered asking her cousin Sumaya as they fell asleep one night and she glimpsed a mark on her forearm. They were about ten years old and Alyson had been slowly realizing how different her life was from the life of her favorite cousin. It made sense that her grandfather would sometimes punish them, since he was the one who was shamed by their misbehavior, but Alyson always tried to be good. Maybe that didn't actually count for anything.

"I shouldn't tell you," Sumaya whispered nervously. "I don't want you to get into trouble."

"Why would I get into trouble?"

"Because... it's shameful." Sumaya looked away. "We could get in trouble and make grandfather angry."

"You made him angry?"

"A lot of times on accident." Sumaya sighed. "I wish I could just learn everything that is bad so that I never do it and I don't have to be afraid of being punished."

"Well, you should tell me what you did so I don't do it." There was something very compelling about Alyson's argument.

"Okay. But don't tell anyone I told you." Sumaya glanced around the dark room to make sure they were alone. "I was at the shop down the road and a boy was there and he tried to kiss me."

At first Alyson thought there was more to the story, but Sumaya was quiet.

"You mean, you got in trouble because of the boy?"

"My dad was very angry."

"I bet the boy got in big trouble, too."

"I don't think so." Sumaya wrinkled her brow as she thought about it. "I don't think his father cared that he tried to kiss me."

Fast-forward six years to the cousins in the dark again. This time they whispered about a friend of Sumaya's who had been caught sneaking out of her house to sleep over.

"Is every family in Pakistan as strict as ours?" asked Alyson in response to hearing that the girl had been beaten.

"No. I have friends who can do almost anything they want. Most families are letting go of the old world views that grandfather has. We're in the minority."

"I'm scared my dad is going to end up like grandfather."

"Your dad?" Sumaya snorted before she saw the look on Alyson's face and grimaced. "Your dad is so different from his brothers. He believes you can have a life outside of marriage. No one else in the family believes that for their daughters."

"I'm sorry." Alyson felt tension grow between herself and the one person on her father's side of the family that she felt was truly her friend. Sumaya's words made her feel guilty.

"It's not your fault. You can post pictures of yourself in your bathing suit and not get in trouble..." Sumaya sighed as she rolled over onto her back.

"Are you kidding me?" Alyson's tone brought Sumaya to her side again to study her cousin's face. "I was in so much trouble!"

"You were? I thought you never were in trouble for anything!"

"I can't tell you how many times my mom has given me speeches about family honor and making decisions based on how it will reflect on grandfather."

"What's it like living in America and trying to be good around all of those crazy teenagers?" Sumaya was intrigued.

"Stressful, mostly. I never know what my friends are going to suggest that I'll have to say I can't do. But I have a reputation now, so I don't have to worry about it as much. Everyone knows me as the boring girl who never does anything. It works."

"Don't you have friends you hang out with?"

"I have Danielle. She's the only person I really spend time with these days. I have a job now, so that keeps me busy."

"I guess maybe our lives are a little bit alike." Sumaya gave Alyson a small smile. "And be careful while you're here; I know the uncles will be watching you extra close now that you're older..."

Alyson was so focused on her deep breathing as the plane landed she almost forgot where she was. The face and voice of Sumaya disappeared from her mind, and she quickly gathered her things together. As she followed the rest of the passengers off the aircraft, she wondered if Sumaya would know how to deal with something like this.

"I can tell you've been crying," said Danielle as she hugged her friend by the baggage claim. The words caused Alyson to break down all over again. Danielle held her tightly as Alyson hid her face in Danielle's shoulder and sobbed. "It's okay. I'm right here."

The girls stood back from each other, and Alyson gave Danielle a heartbreaking frown. Instinctively, Danielle wrapped her arm around Aly's shoulders and led her out of the airport with Aly's one bag. They didn't talk much in the car, both anxious to get to Danielle's apartment and hide within its walls. They knew this visit was not going to be a normal visit.

"So." Danielle came into the living room with two blankets, two bowls, two spoons and one carton of ice cream. "Whatever you want to say, go ahead and say it."

"I don't want to be pregnant." It was the first complete thought Alyson could verbalize. Alyson focused on the corner of the room and bit the knuckle of her pointer finger in an attempt to keep her emotions steady. She cleared her throat and took several deep breaths while Danielle waited patiently. "M-my dad's... My dad's family... I know they will be furious at me for what I've done, but it's possible to keep them from finding out if I can just get myself back together. I'll be fine. Eventually."

Danielle nodded.

"If I am pregnant, though... It's not just me trying to wade through emotional baggage anymore. It affects everyone. I won't stay at my job. I won't go home. I would have to find somehow to just disappear without people worrying about me." Alyson's eyes burned, but she refused to cry. "And I'm only saying this now because if I am pregnant, I don't want to have this conversation ever again."

It was finally time for the tears to win.

"I'm twenty-two years old. I *will* keep my baby. I will be a mother. I want to be a mom!" There was a terrible battle of conflicting emotions that fought in Alyson's soul. "It just wasn't supposed to be like this."

"I know, Aly." Danielle leaned forward to hug her friend. "Whatever happens, I'm going to be by your side."

"Thanks, Elle." Alyson took a deep breath and let it out slowly. "Especially for just letting me come and be with you."

"You didn't actually give me a choice," Danielle joked. A tiny smile appeared on her friend's face. "You know my home is always your home, no matter where I live."

Alyson looked down and swallowed hard, her heart thankful, but terrified.

"Can I ask you a question?"

"Yes! Yes, of course." Alyson quickly returned her gaze to her friend.

"If you are pregnant, will you tell Jamie about the baby?"

Aly's stomach dropped, and she felt herself grow physically light-headed at the question. This was the part of the trip that she dreaded more than anything. The pregnancy test that lay in her duffle bag didn't scare her as much as the full details of that night did.

"Um..."

Danielle waited, twisting the end of her sleeve nervously.

"I... I don't know who the dad will be."

Danielle watched Alyson's face go white. Her breath shuddered as she exhaled.

"You slept with more than one person?"

Alyson nodded hesitantly. Her eyes darted towards the corners of the room in search of a trash can while the nausea washed over her like the waves of an angry ocean. She bolted from the couch and into the kitchen. Danielle could hear her as she threw up. Alyson was careful to avoid eye contact as she walked back into the room.

"So... do you want to talk about it?"

"Not really." Aly gave a sardonic laugh. "But I need to tell at least one person."

Alyson took several deep breaths, and her face twitched while she steadied herself for her story.

"I loved spending the day with Jamie. Everything was... perfect. More than perfect. Nothing happened until we were at the club after the show. We were caught up in the moment and..." Alyson bit her lip and swallowed hard. "He knew I was a virgin. It was a big deal to him to be my first time. I thought that meant something."

Aly fiddled with the spoon that was for the forgotten ice cream as she tried to distract herself from what she was saying.

Danielle frowned. The simple fact that Alyson had agreed to sleep with Jamie told Danielle how strong Alyson's feelings for the young man had been. Jamie had done something to Alyson's heart that no one else had ever done. The story came out haltingly and in spurts. The details were vague, but Danielle let her friend say what she wanted.

"I'm really sorry Jamie did that to you." Danielle watched as Alyson pressed a Kleenex against her eyes. "What he did was wrong, and you didn't deserve that. You didn't deserve anything that happened that night." Danielle reached forward to hold Alyson's hands in her own. "We're going to get through all of this somehow. Together. We're going to figure this out."

"What if I'm pregnant? How are we going to figure out a baby?" Alyson wanted to be comforted by her friend, but her heart drowned in what if's. Her forehead ached from the worry lines that creased it. "What are they going to tell my students? My old neighbors? I've completely ruined my family's name." Alyson's sigh was deep. "This is so much bigger than anything we've ever had to figure out. There could be a child, Elle."

"Yes, there could b-... Wait..." Danielle stopped mid-sentence and looked directly into Alyson's eyes, as if to read her mind and find the answer to her question.

"What?"

Danielle continued to stare.

"What?!"

"What form of protection did you use? I mean... I know neither of us ever planned on having sex before we were married, but the guys... They would think about things like that, but obviously you think you're pregnant."

"Oh!" A light dawned in Alyson's eyes. "Oh, uh... I had this bottle in my bathroom back home." Alyson went over to her suitcase to get the bottle of birth control pills. She walked back to the couch and handed them to her friend. "They had been in there since I moved in, they belonged to the girl who lived there before me. I knew they were there so... so, I told the boys, well Tommy and Jamie anyway... I told them that I was taking it. I did take it when I got back! I did! It was supposed to have worked..."

"Aly." Danielle's face fell. "They could have had STD's, for one. That was incredibly dumb of them. And for two, you have to be taking birth control for months before they help!"

"I-I don't..." Alyson struggled to understand.

"You can't just take these and expect them to keep you from getting pregnant right away." Danielle read the label then looked back to her friend. "Besides, these pills are four years old. They expire after a year, or something! Remember Cassie from high school? That's how she got pregnant! You can't... Oh, Aly. How could you not know? I mean, why would you know? You never needed to know. You didn't even know what condoms looked like until last year..."

All of the color drained from Alyson's face. "Wh-what?"

Danielle drew her eyebrows together apologetically.

"You mean they... like... They're useless?" Alyson's mouth was dry as she forced her words to form into a coherent sentence.

"Unless by some miracle..." Danielle stopped when Alyson shut her eyes and shook her head back and forth forcefully.

"No! No, Elle."

"What?"

"No..." Tears brimmed in Alyson's eyes, and she covered her face with her hands.

Danielle set the bottle of pills onto the coffee table and scooted next to Alyson. She knew how scared Alyson was to be pregnant.

"*Life* is a miracle!" Alyson looked up as she spoke, her hand touching her neck where the lump in her throat was throbbing. "Life. Children. Babies. Those are miracles. Having a baby in your womb..."

She choked on her words and covered her face with her hands as she began to cry again.

"I guess..." Alyson sniffed and pulled back. "I guess if I'm pregnant... it's in spite of... myself."

Her heart was torn when she thought about the possibility of being a mother. It had been a dream since she was a little girl.

"I never, ever wanted to feel this way about a baby. I n-never imagined feeling anything but e-excitement for a child. I can't believe this."

Alyson let her shoulders drop as she exhaled sharply. She allowed Danielle to put an arm around her as she stared down at her feet. She was used to fighting on her own, but she was so, so tired.

"Do you feel better now that you've talked about it?" The question was tentative.

"A little better, I guess. Now I have to own up to it though, and that's hard. Because I always thought I was better than that."

"I wish I knew what to say."

"Just let me cry, and talk, and hug me, and hold my hand while I pee on a stick." Alyson sat back up and felt Danielle's arm fall from her shoulders. "I don't know what to say either. I made a huge mess."

The girls ate their ice cream while they drifted away in their thoughts. Alyson could tell that Danielle was upset by the way she merely played with the food in her bowl. After pretending to eat for five minutes, Danielle took their bowls and put them in the kitchen. Alyson was grateful to be in bed after a long day and lay on her back next to her friend. The bed moved when Danielle flipped onto her side to see Alyson's profile in the dark.

"Do you think Jamie cared about you at all?"

"I don't know." Aly was thoughtful. "I thought he did. All the way up to the moment he walked out the door. I haven't heard from him in six weeks, so I'm guessing that he was just playing me the whole time because I'm an idiot."

"You're not an idiot. He's the stupid one because he let you go. I told you that."

The girls were quiet for a minute.

"He didn't just let me go, though, he..." Alyson didn't know how she could want someone and despise someone so badly at the same time. "I'm dead to him."

Chapter three
"Okay. Breathe."

The next morning Alyson woke up before Danielle and slipped out from under the covers to sit on the couch in the living room. She pulled the pregnancy test out of her bag and set it on the coffee table. She took a few minutes to stare at the innocuous package and grasp the fact that the results from the tiny object inside of the box could irrevocably change everything. It was a little disconcerting to think about such a small thing confirming or denying what the rest of her life was going to look like.

Alyson leaned back on the couch and began typing on her phone. Jamie's face appeared at her bidding, and Alyson sucked in her breath. An ache formed instantly in the pit of her stomach. She set the phone down onto the couch and forced herself to breathe. Inhale. Exhale. In and out. After counting to ten, she retrieved her phone and looked at the screen again.

She stroked his face gently. She missed him so deeply sometimes she was afraid she would go insane if she didn't hear his voice.

"You miserable, horrible man. I miss you."

It had been a few weeks since Alyson last let herself look up the young man, and this time she was doing it in the name of research. If the pregnancy test was positive, she wanted to know what he had been up to before she called him.

"'Having a blast here in Michigan.'" Alyson read the last tweet out loud. She scoffed. "Why such a blast, Jamie? Did you find another girl on another dance floor?"

Alyson's chin quivered as she stared at the words until they became nothing more than blurred lines through her tears. She wiped at them angrily, mad that he was still able to make her feel so much.

"Remember when you tweeted about how much fun you had in Minnesota? Huh?" Alyson questioned the picture of the man. "You're so stupid. So, so stupid. Why do I still want to be with you?"

With a sigh, Alyson put her phone back down and stood to her feet. Her stomach rolled, and she quickly made her way to the bathroom. She knelt by the toilet, throat burning and eyes watering, screaming silently at the man who ruined her life. Had he made her pregnant? Had it been one of the other two? Did her and Garret even sleep together? Whose child could she potentially be carrying?

Alyson heard Danielle get up after she flushed the toilet. The girl stumbled sleepily into the bathroom and pushed one corner of her mouth up into a tired half-smile.

"You okay?"

"Just the normal morning routine." Alyson washed her hands slowly. "But I do need to eat something as soon as I can because I'm starving, and I'm going to barf again if I don't eat something soon."

"Yeah, sure." Danielle led the way out into the kitchen where the two girls grabbed some cereal and took it into the living room to eat on the couch. Danielle flopped down and pulled a blanket on top of her, making Alyson's phone fall to the floor. "Oh, sorry."

"It's okay. It's tough." Alyson was too busy pouring milk over her cereal to notice what Danielle was doing.

"Alyson." The voice was serious.

"Hmm?" Alyson shoved a huge bite of cereal into her mouth and looked over at her friend. She saw her phone in Danielle's hand with Jamie's picture on the screen. Alyson stopped chewing and looked down before she forced her mouthful of breakfast down past the lump in her throat.

"Do you do this often?"

"No." Alyson shook her head. "I was only looking so that I knew where he would be when I call him later. I mean... if I have to call him later..."

"I'm nervous about the fact that you might have to talk to him again." Danielle stared down at the famous singer she had once been a fan of. "I know you still probably have a little bit of feelings left for him."

"Little bit?" Alyson gave a short laugh. "I gave him everything. I feel... I feel everything for him. I don't know if I want to punch him in the face, or have him hug me, if I want to scream at him for being such a jerk or cry on his shoulder. I see these pictures of him, and I read about him, and I want to cry because I'm in agony over the fact that I'm still in love with a man who ruined me."

"In love?"

"I don't know." Alyson let out a sigh and looked away. "Is this love? Maybe it's just me not having any closure. Whatever it is, I feel it everywhere, and I just want it to stop."

"I wish I could help." Danielle's voice was quiet.

"You are helping," insisted Alyson as she put a hand on Danielle's leg. "You're the only one who can help. We're going to do it... somehow. You're all I have right now."

The girls sat quietly, lost in their slowly forming, early morning thoughts.

"So, should we go for it?" Alyson broke the silence and pointed at the pregnancy test on the coffee table. "Sitting here thinking isn't going to help me right now."

"What are you thinking about?" Danielle pressed gently.

"How I have no idea who the father will be." Alyson paused. "How I'll have to leave and go somewhere far enough away that I can protect everyone from knowing what I've done. Keep them from being disappointed and shamed..."

"You can come live with me."

"People would look for me here," said Alyson sadly.

"I could hide you under my bed."

Alyson gave Danielle a look that said she was thankful to not be alone. She took a deep breath and pushed herself up to stand on her feet. With the little package in her hand, she walked down the hall towards the bathroom. She was ready for the moment of truth.

The girls sat side by side on the bathroom floor while the pregnancy test sat on the counter. Alyson held onto Danielle's arm so tightly her fingers left marks on Danielle's skin. She focused on the breath in her lungs to remain calm. For weeks she had brushed the clues aside and told herself to not get carried away. Her period hadn't come, she was constantly tired, hungry and emotional, but this was the most difficult heartbreak she had ever experienced in her life; that had to count for something, right? She chewed on her lips nervously.

"Do you think Jamie will answer if you have to call him?" Danielle asked as they waited.

"I have no idea." The girl kept her eyes on the pregnancy test as she spoke. "He could have my number blocked for all I know."

"Do you think you're going to be okay talking to him again?" She looked over at Alyson.

"Yeah. I'll be fine." Alyson gulped silently.

"Alyson, you don't have to tell him if you don't..."

"I do," Alyson cut in. "I can't just not tell someone they fathered a child."

"That's true, but I'm just worried it's going to be too hard for your heart."

"I know, Elle." Alyson blinked the tears away and leaned her head on Danielle's shoulder.

"One line!" Danielle jumped. She pointed eagerly at the one line that appeared slowly on the test.

Aly sat up. Was this about to happen? There could be a baby, a child, a real live human inside of her. Someone that was half her and half a man she barely knew. For the rest of her life, she would be the mother of this baby and be their family.

For the rest of my life...

"A-Aly... Aly..." Danielle leaned forward and stared. "Alyson."

The girl didn't have to move to see the second line appear slowly on the circle of the test. There it was; she was going to have a baby. Tears of an overwhelming mix of emotions ran down her face as she stared at the two lines. She let go of Danielle's arm and gingerly touched her stomach.

For the past six weeks she had told herself that a child would ruin everything and hurt everyone. Now she could let herself feel the motherly instincts that she knew were inside of her. This truly was a miracle. A terrifying miracle.

"Baby," she whispered and closed her eyes.

Danielle's face was wet with tears as she watched her friend cradle her womb and weep silently. She quickly took a picture with her phone. She wanted her friend to remember just how special of a moment that was forever.

"I'm going to be a mom, Elle." Alyson finally looked up and met her friend's gaze. Her voice was thick as she spoke

"Congratulations!" Danielle hugged her friend tightly. The two cried until Alyson started to laugh.

"Well, I guess that means the throwing up should stop eventually." The laughter stopped, and she sighed. "And I guess that means I'm going to have to call Jamie."

"Are you sure you want to call him right now?" Danielle hesitated. "Maybe you should wait until it's a bit easier for you..."

"No. I just need to call him and get it over with. The sooner I do it, the sooner I can stop thinking about it."

Phone in hand, Alyson pushed the call button next to Jamie's name while Danielle watched over her shoulder. No one answered, and Alyson chickened out of leaving a voicemail. She verbalized all of the millions of possibilities that could keep Jamie from answering her call while she waited another twenty minutes before she tried again. Secretly, Danielle was glad Jamie hadn't answered, but she knew Alyson wouldn't get a moment's rest until she got through to him. The two friends moved themselves and the pregnancy test to the living room before calling again. Again, no answer.

"I have to go to class." Danielle looked at the clock and picked up her backpack from beside the door. "Are you going to be okay? I'm only going to be gone for three hours."

"Yeah." Alyson didn't know if she was going to be okay or not, but she let her friend leave with a smile. She watched Danielle through the window; her knees felt a bit weak as Danielle disappeared from sight. She had to breathe deeply to keep herself from losing control of her stomach again.

Alyson paced the living room, her hands on her stomach and her phone in her pocket. Over and over she whispered to her baby how much she loved it, all the while rubbing her hands over where the baby was with soft, gentle motions. What kind of mother would she be? Would her baby look and act like her? Tears tumbled down from her eyelashes as she pictured a little baby in her arms, seconds old and crying out for food and comfort as bright lights and loud sounds greeted its senses for the first time. She had never seen a baby right after it was born, but she had seen pictures and she could hardly imagine what it would be like to have an infant placed in her arms as her very own.

Her train of thought took a turn towards the three young men who all had a claim to the child, and she wondered how they would take the news of the possibility of being a father. As far as she knew, Jamie wasn't aware of what she had done with the others after he left her.

That's going to be a fun story to tell.

"He probably won't even care." Alyson spoke out loud to help the apartment not feel so empty. "He probably won't care about the baby either. He'll probably be very happy to know that I expect him and the others to do nothing except forget about me."

One hour passed before Alyson tried to call Jamie again. She promised herself that if he didn't answer, she would leave a voicemail this time. The phone beeped, and Jamie's automated message began to play.

"Well, now I won't have to worry about his reaction..." Alyson muttered to herself as she pressed the phone tighter against her ear. The beep sounded, and Alyson began to talk, "Hey, it's me, Aly. I mean, Alyson. Alyson Abidi. Sorry to call you out of the blue like this but..."

She froze. Her mind went blank. How did you casually tell someone over voicemail that he or two of his friends could be the father of your child? With a panicky breath, Alyson quickly pulled the phone away from her ear and hung up. She clutched the phone to her chest and tried to steady herself.

"Okay, Aly. Okay. Breathe."

The phone began to ring in her hands, and she jumped. She looked at the screen and swallowed hard; it was Jamie.

"Aly!" A voice Alyson had been dying to hear for weeks now came through the phone. "Hello!"

"H-hi." It felt all wrong.

"Yeah, sorry you went through to voicemail just then." His tone was too chill for Alyson. "So, you've been trying to get through to me this morning?"

"Yeah." Alyson wondered if she sounded as casual as he did. She didn't want to sound that way; this was important and she wanted him to know that she was contacting him for the sake of the baby, not because of their two-month whatever-it-was they had shared. "I need to talk to you about something pretty important."

"Oh?" There was a slight tremor in Jamie's voice.

"I'm... uh..." Alyson stopped. She closed her eyes and bit her lip.

"You there?" asked Jamie after a moment's silence.

"Yeah," Alyson spoke softly. "I'm here."

"Well... what's going on?" The laugh was nervous.

Alyson went over to the window and stared out into the parking lot that was next to Danielle's apartment building. Nothing and no one looked familiar and she hugged her arm around herself. She looked up at the sky and blinked back her tears. Why did the sky always seem so unchanging when life could turn out so differently than you expected? She had seen that same sun hung in the sky since she was a little girl, and when she was with Jamie they had felt its hot rays touch their skin as fervently as they had touched each other. And then when dawn came the next morning, it was the same sun that rose and saw a broken Alyson getting on an airplane alone.

"Aly?"

"You left me."

Now it was time for Jamie to be quiet.

"What h-happened with you?" All she was supposed to do was tell him about the baby, but she couldn't stop herself. "One minute you're making love to me and the next you're walking out of the room and you... you n..." Her voice cracked and she hated that he could hear her becoming emotional. "You never came back! And I just... I just want to know why."

"Wow. Fair enough." Jamie let out a deep breath. "I did want to apologize to you for that. That was incredibly wrong of me. You're an amazing girl, and I should never have walked out on you... after... what we did."

"Why, though?" Alyson shut her eyes and leaned her head against the window pane. They used to talk together so easily, now it was awkward and uncomfortable. "What went wrong?"

"I went wrong. It was me, Aly, not you. Not you in the least. I was the... I mean, I had been with Beth for years and then you for like, two... two months. You were the first girl I slept with since I left my ex, and I didn't know how... how to feel. Aly, I rushed things. I think you could feel that, too. I was foolish, and lost my head, and... you know what I mean, yeah?"

"I think what you're trying to say is neither of us was ready to sleep together. Is that what you're saying?" Alyson put her free hand to her forehead and rubbed at the places that ached the most. "Are you saying that I reminded you of your ex-girlfriend and you couldn't handle it? Are you saying that Rebound Aly's purpose was completed at the time of taking her virginity?"

"Aly, please," begged Jamie. "I'm not proud of the way I ended things, but I did care about you."

"I cared about you, too. I also really cared about who I gave myself to. I have never regretted a decision or hated myself for something more than what I agreed to do with you that night." The words were so strong, and Alyson felt her cheeks grow hot as she spoke passionately. "You had been so a-amazing, and I felt safe with you! What was I supposed to do when all of a sudden you were done with me without giving me a reason or explanation?"

A sharp exhale could be heard from the other end of the phone call, and Alyson wished she could see his face. Deep down she didn't want to hurt him, she just wanted to hear him say he had been in the wrong, he was sorry for his silence and he would do whatever it took to make it right with her. She waited patiently for him to speak up again.

"Oh, love, I'm so sorry." The cool and casual tone was gone and Alyson couldn't decide if he was crying or if she was just hearing the sound of regret.

The term of endearment he had used on her hundreds of times before struck a chord in Alyson's heart, and she felt a tiny twinge of longing. "I didn't know how to explain what I was feeling to you that night. And I'm sorry for that. I'm very, very sorry."

"Yeah, I understand." Alyson wanted to tell him she forgave him and it was going to be okay, but it wasn't. Not really. Not yet. "It's going to take some time, Jay, but I... I do understand."

"Thanks, Aly." Jamie sounded like he was smiling. Alyson's heart broke a little.

"Yeah." Alyson's voice was low enough that she didn't know if Jamie heard her before he began to talk again.

"I'm glad we've had this talk. I really am. I, uh, have been thinking about it... I mean, just hoping you're okay and... you know? It's good to know you're all right and all is forgiven." Jamie sounded anxious to have the conversation end.

"Jamie, we need to talk about something else." Alyson glanced back over at the pregnancy test and put a hand to her stomach. It didn't feel real.

"Excuse me?" Jamie asked for clarification.

"There are more things we need to talk about than besides just us." Aly rested her forehead on her hand. She sucked her cheeks in and pulled the mouthpiece of the phone away to cover the sound of her crying.

"What's wrong? Are you okay?"

Alyson couldn't stop the tears and she stifled a sob, unable to answer Jamie's questions. She knew he heard her crying when he let out a sigh and a low, "aw."

"I'm s-sorry." Alyson did her best to talk through the lump in her throat.

"No, don't be. What's wrong?" Jamie's voice didn't sound casual or regretful anymore; the same tenderness Alyson had fallen for at the beginning of their friendship was there again for the first time since they started talking.

"Wait, I don't want to do this over the phone. When is a good time to call you over Skype?"

"We'll be leaving for the venue in about three hours so I think now is the best time. What is this about?"

"Are..." Alyson paused. Did she really want to ask her next question? "Can the other guys join you for this call?"

"The others? As in Tommy and Ed?"

"Well, I guess just Garret and Tommy."

"Gar and Tom? What did they do?"

"Just get on Skype."

Alyson went over to her computer and opened it. Her hands shook. She could hear Jamie muttering in the background as he tapped on keys. Finally, his avatar lit up, and he called her.

"H-hi." Alyson waved and put her phone down. She was very aware of the fact that she was in her pajamas with her hair pulled back in a messy bun. Jamie had seen her like that before, but this felt different.

"So good to see your face." Jamie smiled sincerely at the girl who was on his computer screen. He knew he had missed her, but this hit him harder than he thought it would. "And since we're sort of face to face, I want to apologize again for what happened the night I brought you out to L.A. I am very sorry."

"Thanks." Alyson knew what she was about to tell him was going to be hard. "Since the guys aren't with you yet, I'm going to tell you something that... I-I need to apologize for as well."

"Is this what you didn't want to tell me over the phone?"

"Part of it... yes." Alyson spoke slowly. She wasn't so sure that Jamie wasn't going to care about what she had done with the others. At the beginning of the conversation she thought maybe he wouldn't mind, but now he was watching her with those beautiful eyes of his and smiling just enough to let her know that she made him happy. Her heart squeezed at the thought of him still having feelings for her.

"The lads won't be here for another five minutes, so go ahead, love." Again, the pet name slipped out before Jamie could stop it.

"I-I slept with Tommy." Alyson cradled her face in her hands, but forced herself to look Jamie in the eye. He had owned up to his end of the horrible night; she needed to take responsibility for her part.

Alyson watched Jamie's face twitch and his jaw tense up as he looked at his fists that lay in his lap. Her heart pounded, expecting him to lash out at her for what she had done. He looked back up at her face, and she braced herself for the oncoming storm of words.

"I guess neither of us enjoy thinking back on that night." Jamie's voice was quiet.

Alyson's eyes filled with tears as she realized that he wasn't going to take out his anger on her.

"Jamie, I'm so sorry." Alyson tried to keep her tears from falling, but she couldn't stop them. She knew it wasn't fair to Jamie to cry during her apology. "I-I don't know what to say to fix this except that I'm sorry."

"And I forgive you." Jamie's voice was tight as he kept it even.

"I'm so sorry." Alyson sniffed and pressed her lips together to stop them from quivering. There was real hurt in his eyes from her actions, and it made her feel sick. Maybe he had cared about her. Maybe he still did. "I should have never done that, no matter how I was feeling."

"Come now, love. It's all forgiven." Jamie gave himself a little shake and forced a grim smile. She knew he was smarting all over on the inside from the news that she told him, yet he brushed it aside to focus on her.

Danielle was right, I'm not ready for this. I'm not... I'm not ready. I should have waited.

There was a loud knock on Jamie's hotel room door and someone entered. Jamie called out a greeting and patted the bed next to him. The next thing Alyson knew, Garret was on the bed beside Jamie waving hello. He froze when he recognized her. All the color drained from his face.

"Gar, its Aly. You know... You remember her?" Jamie introduced them half-heartedly.

"Y-yeah... I remember."

Omitting the fact that she had maybe slept with Garret was simply because it was his secret, too. If Garret had waited thirty or more seconds to come into the room, she probably would have told Jamie just to have full disclosure, but there he was, staring hard into the computer's camera. She could almost hear him begging her with his thoughts to stay silent, reminding her of her promise.

"Is Tom coming?" Jamie asked.

"Yeah, he's coming." Garret shifted nervously. "Him and Ed stopped for food."

As it stood, only three people knew what had happened between herself and Garret; the two of them and Danielle. If she didn't potentially have Garret's baby inside of her, Alyson would never have dreamed of sharing what had happened with the others.

The three of them sat there in an awkward silence. Garret looked everywhere except for the computer, and Jamie's jaw worked as he pulled at his lip. He was wearing his thinking face. Alyson sat quietly and tried to count her breaths as her mind pondered how Garret was feeling in that moment. Danielle was still in touch with Serenity. She wondered if the girlfriend would ever find out what happened.

"How is the school year going?" Jamie broke the silence abruptly. "You started back in August, yeah?"

"It's been going fine."

"Good. I bet you're a great... I bet you do really well at it."

"Thanks." Alyson looked down at her hands. She hated this.

"Being a teacher sounds cool." Garret sounded absentminded.

"I love being a teacher. It's my most favorite job in the world." A lump pressed against the sides of Aly's throat. It was the dream job she was about to walk away from.

"Are you crying?" Garret asked, peering at the screen.

"I just love my job," Alyson fibbed, forcing a laugh to cover the tears.

A look of inquiry passed across Jamie's face when he heard Alyson's excuse, as if he didn't think it made sense. Still, he kept quiet and smiled sadly at her. The silence came back, and Alyson could feel herself growing sick. Now that it was almost time to tell them about the baby, saying it straight out and hanging up seemed a bit harsh. Her mind scrambled for a good way to go about it; should she go for the serious approach, or a more lighthearted way? Her thoughts were interrupted by another knock on Jamie's door.

"Come in! We're waiting for you!" shouted Jamie. "Aly and I just had a very interesting conversation about what happened when she was in L.A."

"It's Aly?" Tommy's voice could be heard from off camera. "I thought you guys weren't together."

"Well, here we are, and you have some explaining to do." Jamie's glare towards his friend didn't keep him from joining him for the conversation. "What were you thinking?"

"What does it matter what I was thinking? It's done now." Tommy's voice sounded tense. "You weren't there, mate."

"Jamie, it was me, too," said Alyson. "I mean, I was okay with it. We... decided together."

"He should have known better!"

"So should I have." Alyson refused to let the young man take the full brunt for their actions. "But it happened, and I can't change it. Believe me, I would if I could."

The girl looked up to see Garret's face and saw him sitting with his head down. She was afraid he might be sick as he listened to the shouting that was taking place around him.

"Really, Tom? Do you sleep with all my ex-girlfriends?" Jamie was still peeved.

"Jamie, you broke her heart! I was just trying to help!" Tommy's voice was defensive.

"Yeah right!" Jamie spat out.

"You can't just yell at me, Jamie, this was..."

"I can yell if I want!"

"We can talk this out..."

"No! You want to talk? Are you kidding me?"

"Us shouting isn't going to help anything!"

"You were lying to my face! I can't belie-..."

"Stop!" Alyson's shout was closer to a desperate scream. Tears wetted her red cheeks.

Everyone in the room froze.

"I'm pregnant!"

All they could hear was Alyson's heavy breathing as she cried. Jamie hid his face in his hands and shook his head.

"Oh my..." Garret moaned almost silently.

"I took the pills like you said, Jay. I swear I took them." The girl pressed the heels of her hands against her eyes for a moment, then looked back at the guys. "I said that I knew what to do. I thought I did! But apparently, I'm an idiot and had n-no clue! And then I-I found out that th-the pills were expired which means that they don't work anymore. I didn't know. I-I didn't know."

"You're pregnant." Jamie looked up, his eyes watery. His hands clenched in his lap as he shook his head. "I can't believe this. I should have known better."

"Jamie, this isn't your fault any more than it is mine. We all made the choice..."

"I know, Aly, but I told you it was okay! I was the one who made the mistake! I should have never..."

Alyson held her breath as she waited for Jamie to finish his sentence, her heart pounding in her ears. The ache twisted deep as the regret on his face grew more visible with each passing moment. He regretted her, just like she regretted him.

"I should have stopped before I started. Before I started any of this."

The words were like a slap on the face, and Alyson turned away from the camera to try and keep herself together. She didn't want him to see how badly he was hurting her.

"But... who is the father?" Tommy spoke up.

"I don't know." Alyson's whisper was rough. She cleared her throat before she spoke again, "Any one of you could be."

The young men looked around at each other, but stopped when they saw Garret's ashen face. He had the most sincere look of agony that they had ever seen. There was a deafening silence as no one said a word, each one thinking the same thing. Alyson was torn between wanting to feel sorry for Garret and holding tightly to the fact that he had been the one to make her drink. If the baby was his, he only had himself to blame.

"Did you mean Gar as well?" Jamie asked cautiously.

Alyson didn't say anything, waiting to see if Garret wanted to be the one to tell his friends. He had the most to lose in the situation.

"Garret?" Tommy looked to the young man.

He remained silent.

"Yes, I meant Garret as well." The quiet words were barely audible.

She wondered if Garret thought often about what they had done, trying to fill in the blanks with his imagination. She wondered if he was plagued with the same nightmares that chased her down each night as she slept. She had promised not to tell what had happened between them, but there was a possibility that her baby could be his. They didn't know.

"Really?" Garret was Jamie's most trusted friend. There was hurt in his eyes and in his tone as he spoke. "You slept with Aly that night?"

"We, uh... we don't know if... if we did, or, or, or not." Garret wiped at his eyes.

"Wow, I was not expecting that," said Tommy.

The news of the baby no longer seemed happy or important like it had when the second line on the pregnancy test first appeared. Her stomach churned as their discussion went back and forth, growing in volume. She closed her eyes, trying to block it out. The deep breathing did little to stop the tears that slipped down her face. She could hear them continue to talk as if she wasn't there. Someone started swearing, and another shouted defensively.

If only I hadn't gone to L.A. If only I hadn't lost my head. If only I hadn't been so dumb. If only I had known that the pills were bad...

"Jamie, she's crying." Tommy's voice was gruff as he pointed out the girl to his friend.

"Ah, Aly." Jamie turned his attention back to the video call. "I forgot you were there. Sorry."

"D-don't be sorry." The girl took a jagged breath and opened her eyes. "I just gave you all some pretty shocking news."

"I'd say," Jamie agreed, showing his nerves by running his hands through his hair and pulling at the collar of his shirt.

"I just, I just wanted you guys to know. That's all." Alyson clicked the hang-up button before anyone could try to say anything else.

She sat with her hand on the touchpad of the laptop, reeling from what she had just experienced. They obviously didn't care about her or the baby, just like Alyson had known all along. She was alone in this. Her mind remembered how gently Jamie asked her if she was okay before the others joined him, and before he knew what she had done. Just the memory of his tenderness towards her made her heart come undone, and she crumpled into a ball on the floor.

"He hates me now! I kn-knew he would... I knew he would hate me if he ever found out what I did! I knew it!" She sobbed over and over. "I n-never want to see him or hear from him e-ever, ever, ever again!"

Alyson set her heart to move forward with her child on her own. She would figure something out. Danielle said they would. At that point, she was more willing to tell her family about the pregnancy than to ever have another conversation with Jamie. By the time Danielle returned home, Alyson was showered and dressed and watching a movie. She showed no signs of being upset as she mentioned how she had spoken to the guys and they were glad

Alyson didn't want them in the baby's life because they didn't want to be involved.

"Really? What a bunch of jerks," Danielle growled. She had already decided she was never going to talk about or support *Jupiter Waits* ever again.

"I want to be a mom. I want my baby." Alyson's tone was determined. "I don't need or expect them to be the fathers, but they did have a right to know. Now they know, and I'm moving on."

"Are you sure the guys aren't going to change their minds about being involved?"

"No." Alyson shook her head and looked down. "No, they're not."

Alyson knew after their conversation that she was nothing more than a nuisance that they were not wanting back in their lives.

"They're famous. They have successful careers. They live on the other side of the world. I'm just one girl out of a hundred that they met this summer while in the States. I can't imagine they would be interested in keeping me and my baby in their lives."

"Do you want them to give you money or something?"

"No." Alyson shook her head again as she spoke. "No. They have a right to know about the baby, but that's the only reason why I told them. I don't want to be their charity case."

"What are you going to do now?"

Aly shrugged. She was terrified. Tears gathered in her eyes. It was going to cost her to keep the child inside of her.

Chapter four
"You can't just fix this with an apology!"

Jamie marched Tommy and Garret out to the tour bus as soon as Alyson ended their Skype call. They had a concert that evening they had to put on without letting their fans know anything was wrong. It was almost as if they could hear the clock ticking as it counted down the minutes they had to figure this out. They all sat in the back of their bus and stared at each other solemnly.

"Well, thoughts, lads?" Jamie opened up the floor for discussion. His lips were pressed into a thin line, and there was no sparkle in his eyes. His jaw clenched and released as he waited for someone to say something. The more he thought about his friends being with Alyson, the angrier he became. She had been so special to him, and they had known that.

"What's going on?" Eddie walked onto the bus and slowly moved to join them.

"Alyson called him." Tommy was relieved to see Eddie. He motioned for him to sit down beside him on the couch.

"Really?" Eddie eyed Jamie's face and saw anger boiling under the surface. He already knew what Tommy had done, but he didn't know why Garret was there and why he was looking so miserable. Perhaps there was a statement that was going to have to be made. "Wha... What's going on?"

Jamie didn't look at Eddie as he ran his hands through his hair and huffed loudly. Tommy fidgeted and cleared his throat. It was clear that Tommy didn't want to be the one to share the news, but Eddie was looking at him and Jamie wasn't opening his mouth.

"She's... uh, she's pregnant." Tommy choked out the words.

"No!" Eddie looked from Tommy, to Jamie, then stopped on Garret's face. "She's pregnant?"

"Yes, Ed! Now if you don't mind, we've some talking to do," snapped Jamie. "Who would like to go first?"

No one moved.

"Have you got anything you want to say?" Eddie asked after a moment of silence.

"Sure, I've got loads, but I'm way too angry to say anything helpful at the moment." Jamie crossed his arms tightly across his chest, hoping to keep his words inside by holding himself back.

"Fair enough," Eddie mumbled, eying Garret and biting his tongue to keep from asking questions.

"I would pay a lot to know what I actually did with Alyson that night." Garret's tone wavered as he spoke. "We don't even know if we slept together... we don't even know if there's a real chance that I'm the dad or not."

Jamie closed his eyes. He was fuming.

"Have you told Serenity yet?" Tommy asked.

"How am I supposed to tell her? I was drunk one night and woke up next to my best mate's girl with most of our clothes off, and now she's pregnant."

Garret let out a shaky breath as he began to cry. Tommy shot Eddie a side look. Eddie met his friend's gaze and shrugged as he frowned. He hadn't even known that Garret had been alone with Aly until that moment.

"It's my fault. I got us drunk." Garret's throat constricted, and he couldn't talk anymore.

Jamie lifted his hands to his head and turned to face away from the others. He bit the insides of his cheeks and blinked at the watery film gathering over his eyes. His whole body was shaking as he struggled to keep from screaming.

"Did any of you wear protection?" asked Eddie.

Tommy shook his head, cheeks flaming.

"Ren was back in London, why would I have anything on me?"

"So, the baby could be anybody's."

"Thank you, Captain Obvious!" Jamie's words were harsh as he whirled back around, his eyes landing on Eddie and staring at him coldly. He didn't appreciate Eddie's intrusion into their meeting.

"Calm down, Eddie didn't do anything." Tommy gave Jamie a look.

"Good for him! Now he can sit there and gloat!" Jamie shot his words at the young man. "Honestly, Eddie, there's no point in you being here, so please…"

"I was with her that night, too, Jay," Eddie interrupted.

"What?" Jamie froze.

"I didn't sleep with her, but I was with her."

"At least someone cares about the fact that she was special to me!" Jamie's glare was pointed at Tommy.

"Jamie, I'm sorry! Okay? You don't ever look back once you're done with a girl and… and she… she was…" Tommy didn't know how to finish his sentence.

"To be fair, Jamie, you left her in a really bad spot. We were just trying to look out for her." Eddie was the only calm one at the moment.

"Oh, shut up!" Jamie argued back. "You don't have to sleep with someone to make them feel better!"

"You don't know what she went through after you left!" Tommy's voice rose. "You have no idea! Eddie tried to help her! I tried to help her!"

"And who blooming said she needed your help! Huh? Who even asked you?!" Jamie bellowed back.

"She was begging, Jamie!" Eddie stood to his feet, his gray eyes blazing as he stared Jamie down, blocking him from Tommy. "She was begging for help! I walked into that room after you left her and she was slammed, and, and, and in pieces!"

"Drunk?" Jamie's mouth gaped.

"Absolutely smashed, Jay, trying to numb her broken heart! You think I would turn around and leave her to it? She needed me! Needed someone!"

"Fine, but Tom…!"

"Tommy would never take advantage of anyone!" Eddie cut in. "Yes, he slept with your girl, but you'd walked out on her, and she wasn't yours anymore! You can't stand there and pretend as if you've a right to say who she can and cannot sleep with! It was her choice!"

Jamie bit his tongue to keep from shouting back. His head and his heart were throbbing. They didn't understand just how special Alyson was. They didn't know her.

"We didn't do it to hurt you or Alyson," Tommy put in, his voice tentative as he watched Jamie and Eddie glare at each other.

"There is something called respect..." Jamie's words came from between clenched teeth.

"Jamie! We've got to move on from this!" Garret shouted from the couch to break up the argument. "We all slept with the same girl, she's pregnant and any of us could be the father. What do we do?"

"She didn't seem to want us to do anything." Jamie masked the hurt with indignation. He hated that he had burned all his bridges with Aly. He hated that his best friends were now the ones causing him pain.

"Does she plan on keeping it?" Eddie's voice was quiet again as he looked around at the three other young men. He sat slowly back down in his seat. "Do we know if she wants you guys to be in the picture?"

"Why would she tell us if she wasn't going to keep it?" asked Tommy.

"Because she's a decent girl who does what is right," Jamie defended.

"Do you think she'll keep the baby?" Eddie asked again.

"I honestly don't know. Why, Ed? You think you can just waltz in and take care of everything like you did after I left her?" Jamie said bitterly.

Eddie didn't answer, his fingers playing with one of the rings that he wore on his hand. The silence stretched on as the young men stubbornly held onto their thoughts. Tension hung in the air like a thick fog, wrapping around each one and making it a bit hard to breathe.

"I haven't really thought about something like this happening to me before, but it's making me think. I want to do this right... if the baby is mine. I want to change, you know?" Tommy's confession broke the heavy quiet. "If the baby is mine, I want to be a part of his life."

The thought of Alyson's baby being the child of someone other than himself made Jamie's heart pound angrily. He didn't know how he felt about Alyson except he knew he wasn't cross at her. He was hurt, yes, but he had thrown the first blow.

He had spent the last month and a half trying to convince himself that he didn't miss the pretty girl with green eyes and freckles. Sometimes he would stare at his phone for long periods of time and remember how she sounded at midnight when she was tired and her voice turned rough, or how he could hear her smiling through her words. He missed the way she would laugh easily and share deeply, giving him glimpses into her beautiful and shadowed past.

"When was the first time you realized that there were bad things that couldn't be fixed or just go away?" he asked quietly one night as the darkness gave them courage to speak secrets. "Like, the first time you realized that life could hurt you?"

"When I was told that I couldn't cry." Alyson hadn't even had to think about her answer. "All I wanted to do was feel sad and grieve what I had lost, but I wasn't allowed to show how I felt. I was told to just move on and act like it never happened."

"What was it?"

"Someone close to me died." Alyson looked down at her lap and felt her lips quiver for a moment before she steadied them again. She swallowed the lump in her throat and looked back up into Jamie's eyes with a small smile.

"Who told you not to cry?" The young man listened intently.

"My parents. Tears weren't allowed for that kind of thing. It took me a long time to realize I could actually cry if I needed to. I still have to coach myself through letting myself feel things because all I could do as a kid was repress my emotions."

"Wow. That's..." Jamie shook his head and left his sentence unfinished.

"Detrimental?" Alyson offered with a crooked smile. "Yeah. Apparently it's not healthy to never talk about your feelings."

"You seem to be okay talking about your feelings now."

"It's because I trust you."

Jamie felt like someone had sucked the air out of his lungs. He wanted to protect that trust with everything inside of him, and be the one who listened to her late-night whispers forever. He had wanted to be her everything...

She bared her soul to you. Jamie rubbed his hands through his hair and tried to pace before he remembered he was still in the back of the tour bus with his three friends. They all had grim expressions on their faces, as if there was something they could fix if only they looked serious enough. They had shared so little with Alyson, but they were a part of everything now.

"Suppose she can't keep it?" Garret asked, bringing Jamie back to the conversation.

"Then we won't have to worry about anything." Even as the words came out, Jamie knew that he didn't want that to happen. Still, he added, "She has every right to do what works best for her."

"Do you think she would let me have the baby if she didn't...?" asked Tommy.

"Tommy, I don't know!" Jamie snapped. He exhaled sharply and looked away. He couldn't bear the thought of someone else raising Alyson's child.

A baby means that she's going to be in your life again for a long time... The thoughts were swirling. *What if that baby isn't yours and you're forced to watch her with one of your best mates for the next eighteen-plus years?*

Jamie sucked in his cheeks and stared the other direction. They all acted as if they had some sort of claim on Alyson's heart, but what did they know about her? Had they ever seen her laugh so hard she could hardly breathe? Had they ever heard her sing quietly to herself when she thought no one was listening? Had they ever had to catch their breath when they saw her dancing with that little smirk on her face because she knew she was being watched?

"I would imagine that she would let the father have the child if she wasn't going to keep it," said Eddie.

"I agree." Tommy sounded certain.

"You're in a band, and you travel three to four months every year; how would you raise a kid?"

Garret's question made the boys think.

"What makes you think Aly would want screw-ups like us to be in her life? She didn't want to get pregnant! Her whole life is about to change because of us! There is no woman in her right mind that would want guys like us to be anywhere near their child!"

Tommy and Eddie sat quietly. The pained look on his face as he stared at the ground was a hard pill for the lads to swallow.

"I have a headache," Jamie muttered to himself as he rubbed his forehead. "I don't see that there is anything else to discuss until we know what Alyson wants to do with the baby."

"Wait, Jamie." Eddie stood to his feet again and put his hand on Jamie's arm. "Not unless you're good with us. We don't want to leave until you've said what you want to say."

Jamie looked from one face to the next. None of them met his gaze.

"I started it. I was the one who ended things with Alyson. You probably showed her more care and compassion than I did that night." Jamie's voice was laced with bitter regret. "We've never had something like this happen before, and I trust that we've all learned from this."

"Absolutely," Tommy spoke up as Garret nodded.

"I need to have a bit of time to think on my own." He started for the exit of the bus. "I'll see you at soundcheck."

As soon as Jamie was a safe distance away from everyone, he let go of the tears he had been holding back. At first they were angry, burning his eyes as they squeezed out and rolled down his cheeks. Still, they did nothing to relieve the intensity of what he was feeling on the inside. The pressure in his chest was like a volcano, building and bubbling until it threatened to crack him open from the inside out. A yell of outrage tore past the pain and out into the open as he ran as fast as he could to as far away as he could get. He reached forward with his stride in desperation, making them as long as he could. His lungs began to burn.

It wasn't long before the tall, solid walls of the enclosed parking lot loomed in front of him, and his chase of freedom came to a stop. He slammed his body against the wall as he let out another cry. Right then the wall was not a source of protection, but a prison keeping him from escaping his past. He wanted to punch the wall, but knew better, so he smacked his open palm against it. He hit it hard, and his hand stung painfully, the skin turning red and splotchy before his eyes. His chest heaved to accommodate the rise and fall of his lungs as they begged for more air. He could hear himself struggling to catch his breath, blood rushing through his veins.

The throbbing in his hand was just beginning to fade when another burst of anger hit him. He turned against the wall once more, crying out as he beat his hand against the unmoving barrier. There was a slap for Garret, another for Eddie, and one last one for Tommy.

His vision blurred as he leaned his forehead against the gritty surface of the wall, tears and sweat mixing. They ran down his face and neck and into the collar of his shirt. He felt the anger slowly shift and fade into the most horrible feeling of sorrow and regret he had ever experienced. His legs lost their strength and took him to the ground, his fingers clawing at the wall as he fell. The asphalt caught him on his hands and knees. He slumped down, fresh tears welling up in his eyes. The drops tumbled down his lashes and onto the dusty parking lot as he stared at the ground.

"I ruined everything. I ruined it all." The whisper was hoarse as he pushed his confession past the lump in his throat.

He turned to lean back against the wall. His trembling hands covered his face as giant sobs welled up from the pit of his stomach. There was the anger, the regret, the loss, the loneliness, the hurt, the confusion...

He could still hear the breathless way Alyson had told him over the phone that she had finally decided that she wanted to see him again. He could still feel the tight grip of her arms as she wrapped them around his neck when they were reunited. Her smile had been so big when she ran towards him and threw herself into his embrace.

That night she had grabbed onto his arm as they passed through a crowd of people. He turned to make sure she was okay, and she met his gaze with a shy smile pulling at her lips. He drew her closer, keeping the distance between them small, as the look in her eyes told the room that she knew he wanted her beside him. And she was right; he did want her beside him. She was no longer a cute rebound girl he found on the dance floor; she was the one who caught his secret whispers with her gentle touch and stood steady and fearless in the midst of the chaos that whirled around him. He had never felt so safe or understood by someone like he did with Alyson Abidi.

He caught her gazing up at him with eyes that spoke volumes on how much she trusted him. Every time it happened he looked away with a lump in his throat. What he felt towards Alyson overwhelmed him. It made sense to keep their relationship in a safe zone and take their time, but Jamie had never been one to go slow when he knew what he wanted. He adored her, and she trusted him. *She* trusted *him*. Even after all the people in her life that had hurt her, she trusted him. He never intended to break that trust, but he had. He had shattered it like a mirror.

He certainly never planned on walking out on Alyson when she came to see him in California. It wasn't Alyson's job to distract him from the past and keep him from thinking about the girl he had split from, but she had done just that. For the last two months, Beth's spot had been forgotten and the pain of their ended relationship washed away in the newness of Alyson smile. And then, when they were sharing their most intimate moment, Alyson's face was replaced with the face of the girl Jamie was trying to forget. Her smell, her voice, the feel of her skin... it all slammed to the forefront of his brain, and he felt his lungs physically stop moving for a moment. Everything slowed to a stop, and he knew he couldn't stay. He wasn't one to fix problems, not when he could run from them and leave them in his past.

Alyson had just stood there, watching him gather his things and waiting for him to explain himself. He didn't have words or even coherent thoughts in his mind to share with her what he was feeling. He was going to try, honest he was, but when he turned around all he could see were those big eyes telling him that she trusted him. Still. Sometimes he tried to imagine what she must have felt when the door clicked shut behind him, and he never came back.

"I ruined her." Jamie's hands slipped down from his face, and he swiped at his tears with the end of his sleeve. "She gave me everything, and I left her."

Jamie wished he could have a strong drink.

"Now there's going to be a baby..."

Keeping it together on stage that night was a tough job for *Jupiter Waits*. Garret stood by the stage and watched, a knot growing in the pit of his stomach as the evening unfolded. Their concerts were normally filled with little jokes and stories where Jamie interacted with Eddie and Tommy in-between the songs, but that night, Jamie distanced himself from them. He sang and played to the crowd while giving the guys the cold shoulder and shooting several irritated looks in their direction throughout the night. Eddie tried more than once to get his attention and was blatantly ignored. The two musicians shared a concerned look as Jamie strummed a few chords on his guitar to start the next song.

Instead of singing, Jamie stood in a daze, his mind going back to that morning when Alyson wiped the tear off her face as she apologized for sleeping with his friends. The others had been careful not to let him know, but there had been hints that made sense now. It stung to think about. They were friends. The regret had been clear on Alyson's face as her eyes pleaded with him to not be angry at her.

He knew he didn't have a right to blame her for what she did after he left her the way that he did. He also knew that if he hadn't left her, she never would have slept with the others. At the same time, all he wanted to do was shout at her and ask her if she had felt the same spark with the others as she had felt with him? Did it feel as intimate and honest with them as it had with him? A hand touched his arm and he realized that he was still on stage in front of hundreds of people who were waiting for him to sing.

"Sorry, guys. Lost in thought." He tried to chuckle as he stepped away from Eddie and started the song over again.

"You okay?" Eddie stood in front of him, trying to get his friend to look him in the eyes as the music played. Jamie stomped past the young man and began to sing, his voice hitting a wrong note.

Tommy accidentally bumped into Jamie as they squeezed through a narrow doorway while they were leaving the stage between their main set and the encore. Jamie growled out a few words and began to stomp off to the far side of the room, but Eddie's quick reach grabbed him and spun him around.

"Bug off, Ed!" Jamie snapped.

"No! You need to listen!" Eddie's mild manners were nowhere to be seen as he pointed his finger in Jamie's face. "You said everything was okay between us! You can't just come to a show and treat us like this after we tried to fix it with you!"

"You know I have a right to be furious with what happened!" Jamie didn't let Eddie's height intimidate him as he shouted back. "After what the others did to Aly..."

"What *they* did to Aly?" Eddie cut Jamie off. "What about what *you* did to Aly?"

"Shut up, Ed!" Jamie's face grew red. "You don't know...!"

"Listen!" Eddie silenced his friend with the powerful command. "I do know, and you know it! You weren't just some guy on the side of the road to her, Jamie; she bloody gave you her virginity! She wanted to be with you! And then you walked out on her, and you want to be angry at us? Fine, but I'm going to be angry at you because you treated Aly like rubbish! I have known what you did to her since five minutes after you did it, yet I never said a word, and I never got upset at you. You want to know why? Because I could see in your face every day how much you hated yourself for what you had done to her! I knew it! I saw it!"

Garret and Tommy watched Eddie, their mouths hanging open. In all of their six years together, they had never seen Eddie so passionate about something before. Someone came to tell them to go back for their encore, but Eddie dismissed them.

"We're not going back onstage until Jamie is honest with us about how he feels." Eddie crossed his arms.

"Right, Ed! That's a swell idea, let's just ignore the fans while we stand back here and fight!" Jamie's hands were shoved deep into his pockets. He was trying to cover his true emotions by shouting angrily.

"Jamie, you know who we are! You hear their apologies! You see their faces! There is no reason to keep holding this against them. This is unacceptable! We are a band. We're brothers. I will not let you tear us apart because you feel like you have the right to hold a grudge."

Another stagehand ran into the room and motioned for them to get back on stage.

"We haven't finished yet!" Eddie shouted at the man.

They had been through so much together since starting their band six years earlier. It was Jamie's dream, but they had been eager to be a part of it when he invited them to join him as the musicians. Tommy and Eddie were barely out of their teens when everything started. Jamie made it his job to hold them together.

There had been times where they almost walked out on each other, calling it all quits because of a fight, an offense, a mistake; whatever it had been, they were convinced that they would never be able to work through it. Every time it happened, Jamie had been able to do or say something to change their minds. Every time, Jamie kept them from falling apart.

This was the first time Jamie felt this upset and angry at them. He looked around the room and saw the weariness on their faces. They were all ready to go home. This tour had been hard, and they were emotionally drained. Jamie wasn't sure that he was going to be able to hold them together this time, but he knew he had to try.

Eddie looked back at Jamie, and he saw the tears clinging to Jamie's eyelashes. The young man was biting his bottom lip, trying to keep his feelings from breaking through the mask he was wearing. Eddie's eyes went soft, and he lowered his shoulders.

"Jamie, we care about you. We're a bunch of bumbling idiots, and we make horrible mistakes that hurt the people we love the most, but we're fixing it. Aly is special to you, we see that. We're not trying to change that."

Jamie finally gave up. He nodded at them all and took a deep breath.

"Are you sure?" Eddie pressed.

"I'm done. Let's go out there and do an encore."

The guys patted Jamie on the back as he led the way onto the stage. By the time the lights hit their faces, the practiced smiles were in place. They were grateful when the show was over and they were able to leave the stage. There was a quick moment backstage where they reiterated once again that everything was good between them, and then they left to hide away in the privacy of their own rooms.

The carpet in Jamie's hotel room had a path worn into it from one end of the room to the other after two hours of continuous pacing. The covers on the bed were in a heap in the middle from the one attempt Jamie had made at falling asleep before he gave up. His phone battery was about to die from the number of times he had unlocked the screen and typed out a message before erasing it all. There was no way that Alyson would be awake at that time and there was no point in trying to smooth things over when he was overly tired and emotional. Still, he knew he wasn't going to be able to sleep unless he reached out to her.

"Screw it," Jamie muttered under his breath as he whipped his phone out of his pocket and pressed a few buttons. "I'm just going to leave a voicemail."

The phone hummed into Jamie's ear as the call went through and connected his phone to Alyson's. Jamie continued to pace, his free hand running through his unkempt hair. He caught his reflection in the mirror on the wall and turned to take in the bags under his eyes.

"Oh, geez. What a mess..." he mumbled as he poked at the sagging skin and leaned closer to the mirror.

"Hello?"

"Aly?" Jamie immediately straightened and dropped his hand from his face. This wasn't her voicemail.

"Hi." Aly's voice held a tone of hesitancy and worry, but not sleep.

"Oh, Aly! I'm sorry." Jamie slapped his hand to his forehead and groaned. "I didn't think I would wake you. I'm so, so sorry..."

"No, I... I wasn't sleeping."

"I guess I sound silly calling you now. I just wanted you to know that I was thinking about you and hoping you were okay." Jamie's words were gentle.

Alyson shut her eyes and tried to breathe deeply, but her breath kept getting caught on the lump in her throat. The taste of salty tears dripped onto her lips. She couldn't deny the fact that her heart beat faster when he spoke to her like that.

"Yeah, I'm fine." She hid her tears from her voice. "Never thought I was going to hear from you ever again after this morning..."

"I-I'm sorry that, uh, that our conversation ended so badly." Jamie shook his head and rolled his eyes at himself. "We didn't make it easy for you to tell us. We're a bunch of idiots, we are."

"You guys deserved to know." Alyson quietly pushed herself up from the couch and looked at the clock. It was three in the morning. She quickly wrapped herself in a blanket and slipped out of Danielle's apartment and down the hall to the outside exit. She sat down on the front steps of the building, not wanting her conversation to wake Danielle. The door shut behind her louder than she expected, and she cringed. It was nippy out, but she felt comfortable with her bare feet on the sidewalk and the blanket around her shoulders. "I know it won't change your lives really, but I figured it was better to tell you now than ten years down the road when my child wants to know who their father is."

The thought was strange for Jamie. He couldn't imagine going ten years before seeing a little boy or girl that was his own flesh and blood. What Tommy said about wanting to be a part of their child's life made sense.

"That would, uh, definitely be interesting." Jamie made a laughing sound, but they both knew laughing was the last thing he wanted to do in that moment.

"Talking about it this morning was interesting enough for me." Alyson looked up at the stars that spread across the black sky like tiny grains of salt on a table cloth. They were her old, familiar friends that had spent many hours of lonely darkness with her, but she had missed having a voice to talk to in the middle of the night. A breeze blew across her face, and she sucked in the fresh taste of it before letting it out slowly. "Did you guys get it all worked out between you?"

"Ah, yeah." Jamie thought back to their bus lockdown. "A bit. Still angry at the lads, but, we're still mates. We, uh, had a pretty epic row at our show tonight."

"Because... of me?"

"Mostly because of me, actually." Jamie looked out of the hotel window and saw the moon peeking out from behind the clouds. He bit his tongue to keep from asking her if she could see the moon from where she was.

"Are you angry at me?" she whispered.

"No." The answer was immediate, giving the girl no room to doubt that he meant what he said. "I'm angry at myself. I was the biggest jerk in the world to you that night."

Alyson let the silence do the talking as she studied the way her feet looked in the dark on the light-colored pavement. Thoughts rolled through her mind, but never made it to her tongue. She heard Jamie's breathing through the phone, and she wished the sound didn't comfort her. He had broken her heart, yet every piece of it still yearned for his love. She couldn't let herself fall for him again.

"Well, the good thing for you guys is that you're not going to have to worry about anything." The tone was cool. "If you're worried about me telling anyone, don't be. I can't even tell my parents about this, so your secrets are safe with me."

"No, Aly! I'm not... Please, don't think that." Jamie grew frustrated at how detached the girl suddenly sounded. "I'm concerned about you and the baby, not myself."

"Honestly, Jamie, you don't have to worry about it." Alyson pulled the blanket tightly around her shoulders and ignored the ache in her throat. "You don't have to be concerned."

"I think I should though. Don't you?"

"I don't know, Jamie." Alyson laid her head in the palm of her hand and sighed deeply. "I don't know how this is supposed to work. I'm going to have to quit my job and move somewhere where no one knows me and hope I don't run out of money. Life is that simple right now."

"You're going to keep this a secret from everyone?"

"I told you about my dad's family. This... this is major. The wrong person could find out and things could go very wrong. If I got in trouble for posting a picture of myself in a swimming suit online, I can't imagine what they would do if they knew about this."

"You're just going to try to do this by yourself?"

"I have Danielle. I would move in with her, but people would know to look for me here. I have to go somewhere that I've never been to before. Change my number. Delete my information." Another sigh escaped Aly's trembling lips. "But I'm going to be okay. My baby is going to be okay. We'll be fine somehow."

"You're keeping the baby for sure?" The tone was gentle.

"Yeah." Alyson nodded as she spoke. "Yeah, I am."

"I-I wasn't sure... I mean, I didn't know what you had planned. It seems like a lot."

"I'm not saying it's going to be easy." A sad smile appeared on Alyson's face and she looked at her star friends as she spoke. "But there's a reason for this child. You could say that it's just because the pills expired or because I wasn't taking them at the right time, but I think there's more than that. I've been thinking about him or her all day..."

A smile tugged at Jamie's mouth as he listened to Alyson's words. She was opening up to him. He didn't make a noise, afraid that if she remembered he was on the other side of the line, she would clam up again.

"This little person is inside of me, and one day they'll come out and grow up and have friends and know how to talk and think and have dreams and passions... I get to be a part of that. I get to teach him right and wrong, how to love, how to laugh, how to be a friend, how to say they're sorry. It's crazy! I have this chance to love and be loved unconditionally!" Tears made Alyson's voice rough. "I may never have this chance again. I would be stupid to pass this up, even though it seems stupid to keep him."

"You're going to be a great mum, Aly. You really are." Jamie pressed two fingers against his eyes to keep the tears from falling.

"Thanks."

"Aly, I don't know how you are going to react to this, so just... shoot me down if it's something you really don't want." Jamie prefaced his words. "But... the baby could be mine, and if it is, I would like to have some type of role in the baby's life. Tommy said the same thing. We're willing to help you. I understand if you would like us to stay as far away from your child as possible, but I wanted you to know how we felt."

"Jamie, don't think that you owe me anything." The tone was guarded. "I don't need you guys to do anything. I only told you because it was the right thing to do. I'm not looking for favors or to be your pity case..."

"No! No, Aly, tha-..."

"I'm sorry if you thought I was asking you guys to be a part of this. I honestly wasn't meaning to guilt you guys into anything."

"Aly, no! That's not wh-..."

"So, thank you for the nice gesture; you are off the hook."

Jamie sighed. He wanted to keep fighting back and defending himself, to tell her that she was all wrong about their intentions, but he stopped himself. If she wanted them to be involved, she would tell them.

"All right." Jamie let his free hand fall into his lap. "If you change your mind, you are always welcome to contact me."

"Yeah."

"It will be all right, love. I promise you."

A small gasp came through the phone, and Jamie realized what he had done too late.

"Jamie. Don't." The whisper came out as a plea. "Please."

With his head tilted back towards the ceiling and his fist clenched, Jamie bit his tongue to keep from swearing at himself for being so stupid. She had every right to say that to him. After all that had happened between them, those words must hurt the most.

"Sorry, love." Jamie's words barely made it out. "I shouldn't have said that."

"It's late." Alyson cleared her throat. "Thanks for the call. I'm going to be fine. I hope you and the guys work it out. Bye."

Jamie paused for a second before responding, thinking that Alyson might hang up before he could say anything. He counted to five and still heard her steady breathing coming through the phone.

"Bye, Jamie."

It was then that Jamie realized what she was doing; she was letting him get the last word.

"You're very welcome for the call." Jamie spoke slowly, knowing that their conversation was almost over. "Don't worry about the lads and I. We always get it sorted."

He heard a tiny laugh and smiled sadly.

"Good night, Aly."

There was no response, but Jamie knew that Aly heard him.

Alyson slowly slipped the phone down from her ear and ended the call, a lump in her throat. She was physically shaking from all that she felt towards Jamie.

She was angry that he was still able to make her feel things on the inside. He reminded her of what they used to share, and she could never have that back. She wanted him, worse than she did before, but she couldn't have him.

Garret and Jamie were the first ones up the next morning, sharing the silence together over breakfast. They sipped black coffee and stared at their bagels and phones, saying nothing about the tension in the room. Half of his cup of coffee was gone before Garret looked up from his phone and really saw Jamie's face for the first time that morning.

"You look rough, mate. Did you sleep at all?"

"Nope." Jamie's tone was clipped.

"Up thinking?"

"Yup."

"About Aly?"

"Yes, Gar. About Aly. Geez. Is this the Spanish Inquisition or breakfast?"

"Sorry…" Garret looked down at the table and returned to his coffee.

It pained Jamie to have this anger seething up inside of him towards his best friend. He and Garret had gone through the hardest days of their lives together, but Garret crossed the line by being with Alyson, whether they had slept together or not.

"Are you…"

"Garret, shut up!"

Garret didn't say anything. He took a bite of his bagel and chewed it for a long time before he attempted to swallow it down. It nearly choked him, but he managed to keep it from coming back up. He looked at his food and set it back down on the plate. He wasn't going to be able to finish it.

The phone in Jamie's hand seemed to be the most interesting thing in the room to him as he double-tapped a record amount of pictures on Instagram and responded to more people than normal over Twitter. Garret's sigh didn't distract him from his mission of out-sitting Garret at that breakfast table.

"Jay, we need…"

Jamie looked up at Garret with a stony glare in his eyes.

"Jamie, I'm sorry." Garret spread out his hands in front of him. "I can't change it. You know I can't."

"You lied to me."

"You think it was easy for me to go around knowing I may have slept with Aly? Then you told me what went down between the two of you and I couldn't tell you what I had done! Do you think I enjoy the fact that I'm going to have to go back home in a couple weeks and tell Serenity I've completely ruined what we've made together?"

"You're my best mate, Gar! You can't just fix this with an apology!"

"What do you want me to do? I can't make Alyson un-pregnant! I can't make you not leave her! I can't make her and Tommy not sleep together! I can't go back in time and know for sure if Aly and I did anything while we were drunk! I cannot change any of those things and I'm sorry! I'm bloody sorry!"

Jamie looked away, his face rigid and his hand wrapped around his phone tightly. A tiny fly began to buzz around his face, and he swatted at it before turning to look at Garret. His eyes were spilling tears that ran down his cheeks and into his beard.

"Do you remember anything at all?"

"All I remember is seeing her on the dance floor and thinking I should keep an eye on her for you. I didn't know you'd left her." Garret shook his head. "I was just... trying to help her have a good time and get her a couple of drinks."

"But how do you not remember if you slept with someone or not? How drunk were you? How drunk did you make her?"

"I gave her one drink, Jay! One drink and one..." Garret stopped.

"One what?" Jamie snapped.

"Nothing." Garret shoved his chair back from the table and left the room.

The day passed slowly, and Jamie was constantly thinking of the girl from Iowa. Their next show wasn't until Monday evening, so they had a long weekend to rest, and Jamie had time to work on some marketing plans his label had sent to him. Jamie kept to himself, working in his hotel room and hitting up the hotel gym while the other three took advantage of the great weather to see some sites. He pulled his phone out of his pocket every few minutes to look at the picture on his lockscreen that he had set sometime in the night before. Alyson's smile hit his feelings where it hurt, but he couldn't stop staring at it.

Jamie found himself by the window, completely ignoring the email he had started to write over an hour ago. There were budget spreadsheets, charity details, privacy statements and more that needed his attention, but all he could think about was if Alyson was going to be okay. Bits of their conversation floated through his memory, and he focused on one particular phrase she had said, almost carelessly;

"...*I'm going to have to quit my job and move somewhere where no one knows me and hope I don't run out of money...*"

He pulled his phone out of his pocket again, and this time he gave into the temptation to call Alyson. The phone rang once before he quickly pulled his phone away from his ear and hung up, shaking his head at himself.

"No, Jamie. Don't." He hoped that if he heard himself audibly say the words, he would obey them.

He pressed his phone to his forehead and sighed. Everything about their conversation last night had clearly told Jamie that Alyson wasn't interested in his help. He unlocked his phone and went to his voice messages to play the one Alyson had left for him the day before. The way she cut off right in the middle gripped Jamie's heart. She needed him. There was no way she was going to be able to do it all alone.

"I'm doing this for her. Not for me," Jamie tried to convince himself as he set his phone down on the desk in front of him and typed up a text. He pushed "send" and stood up from his spot. There was no telling how Alyson would respond to his words, but he had a little hope as he remembered how she relived their special tradition of letting him say the last word. "I'm doing this for her..."

Alyson sat on the couch in Danielle's apartment scrolling through online listings of cheap apartments in the Midwest. She wasn't sure where she should go, but Danielle was doing research on the best and most affordable health care. They were hoping for someplace within driving distance from Danielle so she could be there if anything happened. Neither of them had been able to find something that suited the situation, and Alyson was petrified of making the wrong decision.

"I don't think Garret has told Serenity about what happened yet," Danielle mentioned softly.

"Why do you think that?"

"Well, I messaged her last night, asking how she was, and she said she's doing great."

Alyson sighed and sucked her cheeks in.

"She asked how you were doing."

"What did you say?"

"Said you were going through a tough time. No details. Told her I wish I could change how hard things are for you right now."

Alyson gave Danielle a sad smile and turned back to her laptop. They could hear the sound of the other tapping the trackpad and typing on the keys as they slipped back into silence. The heater kicked on and the curtains began dancing with the blast of hot air blowing against it.

"I suppose I'm going to have to sell my car." Alyson thought of another thing to add to her already extensive list of things she would have to do.

"You love your car." Danielle looked up from her laptop and frowned at her friend. "Just keep it."

"I can't. I have... I can't just do this halfway. I have to be one hundred percent committed to this." Alyson was vexed. She already knew how much she loved her car. "People find who they're looking for by finding their cars all the time."

"I guess." Danielle looked back at her computer screen and tapped absentmindedly on the keyboard. She didn't look back over at her friend until a few minutes later when she heard a faint hum. "Did you hear that?"

"Mm." Alyson was still looking at her computer. "It was my phone."

Danielle waited for Alyson to pick up her phone and say who it was, but Alyson ignored the text and continued scrolling through apartment listings. The friend drew her eyebrows together and a wrinkle appeared in her forehead.

"Are you going to look at it?"

"Hmm?" Alyson tore her eyes away from the screen and was surprised to see Danielle staring at her. "What?"

"Your phone. You got a text."

"Oh." Alyson shrugged and glanced at the computer for a moment before looking up to see Danielle's eyes still on her. "What?"

"Nothing." Danielle forced herself to look back at her laptop.

Alyson didn't move until she was sure Danielle was actually done watching her. She gripped the edges of her laptop tightly to steady her trembling hands as she waited. Shaky breaths calmed her before she was brave enough to pick up the cellphone. Anger and anticipation danced inside of her stomach as she finally opened the text Jamie sent her. The words flashed onto the screen, and Alyson felt her heart drop.

"Stupid..." The word was barely loud enough to be a whisper as anger won the battle to be the dominant emotion.

"What's stupid?" Danielle's head popped up. She had been waiting for a reaction.

"Jamie texted me..." Alyson swallowed hard. "Said... uh... nothing important."

The words blurred in front of her as she read it again.

"Thinking about you and the baby. Hoping you're both doing well today. Let me know if I can do anything."

Those were the kinds of texts Jamie had sent throughout the day during their two months of being together. Those texts had been special, something no one else had ever done for her. They made Alyson feel like the most important person in Jamie's life, but now she was mad. He couldn't do this to her.

"I thought you were never going to hear from him again?"

"I know." Alyson thought back to the conversation they had had early that morning while Danielle was still sleeping. "He called me last night."

"Did you answer?" Danielle read the look on her friend's face. "Why did you answer the phone? Aly!"

"It was the middle of the night, it could have been an emergency."

"Was it?"

Again, Alyson's face did the talking while she remained silent, biting at her bottom lip and staring at the phone in her hand. A tear tried to escape, but Alyson stopped it.

"He's a selfish jerk, Al. Just... just ignore it!" Danielle frowned as she watched her friend try not to fall apart. "You don't need this."

Alyson was going to do just that when two more texts from Jamie came in, her phone buzzing in her hand as she received them. Alyson's lips quivered despite the fact she was pressing them together so hard they hurt. She breathed unevenly as tears filled her eyes and quietly slipped down her face.

"Okay, it's okay." Danielle quickly set her laptop on the floor and crawled across the couch to be next to her friend. She moved Alyson's computer and pulled the girl into her arms. "I'm so sorry."

Alyson grabbed onto Danielle's sweatshirt and clung to her as she let herself cry. A gentle hand stroked Aly's hair back from her face, and the other pulled Alyson closer. The two girls had cried together before, but Alyson had never melted into Danielle's comfort like this. Alyson was not just sitting tensely beside her, but was crumpled against her side. It made Danielle's heart ache.

"I'm so sorry, Aly."

"Wh-why do I s-still love him... s-so much?"

She felt Alyson's whole body shake in her arms and a tear ran down her cheek. The phone buzzed again several more times before Alyson's weeping slowly stopped, and she pushed herself into an upright sitting position.

"He's asking to, uh..." Alyson paused to take a deep breath and let it out slowly before she finished reading. "He wants to call me on Skype."

"No." Danielle didn't even think about it. "He doesn't need to talk to you. You don't need to talk to him."

"What if it is something, though?" Alyson scanned the other texts the young man sent her and nibbled on her lip nervously, still sniffling. "What if there's something important?"

"I doubt it, Aly. He's just feeling guilty and wants to take advantage of you again."

The thought pained Alyson. She wanted to believe that the Jamie she had fallen for over the summer was the real Jamie, and the man who had walked out on her was a stranger to both of them. She shook her head. It didn't matter which Jamie was real, she didn't have time for him to play around with her heart in the name of caring for her. She had trusted him once, and he had lost her trust. He wasn't allowed to have it back.

"What are you doing?"

Danielle watched as Alyson sat up from the couch and lifted her computer onto her lap. She opened Skype and began to log in.

"No! Aly!" Danielle reached forward to take the computer, but Alyson pushed her friend away. "Alyson!"

"Don't worry, this isn't me being weak." Alyson's words were determined and the resolved glint in her eye was offset by angry tears. She waited for the ringing to start, signaling that Jamie was trying to talk to her. It only took a moment.

"Aly. Are you sure you know what you're doing?" asked Danielle quietly as she watched Alyson's fingers hover over the trackpad, ready to accept the call. Alyson shook her head no, but she clicked on the answer button anyway and connected.

"Aly!" Jamie was close to the camera, his gaze drawn toward Alyson's red, tear-filled eyes as soon as her face appeared on his screen. "Hey! What's wrong?"

"What do you need, Jamie?" Alyson ignored his question and asked her own, aware of the tears slipping one by one down her face. She saw him sit back at her words, surprised at her tone.

"I wanted to, you know, make sure... I just wanted to check on you."

"Why?"

"Pardon?" Jamie looked hard at Alyson's face, but could read nothing in her guarded eyes.

"Why, Jamie? Why?" Alyson let her hands come up from where they had been resting in her lap. They moved as she spoke. "Why do you want to make sure I'm okay? Why are you checking up on me?"

"What do you mean 'why', Aly? I care about how you're doing!" The tone Jamie used was almost snappy.

"Really?"

"Aly, what is going..."

"I don't want you to check up on me, Jamie!" Alyson's voice was strong. "You don't get that right anymore. I have too many things to deal with already because of you; I can't just stop my life and talk to you every time you feel like you want to know how I am."

Jamie sat in stunned silence.

"You're being really, really selfish right now. Maybe you thought it was cute you were able to talk to me last night when you couldn't sleep." Alyson's throat closed up and her voice broke. "But what about all those nights when I couldn't sleep? Hmm? What about the nights that I c-cried myself to sleep because I missed you and hated you so deeply at the s-same time?"

"Aly, I'm..." The gentle voice held no magic this time.

"Stop!" Alyson squeezed her eyes shut and clenched her fists. "S-stop talking! I'm going to have a baby, and I need to be able to get over you. The only person benefitting from you ch-checking up on me is, is, is you!"

Jamie sucked in his cheeks and ducked his head as he rubbed his hands through his hair. He didn't lift his gaze until he heard the hitching in Alyson's breathing fade away. When he looked up he saw her sitting with her eyes closed and a frown on her face.

"Aly, I'm sorry."

"I don't know if I can believe that or not." Alyson opened her eyes and held Jamie's gaze.

"I know." Jamie nodded, keeping himself together as best he could. "I know that, love."

"Do you promise to not talk to me anymore?"

Jamie said nothing.

"Please, Jamie. You have to."

"Can't." Jamie shook his head no.

"Jamie!"

"Aly, stop!" Jamie raised his voice slightly. "Listen. This is why I can't promise."

"No! I will not listen!" Alyson quickly tried to find the cursor on the screen so she could hang up. "You're not going to do this to me again..."

"Aly, you need me!" Jamie broke through Alyson's frantic babbling enough to be heard. "You need me. The baby needs me."

"You're the last person we need!"

"Aly, just listen."

Alyson looked away, but kept her mouth shut. She could see Danielle out of the corner of her eye, taking it all in silently.

"Aly, please, just look at me so I know you can hear me." Jamie watched Alyson stubbornly keep her face turned away from him.

"Just talk before I hang up on you."

"Okay, fine." Jamie took a deep breath. "You're not going to be able to make it on your own with the baby."

Alyson's chin quivered, but she held her ground and continued to look away from the camera.

"Financially you'll never last. You'll need to pay rent, put down a down-payment, get furniture and buy groceries. Maternity clothes, doctor visits, stuff for the baby... It's all going to cost money, Aly, and I know you don't have much of that. You're going to have no job and your savings isn't going to last you enough to get by."

A whisper from off-screen caught Jamie by surprise, and he saw Alyson shrug in response. He looked at the background of the room where Alyson was sitting. She wasn't at her house.

"I want to help, Aly."

"No, thank you." Alyson finally turned to look at him. The pain that appeared in his eyes hit her deep in the pit of her stomach, but she stood firm. "No. I'll have to just struggle through. I would rather live in my car than have you help me."

"But what about the baby?"

The words felt like a slap. She put her hands on her stomach and felt a sob try to escape, but she swallowed it down. Her pride told her to continue to refuse the rock star's help, but her love for her baby made her hold her tongue.

"I know you want to do everything you can for the baby, and I can help you. I can make sure you have enough money for rent and groceries and pay for the hospital bills. Please let me do this to help you."

"What's in this for you?"

"Knowing you're safe, you have a warm place to sleep, that you're not hungry and the baby is healthy." When Alyson didn't say anything, Jamie spoke again. "I'm not pretending to care, Aly. I'm not the type of person who does something for someone if I don't care about them. If I didn't want to do this, I wouldn't have said anything."

"Aly..." The voice belonging to the unseen third person spoke again, distracting Alyson from the young man on the screen.

"I don't know what to do, Elle." Alyson's words revealed to Jamie who her secret companion was.

"Danielle? Aly, put Danielle on."

There was a moment of hesitancy before Alyson complied and handed over her laptop to her friend. Danielle wore a grim expression of deep dislike for the face she saw before her, but she said nothing as she nodded in greeting.

"Hi."

"You're lucky you're not here with me or I would punch you in the face for how you treated my best friend."

Jamie took the comment with a nod and straight face.

"But you know I can help her. You know she's going to run out of money on her own. Danielle, just think about this reasonably."

"Can't someone else give Aly money?"

"Sure, I'll give the money to you, and you can give it to her. I don't care. I just want her to be okay."

"Th-that's not what I meant..." Danielle shot Alyson a look and saw the tortured expression of disquiet in her eyes. There was already so much weight on Alyson simply because of the pregnancy, not including money and trying to figure out the future. She needed to just stay safe and stay hidden, not be stressed about knowing where her next meal was going to come from or if she would be able to afford a doctor. "But if that is what will take care of Aly, I say yes."

"Thank you. Thank you, Danielle." Jamie let out his breath and clasped his hands together in a show of gratitude. "Thank you."

"I'm only saying yes because I love Alyson and the baby. This has nothing to do with you. How am I going to get this money?"

"What is your address and bank info? I can have it there by tomorrow."

Alyson sat on the couch listening to Danielle and Jamie coolly exchange information and talk about details and amounts. He was being generous, and Alyson knew she could live on much less than he was promising to send her. She closed her eyes and listened to his voice, the way his words lilted and danced as they came off his tongue even though all he was saying was a bunch of numbers. The conversation slipped into the background and Alyson's hands went to her stomach. There was nothing to be felt, but she knew her baby was there. Her baby was safe.

I'm going to be able to take care of you. We're going to make it. Alyson did deep breathing and felt her shoulders loosen. *Somehow I will get Jamie out of my head, and we will make it.*

Chapter five
"You've been staring at him for hours."

Saturday morning was cold and gray, a perfect day for staying on the couch under a bundle of blankets with a cup of tea in your hands. A few of the trees were starting to change color early, not unheard of for the cold, northern state. Alyson was sleeping lightly in Danielle's bed when her best friend put a hand on her shoulder.

"Aly, I'm leaving," she spoke softly as Alyson's eyes fluttered open. "I'm going to meet up with those girls from my Psych club. Remember?"

"Oh yeah. Okay." Alyson yawned and pulled the covers closer to her chin. She hadn't slept much the night before.

"Are you going to be okay? I can tell the girls I need to skip if you think you'll need me."

"No, no, go." Alyson shook her head and gave Danielle a reassuring smile. "I'm just going to stay in bed, I think."

"Okay, I'll be back by noon. You're going to be okay?"

"Yes. Don't worry. I'll just be here."

Danielle looked over her shoulder one last time before she finally left the bedroom. Alyson heard her shut and lock the door behind her and then let out a loud sigh. There was no way she was going to be able to get back to sleep now. She had to pee, and there was the familiar rolling in her stomach she had grown accustomed to.

"Okay, baby. Hold on a minute." Alyson pushed herself up slowly into a sitting position, trying not to jostle around too much. With patient steps and careful movements, Alyson found herself in the kitchen five minutes later without losing her supper from the night before. Her hands were reaching for a bowl from the cupboard when there was a knock on the door.

"Hello?" a voice called from outside.

A frown crossed Alyson's face as she looked at the clock; it was 9 a.m. on a Saturday morning. She considered ignoring the visitor and pretending like no one was home, but she knew it could be someone looking for Danielle. She set the bowl on the counter and walked over to the door. There on the other side was Adam with his hand up to knock again.

"Aly! You're here! That's... surprising."

"Hi, Adam. What's up?" Alyson folded her arms across her chest and leaned against the doorframe. She felt her stomach squirm, but she concentrated on her friend and prayed it would settle.

"Sorry to wake you up." The young man raised one eyebrow as he looked at the girl in her baggy pajamas and hair falling loosely around her face. He noted the dark circles under her eyes and gave her a sympathetic smile. "But your friend is outside."

Alyson pulled her eyebrows together and made a face.

"Are you not expecting a handsome stranger to be visiting you this morning?" Adam gave a light chuckle.

"No?" Alyson's expression was perplexed. "Are you sure they weren't asking for Danielle?"

"He said Aly. I told him you weren't here, but he insisted you were, and obviously, he was right."

"I-I'm not expecting anyone. I don't even really know anyone besides you and Elle."

"Well, your friend is here to see you." Adam jerked a thumb over his shoulder at the parking lot that was next to Danielle's apartment building. "And he must be more of a friend than I am because I didn't even know you were here until he asked for you."

"No one knows I'm here, Adam, so don't take it... Wait..." Alyson's face blanched.

"What? You okay?"

Alyson shoved Adam out of her way and rushed down the hallway; her bare feet pounded against the carpeted floor as she ran. The door to the apartment stood wide open behind her, and Adam called her name but all Alyson could think about was the person who was waiting outside. Her vision blurred, her lungs heaved, her hands shook... She threw open the door and stepped outside.

"What are you doing?!" Alyson's voice came out louder and more high-pitched than she had intended. "Why are you here?"

"I told you I would get the money here by today." Jamie stood with his hands in his pockets, a jean jacket shielding him from the cold morning. His shaggy hair was pushed to the side, the very ends tucked behind his left ear to reveal the blue in his eyes.

"No." Alyson's whimper carried on the wind and Jamie's mouth twitched downward, but he stayed in his spot on the sidewalk. "No, you're not supposed to be here."

"I had to come, Aly." Jamie's words were soft.

"No you didn't!" Alyson's voice rose. "You could have mailed the stupid check! You didn't have to come! I-I, I don't want to see you!"

Jamie shrugged and shoved his hands deeper into his pockets.

"This isn't fair, Jamie. You can't keep butting into my life like this."

"You're not the only one still trying to get over what we shared."

The sentence rocked Aly back on her feet, and she put a hand out to catch her balance. The teetering motion was too much for her angry stomach, and there was no stopping it this time. Alyson quickly bent over the bushes by the front steps, one hand clamped over her mouth and the other desperately pulling her hair out of her face. She knelt down and let her stomach empty, panting and grimacing against the bitter taste of bile in her mouth when it was over. The touch of a hand on her shoulder made Alyson jerk away.

"Don't touch..." Alyson's sentence was cut off as she was sick again. She let go of her hair to keep Jamie away, but only succeeded in getting vomit on herself.

"Ah, love." Jamie kept a steady hand on Alyson's shoulder as he pulled back her hair, careful not to touch the soiled parts. "You okay?"

"Stop t-touching me!"

Jamie removed his hand, but stayed close to Alyson's side as she bent over the bushes again. He bit the inside of his cheeks to keep from saying anything as she struggled to do it without his help. She lost her balance and fell into Jamie, who caught her. The vomit on her shirt was soon smeared onto his jacket sleeve, but he didn't seem to notice.

"Here, let me..." Jamie quickly pulled off his jacket before Alyson could even react to being so close to him. He wrapped it around her shoulders and pulled it closed in the front.

"Jamie, leave."

Jamie's hands lingered on the edges of the jacket as it hung on Alyson's body. He was staring at her neck, fingers fidgeting at the closeness of her skin. He shifted his gaze to Alyson's eyes. They were begging him to listen to her. She searched his face and remembered the friend she once had. The somersaulting in her stomach returned, and she knew it was only a matter of time before she was sick again.

"We were together for two months. You left me, it's over! You're being dumb and illogical! You don't need to do this for me! It's not like we were even in a real relationship."

Jamie took a step back and let his hands slip down to his sides as he gave Alyson her space. There was a pained but determined look in his eyes. "I don't let how long I have known a person dictate how much I am allowed to do for them to show them that I care."

Alyson had to look away from Jamie's face as she let out a scoff and tasted a tear on her lips. She knew he was known for being loyal and selfless. He was described by those closest to him as being genuine and someone who meant what he said. Maybe she was the exception in Jamie Donald's life for having been hurt by him. Maybe she would be the only one who ever felt this type of pain because of him, but that didn't matter. The cut from the broken trust went deep and was far from being healed.

"Jay, why did you come?"

"You know why." Jamie's voice was low as he spoke.

Alyson shook her head and stared him steadily in the eye.

"You should have thought about that before you walked out on me." Alyson turned away and walked into the apartment building, her fingers holding tightly onto the borrowed jacket.

Adam was gone, but the door of Danielle's apartment was still open. Alyson sighed as she walked in. Her bowl was on the counter, waiting to be filled with the breakfast she had planned on eating before she had gone running out. She wanted to curl up on the couch and cry herself back to sleep, but she was forced to hurry to the bathroom.

Alyson knew eating something would stay her rolling stomach, but she sat slumped in the corner by the shower. She hugged her knees to her chest and stared at the jacket as it lay on the floor next to her. The scent of Jamie's cologne on the fabric was so strong Alyson could almost imagine him right there next to her, staring at her, touching her...

His hand had touched her. The same hand that she had held and pressed to her lips. The same hand that had snuck down to the waistband of her jeans to feel the warmth of her skin on the dance floor. The last time that hand touched her was moments before he left; he put his hand on her face, caressing it gently as he smiled down at her.

"You're so beautiful, love." His whisper was delicate, and she felt like she was on fire and being plunged into ice-cold water all at once. His fingertips ran down her smooth cheek to the white skin on her neck, pausing at the collar bone to trace its strength and shape. "I could stay like this with you forever..."

She believed him, so she let him touch her. His hands had touched her hands, her arms, her face, her stomach, her hips, her thighs...

"He's touched all of me!" The cry echoed in the bathroom as Alyson scrambled to her feet and stripped off her clothes. The hot water in the shower hit her skin, and she scrubbed as hard as she could, but the memory of his touch and of his love would not be washed from her mind. She leaned against the steamy shower wall and sobbed into her hands. "Please go away! Go away! Please!"

Danielle found Alyson standing by the window in the living room when she returned. Alyson was showered and dressed with a mug of lukewarm tea in her hands.

"How are you feeling?" Danielle called out as she kicked her shoes to the side and pulled off her coat.

"Jamie's here." The voice sounded hollow.

"What did you say?"

"Jamie." Alyson turned from the window to look at Danielle. "He's here. Right out there. In that silver car."

"Why didn't you call me and tell me? I would have come home! Why is he here?" Danielle hurried over to the window to see the young man who was sitting in the driver's seat of the rental car parked near her apartment.

"He came to give you the money."

"I thought he was going to wire it." Danielle bit her bottom lip and watched Alyson continue to stare. Her best friend gave a tiny shrug and took another sip of her tea. "I'm sorry he's here."

"It's okay. I got puke on his jacket." Alyson let herself smile a little at the thought.

"You threw up on him?"

"Technically in the bushes." Alyson motioned towards the bushes that were planted around the outside of the building. "But some of it got on his jacket. I left it in the bathroom."

"Good." Danielle picked her coat up off the kitchen table where she had set it and put it back on. "I'm going to go out and get the money so he can leave."

"Are you going to punch him in the face?"

"He would probably sue me."

"Worth the risk."

"I will give him the most evil stink-eye known to the history of mankind, though. And laugh at his horrible haircut."

"He didn't get a haircut."

"Oh? The magazine at the grocery store said he did."

"Just step on his foot. It could be seen as an accident."

Danielle gave Alyson a sad smile as she left the apartment. Alyson watched from her spot at the window and sipped the last of her tea. She had been standing there for over an hour already. She didn't know if Jamie knew she was watching him, but he had stayed in the car the whole time. Now, as Danielle left the building and walked over towards him, he opened his car door and stepped out.

There were a lot of gestures and Jamie starting to say something then looking away, his mouth pressed into a thin line of frustration. Danielle continued to point and shout, although Alyson couldn't hear anything that was being said. After five minutes, Danielle was given a big manila envelope and a pen. She bent over the hood of Jamie's car and pulled out the papers from the envelope and began to sign them.

"Oh geez, what is she doing?" Alyson breathed, her breath fogging up the window as she tried to get a better look. "Danielle, don't do anything stupid!"

When Danielle was finished, Jamie took the pen and signed the same papers. He then passed a small, white envelope to Danielle and nodded at her. She took it with a grim smile and turned to walk back towards the apartment building.

"What did you sign? What did it say?" Alyson pounced on Danielle as soon as she walked inside.

"It was just to keep things secret and private. I'm not allowed to tell anyone who I am giving this money to or why. It's to keep you safe, Aly." Danielle began to rummage around in her fridge. "What does Jamie like to eat?"

"I don't know. Hamburgers. Why?"

"Hmm." Danielle held up a container of leftovers and looked inside. "Well, I have steamed carrots and a yogurt. Do you think he'll eat that?"

"Why are you feeding him?" Alyson's face fell with a look of dismay. "Just ignore him! He'll leave!"

"He's not going to leave," Danielle grunted as she reached for a container at the back of the fridge. "I told him to, but he said he was going to stay."

"For how long?"

"I don't know, but I promised I would bring him something to eat."

"Why?"

"Because he's giving you a very substantial amount of money to keep you safe and alive, that's why. I may *really dislike* his guts, but he's helping you, and I can't ignore that. Besides, I stepped on his foot and I kind of feel bad because I think it actually hurt."

Alyson returned to her spot by the window when Danielle left to take Jamie the food. She watched the exchange, pleased to see that Danielle didn't smile at Jamie's attempt to make a joke, or whatever it was he was chuckling about. She watched the young man hunch his shoulders as Danielle walked away, leaving the containers of food in his hands. The wind blew his hair into his eyes, and he climbed back into his car. Danielle's steps sounded in the hallway and Alyson turned away from the window.

The girls stayed inside for the rest of the afternoon. Danielle seemed content to ignore the young man and the fact that he was twenty yards away, but for Alyson it was torture. She tried to listen to Danielle read about neighborhoods and birthing centers and preschools all the while trying to decide if she should go talk to Jamie again.

"Did you hear anything I just said?" Danielle peeked over and noticed the faraway look in Alyson's eyes. She was gazing off towards the window, and Danielle knew where her mind was.

"Something about birthing centers and a preschool, I think."

"Okay, you can read this when you're not distracted." Danielle closed her laptop and sat up.

"I'm sorry, Elle. You're being so good to me."

"You have a lot to think about." Danielle smiled graciously.

Alyson stood up and went to her spot by the window. She wanted to pretend that if she stared hard enough, that something would happen. Minutes slipped by and Alyson stayed where she was, her hands on her belly, rubbing it gently. The temperature was dropping with the sun outside when Danielle pressed something into Alyson's hands, rousing her from her deep thoughts.

"What's this?" Alyson looked down at the unfamiliar piece of clothing that Danielle was handing her.

"Jamie's jacket. I washed it so it doesn't have your puke on it anymore. Thought he might want it before it got too much colder out."

A furrow creased her brow, and her mouth quivered ever so slightly as she stared down at the jacket in her hands. She looked back up to meet Danielle's gaze and saw her give a tiny nod.

"But I thought you didn't want me to talk to him?"

"I don't. But you've been staring at him for hours. You can make your own choices, Aly."

Alyson shoved her feet into her shoes and left the apartment, forcing her concentration to focus on her breathing and not on the nerves in her stomach. She looked to the window behind her and saw Danielle in her window spot. Alyson gave a small wave before turning away.

The sound of a car door slamming reached Alyson's ears before she could even focus on the vehicle in the parking lot. The setting sun was almost completely hidden behind heavy gray clouds, making it seem much later in the day than it really was. Alyson had to let her eyes adjust a bit to the growing darkness as she walked closer. She could tell Jamie was smiling at her as she approached him.

"Hey." His greeting caused a twinge of emotion to rise up in her belly, but she pressed it away by hugging the jacket against herself tightly. "You okay?"

"No." Alyson returned his stare. "But I will be. One day."

Jamie gave her a sad smile and pushed his hands deeper into the pockets of his jeans. She looked away, still clutching the jacket against herself. Neither of them said anything for a moment, letting the silence help them pretend they weren't about to have another fight.

"I need you to go, Jamie." Alyson looked back at the face in front of her. "You're on tour. This is complicated, and you just make it worse. What are you gaining from sitting out here in the middle of Minnesota in a rental car?"

"It's helping me know that you know I'm doing everything I can to fix what I messed up between us. That's worth it to me."

"This isn't going to be fixed." Alyson shook her head. "Not by you sitting in this parking lot, not by you calling me every day, not by you looking at me like... like that."

Jamie didn't avert his gaze; his eyes adjusted to the light of the dusk enough to catch the blush that appeared on Alyson's pale cheeks. Her hands gripped Jamie's jacket until her knuckles turned white. She could practically feel how much he wanted to reach out and touch her.

"You're beautiful."

"Stop it!" Alyson was crying.

"I don't know why you expect me to just give up on you!" Jamie's tone was exasperated.

"I don't know why you just expect me to go running back into your arms!"

"I don't...!" Jamie exhaled heavily, cutting himself off.

"Yes, you do. Why else would you be here? You're too late, Jamie. The time to fix this was weeks ago."

"You don't know what happened that night, Aly."

"Oh, and you do?" Alyson's eyes were blazing. "Do you know what happened to me after you left me?"

"You already told me what happened!"

"Are you kid-..." Alyson rolled her eyes and turned away.

"Aly, don't!" Jamie put out a hand to prevent the girl from leaving in the middle of their argument. She whirled back around to face him, her finger jabbing up into his face.

"You think you know what happened after our one little conversation on Thursday? I-I-I barely told you anything!"

"Well, then tell me! Tell me what happened! Let me hear from your own mouth how you begged Eddie to help you because I ruined you! Tell me how you told Tommy how heartbroken you were! Give me every detail about Garret giving you drinks until you blacked out!" Jamie leaned closer as he spoke until he was inches away from Alyson's face, his breath hitting her mouth.

Alyson's lips parted in shock as she slowly realized what Jamie was saying. Her chest constricted, and she couldn't breathe. The young man who had been slowly positioning himself closer to her turned suddenly and began to pace, rubbing his cold hands through his hair and muttering under his breath. Alyson stood trembling in her spot.

"Aly, love, I'm sorry. I shouldn't have said that. Especially not like that." Jamie came back over to the girl, his eyes full of his apology, his fists at his side. "I don't kn-, You're right. You're absolutely right, I don't know what happened to you that night after I left. I'm so sorry I left you. I cannot begin to tell you how sorry I am."

Alyson was rooted to her spot on the sidewalk, the darkness barely covering the guilt and the pain that were etched deeply into the features of her face. Finally she brought her lips together, closing her mouth.

"I don't know what to do to fix this," said Jamie.

"I can't..." Alyson swallowed hard. "I can't let myself trust you again. Not after what happened between us."

"Please don't say that." Alyson could hear the tears in Jamie's voice as he begged her softly. "Please, love."

"I know you're sorry. And I do f-for... forgive you. But trust..." Alyson shook her head and wiped a tear off her cheek.

"I know I don't deserve it, but I don't want to lose you forever."

"I, uh... I brought you back your jacket." Alyson gave him a weak smile. "So you don't get cold."

With a nod of resignation, Jamie gave a sardonic laugh and sniffled. He looked up towards the sky for a minute to blink back the extra tears that wanted to fall.

"There's a good burger place down the road. If you get hungry." Alyson still had the jacket in her hands.

"Aly..."

"Thank you for... for the, uh... for helping."

Jamie didn't say anything, but wiped his cheeks with the backside of his hand. His lips were shaking when he finally looked back at the girl in front of him. She was so tired and sad. He wanted to scoop her into his arms and take care of everything, but she was blocking him at every turn. She was wise to want to keep her distance, but it hurt to watch her hate him.

"Bye." Alyson took a step back, then looked down at Jamie's jacket in her arms. "Sorry, this is yours."

"Keep it," Jamie shrugged, his heart in too many pieces to care.

Alyson bit her lip as she set the jacket down on the ground and walked away. Her hair whipped around her face as the wind pushed against her back, making her walk more quickly towards the tall, brick apartment building. She didn't turn around or glance back over her shoulder as she reached the door, walking right past the place where she had shared her 2:00 a.m. phone conversation with the man who still cared for her. The door shut behind her, and she walked purposefully up the short flight of stairs to Danielle's door. A pair of open arms was waiting for her when she walked in.

"I'm so sorry," Elle whispered as she hugged her friend tightly.

The tears didn't last long. Alyson went to the couch and began looking up apartments in earnest. Her friend brought her a plate of food and sat with her quietly, Alyson's feet on her lap as she used her phone to scroll through articles about personality types and genetic traits that were passed down from parents to children. From time to time, the girls would share something they found interesting and discuss it for a few minutes before relapsing into silence.

"You want to go to bed now?" Danielle patted her friend's leg gently when she saw Alyson's eyelids drooping.

"Yeah. I'm so tired." Alyson shut her computer and struggled to sit up. She batted away her friend's hand when Danielle tried to help her. "I can still get up on my own, thank you!"

Danielle was glad to hear her friend joking and happily took the swat. It wasn't long after the lights turned off that Danielle was snoring softly in the bed next to Alyson. Alyson tried everything to make her brain shut off, but her thoughts insisted on being her companion that night. Before too long, the blankets became uncomfortably heavy and hot for her, so she kicked them down and pushed them onto Danielle's side of the bed. Her hands carefully found her flat midsection and began to trace patterns around her bellybutton. A tiny smile pushed up the corners of her mouth as she imagined her little baby inside of her.

There would be nothing to see yet, but the beginnings of a precious human was there. A tiny shape just waiting for arms, legs, fingers and toes. There would be a face with a cute nose, sweet lips and maybe even hair to cover delicate skin and touch the tops of squishy ears, all wrinkly and pushed against the side of his or her head.

"Will you come out screaming?" Alyson murmured to her baby. "Or will you be one of the quiet ones?"

She moved her arms to position them as if she were cradling a baby. How could a body that tiny be so alive? Her skin prickled with goosebumps as she thought about green eyes and freckles on her son or daughter, proclaiming to the world that she was the mother of a perfect little creature walking around on two wobbly legs and touching the world with ten chubby fingers.

"I can't wait to be your mom."

It seemed safe in that moment. She was safe, and the dangerous journey ahead of her was going to be worth it. A house, money, doctors and other things would fall into place. Wouldn't it? Alyson sat up as the questions came pouring in, pushing the image of her baby out of her head. A wave of nausea reached her, and she quickly stumbled down the dark hallway to the bathroom.

A few minutes later, Alyson found herself in the living room, snuggled into the nook of the couch with a sleeve of crackers on her lap. She had turned on the lamp in the corner, giving herself some light, but leaving the room mostly dark. The curtains were drawn across the window, and she frowned at them. She didn't like curtains. She didn't like that people could live out secrets behind them. She stood up to open them, but stopped just as her hand touched the fabric.

She hadn't checked outside since she came back in from talking to Jamie. She wasn't sure if he was still there or not. They had fought, and she wouldn't blame him if he had changed his mind about her and drove away the second she was back inside.

She fingered the edge of the curtain, debating whether or not she should check to see if Jamie's parking spot was empty. She wasn't sure what she wanted more; to have Jamie still be there, or to find out if he had finally left like she had asked. Both thoughts were unpleasant. Her hand dropped down to her side, and she stepped back to sit on the edge of the couch.

It dawned on her that his presence outside no longer made her angry. The idea of him being close was growing on her. He had won her heart once before and he seemed bent on winning her again. She knew she wasn't strong enough to fight against the way he made her feel for long.

Her phone buzzed in its spot on the coffee table.

"you can't sleep either?"

Jamie was still there. He must have seen the glow of the lamp through the window.

Alyson slipped off the couch and pulled the curtain back a tiny bit to peek through. All she could see was black in Jamie's corner of the parking lot. The street lamp on that side apparently was broken.

Are you safe? Alyson pictured the young man's face. *Are you warm? Did you eat? Are you safe?*

Alyson gripped her phone tightly in her hand before clicking the lamp back off. She sat in the dark, breathing heavily as she struggled to remain calm. At one time, her sleepless nights were a chance to escape into the sound of Jamie's voice over the phone. He was her secret place of retreat, and the reason to smile throughout the day. Being able to talk to him was her motivation to finish quickly and go home instead of stay at work.

He had pressed so deeply into her heart, searching farther and farther into the secrets she carried until there was almost nothing left hidden between them. She believed that if he was so desperate to know her she could trust him. She had never felt that way about anyone before; this meant something.

The lonely night seemed to last forever, as Alyson was forced to sit alone without her star friends shining down on her. Her hands rested on her stomach, as if to shield her child from any negative thoughts that might come against him or her. She was still angry at herself, but she had to let it go and move on. There was a baby to think about and prepare for; how did she expect to be a good mother if she was caught up on the past?

A hand on her shoulder woke her the next morning. She was disoriented and groggy as she pushed her hair out of her face. The familiar urge to throw up hit her before she could even get her eyes open. She rolled off the couch and pushed past Danielle in order to make it to the bathroom in time.

"Why did you sleep on the couch?" Danielle appeared in the bathroom doorway.

"I couldn't sleep." Alyson stood up to wash her hands and face at the sink. "Ugh, my neck! What time is it?"

"Half-past eight."

"When do I have to be at the airport by?"

Danielle didn't answer the question, and Alyson turned to look at her.

"What's wrong? What happened?"

"I'm sorry, Aly..."

It was close to 1:00 p.m. when Jamie noticed Alyson walk out of the apartment building. She was wearing a gray sweatshirt and blue jeans with some chucks, but she had no luggage with her. Jamie had assumed the girl was going to travel back to Iowa that day since she would have school the next morning. He opened the car door and got out. His legs complained about stiffness as he put his weight on them. Alyson was still walking towards him when he was done stretching his cramped muscles, so he met her halfway.

"Hi," said Jamie with a small wave.

"You're still here."

Jamie nodded. He was wearing his jacket again.

"You're still here as well. You're not heading back today?"

"I was supposed to..." Alyson combed her fingers through her hair and looked away. Her green eyes filled with tears that threatened to spill over and run down her face.

"What's wrong? What happened?" Jamie stepped forward before he could stop himself.

"My flight was cancelled. There's too much fog. No planes are leaving from the airport until it clears." Alyson's breath was shaky as she managed to keep her tears safe in her eyes. "I'm pretty much screwed."

"I can get you home." Jamie's offer sprang off his tongue before he could stop it.

"Really? You're going to pull that with me right now?"

"I'm not pulling anything, Aly. I have a rental car. I can drive you to Des Moines in time for work tomorrow."

"I'm not going to stay in a car for five hours with you!"

"Aly, please don't deny my help because you're angry. I won't say a word if you don't want me to. You can lay in the backseat and sleep the whole time. You can drive if you want! I can get you home."

"Jamie, I can't."

"Aly, who else is here to help you?"

"I said I can't!" Alyson's voice rose. "Do you understand?"

"Why can't you?" Jamie fought the urge to match her tone.

"Because I'm not strong enough yet." Alyson looked away as she spoke. She licked her lips before she turned back to face the young man. "I didn't come out here to ask for your help or your pity. I came out to tell you Danielle and I think we found a place for me to live."

"Where?"

"Some place called New Ulm." Just saying the name made Alyson cringe. "It's a good place, I guess."

"You don't want to move there, do you?"

"I don't have many options, Jamie."

"You have a bit of time. You don't have to have it all sorted in two days. You only just found out you're going to have a baby."

"The sooner I find a new place, the sooner I can come up with some way to lie to every single person in my life about why I'm moving away."

Jamie stood, shifting his weight from one foot to the other. He was coming up with ideas and a plan, but kept his mouth shut. Anything he said to Alyson right then would just be shot down, and this plan could be the one thing that would actually work. He didn't hold out much hope for her ever wanting to be with him again, but he would do all he could to make sure she was safe and taken care of, and if the baby was his, that he was a part of his child's life.

"Aly, please let me drive you back to Iowa. I'm just trying to help."

There was a moment of tense quiet, where Jamie was sure Alyson would refuse again, but instead, she nodded and sighed. Her shoulders slumped in a defeated manner, but her weary eyes revealed her relief.

"Let me go tell Danielle and get my stuff together."

"I'll be ready."

When Alyson returned five minutes later with Danielle at her side and her duffle bag in her hand, Jamie could see tear marks on her face. There was a tension between the two girls as they came closer. Jamie stepped forward and took Alyson's luggage from her.

"You better not do anything stupid," Danielle warned, her brown eyes reflecting her fierce love for her friend. "I will punch you in the face if you do anything to her."

"I know."

The two girls hugged one last time, and Alyson cried. They whispered that it would be okay and it would all work out before they loosened their grip and stepped apart. Alyson paused before putting a hand on the handle of the car. Jamie watched, holding his breath and praying Alyson wouldn't change her mind at the last second.

"Go," Danielle urged with a tiny nod. "I'll be praying for you and the baby every day. Call me when you get home safe."

Jamie breathed a sigh of relief when Alyson finally opened the door and slid inside.

The trip was quiet as Alyson slept in the backseat. Jamie stopped to get some food and ran into a nearby Target. He wanted to buy some things for Alyson in regards to the pregnancy and asked a nice woman who was working there to help him choose some items. He came out with a body pillow, a blanket, some pre-natal vitamins, cocoa butter, and bottles of water for his sleeping passenger. Very carefully so as to not wake her up, he covered her with the blanket and squeezed one end of the pillow under her head. He paused long enough to run his fingers lightly across her forehead before stepping back. Just the simple touch thrilled him. His body ached for her, and his heart ached for her companionship.

He shook his head as he thought back to the fateful night in California when his past came swirling down on top of him. If only he had been able to block out the thoughts, or not let them affect him so strongly. But he had been a coward and let his fear of facing the past make him lose one of the most important people he had ever met.

"Sweet dreams, love." Jamie gazed tenderly at the young woman. His heart felt more at ease with her in his care. She didn't have any reason to trust him again, but he was going to continue to be there. It might take years for her to even fully forgive him, but he wanted to be there still when that day came.

After smoothing her hair back from her face, Jamie finally got back into the driver's seat and started their journey again. Only five minutes had passed when he heard a noise from his passenger and saw Alyson sit up in the backseat. He smiled at her in the rearview mirror, but held his tongue.

"I-I really have to pee." Alyson rubbed her eyes and swung her feet down to rest on the floor. She gave a curious look at the blanket that was covering her before bundling it up and setting it on the seat beside her. "And I'm starving."

"Here, I got you a sandwich at the Subway I stopped at a few minutes ago." Jamie reached over to the passenger seat and picked something up. "I think I remembered your favorite."

"You just stopped?" Alyson took the sandwich from Jamie's hand and smelled the tempting flavors.

"Yeah, but I can stop again, love." Jamie saw Alyson hungrily take a bite of her sandwich as he glanced into the rearview mirror once more.

"If you don't mind." The voice was quiet.

"Not a problem at all."

"Thanks for the sandwich. This is what I always order."

"Good." A satisfied smile crossed Jamie's face and he renewed his grip on the steering wheel.

It was dark by the time they arrived at the address of Alyson's apartment complex, but it wasn't late. Alyson had slept the whole ride after finishing her sandwich and using a gas station restroom, leaving Jamie to his thoughts as he drove. Jamie turned off the car, but Alyson didn't stir. Five minutes passed, and she hadn't moved. It didn't take long for him to decide to let her sleep and not wake her. He reclined the driver's seat and wiggled around until he was comfortable.

Jamie didn't close his eyes, but continued to stare at the girl. Her thick, dark lashes were resting softly on her cheeks, pointing down to the freckles sprinkled over her face. The edge of the blanket was bunched up in her fists, pulled up under her chin and covering her tired body. She looked peaceful with no crease of worry or fear to mark her forehead.

A lump grew in Jamie's throat as he realized he could have seen this same face that night in California if he had stayed. If he had stayed. He could have held her tight against him, finding out how perfectly their bodies fit together, her hair in his face and her fingers intertwined with his.

For the second night in a row, Jamie fell asleep in his rental car with nothing more than his jacket to act as a blanket and pillow both. There were texts from Garret and Eddie on his phone, but he didn't respond. It had been strangely exhilarating to have broken free from everything and everyone for a couple days to chase down what he knew was more important than anything his career could give him.

His thoughts slowly faded as he drifted off to sleep.

A splash of sunlight landed on Alyson's face as she lay in the backseat of Jamie's car. She had woken up sometime earlier, but had stayed cuddled under the blanket and against the pillow. She didn't know where the two items had come from, but they had given her a better night's sleep than anything else had in months.

She could see Jamie's face from where she lay, and she watched his serene features light up gradually with the rising sun. His hair hung over his forehead and covered one eye, while his lips parted slightly, allowing him to breathe slow and even. His cheekbones caught the morning shadows, and his strong jaw was covered with stubble from not shaving since before his impromptu trip to Minnesota. He was beautiful in the glowing sunlight.

The peace of the vehicle was broken when she was hit with a wave of morning sickness. There was nothing to do except try to quickly and quietly disentangle herself from the blanket and pillow and make it to the edge of the parking lot. She didn't realize her shoes were off until she was already opening the door. She didn't have time to put them on before running across the cold, damp concrete. She avoided a couple broken glass bottles as she knelt down by the grass and relieved her stomach. It wasn't until she lost her balance as she was trying to stand that she was aware of Jamie's presence.

"Oops, you okay?" His hand barely touched her, just enough to catch her if she fell.

"Oh!" Alyson put her hands over her heart. "I didn't know you were there. You were sleeping two seconds ago."

"I heard you get out of the car. Wanted to make sure you were okay." Jamie eyed the girl warily, unsure of whether or not she wanted to be civil.

"Thanks." Alyson forced a smile and began to retrace her steps back to the car. She knew Jamie was staring at her sock feet, but, thankfully he didn't say anything. She stood by the trunk while Jamie opened it and pulled her bag out. All she wanted to do was go inside and eat some breakfast.

"Here, these are for you as well." Jamie handed her a plastic sack along with the blanket and pillow she had just been using. "I bought you these things. I didn't know if you had anything for the pregnancy yet. The lady at the store told me these were the best things to buy."

"Thanks, Jamie." Alyson didn't know how to respond to the gifts he put in her arms.

"Aly, I was thinking as I was sitting and driving..." Jamie bit his lip nervously. He knew this was the best time to bring it up, especially since she seemed to not hate him as much right then. "If you want, I can find a safe place for you to stay. I'm connected to a lot of charities and I could get you a job, or, uh, a position. Something to transfer you from your job here to a different job someplace else. It might make the transition easier if you could tell people you were moving for a job."

Alyson stared at Jamie's face, trying to decide what she was feeling. On one hand, she was screaming at herself to stay as far away from him as she could. But what if she tried to do it all on her own and she failed? The possibilities of what would happen to her baby were greater than her fear of falling back in love with Jamie. She squinted up at the sun and breathed the fresh, morning air deeply before she spoke.

"Can I think about it?"

The question made Jamie's heart soar. He nodded quickly, doing his best to keep his smile small and polite.

"I will probably be okay, but thank you for the thought. I'll let you know."

"Aly, there are a lot of options for places to live and different businesses to be linked to. I would make sure everything was private and everyone knew this was to be kept hush-hush. Just so you know."

Alyson gave the young man another small smile before grabbing her things and turning away. She could hear him behind her closing the trunk of his car as she walked towards the path that led up to her apartment door. That was probably going to be the last memory she ever had of him; her walking back to her apartment in her socks, the morning sun shining into her eyes and the sound of a car trunk slamming shut. She swallowed hard and kept her eyes focused straight ahead.

It was almost suppertime when Alyson finished unpacking. Alyson gave her room a quick glance and nodded with satisfaction before going to the kitchen to make herself some food. She pulled her phone out of her pocket and decided to call her mother. She had been avoiding her parents for the past few weeks, saying that it was just really busy with the start of the new school year.

"Hello?" Mrs. Abidi answered the phone.

"Hi, mom!" It was good to hear her mother's voice.

"Oh, so my daughter is still alive."

The cold, sarcastic comment took Alyson off-guard and she stumbled to a stop, holding onto the counter with one hand. Her heart began to pound heavily as she searched her memory to find a reason why her mother had greeted her this way.

"What did I do?"

"Well, you failed to show up for supper last night when our important guest was here. I had to assume you had died because I knew my daughter would never shame her family by simply not showing up when she said she would."

"What important guest?" Alyson's voice was breathless as her mind pinpointed a conversation she had with her mother months ago about someone coming to visit... "Do you mean that man who is a friend of Uncle Hassan?"

"I have never been more embarrassed in my life than I was when I promised my guest that my daughter would be coming soon and you never came. How could you do that to your family?"

"I-I... Mom! That conversation was so long ago, I've been so busy! Mom, I'm sorry! I didn't remember."

"What were you so busy doing last night you couldn't think to look at your calendar? I know you have it on your bedroom wall."

"I was..." Alyson licked her lips nervously. She knew things were about to go even more badly. "I was at Danielle's."

"You were in Minnesota? With your friend? You were with your friend instead of making your family a priority? Alyson Abidi, who are you right now? You know better than this! You can't just drive up to Minnesota because you feel like it!"

"I really... needed to..." It all sounded so lame. Alyson loved her mother, but there were certain things that took precedence over Janice's feelings for her daughter no matter what, and one of those things was honoring the family name. She could almost feel her mother's displeasure at the way her daughter tripped and stuttered over her words. "I'm just having a tough time because, uh, you know, uh, because of something, and I needed my best friend."

Tears welled up in Alyson's eyes, and she wished she were with her friend right then.

"If you tell me this is because of a man, I don't know what I'm going to do." The displeasure in Janice's voice was very clear.

Alyson's mouth went dry.

"Did you hear your cousin Sumaya's friend who lives in New York was found after she ran away last month? She was pregnant. Can you imagine finding out your daughter is pregnant? I can't imagine. I tell everyone if my daughter is ever caught with a man, she would never want to look at one again when I was done with her. But you would never do something like that, would you?"

Alyson leaned back against the wall and slid down to the floor, holding her head with her free hand. The words of her mother were like sucker-punches to the stomach. Over, and over, and over. Tears dripped from her chin onto her shirt.

"Oh, I have to go, Aly. There's another call coming in. I'm going to talk to your father and see how you can make this up to the family." Janice Abidi ended the conversation with a cool note in her voice. "And whatever it is you feel like you *must* go through right now, get over it quickly. You've been too emotional lately, and it doesn't suit you. Do some deep breathing, or something."

The girl didn't trust her voice to say goodbye before hanging up. There was a hollow feeling in her gut, and she sat in stunned silence on the floor. Sobs rose up in her throat, forcing her to hear the pain her mother had just inflicted upon her. She buried her face in her elbow and wept for several minutes, grateful her roommate was out for the evening. When she calmed down, she picked up her phone to make another call.

"Hello?"

"Elle! I-I just... I j-just talked to... t-to my m-mom."

"Oh my gosh, Aly! You told your mom you were pregnant?"

"N-no! No! I-I didn't t-tell her... I made her s-so, so angry!" Alyson cried harder.

"Aly, what happened?"

"I didn't remember I had said I would g-go home on Sunday night, yesterday, to have supper with m-my parents and this guy who knows my uncle. I hadn't th-thought about it for months! My mom made it sound like I might as well have murdered someone, she was so upset."

"Because you forgot a dinner engagement?"

"I don't even know the guy! He's just a guy who knows my uncle! He was probably a prospective husband. It's been s-so long since I made my mom upset, I f-forgot what it was like." A tremble crept back into Alyson's voice as she spoke. "She mentioned another girl who knows my cousin who was found after she ran away. She was pregnant. My mom said she knew I-I would n-never..."

"Oh, Aly."

"I'm so scared, Elle. I'm so scared! My family is going to know something is wrong if I mysteriously leave and disappear, and they will look for me! They'll look for me, and find me and, and, and then they'll find out about the baby! My family doesn't mess around when it comes to restoring honor to the family. They take it so seriously."

"I still remember that time Anthony gave you a ride home from school, and I was waiting for you at your house. I don't think your dad knew I was there because when he found out that you were in the car alone with a guy he, like, grabbed you and yelled at you. I had never seen him do that before. I was terrified."

"I was, too." Alyson remembered that incident as well. "There are other things, as well. I forget them sometimes because they're my parents, and I love them. I know they try to love me in a way that I understand, but when I look back and see those times..."

Alyson's mind flashed back to the days of chaos, when there were broken lamps and chairs, glass shattering as a family portrait was yanked off the wall and dashed onto the floor. Screaming and cursing, slammed doors and a weeping mother in the kitchen had been the soundtrack of her life, stuck in an endless loop. Sleepless nights of worry, clouded mornings of wondering what had happened in the dark hours, and heavy evenings as the cycle repeated itself all over again.

Then suddenly, there was silence. Not the silence of peace, but the silence of a tortured soul told to keep quiet. The broken furniture was mended, the family picture was replaced with a new one, but the mother still wept in the kitchen until she, too, was silenced.

"We are restoring honor to our family!" the one in charge of the silence commanded. "Stop crying! We're all better off, and we are no longer shaming the family."

There was no more explanation and the small child was left to feel the empty spaces in her family on her own.

"Elle, I don't think we're going to be able to do this by ourselves," whispered Alyson. "I think we need help."

Chapter six
"I told my mom that you cry a lot."

"I don't know what else to do." Alyson pulled a Kleenex out of the box to wipe the tears and mascara off her face. "My mom just blew up at me for missing supper with a man who doesn't even know me. I can't risk this, and the sooner I figure it out the sooner I'll know my baby will be safe."

"Are you thinking of asking Jamie to help?"

"I don't have many other options, Elle." The words were quiet. "No one else knows about the baby. I know you don't want me to interact with him..."

"He'll be glad to help. He proved that this weekend." Danielle sighed. "I'm just really worried you're not going to handle being in contact with him very well."

"I know. But I'm going to do this for my baby."

"Okay. I'm behind you in this. If you need me to go find him and beat him up or step on his foot again, I will."

"I love you, Elle."

"I love you, too. Let me know what Jamie says."

"I will. Bye." Alyson hung up.

She blew her nose and wiped more tears from her face before she pushed herself up off the kitchen floor. She was no longer hungry, but she knew her baby would be, so she grabbed a banana out of the fruit bowl as she passed it on her way to her bedroom. She slowly changed into her pajamas as she tried to come up with another way to save herself without running to Jamie.

There had been whispered stories of other girls from her father's country who had disappeared for a few months, and then returned to their homes with the ghosts of their choices haunting their every step. They didn't laugh. Their eyes never seemed to smile when their mouths tried to, and whenever a baby cried, they cried, too. Alyson was now faced with the choice those girls had to make; baby, or family?

Some girls held onto their child and ran, leaving all they knew and loved behind. Some of them survived. Some were drug back home without a baby, and without hope of mercy. Other young ladies knew they didn't have a chance on their own and took matters into their own hands. The blood of the tiny, living child ripped from their wombs may have been washed away long ago, but to them, the red still dripped from their fingers. Then there were the ones that didn't make it. Sumaya told her about the girls from her school who had gotten caught.

"They were stoned in front of their houses," her cousin whispered. "I could hear them screaming from my house three streets over."

Alyson sat on her bed and cried. She had never anticipated a moment like this, a feeling like this, a choice like this. Nothing she had ever learned from school or her past could have prepared her for the moment when she realized her bad choices were endangering another person.

"God, I don't even deserve to pray to You right now." Alyson's chest shuddered as she breathed. "I-I know I've done something unforgivable. But please, God, don't let my baby get hurt because of what I've done. Protect us."

After a moment of silence from heaven, Alyson stood up and grabbed her new pillow and blanket. Since her roommate was gone, she could snuggle down in the corner of the couch in the living room for a while. It was her favorite spot in the apartment.

Alyson pulled up Jamie's number and noticed that her hands were shaking. The memory of her mother's disapproval made her gut twist. She bit her lip as she tried to imagine what her mother would do if she discovered the truth. Missing a meal with her uncle's friend was trivial to the existence of an illegitimate child. What would her mother actually do?

No, Aly. Don't go there. Alyson shook her head and focused on the buzzing from her phone. *She's never going to find out.*

There were several rings before the call was answered.

"Hello?" a voice yelled loudly. Alyson pulled the phone away from her ear.

"Jamie?"

"Aly! What's wrong?" shouted Jamie.

"Where are you?"

"Backstage. I've run offstage to answer this. Sorry if I'm loud, my ears are ringing."

"I can call back..."

"No, you're more important than a show. I told Garret to tell me if you tried to get ahold of me."

The words slid off his tongue easily, despite the meaning behind them that came barreling into Alyson's stomach. She had shouted and screamed at him, blaming him angrily for all the pain she was feeling, yet her phone call was so important to the singer that he had left his audience, his stage, and his concert to spend his time talking to her.

"What's up?" asked Jamie.

"I want to take you up on your offer." Alyson hoped her voice was loud enough and strong enough for him to hear her. She hugged her blanket around her shoulders and breathed deeply. The lump in her throat ached. "I need you to find me a safe place."

"Absolutely, I'll get working on that right away." Jamie didn't even skip a beat or sound surprised. "Gar, get that list of things from my bag, no, n- yeah, that one. Start highlighting things you know would work for Aly. Okay, love, this is my last show of the tour. People are expecting me to head back to London right away, but I can push that back and stay in the States to figure things out with you. Does that sound okay? We'll figure something out, yeah? We'll get you someplace safe."

Alyson nodded with tears of relief brimming in her eyes, the ache growing stronger. She grabbed another Kleenex from the box, but wadded it into a ball in her fist before she could use it.

"You okay? Everything okay?" Jamie asked with concern in his voice.

"I talked to my mom tonight... I didn't even tell her anything about you or the baby, but something else came up, and she got really, uh, mad. So that was hard." Alyson's voice cracked.

"Oh, love." Jamie sighed. "I'm so sorry. Do you want to talk about it?"

"No. No." Alyson shook her head and remembered the fact she was talking to him when he was supposed to be on stage. "I'm done. Just let me know when you've come up with ideas or whatever."

"All right, Aly. I'll talk to you very soon!"

"Bye."

Once the phone call was done, Alyson cuddled into the corner of the couch and cried until she fell asleep. Nightmares of not being able to run fast enough or hide well enough roused her from her slumber. The light was on in her roommate's room, warning Alyson to weep silently into her pillow. She wrapped her arms around her stomach and held her baby. Again, she prayed through her tears.

"God, I don't even know why I'm praying. I know this is my fault. But please, keep my baby safe. Please."

Alyson didn't know if her prayers were being answered over the next two days, but she began to feel safe with the future of her child in Jamie's hand. She built the walls around her own heart tall and strong, protecting her emotions; however she let herself trust Jamie's intentions towards her child. In between the mad dashes to the toilet and crying over how on earth she was going to make it another day, Alyson felt the tension and a bit of the anger ease up. Two days later, though, it all came rushing back with renewed vigor.

"Aly, Jamie's in London." Danielle's early morning phone call had woken Alyson from a fitful night's sleep.

"What?" Alyson sat up, her morning voice rough and groggy. "H-he said... he said he would stay!"

"I don't know what he's doing, but it's showing up online."

"No, no, no...! No! This... this can't be happening!" Alyson swung her feet to the floor and stood up. She wobbled for a moment, then reached for the trash can next to her bed.

"Maybe he's there trying to find something to help you?"

"Or what if he just wanted to see me beg for help so he c-could..." Alyson's voice cut out.

"Aly..."

"I can't do this alone!" Alyson began to feel lightheaded at the thought. "I-I... I can't. I just..."

"Aly, calm down. It's going to be okay."

"No..." Alyson couldn't say anything else. She had been putting so much faith on Jamie pulling through for her and the baby; the thought of him breaking his promise was too much for her to bear on her own. All she wanted was for her baby to be safe. "Elle, I c-can't talk..."

Shaking fingers pressed the red hang-up button and quickly navigated through the phone book, until she found the desired number. Alyson put her phone back up to her ear, tears tumbling down her lashes as she waited for Jamie to answer. He had offered her the one thing she truly needed, and then he snatched it back and left her alone. The longer the phone rang, the angrier she became.

"Aly!" Jamie's voice was cheerful as he answered.

"You left me!" Aly screamed her accusations into the mouthpiece of the phone. She didn't care that her roommate was still sleeping. "H-how dare you! H-how d-dare you!"

"What in the world?" Jamie hadn't been expecting an outburst when he picked up the phone. "Aly, what ar-"

"Y-you said! You said you would stay after your tour ended to help me! Y-you said that!" Alyson sobbed out her words angrily.

"Aly, I *am* helping you!"

"Then why did you leave me?!" The question was an echo of what she had been chanting in her mind over and over since she watched him walk out on her in L.A. "Why? You have to tell me why!"

"What do you mean I left you?"

"You're in L-London!"

"Aly! Please calm down! Who told you I was in London?"

"I can't calm down!" Her stomach was in so much pain, she wasn't sure if she was going to be able to go to work that day. She pulled the trash can closer, just in case.

"I can't understand you when you're carrying on like this." Jamie's tone was tense as he struggled to sound patient.

"Danielle told me. You lied to me, Jamie! Right after I was starting to think I c-could trust you again!"

"Aly, you can trust me! You can! I'm in London to meet with some people who I think are the best fit for you and the baby!" Jamie was defensive as he told the young mother the truth behind why he had left. "I didn't tell you because I didn't want to get your hopes up if it didn't work out. I'm not in London because I changed my mind about helping you!"

"H-How am I supposed to believe that?" Alyson tried to calm herself. She was going to be sick otherwise. Her eyes burned.

"Well, if you're not wanting to trust me, then just wait three days, and you'll know."

"Why? What's in three days?"

"That's when all the details are supposed to be finished, and I can tell you about it."

Alyson said nothing.

"Okay?"

"O-okay." Alyson's voice came out quiet. Her breath hitched as she inhaled. One hand slipped down to her stomach and she stroked it, imagining she was comforting her child, even though she knew the act was more comforting to her own frayed emotions.

"Can you give me three days before you write me off again?"

"I guess." Alyson wiped her cheeks. "I don't have many other options at this point."

"I'm sorry finding out I was gone hurt you." The gentle voice calmed the girl's pounding heart. She closed her eyes and leaned her head back against the wall as she listened. "I didn't even think you would find out."

"I-I just... I can't do this on my o-own."

"I know, love. I'm not going to let you down." Jamie's voice grew rough for split second. "We're going to get through this."

"Thank you." Alyson let out a shaky breath. "I'll hear from you in three days?"

"Three days."

He kept his promise, and Alyson began to breathe easier about trusting Jamie again. Not with her heart, of course, but with her future. The proposition Jamie gave her was a position at a school training new teachers. She would maintain her teacher status while helping train young people who wanted to teach.

"Do you think your mum and dad would be happy with you for being chosen for something like that?" Jamie was glad to have a conversation with Alyson when she was calm. He had worked tirelessly to get everything ready by the three-day deadline he had promised the girl, and he was exhausted from not getting a chance to recover from jet lag yet.

"Yeah. They would be over the moon. For me to be a teaching instructor, I mean... Anything that makes me more important and get more recognition. It's their dream for me to do stuff like this."

"They should dream bigger things for you." Jamie gave a short laugh.

"Well, I'm sure they do, but they've always pushed academics with me. They made it my thing, you know? It went really well with my good girl image. Brainiac nerd with prudish values, that kind of thing." Alyson heard Jamie give a little laugh. She shook her head and refocused on the original intent of the conversation. "Anyways. You don't get to be the valedictorian of a class of 350 students and graduate early just by being a little smarter than the other kids. You have to fight for it. That's why I became a teacher, because teachers are the ones changing the world and helping shape minds."

"Then I think this is the right spot for you. Even if all you do is sit there and talk about how much you love being a teacher, I guarantee you will inspire someone." Jamie knew the girl couldn't see him, but his eyes were shining.

"How will this work out? Do I go to my boss and give her my two weeks' notice?" Alyson nibbled on the knuckle of her pointer finger nervously.

"No, I'm making plans for that right now. Don't worry about any of that. I'll keep in touch and tell you things as we find them out."

"Thanks."

"How's the baby?" Jamie's voice was soft again, making Alyson smile in spite of herself.

"Good, I guess. I'm still not showing at all, which is good. I just don't know how you're supposed to feel when you're pregnant."

"I don't either." Jamie smiled when he heard the girl chuckle. "We'll figure out doctors and such once all of this is settled, all right, love?"

"All right."

"Everything else okay?"

It was midnight for Jamie, and he was pacing the floor of his bedroom in his mother's house. He had his own place in London, but he liked to spend a few days with his family after a long time away. His father had left them years ago, and he took the role of being the man of the family for his three younger siblings very seriously. They had been excited to see him, then confused when he told them he wasn't going to be home for long. His mother pressed for answers, but all Jamie could tell her was that he needed to help take care of a friend. He had waited for everyone to go to sleep before he made the international call to Iowa.

"I don't even remember what okay feels like."

"Hang on, love. Just a bit longer, and it'll all be worked out."

"Mmm." Alyson nodded. She couldn't wait for it to all be settled so she could sleep through the night and not feel like her life could be jeopardized at any second.

The call ended, and there was silence from Jamie for the most part over the next week and a half. She received a handful of texts saying things were working out nicely and he hoped she was doing well, but that was all. Alyson was grateful for the space. Tough days at work drained her long before the weekend and she had to push hard, but she didn't let up. She needed to put her all into it before she left. She owed that much to the children that held her heart.

October first dawned bright and sunny, the rays of the sun making the orange, yellow and red leaves glow. Dew sparkled briefly, and then disappeared. It was still warm enough to wear short sleeves without a jacket, but Alyson donned her baggy sweatshirt to hide the little bit of tummy that was starting to show. It was out of paranoia more than necessity.

There was a hum of activity at the school when Alyson arrived, pulling into the parking lot with the familiar sense of trepidation she carried with her throughout each day. Vehicles she had never seen before were parked in the visitor spots, and a crowd of kids were trying to see through a window into the principal's office. She took her bag into her classroom, then left to find out the news from the staff resource room. Before she could enter, two familiar voices reached her ears. She stopped just outside the door, still hidden from view. She put her hand on the wall to steady herself as she listened.

"We heard you're one of the best schools in the area," Jamie was saying. "We would love to have one of your teachers come and train the new teachers starting at the school we sponsor in Bedford."

"It's a year-long commitment, but we provide them with food and lodging and make sure they have everything they need," Garret added. "We're very passionate about this project, and we want schools like you, private schools with excellent reputations, to be able to train others."

Alyson knew if she tried to walk into the office she would give away everything. She slipped quickly back to her classroom, her arms crossed over the twisting inside of her stomach. She heard enough to know they were there to put their plan into motion, but she was more angry than excited. Garret was in there, and she wasn't ready to face that man again. She sat down in the chair at her desk and cradled her head in her hands.

"Breathe, Aly," she whispered. "In... Out..."

Thirty seconds later there was a knock on her door.

"Aly, we have a proposal for you." Alyson's boss stuck her head around the door and smiled at her. "A very exciting proposal."

Heart pounding and head spinning, Alyson nodded and motioned for her to come in. She stood up and leaned against the edge of her desk. She held onto it tightly, her knuckles aching against the hard surface. How had Jamie gotten her boss to choose her? They had to have said something to make Alyson the obvious choice without saying her name. Whatever he had said, he looked very pleased with himself as he filed into her classroom behind the principal. Three young men trailed in after him. Alyson licked her lips nervously.

"This is our third grade teacher, Miss Aly."

"Good morning, Miss Aly." Jamie stepped forward and shook the teacher's hand. He gave her a quick wink and squeezed her fingers as he flashed his bright smile. "My name is Jamie Donald, we're here at your school looking for someone who could move to England for the rest of the school year to train some teachers at a school myself and my friends are sponsoring."

"O-oh?" It was all Alyson trusted herself to say.

"Yes. We like to give back to the community, and this school is one that would impact our society in a big way." Tommy nodded, trying to get Alyson to smile at him as he spoke. When the girl barely made eye contact, he frowned. He looked to Eddie and saw his friend observe everything with an expression of concern on his face.

"They're going to sit in the classrooms today and just see who they think would best fill the position. They'll be in and out, so just teach like you always do. I know you'll impress them." Having one of their teachers be flown across to the other side of the world as a teaching instructor was a thrilling idea for the principal. She wanted one of her own chosen, despite the fact that any teacher she lost would be almost impossible to replace, especially two months into the school year, and especially Alyson Abidi. She might be young, but she was one of the best teachers they had ever had.

"Perfect!" Alyson grinned after getting a hard look from her boss. She hoped no one else could hear that her heartbeat was roaring in her ears. A nervous sweat broke out all over her body, and she was afraid she would throw up.

"Let me know if you guys need anything!" The principal left the room with a satisfied smile.

"You okay?" Jamie was by her side in an instant, gaze focused and hand touching her arm before he could stop himself.

"Are you serious right now, Jamie?" Alyson snapped in a low but serious voice. She yanked her arm away from him. "I haven't seen the others since I had sex with them! I can't deal with this right now!"

"I'm sorry, Aly. I didn't know they were going to come with me until last night." Jamie put a light touch on Alyson's shoulder. He had been opposed to the idea, knowing Alyson would react to it negatively, but he had been overruled. "My management team wanted them to come with me."

"What in the world does your management team have to do with this? With us? I mean, me?"

"Things are... going to be a bit different," Jamie spoke slowly. "It's a little complicated, but to have this work out properly, I had to bring them into the situation."

"You told someone else about the baby without asking me?" Alyson leaped back, eyes wide.

"I had to!"

"You should never have done that!"

"I'm sorry, I was forced into it!"

"You never told me this was part of the plan!"

"I'm sor-..."

"Jamie, this is too much," Alyson cut him off, glancing over at the three silent young men who were standing to the side and watching the couple argue in hushed tones.

"If I could have made this happen any other way, I would have, you have to believe me." He moved his body to stand between Alyson and the others. He watched her peer over his shoulder and look away quickly.

"Does Garret have to be in here?" She couldn't look Jamie in the eye as she spoke.

"Yeah." Jamie's face was tense. "He has to be with me so he can help with the decisions. Management said."

"I hate your management."

"It is going to get you out of here, though. We just have to get through today." Jamie dared to put an arm around Alyson's shoulders to give her a side hug.

A student came running into the room and stared at the four strangers with an open mouth. Jamie quickly stepped back from Alyson and smiled at the young child.

"Miss Aly, who are these people?"

"This is Mr. Jamie, and these are his friends." Alyson leaned forward to speak to the girl. She gave her a smile, comforted by the familiar face and voice.

"Hello!" Jamie waved and watched the interaction with interest.

"Do you guys like each other?"

"Sometimes grownups hug each other when they are saying hello."

"He looked like he wanted to kiss you." The girl made a face. She was in third grade and very opposed to the thought of anyone wanting to kiss someone else.

"He doesn't want to kiss me. Can you put your backpack on your chair for me? Class starts in five minutes." Alyson didn't have to look at Jamie to know his cheeks were as pink as hers from the child's accusation.

More children began to trickle in, and Alyson was able to put all of her focus on them. Garret slipped into the corner and settled into a chair, looking as miserable as Alyson felt on the inside. She didn't know that in his mind he was reliving the argument he had had with Jamie the night before.

"Believe me, I like this less than you do," Jamie retorted when Garret came rushing into Jamie's hotel room with his fists clenched. "Do you know how awful it's going to be for Aly to see you again?"

"Sure, mate, and me as well!" Garret huffed. "I'd really like to forget the whole thing."

"I know, but we don't have a choice, Gar. We're going to just have to roll with it. If we're going to help Aly, this needs to happen."

"I understand wanting to be a stand-up guy and helping her because she might be carrying your kid and you used to be with her, but why do you have to drag all the rest of us into this? This doesn't have to be a massive ordeal! Just send her money or something!" Garret paced the room.

"I'm not having this conversation with you. Not now."

"Listen, the best thing for her may be to just move on from us!"

"You don't understand; her life is at stake. Her being pregnant could get her into loads of trouble."

Garret stopped and shot his friend an incredulous look.

"This is a real thing, Gar. Giving her this job will get her to a safe place where people assume she's working and leave her alone."

Garret sighed and leaned back against the wall. Jamie tried to ignore him, still plagued by thoughts of what may have happened between Garret and Alyson. They had moments where they slipped back into their old roles as each other's best friend, but those moments didn't last for long. Jamie was already planning on using the whole situation to inspire writing for his next album.

"Why did you choose Bedford? Why did you choose a place so close to us?"

"The closer she is, the better I can keep an eye on her. If something happens and she's still in the States, it would take a whole day just to travel here to get to her."

Garret glared at the carpet, saying nothing.

"You went over the lists with me, the school in Bedford is the best fit!" snapped Jamie.

"What about that place in New York? You thought that would work!"

"I looked into it; the people who run it are two young men, and there are no other full-time women on staff. She would have been uncomfortable."

"Jamie, I can't go home and tell Serenity what I've done and add on, 'By the way, darling, I helped move that same girl to live an hour down the road.'"

"Stop your moaning for two minutes and realize how important it is to get Aly out of Iowa, okay? Thanks."

"I just know I'm going to get there, and Aly is going to be upset. I'm going to be upset. I'm upset just thinking about it." Garret swore as he ran his hands through his hair. "If I could erase one night from my life, it would be that one, Jay. I would make everything about that night disappear."

Jamie sat on the edge of his bed silently.

"Does she talk about it?" Garret was sniffling as a few tears ran down his red cheeks.

"About what?"

"About what happened with me?"

Jamie shook his head no. Their conversations, or arguments rather, had all been about themselves.

"There are no answers. None. There's absolutely no bloody way to find out what we've done." Garret swore again.

"You danced with her, got too drunk and then slept with her, okay? People do that sometimes." Jamie gestured with his hands to show his resignation to the idea.

"But I didn't, Jay! One minute I was fine, the next minute we could hardly stay on our feet! Something happened. You know I don't get sloshed easily! I don't know how I couldn't see it coming. I just... I don't know."

"It's done now, mate. Stop letting it pull you down." Jamie watched Garret roll his red, watery eyes at Jamie's words. "Did you ask Trent if you could sit back from the school meeting tomorrow?"

"I did. I offered to do anything he wanted." Garret resumed his pacing. "But he says I have to be there, doesn't understand why I'm so worked up about some random girl Jamie is keen on."

"He said that? Said I was keen on her?"

"I don't know, something like that."

"No, no, no! I can't just have it be 'something like that,' because if people are talking about me being keen on Aly, we could potentially have a problem! This charity move is supposed to be us making an unbiased decision to bring a qualified teacher to work at a school we sponsor! I don't want people whispering about who she is, or who I like."

"Is she actually qualified?"

"She graduated at the top of her class, got her teaching degree by the age of twenty-one and has a job teaching. I'd say that's pretty qualified."

"At least we don't have to lie about that," muttered Garret.

"We don't need her linked up to me and creating headlines. The news that she's expecting is to be kept top secret; we don't need a love affair story coming out of this. We have enough drama going on."

Garret turned away. He knew Jamie was talking about him and Tommy.

"Management knows she's pregnant, but they don't know the baby is connected to any of us. We have to keep it that way."

"Jamie, how is all of this supposed to work out? Really."

"What do you mean? We'll choose Aly, get her into the school..."

"No, with the baby, Jay."

Jamie shifted uncomfortably.

"What about the baby?"

"You're acting as if you're the dad, but what if it's Tommy? Or me? Tommy wants this baby. Have you heard him talk about it? He's changing. Trying to really get himself together because of this."

Jamie stood up and exhaled deeply.

"How is this going to work with all of us? We understand Alyson is special to you, but the baby..."

No response.

"She's going to live right down the road from us, we have to communicate about this." Garret moved to stand in front of his friend, forcing his gaze to focus on him. "What is going to happen? Who is going to do what?"

"We let Aly decide. She should be the one in charge. It's her body and safety that are affected the most by this."

"Mate, you've stalked her in another state. She didn't ask for that."

"That had nothing to do with you!" Jamie's eyes flashed. "You have to come to the school tomorrow, and you're going to do it. I know this blows for you, but we don't have any other options!"

Garret left the room and Jamie sat on the edge of his bed with his head in his hands. It was still a struggle for him to think about someone other than him being the father of Aly's child. He knew he had to think of the big picture. He had to be realistic. He only had a one-in-three chance of being the father. All Aly had asked him to do was get her to someplace safe. She didn't invite him into her life as a friend, or as the father of her baby. If Aly didn't want them to be a part of her pregnancy, she had that right.

Later that evening he joined Tommy, Eddie and Garret in Eddie's room to tell them about the next day. When the conversation was over, Jamie stood by the door, wanting to simply walk out and ignore the fact there was another topic they needed to discuss.

"Jay." Garret's low voice urged him to do what he knew he had to do.

"What else are you not telling us?" asked Eddie.

"Is everything okay?" Tommy watched Jamie closely.

"There's something we need to talk about." Garret spoke for his friend.

"It's not going to be easy being in this situation, you know, as potential fathers, or whatever term you want to give it." Jamie hurried through his words. "But, at the end of the day, Aly gets to say who does what, and if she wants none of us to interfere, we will respect that."

Garret stared down at his hands and said nothing.

"Are we going to see her tomorrow when we're at the school?" asked Tommy.

"I certainly hope so. She doesn't know anything about it, so I'm not sure how she's going to react."

"Can't you tell her now?" asked Eddie with concern. "She should know we're going to be there."

"But what if she finds out we're coming, and then doesn't show up to work? Then we're there asking for someone we're supposed to not know about and having to choose a teacher we don't want. The only sure way to guarantee she's going to be there is to just let it happen." The thought made Jamie sick, but he couldn't take any chances...

Looking over at Alyson as she interacted with her students as they entered the classroom, Jamie finally stopped holding his breath. The third grade class quickly discovered his presence and formed a crowd around him. He pulled out his funniest jokes and stories and basked in their giggles and smiles. They were enamored by his accent and antics and begged him to tell "just one more" story as they waited for the bell to ring. Jamie loved kids, and the children in Alyson's class were charming and engaging. His smile dropped when he remembered these were the kids Alyson was going to have to leave very soon. He glanced at her again, but she was distracted by the two other members of his band.

"I wanted to tell you I'm sorry we had to surprise you like this." Eddie kept his voice low. "Tommy and I are a part of the charity as well so people thought it would look better if we came with to help choose the teacher."

"I'll be fine. Thank you." Alyson was genuinely at ease with Eddie. He had been watching her since he walked into the room, ready to nod or smile at any moment of eye contact.

"You look great," said Tommy.

"Thanks." Alyson gave a weak smile.

"Are you doing well?" asked Eddie.

"I'm just anxious, you know. I just want to get out of here and settle down where it is safe."

"Don't worry." Tommy was quick to reassure the girl. "Jamie and Garret are working hard to get this all taken care of."

Alyson gave a quick look over her shoulder at the young man who was in the corner. He was busily typing something out on his phone, a pen in his teeth and a stack of papers on his lap.

"Just teach." Eddie saw the way Alyson's eyes began to fill with disquiet at the sight of Garret. "And pretend like you don't know us. Don't even look at us."

"We won't bother you at all. This is all for looks in any case," said Tommy with a quick reach to her arm. He only let his hand rest on her for a second, before he pulled it back. Jamie had warned them to leave her be and let her have her space.

The last student walked into the classroom as the bell rang, and the members of *Jupiter Waits* took their spots at the back of the room.

"We look forward to watching your teaching methods, Miss Aly," Jamie said in a mock-serious voice that made Alyson's lips move into a smile before she could catch herself.

Class started, and it was as if Alyson transformed into a new person in front of the eyes of the young men. The scared mother who was trying to save her baby was stripped away, and there stood a young woman, full of confidence, sure of her abilities to lead a classroom. She gave out smiles and compliments to each child as she taught, giving misbehaving students a raised eyebrow to quiet them without saying a word. More than once her clear laughter rang out, endearing her to her students and the visitors in the back of the room. Before Alyson knew it, her day was halfway over, and her boss was motioning for the guys to follow her.

"I didn't realize you would all stay in Alyson's room the whole time." She looked anxious. "Let me take you to another classroom."

"I'm going to stay in here," Jamie told the others quietly as they left the room. He stayed at his spot in the back with his hands shoved into his pockets and eyes riveted on the teacher in the front. He had fallen for the girl once before, now he was watching her do what she loved the most, and he couldn't take his eyes off her. His mind began to paint a picture of where they would be right then if their night in L.A. had gone differently.

Alyson was very aware of Jamie's presence as she continued to teach spelling, handwriting and all through reading class. Their eyes met once, and Alyson felt every thought in her mind unravel in the split second she let herself soak in his adoring gaze. He pushed one side of his mouth up into a crooked grin. She had to remember how to move before she could give him a quick nod and turn away. She spent the next five minutes with her back towards Jamie to hide how red and hot her cheeks were. She wanted to scream and cry because she wasn't supposed to feel that way about Jamie again, but all she could do was breathe in and out, over and over, focusing on the movement of her lungs and hoping none of her students would notice how upset she was.

"Miss Aly, are you crying again?" one of her students asked as Alyson stood nearby helping with a difficult math problem.

"I'm fine, honey." Alyson gave the child a sad smile. "Do your work."

"I told my mom that you cry a lot," one boy turned around in his seat and said, "and she said you were probably going through a really tough time."

Jamie stood there listening to the kids all speak up about their teacher's recent fragile emotional state and watching Alyson try to hush them, humiliation heating up her cheeks. He wanted to tell her it was fine, she didn't need to be embarrassed, and crying was okay, but he couldn't, so he stood along the wall and looked down at his feet. At lunch break, Jamie finally left his spot and walked towards the front of the room where Alyson was cleaning off her whiteboard.

"You are amazing." His words were coupled with a smile. "I knew you'd be a great teacher, but this is beyond what I imagined. I can't wait to get you into the school in Bedford."

"How long until I'm chosen and get out of here?" Alyson looked exhausted.

"You'll have a couple weeks to train a replacement and write up a curriculum to use. It's not a posh job, but it is actually a great need, and the community really wants this," Jamie explained as he watched Alyson pull her lunch out of a desk drawer and start to eat it. "And this way you'll still have a job to come back to if you want to come back sometime in the future."

The fact that Jamie had thought of that meant more to Alyson than she knew how to say "thank you" for. Her eyes teared up, but she quickly blinked them away and cleared her throat. She had thought she would have to give up a teaching career forever to take care of her child, but Jamie had given her an open door to come back one day.

"Is this something you're interested in? You're awfully quiet." Jamie's voice turned gentle.

"Oh, yes!" Alyson blurted out quickly. "I just... I'm overwhelmed. I thought we would never find a solution."

"I'm just taking care of you and the baby." Jamie flashed a smile. Alyson could tell he wanted to touch her, but he kept his hands safely in his pockets. "We'll make this work."

At the end of the day, the four young men promised they would be in touch after they discussed with their people back in England what they thought.

"We definitely have who we need at this school," insisted Garret. "All we need to do now is figure out which person will best fit our needs."

"I'm so excited to see who they choose!" The principal smiled at her team of teachers after the young men left. "How do you guys feel?"

"I feel like my classes went well," one of Alyson's co-workers said. "And Tommy, the guy who sat in my classroom, he was so sweet."

"Yeah, I feel like they were impressed by us, and by the kids," the high school science teacher put in.

"Me too!" The principal was pleased to hear the reports. "How did you feel like it went for you, Aly?"

"They were... nice. I think they liked what they saw. It's hard to know because they're just so nice, you're not sure if they like your work or if they are just trying to not make you feel bad."

Those listening to Alyson seemed confused by the remark, but didn't question it. The teacher meeting was dismissed after the principal discussed how the person who was chosen would have to finish out the month to train someone to take their place before they could go. The younger teachers twittered excitedly about the guys and their day and how they hoped they would get chosen. The only one who didn't seem worked up by the opportunity was Alyson. Her boss pulled her aside as they were leaving the office.

"Alyson, do you think they didn't like your work?" She seemed concerned.

"No, I-I just... I know I work with amazing people. I don't want to think I'm so impressive and they loved everything I did. I honestly don't know." Alyson knew the job was hers. She knew she was the one chosen. She knew it wasn't because of her teaching.

"Okay, because I specifically suggested you when they said they wanted someone who was young, but mature, in their twenties and who had experience traveling and living outside of the States. Not only are you academically well-qualified for the job, but your dad's family is from Pakistan, and you have traveled. You're twenty-two, and you're an amazing teacher, and I know you would represent us well overseas. That's why I told them they should start in your room."

The glowing report warmed Alyson's heart, and she gave her boss a side hug before leaving. People didn't notice the baby when she hugged them, but she was aware that one day she could wrap her arms around someone and they would feel her secret growing inside of her. Alyson got into her car to leave and smiled to herself over the fact that even without the baby, she was chosen for the job.

Alyson pulled up to the address Jamie texted her after he had left the school building and looked up at the fanciest hotel in Des Moines. She took a deep breath as she climbed out of her car, glancing around quickly to make sure no one was paying her any attention. There was the normal amount of hustle and bustle on the street, and no one appeared to notice the girl hurrying towards the entrance of the hotel.

It had been Jamie's idea to meet up and discuss the details and conditions they wanted before they met with his management team. Alyson had only agreed because she was more scared of the management team than Jamie and Garret.

Jamie opened the hotel room door for Alyson when she knocked.

"Hey! Glad you could make it!" Jamie stepped back to let her in.

Alyson saw Eddie, Garret and Tommy as she walked into the room. Tommy and Eddie waved and smiled while Garret stared at the computer on his lap, refusing to acknowledge her presence. Jamie led her over to an empty chair and offered her a cup of tea.

"Oh, thank you." Alyson gave a little smile. She didn't want to fight with the guys. Not right then.

"Jamie is always making tea." Tommy gave the girl a grin, excited to see her seem a bit more at ease with them. "Pretty decent at it, too."

"When it's not so hot that it's going to burn my tongue off, I will tell you if I agree."

The smile on her face was not lost on Jamie as he watched her out of the corner of his eye. She was trying. He wanted to blurt out how brave she was being, but instead he plopped down on the couch next to Garret, startling his friend and receiving an annoyed look.

"Budge up, Jay." Garret jabbed his elbow into Jamie's side.

"Shall we get started then?" asked Eddie as he looked at the two on the couch.

"I..." Alyson began, and then stopped.

"What?" Jamie and Eddie asked at the same moment.

"I don't know how to do this." She was holding her tea cup so tightly the hot liquid was burning her fingers from the other side of the glass. "What is this going to do? How is this supposed to help? And I thought your management team was supposed to be on our side?"

"They are." Jamie's voice was serious as he answered. "But I want you to have everything you want and need. They have an idea in their minds about what this should look like, and I don't want you to be taken by surprise. Garret and I thought this would be a good way to make sure the meeting on Friday benefits everyone."

"So, wh-... what do I do?"

"You just tell us what you want, Alyson." Tommy's voice was strong and confident, telling the girl she didn't have to be afraid. "We'll take care of the rest."

Jamie watched the way Alyson responded to Tommy's words and shifted uncomfortably on the couch. Tommy had said such a simple phrase, something Jamie could have easily said himself, yet he knew he would have never gotten a response like that. Alyson's shoulders loosened and the lines of worry on her face faded away, transforming her from tense to trusting. A little smile passed between Alyson and Tommy before they broke eye contact and returned to the conversation.

Figuring out the details of what Alyson wanted was a slow, uphill climb. It was more than just writing down the first thing that popped into their heads; they needed to think of every situation and what each one might entail. Each question bought up a million little things that started a whole new discussion.

At first Alyson's requests seemed very straightforward, but as they dove into the specifics, they became much more complicated. She wanted limits on and control over all the contact people from back home had with her, she wanted absolutely no media attention over the job in Bedford, and she wanted to live in a place that seemed proper for a single girl who was a simple school teacher. She wanted to appear as normal as she could to anyone watching her life.

Jamie and Garret sat huddled on the couch over the laptop where Garret acted as the scribe. Everyone put in their ideas, but Jamie and Alyson were the ones who settled on the final decisions. They slipped into the rhythm of being on the same team so effortlessly Alyson forgot about everything else as they worked. Suppertime came, and they ordered room service.

"Do you have enough to eat?" asked Eddie as they divided the dishes into fifths.

"Yeah, I'm fine." Alyson dismissed his concern with a smile.

"Here, have some of my chicken. Chicken is good for the baby." Tommy generously shared a portion of the meal he had on his plate.

"Oh, thank you." Alyson was grateful for the extra food. She hadn't realized she was starving until they stopped to eat.

"Here, there's one dinner roll left." Eddie put it on her plate.

"Thank you."

"More salad?"

"We can order more food."

"I'm fine. I promise."

"You sure?" asked Tommy.

"She said she's fine." Jamie had been watching his two friends with Alyson closely.

Alyson sensed the mood in the room immediately turn tense. No one said anything else, and Alyson's food felt dry and tasteless in her mouth as she tried to chew and swallow. The food barely made it down her throat, but she managed to wash it down with a drink of water. Tommy and Eddie took their plates and returned to their spots. After a few minutes of silverware clinking on their plates, Eddie broke the silence.

"Aly, are you feeling okay with how things are going so far?"

"Yeah." Alyson didn't sound convincing. "It's a lot to think about. It's all very heavy."

"Why does all this matter so much?" Tommy's interest was piqued by the intense amount of detail Jamie and Alyson were working into each paragraph.

Alyson looked over at Jamie, and he answered her silent question by shaking his head no. She put her fork down on her plate, took a deep breath, and gently laid her hands on her stomach.

"My decision to keep my baby means I don't really get to keep my family."

"What do you mean?" Tommy leaned forward to catch every word Alyson said.

"To have a child before marriage is a huge deal for girls in some countries, including Pakistan, where my dad is from. Depending on where they are from and what kind of family they have determines what happens to them when they are found. I don't know if this would happen to me, but..." Alyson's brow wrinkled with consternation as she struggled to say the words. "My cousin had friends who were stoned to death because they were caught in a situation just like this."

"Stoned?" Eddie's eyebrows were raised as he spoke.

"Sometimes they're drowned." Aly's stomach twisted at the thought. "Or burned."

"You're saying you could be killed because of the baby?" Tommy almost whispered.

Alyson shrugged and pressed her hands against her womb even harder, as if that would protect her unborn child. Garret sat at the laptop, his fingers resting motionless on the keyboard. His eyes seemed to be glazed over and watering, but there were no discernible tears. Jamie sat with his hands folded in his lap, and his eyes focused on the carpet by his feet. Every once in a while, he would look up at Alyson and frown. He never let himself forget that Alyson was in this situation because of him.

"Do you think you would be killed?"

"I just don't know. Things like this are taken very seriously in my dad's family. They've mentioned things before, and I-I... I can't risk it. I have to keep this a secret from everyone."

Silence enveloped the room as Alyson's words sunk in. She stared at the plate of food next to her and wished she didn't feel so sick to her stomach so she could finish it. Someone in the hotel room next to them laughed loudly, and the elevator dinged, but no one moved.

"Should we get back to our work?"

Alyson nodded at Jamie. They were just getting back into their work when Eddie and Tommy quietly left the discussion and took a deck of cards into the corner of the room. Perhaps they felt as though they didn't have anything left to add.

Alyson glanced in their direction a few minutes later and caught them watching her. They smiled and gave a little wave. She smiled and lifted her hand in return. After a while, she heard them chuckling and saw them writing on a piece of paper. She wished she could be in the corner with them, instead of on the other side of the room with Jamie and Garret trying to rewrite the same sentence for the seventeenth time. Alyson could hardly keep her eyes open.

Jamie was stressed. He had pushed his hands through his hair so many times it was sticking up in places. There was a hard look in his eyes as he stared down at the laptop and snapped at Garret for missing the critical word. Alyson couldn't believe Garret took the comment without a reaction. He didn't even flinch. As soon as Jamie looked in her direction, though, his expression changed, and his voice went soft.

"You okay, love? You must be exhausted. Can I get you anything?"

"No." Alyson was in denial over the fact she had butterflies in her stomach when their eyes met. "I'm fine."

"Can I get you a blanket? A pillow?" He stood up and walked over to her chair. His fingers brushed over Aly's arm as he passed her.

"No." Again, the girl shook her head, rubbing her hand over the place where Jamie had touched. It wasn't to make her skin forget what he felt like; it was because she wanted the touch to last longer.

"Here." He handed her a water bottle. His strong hands twisted the cap off before she took it. "Don't worry, love, we'll get you out of here soon so you can sleep."

The young man returned to the couch and sat down. This time, he pulled the laptop off Garret's lap and began to type. Garret leaned his head back against the back of the couch and sighed, rubbing at the kink in his neck that was killing him.

"Cheers, mate." The words came out as a groan, and Garret closed his eyes to rest them.

The sound of humming reached Alyson's ears, and she realized Jamie was humming their song. It was the song they had listened to when they missed each other, it was the song they danced to in his dressing room before his concert in L.A., and it was the song she screamed at when the radio played it after Jamie left her.

She stared at him with every nerve in her body tingling. She wanted to pretend she was allowed to feel the way she wanted to feel about him. But she couldn't. He didn't deserve it; he had lost her and he wasn't going to be able to have her back. Back and forth her thoughts flew, her heart screaming from wanting to love and hate Jamie all in the same breath. Suddenly, she knew...

"I can't do this." Her words were quiet and desperate.

Jamie quickly looked up at Alyson. His heart started pounding; she had that look in her eyes again. The look that said she was terrified and was about to run away. No one else in the room seemed to have heard her, and he wondered if maybe he had heard her wrong. He didn't breathe as he waited for her to speak again.

"I'm sorry." She looked away, her face hot and her throat tight. "I thought I could do this, but I-I can't."

"What are you saying?" Jamie's mouth was dry.

"I'm saying I can't do this!" Alyson's voice grew louder, and this time the other three looked at her, their faces registering their surprise at the frustrated words.

"Can't do what?" asked Tommy quickly, looking over from the corner of the room.

"This whole situation!" Alyson waved her hands out of frustration as she spoke.

"I thought you needed us to help you! Jamie said you needed us." Garret sat up and gestured towards his friend as he spoke directly to the girl for the first time all evening.

"Yeah, why are you changing your mind all of a sudden?" said Tommy.

Her eyes darted in Jamie's direction and changed from agony to rage in a moment. She hated herself for not being strong enough to sit in the same room with him without falling apart on the inside. How did she expect to save her child if she couldn't even save herself? She was failing her baby before it was even born.

"Is something wrong?" Jamie's voice sounded strange as it came off his tongue. "Did I do something wrong?"

Alyson shook her head and looked away, tears smarting in her eyes.

"You're not making sense!" Jamie blurted before he could stop himself.

"You're moving me to England, Jamie! I just said I wanted to get away from Iowa. I easily could have been relocated within the States, and you know that!"

"It was Jamie's idea." Garret lifted his hands in a show of innocence.

"It was a brilliant plan, though!" Tommy defended the choice, sitting up on his knees. "He wanted you to be close to us so we could take care of you and keep an eye on you once we go back home. We didn't want you on your own in some place where it would take us hours to get to you."

"We thought it would make more sense to move you to Bedford since we're headed back home in the next couple of weeks." Eddie glanced around the room nervously.

"I want you to be safe." Jamie's tone was taut. "Isn't this what you wanted?"

Alyson slowly shook her head no, as tears spilled over onto her flushed face. Her shoulders shook from repressed sobs, but she sat up straight, the way her mother had taught her. She could hear her mother's voice in her head telling her to be strong, to hold herself together.

"Aly! Why didn't you speak up hours ago?" Jamie threw his hands up into the air and pushed the laptop onto the couch. She didn't flinch or move away when he walked towards her, so he knelt on the carpet by her feet and watched her face. "Aly, what's wrong?"

"I can't be that close to you guys." Alyson avoided Jamie's eyes. "I didn't ask for you guys to be close to me, I asked you to help me keep my baby safe."

"Bedford is a place to keep your baby safe!" Jamie insisted. He didn't have to see behind him to know everyone else in the room was watching them. "And the job is the best fit for you!"

"Jamie, stop lying to me!" Alyson finally looked at him. "They just told me it was so I could be close to you!"

"There were a lot of different factors tied into picking that location, Aly!" Jamie shook his head and rubbed his forehead, his heart reeling from Aly's words.

"You did this on purpose! I know you did!" Alyson's hands moved wildly as she shouted at him. "Once I'm over there I'm stuck there! With you!"

"Are you serious right now?" Jamie's eyes snapped at her.

"Jamie." Eddie's voice came from the other side of the room. He stood to his feet.

"Aly, I'm trying to help you! I-I'm here, spending my time and energy to get you someplace that is safe. I'm trying to get you someplace that feels nice for you! I'm not trying to manipulate you!"

No one said a word as they watched the girl in the chair stare down at the boy on the floor, her chest heaving with the angry breaths she pushed in and out of her nose. Her chin quivered as tears slowly painted their wet trails down the sides of her face.

"You have to tell me what you're thinking!"

"I can't trust you! I'm not strong enough!"

Jamie closed his eyes and exhaled slowly. His hands and jaw ached from being clenched so tightly. He wanted to shake some sense into her silly head, then hold her until she never felt like crying again. She slipped her hands over her face to hide from them. Jamie took several deep breaths to calm himself, then cleared his throat.

"Aly, there is a nursing job in New York, an animal shelter I'm connected with in L.A., and a few places in France and Germany that have to do with starting businesses, as well as many more in London. If you want to choose one of those places, you can. Let me know by tomorrow." He spoke softly before he stood up to his feet and walked out of the room.

The girl's hands slipped down as she heard Jamie's retreating footsteps. The defeat she was feeling was written clearly in the traces of her tears. Eddie and Tommy were by her side before the door closed all the way behind Jamie; worry and sympathy on their faces.

"I just messed everything up, didn't I?" Alyson's voice caught on the lump in her throat as she spoke.

"You don't have to apologize or be sorry for anything." Eddie knelt with his hands in his lap, but he would have gladly hugged the girl if she had asked for it.

"Are you okay?" Tommy put a hand on her knee and left it there.

"No." Alyson's lips trembled again, and she bit the inside of her cheeks. "I'm terrified."

"We're here to help you, Aly." Eddie's voice remained calm as he spoke. "We're not here to hurt you or try to make you do anything you don't want to do."

Alyson nodded and wiped her eyes. She knew her makeup was ruined. She felt self-conscious about the fact that they were seeing her in such a vulnerable state. A box of Kleenex dropped into her lap, and Alyson looked up to see Garret turn and walk back to the couch.

"Jamie really does care about you," Eddie put in. "We want to just be there to help you through anything that might happen."

"We know this is a huge deal to you, especially with your family situation, and Jamie felt that being close in location would help you feel more at ease."

Back and forth the soothing voices of reason calmed Alyson until she was breathing evenly. When they had finally conciliated her, Eddie called Jamie back into the room.

"I'm so sorry." Jamie approached her and knelt before her chair. His hand brushed over her knee, begging for her forgiveness with a touch. "I'm so sorry I lost my temper."

Alyson could see traces of tears on his face. She moved her hand an inch closer to where Jamie's rested on the arm of the chair, but stopped herself before their fingers touched. The tiny reach was enough for Jamie, and he nodded with a grateful smile.

"Are we settled yet?" he asked gently.

Alyson nodded, noticing Eddie's attentive gaze watching the interaction from the side. He stood with his arms folded across his chest, ready to be the peacemaker at any moment.

"What would you like to do?" Jamie continued to speak soft and low, his eyes tracing Alyson's face from her eyes to her mouth and back again.

"I think..." Alyson paused to lick her lips and take a deep breath. "I have decided that moving to Bedford is the best, most safe place for the baby and I. I think being close to where you and the others are will be beneficial in case of any emergency that might arise."

"Are you absolutely sure?"

Alyson nodded.

"I can make another place work for you, Aly. I told you there were many options."

"I know. But Bedford is the best fit for what I need."

"All right." Tommy clapped his hands together, and Garret began to type again. "It's all settled. Alyson and the baby will be our neighbors."

"I really am sorry. I should never have spoken to you that way." Jamie waited until Alyson gave him her eyes before he apologized again in a hushed tone that was ignored by everyone else in the room.

"I know." Again, Alyson reached with her fingers. Again, she stopped short of making any physical contact. "You are doing a lot to make this work. Thank you."

"It's a pleasure to help you." Jamie's smile was small, but it looked genuine. It was enough to make a butterfly flutter in Alyson's stomach before it flew away.

Chapter seven
"Bambi."

Alyson got home much later than her bedtime and cried herself to sleep. Tears of gratitude were mixed with guilt, fear and exhaustion. Two days later, the young men returned to the school and announced they had chosen Alyson for the job in Bedford.

Co-workers and friends congratulated Alyson the day the announcement was made. It spread quickly and became overwhelming for Alyson. They all said how they knew she could do the job and how exciting it would be for her to live abroad for a year. Everyone seemed to know someone or heard of someone who had lived in England at one point and had an opinion on what Alyson should do and see while she was there. She nodded politely as she listened, disregarding each tourist attraction with an aching heart.

Alyson was exhausted when she got done with work that day. All she wanted to do was hide away in her room alone with her baby where she wouldn't have to tell lies and smile. Her phone dinged as she unlocked the front door of her apartment, and she sighed. It was probably another well-wisher or someone asking if she wanted to get together before she left. When she opened it, however, she was pleasantly surprised by an invitation to join Eddie for dinner. Alyson decided to accept his offer and drove to her favorite Mexican restaurant.

"Hi, Aly." Eddie's deep but cheerful voice greeted her as she approached the booth he was already sitting at. He stood to kiss her cheek and help her slide into her spot. "You're looking well."

"You don't have to lie." Alyson gave a chuckle. She had tried to cover the dark circles with foundation, but she knew they were still visible. "I haven't looked well for a couple months now."

"You do look well. A lot more settled." Eddie's voice was firm as well as gentle.

The young man was wearing a black button-down shirt. His blond curls brushed against the collar when he moved his head. His gray eyes rested on his dinner companion, making sure she knew she had his complete attention. He rested his interlocked fingers on the table, fiddling with the two rings he wore.

"Ah, well, that I believe. I'm very relieved everything is working out." Alyson let out a sigh. "I just have to hang on one more month, and then everything will be fine."

"Not too bad." Eddie's little smile playing with his lips made Alyson smile as well.

"No, not too bad."

"So, the reason why I wanted to spend some time with you this evening is to give you a chance to talk about how you're feeling, let you have a chance to process and ask questions. I know things have been hard and crazy for you since you left L.A. and I know you don't have many people you can talk to about all of this."

"Thank you." Alyson was touched by Eddie's thoughtfulness. "That's very kind of you."

"Things are going to be crazy for a bit, and it's helpful to talk about things."

"You sound like my old therapist." Alyson chuckled. "She never gave me Mexican food, though."

"That makes me the better therapist then, eh?" Eddie smiled.

"I'm not positive, but I'm thinking chips and salsa help me deal better with life's problems."

"Oh, I am positive about that. Unless I have chips and salsa, my life is not going to go well."

Alyson laughed.

"I should just carry a bag of chips with me everywhere I go for the next seven months."

"I'll follow you around with a bowl of salsa. We'll be unstoppable then."

"Not even Jamie would be able to ruin anything." The smile on Alyson's face turned to a grimace. "Well... that would have to be very powerful salsa."

Eddie's face sobered and they sat quietly for a moment. The mariachi band playing over the speakers continued to sing and trill, and the family on the other side of the restaurant was talking loudly about football. A toddler cried. Alyson took a sip of her water, trying to think of what to say next. Eddie beat her to it.

"That was quite the fight you guys had the other night."

"Yeah, well... I shouldn't have been surprised by it. We fight constantly now." Alyson shook her head and drew her brows together. "It's so weird because I-I don't fight with anyone! Ever! But he's just... He makes me so angry sometimes. We were never like this when we were together."

"He hurt you a lot when he left you."

"Yeah. You would know, too. You were there."

"I think you getting angry at him is to be expected."

"It's not even that he's provoking me, or trying to get a reaction out of me, I just get angry at the fact that..." Alyson stopped. "I mean, my heart is still broken."

It grew quiet between them again as Eddie simply nodded and waited for the pensive look to leave Alyson's face. She took a deep breath then tried to smile. Eddie returned the look and pushed the bowl of chips from the middle of their table closer to her side. She chuckled softly and took one.

"See, chips and salsa."

"If you ever decide to leave the band, you could make it big as the only therapist that serves chips and salsa to their clients."

"If I leave the band? Don't say things like that! I love the band! I love playing with my mates!"

"Aw." Alyson smiled at Eddie's declaration. "I'm glad you're all still friends."

"Well, it's definitely not the same as it was before. It was hard for me to be with Jamie at first, knowing what he had done to you. And when I found out about Garret..." Eddie's forehead crinkled and he put his hand around his cup for something to hold onto. He rubbed at the condensation that was running down the outside of it. "He carries this so heavy because he knows this affects you for the rest of your life, and it also affects Serenity. Sometimes I watch him sit and stare at nothing, and I know he's trying to figure out how to fix it all. That's what he does, you know, for everyone. He fixes problems. The fact that he has caused a problem eats at him."

"I'm sorry you're stuck being with them for longer on my account." Alyson frowned. She pushed the chips and salsa back over towards Eddie and saw a small smile play on the corners of his lips. "You could be back home in London by now if it wasn't for this whole charity job thing."

"Shush now! I don't regret this at all. I'm just very happy we can do something for you after all you went through because of us."

"It wasn't you." Alyson dismissed Eddie's words. "It wasn't really Tommy, either."

"It was Tommy, though!" Eddie's voice rose as he dipped his chip into the salsa bowl. "I couldn't believe he had slept with you when he came back and told me."

"I mean, yes, we shouldn't have done it, but..."

"No, Aly, you need to understand something," Eddie interrupted, lifting up one of his hands to quiet her. "Tommy can be a bit of what you call a player sometimes, but you're not just some girl. Just because you agreed to sleep with him and he didn't force you to do anything doesn't mean he didn't take advantage of you. He knew you were with Jamie and that both of you were still drunk. He behaved badly towards you."

"Well, yeah." Alyson looked down and noticed crumbs on the table in front of her. She used her napkin to wipe them to the side before she looked back up at Eddie and exhaled. "I mean, I wish we hadn't because it just made things more confusing and I do regret it, but I regret everything from that night, so..."

"I just hate that so much happened to you and I couldn't stop it. I thought I could help you, keep an eye on you and make sure you got off safe after

Jamie left you, but I completely failed at all of those things. I didn't stop anything."

"Oh, Eddie." Alyson gave him a sad smile. "I don't blame you for what happened. You didn't know."

"No, but I shouldn't have let Tommy take you off by himself, and I should have stayed to just make sure you didn't get bothered, but..." Eddie let out a heavy sigh. "Instead I took Tommy back to the hotel so I could yell at him."

"How did he take it?"

"Told me I was right. Told me he knew he should've thought it through better. I mean, he's my best mate and we've done everything together. We can call each other out on things like that and still be best friends."

"I'm glad." Alyson smiled. "Elle and I are like that."

"How is Elle, by the way?"

"Good." Alyson's smile grew bigger. "Worried about me, of course, but she's good. She still loves me despite the fact I completely ruined my life."

Eddie frowned. A waiter rushed past their table, distracting them both for a moment. When they turned back to each other, Alyson was clearly trying to keep her lips from shaking and one hand was pressed against her throat. Eddie didn't say anything, just watched the way Alyson's brow furrowed. A forced smile appeared, and she looked back up at him with a stubborn light shining in her eyes.

"You're a good person, Aly."

The words seemed to come out of nowhere, but Alyson believed he meant them. She didn't want to hear him say it, and she didn't want to acknowledge what he had said, yet the look in his eye forced her to take the compliment and swallow it down. He knew what she had done. He had held her as she sobbed and screamed in drunken agony and he still said she was a good person.

"You're a good person, too." Her voice was rough.

Their food arrived, lightening the mood. They thanked their server and looked over the food. Eddie's steak tacos were loaded with meat, cheese and lettuce, while Alyson's chicken enchiladas steamed in front of her. The side dishes of rice and beans were placed in the middle of the table while their bowl of salsa was replenished. They waited for the woman to be done at their table before they started eating.

Alyson was about to pick up her fork so she could take her first bite when Eddie took another chip and held it out towards her. He nodded at her to pick up a chip of her own.

"A toast." Eddie's voice was serious. "To chips and salsa for helping us get through life's hard times."

"I'll toast to that." Alyson tapped her chip against Eddie's. "To chips and salsa."

"Cheers."

Eddie's genuine compassion set her heart at ease, and she wished for a moment that her baby would be born with gray eyes and curls. She could trust this man to help her raise her child, but he wasn't the father. She sighed.

For most of the meal they avoided anything that had to do with the night in California and simply enjoyed their food. Eddie's dimples worked wonders on Alyson's mood, and she found herself enjoying the evening more than she imagined she could.

"Thanks for hanging out with me tonight," said Alyson gratefully.

"I'm looking forward to many more hanging out times once we're both over in the UK. We'll get to be neighbors and do neighborly things."

"Like eat chips and salsa together?" Alyson raised her eyebrows.

"I'm offended you even feel like you had to ask that question."

Alyson tried to keep a straight face at Eddie's words, but couldn't keep her lips from pushing up at the corners.

"In all honesty, though, it feels surreal to me that you guys are willing to help me like this, and spend time, you know, making sure I'm okay. I'm very thankful for it. I'm not even an old friend or anything, yet you've all been so happy to help. It means a lot."

The young man looked down at the table with a smile. Alyson watched, wondering what he was thinking. She moved her empty plate out of the way and leaned forward on her elbows as she waited for Eddie to talk. He looked back up at her, his grin leaving a dimple indented in his cheek.

"I have known Jamie for six years, and I have never known him to keep bad company. He has this way of finding people who are honest and genuine and really care about others. He meets thousands of people in this job, and we always pay attention to the people he decides to keep close. You're one of them, and that means something to me."

"You trust Jamie's intuition about people that much?"

"He picked me as a friend, didn't he?"

Alyson chuckled and shook her head. She hadn't been sure what having a meal out with Eddie would look like, but this was nice. It was comfortable. They talked about the baby, they talked about the move, and they talked about the others, but only briefly as the chips were almost gone and Alyson didn't want to talk about anything too problematic without having chips and salsa on hand.

"So, I think we need a name for the baby," Eddie said suddenly. "Like a pet name, or something. Tommy and I were talking the other day while you guys were working on the papers, and we came up with a list of suggestions."

"Oh?" Alyson felt her own smile begin to grow. "I don't have a name for the baby yet. I was thinking the other day that I'm going to have to call it something."

"Well, don't bother yourself over it any longer, I have the perfect name on this list, I am sure of it. Hundred percent." Eddie pulled a piece of folded up paper out of his pocket and laid it out on the table, smoothing it with his hands. He pushed up an imaginary pair of glasses as he made a show of clearing his throat before reading it off. "Fortescue."

Alyson's mouth fell open.

"Snippy, Black Mamba, Chop Sticks, uh... Cha-Cha Slide, what's that say? Oh, Fire-breather..."

Alyson couldn't hold back the laughter that was bubbling inside of her.

"Taun Taun, Flappy Bird, Ricardo, Spatula, Papa Smurf..."

"Papa what?!"

"Rocket, Launch Pad 7, Potato..."

"No! You can't name a child potato!" Tears were running down Alyson's face as she gripped her aching stomach and tried to calm her hysterical laughing.

Eddie put the paper down, giggling at Alyson's red cheeks and the happy crinkles by her eyes.

"How did you come up with these?"

"People hire me to name their children all the time. This is my job. Playing in *Jupiter Waits* is just a side gig."

"And you name them Spatula? You're a horrible person!"

"Well, baby Spatula is very pleased with his name!"

"Okay, you are not allowed to name the baby when he or she is born! Neither of you. I might let you name a houseplant. Maybe. But I wouldn't even want you guys to help me name a dog." Alyson took the paper Eddie handed to her and wiped her eyes as she looked it over.

"Hey! These are quality names!"

"I think the only names you've missed on this list are 'Kitchen Sink', and 'Bon Jovi.'"

"Oh man! We did! Bon Jovi is a legend, we have to have that name on the list." Eddie reached for the paper, but Alyson held it away from his grasp.

Alyson smiled as she read the rest of the names quietly to herself. Her gaze landed on one name in particular, and she looked back up at her friend who was busy fiddling with the napkin dispenser so the napkins were easier to pull out.

"What?"

"Look at this one." Alyson pointed at one of the names that had been scribbled down with a pencil.

"Bambi," Eddie read. "You like it?"

"Well, I just got a text the other day where Danielle called the baby a bambino... Bambi, Bambino. I don't know... it kind of sounds right."

"Bambi." Eddie tested how the name sounded with his own voice. "Bambi. Hello, Bambi. Come here, Bambi."

"No! Stop! Bambi is just what we will call it while I'm pregnant." Alyson giggled. "Do you like the sound of it?"

"Yeah, I like it! It's on the list I made, isn't it? But honestly, it's your child. You can choose whatever name you please. You don't need my permission."

"I'm going to try it out for a few days. See if it fits. It's a cute name, and it reminds me of cute baby animals, so all around it seems like a win."

"Tommy is going to be so chuffed you picked one of our names. We were just doing it for a laugh, to be honest."

"I'm glad. I needed that laugh."

The night didn't last as long as the night before it had. Alyson yawned once, and Eddie refused to let her stay out with him any longer. He walked her to her car, careful to avoid being spotted by anyone as he opened Alyson's door for her. The small gesture was just another thing he did to help her feel like she was going to be okay.

"Thanks for everything." Alyson gave the young man a side hug before she climbed into her vehicle. "I really mean that."

"I know. And you're very welcome. It was an absolute pleasure." Eddie's smile made his eyes sparkle.

After school ended on Friday, Alyson drove back to the hotel where Jamie and the others were staying for the meeting with the management team. She had been told she didn't need to be afraid, but she could tell Jamie was nervous about it. All the things she had discussed with Jamie and Garret earlier that week crowded into her mind as she walked into the hotel lobby. She bit her bottom lip and worried they hadn't thought of everything. Her fears eased up a little when she saw Jamie and Eddie waiting for her.

"Hi, love." Eddie gave the girl a side hug and studied her face. "You look a bit jumpy today."

"Nervous," was all Aly said as she turned to give Jamie a brief smile.

"You okay?" Jamie asked in a whisper as the three of them trekked down a long hallway to a meeting room.

"Let's just get this over with."

Jamie barely let his hand touch the small of her back as he ushered her through the doorway and toward a long table. Garret and Tommy were already in there, along with four or five other men dressed in suits. There were shiny, black briefcases at several of the spots, but Jamie guided Alyson carefully to the other side of the table where she would sit beside him. Garret sat on his other side while Eddie and Tommy took chairs at the end of the table. The girl shot Eddie a silent cry for help, and he gave her an encouraging nod.

Okay. I'm going to be okay. I'm doing this for Bambi. Bambi. Bambi is worth it. The girl put her hands on her stomach and took a deep breath.

The beginning of the meeting was filled with vocabulary and terminology that Alyson had no comprehension of. She sat quietly, listening to Garret and Jamie read off the things Alyson had requested. The men in suits wrote words down on notepads while they stroked their chins thoughtfully. Halfway into the list, one of the men held up his hand to stop Jamie mid-sentence. Alyson's stomach dropped, her sweaty palms covering it instinctively as fear enveloped her.

"This is not going to happen." The man shook his head. "We can't make limits on who contacts her or when. Really? This is absurd."

"Excuse me, but this is something that Alyson wants, and we will do it." Jamie's voice was just as firm as the man on the other side of the table. He never used her full name, but it seemed important to use it right then.

"It's a very difficult process and I don't see that it is necessary," another suit spoke.

"Not only is it necessary, it is what's going to happen."

"And you say that she needs to be completely out of the papers? No mention of her name at all?" A third man looked down at his notes as he spoke.

"Yeah, we can't have this." The first man spoke again. "How are we going to make this into a PR stunt if we can't publicly talk about it?"

"Trent, this is not a PR stunt!" Garret spoke angrily, surprising everyone. "This is a girl we're helping and it just so happens that she's going to be able to help this school as well!"

"See, now, this is where we need to insist you listen to what we're saying, and make this into a PR stunt." Trent seemed disinterested in the conversation.

"No." Jamie shook his head adamantly. "You will do as she is asking. No phone calls. No publicity. No interference in her plans once she's in Bedford. It's really that simple!"

"Jamie, you're being very foolish right now."

"No, Trent! You're being lazy! Now snap out of it, and let's finish this!" Jamie was annoyed at his management team.

Alyson watched the exchange with wide eyes. Jamie looked her direction and frowned apologetically. She tried to smile and shake the look of terror from her eyes, but he could see plain as day she wanted to be out of there.

"Okay, we can do the phone calls," one who hadn't yet spoken finally weighed in. "But there has to be PR for this."

"Yeah, you need to be seen as the charity man; giving time, recruiting people, paying it forward..."

Jamie was about to shout again, but Garret beat him to it.

"Are you guys bloody thick?" Garret smacked the table with his hands as he stood up from his chair. "This is not for negotiation! This girl is pregnant with a child, and their lives are in danger! You know that! We're not doing this to feel better about ourselves, this is legitimately a situation where helping someone needs to go unnoticed!"

"Alyson's safety is much more important than fame or recognition. What is that worth anyway?" added Jamie. "Just do as we're asking!"

"Then why is she even taking this job in the first place?" Trent shot back angrily. "Why should we be involved?"

"Because this keeps her safe! We've done a lot of thinking and weighing out of pros and cons, and her taking a job is the best cover for her."

"I suggest you get out of this mess, Jamie." The one who wanted to press for the PR shook his head. "She's not your responsibility. Cut her loose. Find someone else."

"You've got to be kidding me."

"Jamie, we're talking as your friends, not just your management team. We suggest you forget this whole plan. Let Alex get help somewhere else, and find a new thing to sponsor." Trent's words were slow and measured, as if he were talking to a small child.

A gasp escaped Alyson before she could stop it. Her heart was pounding so heavily it felt like it was shaking her insides. She sat with her hands twisting in her lap as she took in every word and expression. The young man sitting next to her saw the tears beginning to trickle down her cheeks, and his face grew red with rage.

"I am not looking for your advice or your permission!" shouted Jamie. "There is nothing in my contract that keeps me from helping Alyson the way I am helping her! You're here to make sure we have what we need to keep her safe! Is this clear?"

The men in suits considered their options and finally gave in. There was some more grumbling and a few muttered protests, but at long last, Alyson's terms were drawn up and everything signed. The girl never said a word, but let Jamie and Garret continue to fight for and defend her until the very end. She hadn't expected it, especially from Garret.

"All right, Alex, sign on the line," Trent sighed.

"Her name is Alyson," Garret corrected, his voice snapping.

Alyson stood to take the pen, braving a look towards Garret. He saw her eyes turn towards him and looked away. She wanted to thank him, but he stood up and left the meeting as soon as it was done. Jamie grabbed Alyson by the hand and pulled her out of the room as fast as he could.

"I'm so sorry you had to sit through that!" Jamie dropped her hand and raked his fingers through his hair.

They were in the hallway with Tommy and Eddie, walking away from the meeting room and towards the lobby. Eddie reached over to pull Alyson into his arms and give her a hug, calming her trembling body with his touch. She was thankful for the physical act of affection, but she felt bad hugging Eddie and not thanking Jamie with some sort of embrace as well. He seemed to assume he wasn't going to receive one, as he continued to walk without so much as a look in her direction. Tommy slipped an arm around her shoulders quick, but Alyson was too busy trying to keep up with Jamie to properly return it. She gave him a smile as he fell into step next to her, his hands in his pockets.

"I've never seen Trent go off like that." Tommy's eyes had been nearly as wide as Aly's during the entire argument.

"Anything that makes him actually work makes him a proper menace! I should have seen it coming."

"We won. In the end," Eddie pointed out.

"Barely. Couldn't have done it without Garret though." Jamie sighed and looked over at Alyson. "You okay, love?"

"Thank you." Alyson reached out and grabbed hold of his arm with her hand. It wasn't timid or uncertain; it was absolutely what Alyson wanted to do in that moment. "Thank you so much."

"Course." Jamie's voice softened, and he put a hand over Alyson's. "I promised I would take care of it."

Their hands slipped apart, and Alyson looked down at the carpet until they reached the lobby. The young men invited her to stay and eat with them, but Alyson said she needed to get home to rest and call Danielle. She waved before turning to walk out into the early evening twilight.

"I'm really glad Garret was there to help as well. Tell him how grateful I am, please." Alyson hoped he knew how deeply she meant those words. "Bye, Jamie."

Jamie's mouth turned up in a smile when he heard her say his name. She waved one last time, and then was gone. The plan was official; Alyson and her baby would be safely moved to Bedford, UK for the remainder of her pregnancy and for several months after under the guise of teaching for charity. Now all she needed to do was make it until she could leave.

Besides training the new teacher and planning a goodbye visit to her parents, Alyson's sole focus was getting packed and creating a curriculum she would use once she got to Bedford. She met with friends who asked to spend time with her before she left, faking smiles and excitement as they wished her well and told her what a great opportunity it was going to be. They were all proud of her.

Every day the baby grew a little more, and every day Alyson became more worried she would be too big to fit into her regular jeans. At the same time, she worried she was too small and that the baby wasn't growing right. Each night Alyson would rub her belly and sing softly to her child.

"Mommy's going to make sure you're safe, Bambi," she promised.

Phone calls home to her family were the hardest. Alyson wanted nothing more than to have her mother tell her she was going to be okay. The disappointment her parents had felt over her missing the special meal with their guest was forgotten when she told them about her "promotion" and new location.

"We've told everyone about your move. The whole neighborhood is so proud of you." Her parents called one evening to talk. "Do you know when you'll be coming home to visit before you leave?"

"Not quite sure yet. I've been trying to figure out when it will work best." Alyson had to make the trip happen soon, before the bump could be seen as more than extra food for supper. She was thankful she was still relatively small for how far along she was.

"Why don't you come this next weekend?" Mrs. Abidi asked. "That way, you'll come before you're in the last minute push, and you will enjoy your time more."

"O-okay." There was nothing stopping her from going home on the dates her mother proposed. She would simply have to be quick about wrapping her head around it all.

The next phone call she made was much more serious. She had spent a long time staring at her phone before she pushed the call button. There was nothing to be afraid of, she told herself. They hadn't talked since the meeting with his management team. He hadn't even texted her.

"Hi, Aly." Jamie was careful to keep his voice from sounding too excited.

"Jamie, I need to see a doctor, but I can't go to my normal doctor."

"Why? Is there something wrong?"

"I-I don't think so, but I just want to get an examination. I've never had a baby before, and I want to make sure everything looks good." Alyson had debated making that phone call for days, but she just didn't know how to pull the strings to get what she wanted like he did.

"All right, when do you want to go?"

"I'm free Thursday after school."

"Thursday after school. On it. Anything else, love?" He hadn't been able to break himself of the habit of calling her love, even after their arguments and the distance Alyson put between them.

"Are you back in London?" asked Alyson, remembering the boys had said they would be going back home after the meetings were over.

"Not yet. I'm sticking around for a while longer."

"Okay, well, just send me the details for the doctor when you have them."

"Absolutely. I'll talk to you again soon."

"Oh, Jamie..." The casual sound in her voice piqued Jamie's curiosity. She never sounded casual.

"Yes?"

"I'm, uh, going to see my parents this weekend."

There was a pause before Jamie said anything.

"Are you going to be okay?"

"I think so, but I wanted to let you know. Just in case... you know."

"Thanks, Aly. Let me know if you need anything."

"Bye."

Alyson let out a huge sigh of relief when the phone call ended. They hadn't fought, and he hadn't tried to wiggle his way back into her heart. Maybe things were finally going to be different. The doctor's appointment was a huge weight off Aly's mind, and she was glad Jamie was going to take care of it. She marked it on her calendar with a tiny x.

"Just a few more days, Bambi." Alyson placed gentle hands on her womb. Her stomach was firm under her fingers, and she massaged it gently. "Jamie's going to make sure we're both okay."

Alyson was straightening up her classroom at the end of the day on Thursday with her mind a million miles away in a cloud of thoughts. The doctor's appointment was in an hour, and the next day she would be driving home to see her parents for the first time since she met Jamie. Both things scared her and caused her stomach to knot nervously. There were a lot of unknowns tied into the doctor's visit, and Alyson wished someone could go with her. She looked at her watch again and hurried to finish so she could leave.

"Do you want to come out to eat with us tonight?" asked a co-worker as she stuck her head around the corner.

"Sorry, I have a doctor's appointment," Alyson answered with a smile.

"Oh no, what for?"

"Oh! Um..." Alyson couldn't believe she had let herself slip up like that. "It's just... a normal checkup."

"Oh, whew. I was getting worried! I mean, I know you have been pretty stressed about moving to England, and I noticed you're not working out anymore, so I thought maybe something was wrong."

"Wait... What do you mean?" Alyson didn't understand what her friend was trying to tell her.

"Oh, you lifted up your hands the other day, and I saw you didn't have your tight, little tummy that you normally have anymore. Don't worry, my stomach has never been awesome. You can get it back if you work on it."

The words of Aly's co-worker pounded in her mind as she got into her car to leave school. If one person had noticed, how many other people had noticed? Would she be able to play it off as letting herself go? She still had two weeks left in October, and her boss was dropping hints about having her stay for at least the first half of November. Her phone beeped, interrupting her thoughts; it was ready to direct her to the address she had gotten from Jamie the day before.

As she drove, her thoughts transitioned to the examination she was about to have. A million illogical fears about what could go wrong with her and with Bambi popped into her head as she drove. She had spent hours researching what the procedure she was going to have done would be like. It was more the fact that she would be alone with a stranger in a room during it all that made Alyson panic the most. She reminded herself that the doctor was a professional and had nothing but her health and safety in mind, but her heart continued to pound against her ribcage.

Breathe in, breathe out. You need this. Bambi needs this. It's going to be okay.

Alyson was still doing her deep breathing when she found the office. She typed up a quick text to Danielle, asking her to pray and that she would tell her how it went as soon as it was done. She wrapped her maroon-colored, oversized sweater around her tightly and rushed inside to get away from the cold wind.

"Aly! Here!" A familiar voice called out as the girl entered the dark foyer and looked around to get her bearings.

"Jamie!" She was surprised to see him standing off to the side, his phone in his hand.

"Hi." He walked over to her. His expression changed to concern when he saw how pale her face was. "You okay?"

"I'm fine." Alyson's words were tense.

"What's wrong?"

"I'm really nervous about seeing the doctor." The words were quiet and Alyson looked away as she spoke.

"It's going to be fine. The doctor is a nice man, I met him before I set up an appointment for you." Jamie put a hand on Alyson's shoulder and gave it a squeeze. He was surprised when she leaned into it and slipped her arm around him for a quick second. "Honest, Aly. You don't have to be nervous."

Alyson breathed in deeply as she pulled her arm back towards her, and she inhaled the smell of Jamie's cologne. It was the same one he had worn the night she met him.

"What are you doing here?"

"I thought you might want some support," he offered. "If you don't, I'll leave, but I wanted to let you know that I was here for you if you needed someone."

"Thank you." Alyson couldn't disguise her relief to have him with her.

He gave her a small smile and felt for her hand to give her fingers a little press. "I know doctors can be scary sometimes."

Alyson swallowed hard and made the choice to let her hand slide effortlessly into Jamie's. It was only because she was nervous about her examination. When the visit was done, she would be fine. It was fine. Holding his hand for one afternoon was fine. She knew he was giving her a hard look as he tightened his grip on her, but he didn't say a word about it.

"All right, we go up here." He led the way to the reception area and approached the nurse behind the desk, asking about the appointment he had set up a few days earlier. As they waited in the waiting room, Jamie explained how he had found this place. "I wanted a place that would be fairly empty. The end of the day is a good time to come, but some places were still quite busy until the very end. This place is small, but nice enough, I figured we'd give it a go. If it becomes too sketchy, let me know, and I'll get us out of here."

Alyson looked at him. His high cheekbones and expressive eyes caught her attention, reminding her of how handsome she had found him the first time they met. It had been a long time since she had really studied his face. She remembered tracing her fingers through the stubble he let grow on his chin, and laughing at him as he told her he grew it out to appear more rugged and manly. Then he had kissed her forehead and ran his hand down her cheek to her neck, slipping his fingers through her hair to touch the warm skin. She had never been touched there before. Alyson came back to the present with her breath still stuck in her lungs from the memory.

"Yeah, k." She swallowed hard.

Alyson's smile was all the thanks the young man needed.

Jamie kept hold of her hand and rested their interlocked fingers on his lap, stroking the back of her hand with his thumb. She didn't pull away, but let her hand stay in his, too anxious to fight it. Her leg bounced the tiniest bit, giving away her nerves. The girl seemed content to wait in silence, however Jamie knew then was the best time to talk with her. He didn't want to start another fight, but this could be the only time they had a chance to talk privately for a while.

"Aly. Do you mind if I tell you some things I've been thinking about?"

"Sure."

"I haven't been handling us very well." Jamie pointed at the both of them. He left a little pause at the end of each sentence. "I haven't handled it well since the beginning. I was impatient and pushed us too fast, and then I was stupid and hurt you. I don't have much practice in going slow and doing things right."

Aly looked back at her lap as she listened to Jamie's words.

"When I first saw you, I liked the way you were dancing, so I decided to meet you. My plan was if you were boring, I could at least have fun dancing with you before moving on. But then you showed me a little bit of who you are, and I just, I just couldn't let that walk away. You were honest and kind, and when you meet people like that, people like you, you hold onto them."

Alyson listened quietly. The lights in the waiting room glowed softly and the gray carpet under their feet looked worn, just like the padded chairs they were sitting in. There was one other person sitting on the other side of the room busy reading a book. A nurse came and went from behind the desk. Otherwise the room was quiet.

"But I didn't know how to hold onto you and not crush you." Jamie ran his free hand through his hair. He looked down at Aly's hand in his own and wondered how long she would leave it there. "Instead of letting you tell me what you wanted to tell me, I pressed you to tell me what I wanted to know. I was trying to get as deep with you in two months as I had with Beth in two years. I don't know why you let me in so far, but I should have been much more careful."

The young man dared to glance over at Aly as she sat with her head bowed. She had one side of her bottom lip tucked between her teeth and there was a furrow at the top of her nose. Still, her hand remained in his.

"When I left you in L.A., I was caught completely off-guard by feelings for Beth." Jamie's voice was the most gentle and honest Alyson had ever heard it sound. "I wanted to tell you, but I looked at you, and I-I couldn't even breathe. You trusted me enough to give me everything because I promised you the world." Jamie stopped to give a soft, yet bitter laugh. "You deserve the world, Aly. You deserve so much more than I can give you."

Alyson shifted in the chair next to him. Jamie felt her fingers loosen their hold on his, but she didn't let go. He felt the beginnings of a lump begin to grow in his throat.

"I was a coward. I made a mistake, and I knew it, but I didn't know how to fix it, so I ran away."

Nothing was said for a long moment, as Jamie let Alyson mull over his confession. It had been a risky move, but he felt better for having put it out there. Now she would know. Now she could decide if she wanted to continue to push him away or let him back in, but at least she would know his side of the story.

"I should have been wiser." Alyson's words were quiet, a hint of regret in their tone. "But I decided to be foolish. I knew how fast and deep we were going, but I didn't try to stop us."

"Aly, what I did is not your faul-..."

"It is." Alyson shut her eyes as she cut him off. "It is my fault, because I made choices. I chose you. I chose to trust you without knowing you. If I didn't want to get hurt, I shouldn't have made those choices."

Jamie watched Alyson earnestly, his eyes taking in every minute move of her mouth and shift of her eyes. He wished he knew what she was thinking.

"I'm sorry I hurt you. Not just that night, but every day after that."

"I know."

Alyson looked up and met his gaze at last. She wanted to tell him she forgave him and it was all going to be fine, but she couldn't make the words come off her tongue. Instead, she squeezed his hand and hoped he would understand what she wasn't saying.

"Aly, you're one of the best people I have ever met." Jamie looked her in the eye. "I know you weren't planning on having a baby, but I don't think I would have ever had another chance to get to know you if it wasn't for this little one."

Alyson was surprised when Jamie let go of her hand before she decided to let go of his. He missed the look of inquiry she was giving him as he leaned over her lap. His hands settled on her stomach and for the first time, someone other than Alyson put their hands on her womb. She shivered at the warmth of his touch. Her eyes drank in the moment, watching Jamie's face as he tenderly and sweetly gazed down at her belly. Tears began to form in her eyes.

"Thank you, little baby. You're going to have one of the best mums in the whole world."

The words made Aly's tears slip down her cheeks, and she bit her bottom lip to keep herself from losing complete control over her emotions. She put her hands over Jamie's and smiled at him when he looked up at her. The tears on her face surprised him, and he quickly reached up to wipe them away.

"Hey now. What's all this about?" he asked.

"I never had anyone else put their hands on the baby before," said Alyson. "It's a beautiful feeling."

Jamie didn't look away from Aly as he brushed another tear from her face. A smile appeared there, and she moved her hand to rest on his arm. She breathed deeply and felt her heart beating steadily, telling her over and over she was alive.

"Thank you for staying."

This time it was Jamie's turn to respond with a smile. They finally settled back into their seats, Jamie's hand resting protectively over Aly's, while her other hand stayed on the baby. The safe silence they were sharing with each other was what Jamie had wanted.

"I'm calling him or her Bambi while I wait for him or her to be born."

"The baby?"

"Yeah. I call the baby Bambi now." Alyson smiled when Jamie looked at her.

"Bambi? How did you pick that name?"

"Eddie and Tommy made a list of ridiculous names that were all dumb, but Bambi was on there and, I don't know. I just like it."

"Bambi." Jamie put a hand on Alyson's stomach again. "Do you like being called Bambi? Or do you think it's embarrassing?"

"Stop!" Alyson laughed and gave Jamie's shoulder a playful shove.

"I think, what the baby said, is Bambi is a girl's name."

"It is not! It's for boys and girls!"

"Hush, the baby is still talking!"

Alyson bit her lip, waiting. Her eyes danced as Jamie pretended to listen to her stomach.

"Ah, the baby also says that you're so beautiful and sweet, you may call it whatever you want, just as long as you don't share bath pictures after he or she is born."

"Okay! Deal," Alyson laughed. She purposefully dropped her hands on his arm to touch him before she placed them safely in her lap.

It was only a few more minutes before they were called back to see the doctor.

"Is this the dad?" the doctor asked as the couple walked hand-in-hand behind him to the examination room.

"Yes." Aly didn't feel like going into all the details with a doctor she was only going to see once. She felt Jamie squeeze her hand in response to her words.

"Okay, well, some dads stay out of the room for the examination part."

"I-I want him to stay." She knew there was an edge of panic in her words. This was why she was holding his hand. This was why she had let him be with her.

"Are you sure?" Jamie had no idea what the examination consisted of and wondered if he shouldn't leave the room.

"Please?"

"Sure. Whatever you want." He dutifully held her purse and jacket as she got ready to get onto the examination table. When she was settled on the padded surface, he pulled a chair over to sit by her head, facing away from where the doctor was. He grabbed her hand and stared steadily at her face.

She made eye contact a couple of times, but otherwise kept her gaze on the ceiling, grimacing at intervals when the internal examination was uncomfortable. The doctor asked more questions and Aly answered them, holding tightly onto Jamie's hand and focusing on her deep breathing.

The procedure finished, and Alyson was given a moment to get her clothes back on. Jamie came back in when the girl was done. She opened the door for him to enter and smiled shyly as he walked past. She thought she saw him blush, but by the time he had turned back around to face her, the ruddy tinge was gone.

"You okay?"

"Yeah, it was just really uncomfortable." Alyson's face was still red. "I wouldn't have done it, but I wanted to make sure everything was okay. It's my first baby, I don't know how everything is supposed to feel."

"Well, he said it all looked good and healthy," Jamie smiled.

"I'm glad for that."

The doctor returned and nodded towards the table again.

"Ready to hear your baby?"

"Hear my baby?" Alyson's face lit up.

"Yeah, your little guy is big enough to let us listen to his heartbeat if you'd like."

"Yes, please!"

Jamie helped Alyson get back onto the table and slipped his hand into hers, but his attention was more on what the doctor was doing than on the mother. His eyes watched everything intently, not wanting to miss a single detail about what was happening. He had a flashback to his mom's last pregnancy and the time when he got to go with her to see his youngest sister on the sonogram. That had been special, but this made his stomach feel like it was on fire. The baby he was about to hear could be his own. He nearly cried at the thought, but he pressed the feeling away.

The doctor measured Alyson's stomach first, telling her she was small, but allaying her fears by saying that she was perfectly fine and the baby should be as well. Next, a squirt of the cool gel onto her stomach made Aly suck in her breath. She squeezed Jamie's hand tighter, and he smiled down at her briefly before returning his sights to the screen that was going to show the heartbeat. They waited breathlessly to see what the doctor would find.

"All right, I think he's over on this side..." The doctor moved the instrument over Alyson's stomach until he thought he had found his mark.

A moment later, the sound of a ten-week-old heart pumping blood reached their ears, and Alyson melted. Tears ran down her face as the heartbeat grew louder.

"That's my baby." Alyson's whisper was filled with awe. She felt Jamie's other hand cover theirs and his lips press softly against her temple. To share that moment with him was incredible.

"Well done, love." The young man was on the verge of tears as he looked at the mother.

"Nice steady heartbeat. Sounds good and strong." The doctor interrupted the interaction between Alyson and Jamie with his words. "If you're right about the date of conception you should be having this baby by the middle of April."

Alyson had known the date from looking it up online, but hearing it from the doctor was a shock of reality. For six and a half more months she would be nurturing and carrying a tiny little human in her womb. "Wow."

"Six more months." Jamie smiled down at the girl, his face close to hers.

The look on Jamie's face brought more emotions into Alyson's stomach than she had felt in a long time. Fuzzy thoughts began to warn her she was feeling more for him than she should as his fingers brushed an imaginary hair off her forehead. Alyson's lungs constricted in her chest. She knew he felt the spark by the way he gripped her hand and used his other one to brush against her bare shoulder where her shirt had slipped off.

"I hope things continue to go well for you both. Congratulations!" The doctor felt the chemistry between the two as much as he saw it.

The two young adults took their time leaving the office after the appointment finished, reluctant to have the magical moment end. The familiar rush of being next to him washed over her, and she couldn't breathe. Impulsively, she leaned forward and kissed his cheek, interrupting him from what he was saying about the baby. The unexpected action made the young man look down at her.

"Thank you for everything," she whispered. Her heart pounded fast.

"You're welcome." Jamie glanced at her lips, wanting nothing more than to kiss them. Instead, he wisely took a step back. "I'm glad I can help."

The moment their bodies broke apart and space came between them, Alyson knew she had made a mistake. She made a mistake the second she decided holding his hand was going to be okay for one afternoon. Her head was spinning as she realized all she had allowed herself to feel for him. One of her biggest fears was confirmed; Jamie Donald still made her go crazy.

"I-I... I need to go home and keep packing." The words sounded lame in her mouth, but she didn't know what else to say. They were by the door, and the sun was setting.

"Will you let me take you out for dinner first?"

Alyson was about to say no, the word on the tip of her tongue, when she saw Jamie look away. He looked down at her hands and reached forward slightly. She remembered the feeling of comfort the touch had given her. She had felt the assurance of Jamie's feelings for her in that touch, and it had felt good. It felt better than holding herself away from him and trying to fight him.

"Okay. Let's get dinner." Alyson closed the distance between their hands.

"Are you sure?" Jamie was surprised at her actions and the smile on her face.

The girl nodded, and Jamie led them out to his car. They drove to a small burger joint that was down the road and slid into a private booth in the corner. Their conversation was about nothing important, and the couple laughed together more than once. Jamie let his hand slip over Alyson's, and she smiled at him with flushed cheeks. She listened to his stories and then brought up a few of her own, keeping herself distracted so she wouldn't think about the consequences of their actions. The only thing that interrupted their pleasant evening was Alyson's phone ringing.

"Oh! It's Elle!" Alyson quickly let go of Jamie's hand and stood up. "I'll be right back."

Alyson answered the phone as she walked towards the back of the restaurant where the bathrooms were located.

"Hi, Elle!"

"You never called me!" Danielle exclaimed before saying hello. "I thought maybe something horrible had happened and you didn't want to tell anyone..."

"No! No, it's all fine. I'm good." Alyson had forgotten she had promised Danielle she would call after the appointment. "I'm with Jamie and I for-..."

"What the heck, Aly." The words shocked the smile off Alyson's face.

"Excuse me?"

"You're with Jamie! Why are you with Jamie?" Danielle knew her best friend well enough to know she needed to say something. "Do you not remember why you are pregnant right now? Because of him!"

"I... Elle! He was just helping me!" Heat flooded Alyson's face, and she knew Danielle was right. "He was the one who made the doctor's appointment, I'm just trying to say thank you."

"Then say thank you and get the heck away from him! Alyson, you know you're going to regret going down that road again!"

Alyson felt tears stinging against her eyes, and she sighed deeply. Her spot in the hallway kept her out of Jamie's range of vision, hiding her tears from him. She knew Danielle was right; her focus needed to be on her baby. Trusting Jamie came with a high price.

"You're right. Thank you." The words came out as a whisper.

"Besides, you need to be in the right head space before you go home and see your parents tomorrow night."

"I'm so nervous, Elle."

"I know. I'm nervous for you. But you're going to be okay. Just love them and tell them all you can and know you'll get to see them when you come back." Danielle's calm voice helped steady some of Alyson's raging emotions. "Love you, Aly."

Alyson had to take several deep breaths before she could make herself walk back over to where Jamie was sitting at their table. He was busy looking at his phone as she approached him. Her stomach churned a bit as she realized how out of control she had let herself become. It had been nice, for a few minutes, to pretend like things were safe.

"You okay?" Jamie looked up when she reached the table and quickly set his phone down when he saw the look on her face. "Love, you all right?"

"Yeah, thanks." Alyson brushed away his helping hand. "I was just talking to Danielle about visiting my parents this weekend. It's going to be hard."

"Are you going to tell them anything?"

"I could never... there would be no way to explain this to my parents. That would bring so much shame to the family." Alyson shook her head. "And besides that, my mother raised me to know how to be a respectable young lady."

"I know your dad is from Pakistan, and I know that this situation is serious for you, but that's all I know about this." His words were an invitation to explain.

"My dad moved to America when he was eighteen and married my mom a few years later. She's from Chicago. I feel like..." Alyson licked her lips and wrinkled her brow as she found words to explain. "When I was younger it felt a lot more normal. I didn't really feel that different from my friends at school. I was in dance class, and I could be friends with boys, and we would do fun things together, and I just felt... I guess typical is a good word."

Jamie nodded and waited for Alyson to continue.

"My dad's family is all still in Pakistan, and we go visit them sometimes. One of my cousins, her name is Sumaya, she is around my age and we grew up close. She taught me a lot about the culture and how to act while I'm there."

"To be respectful, yeah, sure, that makes sense," murmured Jamie quietly.

"Right. But it is my culture as well, because I am my father's daughter. There are beautiful things about Pakistan that I love that are a part of me. Not everyone gets to say that."

"So what changed?"

Alyson hesitated.

"After we moved to Nebraska, uh... some things happened, and my dad started to become really cautious and protective. By the time I became a teenager he seemed like a completely different person in a lot of ways. He was still my dad and we had our special things, but he started to become more like his dad."

"What is his dad like?"

"Old-fashioned. Strict. Even compared to the people in the city he lives in, he's much more closed-minded to changes in society. Honoring the family is a very big deal. That's one of the reasons why my dad left Pakistan; because of my grandpa. But now he's a lot like him."

"What is his name, your dad?"

"Zaheer." The name sounded musical as it came off Alyson's tongue.

"Do you look like him?"

"We have the same nose." Alyson touched her nose with a little smile. "The green eyes come from my mother, though."

"Does your mum like your dad's family?"

"Oh yeah, very much. She raised me since I was little to think about my grandfather and make sure I didn't shame him. Even when my dad was lenient and didn't mind what I did as much, my mom would punish me if I did something she didn't think my grandfather would like."

"Really?"

"I think it has something to do with the fact that when my mom and dad got married, my grandpa paid a debt or something for her. She's always spoken highly of him, even though he... I mean, he has a backwards way of thinking. You never know what would set him off."

"Your grandfather paid off a debt for her? He must be well-off."

"Apparently. You should see how beautiful his house is. He works for one of the big bank chains in the country. It's one of the best jobs, which is why he's so honored and respected in society."

"Wow."

"I don't know if this is what you wanted to know." Alyson tried to smile away the knot in the pit of her stomach. Every time she opened up to him, she was afraid he would treat the information as trivial and hurt her.

"No, I find this fascinating. One of my good mates from secondary school was from Pakistan. He was a legend at footie, and I could never beat him. It was the worst!"

Alyson laughed.

"Are your cousins amazing at football as well?"

"I never really played soccer with them. I danced with them, though. My cousins are the ones who taught me how to dance. But then I got better than them."

"Really now?" Jamie raised an eyebrow at the girl's boast. "I guess I will just have to go to Pakistan sometime and make you prove it."

"I don't think my cousins would dance with you."

"Do you think? Why not?" Jamie asked incredulously.

"Because... well, because you're a man."

"Ah." Jamie chose his next words carefully. "But you're allowed to dance with me?"

There was no answer as Alyson looked down at her hands on the table

"Are you even allowed to be in a relationship with someone like me?"

"Yes." Alyson looked up quickly, but her eyes shifted uncertainly. "I mean, I can't imagine why I couldn't. I guess... I guess I've never... asked."

"Too afraid, or never wanted to?"

"Like I said before, my dad became very cautious and protective of me. He wants me to be the best at everything and do anything I need in order to achieve my dreams. I felt like trying to be in a relationship with someone that was good enough for my dad while I was in high school just wasn't going to happen."

"But now that you're an adult, surely they wouldn't mind who you fancied, as long as you loved him, yeah?"

Alyson shrugged. She didn't know, and she didn't like Jamie bringing it up and making her think about it. It was easy to pretend she was a normal girl who could do normal things when no one else was around.

"What other kinds of things are not allowed?"

"Sleeping around, obviously, drinking..."

"Drinking?"

"Yes, drinking. The girls have to be modestly covered at all times and careful in their interactions with guys."

"What happens if you do something that brings shame?"

"Depends on what it is."

"Do you honestly think your parents would kill you if they found out that you were pregnant?"

"I want to say no." Alyson spoke slowly. "But there are things that have happened in the past that tell me it is possible."

"Well, I'm glad we're able to give you a way to keep both you and Bambi safe. I know how badly you want him, and how badly I want him, too."

"Really?"

Jamie tried to read Alyson's eyes.

"Did you think I didn't want the baby?" he asked softly.

"You never really came out and said it, so I-I didn't know."

"Why would I not want Bambi?"

"I don't know! Babies change everything!"

Jamie didn't speak right away. He could tell Alyson felt a bit uncomfortable with his silence, but he didn't have the words. Not the right ones, at least.

"Is it hard to talk about this with the other guys?" Alyson was quiet. There was a weight to her question; she was the reason a conversation was needed.

There was silence as Jamie rubbed the back of his neck. Alyson waited for the answer.

"I love the guys. We've had our rough spots, for sure, but we've gotten familiar with each other and the way everyone processes life. So..." Jamie didn't sound like he knew where he was going with what he was saying.

"Does that make it easier?" prompted Alyson.

"A bit. But mostly harder."

Alyson looked at Jamie with surprise.

"If they were just blokes I didn't know, or that I didn't like I wouldn't care if they got to be the father or not. I would do what I could to push them away from you, so I could be the father in the end. If I'm honest, I've thought about doing it with these guys as well, even though I know that they are all great guys and will be brilliant dads one day." Jamie didn't look at Aly as he spoke. "But I know their friendship is valuable and I know whoever the father is, is more than capable and ready to be there for you and Bambi."

"You guys really want this baby."

"Mmm." Jamie nodded. "I really want this baby."

To Jamie that night in L.A. seemed like a blur, and all he could fully remember was dancing with Aly and then asking if she wanted to go somewhere they could be alone. He whispered his intentions, and she stared at him for a moment. She had spoken her answer with slight hesitation, but she had said yes. If he had never asked, she would have never said yes, and the night would have ended very differently.

"I should have known this about you before I brought you out to L.A., but I didn't even think." Jamie's voice was quiet. "You took my heart by surprise, Aly. I never planned on getting close to you. But here you are..."

"Thank you for everything, Jamie." Alyson let her fingertips brush across Jamie's arm.

Jamie covered Alyson's hand and held it.

Oh God, help me. Jamie's hand fit around hers so perfectly.

"I need to get back to my car now. I have a long day tomorrow." It was all Alyson could manage to say.

"Yeah, course, love." He stood up and grabbed the check that had been sitting on their table for the last fifteen minutes. "You need your rest. The baby needs to rest."

"Bambi," Alyson reminded with a smile.

"Bambi. Of course." Jamie gave her a crooked grin.

Alyson's free hand moved towards the baby and settled there for a brief moment as the couple walked. The doctor had said everything had seemed to be healthy and going well. Bambi was healthy. She smiled at the thought of her baby growing and developing perfectly inside of her. The memory of what her baby's heartbeat sounded like rushed through her mind, and she tightened her grip on Jamie's hand.

Jamie parked his car next to the only vehicle left in the parking lot of the little clinic. He unbuckled and climbed out before Alyson could even get her own buckle undone. Her seatbelt was still slipping up over her shoulder when her door opened. A strong hand reached in to help her to her feet.

"You going to be all right, love?" It was that voice that got to Aly every time.

"Hmm." Alyson nodded.

"I'll call you again tomorrow to check in on you."

"Wa-..." Alyson had to shake herself to get her mouth to remember how to talk. "No, I'm going home tomorrow. I won't be able to talk."

"Not even for a minute?" Jamie drew his eyebrows together.

"I-I don't know. I won't know until I get there." Alyson knew her words and her body were sending him mixed messages. She was in his arms, but her eyes refused to look at him

"You're not saying what you really mean, love. Please, tell me what you're trying to say." The young man was very aware of the fact the spell between them was about to be broken.

"Jamie, this is a bad idea." Alyson struggled to push away from him. "I have to focus on my baby. This isn't about us, or how we may or may not feel about each other. Yes, we talked things over today, and I-I'm glad, I'm glad for that. But I'm not sure how smart it was for me to let you stay with me. This isn't what I need in my life right now."

Jamie wiped a tear away from Alyson's red cheek. He smiled sadly, then leaned his forehead against her shoulder and breathed for a moment. She sighed and felt an ache in her heart. She could give him one more moment. Her hands found his shoulders, and she pulled him close.

"Thank you. I'll see you again soon," she whispered in his ear.

The young man didn't respond, but stepped back and looked Alyson in the eye before letting her go. He waited until she was in her car and ready to pull out before he got back into his own. She saw him wave at her through the window, then start his own vehicle to drive back to wherever he had come from. Tears blinded her as she drove in silence.

She tried to be angry at him for making her lose her self-control again, but she couldn't. It was the fact she had to pretend like she didn't want to be with Jamie that made her angry. She didn't want to feel the longing that was quickly growing stronger than the memory of his leaving her.

Every day she thought about how Jamie stood up and fought for her and Bambi in the meeting with his management team. His advisors told him to cut her lose and let her sink or swim on her own, yet his commitment hadn't budged and he fought even harder. He hadn't even taken a moment to reconsider it as an option.

"I hate emotions!" Alyson slammed the heel of her hand against her steering wheel as she drove. "I hate them! They're so fickle and, and, and do nothing but cause trouble! I wish I was still like my mom. I wish I never felt anything!"

More tears came as she tried to dissuade her heart from wanting Jamie. She rested a hand on her womb and stroked it, hoping her baby knew that even through all the tears she never wanted to lose the gift of life inside of her.

Chapter eight
"It's cold, sweetheart."

The drive home to her parent's house never took as long as Alyson wanted when she was nervous. The cars in front of her were in a hurry to get to their destinations and left the road wide open for her. She tried to get in the mood by listening to old CDs she and Danielle had made when they were in high school, but none of the songs soothed her restless spirit; so she chose silence. The quiet felt almost as uncomfortable as the music had.

Alyson grimaced and readjusted her grip on the steering wheel when her phone began to ring on the passenger seat. Again. She knew it was the same person who had already called her twice in the last twenty-four hours, not that she had answered those calls either. The last thing she needed was to have a conversation with Jamie, especially after their time together the day before. A nagging thought in the back of her mind was that he could be calling to tell her something important, but she ignored that, too. There was no more mental or emotional energy left for her to give him at that moment.

"Jamie, stop. I can't be dealing with you and my family at the same time." Alyson felt better saying the words out loud in the empty car. She sighed when the ringing stopped and silence surrounded her again.

Her weekend at home was going to be a huge act for Alyson. Her lies and her masks were going to have to be flawless, and her emotions so detached that no one would suspect a thing. This wasn't what she had imagined for herself; saying goodbye to her parents in the midst of secrets and lies. She dropped one hand from the steering wheel and began to stroke her stomach.

"We got this, Bambi. We'll be okay. Just please don't make me sick. And please don't let my parents find out about you." Alyson chewed on the inside of her cheek. She nearly jumped when her phone rang again. "Ugh! Jamie, stop!"

The girl picked up her phone and rejected the call. She didn't think she would be able to listen to her phone ring for sixty seconds without going crazy. Alyson found herself calling her best friend, putting the call on speakerphone. She hoped Danielle wasn't out with friends to start the weekend, something Alyson never did any more. Danielle answered the call, and Alyson was relieved that there was no loud chatter or music in the background.

"Hello?" Danielle sounded hesitant.

"What's wrong?"

"Oh, nothing! I just... I always have a mini-panic attack when I see you're calling 'cause I'm never sure what has happened, or if you're in trouble."

"Ah. All is well. I just needed to talk to someone."

"What's up?" Danielle's tone relaxed. "Aren't you on your way to see your parents right now?"

"Yeah, I'm driving."

"You must have something on your mind. You never call people when you're driving."

"I'm avoiding Jamie." Alyson did her best to sound indifferent as she spoke.

"Taking my advice from last night? I'm very proud of you, Alyson."

"I'm going to try at least. I told him when we said goodbye that we couldn't be in a relationship right now."

"Wait, wait, wait! 'Right now'? Would you ever want to be in a relationship with him again? Aly, he left you after you slept with him. You shouldn't get back together with a guy like that."

"I know! But, Elle!" Alyson sighed with frustration. "It's different now. He stood up for me when his management team tried to tell him to dump me."

"You already told me..."

"There have been so many things put into this move, and he's doing them all. Everything. Without complaining. He's being... really nice."

"Okay, so he's being really nice now because he realized how much of a jerk he was. Good for him. Just stay away, and don't let him get to you."

"I'm trying." Alyson let out a loud sigh. "Hence, I'm talking to you on the phone right now."

"I'm very proud of you." Danielle grunted as she rolled over on her bed to get into a more comfortable position. "What else do you want to talk about?"

"I don't really know... I mean..."

"Spit it out."

"My baby has a dad."

"That's always how it works, Aly. Please tell me you knew that."

"They want to be in Bambi's life." Alyson ignored Danielle's teasing. "H-how... I mean, how does that even work? I know people do it, raise a kid with someone they're not married to, but I feel like it's such a bonding, intimate thing. How do people do that?"

"They just take turns, I guess."

"What kind of things do you talk about with someone to know what kind of parent they are going to be? What if they want Bambi to grow up, I don't know, vegetarian, or, or, or let Bambi watch horrible movies I don't like?"

"Aly, you still have six months before Bambi is born to get to know the guys better and come up with rules and stuff."

"I know..."

"You know, but...?"

"If my family found out, assuming they don't just kill me on the spot, I would be forced to marry the man who fathered my child. D-do I try..."

"Aly! No! Don't even start thinking about that!"

"I'm not! I just... I went from thinking they wouldn't even care that I was pregnant to slowly realizing this is a big deal for them, and whoever the dad is is going to raise this child with me. How do you prepare for something like this? Don't say go to the library. I already checked and they didn't have any parenting books for situations like mine."

"Did you actually go to the library and look?"

"I'm just trying to figure out how to do this!"

"Okay. So, is the thing you're unsure of whether you want them to help you, or that you don't know how to let them help you?"

"I want Bambi to have a dad." Alyson had thought about it late into the night. Dads were important, and she wanted to give her child a father. She could go through the potentially hard and awkward situations to give her baby what it needed. "Especially if that dad is going to love and take care of Bambi. You know really love them in their heart like a true father."

"Then just start making a list of everything you feel like is a big deal or a fear you have and bring it out from time to time when you're with them and just have discussions. If they don't want to listen to what you want, then kick them in the face."

"Oh, thanks, Elle. Super advice."

"You're so welcome."

"I hope they listen to me then, because I don't know how much longer I'll be able to do a high kick."

"I guess you could have them sit down first. Then you wouldn't have to kick so high."

Danielle had always been able to get her to laugh, somehow, no matter how tense or stressed she was. That was one of the reasons why she valued Danielle's friendship so deeply. Alyson let herself laugh and release some of the tension she was holding in her shoulders. She knew it would be back before long, but it was nice for the moment.

"You know, I had it in my mind it was going to be just me and Bambi on our own. I would have you. Obviously. But whoever the dad is, he is going to be a dad for my child... for forever. They are going to look like each other, and be like each other, and there's going to be me in there, too, but... my baby has a dad, and he's going to be family to Bambi as much as I am."

"Mmhmm." Danielle pulled out her nail polish and began to do her nails.

"In the beginning I thought Bambi would never get that."

Alyson saw empty fields slip past her window as she drove the familiar route to her parent's home. She had driven that road hundreds of times since she moved away, and it was almost automatic; knowing how to get to her destination without thinking. She had grown so used to the view that she took for granted that you could see for miles across the flat Nebraskan fields. The sun was getting lower in front of her, its rays blazing red and orange, fading to yellow in certain places. The sunset matched the leaves of the trees by the old farmhouses that stood back from the road.

This is my last time to drive this way for a long time... The thought came out of nowhere, and it hit her like a punch in the gut. There would be no trip home for Thanksgiving, or Christmas. There would be no special weekends with her parents to get some of her mom's home cooking or to play card games with her dad by the fireplace. She would be thousands of miles away with her baby and four young men she hardly knew. Tears welled up in her eyes, and she blinked them away so she could see the road.

"Who do you hope the dad is? Who do you think will be the best?"

"Oh, geez. I don't know." Aly sniffed and gave a little laugh, thankful Danielle had broken the silence. "It's such a weird thing to think about."

"The craziest thing is that there are going to be three dads."

"Yes, but not technically," said Alyson. "I'm sure once Bambi is born it will feel less like that, and more like one dad and two uncles. Three uncles if you include Eddie."

"They might take over the baby duties completely. You won't even have to be a mom, they'll just raise Bambi on their own. They could start their own TV show."

"I would never allow that," Alyson chuckled. "I'm going to keep my baby."

"Three dads, one baby, the whole world to discover..."

"Here we go..."

"Which dad will win the best nighttime duty award? Find out on this episode! Which dad can keep his composure after being pooped on? Tune in next..."

"Danielle!" The girls dissolved into laughter. "You're being so weird!"

"They could be super-weird! You don't know yet."

"I know they could be super-weird, but Bambi deserves a father. We'll just have to figure it out. Or, like you said, high kick to the face."

"I feel like that is solid advice for a lot of situations in life."

"Please don't ever write a book. Besides, all this talk of them being weird with my baby is starting to scare me."

"Okay, here's a happy thought; there will always be Auntie Elle to take care of him or her whenever you need a date night with your hot husband that you will meet when you're in England."

"Whoa! Husband! Slow down!"

"It's inevitable. You're a babe."

"Yeah, a pregnant and severely complicated babe! I guess it could happen."

"I'll be waiting for the wedding invitation."

"Okay, but don't hold your breath."

Alyson saw her exit coming up in a few miles. She wanted to have the last little bit of the trip to think on her own, so the two friends said goodbye and promised to talk again soon.

"Remember, if anything happens and there's an emergency, text me, 'Bambi in the woods.'" Danielle's voice grew serious as she reminded her friend. "Even if it's just too much emotionally, get out. I know you're strong and brave, and that your parents love you, but do not risk your safety."

"Thanks, Danielle. I'll remember."

It was dusk outside when Alyson pulled into the familiar neighborhood. She smiled softly, looking at the porch lights and street lights and headlights she passed. The streams of light pouring out into the oncoming night reminded Alyson to hold onto every type of illumination that entered into her seemingly dark world. Light was strong and always overpowered the darkness. She put her hand on her stomach and said a tiny prayer of protection for herself and her baby. Then, she was home.

It was a big, white house with a full front porch and a sidewalk leading up to the front door. The forest-green shutters matched the well-trimmed bushes that grew around the front of the house and accented the many, large windows. It was one of the prettiest houses in the neighborhood, especially in the spring when the lilacs and lilies were in full bloom and spread color throughout the flower garden that hugged the foundation of the house.

"Oh, my girl!" Mrs. Abidi had been watching for her daughter from the window and ran outside to Alyson's car before the girl could even get out of the driver's seat. She usually held herself back, giving love in a reserved and calm manner. Her overt show of affection shocked her daughter. "I'm so excited to see you!"

"Hi, mom!" Alyson was grateful for the welcome from her mother and for the thickness of her fall jacket. "Wow! You look happy!"

"It's not everyone's daughter that was chosen to travel to the United Kingdom for a year to train other teachers at the age of twenty-two!" Janice smiled down at Alyson before leaning in to kiss her daughter's cheeks.

"It's so good to be back home for a little while before I go." Alyson was encouraged by the warm greeting. She hardly received a hug from her mother that involved both of her arms since she moved away. Every once in a while, Janice would give her a quick squeeze, but a full-on embrace was rare, and Alyson was almost moved to tears by the feeling of being completely enveloped in her mother's arms.

"Come in, I have so many things to tell you. Oh, let your father carry your bag. Zaheer, come get Aly's bag from her car! I don't know if he can hear me, he's in the workshop. Zaheer! Aly's home!"

The talking didn't stop as the two women entered the Abidi family residence, Alyson carrying the bag her mother had told her to leave in the car for her father. For five minutes, Alyson listened to her mother go on excitedly before excusing herself to her room to settle in a bit before supper. It had been years since she had seen her mother so happy and bubbly.

"Oh, there's a new dress I bought for you on your bed. It's for the going-away party we're having for you. It's on Sunday, and I think everyone we know is able to come. Go try it on, and see if it fits."

That was when Alyson began to grow nervous. She walked quickly up the stairs and into her bedroom, shutting the door behind her. Before she even looked for the dress, she let out a deep sigh and breathed in the smell of home. This small room had been her sanctuary for years. From the faded white-and-pink-flowered wallpaper that used to be her favorite, to the pink dresser she had received for her tenth birthday, there were signs of Alyson's childhood everywhere. She walked slowly across the white carpet; the stain from the time Danielle had spilled her red Kool-Aid was still there in the middle of the room.

Most of her things had moved with her to Des Moines, but there were still a few items left to keep her old bedroom homey for when she visited. In the bottom of her closet were trophies, plaques and certificates she had won for one thing or another. Dance recital costumes hung on old hangers above them, all of them too small for Alyson to wear anymore. She had been told she couldn't dance in recitals once she reached her thirteenth birthday.

A dusty picture frame sat on the bedside table next to the pink ballerina lamp Alyson had used all through high school despite the fact she picked it out in second grade. Alyson stood in the middle of the room and turned slowly in a circle. She stopped to stand in front of the full-length mirror that hung on the back of the closet door. Behind her was the window. Her mother had insisted on there being curtains...

"Well, Bambi. This is it. This is my room. I was a very big fan of pink at one time." Alyson turned to the side to get a better view of her profile. There was hardly anything to see as she pulled her shirt tight over her stomach, but it was strange trying to see the outline of her baby in the mirror she had used as a little girl. "I have a feeling this is the only time you'll ever get to see it."

There was the dress on her bed, just as her mother had told her. The material looked stretchy, but the style was all about hugging her midsection and hips. It was the worst possible type of dress Alyson could have tried to wear at that point in her pregnancy.

"Oh, God. Help." Alyson shot up a prayer as she dropped her bag onto the bedroom floor and herself onto her bed. The springs squeaked from her weight. "I hate lying."

A few moments later, Alyson got up and changed into her sweatpants and baggy sweatshirt, claiming to be ready for bed as soon as supper was over. Her mother asked about the dress and showed her surprise when Alyson said she didn't think she would wear it. That was the first time Alyson had ever turned down clothes her mother bought for her.

"I just don't like the color." Alyson knew if she complained about anything else, her mother would force her to try it on and model it for her.

"Really? Didn't you have a dress that same color a couple years ago?"

"I don't remember. Sorry, mom. You usually pick out the best stuff." Lies. Lies. Lies. Tears started to prick at the back of her eyes, and she knew she was moments away from bursting into tears. She looked around the room to find an escape. "Hey, can I give Casson a walk quick before supper?"

The family's old basset hound lifted up his head from under the table at the sound of his name. He was slow and fat, and loved by everyone who knew him. He was not a fan of the cold, but Alyson didn't care.

"It's cold, sweetheart."

"I'll be okay. I have a sweater."

Alyson was thankful for the cover of night to keep her tears hidden as she quickly left the house, pulling her dog behind her. The family pet didn't seem to notice the sniffling coming from the girl as they passed the houses of neighbors and family friends. Some of them had watched her grow up from a skinny little eight-year-old with huge freckles and warm smile, into a bit taller and self-assured young woman. They had all been there the day she had loaded up her car with most of her things and driven away to a new adventure as a teacher in Iowa. She knew they would all be at the party on Sunday expecting to see her off on her next adventure.

The thing with her neighbors was that everyone loved her. They were continually gushing about how smart and kind and talented she was, but no one really cared about her. They cared about the articles in the newspaper after she won the spelling bee, and the short-story contest. They cared about her being on the winning basketball team, but they never cared what happened when the curtains were closed. When she had gotten first place in the dance competition, they couldn't stop talking about her and telling anyone who would listen that she was the little girl from their neighborhood. However, when the curtains remained shut for two days and she didn't appear, there was no mention of her. No one knocked on the door to ask if she was okay, or if they could help. They simply waited until the curtains opened and their hero emerged once more.

The memory still made her angry, and her hand went to her belly. She wished she could hold her child in her arms and gain comfort from a warm body pressed against her chest, and covering her aching heart. A fresh wave of tears was about to fall when her phone buzzed in her back pocket. She wiped her eyes as she pulled her phone out, hoping it wasn't her mother or Jamie; it was neither.

"Tommy?" Alyson felt a surge of panic rise up in her when she saw the name on her phone. Tommy had never called her before, and Alyson quickly answered. Something had to have happened. "Hello?"

"Haha! I knew you would answer if I called you!" Tommy laughed on the other end of the phone.

"Wait, what?" Alyson stopped walking.

"Jamie said he had tried to call you, and you hadn't answered, so I said I could probably get you to answer my call."

"Are you serious right now?"

"He's going to be so upset when he hears that you answered!"

"So everything is okay? There's nothing wrong? No emergency?"

"No, everything's right as rain. More so now 'cause Jamie owes me a hundred quid."

"I'm sure that is a very desirable amount of quids." The remark was supposed to sound annoyed, but she received another laugh.

"Well, since we're on the phone, tell me how you're doing. Thanks for the update on the baby yesterday, by the way."

"You're welcome." Alyson let her vexation show in her voice.

"Whoa, you okay? You sound grumpy."

"I'm fine."

"Why only fine? I know that means something is the matter."

"Well, right now I'm at my parents' for the weekend to say goodbye, and my mom bought me a dress to wear to my going-away party. I love the dress, but it is the worst possible type of dress for me to wear right now. Everyone would see my bump and know exactly what is going on. I feel horrible because I know my mom really wanted me to wear it, but I can't! I don't have any other dress to wear so it's just, ugh, complicated."

"You don't own any dresses?" Tommy sounded incredulous.

"No! I do own dresses, they're just all at my house. I didn't know there was going to be a party. At any rate, I don't know if any of those dresses would have worked either."

"So, buy a new dress and just wear that one." Alyson could picture Tommy shrugging his shoulders as he spoke.

"I can't! I don't have anyone to go with me. Besides, I have too many other things I need to spend money on to just go buy a new dress."

"Why can't you go buy a dress by yourself?"

"How could you go dress shopping by yourself? What if you need someone to zip you up in the back? Who is going to tell you if it looks good? What if you can't get it back over your head? I'm not just going to ask some stranger, and I sure can't bring a friend."

"Sorry, I never knew dress shopping was so complicated," he muttered quietly.

"It's fine. I'm just frustrated." Alyson kicked at a rock with her shoe and realized she was several blocks away from home. She turned around to retrace her steps to get back before she was gone for too long. "I'll figure something out."

"What are you going to figure out? You don't have anyone there to help you dress shop!"

"It's just a dress. I mean, yeah, it sucks, but I don't need to be crying over it."

"What are you going to do about it?"

"I don't know, Tommy. But something will get figured out. It's fine."

"How about I fly out and help you go dress shopping?"

The invitation hung in the air for quite some time before Alyson fully grasped what Tommy had suggested. Casson pulled on his leash, eager for the girl keep up with his waddling and get him back to his warm home again.

"Are you... is this a joke?" she said hesitantly.

"Absolutely not! I'm bored out of my brains here in L.A. waiting for my cousin to fly in on Sunday. He's gonna hang out with me for a few days before I go back to London, and I have nothing to do. Flying to Iowa to go dress shopping for a day sounds like great fun, actually!"

"I'm not in Iowa right now, I'm in Nebraska," Alyson corrected. "My parents are from Nebraska."

"Is there an airport there?"

"Well, yeah..."

"Perfect, then I can come. When do you want to go shopping?"

"Um, tomorrow morning? My dad has bowling club, and my mom will be meeting with the ladies' committee for breakfast. I was just going to sleep in and cry and wonder what happened to my life."

"No. That sounds like the worst idea ever."

Alyson nodded and exhaled. She knew it was the worst idea ever.

"I'll fly to Nebraska, and we can go buy you a dress. It's settled. I'm phoning my friend at the airport as soon as I get off the phone with you. He'll get me on a redeye in the morning."

"Okay, but first, do you even know where you're going to be flying to?" Alyson wondered how often Tommy planned things like this.

"Nebraska." The simple answer made Alyson start to laugh. "What? That's where you said you were!"

"I know, but, Tommy, Nebraska is an entire state! You need to fly to Omaha. I'll pick you up from the airport, and we can go to the mall there." That seemed like the safest plan since her family was so widely known in her town. "When will you fly in tomorrow?"

"I'll text you the information when I get off the phone with my friend. Let me look up flight times... Oh! There's one that leaves at four in the morning here, that would get me into Omaha at... let's see..."

"Four in the morning? That's so early!"

"Yeah, but it would get me in at about ten-twenty. That's a good time."

"So I just go to the Omaha airport a little after ten, and you'll be there?"

"Yeah, I'll have to text my friend, but I don't see why I shouldn't be able to get on that flight."

"Great. So, I'll just see you sometime tomorrow."

"Yeah, I'm buzzing now! I've never been to Omaha!"

"Well, I hope you're not disappointed." Alyson chuckled lightly. "Let me know if you realize in the morning you're too tired and don't want to come. That's fine, too."

"I'm not going to change my mind." Tommy sounded offended by the idea. "Alyson! Really? I wouldn't ever do that to you."

A flashback to the night in L.A. slipped into Alyson's memory, and she remembered how he had held her as she cried after they were done. Alyson remembered the smell of his aftershave and the smooth feel of his skin under her hand as she laid it over his heart. She wanted the steady thumping to slow down the racing of her own heartbeat. Their breathing fell in sync as they lay in their dark hotel room. Inhale. Exhale. And again. And again.

The kisses he placed on her forehead eased the throbbing headache the Tylenol seemed to be unable to touch. In the light of day he was personable and outgoing. Most people only knew the funny, young drummer from his concerts or nights out at the club, but Alyson had gotten a glimpse of something else there in the dark.

"Okay, so the plan is you come in at ten-ish, we shop for a few hours, and then I just take you back to the airport, and you fly back to L.A.?"

"Is that a good plan?"

156

"Yeah! I guess!" Alyson wasn't sure what else to say. It was all so spontaneous. Casson began whining louder and tugging at the leash with more strength. She looked up and saw her house in front of them. "Oh, I have to let you go."

"All right, Alyson. I'll see you in the morning. No more crying over dresses."

"Got it." Alyson ended with a smile on her face, but it slowly faded as she realized what she had just gotten herself into.

Casson didn't care how slowly Alyson wanted to walk as they reached the front door; he was ready for his nice warm bed by the heater vent. She managed to make him wait while she took a couple deep breaths and calmed herself. She shivered at the thought of Jamie being upset when he heard about this. What had she been thinking?

Things hadn't been awkward between herself and Tommy, per se, but they had always been with the others. With Jamie and Garret her emotions were very clear, and very strong. At least, they had been in the beginning. So many things from that night had been a drunken blur, but with Tommy she remembered it. She remembered it all, and she knew he remembered, too.

Alyson opened the front door and let Casson off his leash, freeing him to scurry across the room to his bed. She quickly ran up the stairs before her parents could see her. The meal was ready by the time Alyson had finished washing her face, hiding all evidence of how emotional her walk had been.

Conversation around the table was mainly about the curriculum Alyson was writing for her new job. It was an easy topic that Alyson didn't have to make up as she went along. She went to bed that night rubbing her hands over her belly. One night down. Two days and one night to go.

It was just after ten when Alyson wandered into the Omaha airport. She looked at the signs and found directions to the baggage claim. Tommy wouldn't have any bags since he was only staying for the day, but she figured it was as good a place as any to wait for him to arrive. She had spent the whole drive to the airport telling herself it was okay to spend a few hours getting to know Tommy. She was almost convinced.

She hadn't slept well the night before, unable to get comfortable on the twin-sized bed she had used as a teenager. She wished she had brought her body-pillow from home and grabbed a cup of coffee before she left her parent's house.

"Where is that boy?" Alyson looked down at her phone and realized it was just barely past ten, and she had only been waiting for five minutes. She stood up from the bench and began to walk around, afraid that if she sat she would fall asleep.

She stood along a wall and watched a family with three young children juggle luggage and jackets as they left the airport. Next there was an elderly couple with two huge suitcases each. Their Hawaiian-style shirts revealed where they were arriving from. After watching the couple totter slowly out of the building, a group of young teenagers dressed in matching soccer uniforms ran past, their happy chatter and laughter drifting behind them to where the lonely girl stood. Finally, her phone began to ring in her hand.

"Alyson! I'm here! I'm in Omaha!"

"Oh, good!" Alyson couldn't help but smile at the excitement her friend had over visiting such an overlooked city. "Where should I meet you?"

"Well, I'm coming down the tunnel thing now, and I'm about to run out past the baggage claim."

"Perfect. Don't die."

"Wait, what kind of car do you have?" asked Tommy.

"It's silver."

"Do you have the only silver car in all of Nebraska?"

"Don't worry, I'll be watching for you."

A few short minutes later, Alyson spotted the blond-haired young man, who was wearing a gray jacket and tight, light-blue jeans walking quickly towards the exit. She would have to move fast to catch him before he left the building without her. Careful to dodge the many people crowding around the baggage carousel, Alyson jogged to catch up.

"Tommy!" she shouted over the din of voices. "Tommy! I'm here!"

Not only did Alyson get the attention of the young man who was looking for her, but also caused several people around them to turn and take notice. For a split second, Tommy's expression became panicked, but he acted quickly, grabbing Alyson by the hand and hurrying them out of the building. He kept his head down and pulled up the collar of his jacket, making Alyson run to keep up with his long legs. They crossed the road and looked behind them to see that no one had followed.

"Oh good. No one noticed." Tommy let out a sigh of relief.

"Sorry." Alyson made a face. "I wasn't thinking about the fact that people might recognize you."

"No harm done. That would be a rotten start to the day, being followed everywhere. By the way, you look lovely." Tommy finally stopped and was able to get a look at her.

She was dressed nicely in a long, loose fitting, cream-colored shirt and black skinny jeans with some black boots. Over the top she was wearing her maroon-colored sweater she had worn to the doctor's appointment two days earlier. She hadn't dressed up in the past couple months, and she appreciated the opportunity to look nice and be out with a man.

"Thank you. You look nice as well. I wish my jeans were as tight as yours, they might make my legs look longer." Alyson admired her companion for a moment. "Welcome to Omaha."

"Thank you! This is my first time here!" His face lit up like a small child's on Christmas morning. "I can't wait to be a tourist!"

A truck rumbled by the young couple, and the exhaust fumes hit Alyson full in the face. She grabbed Tommy's arm to steady herself, her head spinning and nausea gripping her stomach. Her other hand flew up to her mouth.

"Alyson!" Tommy felt the reach and turned around to see Alyson nearly doubled over. "What's wrong?"

Unable to speak for fear of throwing up, Alyson gestured to her stomach and frowned.

"Are you gonna be sick?" Tommy steadied Alyson by her elbow and looked around for a trash can. "Are there toilets nearby?"

The girl mumbled unintelligibly and pointed straight ahead. If she could just get to her car she could use one of the empty trash bags she kept in there for that exact reason. There had been more than one morning on the way to school where she had pulled over to use one.

"You okay now?" he asked, still holding Alyson's purse after they had reached the car and Alyson found a bag.

"That was not the greeting I was planning on giving you." Alyson sighed and took her purse from Tommy's arm. "Are you still excited for Omaha?"

"As long as you're feeling okay!"

"I'm not sick. I just smelled too much exhaust when that truck drove past." With a wave of her hand, Alyson dismissed his fears. "But, do you mind driving?"

Tommy's concern didn't stop after they arrived at the mall and began to try on dresses. They watched their surroundings, glad to find many of the stores they went into relatively quiet. The young man kept a hand on Alyson's elbow or back as they walked, ready to whisk her away from wherever they were at the first sign of being noticed. Alyson rummaged through several racks of dresses, shared a pretzel with Tommy, then searched through two more stores before they finally found a dress that suited Alyson's taste and growing stomach.

"I really like this one." She came out from the dressing room with a grin. "Do you like it?"

She spun around, modeling every side of the light blue dress that brushed against her knees with its hem. The sleeves were loose and the waistline hit high on her midsection. Her smile made her appear to be almost glowing as she swished the flowing fabric and pranced around the store. Tommy watched, his own smile tugging at the corner of his mouth. He remembered that smile from watching Alyson with Jamie before they broke up. She danced past him, and he caught her wrist with his hand.

"Shall we dance?"

With a laugh, the pair of them waltzed around the store until they were laughing too hard to keep going. Two teenage girls entered the store, and the couple slipped into a corner behind some clothes racks to hide. They smothered the last of their laughter and gave each other a knowing look.

"I think it is a lovely dress," Tommy whispered through his slightly labored breathing, enchanted by the way Alyson's eyes were sparkling up at him. "Much better than the red one."

"Which red one?" Alyson giggled softly before peeking around the clothes to see if the coast was clear to return to the dressing room.

"The... the red one. You know..." Tommy sputtered.

"You sound like me trying to describe my car." A cheeky smile made Tommy roll his eyes. "This is the dress I want. I'm starving. Are you ready to go eat somewhere?"

"I thought we'd never get to eat! How quickly can you change?"

"So fast!" Alyson made a mad dash for the dressing room, leaving Tommy behind.

It was risky to take Tommy to a place closer to her hometown, but Alyson knew this was her last chance to eat at her favorite diner before she left. She leaned her head back against the headrest and rubbed her stomach as she listened to Tommy's stories and comments about Nebraska, a little smile pulling up the corners of her mouth. It was easy to be with Tommy. She liked it.

"Here! This place!" Alyson pointed at her old favorite place to eat. She used to beg her parents to eat there all the time as a young child, but it had been years since she ate there last. It was half an hour away from her hometown, so the few times they had been able to go were special memories to Alyson.

Tommy put a hand on her elbow as they walked in through the glass doors. A bell dinged to announce their entrance, and Alyson gave the main floor a sweeping glance. As she expected, she saw no one she knew. The place seemed to have cleared of most of their lunch guests, and there were only a few patrons left in the afternoon lull.

"Come this way!" The hostess smiled at them cheerily.

Tommy's hand remained on Aly's arm as they walked carefully around tables behind the young woman. They were halfway through the restaurant when someone called out Alyson's name.

"Aly!"

The voice was like ice to Alyson's blood stream, and she froze. The bottom of her stomach fell to her feet like a rock to the ocean floor. She quickly pasted on a smile as she turned to face her mother. In that moment the hand on her arm felt too close for comfort. The girl knew her mother had already seen the intimate gesture and was not pleased. Mrs. Abidi stood up from her spot at the small table she was sharing with two other women. The daughter recognized them as her mother's colleagues she had met at Christmas parties in the past.

"Mom!" The fake smile hurt her face.

"When you're done saying hello, your booth is the one on the end by the back exit." The hostess excused herself politely.

"Thank you." Tommy nodded at the woman who then walked away to fix up their table.

"I thought you were in Omaha." The mother looked from her daughter to the tall young man and back again.

"I was." Alyson was grateful to have one chance to tell the whole truth. "We were. I had to pick him up from the airport."

"And this is?" Frown lines pressed around the mother's mouth as she took in the stylish apparel of the man who was standing next to her daughter. Alyson knew her mother would put up a fuss about her being with a young man alone, but it was too late now.

"This is Tommy. He is one of the sponsors of the school in Bedford. He was part of choosing the teacher."

"Oh!" Mrs. Abidi raised her eyebrows. "So, this is a business lunch?"

"Yes. Yes, it's about the school." The lie was the only way to salvage the situation.

"Very nice to meet you, Mrs. Abidi. I've heard a lot about you." Tommy's smile was genuine as he shook hands and leaned in for a hug.

"Hello." Mrs. Abidi stuck out her hand and declined the hug. "I thought you were a secret boyfriend with the way you were holding onto Alyson's arm."

"Ah! Well, I can only wish I'd be lucky enough to date your daughter. She's a great kisser!" The last sentence was supposed to get a laugh, but instead made Alyson's face go white.

"Don't worry, Aly, I know you would never kiss him." Mrs. Abidi put a hand on her daughter's arm to calm her, seeing her daughter's livid reaction to the joke. "You'll never pull that one on me; my daughter isn't one to kiss strange men because she feels like it. She's very smart and confident in who she is, which is why, I believe, you guys chose her for the job in Bedford."

"Oh, absolutely." Tommy knew he had said the wrong thing. His cheeks turned red. "All of us lads know Alyson is the most respectable young woman we have ever met. We are very excited to have chosen her."

"I knew she was made for more than Iowa." Mrs. Abidi looked at her daughter's face and saw the girl's eyes becoming watery. "No tears, honey."

"I know." Alyson tried to play off the rising emotions as happy. "I'm just overwhelmed."

"That's no reason to cry." Mrs. Abidi gave her daughter's shoulders a squeeze. "You know, Aly, you should have had another person join you for the meeting. It doesn't look good to have the two of you alone together."

"I know. I tried, mom. Everyone else is busy with other things. I'm very, very sorry."

"How long are you staying in Nebraska, Tommy?"

Alyson was about to say he was leaving that evening, but couldn't speak fast enough.

"I was planning on staying for the party tomorrow night. Alyson told me about it, and I wanted to come say a few words about what she'll be doing and how much we're looking forward to her joining us over in England. Give her an official send-off. Thought that might be nice." Tommy didn't have to look at Alyson to know she was taken aback by his words. "As long as that is okay, of course."

"Oh, yes." Janice's eyes lit up. She was pleased by the idea. "What an honor to have one of the sponsors say a few words about the job. Aly, bring him to the house when you're done here."

"Are you sure..."

"Aly. As soon as you're finished." Janice's tone told her the conversation was over.

"Yes, ma'am." Alyson nodded and wiped her eyes. She looked and saw she had a line of black on her pointer finger from her mascara. And just like that, the weekend was ruined.

Tommy shoved his hands into his pockets as they walked over to the booth that had been prepared for them. Alyson continued to cry silently as they settled into the secluded corner. She used a napkin to wipe the makeup off her face. Neither of them said anything for a while; Alyson looking down, and Tommy looking at her.

"Sorry for what I said to your mum. Calling you a great kisser. I wasn't thinking." He apologized first.

"No, Tommy, I know. That's not what made me cry." Alyson sniffled. "I'm crying because of the fact that my mom still knows me as the girl she raised; the one who doesn't kiss random men. The girl who was going to bring honor to the family name. And here I am, pregnant."

"Ah." Tommy reached over and put a hand on Alyson's arm as she began to cry again.

She moved her arm away, glancing over her shoulder to where her mother was still sitting with her friends. They weren't paying attention, but she knew that the wrong thing at the wrong time could bring the whole cover-up crashing down.

"And you sai-..." Alyson could hardly make it through a sentence without her voice failing her. "You said that you and the boys all know me as the most... the most respectable woman you guys had ever met! And that kills me because that's who I was. That's who I used to be. That's who I w-wanted to be! But you guys know the most ugly, unrefined side of me. You know it better than a-anyone else in the world!"

"But I didn't just make that up, Alyson! Everyone who knows you and who has worked with you has nothing but good things to say."

Alyson gave a scoffing laugh as she wiped her eyes again. Why was everyone so bent on seeing the best in her? She didn't earn the right to hear Tommy say those things about her.

"We respect you."

"Thank you for saying so." Alyson nodded and looked down. "I don't deserve your respect, but I am thankful for it."

His jaw tensed and he licked his lips, ready to say something else, but stopped when the server brought over drinks and asked them for their order. Tommy asked for some more time with a big grin, hoping to distract from Alyson's tears. Tommy dropped his smile after she left, and he focused on his friend again. Alyson stopped to press the napkin against her eyes, and she let out a shuddering breath. Tommy watched, his brows drawn together in concern.

"And if they knew the truth, they could have me killed." The words were heavy. "My mom just praised me to your face, and my mom never does that. If only she knew..."

"She's not going to know. We're taking care of that."

"It's almost enough to make me want to call the whole thing off."

Tommy silently thanked his lucky stars he was with Alyson in that moment. He could only imagine what would happen if Jamie got the call saying Alyson had changed her mind again.

"Alyson, I want you to listen to me." Tommy's voice was low as he waited for her to look him in the eye. "You don't want to call this off. I know you don't. You're scared, and you're emotional, and I understand that, but you need to keep yourself together."

Alyson took a deep breath and closed her eyes for a moment. Tommy was right. Her mother was right. No tears. She needed to keep herself together.

After their server took their orders, she asked for a picture with Tommy. He obliged but asked for her to not post it until Monday when he would be gone. She agreed and smiled as she left.

"Do you think she'll talk?" Alyson asked quietly, watching the girl walk away.

"Nah. They usually don't care who I'm with, they just want a picture. Besides, we're on a business meeting. Nothing wrong with that, right?"

"Well... no." Alyson sighed. "I just have to make sure no one becomes suspicious and tries to find out about Bambi."

"Bambi? Is that what you're calling the baby?" A crooked grin appeared on the young man's face. "Isn't that from the list Eddie and I made?"

"Yeah." Alyson smiled.

"That's hilarious! I love it!"

"I feel like it suits him. Or her."

"You want to know something." Tommy leaned his elbows on the table. "I was listening to our first album the other day, and one song just jumped out at me, and I couldn't stop thinking about the baby."

"Really? Which song?" The first album was Alyson's favorite, and she knew every song by heart. That was the album that had introduced her to *Jupiter Waits* and Jamie Donald, the only famous person she had ever wanted to meet in her life.

"'Sweet Dreams.' I don't know why, but it just seemed to fit how I feel."

"I love that song." Alyson's smile was genuine. "I remember listening to it for the first time and promising myself to go to the concert so I could hear you guys play it live."

"Wait, did we?"

"No." Alyson frowned and shook her head. "You guys never played it in concert."

"Shame, that. Jamie should have done that song."

"Meh." Alyson shrugged good-naturedly. "I learned it on the piano so I could give myself concerts whenever I wanted to hear it live."

"You play?" asked Tommy with surprise.

"Not well, but Danielle had a keyboard in her bedroom that we would fool around with all the time. I wasn't good enough at it for my parents to buy a piano for me."

"That's how you get better, though, by playing it!"

"I was better at other things, and they wanted me to stay focused." Again, Alyson shrugged, this time without a smile.

Their food began to arrive and the pair kept their conversation going between bites. Alyson stole so many of Tommy's fries he ordered more and put them in the middle of the table to share. The lighthearted conversation was interrupted by Alyson's mother walking over to their table and telling them she was going.

"Tommy, do you prefer coffee or tea?"

"Oh, tea, please." Tommy flashed her another winning smile.

"I'm going to set on the kettle. Don't let the tea get cold."

"Yes, ma'am." Alyson gave her mother a weak smile.

"It would probably be better if your father didn't know about this lunch," said Janice before she turned around and walked away. Alyson watched her, her heartbeat pounding dangerously close to the tight knot in her neck.

"You ready to go back and face everything?" asked Tommy quietly.

"You'll be there to distract them. They'll be fine as long as you're there."

"Good. I'll do what I can."

The food settled nicely in Alyson's stomach as she sat in the passenger side of her car again. Tommy hummed quietly as he drove along, providing a nice distraction from the silence Alyson was used to. She watched out of the window, her eyes taking in the familiar sights and trying not to get too sentimental about it all. This was the stretch of road she and Danielle used to drive down when they wanted to pretend they were running away. She turned back to look at the driver when he began to talk.

"We were talking the other day, Eddie and I, and I realized how thankful I was that you were willing to keep the baby. You could have decided to just not keep him, you know? I want to be a dad, and there's a chance Bambi is mine, and I'm happy you're a part of this."

The words made Alyson smile.

"I'm glad you want to be a dad." She thought back to the last conversation she had with Jamie. "Bambi is going to have a really great dad."

Mrs. Abidi had the tea ready for them when they arrived home and settled them in the living room. Tommy and Zaheer talked sports while Alyson sat on the other side of the room, trying desperately to stay awake. It surprised her that Tommy seemed to get along with her father quite well. The passionate conversation about the World Cup lasted for close to an hour before Alyson slipped out of the room.

Alyson could hear her mother preparing the evening meal in the kitchen as she started to tiptoe up the stairs. A little voice in the back of Alyson's mind told her to go help her mother cook, but the daughter could hardly keep her eyes open. She crept silently to her bedroom and lay down on her bed. She was almost asleep before her head hit the pillow.

Two hours passed before Alyson woke up needing to use the restroom. She stared at herself in the mirror and took a couple deep breaths after washing her hands. She found her stomach and stroked it softly.

"Well, Bambi. So far, so good. Very glad my mom is feeling forgiving this weekend. I just really hope that Tommy doesn't do anything stupid."

Alyson opened the door to see Tommy standing at the end of the hallway staring at a picture hanging on the wall. Her hand froze on the doorknob, and she gave him a hard look when he turned to smile at her.

"What are you doing up here?"

"Your dad needed to go meet with someone and your mum is in the kitchen, so I was just admiring this family photo. You're really cute in this picture."

Alyson's feet skipped the squeaky floor board without any conscious effort as she walked to the end of the hallway to stand beside him. She noticed that the same tiny nightlight that had lit up the hallway since she was little still glowed near the staircase. No one had slept upstairs for years, yet her mother still kept the light on.

The braided rug kept their feet from touching the cold hardwood floor as they stood in front of the family picture. She had been seventeen when the picture was taken. So young. It was the end of a very hard season, and life was slowly coming back into her eyes and her heart. She could see a shadow of it peeking through in the picture.

Alyson turned away from the image, aching from a growing feeling of nostalgia. Sometimes she felt like she had lived so much life already. Tommy watched her turn around and waited to see what she would do next. She looked uncomfortable as he followed her into the first bedroom at the top of the stairs.

"Is this your room?"

"Guest room." She eyed him carefully.

The shade was up, and Alyson walked over to the window. No one had ever made the time to hang curtains for that window. It was the only room in the house without them. It was also the only room in the house Alyson had never seen her father go into.

Tommy flopped onto the bed and stretched. He closed his eyes for a moment, his arms folded behind his head. The light of the setting sun splashed onto his face, highlighting his soft hair that lay every which way as he rested. It was a little brighter than their hotel room had been, barely enough light to cast dim shadows onto the wall before they slipped away into the darkness. She had felt the sweat on his skin, and his hot breath on her face, but she hadn't seen his eyes, and he hadn't seen hers.

If my parents knew what you've done... What we have done... Alyson didn't let her thoughts go any further.

She turned her back on the young man, grabbed the string of the shade and let it down. The room was thrown into a deeper darkness, and Alyson took a deep breath before she turned back around. Tommy stood up slowly. He smiled before he reached for Alyson to put his arm around her shoulders. Alyson was stiff in his arms, and she pulled back quickly. He was about to ask her what was wrong when she put a finger to her lips and motioned below them.

"My mom can't hear us together. You should go back downstairs."

"Will you get in trouble if you're found with me?"

Alyson shrugged and nodded at the same time.

"Right. I just have to use the toilet quick."

Alyson pointed Tommy to the bathroom at the end of the hall. She slipped into her bedroom once he was out of sight, closing the door behind her and leaning back against it. Her hands pressed over her heart before she dropped them to her stomach and began to cradle her tiny bump there. Tears formed quietly and fell without making a sound.

"Being in this family is hard, Bambi." The young mother slipped down to the floor and sat with her back against the door. "There are so many rules, and no one to tell you what they are. There are so many things."

Tommy heard Alyson talking softly as he walked past her bedroom, drying the last bit of water from his hands onto the lap of his jeans. He couldn't make out what she was saying, but he pressed his ear against the door and heard her sniffling. His mouth twitched down into a frown. The soft voice drifted out from the under the crack between the door and the floor; loud enough to tease his hearing, but not loud enough to share with him what her secrets were.

I can't even imagine if I was her right now... Tommy's thoughts went to his own family.

Every holiday he had off he spent with them. There was always laughter and plenty of unconditional love whenever they were together. Tommy treasured those times. He couldn't imagine leaving all of that behind not knowing if he was going to get it back.

She is so brave. Tommy pressed his hand against the door, wishing he could tell her what he was thinking. *She is so, so brave.*

Tommy left the hallway and walked quietly back downstairs. It was strange to be in the Abidi home and see Alyson around her parents. She was such a strong person, but when she was with her parents it was as if she didn't have a voice of her own. He could smell the food that Janice was cooking in the kitchen and wondered if he was allowed to go ask her if he could help. The sound of Alyson's footsteps on the stairs made him decide to risk it.

"Hello! Smells good in here!" He smiled when he saw the pleased expression pop into the mother's eyes. "Can I help?"

"Oh, no..."

"Please? I love cooking with my mum when I'm at home. Reminds me of being with my family."

Janice let him come into the kitchen and handed him a spoon to stir the pot of sauce on the stove. She kept on her side of the room, making a few comments now and then about what she was making and cooking tips. Tommy listened respectfully and shared some of the cooking lessons he had learned from his mother.

They were in the kitchen when Zaheer came home. He said nothing about Tommy standing by the stove, but instead asked where Alyson was. Tommy was careful to say nothing and let Janice do all the talking. Zaheer left in search of his daughter and took the heavy atmosphere with him.

"He's happy because I'm making his favorite meal," said Janice with a smile. "That's the best way to keep your husband happy."

"Sounds like solid advice. I know my favorite meal makes me happy."

"I was going to make Alyson's favorite meal, but I knew things would need to be smoothed over after today."

Tommy didn't know what to say as he stirred the bubbling concoction of vegetables and meat. He had wanted to be helpful to Alyson and spend more time getting to know her, not get her in trouble and ruin her weekend with her parents. He supposed he was getting to know her more, just not in the way he had imagined the night before when he offered to help her buy a dress. It made sense now why Alyson needed to get out of Iowa and away from her family.

"**Y**ou're awake." Zaheer's deep, strong voice vibrated in his throat as he walked into the sunroom where his daughter was sitting on the love seat.

His brown eyes and dark complexion were familiar and dear to the girl, although she looked very little like him. He settled into the armchair that sat across from her so he could see her face. His broad shoulders and muscular body hid the fact he was a few years past the age of fifty. Decades of working as a bricklayer when he was younger had made him strong. She smiled at him when their eyes met.

"How's my daughter?"

"Good. It's good to be home. It's nice to see you guys before..." Deep breath and forced smile. "Before I leave."

Zaheer noticed his daughter didn't have the same glow as she usually did. His wife had noticed as well. She seemed edgy and nervous, unable to fully relax. There were traces of tears on her face even when she pretended to to be happy. Perhaps the pressure of pushing herself too hard and too fast was finally catching up with her.

"Are you ready to move all the way to London?"

"I think so." Alyson's tone was thoughtful. She looked hard at her dad's face. He didn't have any hint of anger or disapproval in his expression. Even his frown lines were shallow as he gave her another smile. She let out her breath in relief. "I'm really thankful for the opportunity. I need something to shake me up a bit, give me new direction, introduce me to new people."

"That's my girl." Zaheer smiled. "How do you feel about leaving your job in Iowa?"

"It's my dream job, dad." The sun shone against her face and made it hard for her to make out the face of her father, but easier to share her heart. "I love those kids and the people I work with. I feel terrible because I..."

Alyson stopped herself. For years, their favorite thing to do had been to sit on the back porch and stare at the clouds. They would watch the birds eat at the bird-feeder she had made in kindergarten and throw stale bread to the squirrels. Some of the time they sat quietly, but every so often Alyson would share a dream or a passion she carried inside of her, and her dad would turn it into something she could reach. It didn't matter how big or impossible the thoughts seemed, he always found a way to make it sound attainable for his daughter. That's what he had been her whole life; the one who set the steps in place for her to reach the stars.

"Why?" asked Zaheer when she didn't finish her sentence.

"They need me there. I trained a new girl, but it's not going to be the same," said Alyson. "This new job could be even more of a dream come true, though. I just have to trust that everyone knows what they're doing and go for it."

"You're going to do great. I'm so proud of you." Zaheer's voice turned gruff. "I know how hard you've worked."

"Dad, don't cry." Her throat constricted and began to ache.

"You have brought so much honor to your family. I don't know how I ended up with such a wonderful daughter." His face sparkled with tears. Alyson couldn't remember the last time she had seen her father cry. Had she ever?

"Dad." The name came out as a hoarse whisper. Alyson stood up and went to kneel at her father's feet. She rested her chin on his knee and gazed up at him. How many other times in her life had she ached for this kind of moment with her dad? "I wish I did more to make you proud."

"Aly! I am so proud!" He reached down and cradled her face in his big, rough hands. "I talk about how wonderful you are to anyone who will listen; that's how proud I am of you."

There were no words left to say as Alyson tried her best to hold herself together. Her heart was breaking as her father declared his love and pride, and she sat at his feet with his illegitimate grandchild in her womb. She was hiding behind the guise of a promotion to sneak away from everyone who knew her, leaving them to think she had been given the world.

"I love you, dad. Always," she managed to choke out.

"My precious daughter. My pride and my joy."

Alyson bit her lip as she heard the words. She had seen his face red with rage a hundred times as he shouted down at her for acting in an unacceptable fashion. Days of silent treatment would follow each time where Alyson would be forced to act like a stranger in her own home.

But then there would be a report card or some sort of award. With trembling and trepidation, Alyson would tiptoe up to her father and lay her offering at his feet, hoping it would be enough to regain his favor. Each time, Zaheer Abidi would smile broadly at her as if nothing had happened and remind her of how proud he was to have her as his daughter. And so she would be safe again, until the next time she did something wrong. She never doubted his words of praise, but his words of affection were never something she could hold onto very tightly.

Alyson excused herself and left for the bathroom. She heard him sniffling as he made his way into his study and shut his door behind him. She stayed in the bathroom for a long time.

Chapter nine
"Just don't ever forget how much I love you."

It was strange that Mr. and Mrs. Abidi continued to keep their big, two-story house with full basement and attached garage when it was just the two of them. There was no need for the three bedrooms and full bathroom upstairs when they had the master bed and bath on the main floor. They didn't entertain guests enough to justify their large living room with hardwood floors and beautifully decorated fireplace. Forest green and a deep maroon were on the couches, pillows and in the artwork on the walls. The same color themes leaked into the dining room that stood next to it, separated only by a wide doorframe. Tall windows let light fill the big house throughout the day, each one flanked by thick curtains of various colors, ready to be drawn across the glass in a moment's notice.

Alyson could smell the evening meal as she walked through the narrow hallway towards the brightly-lit kitchen where she was greeted by pale-yellow walls and white cupboards. The kitchen had always been the cleanest and happiest part of the house with a vase of plastic sunflowers in the corner by the window that gave a clear view of the western horizon. The curtains in the kitchen were white lace and hardly ever closed. It was the only room in the house that wasn't filled with the darker shades of green and red. Even the sunroom didn't compare to Janice's kitchen. Alyson stood in the doorway, leaning against the frame with her shoulder.

Tommy saw her out of the corner of her eye and turned to give her a questioning look, asking with his eyes if she was okay. She had her hands pulled into the sleeves of her sweatshirt so he couldn't see anything except the tips of her fingers. She looked cozy, and he bit his tongue to keep from coming out and saying so. Alyson gave a little shrug and smiled her silent answer back to him.

"Will you set the table, honey?" Janice turned around a moment too late to witness the wordless interaction. "I'm going to get your dad and tell him that it is time to eat."

Once plates, silverware and cups were on the table, the family sat down together for their meal. Alyson sat across from Tommy, and her parents sat on either end of the table. It was then that Alyson realized that they were eating her father's favorite meal. Her stomach churned, and she shot a quick glance in her mother's direction. Janice pretended to not notice.

"So, Tommy," Zaheer began, wiping the corners of his mouth with a napkin.

Alyson froze with her fork halfway to her mouth.

"Yes, sir." Tommy's eyes were bright and respectful as he looked Zaheer full in the face.

"Janice told me you were one of the young men who chose Aly to travel over to Bedford."

"Yes, sir." Tommy nodded, careful not to look at Alyson as he focused on her father.

"What kind of process did you guys go through to choose schools to look at? How did you settle on Aly? She's an excellent teacher, for sure, but she's very young."

"Well, we looked into schools that were connected to charities we supported, or similar ones, you know? Things that we stood behind. And, uh, as we looked down the list, we looked into schools that had good reputations and had good students come out of them. Things got narrowed down, you know, and next thing you know we're in a classroom with this young lady and she's, uh, just blowing us away with her natural talent and ability."

The girl didn't know Tommy had been given a script to read in situations like that. A list of facts that sounded believable and would hopefully stave off any other prying questions that could blow the entire cover. She didn't fully realize her father was insinuating she had been chosen because of her gender and looks.

"She's an amazing young lady, I'm sure you've noticed." Zaheer didn't miss the red that crept up Tommy's neck and into his cheeks as he gave the young man a hard look.

"I have, sir. She's one of the best girls I've had the pleasure of meeting."

"We are very proud of her. She has more dreams and passions than most girls her age, and we don't want to see anyone come between her and achieving her goals."

"Absolutely." Tommy's face was still red as he reached for his water cup and took a gulp.

"Zaheer, she's twenty-two," said Janice softly from her end of the table. "She'll have to get married eventually."

"Not my daughter. She has no need for a husband."

"Your father thinks..."

"My father is not the father of my daughter," Zaheer hissed through clenched teeth. This was not the first time they had had this argument. "Now please, pass me the bread."

His wife understood the conversation was over.

The two young adults on either side of the table didn't dare look at each other for the next twenty minutes. It wasn't until Alyson quickly excused herself to use the bathroom that the conversation started again, and Janice cleared the table for dessert.

After supper was finished, Zaheer brought out the Uno cards and his playful grin lightened the mood of the room. Alyson wanted to retreat back to the safety of her bedroom, but Uno was their tradition and this was the last time she would have this opportunity. Laughter rang out from around the table as they reminisced about other evenings they had played together when Alyson was younger.

Alyson felt her throat tighten during a pause in the game as she considered the fact that her child would never get to share moments like that with her parents. She would never watch her son or daughter at the dining room table laughing with their grandfather, or squealing with excitement as they won for the fifth time in a row. The things that had created her happiest memories were things that Alyson could never give. They were about to play another game when Alyson noticed Tommy's eyelids drooping.

"We should call it a night." Alyson gave him a smile.

"I can hardly keep my eyes open." Tommy yawned and stretched in his seat.

"Aly, can you go get an extra set of pajamas out of the guest room." Janice nodded at the two of them.

"Where is Tommy going to stay?"

"The nice bedroom, of course," said Janice.

Alyson knew that they put Tommy in that room because it was the furthest from the stairs, and he would have to pass their room to get to anything in the house.

"Good night, Aly," Zaheer said gently to his daughter.

"Good night, baba." Alyson leaned forward and kissed her father on the cheek. She hadn't called him that since she was little. The chair scraped loudly across the floor as he stood up quickly and left the room. Janice wasn't looking as Alyson stood to her feet as well. "See you in the morning, mom."

Alyson didn't know that Tommy had followed her up the stairs until his weight caused the creaky part of the floor to moan under him. She cringed before looking over her shoulder and giving him a smile.

"You survived a day with my parents. Congratulations."

"Well, it was much different than I was expecting, not going to lie." Tommy leaned against the dresser as Alyson opened a drawer and pulled out clothes that smelled like her dad.

"They don't seem to hate you. That's a good thing."

"Did Jamie ever meet your parents?"

"No. No, never." Alyson paused, trying to picture it in her head. "My parents would know right away that we liked each other, and that would be the end of it."

"What would they do?"

"I don't know." Alyson straightened and handed Tommy the pajamas.

Alyson hadn't realized until she saw the clothes in Tommy's hands that Tommy and her father were similar sizes. When she was little, her father was the tallest and strongest person she knew. Even then, the thought of anyone being able to wear the same clothes and fill them with as much muscle and broadness of shoulder as he did was strange.

"Well, I'll see you in the morning." Alyson looked up into his eyes and saw a fond, soft expression there. She smiled the tiniest little bit and remembered how easy it was to be with him when it was just the two of them.

"Going to bed now?" he asked, noting how Alyson looked away quickly, red in her cheeks.

"Yeah. Gotta rest up for tomorrow. Big day."

"Hey. Don't worry about a thing."

Alyson looked up at him, her lips pressed into a frown. "I wish I could just stop from worrying. You don't know how much I wish that."

Tommy's forehead creased with empathy as he wrapped his arms around Alyson. He felt her lean into him, just like she had when they had kissed for the first time. Their breathing fell into a rhythm; her lungs exhaling as he inhaled, the line where their bodies met shifting as their diaphragms worked together. The hug was a risk, but Alyson could hear her mother on the phone with her sister as the water ran in the kitchen sink.

"You smell like my dad." Alyson gave a little laugh as she smelled her father's familiar scent on the shirt Tommy was holding.

"Is that a good thing or a bad thing?"

"I dunno." Alyson let her arms fall as she stepped back from Tommy, her smile fading. She looked up at him and watched him cross his arms over his chest. "It depends on if the curtains are closed or not."

"What does that mean?"

"Maybe I'll tell you later..." Alyson gave a little wave, dismissing the question. "Good night, Tommy."

Aly got ready for bed slowly. She thought about all the love and affirmation her parents had poured out onto her since she had returned home. It made the visit easier and harder at the same time. She wanted to please them, but she didn't want them to be proud of a lie. She pulled the jar of cocoa butter out of her suitcase and rubbed it on her stomach. The words to the song "Sweet Dreams" came to mind, and she sang softly to her baby.

"Sleep well, sleep tight, you will be in my arms in a little while..."

The words did fit perfectly.

With her nightly routine finished, Alyson put her things away and reached to turn out the light. The edge of a photograph under her mattress caught the corner of her eye and she stopped. Her nerves began to tingle as she leaned closer to get a better look. She remembered that face. She remembered that picture; it was the last one. She had barely rescued it in time from the burn pile her father had made one night over a decade ago.

"Oh, Amir." Alyson sat down heavily on her bed, the photograph in her trembling hands. It had been so long since she had seen his face.

For the past fourteen years Alyson had been an only child, but for the first eight years of her life she had grown up with the most devoted and loving older brother. He had been eight years old when she was born, making him the perfect age to take care of the baby when she arrived. When their mom went back to work six weeks after giving birth to Alyson, Amir had been the one to take care of her at the neighbor's house. Their bond was deep.

"He would be thirty this year." Alyson put a gentle finger on the figure in the picture and felt a twinge in her heart. "I still miss him."

It was because of Amir that Alyson knew the severity of her father's temper, and her grandfather's dedication to purging the family of shame. It was because of Amir that Alyson had learned to stay quiet and good. They had started off as such a happy little family when Alyson was a baby, but she grew up and so did her brother, and Amir's friends began to change. Amir began to change.

The summer before Amir had been taken away, Alyson learned to drown out the sound of her father and brother fighting by listening to the radio. Every day something new was broken in the heat of a rage. It became harder for Alyson to see the boy who had once spent every waking hour doting on her in the face of the young man living in her house. Sometimes he would smile at her when he caught her staring, but the guilt on his face broke her heart, so she tried to stop staring. They had moved to a new house in a new town in a desperate attempt to save their son from the dark future he was hotly pursuing. It didn't matter; the secrets and rebellion didn't stop, and Mr. and Mrs. Abidi didn't know what to do.

One night in the middle of the summer when Alyson was eight, Amir snuck into the house well after the time he was supposed to be home. He took his normal route; climbing in through the unlocked window in Alyson's room. The tree beside their house grew near it, and he could shimmy from the branches to a little ledge he stood on while he pushed up the sash. He knew Alyson checked her window every night before she went to bed to make sure it wasn't locked in case he needed to come in that way. She was too good to him, and he hated the fact that his life was about to ruin hers.

"Miri?" The soft voice of a child reached him through the dark as he tiptoed towards the door.

"Did I wake you up?" He crept back over towards her bed and knelt down beside it. His fingers found the pink ballerina lamp on her bedside table and turned it on. Her eyes squeezed shut against the sudden burst of light. "Sorry. I'll turn it back off."

"What time is it?" Alyson yawned as she spoke.

"Doesn't matter." He waved off the concern. He was about to stand up and leave the room, but Alyson blinked her eyes back open and stared up at him. He had forgotten how green her eyes were, and how many freckles she had on her face. When was the last time he talked to her about life? They used to be best friends.

"You're probably going to be tired in the morning."

"Yeah, maybe." Amir nodded. "Aliya, I'm sorry I don't always know how to be a good big brother."

"It's okay." Aliya had been Amir's special name for Alyson since birth. The "ya" on the end acted as a possessive term. "Are you sad?"

"Yes. I am." Amir's expression was stoic. His deep-brown eyes stared at her with clarity; no sheen of tears to blur his vision. "But I want you to be happy. Okay? I-I haven't been here for you a lot since we moved, I know that, but I'll always be there if you need me. K? I mean... i-it's just going to be different."

"Miri, what is going to happen if mom and dad send you to grandpa like they say sometimes when you're fighting?" The children had two views of their father's father; one was that he was extremely generous and loved to be happy. Two, was he had absolutely no tolerance for foolishness and indecency. "What if you get punished?"

"Then I'll just have to live through the punishment." Amir put on a brave face for the child. Alyson looked at him like he was the most important person in the world, and it ripped his heart out. The fact that she had to listen to the screaming and swearing when she did nothing wrong suddenly weighed on his conscience for the first time.

Amir knew he was pushing too hard against a weak line, and everything was about to fall to pieces. The threats his parents made about sending him to his grandparents in Pakistan were not idle, and the punishments for what he had been doing would be severe. What was Alyson going to think when she woke up one day and found out he wasn't there? He wasn't sure how long he would have to suffer through living in his grandfather's house, but he knew it would be a good chunk of time. He would miss birthdays, Christmas, tough days at school, dance recitals, soccer games, and bad dreams in the night when she just needed someone strong to protect her from the imaginary demons that haunted her. He would miss everything, and Alyson would never forget it.

"Do you know how much I love you?" His whisper almost got lost in the dark.

"A lot?" Alyson knew her brother adored her, but his behavior was putting a strain on the once-thriving relationship. "Sometimes I feel like you forget about me."

"Oh, Aliya." Amir leaned forward and kissed his sister's forehead, suddenly aware of the smell of cigarettes, perfume, and drugs on his clothes. He hadn't gotten high that night, but his friends had. "I know. I'm so sorry. But I do love you very, very much. I'm going to get better and come back, okay? Just don't ever forget how much I love you."

"I love you, too, Miri." A smile lit up the little girl's face in the dark bedroom. "Will you hold my hand until I fall asleep again?"

"Of course."

Alyson didn't know how much he wept after her eyes fluttered to a close. She breathed deeply as she slept, knowing nothing of the explosive situation her brother had created and the toll it had taken on their parents. Self-control had never been Amir's strength, and the lack of patience and gentleness he had shown in every area of his life was now coming around and causing consequences Amir had sworn would never reach him. Her tiny hand in his rough palm brought him hope and peace for a few moments in the last hour of the night. They didn't know it then, but that would be the last time he would ever feel those hands or see those dark lashes resting so daintily on her sun-kissed cheeks. When they both woke up the next day, the decision had been made. A plane was waiting to take the wayward teenager away during the middle of the younger sibling's dance lessons, and he wasn't allowed to tell her goodbye.

"We're not going to talk about Amir anymore." The stern command came from Zaheer Abidi. The angry and hurting father told his wife and daughter to keep their tears in check and the name of the exiled son from their lips. "He will come home if he decides to honor his family."

Alyson prayed daily her brother would be returned to her, but he never came back. She wasn't allowed to ask about him or inquire after when he would be done with his punishment. Her mother would cry quietly in the corner of the backyard from time to time when she thought no one was looking. Alyson would stand at the window and watch her mother's shoulders shake as she wept, too far away from the house to be heard.

It wasn't until Alyson herself was sixteen that she found out her brother would never be coming back. He wasn't dead, but to them he would be. They assured her that no one had heard from him for years and Alyson wouldn't be able to find him even if she tried, but she was not to try ever. Once again, the old memories and emotions were brought back to the surface, only to be shushed and deemed shameful by her parents. While she continued to repress them at home, she found ways to work through what she was feeling in the safety of the classroom of a kind and wise teacher, and after the lights had been turned out at Danielle's house.

Thoughts about Amir were few and far between, but the little girl inside of Alyson still ached for her big brother to come back. She didn't notice his empty spot, or the absence of his presence at family events, yet in the back of her mind she always knew he was missing.

"Oh, Bambi." With a hand on her child, Alyson continued to stare at the face that had been so dear to her at one time. "If they sent away Amir for what he did, then how much more would they punish me for what I have done? He was the heir of my father, yet they disowned him. I'm only a daughter..."

She lay down on her bed, the picture placed where she could stare at the face of her brother. He looked so much like their father with his dark eyes and the jet-black hair shaved close to his head. He had taken up carpentry in the last couple years before he left home and worked muscles and callouses into his young body. It was his escape, he told Alyson. Alyson wondered what the last fourteen years had done to change his looks. He hadn't reached their father in height before he left them, and his shoulders had still been narrow and boyish. A strange image came to Alyson as she tried to picture what he would look like if he had a beard. She wondered if she would instantly know it was him if she ever saw him again, or if he would even want to see her if she found him.

Alyson was alone at the house for a few minutes on Sunday evening after her goodbye party ended. Her parents and Tommy were on their way, but she had arrived first. She stood in the living room with her hands on her stomach, letting her baby experience her childhood home through the womb. She didn't say a word; she just stood, her heart pounding. She looked at the picture of the dark green, forest-covered mountains of Vermont her dad bought at a garage sale years ago. It was her favorite picture in the house, and she always felt like it was calling her to keep dreaming and pursuing bigger adventures. The trees murmured their invitation again as she stood with tears running down her face.

"Well, here I go." Alyson heard her parents pull into the driveway as she whispered to the trees. "Biggest adventure of my life."

She ran up the stairs to pack up her bag, making sure to slip the picture of her brother in-between her clothes. She looked around her room one last time and felt the lump grow in her throat. Her hand pressed against her baby gently as she said goodbye to her childhood, and possibly her home, forever. She shut the door behind her as she left. The clicking sound of the latch echoed in her ears. Her hands found the railing at the top of the staircase, and she gripped it tightly, though she had never needed to before. Her legs felt weak, and the stairs seemed endless as she walked down them one last time.

Zaheer and Janice stood at the front door, watching Alyson as she walked slowly towards them. Janice remembered the way Alyson's smile used to light up her face when she was little. She wished she could see that smile one more time. She knew she wasn't supposed to cry, but she had already lost one child. Her home would seem so empty.

"Well," Alyson choked out as her eyes filled with tears. She couldn't help it. "I guess I'm ready."

"You're dropping Tommy off at the airport on your way back?" Zaheer looked down at the young man who had spent two days in his home.

"Yes, dad." Alyson didn't tell them that it was the airport in Des Moines.

"We're so proud of you, honey." Janice blinked tears from her own eyes.

Alyson nodded, her lips trembling as she tried to smile. They were never going to know what this trip was really about.

"Love you, Aly." Zaheer hugged his daughter tightly, feeling her body tense up in his arms. "Take care of yourself. We'll see you when you come back."

The dog whined behind them, asking to be let back inside so he could escape from the cold wind. The family laughed, and Alyson knelt down for a moment to scratch him behind his ears. He looked up at her with his mournful eyes and wagged his tail. She gave him one last pat on the head and straightened. Zaheer and Janice watched her, eyes shining with tears and pride. She had never seen them so delighted over her achievements.

"Love you guys so much it hurts." Alyson memorized what her parents looked like standing on the front porch, their arms around each other. The family resemblance she shared with them was suddenly the most important thing to her. She would always have her mother's freckles and her father's nose no matter where she lived. She would still have the dark eyelashes and the big bright smile everybody said she inherited from them. It was one of the few things no one could take away from her. "Thank you for this weekend. I'll never forget it."

It was almost unbearable to turn her back on them and continue the rest of the way to the car. She swallowed hard as she walked away. Tommy's eyes filled with sympathy as he took her bag and opened the car door for her. She turned and waved at her parents, her hand trembling.

"Bye, honey!" Janice had already masked her tears and was forcing a smile. "We love you!"

Nothing could get past the lump in Alyson's throat. She shut the door and buckled her seatbelt. Her parents remained on the porch, waiting until Alyson and Tommy were gone to go back inside. Alyson stared steadily at the sight of her family and her home as Tommy backed out of the driveway and started them on their journey to Iowa. When they had finally been lost from sight, Alyson hid her face in her hands and wept. She never would forget the last weekend she spent with her parents as their pride and joy.

Empty corn fields blurred together as she stared out of the window. She had grown up seeing the wide, flat expanse of the Midwest as her home. Soon there would be very different sights outside of her windows. Tommy's hand rested on her leg as he drove.

"Alyson," said Tommy after half an hour of driving without talking. "This is a huge sacrifice that you're making for the baby. I know Bambi doesn't know what is going on, but one day I will make sure he or she knows exactly how much you sacrificed to keep him safe."

"Thank you." Alyson looked over at Tommy as he drove.

"You're welcome." Tommy nodded, taking his eyes off the road for a moment to see Alyson's face. "This baby could be, you know, mine, and I'm never going to forget how much you're giving up for my baby."

Of course Alyson had thought about Bambi belonging to each of the different boys, but it was different hearing the words come out of one of their mouths. This baby could be Tommy's. He could be the father of the child in her womb and spend the next two decades sharing everything that had to do with Bambi with her. Alyson put one hand on Tommy's and the other on her baby. This... this could be her family one day.

The farther they got away from Alyson's childhood home, the more relaxed Alyson became. Tommy worked hard to bring the smile back to her face, wanting nothing more than for Alyson to laugh. Jokes and stories brought out giggles and eye crinkles, but the deep laughter didn't come until they were stopped for supper and he pulled out his best stories from his high school days.

The pair was in the middle of a game of 'Would You Rather' when they entered Des Moines. Aly let out a sigh of relief as she realized the weekend was over. She had survived. Jamie was waiting for them in the parking lot of Alyson's apartment building. The sight of him made Alyson's heart pound a little harder, and she felt her cheeks flush scarlet as she took his hand to get out of the car.

"Ah, love." Jamie wrapped her in a hug and buried his face in her neck. Alyson quickly responded by wrapping her arms around him tightly. All the stress she had accumulated that weekend slipped away as she inhaled the cool, evening breeze and softened into Jamie's touch. Her hair blew into his face, hiding the smile he wore as he felt how desperately Alyson held onto him. He didn't pull away until Tommy got out of the car and walked around to stand next to them. "How was the visit?"

"It went so much better than I thought it would." Alyson used both of her hands to push her hair back behind her ears, giving the boys a full view of the grin on her face. "Thanks to Tommy."

The news of his friend flying out to Nebraska for the weekend had angered Jamie, but Garret had talked him through it, reminding him that Alyson was the one who got to say what she wanted them to do. She had said yes to Tommy being with her, so Jamie had to be okay with it. In the end, he knew it was best for it to be Tommy and not himself. Tommy was good at keeping situations from becoming too heavy. Alyson needed that.

"I'm glad you were there to help." The words were delivered with a small nod.

"It was my pleasure." Tommy knew Jamie was jealous. "It was great to get to know Alyson a little bit more, talk about the baby, and meet her parents."

"How are you feeling about leaving November fifth?" Jamie asked her, forcing himself to ignore what Tommy was saying. "Will you be okay to wait three more weeks?"

"I should be able to. I know my boss really wants me to be at school for our harvest party the last Friday in October." Alyson knew Bambi wouldn't be the size of a lemon forever, but he or she seemed content to remain so for the time being. "I think we can make it to the second trimester before we run into any belly problems. Bambi likes to be little, I think."

"Speaking of Bambi... hello, baby." Jamie smiled and put his hands on Alyson's stomach, his face shadowed in the dying light of the evening. "Were you good for your mummy this weekend?"

"She was throwing up the whole time, almost." Tommy noted how comfortable Jamie seemed with Alyson and wondered if there were still feelings between the two of them. He looked away and sucked in his cheeks.

"Ah, bless. Bambi, be nice to your mum." Jamie gave Aly's stomach one last rub before blowing the baby a kiss. "Sorry the weekend was rough."

"It went better than it could have." Alyson smiled.

"Is there anything you need me to do before I fly back to L.A. for the week?" Jamie put his hands on her shoulders. "Groceries? Clothes? Money? Cars? Houses? Diamonds?"

Jamie's list made Alyson laugh and shake her head. "No, I'm fine. I got what I needed while I was at home. Thank you for coming to say hi."

"I couldn't stand the thought of not getting a chance to see you again." Jamie pulled Alyson in for a goodbye hug.

Alyson let Jamie's hug linger, resting her head on his shoulder.

Tommy hung back, waiting for his turn to say goodbye. Seeing her with Jamie was strange, reminding him of the fact that Jamie had been there first. Still, the way she smiled at him made him think she felt something special between them. Jamie let Alyson go and gave her one last look before he turned away to get back into his car. Tommy stepped forward, not ready for his time with Alyson to come to an end.

"Tommy, I will never be able to thank you enough." Alyson could see Jamie out of the corner of her eye watching them closely. That didn't keep her from hugging Tommy and letting him rest his chin on the top of her head for a moment. "Thank you for everything."

"Thank *you* for everything," whispered Tommy.

"I'll see you both soon enough." Alyson had her duffle bag by her feet and her purse draped over her shoulder as she waved to them. They had wanted to help her carry her stuff inside, but she said her roommate would ask too many questions. She wanted a quiet homecoming. "Have a safe trip back to L.A."

The two young men climbed into Jamie's rental car and drove off into the night, leaving Alyson to walk through the quiet evening to the apartment that she would call home for only a few more weeks. She had spent two years in that building, making memories and creating an identity for herself. Fresh starts had been an exciting thought to the hardworking young woman, but with the impending move into anonymity, Alyson felt herself needing to breathe deeply. Everything was about to change.

The first of the three weeks Alyson had to get through before the move went by smoothly. She packed boxes and put them in storage, gave things away and posted items on craigslist. Danielle joined in the process of sorting and packing via Skype, helping her sentimental best friend with the tough decisions.

"What about summer stuff? I don't even know where I will be when it is summer time," Alyson groaned, pulling out a stack of clothes she had put away for the winter. "But it seems dumb to take it all with me. I can just buy new clothes in London, I guess."

"So, pick your five favorite summer things and take those," Danielle said. "Like that t-shirt you wore the whole time you were here last summer. You love that shirt."

Alyson agonized over each item, but ultimately ended up doing as her friend suggested. As she folded clothes and stuck them into her suitcase, she noticed that Danielle was blowing up a balloon.

"What are you doing? Are you hosting a party?"

"No, I'm making Bambi."

"Wait, what?" Alyson started to laugh.

"See, it says that a baby is about the size of a pea pod, or a lemon, I saw both of those things mentioned on the pregnancy websites, so I'm blowing up this green balloon until it's about the size of a pea pod to help me watch Bambi grow."

"That's an awfully big pea pod."

"I... well, Bambi's on the bigger side."

"Actually, he's quite small. Or she. He or she."

"Well, here's the thing about balloons." Danielle pointed her finger at her friend over the computer screen. "The thing about balloons is that I can just let a little of the air out. Watch."

Danielle released a little bit of the air from the balloon before she tied it. Once it was tied securely and a tiny face was drawn on with a sharpie, Danielle stood up on her bed to tape it to the wall.

"There, now I can remember to pray for baby pea pod every time I look up."

"You're such a good aunt." Alyson smiled.

A care package from Jamie came under the name Mr. Smith and contained a box of tea and a note that said, "Some tea for a tea-loving girl from a tea-loving boy." Each morning Alyson would make a cup of tea and spend a half hour alone, singing and talking softly to Bambi.

The second week, however, had a rough start. On Sunday Alyson pulled on her favorite pair of jeans and realized she could no longer button them. She texted a picture of her unbuttoned pants and her frowning face to the guys saying, "Officially grown out of my pants." Eddie was the first to respond with a, "Trousers*", and Jamie gave her a call, asking if she was still going to be able to wait two more weeks.

"I think so," she replied hesitantly.

Eddie and Garret had furniture delivered to Garret's apartment to move to Alyson's new place, and she felt the reality of the move hit harder than it had been. She spent twenty minutes before bed doing deep breathing.

On Monday morning one of her students hugged her, then looked up into her face and said, "You feel like my mom does when she has a baby in her belly." Panic struck hard and fast. Her heart was calmed when Danielle talked her through it over her lunch break.

The teacher's heart was worn and aching when she reached home after work. She wanted to sleep well that night, her body tired from the hours of packing and planning, but she had to get up and use the bathroom every few hours. The next morning came too quickly for Alyson's liking. She sat with a cup of tea, stroking her belly and reading over the lesson plans made the day before.

Her day went as Tuesdays normally went; a few laughs in the classroom and fights on the playground, but otherwise it was nothing special. The children finally left, and Alyson went into the teacher's resource room to get started on her last batch of lessons she had to plan. She had just sat down when her cellphone rang.

"Hello?" The call was from an unknown number.

"Aly? Is that you?"

"Who is this?" Alyson froze in her spot. It sounded just like Sumaya, but why would her cousin be calling her out of the blue like this?

"It's Sumaya! How are you? You okay?" The voice sounded distant and worried as it stretched a thousand miles around the world.

"Hi! I-I'm fine..."

"Aly, your mom called me."

Alyson quickly stood up and left the room. She felt her blood begin to pound through her body as her heart rate increased. Her hand found the handle for the door of the back entrance, and she slipped out into the empty parking lot. The scent and feel of fresh fall air hit her full in the face.

"She told me to call you. Said something was wrong," Sumaya continued.

"Sh-she said that?" Alyson tried to lick her lips, but her mouth was dry. She walked further away from the school building, a few orange leaves crunching under her feet as she paced. A chill wind blew around her, and she shivered. Her jacket was still inside.

"She said she's afraid you've been lying to her, and she wants me to find out."

Alyson leaned against the side of the school building to keep herself from falling over. She looked down at her hand; her fingers were shaking and the ground was spinning.

"Aly, what's going on? Your mother is asking questions. If the family gets involved..."

"Shoot..." Alyson's stomach churned.

"Have you done something?"

"No one can know, Sumy. What do I do? What should I do? I don't know what to do!"

"What have you done?" Sumaya's voice was low.

"I c-can't... I can't tell... I don't... It's too shameful."

Alyson's hair swept around her face in a gust of wind and stuck to the tears on her cheeks. She could hear Sumaya breathing on the other end of the line, but she said nothing. Her knees felt weak at the thought of opening her mouth and telling Sumaya what situation she was in. She knew she could trust her cousin, but her baby could be killed. She didn't want to say a word.

"Aly, your mother is suspicious. You're not doing a good job keeping your secrets."

"I tried." Alyson shook her head and bit her lip. "I tried so hard."

"The next step is the uncles. You know what they would do to you if they find out you've been hiding something bad that you've done."

"Sumaya, you can't let them get involved. Please, you have to help me."

"I can't unless you tell me what you did."

Alyson sighed and looked up at the bright blue sky.

"Aly..."

"Are you alone? Is this conversation safe?"

"Of course. I wouldn't ask you to tell me if it wasn't safe." Sumaya's voice was gentle. "You can tell me. I'll do what I can to help."

Alyson remembered the last time the uncles got involved with their family. It had ended with Amir being sent to Pakistan, and then out of their lives forever. She swallowed hard. How long had her mother been pondering this phone call to Sumaya? What would the next move be? What in the world was she going to do if her family found out about Bambi?

"Sumy, I'm... I'm pregnant."

There was no immediate response and Alyson wondered if her cousin had heard her. She didn't want to say it again, but Sumaya was silent. Finally, she heard a shaky voice.

"How far along are you?"

"Fourteen weeks."

"Oh, Alyson," Sumaya groaned under her breath. "Is that why you're leaving?"

"Yes. My parents can't find out. The uncles..."

"Yes, they must never know about the baby. When do you leave for England?"

"Almost two weeks." The time seemed like an eternity. "What should I do?"

"Be very careful, Aly. Don't tell a single person about the baby. When you get to England, trust no one. Keep hidden."

"Jamie is making sure everyone involved signs a confidentiality agreement. No one is allowed to talk about it."

"Good. I'll do what I can to keep everyone from finding out."

"Thank you, Sumaya." Alyson knew how much trouble Sumaya could be in if they ever found out she was helping her keep this secret. "Thank you."

"Never thought you would be the one, Aly."

"Me either." Alyson's eyes watered again.

"Stay safe, Aly. Bye."

Alyson walked slowly back into the school. She was glad that most everyone had already left for the day or was busy in their classrooms. They didn't notice the faint traces of tears on her face, or the wobble in her smile as she gathered her stuff together. She had planned on working at the school, but she was too shaken up to stay anymore.

All of her things were packed up into her backpack and she was about to leave when her phone vibrated with another incoming call. This time she knew the unknown number was her cousin. Alyson sat down and stared at the phone in her hand. Something had to have happened. With a deep breath, she put the phone up to her ear.

"Alyson, you have to leave now. Don't wait for the job, or the people from the charity, you have to leave."

"Why?"

"The uncles found out."

"What? Wh-what did they f-find out?"

"That Aunt Janice thinks you're hiding something. They want to get to the bottom of this. If they find you, they'll find the baby. That's the first thing they'll look for. If you want to keep your baby you have no choice, Alyson. You must leave."

"Are you sure? Are you sure they know?" Alyson found a tiny thread of hope and clung to it.

"My father is ready to fly to America. Grandfather is furious."

"No..." Alyson could hardly breathe. "Wh-what do I do? I-I can't just leave! People will want to know what is going on! That will only confirm I'm hiding something!"

"Tell them your plans changed! Tell them you have an emergency! Go somewhere that no one knows about! I don't care, think of something, but leave today."

Alyson put a hand over her mouth as she started to cry.

"Aly, I don't want to lose you."

"I don't want to lose my baby."

"Then leave," Sumaya whispered. "Run, and keep your baby safe."

Tears ran down Alyson's face as she drove. Her hands gripped the steering wheel so tightly her hands ached almost as much as her heart. The sun was setting in front of her, and miles had gone by between her past and her future. There would be no going back now, there was only straight ahead. She felt like there was something missing in her chest as she sped down the interstate, but she knew she couldn't look back. They had never planned for something like this.

Alyson flicked on her headlights and stared at the blurry road in front of her. There were very few people driving near her that Tuesday evening, but enough to warn Alyson that she shouldn't be driving and crying. She couldn't stop, though. Fear drove her on towards the only place of safety she could think of. It was a long drive, but there was no distance too far for her if she needed to keep her baby safe.

The phone rang on her lap, and Alyson jumped.

"Geez."

She was shaking so badly she pulled off to the side of the road, her hazards blinking. The caller ID showed a picture of her best friend, and relief flooded her body. She was terrified that Sumaya would call her at any second and tell her that her secret was out. Before she could even say hello, she heard Danielle's panicky voice coming through the phone.

"Aly, where are you? Did you leave?"

"Yeah, I-I left." Alyson's breath was ragged from crying and shaking.

"Do you know what you're doing? Where are you going?"

"I don't know." The lie came out as a whisper. She couldn't tell Danielle where she was; it was the only way to make sure Danielle stayed safe.

"Did you tell your boss you were leaving?"

"Yeah." Alyson took a deep breath and stared out of her windshield at the cold, dead wilderness around her. A truck zoomed past, and her car shuddered from the rush of air. "I told them it was a family emergency."

"Did you tell your parents?"

"No." The word came out quickly. "I don't know what to tell them! I have to just... I have to keep Bambi safe. I can't keep him safe here anymore. People will notice, and all it will take is one person! Danielle, no one can know about Bambi!"

"Sh, calm down!" Danielle tried to keep herself calm for Alyson. "You're going to be safe, I promise!"

"But what if they find me!" The young woman leaned her head against the steering wheel of her car and shouted in frustration. "You can't promise me that, Elle!"

Danielle sighed. She didn't know what to say.

"I'm sorry, Elle. I shouldn't shout. I'm just so scared."

"Do you want me to pray for you?" Danielle offered.

Alyson thought about it. She almost said yes, desperate for anything that might help, but she was stopped by the beeping of an incoming call.

"Someone else is trying to call."

"Ok. I'll call you later. I love you."

"Love you."

With a deep breath and all the courage she could muster, Alyson answered her new incoming call.

"Hi! You okay, love?" Jamie's voice came through the phone. "Danielle just called me. Said you had a bit of a scare, and she was worried about you."

Alyson bit her knuckle to keep herself from crying like a baby at the sound of Jamie's strong voice. It was the sound she hadn't known she was craving. She ached for his protective hand to hold onto, and for him to tell her she was going to be okay. It was several seconds before Alyson could calm herself enough to answer him.

"Danielle called you? She... When did she call you?" Alyson knew Jamie could hear the way her voice shook unsteadily.

"Where are you?" An edge of concern crept into Jamie's words.

"I don't know." Hot tears burned as they fell quickly down her cheeks. "I stopped driving because I couldn't see."

There was a pause. Alyson squeezed her eyes shut as she waited for him to respond.

"Sorry? You left? Aly, did you leave Des Moines?"

"I h-had to."

"What the heck happened? Where are you?"

"You know how my dad's family is Pakistani?"

"Yeah, course I do."

"They c-can't find out about Bambi." She couldn't make herself say anything about her cousin. "So I left today."

"What about your job, and your boss, and your parents?!" Jamie was clearly upset. "We had a plan, Aly! You said it was all okay! What are you trying to do?"

"D-don't be angry. P-please, Jamie." Alyson cried harder.

Jamie exhaled loudly. "Where are you now?"

"I'm outside Lincoln." Alyson saw fuzzy headlights race past her.

"Where in the world is that? Are you driving up to Danielle, or..."

"I'm driving west, Jamie! I didn't know where else to go so I started... I started driving towards you." Tears made her voice hoarse as she spoke. "I'm in the middle of nowhere Nebraska, but I will keep driving until I get to where you are because I, I need you. I need you to keep my baby safe."

There was no reply. Alyson cleared her throat, dried her tears, and turned off her hazards.

"I know I ruined every-..." whispered Alyson.

"I'm coming. I'll meet you halfway." Jamie's voice was thick. "I'm on my way. I'm coming to get you. I'll call you when I land. I'll find you somehow. I promise, I will find you, and I will keep you safe."

Alyson blinked until she could see again as she pulled back out onto the highway. She dropped her phone into her lap and kept her foot pressed on the gas pedal. There were fewer cars the further she drove, and the distance between them was longer. Alyson's eyes burned, but the adrenaline rushing through her kept them open. She drove for almost four more hours and was an hour away from the Colorado boarder when her phone rang again.

"Where are you, Aly?" The sound of engines roaring and vehicles beeping filled the background noise of Jamie's phone call. "I'm just landed. I'm getting into a car to meet you."

"I'll share my location with you." Alyson's gas light turned on. "I'm stopping to get gas."

"I'm coming. Stay there." A car door slammed and an engine turned over. "Stay right where you are."

Alyson pulled into a gas station and filled the tank with a few dollars of gas. With the last of the money in her wallet she bought a sandwich and a bag of trail mix. She walked slowly back out to her car, passing strangers and avoiding their gaze. No one gave her a second look or a second thought, proving to her that she could hide away in the country of America.

She moved her car to one of the parking spaces in front of the building to free up the pump she had used. Alyson wrote a message to Danielle saying she was safe and Jamie was on his way. She was too tired to cry as she sat in the front seat of her car eating her food. Her body moved automatically. Twenty minutes passed before Alyson realized her food was gone, and she was still holding her empty bag of trail mix.

Looking for a reason to stretch her legs, Alyson got back out of her car and walked into the gas station. She meandered up and down the short aisles, hands in her hoodie pocket and feet scuffling along the linoleum floor. Her phone buzzed in her hand with a text saying that Jamie would be there in a couple minutes. She didn't bother to text him back, but stuffed her phone into her pocket and rubbed her hands carefully over her stomach.

The tiny gas station had a steady flow of customers come in and out, despite their location on the edge of town. Each one ignored the girl pacing the store as they made their purchases and left. Alyson turned down the next aisle, and a man standing at the end looked up at her to smile politely. She knew he was a worker by the company shirt he was wearing as he restocked a shelf of Twizzlers and chocolate bars.

Not wanting to be noticed, Alyson quickly turned to go to the next aisle. She was stopped by someone calling out her name.

"Hey, are you Alyson Abidi?" he asked haltingly.

Alyson's face blanched and she froze with one foot about to leave the ground. She turned on her heel and rushed towards the exit without looking over her shoulder at the man who had spoken to her. She bumped into a rack holding post cards and nearly made it fall over. Her quick reflexes kept it upright, but not without several of the cards falling onto the tile floor. The teacher inside of her told her to stop and pick up what had fallen, but the sound of the young man calling her name again forced her to leave it.

"Alyson Abidi! Wait!" The man sounded sure that he had identified her correctly as he hurried after her.

"No!" It was the only word the girl could think of. The loose gravel under her feet crunched loudly as she ran as fast as she could towards her car. She pressed the unlock button on her keychain as her hand reached the handle. She jerked open the driver's door, nearly losing her balance from the force she put into the motion. She slid into the seat and was about to slam the door shut behind her when a body appeared out of nowhere, blocking the way. "No! No!"

"Aly! It's okay!" Jamie shouted as he reached in through the flailing arms and legs. "Love, it's me!"

"He's going to kill my baby!" Screaming as tears ran down her face, she pointed at the man who had followed her outside.

"Calm down, love. You need to just calm down." Jamie was genuinely frightened to see Alyson so worked up. His hands held her arms still by her sides, feeling them press against the force he was using on her. "Calm. Down."

"Don't... don't let him!" Alyson whimpered like a child.

Jamie let go of Alyson's arms and stood up to face the bewildered man who stood a few feet away. He was far enough from the vehicle that Alyson didn't hear what he said as he handed something to Jamie and hurried back inside. Alyson watched, her breath catching as she inhaled slowly. Jamie turned and walked back over to the car. He crouched down beside her seat and looked up until he could see into her red-rimmed eyes.

"He found your license, love," Jamie explained gently. "Apparently it dropped on the ground by the pumps, and he found it. He was chasing you to return it to you. He doesn't know who you are, or anything about the baby."

"Are you s-sure?" Alyson looked like a small child who was asking her dad if there were no monsters in the closet. The tears had stopped, but the shaking hadn't.

"I'm positive." Jamie handed the license back to its rightful owner and waited quietly. The whole plane ride to rescue Alyson had been filled with Jamie trying to figure out what exactly had happened that made today so different from the day before. Her family had always been a threat, and the safety of the baby had always been top priority; what had changed to make Alyson become suddenly so afraid? "Do you mind telling me what happened today?"

Alyson sniffed and hiccuped softly, shifting in her seat before she opened her mouth to talk. She stared straight ahead through her windshield, seeing the bright lights of the gas station through the windows. Jamie's strong and steady hand slipped over her shaking fingers and held them still. With quivering lips, Alyson looked at her friend.

"My cousin called me from Islamabad today. She's m-my age. We're really close," Alyson explained. "Her name is Sumaya."

Jamie didn't say anything as he kept his eyes on Alyson's face, watching every change of expression.

"She told me that my mom called her."

Deep breath in.

Deep breath out.

"She said my mom thinks that I'm hiding something from her, and she wanted Sumaya to find out what it was. I-I told Sumaya I'm pregnant and,

and, and she said, she said it was okay t-to stay until it was time to leave. But then my uncles... they found out my mom thinks I'm lying and they all, they all wanted to come find out. So Sumaya told me to leave."

Jamie kept his hand tight on the girl's as he felt his stomach twist.

"She said I have to be careful. I have to hide. I can't tell anyone about the baby."

"Does anyone else know about Bambi?"

"No." Alyson shook her head. "I haven't told anyone. Just Danielle, and you four."

"Okay, so, you and the baby are safe." Jamie tried to reassure the girl. "We'll take care of this. It's all going to be okay."

"Jamie, I have to find a way to get my family to not worry about me."

"I know. I'll figure something out."

"I need to hide."

"All right." Jamie stood back up to his feet and helped Alyson out of her car. He opened the trunk to get the few things she managed to finish packing before she left and put them in his car. "I'll have a tow truck take your car to your parent's house. Leave a note inside."

"Is this part of the plan?" she asked him as he handed her paper and a pen.

"Yes. Don't worry, I'm going to make sure you stay safe."

The note was short and simple, saying she had finished her lesson planning and decided to do a little traveling before she moved and started work in Bedford. No mention was made of Sumaya. No one would know they had spoken. She signed the note with her name and a heart, hoping that one day she would be able to come back for her car. The thought of what her life would look like after that day spun through her mind as she watched the man with the tow truck secure her car onto the back of his big vehicle. It felt like he was taking away her old life as he rumbled off down the road. There were things that were going to be gone forever now. The unknown crashed like the heavy waves of the ocean, but Jamie's hand never let her drift away.

"We'll stay in L.A. a couple of days until I'm done with work, and then we'll fly over to London. Is that going to be okay for you, love?" His voice was so tender.

A tiny smile was his answer yes.

The trip back to the private jet Jamie had hired was a quiet one. Jamie let Alyson have her space and kept his questions to himself. Every so often a sniffle would come from Alyson's side of the car, but he said nothing. She leaned on the arm rest and let her head drop to her shoulder. A gentle hand reached over and settled on the back of her head, fingers intertwining with her silky tresses.

"You're going to be okay, love."

"I can't believe Danielle called you. Do you know how huge it is for her to do that?"

Jamie said nothing.

"She trusts your intentions enough to know you'll keep me from getting killed by my family." Alyson reached up to where Jamie's hand was still caressing the back of her head. She moved his hand to her lap so she could trace the pattern of his veins that went through his palm and up his wrist. "She knows you'll at least keep me physically safe."

"I'll keep you safe every way I know how." Jamie took Alyson's hand in his own, keeping her fingers still. "Especially from your family."

"And Bambi?" Alyson looked to the young man behind the steering wheel.

"Whatever it takes to keep you and Bambi safe from your family, I'll do it."

Alyson squeezed Jamie's hand and let out a deep breath.

"I don't know what they would do to me, but they don't play around. First my brother, now me..."

"Wait, your brother?" Jamie shot the girl an inquisitive look, before turning back to the road. "You told me you don't have a brother."

"I-... I don't. I mean, I don't know where he is. They sent him away when I was eight."

"Why didn't you tell me?"

"I never tell anyone." Alyson shrugged. "How do you casually tell someone that your only sibling was exiled from your family fourteen years ago, so technically you have a brother, but for all intents and purposes, you really don't."

"Why are you talking about him now, then?"

"I found a picture of him when I was at home. Reminded me of him." Alyson paused and looked down at her and Jamie's hands in her lap. "I miss him."

Jamie bit his lip to keep from saying anything. The girl next to him was so full of mystery. He wanted to know them all so he could protect her from everything that might try to hurt her.

Jamie sat Alyson beside him on the airplane and let her lean her weary and aching head on his shoulder as they took off. Jamie laid her down on the seats when she fell asleep. He moved to a spot nearby, keeping a close eye on her. When the sound of a gentle sob reached his ears, he knelt down by her head and pulled the blanket back. Tear-filled eyes greeted him.

"Love, what's wrong?" His hand reached up to push her hair back from her face.

"I'm leaving. I'm actually leaving."

"Yeah. You are." Jamie adjusted himself to get more comfortable on the floor of the plane.

"I'm never going to get that part of my life back." Alyson reached up to wipe at the tears. "A part of me is dying to keep Bambi safe."

Jamie didn't say anything, just leaned forward and kissed Alyson's forehead softly. One corner of Alyson's mouth twitched up for a moment, and he ran a finger softly down her cheek. She reached up from under her blanket and put a hand over his, helping him hold her face.

"My heart hurts."

"I know."

"Do you think this is going to work? Do you think Bambi will really be safe?"

Jamie shook his head and lifted his shoulders as he mulled over her words. He wanted to tell her that he knew everything was going to be great, but he couldn't and she knew it. They wanted this to work out. This was the best plan they could come up with, but all they could really do was be smart and watch carefully. There was no guarantee that their location and the purpose of her job wouldn't be exposed and everything ruined. They just had to try their best.

Chapter ten
"Sweet Dream Baby"

"**A** couple days in the sunshine will be good for you," said Jamie as they arrived at his L.A. home.

She was introduced to Jamie's house staff, told to make herself at home, and left to do as she pleased while Jamie worked furiously to tie up all the loose ends he had planned on having two more weeks to finish. The private backyard became Alyson's safe haven, and the furnished patio the perfect place to rest and soak in the warm rays despite the fact that it was the very end of October. Going from Iowa to California made the sun seem like a treasure.

"Look at how tanned you are!" Jamie laughed when he saw her at the end of the first day. "You look great! You're going to make everyone in London so jealous!"

"Well, my Pakistani roots do come in handy for something." Alyson smiled and almost leaned in to hug her host. He seemed to sense her desire for physical contact and put a hand on her arm for a moment. It was safe and gentle. Alyson felt her heart relax.

"Did you have an exciting day?" asked Jamie as he walked into a large room that had a paper-covered desk at one end, a big, leather couch in the middle, and a pretty view of the back garden from the window. He seemed preoccupied as he pawed through a few stacks of letters and such. When Alyson didn't answer, however, he looked over at her. "Is that a no?"

"Oh, I just... I can see you're doing something. I didn't want to distract you."

"No, not at all!" Jamie smiled as he turned back to the papers. "I enjoy company whilst I work."

"Let me help you with something. Please."

"Okay." Jamie nodded at the girl, his eyes smiling as he spoke. "Look through this stack of papers and see if you can find any receipts. I need anything that looks like a receipt."

"On it."

She took the stack of papers from Jamie's hands and settled down on the couch. She looked at each paper carefully, a line of concentration on her forehead as she skimmed letters and numbers. Jamie stood by the desk, his hand on his task, but his eyes on his guest. He had never seen that expression on her face before, but he loved it already. It was almost a day-and-night difference between the girl on his couch and the girl had he picked up from the gas station the day before. One day of sunshine and safety had erased almost every sign of tension and worry. This was the Alyson Jamie wanted to see. He didn't realize how long he had stood there staring until Alyson looked up, a smile on her face saying she had completed her task.

"You're finished already?" Jamie walked over to the couch to take what she had found. "You looked through all of those?"

"Give me another stack, slowpoke." The teasing look in Alyson's eyes made Jamie smile. He obliged by handing her another pile of papers. "I'll race you."

"I'm sure you'll beat me, but tell yourself it's a race if you'd like."

The two sat closely on the couch, shuffling papers and licking their fingers to give them a better grip as they tried to beat the other. Alyson won by a long shot and smiled triumphantly at Jamie who would have lost a thousand times in a row if it meant Alyson would smile that big every time.

"What's next?" Alyson leaned back against the couch and tucked her feet under her. Her hair was down and swished over her shoulders as she turned to look at Jamie's face. He was watching her with a smile. She smiled back, feeling her cheeks turn pink. Her hands settled on her baby, and Jamie's attention was distracted from her face.

"How's Bambi? Did he or she make you sick today?"

"No, thanks to the food you left by my bed this morning." Alyson stroked her stomach, but stopped when Jamie's hands covered hers.

"Well done, Bambi! Do you like California, huh? Do you like the sunshine?" Jamie cooed as he leaned close to Alyson's stomach. Alyson's giggle met his ears, and his hands tightened their grip over hers for a second before he removed them. "Bambi says you're the best mum ever."

"Well, thank you." She smiled shyly as she looked down at her hands still on her womb.

Jamie spent a moment admiring his beautiful companion again before she looked back up at him and repeated her question about another task to do. Jamie pulled out his laptop and started up Skype.

"Are you going to call Garret?" Aly's voice was a bit hesitant.

"No." Jamie shook his head, not looking at the girl on his left. "I'm going to call Ed."

"I-I didn't mean... I'm okay with talking to Garret," Alyson hurried to explain herself. "I just don't think he likes talking with me."

"He's still pretty gutted about not knowing what went down between you and him." Jamie paused before adding, "I think we all are."

The two on the couch sat in silence for a minute. It was hard for Jamie to think about the fact that his best friend had hurt the girl he loved. He and Garret had worked through a lot of their tension, but there were times when it would hit Jamie all over again that Garret may have slept with Alyson.

"I'm really thankful," Alyson broke the silence. "For all that he's been doing for me, you know. I don't know if he knows that."

"I'll make sure he knows." With a quick smile, Jamie looked over at the girl. She was looking down at her hands, her lips pressed together. "Should we call Ed?"

"Yes." The worn expression lifted from Alyson's eyes as she returned his gaze. "Is he still awake?"

"Eddie is always awake. He has his own time zone."

The Skype call rang through and connected.

"Hi, Eddie!" Alyson waved at the handsome young man who appeared on the screen. His long curls were pulled back from his face with a headband, and his simple gray sweater reminded his two friends that the weather was not the same in London as it was in California.

"Well, hello, gorgeous! You're looking very tan and beautiful. Is Jamie behaving himself?" Eddie's dimples were deep as he smiled at her.

"So far." A laugh accompanied Alyson's words, and Jamie only scoffed at the question, wishing he could make a snarky comment, but he knew he would pay for it if he did. "He's been very good to me."

"Well, you're in good hands."

"Thanks, Ed." Jamie nodded at his friend. "So, here's the plan. Alyson and I will be flying into London on Saturday, yeah, so we need someone to come pick us up from the airport and take us to the apartment."

"Saturday?" Eddie's brow furrowed. "I thought you guys were going to be coming back in two weeks! The apartment isn't ready yet."

"Something happened, and we need to come early. Just get the apartment ready and pick us up on Saturday." Jamie's tone became snippy.

"Something happened? What was it?"

"It..." Jamie looked over at Alyson and saw her pale face, her pink lips trembling. He put a hand on her knee and shook his head at Eddie. "It doesn't matter. We're here in L.A. now, and we're going to be flying out on Friday."

"If it means you pushed up your trip by a whole week, it does matter." Eddie stood his ground.

"Ed!"

"Eddie, I will tell you." The girl spoke and Jamie fell silent. "I just don't think over the computer is the best way."

"Are you okay?" asked Eddie. "Are you safe?"

Alyson nodded and frowned.

"I'm sorry about whatever happened."

"Thanks."

"All settled now?" Jamie was anxious to change the subject and get Alyson's mind off her family.

"Yes. Settled." Eddie nodded, glancing back over at Alyson, who put a brave smile on her face and nodded.

Her side was tight against Jamie, pulling comfort from his nearness. She resisted the urge to rest her chin on his shoulder. Jamie's hand was still on her knee, and he gave it a little squeeze as she shifted towards him.

"What is the plan now?"

"Saturday morning, airport. Get the apartment ready."

"Yeah, would do, but I can't. Garret is supposed to help me on Sunday when he comes back from his trip with Serenity."

"You're a grown man. You don't need Garret."

"I can't carry a bed and a couch by myself, Jamie!" Eddie retorted. "Why can't we just have movers do it like normal people?"

"Alyson's apartment has to be kept secret. People buy information like that, Ed."

Alyson wanted to disappear into the couch as she listened to the stress in Jamie's voice grow. She felt like she was asking for them to do more than she had a right to, and she kicked herself on the inside for taking advantage of their kindness. Her body moved to put space between herself and the man sitting next to her.

"You're acting mad, Jay! There's no way that I can get the apartment ready before Saturday."

"Figure it ou-..."

Alyson stood up abruptly from her spot on the couch and started for the door. Jamie stopped what he was saying and watched her walk away quickly.

"Aly, what are you doing?" he called after her.

The girl didn't answer or stop. Jamie set the laptop on the floor and jumped off the couch to cut Alyson off from the exit. He reached the doorway before she did, and he blocked her way out with his arm. She looked down, crossing her arms over her chest. She knew she couldn't make it past Jamie.

"Aly, what's wrong?"

"I'm fine."

"You just boldface lied to me." Jamie put a finger under Alyson's chin to make her look at him. "You're not fine."

"I'm fine." She couldn't meet his eyes.

"But, love... you're not fine." Jamie put his hands on her arms, slipping his fingers under the sleeves of her t-shirt to feel her skin. He rubbed the girl's arms comfortingly.

The touch made Alyson's mind spin to a stop, isolating one potent memory of Jamie's hands on the bare skin of her arms to calm her. She closed her eyes and sucked in her cheeks as his words filtered through the past.

"It's okay, love. I promise you. You okay? You ready?"

"I need a minute." Alyson pushed past Jamie, breaking free from his intoxicating touch. She felt her gag reflexes acting up as she ran towards the door that led to the back garden.

"Aly!" Jamie started after her when he saw she was going to be sick.

"Stop! I'm fine." Alyson won against the food pressing against the back of her throat and disappeared out of the house.

She didn't stop running until she had left the patio and houselights behind. She stood on the far side of the lawn, her hands gripping the cold, metal fence and her forehead pressed against the strong bars. The moon rose in the sky and her star friends twinkled down on her as she shuddered from the cool evening breeze and the memory of Jamie's hands on her body. It was that touch— those hands, those calloused but gentle fingers— that had convinced her so thoroughly that what they wanted to do was right.

Her hand went up to her collar bone. She felt its hardness under her cool skin. Jamie had kissed there. His lips had tasted parts of her skin and stirred feelings deep inside that she had never imagined existed; just the memory of them still turned her feelings inside out.

"It wasn't worth it." Alyson shook her head as she stared up at the sky. "Not even a moment of that pleasure was worth it."

She rubbed her hands over her arms, still feeling the heat of Jamie's touch amidst the goosebumps that prickled on her skin. There was nothing she wanted more than to close her eyes and wake up to find it had all been a bad dream; Jamie, her trip to L.A., Tommy and Garret, the excruciating ending to her relationship with the man she gave her body to. She wanted to forget about the weeks of horrible emotional turmoil that had nearly cost her her job and made her take a trip to Minnesota, and... Alyson stopped. Tears filled her eyes as she remembered the part of the story where she found out she was going to have a baby.

There was a soft swishing through the grass as Jamie made his way towards Alyson where she sat on the edge of his large property. It had been quite some time since she ran out of the house, and Jamie could only hope she was ready to talk. She was looking up at the stars with her hands over her stomach. Her mouth moved with silent, yet fervent words. It wasn't until Jamie was right next to her that she turned her head to look at him.

"Hi." He gave her a sad smile and found a spot on the ground beside her to sit down. He couldn't see her face very clearly in the dark, but he could guess she had been crying.

"Hi." Her voice was steady, despite the occasional catch in her breathing that Jamie had heard before.

He sat without saying a word, wanting to let Alyson speak in her own time. She shivered, and he slipped his light jacket off his shoulders and handed it to her. She took it with a weak smile and pulled it around herself, then looked away. He wasn't sure what he had done to make her leave him; first from the couch, and then in the doorway. His fingers scratched lightly over the scruff on his chin, and he worked his jaw silently as he waited.

"That wasn't the first time you put your hands on my, on my arms like that." Alyson's gaze returned to her star friends. "You did that another time... just once..."

"I-I don't remember..." Jamie stared at the girl's face.

The young man was surprised Alyson remembered something so specific. They had been physically affectionate in many different ways, and there was no way he could remember all the times his hands had touched her. He wanted to memorize everything about her, the way she sounded, the way she felt, the way she smelled... but his memory could only remember the tremor of nerves that rushed through him whenever their bodies collided, even for a moment.

"It was right before..." her voice cut, and she squeezed her eyes shut. "Right before we slept together. I said yes because I trusted you."

Her whisper seemed loud enough to reach up to the moon.

"And I was sitting here hating myself and wishing that none of this had ever happened, but then I stopped..." Alyson's tears reflected the lights in the sky as they trickled down her cheeks. "Because I want my baby."

The ache in Jamie's throat was painful as he listened to Alyson talk. Her words seemed magical and heartbreaking as they sat in the moonlight, the cool breeze washing over them and the fence bracing them from behind. Her eyes appeared to be the same color as the light in the heaven that shone down on them.

"I have never felt so much love and desire for someone like I do for Bambi. And to think, I was purposefully trying to get rid of him with those pills..." Alyson's face crumpled into a look of agony and her shoulders bounced against the fence as she wept. "I can't believe..."

"Shh. Love. Shh." Jamie scooted closer and slipped an arm around Alyson. She leaned into his warm body, her forehead pressed against the pulse in his neck, and her shoulder tucked under his arm. "You didn't know, love. Bambi knows that."

"But what if those pills hadn't been bad?" Alyson choked out quietly. "What if I had really killed Bambi without knowing it?"

Jamie's hand stroked back the girl's hair as she cried.

"What if Bambi never existed?"

"But Bambi does exist, Aly. It's okay. Bambi's safe." Jamie tightened his grip on the girl. "You're both safe. It's all okay."

"I can't regret that night." Alyson spoke up after a moment's pause. "I can't regret my baby."

"I regret very much how much pain I put you through." Jamie's words were muffled as he spoke into Alyson's hair. "But I don't regret you in any way. And I am very thankful Bambi gave me another chance with you."

"You told me that at the doctor's office," said Alyson quietly.

"I still mean it." Jamie's hand slipped down to the girl's stomach.

Alyson shifted her head so she could look at the hand that was gently stroking her baby's home. She smiled and wiped a few tears from her chin with the sleeve of Jamie's jacket. His hand rose and fell with the movement of her lungs.

"I know God doesn't hate me completely." The words seemed to come out of nowhere as Jamie listened to his companion speak.

"Sorry?"

"If He hated me, He wouldn't have given me something as precious as a child."

Jamie wasn't sure what to say in response, but he kept his hand on the baby and pressed his lips against the top of her head. He only held her for one moment longer before she traded his body for the fence to lean against. He cleared his throat and looked away, his hands picking at the grass beside him, and feeling suddenly quite cold.

"What did you and Eddie decide?"

"Hmm? Oh, Eddie insisted you stay with him for a few days after we get to London so we can set up your flat. If you don't want to stay with Ed, you can always stay at my place..."

"You've done so much, Jay. I don't want to put you out anymore. I'll stay with Eddie."

"You sure?"

"Yeah, I'm sure. He's been a good friend to me."

Jamie was quiet for a moment, rolling Alyson's answer around in his mind before spouting out his question.

"Why did you leave all of a sudden? What happened?"

"Don't worry about it. It's over now." Alyson shook her head and looked down at her hands. They had been rubbing her belly without her even realizing it.

"Well, we have one more day here and then we leave. You ready for it?"

"I'm ready to be where I can give my baby a home."

"Me too, love." One side of Jamie's mouth turned up into a smile.

It was Alyson who stood first, looking down at Jamie with a smirk as she offered him her hand. He swatted it away with a soft laugh before hopping easily to his feet. There was distance between them as they walked back towards the house in the dark, their hands by their sides. Alyson heard Jamie begin to hum a song, and she listened closely. She was surprised when she realized it was one of his own songs.

"You're humming 'Sweet Dreams'!"

"What does that mean?" he asked with a laugh.

"I just... You've never sang that song before."

"Sure I have! Loads of times!"

"No, you have not!"

"I sang that song on the radio probably a hundred times when I was first starting out."

"In America?"

"No, I didn't do that song in America. I was already singing 'March Forward' by the time I was in the States."

"I remember wishing you would randomly play that song every time I heard you at your concerts. It's such a sweet song."

"Do you know what I wrote 'Sweet Dreams' about?" Jamie's eyes went soft as he turned to Alyson.

"An old girlfriend?"

"No." Jamie shook his head. He could see Alyson much more clearly now as they were almost back to the house. The lights were shining through the windows and lit up the yard in patches. She shrugged and waited for him to tell her. "Here, come inside. I'll tell you in there."

Alyson walked behind Jamie as he led her down several hallways and a flight of stairs to a lower level. She could hardly keep her eyes from growing wide with awe when she walked into a large room filled with musical instruments. Her hands went to her face to try to cover her gaping mouth as she saw lines of guitars hanging on the wall and a beautiful grand piano in one corner. There was a drum set, a few stringed instruments, and even a trumpet setting on a shelf.

"Wow!"

"This is my music room, if you can't tell." He walked over to the piano.

"You play all of these?" Alyson's voice was filled with wonder.

"No. Not yet, anyway. I just like to mess around. It helps the creative process to be able to hear different things to know if I want to add them to a song." He sat down on the bench and patted the space beside him before resting his fingers delicately on the gleaming white keys.

"You play piano?" Alyson hurried over and slid onto the bench, her body leaving space between them.

"Sh! It's a secret." He winked at her as he started playing the familiar melody Alyson had been in love with for years. His voice was quiet as he began to sing. "One day last summer, I got the news, we had a little girl and that was you..."

Alyson gasped. These were not the words of the song she knew, but it fit the melody and Jamie's voice like a familiar friend. He smiled as he noticed her look of surprise out of the corner of his eye.

"You were sleeping, I said your name and I promised that I'd keep you safe. Sweet Dream Baby."

The single audience member was enchanted as he sung the story for her and her alone. She could tell how meaningful the words were to Jamie as he sang and played. He had never once mentioned or been seen playing anything other than the guitar. His fingers skillfully worked the keys of the piano, but it was the lyrics that had Alyson enchanted.

"That song is about a baby. A little girl." The song ended, and Alyson wished she could hear it again.

"I wrote it for my little sister. It was one of the first songs I wrote. I sat down and played it straight away after my mum called and told me she'd had her."

"What's her name?"

"Beatrice Rose. We call her Bea or Beatie for short. She's seven now." Jamie reached for his phone and pulled up a picture. The little girl on the screen had the same sparkling eyes and sandy brown hair as her older brother, but her cheeks were round and rosy, giving them a striking difference. "We're pretty good chums, despite the fact I moved out a year after she was born."

"The words you wrote for her are beautiful! Why did you change the words?"

"No one wanted to sing songs to their little sisters," scoffed Jamie lightly as he shook his head. "It was personal, I didn't want to share that with a million people. That's why I never sang it at concerts."

"You sang it on the radio!"

"Yes, because that was the only song I was able to play without going completely blank because of nerves!"

"That was beautiful." Alyson nudged him with her shoulder and gave him a smile. "I really love it."

Jamie nodded and put his hands in his lap, leaving the piano open. He was surprised when Alyson slid her fingers over the keys and pressed a chord. She quickly removed her hands and blushed as she looked away.

"No, it's good! Please! Play something!"

"I'm not good."

"I didn't ask if you were good. I said you should play something."

Alyson straightened and slid closer to the middle of the bench, her hip connecting with Jamie's. He scooted off the seat and stood to the side where he could watch the girl play. He was smiling without even realizing as he watched her start again. "Please don't judge."

"Never!" Jamie nodded at her encouragingly.

"This is the only song I ever really played on the piano." Her fingers retraced the notes her friend had just played for her. "But I don't know your original lyrics... the ones for Bea..."

"Sing the album version."

The girl's soft voice filled the room as she played Jamie's song back to him. She wasn't an accomplished singer, but she had a sweet voice and filled each phrase with emotion. Her face flushed as she performed, but she stayed steady until the end. When the last note dropped off she could hardly look at Jamie.

"Well done, love!" Jamie applauded the girl. "I didn't know you had that in you!"

"I never took lessons. Elle and I found some stuff on Youtube. That's why I only know a couple songs."

"I can send a piano over to your flat in Bedford if you'd like," he offered.

"You don't have to do that. I don't really play, I just fool around." Alyson stood to her feet and took a few steps back. She was suddenly very aware of the fact that it was only her and Jamie in the house for the evening. Her mind began to warn her of the potential danger of the situation, and she looked towards the door.

"I'll see if I can find one for you."

"I doubt I'll have time to play it." Alyson's hands moved nervously to her stomach. When Jamie didn't say anything else, she gestured towards the exit. "I-I should go to bed. I'm tired, and it's getting late."

Her nerves weren't lost on Jamie, though he thought them strange, and he followed her at a respectful distance. She smiled and gave him a little wave as she disappeared up another staircase that led to the room where she was sleeping while he stayed below. She didn't know that he would probably have to pull all-nighters until they left to make sure everything was taken care of. As he returned the smile and the gesture Alyson had given to him, he knew it was worth it. Alyson was safe. Bambi was safe.

The sun was high in the sky when Alyson finally opened up her eyes again. She wondered how her body had allowed her to sleep that long. Perhaps it was because of the sense of safety she had in Jamie's big house where she was hidden away from anything and anyone that could hurt her. The housekeeper brought her bottles of water and fresh fruit as she sat on the patio to wake up.

Everyone working in the house knew about Alyson's presence, even more so than the first day. She thought she heard whispers of her name going around, but it was all in her head. Just like when she thought the man at the gas station was trying to hurt her. She paced the hallways and sat against the fence at the far end of the yard, her eyes serious and her steps quiet.

Time ticked by slowly. The sun was the only one telling Alyson that the world wasn't frozen as it traveled across the blue, cloudless expanse overhead. She was lonely. She mentioned deep thoughts and fears to Bambi, whispering them just loud enough for her secrets to reach her own ears. Her thoughts wove in and out of confidence and doubts, each thread pulling a little tighter than the one before it, until Alyson felt like they would snap and everything would become unraveled.

"God, help me." Her words shot heavenward as she clutched at her head with her hands. "Please. Help me."

Even as the prayer left her lips, she knew she didn't have any right to talk to The One who created everything perfect and good. She used to think she fit in that category, or that she would be able to squeeze by just enough to make it. People talked about second chances and she knew He saw her heart, but she had chosen sin after promising Him her life. How could she even dare speak His name?

"I'm sorry. I know I'm nothing to You. But for the sake of Bambi, for the sake of this child, please let this whole plan work. Please." Tears formed in her eyes, and she wiped her sleeve across them. They left a wet stain as she pulled her arm away. "I did everything I promised I would never do, and I know You have to punish me. I know... I know that. But, God, please take care of this baby."

That was the prayer she carried in her heart throughout the day.

One of the gardeners saw her yawning early in the evening and asked if she would like to see the secret koi pond Jamie had just put in a few weeks earlier.

"Yes, please!" Alyson was glad for anything that would keep her distracted.

The pond was lovely, and Alyson sat on a marble bench next to it, her shoes off and her sweater slipping off one shoulder. The last of the sunshine was pouring over her from behind, soaking deep into the tense muscles of her back. A few of the fish poked their heads to the surface and nibbled at food that had been thrown to them. She breathed deep and closed her eyes. The smell of earth and flowers filled her senses.

"There you are!" Jamie's cheerful voice rang out from behind her. "You found my little secret, eh?"

"I love it." Alyson smiled at Jamie, thankful to see her friend after a day alone. He had bags under his eyes, but there were deep smile lines etched there too. "How was your day?"

"Fine, love. Yours?" Jamie took a seat next to her on the bench, letting out a big sigh as he did. He stared out at the pond and gave a little laugh as the fish swam aimlessly and poked their big mouths up to the very edge of the water.

"All of your staff are very kind."

"Oh, good. I told them if they were rude to you I would have them executed. Glad to know my threats work."

"No executions. Everyone deserves a gold star."

"Gold star? Wow. Their service to you must be so much more than what they give me!"

"Maybe they like me better?"

Their teasing exchange ended with Jamie staring at the girl as she smiled and looked off into the distance. Her whole face was glowing in the setting sun, and her dark hair gleamed so brightly it seemed like gold until second glance. The smile on her lips was inviting, but Jamie knew better than to steal a kiss. Her eyes reflected the light of the heavens, just as they had the night before. He fought to remember how to breathe at the sight of Alyson wrapped in sunshine.

"Spent most of the day thinking," Alyson offered, breaking the silence and looking over at the young man who was already staring at her. "About the move and life and stuff."

"Good, good." Jamie nodded and looked away. "Feeling okay about everything still? Still want to go for it?"

"Oh, yes." Alyson answered quickly. "I wasn't thinking about it like that, I was just realizing how different life can become in such a short amount of time. Six months ago I never dreamed I would be pregnant, or moving, or changing jobs, or leaving my family. It was only five months ago that you were just my favorite singer. Now I'm... I'm..."

"My friend?" Jamie's voice was gentle as he spoke.

"Yeah." Alyson smiled, but looked straight ahead. He was so much more than that. She had thought about him a lot that day, how she knew him, but there was so much about him that she didn't know. There she was, entrusting her life and the life of her baby into his care. She was putting faith into his promises just weeks after vowing she would never trust him again. The thoughts made her uncomfortable.

She tried to imagine what life would have looked like if her situation had played out differently and she hadn't needed Jamie. She couldn't picture it. It felt as though she had been planning to live in Bedford all along; it was the only future she could imagine.

Her mind had grown accustomed to the idea of leaving everything and everyone, but hadn't slowed down enough to soak in the hard details of starting all over again on her own. There would be no one there to greet her as a neighbor or a co-worker, assuring her they would be happy to drop everything and help her if she needed them. There would be no family. It would be her on her own finding the nearest grocery store, the safest route to and from work, the best park, the bus stops, and places to eat. She would be surrounded by strangers. The thought made her heart fade a little.

"Will I get to meet your family?" Alyson broke free from her thoughts to ask.

The question made Jamie give the girl an inquisitive glance. He hadn't been expecting her to say anything about his family. She had never mentioned them before.

"I'm not sure. Just 'cause the less people who know about you and Bambi the better."

"Right." He spotted Alyson's frown before she looked away and pushed her hair behind her ears. "That's smart."

"I'm trying to be." Jamie watched Alyson closely. "Trying to keep you safe."

"I know." A smile pushed the frown away, and Alyson looked to the young man briefly. "Thanks."

The sounds of nature were soft as the wind blew the bushes and trees, the water stirred in the pond and the birds flew home for the night. Everything was so calm. Most nights the garden was empty, used mainly for when Jamie was hosting parties, but it suddenly seemed much more appealing with just one special person to soak in the sunset with. Alyson let out a breath from someplace deep inside of her, and her shoulders slumped.

"You okay, love?" Jamie reached out a hand and let it brush lightly over the skin on her shoulder. She leaned into the touch, and Jamie let his hand trail over her shoulder and down to the smallest part of her back.

"Hm? Yes. Yeah, I'm okay. I think I'm just tired from thinking so much."

"You sure?" Jamie's hand followed her spine to her neck and massaged it lightly. There was so much tension behind the skin.

"That feels good." The girl let her head fall forward, giving Jamie better access to her neck. "It aches."

"Ah, love. Stop being so tense." Jamie shifted to get both hands on her slim neck. He pressed his fingers into the muscles.

"How far away from London is Bedford?"

"Not quite two hours, I think. I don't know, I've only ever made the trip up there from my place."

"How far from where you and the others live?"

Jamie's lips twitched into a sad smile. Alyson sounded so lonely. He stopped massaging and let his hands rest on her shoulders.

"Little over an hour. Not too far. Easy distance if you needed us."

"An hour?" Alyson turned to look at her friend.

"And for Eddie it's half that 'cause he usually stays with his gran who lives further up north than us. He could get to you in, let's say, twenty minutes if it was an emergency."

Alyson pondered the new information. At first she had been afraid Bedford would be too close. Now that it was time to actually leave, it seemed so far away from the only people she would know. She could feel Jamie's gaze on her, so she quickly smiled in his direction before looking back to the koi pond and distracting herself with the fish.

"We'll pop by and visit you, Aly. Don't think I'll just be leaving you up there alone. I know this is a big move and loads of things are scary. There's a nice bed and breakfast place down the street from your place, I can stay there if you need me close."

"Really?" Alyson knew she should insist that she would be fine, but there was nothing inside of her that believed that. Jamie would know the second the words came out she didn't believe them.

"I'm not just going to dump you in some strange town and wait for you to ring us up and tell us that Bambi's been born. I'll be there to check in on you."

The moment was disrupted by the housecleaner coming up behind them with a somber expression on her face.

"He's here, sir. I left him in the office."

"Thanks, Mary." Jamie stood to his feet at once and started back towards the house. "I'll be back. Don't leave."

Alyson watched Jamie's retreating form until he disappeared into the house. Her first plan was to stay by the edge of the pond with the fish until he came back like he said he would, but the sun set lower, and its rays were no longer warming her body. She stood to her feet and walked slowly back to the house. She didn't know where the office was, but she guessed she had found it, or the outside of it at least, when she heard two angry voices drift out through the open window and into the garden.

"I'm sorry, Jay. I didn't get it." The tone seemed nonchalant.

"What? That's not what I paid you to do. I didn't pay you to not get it! Are you having a laugh right now?" Jamie's voice was angry. Not upset like he sometimes sounded when he fought with Alyson, but actually angry. "This was important to me, which is why I gave the job to you! Now you've gone and not done what I asked, so, cheers for that, I guess I don't have to pay you."

"No, man! I need the money!"

"I needed that information! So I guess we're even!" Jamie shouted back. "I trusted you. And you mucked it up big time."

"Bro, come on!" the other man begged.

"No, bro, *you* come on!" Jamie's tone said he was done with the conversation. "Get out of my house. Don't come back."

"Jamie! Man!"

"I needed you to do your job, and you didn't. You were out in the club last night, mate! Pulling birds and getting plastered. Was it worth it, eh? Because we're finished."

There was the sound of doors slamming and furniture being shoved. Alyson cringed. An aggravated growl came from the office before silence. Alyson crept forward to the window to see Jamie leaning over his desk with his hands pressed against the flat surface, his head hung in defeat. Jamie needed her.

Alyson walked into the office, her footsteps light and undetected by the young man whose back was towards her. He was still in the same position as he had been when Alyson saw him through the window. She could see his shoulders moving as he breathed heavily, deep breaths in and out. He was wearing skinny jeans and a simple t-shirt; however, Alyson knew that underneath the clothes and the tanned skin was a heart that beat wildly and passionately for those he loved.

"I'm sorry." It was all Alyson knew to say as she placed her hands on Jamie's back. She felt him stiffen then relax to her touch as he realized who it was. He turned around slowly, wiping at his eyes as he did so. The desk behind him served as a support and he leaned against it, his arms crossed over his chest.

"Did you hear the whole argument?" Jamie asked quietly.

"No." The girl shook her head, her arms hanging down at her sides awkwardly. "I just know he didn't do what he was supposed to."

Jamie looked down and kicked at the carpet with the toe of his shoe.

"What he was supposed to do was find out if anyone was looking for you. All I wanted was for him to make sure no family or friends took it upon themselves to find out where you went. Just to make sure." Jamie drew his eyebrows together as he watched Alyson's face. "Obviously, he didn't do as I asked."

"I'm sure it'll be all right." Choosing to be the optimist, Alyson reached out to take Jamie's hands in her own.

"No!" Jamie's voice was louder than it had been before, causing the girl to jump. He grimaced as he realized he had startled her. He squeezed her hands and pulled her against him. "No, Aly. Your safety and the safety of your baby is more important than just assuming it'll be all right! It's not all right."

Alyson's heart was still pounding from the suddenness of Jamie's objection. She knew the man holding her could feel it racing, and he pressed his lips to the top of her head. She didn't let herself relax against him, but rested her forehead on his collar bone.

"I don't think you know how important you are to me." Jamie's voice was low. Those were the words he had kept himself from saying while they were outside.

Alyson didn't say anything as Jamie moved his hands to her back and rubbed softly, his fingers pressing into the knots that were aching there. She tucked her arms in-between their bodies and their heartbeats, feeling the separate rhythms of the two hearts on the skin of her arms. She could smell his cologne on his shirt and it reminded her of the day at the doctor's. The memory of Bambi's rushing heartbeat filled her mind, and Alyson focused on the sound. The three heartbeats melted together in Alyson's senses.

The young man knew Alyson was crying when she reached up to wipe the tear off her cheek with the back of her hand. He didn't say anything, only wrapped his arms more tightly around her. After letting out a deep breath, Alyson lifted her head from Jamie's chest and looked up at him. He didn't shift from his pensive stare into the distance, but his lips twitched as she moved. His dark brown stubble was so close to Alyson's face she almost reached up to brush against it with her fingertips.

"I don't take that lightly, Jamie." Alyson studied her friend's face. She noticed a glistening on his cheekbone, and her heart thudded with compassion. "Don't cry, love."

The term of endearment brought Jamie's gaze down quickly to the girl in his arms, showing her the surprise written on his face. When Alyson turned away and laid her cheek on Jamie's shoulder, she felt him exhale deeply. Her arms left their place from the middle of the hug and slipped around Jamie's waist.

Alyson swallowed hard. She already knew her two days with Jamie at his house were going to make their relationship harder than she wanted to admit. Her hands found Jamie's chest, and she pushed herself away from him. His arms fell easily to his side, and he gave her a sad smile.

"It's going to be hard."

"Hmm?" Jamie tilted his head inquisitively.

Alyson didn't even know what she was referring to as she said that. Her relationship with Jamie? The pregnancy? The move? All the changes? Sharing with the other potential fathers of her child? She supposed she could be talking about all of it. It was all going to be hard.

"All of it."

"Yes." Jamie's hands found the tiny baby bump and felt a tremor run through Alyson's body. "But it's going to be worth it, Bambi."

That evening was mostly quiet. Alyson sat in the den with a bowl of popcorn watching old TV reruns of NCIS while Jamie stayed for the most part in his office. Every so often he would look in to make sure Alyson was okay and steal a handful of popcorn. Each time he came in, it seemed that his eyelids were drooping lower and lower. They told Alyson that he was fitting much more than two days' worth of work into forty-eight hours.

"Can I get you anything?" Alyson asked as he turned to leave the room.

"No, love. I'm fine." He turned to give her a weary smile. "Thanks, though."

The answer didn't satisfy Alyson. She clicked off her show and stood slowly to her feet. Jamie stopped in the doorway and turned. A confused smile crossed his face as he looked at her.

"Tea?" She walked towards him.

"Yes." Jamie's grin went from cheek to cheek as he held out his hand to his guest and led her towards the kitchen. "I'll make you my favorite kind."

Alyson tried to help, but Jamie made her stand back, claiming it was his pleasure to make her a proper cuppa. They were soon settled at the small kitchen table with their tea and some cookies Jamie found in the pantry. Their spoons clinked lightly against the edges of their cups as they stirred in the milk. The kitchen was large and had brick accents, making it feel homey and rustic. The large window beside the table showed a dark sky and a million tiny specks of light shining through the atmosphere. A hint of warm sugar permeated the air, making its way from the oven to the high ceiling.

Jamie's laugh came easily as he listened to Alyson share a few of her favorite stories about her students. She watched him with shining eyes, her heart growing lighter as she pushed past how she felt and focused on someone else. It felt good to help him feel better.

"Look at us." Jamie chuckled. "Talking over a cup of tea in the kitchen like an old married..."

Jamie stopped and looked to the girl to gage her response to his words. She gave him a little nod.

"You can say it," said Alyson with a soft smile. "Like a couple."

"Do you ever think about if we'll end up like this further on down the road?"

Neither of them said anything for a long moment. Alyson fiddled with the edge of the table as she tried to find words to say. She looked up to see Jamie staring hard down into his drink and gripping his cup tightly, his knuckles white. It dawned on her that Jamie didn't know how she felt about him. Her actions went from hot to cold depending on her emotions, and he was left to meet her where she was, guessing at everything. Even so, he had done nothing but support her as best as he could.

"I guess... I've thought about how a lot of different things could end up down the road. Sometimes I think about us... but I try not to. I'm afraid if I try to imagine anything we'll spin out of control again, and I... I don't... I don't want that." *I don't want to lose you again.*

Jamie's intense gaze softened at her words. They were subtle enough to keep his feelings at bay, but they confirmed there was still hope for him. He didn't like waiting, but for her he would try. Together they were a combustible force of passion and chemistry; they needed to learn how to hold on without crushing each other. If that baby was his, he was going to do everything he could to make them a real family, but that could only happen if they stayed steady while they waited.

"I don't want that either."

"My first priority is Bambi. Everything else has to come after being a mom."

"Absolutely. Who knows what the next few months will be like?"

Alyson smiled wearily. Thoughts of the future were always heavy, no matter how rested and safe she felt.

"Do you think about who the father could be?"

"Yeah, all the time! I think about all the different possibilities of the future. I think about the personality and looks Bambi might have."

"Well, I hope Bambi looks like you," said Jamie.

"Why?" A tinge of crimson started to blossom in Aly's cheeks.

"I can't think of a more lovely and wonderful person for a child to be like." Jamie was serious as he spoke. "I want to look at Bambi when he or she is grown and still see you in them. Green eyes that sparkle. A smile that lights up a room. Those adorable freckles all on your cheeks. When I talk to them I want to hear your voice, hear words you would say yourself. There's so much love inside of you to pour out into Bambi, it seems right that your baby would look like the one who is giving up everything to make sure it survives."

The ache in Alyson's throat burned worse than the tears that were burning against her eyelids. She couldn't look at Jamie as she heard him describe the dreams he had for her baby. In some ways, it felt like Bambi was already Jamie's and the others were simply along for the ride. He had been the first to put his hands on her belly, been there to hear the heartbeat and the doctor say that everything looked good, been the one to pick her up in the middle of nowhere to make sure they stayed safe...

"You're going to be a brilliant mum."

"I really don't feel that prepared to be a good mom." Alyson swallowed hard as she finally returned Jamie's gaze. Everything in front of her blurred from the tears she was trying so hard to keep from falling.

"You're a great mum right now! You're keeping Bambi safe and healthy. You're doing amazing, Aly. I know when he's born you two are going to be inseparable."

"Well, Bambi is the only family I have left now," she said quietly.

"Oh, love." Jamie could hear the ache in Alyson's words. "You still have us lads. I know it's not the same, but we're here for you. Okay? Don't be scared. We'll try our best to make sure this goes well for you."

"Thank you."

A smile crossed Jamie's face, and he reached across the table to touch the back of Alyson's hand with his fingers. The simple gesture was the end of their conversation. He excused himself from the table and told his guest to get some sleep. He knew the long journey they were going to make the next day would be hard on the mother-to-be.

"Thank you for letting me stay in your house, Jamie."

"You're always welcome in my home. Any home of mine is open to you."

"I'll remember that." Alyson's smile was weak, but she pushed the corners of her mouth up with a little determination.

The look on Jamie's face softened, and a satisfied grin appeared. With a nod, he left the kitchen. Alyson finished the rest of her tea slowly. It reminded her of her quiet mornings with her baby where she would sit and sing lullabies at the start of each day. Her stomach was still quite tiny, but it was finally to the point where someone could see it. Now that she was far away from everyone who knew her, the physical changes in her body were exciting. With her hands stroking her belly, she began to sing.

"Sweet Dream Baby..."

Chapter eleven
"Life sucks, apparently."

The cold London air bit at Eddie's cheeks and nose as he stumbled out of the taxi and shoved a wad of bills into the driver's hand. He could hear the old man saying he was paying too much, but Eddie didn't care.

"Keep the change," he slurred.

His eyes were bloodshot as he knocked on the door of his sister's house, his knuckles throbbing from the cold and the hard structure of the door. He waited for her to answer, stomping his feet and breathing on his hands to warm them. After waiting for a minute, he knocked again, this time using the heel of his hand. There was a shuffling sound and a light clicked on in the hallway, then a pause of footsteps right inside the door. It was two in the morning, a good enough reason for any single girl living alone to hesitate before opening her door.

"Gi! It's me!" Eddie shouted, much more loudly than he realized. "Let me in!"

The door opened and one hand snaked out. She grabbed Eddie by the wrist and pulled him inside.

"Geez, Ed! What are you doing? It's the middle of the night!" Gianna Mallory shut the door with enough force to make it slam. The sound echoed in the quiet entryway. She shivered from the blast of cold night air that rushed in with Eddie.

"You're still awake."

"But I'm not making house calls!"

"I just... I needed to talk. I need your help." Eddie clumsily slipped off his shoes by the door and walked into the dark sitting room. He flicked on the light and slumped onto the couch. The room was cold, but it was a step up from the backseat of the taxi.

"Eddie, can't this wait until a reasonable hour when you're not drunk?" Gianna stood in front of Eddie and looked down at him with her arms crossed. He was tall and lanky and broad all spread out on her couch, looking very much like their father. Her own blonde hair was a shade darker than his and long enough to reach past her shoulder blades. It didn't curl like Eddie's.

"Life blows." Eddie closed his eyes and ran his hands through his hair.

"Really, Ed? You had to come talk about this right now?" Gianna huffed and shook her head, her blue eyes rolling in annoyance. He was two years her junior and had been giving her reasons to roll her eyes at him for years. She was tiny next to him, but she never let him forget that she was the oldest. "What even blows? You're in a band, travel the world, friends with everyone you work with, handsome, loved by girls..."

"No! Gi! It blows! Everything is stress, stress, stress! Jamie is angry. Tommy wants to be the dad. Garret has to tell Ren... It all sucks!"

Gianna sat down on the couch next to her brother and let out a heavy sigh. Having him show up drunk on her doorstep wasn't common, and she knew there had to be a reason for his actions that night, but they were unclear and she was exhausted. They hadn't had much time together since he came back from tour to catch up, but this was not what she had in mind.

"I don't, I do-… I don't even know Aly. Hardly. Not really. How am I going to help her with Bambi if I don't even know them?"

"Pardon? Who is Aly? What is Bambi?"

"Aly is the girl that is pregnant! Bambi is her baby!" Eddie yelled, clearly distressed by the situation. "I have to take care of them for Jamie."

"Absolutely nothing you are saying is making sense! What does a pregnant girl and her baby have to do with Jamie? Did he get her pregnant?"

"Well, she's pregnant, but we don't know who the dad is yet." Eddie cradled his head in his hands as he braced his elbows on his thighs. "I don't know what to do. I don't know all the things. I-I don't know. There are so many things, and it all blows."

"Why do you have to watch her? Ed?" Gianna put a hand on Eddie's shoulder and tried to see his face.

"I was just trying to help her. I just wanted to help her."

The older sister was having a very hard time putting together all the pieces of the story. She listened to him list off the things that had to be done before the girl named Aly came over to stay, not sure why there was such an intense emphasis on her safety and protection. She assumed it was another irrational fear caused by the alcohol.

"Gianna." Eddie was leaning back against the couch, his head resting on the pillows and his eyes closed. He looked like he was about to fall asleep in that position.

"Yes?" She glanced at the clock on the wall and saw it was almost three. Eddie had been rambling for close to an hour. Her jaw ached from yawning.

"Will you be angry like Jamie if I help Aly and Bambi?"

"Ed, I don't…" Gianna started, then sighed and shook her head. "No. Eddie, I will not be upset, but I really doubt that you'll remember this in the morning. Come on, it's bedtime."

The siblings staggered up the stairs, and Eddie was soon asleep in Gianna's guest room, still fully clothed. She pulled a few blankets over him, and then left him to sleep off his drinks.

Gianna didn't have work the next day, so she was sitting in the dining room working on her laptop when Eddie stumbled down the stairs in his sock feet and wrinkled jeans. He couldn't believe he had slept in his clothes. His eyes were squinty and sleepy-looking as he groaned and sat down in the wooden chair next to the table.

"Morning, sleepin' beauty," Gianna hummed with a smile. "The cure for your hangover is on that counter."

With another groan, Eddie pushed himself to his feet. Gianna continued to type, but she wasn't putting much thought into her words. She wanted Eddie to sit down and sober up so she could grill him about what he had said the night before. He was moving slowly, and she had to bite her tongue to keep from urging him to hurry.

Her dining room was connected to the kitchen and filled with splashes of light that came in through one of the two windows. It wasn't big or fancy, but she enjoyed having a nice place to fix her meals and entertain her friends. She could have easily asked her brother her questions while he stood in the kitchen, but she wanted him to return to the table. He drank his coffee and stared at the hardwood floor.

"Ed, come sit." Gianna motioned to the chair across from her.

"Mmm." Eddie grunted and sipped the black, bitter liquid in his cup.

"Come over here."

"I'm fine, thanks." His morning voice was deep and raspy and Gianna couldn't believe how much of a man her little brother had become. Even two years ago when he was twenty-two, he had some boyish looks still clinging to his body, but now he was fully a man in every way. There was even a bit of stubble growing on his chin that reminded the girl of when their father would wake up on Sunday mornings after a weekend of not shaving.

"Ed, we need to talk about last night. Come sit."

"Yeah, we do. For starters, how did I even get here?" Eddie rubbed one of his hands over his face and yawned. "And how much did I drink?"

"I have no idea. You just knocked on the door at two in the morning, and you were really upset."

"Upset?" Eddie's body tensed. "A-about... about what?"

"Life sucks, apparently." Gianna could see Eddie was nervous. He shifted his weight from foot to foot before he set down his coffee cup and rubbed his face again.

"I-is that all I said?" His eyes were watery as he looked at his sister. "I didn't say anything else, did I?"

"You mean about Aly and Bambi?"

Eddie muttered a swear word and hung his head. When he finally looked back up Gianna could see his lips trembling, but there were no tears.

"What's going on, Ed? You can talk to me about this!"

"No. No, I can't." Eddie shook his head. "I can't believe I got drunk and ruined everything. Jamie is going to kill me."

"Eddie, you came to my house last night and told me you needed to talk. Obviously something about this is really bothering you."

"I can't talk to you because I signed the contract saying I wouldn't tell anyone about Aly. No one is supposed to know about Aly, and especially about Bambi. If Jamie finds out you know..."

The story still didn't make sense to her as she watched Eddie pace back and forth in the short space the kitchen allowed. He muttered things under his breath and shook his head, his tangled curls falling around his face, forcing him to reach up and push them back with his long fingers.

"Can't you tell me anything? You're worrying me."

"You already know too much."

Gianna sighed and let her hands fall into her lap. "Is someone going to die if you tell me?"

"Yes! Someone could die!"

"Great." Gianna's tone was sarcastic as she threw her hands in the air. "Can you at least tell me what Garret, Ren and Tommy have to do with this? I sort of understand Jamie's part, but you mentioned Garret having to talk to Ren?"

Eddie sighed again and rubbed his hand across his forehead. He leaned over the counter and bit the inside of his cheek.

"Okay, fine. I get it. You can't tell me."

The sun was still filtering through the windows, laying a pretty pattern on the carpet from the trees that stood near the house. Leaves and branches crisscrossed and left shadows in the room. The sky was blue, but Eddie could tell it was going to be another chilly day. He would have to take a taxi home unless he wanted to walk half an hour to his flat that was in a different neighborhood.

"I just wish you could talk to me more about it all. I don't feel like I can give you very good advice without knowing the whole story."

"I know. I wish I could, too. I could do with the wise words of a university graduate."

"I'm hoping you'd want the wise words of your sister, as well."

"It helps when they're one and the same." Eddie gave a tiny smile.

He grabbed his coffee and walked over to the table. He sat down in the chair across from his sister and studied his hands as they lay on the blue and white checkered tablecloth. In some ways he was glad he had slipped up and told his sister about Alyson, but he was also nervous about what would happen if anyone found out what he had done.

"It's a shame you can't talk about what's bothering you just because people can't know about Aly. I don't see why she's so special that you have to be stressed and bothered by all of this."

"Gi, it really is a matter of life and death for her." Eddie's voice was low. "Keeping her baby is a huge risk and she's having to leave everything behind to keep her baby safe. I have to do my part to help as well."

It was hard for Gianna to not force Eddie to say anything more as she watched him bundle up in his jacket and a borrowed scarf before heading out into the cold. He walked for about five minutes before he caught a taxi and rode the rest of the way.

"Got any exciting plans for the weekend?" the driver asked, trying to make some polite conversation.

"Uh, yeah. Picking up a friend from the airport in the morning."

"Ah, very good. I hope you enjoy their visit, mate."

"Thank you, sir."

In less than twenty-four hours Alyson would be there to stay with him for a few days. He was nervous about seeing Jamie again. They had ended their Skype call on friendly terms, but his patience with both him and Tommy was as thin as a sheet of ice in April.

Jamie turned to look at Alyson as their plane landed in foggy London early on Saturday morning. He had looked at her many times since their journey started. He saw the rumpled clothes and cheeks pink from sleep under the red-rimmed eyes and tussled hair. He couldn't help but feel the tightening in his stomach as he realized he was the one to take care of her now; every other person in her life had been left behind.

They didn't say a word as the plane taxied to the gate and stopped at its destination. Alyson stood behind Jamie, waiting to deplane. He couldn't see the tears slipping slowly down her face, but he felt her as she leaned against him in a silent plea to be held. Her stomach pressed into him for the first time and he was thankful she was safe and sound, away from anyone who would share her secret.

Sumaya had called them right before they left for the airport in California and told Alyson the uncles had been convinced that everything was fine. Their favorite aunt had defended Alyson by bringing up her history of being a good girl, insisting Alyson would never do anything to shame the family. Together, they had been able to convince Alyson's uncles that there was no need to investigate the situation. It seemed that Bambi and Alyson were safe for the time being.

"Shh, don't cry." Jamie turned and pulled her close. He whispered against her hair and felt her swallow hard against his shoulder. "I'm right here. I'm not going to leave you."

"I-I know." Alyson struggled to steady her breathing. The exhaustion made her limbs feel shaky, and she leaned heavily on her companion as they descended from the aircraft. She felt his hand on the small of her back.

"I've got you."

"Thank you." It was a whisper, but it was honest.

The cold hit their skin, and they noted the heavy, low clouds in the sky. People in brightly colored vests and thick gloves and hats were there to fuel the plane and unload all the luggage. Jamie led her carefully through customs, security and to baggage claim. The frigid wind took Alyson's breath away when they exited the building.

Eddie stood by his car in the carpark. He held a cup of coffee in his hand as he snuggled into a thick, wool scarf and shivered from the early morning chill. It wasn't his favorite time to pick people up from the airport, but it was the best time to fly in and not get photographed. His friends entered the carpark and Eddie noted Jamie's protective stance. He instantly left his coffee and walked over to greet them.

Alyson saw him coming, and relief flooded her body. There he was, the one who was steady and kind. She reached for him, leaving the strength of Jamie's support. The reach made Eddie pick up his pace and he wrapped his arms around her, cradling her head against his chest as she melted against him. Her shoulders shook, but his jacket muffled the sound of her weeping. She felt his chest rumble against her forehead as he spoke to Jamie in a low voice.

"What happened?"

"She's running for her life, mate, and she hasn't slept in a bed for over twenty-four hours."

"Oh, love." Eddie rubbed his hand on her back, and then pulled away to see her face. "Come on, let's go back to mine. I've got tea and blankets and biscuits and anything else you want."

"Thanks, Ed. Take care of her." Jamie watched the pair turn towards Eddie's car with a twisting pain in his heart. He gave a halfhearted wave and began to back away from them. He was going to miss her.

"You're not coming with us?" Alyson whirled around when she heard his farewell.

"Nah, I'm going to go to my own flat. I'll let Ed take care of you for a couple days so I can rest up after being your nursemaid on our way over here." The last sentence was spoken in jest and in hopes of seeing Alyson smile.

"Oh." Aly's forehead furrowed. "When will I see you again?"

The look on Alyson's face reminded Jamie of a small child who was about to watch their dad leave on a trip.

"Tomorrow, love." Jamie gave her a smile and waved again. "You'll be with Eddie. He'll take good care of you."

Alyson stared after Jamie for a moment, watching him walk rapidly towards another man who was waiting next to a black SUV. He was smiling as he spoke, but he glanced over at Alyson with a frown. He tried to smile again when he saw her watching him, but his eyes didn't look happy.

After a shower, change of clothes and a seat next to the fireplace, Alyson felt the tension of traveling slowly seep out of her weary body. She wanted to stay awake and adjust her body to UK time, but she wasn't sure how long she would make it; she was exhausted. Her hands rubbed her stomach while she waited for Eddie to join her with their tea. She had chosen to sit in the rocking chair and wrapped a huge quilt around her shoulders for warmth and comfort. The blazes of the fire leaped playfully, mesmerizing her.

Thoughts of her home and her parents flitted from the corners of her mind and reminded her of how alone she was. In a few days she would call them and tell them she made it safely and everything was perfect. They would believe her because she would smile and wave and act like nothing was wrong while below the camera, one hand would be on Bambi. Then she would say goodbye for another two weeks when her next scheduled phone call was. Her calls home would be as regular as her doctor's appointments in the last trimester of her pregnancy.

"Still awake?" joked Eddie when he saw the glazed look in her eyes.

"Yes." Alyson quickly snapped back to focus and reached for her mug. "Thank you so much, Eddie. I'm sure you don't spend most Saturdays waiting on young, emotional pregnant women."

"No, but I'm hoping to make a habit out of it." Eddie's dimples flashed as he took his seat in the armchair that sat across the fireplace from his guest.

Eddie's flat wasn't anything fancy, a definite difference from Jamie's L.A. home, but it had three bedrooms, and the sitting area with the fireplace was spacious, accented with dark wood and rich red colors in the furniture. There were two windows that showed the sky outside. Long ruby-red curtains hung beside them, pulled back to reveal sunlight and the tops of trees.

Aly smiled in response to Eddie's words. The friendship that had started over their chips and salsa in Iowa the month before was still there. She let out a deep breath and inhaled slowly. The steam from her tea rose to her face. She smelled the sweetness of the flavor.

"Sorry to take you away from Jamie, though. I'm sure you two enjoyed your time together."

"It was nice." Alyson looked uncertain as she spoke. "But I guess it's probably better that we're not together all the time."

"What do you mean?" Eddie's eyes locked onto Aly's in a concentrated stare.

"I just don't want things to get out of hand." Alyson blushed as she remembered the hugs, the kisses on her cheek, the way he had spoken so tenderly to her, the songs in the music room, and their conversation in the back yard under the stars. How could she explain to Eddie the way he had dropped everything to take care of her? They still had enough chemistry to light up a room, but there was also a healthy amount of fear.

"You still have feelings for each other?"

"Yeah." She looked down into her tea and licked her lips. "I definitely still have feelings for him."

"What's your plan? Besides eating chips and salsa, of course."

"Right, besides that." Alyson smiled. "Try to be smart. Wait for Bambi to be born. Get ready to be a mother. Do my job. Not let my emotions get the better of me. Probably mostly just eat chips and salsa, though."

"That's quite a list." Eddie watched Alyson's hands settle comfortably on her stomach. "What's Jamie's plan?"

Alyson shrugged. They hadn't talked about it.

"I'm sure it'll all work out. You're here now. It's not too bad, yeah?" He smiled before taking a sip of his tea. A little grin appeared on Alyson's face.

"Not too bad."

The fire crackled, and Alyson looked around at the pictures that hung on the walls. There was a painting of a ship on the rolling waves of a storm on one wall and another beside it that seemed to be of a huge wave breaking on the foot of a mountain. Over the fireplace was a family picture. That was the one Alyson was the most interested in. An older couple were in the background of the photo, but her eyes were drawn to a younger version of Eddie's famous grin. A girl sat next to him with a smile just as wide as his. Eddie couldn't have been older than fifteen when the picture was taken.

"You have a sister?" Alyson motioned towards the photograph.

"Yes. Gianna." Eddie smiled fondly as he spoke. "She's two years older than me. She's all right, I guess."

Alyson saw Eddie's expression fall out of the corner of her eye as she turned back towards the picture. He fidgeted in his chair and rubbed his fingers across the lines on his forehead. It was clear to the girl that he didn't want to share his feelings with her right then, so she kept her gaze averted and pretended not to see.

"I would ask to meet her, but I think Jamie has me on a pretty short leash when it comes to people."

"You'd like her."

"It's going to be strange..." Alyson stopped talking for a moment, her eyes still studying the face of Eddie's sister. "Not being able to make friends while I'm here."

Eddie sat watching Alyson stare at Gianna's smile with longing written on her face. The parts of her heart that had been emptied of friends, family and familiarity were calling to be filled, begging to not be ignored, but she had nothing to put inside of them. She knew over the next days and weeks, little by little, she would shut those parts off and let them die. She didn't have a choice. Alyson finally turned back to face Eddie. Her eyes were sad.

"You'll still have us," he said as he forced a smile. "We'll be your friends."

"That's what Jamie said." Alyson smiled down at her tea. "I'm glad for the three of you. Well, four of you... I guess."

"We're not much, but we'll try our best." Gianna was wiser and kinder than he was; Gianna was the one Alyson needed in her life right then. "I wish we had more to offer you."

"Oh, please don't say that!" Alyson's eyes flashed a sincere look of regret. "I'm extremely thankful for everything! I'm going to be fine. Bambi will be safe. I will be safe... You guys have done more than enough."

"Believe me, it was mostly Jay and Garret."

The last name that Eddie said made a shadow cross over Alyson's face. She put her fingers up to her mouth and traced her lips as she stared thoughtfully at the fire. She could feel the chapped skin as she rubbed her soft fingers over them in an endless circle. Hazy thoughts about her encounter with Garret simmered in her mind. Sometimes it was easy to separate the man from the incident, and other times the two were so intertwined that they were one black memory in her past.

"Does he want to be a dad if Bambi is his?"

"Haven't asked him."

Alyson nodded and went back to staring at the fire.

"How do you feel about it?" asked Eddie.

"About Garret?" Alyson's eyebrows hooded her eyes as she put her feelings into words. "You remember how you told me that you knew I was a good person because Jamie didn't keep bad people in his life?"

"Mmm." He nodded.

"I keep reminding myself of that. That if he's Jamie's best friend, I can believe him when he says he doesn't remember what happened. He wouldn't lie."

The words soaked into their easy silence. Alyson remembered her tea and took a drink. It was the perfect temperature, and the liquid felt good going down her throat. She hadn't even realized that it had begun to hurt until just then. She took several more drinks before she rested it on her lap again. Eddie met her gaze when she peered over at him.

"I know it probably seems stupid for me to wish that I knew, even if it means knowing we did actually sleep together. That probably doesn't make sense to you."

"Yeah, course it does." Eddie nodded and set his empty teacup on the floor next to his chair.

"I just hate not knowing if he even has a chance of being Bambi's dad. It could save us so much extra stress if we just knew. We wouldn't have to tell Serenity, you know? I keep trying to convince myself we didn't do anything, but why else would we have taken our clothes off?" Alyson's face was tense as she used all of her strength to keep from crying. "I had already slept with people that night. Maybe that's just who I am."

"Oh, Aly." Eddie sat up in his chair. He saw his friend slowly crumbling under the weight of secrets that tore her heart open every time she thought of them.

"I..." Alyson started to talk, but her voice refused to share the vulnerable thoughts. She closed her eyes and tried to deep-breathe her tears away, but they turned into heavy sobs. Her hands felt Eddie's cover them as he came to kneel on the floor in front of her.

"I'm so sorry, love." He stroked the backs of her hands with his thumb.

Alyson pulled one hand away to cover her eyes. She felt Eddie's chest press against her knees as he shifted closer. His hand tightened over hers. It wasn't until her tears had run out that she realized his chest was shaking as he breathed. She opened her eyes and saw tears running down his face.

"Are you okay?"

"I will be." Alyson believed the words. "Thank you for letting me cry."

"You're part of my family now."

It was strange and wonderful to hear the word family come out of Eddie's mouth as he stared up at her with serious gray eyes. He meant it. When he looked at her, he saw a sister. Alyson could hardly remember what it was like to have a brother; a close confidant who could be trusted to have your back and call you out on your foolish decisions, all the while loving you fiercely and protecting your honor.

"I promise I will do everything I can to help you. Including provide you with chips and salsa when life is hard."

"Thank you." Alyson finally smiled. "Thanks, Eddie."

He gave her hand one last reassuring squeeze before pushing himself back up to his feet and returning to his chair. Alyson waited for Eddie to be settled before she said anything else. The fire still crackled merrily, warming the room and distracting the pair from the heaviness of the mood. The girl sipped her tea as she gathered her thoughts.

"Ed, can I ask you to do a favor for me?"

"Of course."

"I-I need someone who is able to be honest with me. Someone who isn't going to let me forget what's important or get caught up in the past. And with Jamie..." She looked down. "I'm so emotional and I c-can't... I can't trust myself to get through this without someone just being honest. Danielle used to be the one who kept an eye on me, but she's not here."

Alyson felt the homesickness wrap around her. Every mile between her and her best friend was tearing her heart down the middle.

"I need someone steady, and who knows me, and just, I don't know, who will keep me from being stupid." Alyson's voice was broken with tears as she finished her request. She pressed two fingers against her eyes, forcing herself to stop crying. When she looked up again, Eddie was frowning at her empathetically.

"I wish I was better at being clever, but I will do my best." He sighed and glanced up at the picture of his family, his eyes resting on his sister's smile.

Relief showed on the girl's face. She whispered her thanks and leaned her head back against the chair for a moment. She didn't even know she had drifted off to sleep until she felt Eddie gently waking her. He had her nearly empty teacup in his hand and an apologetic smile on his face.

"I don't want to bother you, but you can rest in the bedroom if you like. It would be more comfortable."

"I didn't even know I fell asleep," she mumbled sleepily, reaching out to take the helping hand Eddie was holding out to her. He carefully helped her stand. "I forget how tiring it is to travel."

She was led to a guest bedroom and left to snuggle under the thick comforter. It felt good to lay out flat with a pillow under her head. Her thoughts kept her company for a few minutes as she felt her eyelids close, thinking about Jamie, and Eddie, and how she was finally safe on the other side of the ocean.

"We're going to be okay, Bambi," she mumbled sleepily before she finally drifted off.

Nothing disturbed Alyson's slumber until something cool rested on her forehead and Eddie shook her shoulder for the second time. The only two thoughts in Alyson's mind as she awoke were how hot she felt, and that her bladder was about to explode. Her arms shoved at the covers, and she struggled to push herself up into a sitting position before she could even get her eyes open.

"Bathroom..." She felt the hand shift on her face as she blinked her eyes open. The ceiling light hurt her eyes, but she continued to work towards the edge of the bed. "I have to pee..."

"Easy now, love. Are you feeling okay? Your face is burning up right now." Eddie's deep voice met her ears.

"No..." Alyson moaned as her feet hit the floor, and her head began to spin. She forced her eyes open, but couldn't manage to stand upright. "My head."

"Easy, Aly." Eddie put an arm around Alyson's shoulders and half carried the girl to the bathroom at the end of the hall. "Let me know if you need me."

Alyson let her head hang weakly as she went to the bathroom. She didn't have any idea what time it was, but she was starving. Feeling the familiar rolling in her stomach, Alyson reached for the dust bin that was in the corner of the bathroom and held it close.

"Aly, you done?" Eddie knocked lightly on the door.

"I need food." Alyson struggled to hold her head up.

"What do you want?"

"Toast." Alyson tried to think of what would help the most. "Toast and orange juice."

Eddie was waiting on the other side of the door when Alyson finally managed to shuffle her way out of the restroom, one hand bracing herself against the wall and the other clutching at her nauseous stomach. She felt Eddie grab her and lead her carefully down the hall and back into the bedroom. She sank onto the bed she had just left as if she hadn't slept for days. Her head throbbed with pain, and her stomach swirled.

"Here, I have your orange juice. The toast should be up in a minute." Eddie sat the girl up against the pile of pillows and held the cup to her lips. "I think you have a fever. You look proper ill."

Again, his cool hand touched her flushed face, and she leaned into the relief it gave her. A sip of orange juice went down her throat, settling her insides. She leaned back and let her head fall to the side, too heavy to hold upright.

"I'm going to fetch your toast, love, I'll be right back." The sound of Eddie's feet pounding on the floor as he jogged down the hallway filled the quiet apartment. Moments later, Alyson heard the same sound returning to her. "Do you want anything on it? Jam? Butter? Marmite?"

"Ew." Even with the fever raging in her body, she still knew she didn't want the salty spread on her toast. "Just plain."

A few bites made it down, and Aly's stomach calmed. Eddie found a thermometer and stuck it into her mouth. She didn't make a noise as she waited for the result to show up. When Eddie pulled it out, he drew his eyebrows together in concern.

"You've definitely got a fever. Almost 38 degrees. I should take you to the doctor." Eddie glanced at the clock on the wall and sighed. "He's not open anymore; we'd have to go to A and E."

"What's that?"

"What we call the emergency room."

"Oh. What time is it?"

"Eight-thirty. I heard you calling out in your sleep, that's why I woke you. You must have fallen ill after laying down."

"I think it's jet lag and from being on such a long flight. I have vitamin C in my bag..." Alyson gestured weakly towards her purse that sat next to the bed. "I just need to have lots of water and rest... and if it doesn't go down, then you should take me."

"Are you sure?" asked Eddie. "The lads will kill me if they knew you were sick and I didn't take you to A and E."

"I'm sure."

"How can you be sure?"

"I researched this kind of thing."

"You read it online, didn't you."

"It was a reliable source, and I double-checked it. Going to the emergency room just gives me a chance to catch all the sicknesses there." Not to mention all the questions and paperwork and people seeing her and Eddie Mallory in public together.

"Fine," Eddie conceded. "All right, well, let's have you drink all this up and stay in bed. We'll check your temperature again in half an hour."

"You're an awesome doctor." Alyson gave her caretaker a smile.

Every half-hour throughout the evening, Eddie took Alyson's temperature, and made her drink another cup of water. In between times he would watch her doze off, her hair spread out softly over the pillows as her breathing slowed.

"Mum, is it bad if someone who is pregnant has a fever?" Eddie held his phone in his hands, ready to press the 'call' button and ask his mother that very question for real. "How do I make it go away?"

He hung his head, holding it up with the palm of his hand on his forehead. His fingers hovered over the 'call' button several times that night for Jamie as well, but he was terrified he had already done something wrong and Jamie would hate him forever for not doing the right thing. He jumped at every sound that came from the bed, and he placed his hand on Alyson's forehead to check the temperature more often than she knew.

"I'm never going to be able to forgive myself if something happens to Aly or Bambi." Eddie rubbed his hands over his face. Alyson shifted as she woke, and her eyes fluttered open. "How are you feeling?"

"A bit better." Her voice and smile were tired.

He helped her to the toilet before getting her another piece of toast. She laughed when he started singing the song from *Mary Poppins* about a spoonful of sugar, except he changed the words and sang, "Just a spoonful of marmite." Even though she was hot with a fever, her worry lines were relaxed and she smiled easily at him. Her hand rested on his arm as he sat on the edge of her bed and listened to her soft voice tell him a story about one time when she was sick with a fever when she was a little girl. He chuckled and pulled the covers back up to her neck.

Once the clock hit midnight, the pair finally let out a deep sigh of relief; the fever was going down. The girl in the bed smiled and said she knew it would be okay, while Eddie exhaled deeply and massaged the back of his neck with one hand. He met eyes with the girl and saw her staring at him, one side of her mouth up in a type of smile.

"I think we're officially out of the woods."

"Thank you, Eddie."

"You're very welcome." He stood from the chair and stretched. He had moved the recliner in from the living room to sit in while watching over Alyson. "It's what family does for each other."

Alyson's smile faded at the words, and a quizzical look formed on her brow. She blinked as she looked away. The edge of her bed sagged down when Eddie joined her there.

"What's that look for?"

"I-I'm not used to having a family like that. I've always just had to take care of myself best I could. Hearing you say that just... I don't know. Elle is the only person who has ever really taken care of me, and it took me a long time to let her get that close."

"Well, I'd be more than happy to show you how my family takes care of each other." Eddie placed a steady hand on Aly's forehead.

"I think I would like that."

They set their alarms to wake them in an hour and check Alyson's temperature again. This time, Eddie actually allowed himself to close his eyes for a bit. The alarm startled him and he jumped up, worried that Alyson had fallen back into the clutches of the fever while he slept, but his hand touched her forehead and proved to him that she was fine. He carefully stuck the thermometer into her mouth and waited for the numbers to tell him if she was still going to be okay. The numbers appeared, and Eddie let out his breath.

"Getting there. Well done, Aly," he whispered to her, even though she hadn't woken for the checkup. Her face was more pink than white, encouraging the young man to let go of his concern for her health.

As Alyson slept, Eddie finally let himself look down at her tummy. The blankets were tucked in around her, showing the tiny lump that Eddie now stared at. Inside, under the blankets and Alyson's shirt and her smooth skin, was a baby. A real, live baby.

"I know I'll love you." Eddie whispered to Bambi. "I already do love you in a way."

Eddie fell asleep in the chair until his alarm woke him again, telling him it was time to check on his patient. Alyson woke up this time and was eager to have him see how much better she was doing. She obediently sipped on her water and took another packet of vitamin C, though she said her throat didn't hurt when she swallowed anymore.

"You must be exhausted." The night was almost over, and Alyson could see bags growing dark under Eddie's half-opened and bleary eyes. "I feel so much better, though. I must have just been dehydrated and worn out."

"Your fever is almost all gone." Eddie squinted as he tried to make out the little numbers on the thermometer.

"This isn't going to help me with my jet lag."

"I'm not worried about jet lag. Jet lag isn't life-threatening." Eddie stifled a yawn as he spoke.

"Why don't you get a couple hours of sleep, and I'll wake you if anything happens. I promise."

Reluctant to leave his patient, but unable to stay awake any longer, Eddie complied. His head was aching as he slipped between the blankets on his bed and lay down. He was sure he wouldn't sleep for long, knowing that Alyson was there and might need him, but it was several hours later when he opened his eyes again.

Sunshine was flooding into his bedroom. He hadn't shut his curtains before falling into bed, and now he was paying the price for it. He blinked and stretched before forcing his eyes to stay open. Alyson's shadow flitted past his door and he called out for her. She walked to the doorway of his room and leaned against the doorframe. She still appeared a bit peeked, but she was standing.

"How are you feeling?" Eddie sat up hurriedly, his covers falling down from his shoulders and onto his lap. He motioned for her to come closer so he could press his hand on her forehead.

"No fever." Alyson smiled at the look of concern she saw on Eddie's face. "Still a little on the shaky side, but much better. I'm sure after another day of resting I'll be back to one hundred percent."

She took a seat on the edge of the bed and pulled her feet up to sit cross-legged.

"Good. And Bambi?" He reached out to touch Alyson's stomach before pausing and looking to the mother for permission.

"Go ahead." She guided Eddie's hand to her bump, smiling broadly. She laid his hand flat over her stomach and laughed as it nearly covered her entire belly. "Look at how big your hand is compared to the baby!"

"I guess I do have rather large hands." Eddie chuckled, his muscles slowly relaxing as he felt the warmth of Alyson's skin fade into his touch. "But you're not that big."

"I am bigger than I was two days ago. You could hardly tell it was a bump when Jamie picked me up in Nebraska."

"Really? How much did you eat while you were in L.A.?" asked Eddie with a smile, pulling his hand back slowly.

"I did eat very well while I was there. Mary fed me all the fruit I wanted. Mmm! California is the place to live in the winter."

"Sorry we moved you to London then!" Eddie gave a little laugh.

"Probably safer here." Alyson dismissed it easily. "Right, Bambi?"

She put her hands where Eddie's fingers had rested and looked down as she spoke to her child. Her eyes grew soft and her voice calm and sweet. A warm look filled Eddie's eyes as he took in the moment of the mother adoring her unborn baby. She was so sure of how she felt towards the little one. Eddie was awestruck.

"You can talk to him. Jamie does it all the time." Alyson put her hand over Eddie's and gently brought it back to her belly.

"Are you doing okay, Bambi? Are you feeling better today?" Eddie tried to imagine a tiny baby hearing his words on the other side of the womb. "I hope you're okay in there."

He paused, and Alyson waited quietly for him to say something more.

Eddie's next question was directed towards the mother. "Do you feel it moving yet?"

"No. Not yet. It will be a few more weeks, probably."

Eddie slid his hand off Alyson's stomach and leaned back against his headboard. He was still exhausted, but the sun was up and he knew he needed to get out of bed. At least he didn't have to continue worrying about Alyson's health. She looked peaceful and relaxed as she perched on the edge of his bed in her pajamas.

"I hope you were able to rest enough."

"I'll be fine. I'm used to getting little sleep most days. I'll work hard today and sleep harder tonight."

"Oh! The apartment!" Alyson's eyes widened. "When are Jamie and Garret going to come over to pick us up?"

"Us? No. Not after last night." Eddie shook his head. "You're going to stay right here, you nutter. You can watch the telly, and I will buy you all the fruit you want, but you are not going to leave your bed for any other reason than to use the toilet."

"But I... I want to help. I feel badly to make you guys..."

"Ah!" Eddie stopped the girl with his finger and a look. "Family."

Alyson obediently followed Eddie back to her bedroom and waited for him to set up the television in the corner and cover the bedside table with food. She couldn't deny that her body felt better all snuggled in the bed with the pillows and blankets Eddie had provided for her.

"Hey, can you bring some fruit when you come?" Eddie asked as he pressed his phone up to his ear. "I don't have much to give Aly."

The answer must have been yes because Eddie hung up the phone and left to get dressed. He returned with a hat pulled snugly over his curls and a thick, gray sweater over his shirt. An old pair of jeans with a rip in the knee matched the scuffed-up boots on his feet. He dropped easily in the recliner that hadn't been moved back to the living room.

"Movie?" he inquired.

"Sure."

"Which one?" Eddie grabbed a couple DVDs off the shelf and held them up.

"You own *Love Actually*?"

"What's wrong with *Love Actually*?"

"Nothing." Alyson smiled.

"Listen, I don't want any of that cheekiness, young lady. Keira Knightley is in this movie. I have no shame in owning this film."

"Fine then, Mr. Defensive. Just put it in."

The two friends watched their movie and munched on the snacks for another half-hour before anyone else arrived. A voice from the front door called out a greeting.

"Knock, knock," Jamie shouted. "I used my extra key. Where is everyone?"

"Back bedroom."

"Bedroom?" Jamie sounded suspicious. When he appeared in the doorway he stopped to take in the sight of Aly in bed and Eddie in the armchair. "What happened?"

"Aly is not allowed to get out of bed," Eddie informed his friend. He gripped the arms of the chair nervously. "She was feeling poorly last night."

"Is she all right? Did you take her to the doctor?" Jamie's questions came tumbling out as he rushed into the room to stand by Alyson's side. "Where's her medicine? Have you called someone to ask if the baby is okay?"

"I'm okay. We got the fever down." Alyson grabbed Jamie's hand to reassure him. "Eddie did everything I told him to do. And look, no fever."

She put Jamie's cold hand on her forehead and smiled up at him. He finally dropped the look of concern from his face and exhaled sharply. Alyson's smile was enough to warm his fingers from the cold wind outside, and he moved his hand from her forehead to her cheek. Her smile deepened, and she leaned into the way he was cradling her face. His eyes sparkled at her, and he sunk down to the edge of the bed. He could feel peace radiating from her as he leaned closer.

"I promise I'm all right, Jamie," she whispered, leaning forward to meet him halfway until her forehead was touching his.

"You sure?" He reached up with his other hand and felt for her neck. It was warm and soft.

"Mmm." Butterflies swarmed in a hot bunch in Alyson's stomach, but she loved it.

Jamie leaned back and took in all of the features of Alyson's face, stopping at her pink and freckled cheeks longer than anything else. Her face was beautiful to him. It wasn't until he let his hands fall from Alyson's face that he remembered Eddie was still there. He cleared his throat and stood to his feet.

"Eddie's right, you're not to leave this bed. Here, I brought you your favorite fruits." Jamie held up a bag. "You stay right here and watch television and... are you watching *Love Actually*?"

"It's Eddie's movie."

"Course it is, it's his favorite. Has been for years." Jamie grinned as he shot Eddie a look.

"Are you sure I can't go with you guys?" she asked one more time.

"Positive."

"Absolutely."

The next knock on the door was Garret. Eddie looked over at Alyson as Jamie ran down the hall to let their friend in. Alyson sat quietly, breathing deeply and gripping the blankets of her bed in her fists.

"Here's Garret. Fresh from his holiday." Jamie picked up his jacket from where he had discarded it on the end of Alyson's bed. "Shall we go?"

"Yes, let's." Eddie started down the hallway.

Alyson looked up and met eyes with Garret. They were strangely different than normal, somehow. Not in color and appearance, but what was behind them. He didn't seem like a hunted animal, but more settled. Sad, but calm. He gave her a polite smile and nod.

"Hi, Aly."

It was the first time he had ever voluntarily spoken to her since California.

"H-hi." She waved back.

"Jay says you were sick last night."

"Yeah, I had a fever."

"I'm sorry." He smiled sympathetically. "You need anything before we leave?"

Alyson shook her head no and forced her mouth up into a smile.

"Call us if you need anything," said Jamie. "I'm going to leave the phone I bought you this morning just there on the bedside table. My number and all the others' numbers are in there."

"I'll be fine." Alyson rubbed her belly. "I have everything I need."

"All right. We'll see you when we get back." Jamie winked at the girl before turning to leave.

"Bye, guys. Stay safe," she called after them. The door shut, and Alyson was alone.

The day passed slowly and quietly. Episodes of *The Inbetweeners*, some British television show that Eddie promised she would enjoy, blurred into each other until Alyson wasn't sure of the storyline anymore. She thought often of her interaction with Garret and pondered the fact that he seemed so different. The sun was beginning to set when her thoughts faded, and she let herself drift off to sleep.

It was dark in the bedroom when Alyson finally opened her eyes again. The TV was switched off and her door was shut most of the way, letting in only a sliver of light from the hallway. She yawned and took a deep breath before rolling over to reach for her pre-paid phone. The time was seven in the evening.

"Well, it's not like I planned it that..." Jamie's voice was loud as he walked past Alyson's bedroom, then died away as he entered the living room.

"Jamie is here?" Alyson muttered to herself as she yawned again. The pang in her stomach told her it was about time to eat, and she was going to need something more substantial than fruit and toast. She stood to her feet and waited for a moment, checking her balance and her strength. Her body proved it was up for a journey to the kitchen, so off she went.

"Well, look who is awake!" Jamie noticed her first from his spot on the couch that faced the entrance of the hallway. "You look lovely and rested! Come. Sit."

He patted the cushion next to him. Eddie grinned from the rocking chair and the third young man, Garret, simply nodded politely and smiled at her from the far end of the second couch. Alyson made sure to look him in the eye to confirm what she had seen that morning. It was true, there was something very different about him now.

"I'm actually really hungry." Alyson stood awkwardly as all three men stared at her.

"You're just in time for some marmite and toast." Eddie winked as he jumped to his feet.

"Mmm, I was hoping I hadn't missed it."

"Marmite on toast? Really?" Jamie looked disgusted by the idea. "Is that what he's feeding you, Aly? I'm so sorry."

"Didn't Eddie tell you? That was my cure last night."

Eddie gave Alyson a knowing smile over his shoulder right before he disappeared into the kitchen whistling the song from *Mary Poppins*.

"One day together and you two have jokes between you, eh?" Jamie hoped his remark seemed innocent and light-hearted, not serious and bordering on jealousy.

"Just toast and marmite," Alyson said casually, sensing the true feelings behind Jamie's words. She sat gingerly on the other end of the couch from Garret, making sure to keep as much space between their bodies as possible. She flitted her eyes in his direction and saw he was distracted by his phone and didn't seem to notice at all. "How did the apartment setup go?"

Again, Jamie had to hold back the words he wanted to say as he watched Alyson sit down. Logically, it made sense for her to sit on Garret's couch as it was the closest empty spot to her, but he had invited her over to him and she hadn't even responded. Questions and emotions sifted through his mind, and he shifted uncomfortably as he wondered if her feelings for him had changed since she arrived at Eddie's apartment. Flashbacks to when they were in Iowa came to mind and aided him in his theory that Alyson could easily fall in love with Jamie's friend. He felt panic start to shake his confidence.

"Oh, it went good." Garret nodded and looked up from his phone when he realized that Jamie wasn't answering. "Jay, you want to tell her about it?"

"Sure, yeah, I mean, not much to say. Everything's in and looks great. Really great." The edge in his voice slowly disappeared as he realized Alyson was gazing warmly at him. "The furniture all looks nice in it. We picked up some more things while we were there to fill up the empty spots so it doesn't look quite so big and empty."

"Thank you." Her voice was gentle as she spoke.

"Yeah, course, love." Jamie did his best to seem unaffected by her tone. His confidence restored, and the shaking of his insides steadied. "It looks great, although you don't have any curtains yet. We'll have to get you some."

Eddie returned to the living room with a plate full of food as Jamie was talking. Alyson took it gratefully, smiling. She was about to put a bite into her mouth when she heard Jamie's comment about curtains.

"I don't like curtains." Alyson shook her head. "Eddie asked me if I wanted some the night that they were shopping at the furniture store. I-I don't... want curtains."

"Yeah, she said she didn't want any," Eddie said casually as he sat back down in the rocking chair.

"That's ridiculous! You need curtains! You don't want people looking in through your windows every day."

"I'd rather not have curtains." Alyson's adamant expression was a thin veil over her anxiously pounding heart.

"You don't have to have curtains," said Eddie quickly, giving Jamie a look.

"I guess if you really don't want them, it's up to you."

The conversation about curtains was far from over in Jamie's mind. He would keep that for a time when it was just him and Alyson. She looked troubled as she returned her focus on her food. He couldn't imagine why she had such a violent reaction to a simple household item.

"Wait, what about curtains?" Garret looked up from his phone again and put it back into his pocket. He quickly took in the others' faces as he attempted to jump into the conversation.

"No curtains for Aly's house," announced Eddie, giving the girl a little smile.

"Fine." Garret was curious about Jamie's ruminative expression, but said nothing.

"I'm very thankful for all the work you put in for me today." Alyson hoped her smile could break the tension that had built up subtly around them.

"Our pleasure." Garret spoke up for the lads. "It's a nice place. I hope you'll like it."

"Nice neighborhood, we made sure of that." Eddie pointed at himself and Garret as he spoke.

"You'll have plenty of room for your growing stomach," said Jamie with a nod in Aly's direction.

She rested her hands on her belly and stroked it softly out of habit, her eyes fading to an enamored glow as she looked down. Garret and Eddie were watching Alyson's hands, while Jamie couldn't take his eyes off her face. He wanted to stare at her for hours to make up for the time they had spent apart since coming to London. It had only been two days since they left L.A., but it felt empty to not come home to her bright smile.

"It's so tiny, though," Eddie said of Bambi's current size.

"I promise you it's bigger than it was when we were in California. It seems bigger, doesn't it, Aly?"

"Is it really?" Garret looked over at Jamie as he spoke.

Alyson glanced up and watched the two friends begin to dialogue about *her* baby that was inside of *her* body. Her heart was torn as she heard Jamie talk excitedly and Garret engage with interest. Jamie had earned the right to talk about Bambi, but Garret... She didn't want Garret to talk about Bambi. Not yet. She didn't know him.

"How far along is she?" Garret asked Jamie.

"Fifteen weeks, right, love?"

With a nod, Alyson returned her gaze to her stomach. Her hands gripped tighter, possessively, over her baby. She didn't understand how this could be the same man who had hardly been able to look at her face. The Garret she knew had remorseful, haunted eyes and had forgotten how to smile. His laugh reached her ears, and she cringed. She didn't know how to interact with this new person.

"When is the baby due?"

"We call the baby Bambi, Gar," said Jamie with a grin.

"I know..." Garret drew out his words slowly, looking sideways at the girl to his right. "I just didn't want to assume I could... use that name."

For a split second, the shadow of the burdened Garret returned, and Alyson saw the apologies written on his face. She didn't know how to respond to the obvious show of respect to her wishes. His posture changed from relaxed to repentant, his shoulders falling forward. Jamie and Eddie watched the interaction quietly.

"I'm due April twenty-second." Alyson's softly spoken words were a compromise. What she didn't say filled the silence.

"Well, I hope things continue to go good for you both." Meek words. A contrite frown. Yet, at the same time, peace. Alyson didn't know how to explain it.

"Thank you."

"I took Serenity on a trip this week." Garret's eyes watched Alyson closely as he spoke. Alyson couldn't look at him. She felt her food turn sour in her stomach.

"Did you tell her?" asked Jamie.

"Yeah." Garret turned to him as he spoke. "I told her. Well, everything I could."

'Everything I could'? What does that even mean? Alyson sucked in a nervous breath.

"Good. That's good." Jamie's gaze rested in Alyson's direction. She wanted to melt away from sight; she was so embarrassed.

"Aly?" Eddie's low voice shook her from her thoughts.

Alyson swallowed and cleared her throat. She blinked her eyes rapidly and pushed her mouth up into a hurried smile.

"That's great." She quickly stood up from the couch and walked out of the room, her hands balled into fists at her sides. Thirty seconds later the men in the living room heard the door to her bedroom click shut.

Chapter twelve
"Be kind. Forgive. Love others, even when they hurt you."

September 28th

Serenity was upset. So was Garret, but he couldn't tell her that; not after telling her what he just had. Her family was going on a two-week long holiday to Australia in October, and Garret wasn't going to be returning to London until after she left.

The holiday was for her dad's birthday, and everyone was making the trip; her aunts, uncles, cousins and grandparents. Garret had planned his return home that way on purpose. He knew that once he saw her, he would have to tell her about Alyson, and he didn't want to ruin her trip.

"Garret, you've got to be kidding me!" Serenity never raised her voice, but that night she was shouting through the phone. "You're coming in less than twenty-four hours after I leave! Why?"

"It's just how it is right now, darling. I'm so sorry." Garret sat on the floor of his hotel room, his back against the wall. The lights were off and only the red and orange glow of late afternoon was filtering through the half-drawn curtains and lighting the room. He was thankful his voice didn't give away how he felt as tears ran down his face. "I'll see you when you get back."

"Really? That's all you've to say about it?"

"It is what it is, Ren. It's just a fortnight. We'll make it."

"Oh, come off it, G! I haven't seen you since July! Tell Jamie you're coming home to see me before my trip."

"Ren." Garret let out a deep breath. "If I leave now, Jamie will have to do all the extra work on his own."

"You're only his tour manager, you don't have to do everything!"

"He's my best friend. I have to stay and help with this charity deal. There's a million things that need to be finalized before we ca-..."

"Garret, please." Serenity's voice broke as she began crying. "You sound like you don't even care! Are you breaking up with me?"

The stab made Garret cover his mouth to smother the sobs that shot up to the surface like lava inside of a volcano. His stomach turned as he gulped and tried to steady his voice enough to continue. The silence screamed into his ear, and he had to break the quiet whether his voice was ready or not.

"I promise you, I don't want to break up with you. I-I... I can't imagine... Ren..." Garret's words were thick as he spoke.

"I feel like I never get to talk to you anymore." Serenity's soft voice was still trembling.

Garret pictured his girlfriend sitting in the armchair in the living room of her apartment, her hair pulled back into a silky ponytail, the sleeves of her sweater pulled down to the heels of her hands and her feet covered in a thick pair of wool socks to stay warm. He could remember the view from her living room window, and how her television set was old and muffled the soundtrack of movies when it was turned up too loud. He had memorized the position of the button to her floor in the lift and would push it without looking. His heart still pounded wildly in anticipation of seeing her during that ride up to the seventh floor. She would always answer the door with a smile and a gentle kiss to the cheek, her lips warm and soft against the stubble of his beard. If he was lucky, he would snag her elbow before she could pull back, and he would stare down into her eyes for a moment and drink in the steady calm that pooled inside of them.

"I miss you." The words were choked and shaky, but he didn't care. He couldn't have held them back if he had tried.

"Are you sure you can't come home sooner?"

"I can't." Garret could barely get the words out past the lump in his throat. "But when you get back, let's take a little holiday ourselves. Just the two of us. Give us some time to really be alone and talk about things."

"I'd like that."

"All right, darling. I can't wait."

"Garret."

"Mmm?" Garret's heart thumped as he waited for Serenity to say what she was thinking, afraid that maybe she already knew his secret.

"I love you."

The declaration brought a flood of guilty tears to Garret's eyes. He pinched the bridge of his nose so hard it hurt, but there was no stopping them. He missed her so badly. It made his head, his heart and his body physically ache to think about Serenity leaving him. He wouldn't make her stay if she wanted to go after she knew the truth. The thought killed him on the inside.

"I love you, too." The words were mumbled, and Garret quickly hung up after confessing them. He didn't have the right to be loved by the most beautiful and kind person on the face of the earth. He didn't have the right to love her back, but he knew he would for the rest of his life.

October 25th

There was a very good reason for the twisting feeling in the pit of Garret's stomach the day Serenity flew back into London, just one week before Aly and Jamie did. Their special trip was scheduled to start the next day, but he wanted to see her. He usually bought her a gift whenever they were apart to give her when they were reunited, but he disliked the idea of giving her something that would be tainted by whatever happened between them next. He hoped she wouldn't notice and ask about it. The taxi pulled to a stop in front of her apartment building, and Garret saw the familiar smile light up the backseat through the window.

"G!" Even with the door shut, Garret heard her squealing happily.

Within moments, she had opened the door and flung herself into his arms. Shaking as her face pressed against his warm neck, she inhaled deeply, as if he was her oxygen and she hadn't been able to breathe for too long.

"I missed you." Garret wrapped his arms around her as tightly as he could, until he was afraid she couldn't breathe, and even then, he didn't let her go. His heart was pounding out of his chest at the familiar smell of her perfume and lavender shampoo. Tears were beginning to burn at his eyes, but he refused to cry. "I missed you so much."

"Me too, babe." Serenity finally let her arms fall from his shoulders, and she stepped back to look at his face. Her long, tender fingers pressed against his red cheeks and she saw the tears he was trying so desperately to hide. "Don't cry, I'm here. We're together. We made it, just like you said."

"Let's, uh, get your bags." The taxi driver had unloaded the girl's two suitcases and set them on the sidewalk. "Here, I'll pay the guy."

Once the taxi had pulled away, Garret took a suitcase in each hand and walked behind Serenity into her apartment building. His knees were knocking the whole way up in the elevator, and he licked his lips nervously as Ren wrapped her hands around his arm. She smiled up at him with an adoration Garret told himself to never expect to see again.

"You seem quiet, babe." Serenity finally emerged from her bedroom, changed out of her travel clothes and into some sweatpants and a sweater. She sat down at the chair across from Garret in front of the cup of coffee he had made for her.

Her small eating nook stood right outside her kitchen and open to the living room, tan-colored carpet on the floor and surrounded with light purple walls. The little circular table sat four people, but she had one side pressed against the wall, allowing only three chairs to sit around it.

"A lot on my mind." Garret stared down at his cup, knowing that if he looked back up he would break into tears.

"Tell me." Serenity reached over and put an encouraging hand on his wrist. She rubbed over the back of his hand with her thumb, feeling the thin layer of skin shift with the pressure of her touch. "I've missed our talks."

"This... this isn't a good thing to talk about right now." Garret grimaced and stared down at Serenity's hand on his arm. He wanted to catch those fingers and lace them between his own, pull her against him and just hold her, pretending that nothing from the past or the future could hurt them.

"Why?"

"I want to wait until we're on our trip tomorrow."

Serenity nodded and pulled her hand back to her side of the table. Whatever it was that her boyfriend wanted to tell her couldn't be good. She sipped on her coffee and watched him stare down at the table. The steam disappeared from his drink, but he made no move to pick it up and taste it.

"G." Serenity saw him start at the sound of her voice. "What's wrong?"

"So much." Garret shook his head and rubbed his hands over his face as he straightened his back from his hunched position. "I... I..."

"Garret, please tell me." Every horrible possibility filled her imagination. Her throat began to close.

"I'll pick you up in the morning at seven." Garret pushed his chair back.

There was a silent plea in Serenity's eyes as she watched him stand to his feet and lean over to place a kiss on the top of her head. He let his hand brush against her cheek before he pulled away and stepped towards the door.

"I'll see you tomorrow, darling."

"Do you promise?" Tears rolled down Serenity's cheeks as she saw Garret's hand on the door handle.

Garret pressed his lips together and returned to Serenity's side. He pulled her to her feet with unsteady hands. He pressed her head against his shoulder and wrapped his other arm around her waist. She cried as Garret swayed gently with her in his arms.

"I absolutely promise, my love," he whispered against her hair.

She let him step back and return to the door without stopping him. He could see on her face how upset she was to see him go, but he knew he had to. It wasn't fair to her to spend time together pretending like he wasn't going to break her heart the next day.

Serenity waited a few minutes after Garret left to pick up her phone and call the person she always turned to when she needed wisdom. She put the phone to her ear and stood up to grab a Kleenex from the tissue box in the living room. The phone was still ringing when she reached the table and sat down again.

"Hello?" A woman's voice called breathlessly through the mouthpiece right before the call went to voicemail.

"Aunt Becky?" Serenity's voice was shaking.

"Ren! Dear! How are you?"

"Is now a good time for you?"

"Of course, dear. The children are all at school and Joel is at work. What's the matter?"

A tiny sob escaped, and Serenity quickly pressed the tissue against her eyes.

"Ren, dear. Tell me what's happened." The voice was steady and patient.

Aunt Becky had always been Serenity's favorite. As the youngest sister of Serenity's father, Becky was closer to Serenity's age than her brother's. When Serenity was little, she would toddle after Becky and mimic every word and action the teenager did. No one minded, though, as Becky was the epitome of sweet and kind. Her heart was set on being like Mother Theresa, despite her family's attempts to dissuade her. It wasn't that the Fitz family didn't want their daughter to be sweet and kind, but they wanted her to be sweet and kind with them in London, not on the other side of the world.

Serenity remembered well the day her aunt told her she was going to fly to Africa and live in a country called Cameroon for a long time. She was seven, Aunt Becky was eighteen, and they were both very emotional when it came time for them to say goodbye.

"Remember what I taught you, Renny," Aunt Becky whispered to the weeping child. "Be kind. Forgive. Love others, even if they hurt you."

Those were the words that had guided Serenity's entire childhood. It was hard to no longer have Aunt Becky there to talk to and do things with, but the letters from Cameroon were as regular as the tide. Every two weeks one would arrive in the mail and Serenity would carry it with her until the next one came. Each handwritten note ended with a reminder to be kind and forgive.

After a year and a half, the letter bearing the news that Aunt Becky was returning from the hot country of Cameroon arrived in the mail, and Serenity was over the moon. She didn't understand why her parents and grandparents weren't pleased. Hadn't they all missed her terribly while she was gone? Grandpa Fitz had cried at their first Christmas dinner without her. But even her other aunts seemed to be tense as they waited for Becky's return.

Serenity overheard the angry voice of her grandmother on the day of Aunt Becky's arrival. The whole family was there waiting for Grandpa Fitz to come back from the airport with his youngest child. Serenity heard whispers of a special guest coming with, but no one would answer her questions when she asked about it. The welcome home feast Grandma Fitz and Aunt Sylvia had cooked up smelled delicious. Serenity was sitting in the hallway pulling at the edge of her t-shirt and watching the driveway like a hawk when her sharp ears picked up the hushed conversation.

"I don't understand why she had to choose to marry a man from there. Being a missionary is one thing, but marrying a man from there is completely absurd!"

"Mum, please don't embarrass her when she gets here." Aunt Sylvia sighed heavily. "And please try to be polite to him."

"I can't make any promises. I doubt I'll even recognize her when she comes through the door."

"Mum, honestly! She's still Becky!"

And she was. She scooped Serenity into her arms as soon as she walked through the door, trailing a nice young man with beautiful dark skin, white teeth and happy smile behind her. He shook everyone's hand and introduced himself in broken English.

"My name is Joel. Is very nice to meet you."

"Hello, I'm Ren." Serenity had been the only one to smile back.

"Ah, yes! I know you from your letters." He leaned over to pat her head, but she was snatched back by her mother. Serenity was appalled by the hurt look that filled the eyes of both Joel and her beloved Aunt Becky.

Life after Aunt Becky's return was nothing like it used to be before she moved away. Serenity wasn't allowed to spend time with, or talk to her aunt on the phone unless someone else was there. Visits were short and rare, and Serenity was old enough to know that her father left on purpose if Joel ever came up in conversation.

"I like Joel, Aunt Becky," Serenity whispered to her aunt one time after her father walked out of the room.

"Me, too." Becky's green eyes were swimming with tears, but she blinked them back.

"Is it hard to have everyone mad at you?"

"They're not mad, baby, they're just worried something might hurt me." Aunt Becky's smile crept back onto her face. "And if they do get mad at me, I forgive them and love them anyway. That's the most important thing to do when people get mad or angry at you."

"I remember." Serenity smiled back. "Mummy said I might be able to come to your wedding."

The whole Fitz family ended up going to the wedding that took place a year after Becky and Joel's arrival to England. There weren't many smiles, but they were all determined to look on the bright side of having a Cameroonian son-in-law. The idea had been able to settle for a while and they were learning that Joel was a very nice young man who loved Becky very much.

After the wedding was the endless paperwork with immigration as Becky worked hard to make her new husband a resident of her home country. Things worked out slowly, but the newlyweds persevered through it all and embraced their life together with joy and confidence. The same sweetness that Becky had exuded all throughout her life was still there, and Serenity soaked it up as often as she could.

Little by little, the reins were loosened as the family grew more comfortable with Joel and Serenity grew older. Serenity was staying with Aunt Becky for a sleepover shortly after her thirteenth birthday when the call came in and changed everything...

"Ren." Aunt Becky's voice brought Serenity back to the present.

"I-I think something's wrong with me and Garret." Serenity wiped at her eyes again with the tissue. "I don't know what, but h-he's acting off, and, and, and he won't tell me why! I asked him what was wrong but he doesn't want to tell me until we're on our t-trip tomorrow, and I'm so scared! Whatever it is isn't going to be good, or he would tell me, right?"

"Renny, dear, calm down. Sh, all right, love. Calm down." Aunt Becky's voice soothed her niece over the phone.

"But what if he has done something really bad!"

"Do you think Garret doesn't love you anymore?"

"No, he says he does! H-he says he doesn't want to break up with me, but I don't know what is going on!"

"Do you think he would do something to hurt you on purpose?"

"No! Absolutely not!" Serenity found herself saying with conviction.

"Dear, if he says he doesn't want to leave you and you know he wouldn't purposefully hurt you, then I know you can work through whatever has happened."

"I-I know, but..." Serenity tried to calm her shaky breathing. "I don't want anything to change between us!"

"Renny, things have to change. If things never changed, you would never fall deeper in love and you would never get to know each other more."

"What should I do?"

"Love him. If he has done something that hurts you, forgive him. And above all, listen to his side of the story. I know how much you two love each other; don't let anything break you apart."

"Okay."

"But Ren..." Aunt Becky's voice grew serious. "If he has done something to purposefully hurt you, you can end things. Don't let him hurt you on purpose. If you don't know, then talk to someone about it. Your mum, Aunt Sylvia..."

"Like I would tell them if Garret did something bad after my track record with boyfriends." Serenity laughed and let out a deep breath. "All of the other boys I dated were such losers, and I thought I could love the bad out of each one of them. Then Garret showed up, and he was so wonderful..."

"And he still might be, dear."

"I know." Serenity nodded as she held her phone up to her ear. "Thanks for calming me down, Aunt Becky."

"Absolutely, Renny. You know I'm here for you any time you need me."

"How are things in Marseilles? Joel and the kids all good?"

"Yes, dear. How's mum and dad? The others? Did the trip for your dad's birthday go well?"

"Yeah, it was great. Just arrived back home today, actually."

"I'm sure it was lovely to have the whole family all together."

"It wasn't the whole family. You weren't there."

"It's been a long time since I was considered part of the family, Renny."

It had been twelve years since the incident that changed everything for Becky and Joel. He had been at the wrong place at the wrong time, trusted the wrong people, said yes to the wrong thing. The next thing he knew, he was being framed for having stolen thousands of pounds from the company warehouse where he was employed. No one wanted his side of the story, they just wanted him gone. The phone call from prison came while Serenity was with her aunt, and she remembered the way Aunt Becky's face went white and she fell to her knees, the phone still pressed against her ear.

Joel was sent back to Cameroon, and Becky went with him. She was told that if she did, she would have no family to return to. They didn't trust Joel's side of the story, and told her to leave him before he dragged her down even more. Before she left, she managed to catch Serenity on her way home from school and tell the girl goodbye.

"Forgive them, Renny. Love them, even though it's hard."

"But they hate you and Uncle Joel!" Serenity sobbed into her aunt's shoulder.

"That doesn't matter." Becky's heart was breaking. "We still get to choose to love them and be kind."

As Serenity hung up after her conversation and put the two mugs in the kitchen, she remembered the values her aunt had instilled in her. She remembered deciding that she didn't care if everyone else she knew was mean or rude, she wasn't going to let them change the way she walked out her life. She wanted to be kind. She wanted to love others, even when it was hard. Even Garret. Even if what he did had hurt her, she wanted to love him.

Serenity sat on the bed of their hotel room with her hands over her face their first night in Brighton. Garret had picked a place they had never been to so there would be no memories ruined, but everything was ruined anyway. He had ruined it three months earlier. She sat hugging her knees to her chest and staring at him as he shifted on his feet, tried to sit down, rubbed his sweaty palms on his jeans...

"G, please just tell me. I need to hear what's going on."

All of the words he had been rehearsing in his mind for the last three months left him, and he was left staring at her blankly. Her eyes were hesitant, masking the trust that Garret usually saw reflected there when their eyes met.

The first time he had laid eyes on her, she had smiled at him from across the room, and Garret's heart pounded like the hooves of a race horse against the track in the homestretch. From the very beginning of their relationship, just one quick glance into Serenity's eyes was all he needed to get his world back in motion when he lost himself. No matter how many times a day had tried to break him, all he had to do was look to his side and see those brown eyes staring back. They grounded him, anchored him, held him gently yet fiercely to what mattered most. Now he was about to watch them fill with tears.

She crumbled as he choked out his confession, the look of betrayal in her eyes was enough to make him sick. The tight control over his emotions for which he was known had slipped from his grasp, and he had nothing left except hollow sounds and incoherent words. He wasn't even sure if he was speaking in complete sentences, but as he watched Serenity's expression break apart, he knew he was saying something that was true.

"So?" he asked at the end of his horrible monologue.

She gave him a look that pleaded with him not to ask her to speak. The red around her eyes grew from pink to scarlet as tears poured down in quick succession. They stayed in silence for hours, neither of them saying anything. Serenity lay on the bed quietly, and Garret sat on the window seat with his hands balled into fists. The space between them was only about twenty feet, but it felt like the ocean.

"I'm so sorry." They were the only words Garret had to offer. Tears ached in his throat and made it hard to see. "I can't tell you how sorry I am."

"Is she all right?" Serenity spoke up after another long pause.

"Sorry?"

"The girl. The one you might have slept with."

"Oh... Well, no."

"G, what happened?" Serenity sat up and braced herself against the mattress. Her hair fell over her shoulder in a messy ponytail. Her face was covered with red splotches, but her eyes were clear and intent.

"She slept with two other lads that night. And, uh..."

"Garret, what happened to her?"

"She's pregnant, and she has to leave her job. She has to hide from her family because they could hurt her or the baby. It's a very complicated, dangerous situation."

"She's..." Serenity couldn't talk, her mouth was dry. "She's..."

"Yeah." Garret nodded and looked back out of the window, biting his lip as tears fell.

"Wow. She's pregnant." Serenity moved to sit cross-legged on the bed. She could see Garret's profile as he kept his eyes on the rain drizzling down outside. "And you might be the dad."

"We won't know whose it is until the baby is born."

"When will that be?"

"I don't honestly know. Spring or something."

"Are you going to be able to help her? You have to make sure she's getting taken care of."

"I am. She is. I promise you, I'm doing everything I can for her right now." Garret finally turned and made eye contact again. "That's one of the reasons why I had to stay in the States for so long."

"And she's going to be all right?"

She spoke the question with genuine concern, and Garret was in awe of Serenity Fitz all over again. She had just found out that he may have slept with someone, and the girl was pregnant, yet the question she needed to have answered was whether or not Alyson was going to be okay. She needed to know that Alyson was being taken care of.

"I think so. Me and a few other people helped her get a new job... new home. She's safe from her family at least."

"Good." Serenity sat with her fingers running through the end of her ponytail as she thought quietly. "What are you going to do if the baby is yours?"

Garret shrugged and took in a jagged breath. He didn't know yet.

What am I going to do if Bambi is mine? he asked himself. That question was constantly in the back of his mind, begging to be answered.

November 1st

Garrett looked around at his two friends as they sat in Eddie's flat. Jamie was still staring down the hallway toward Alyson's room, and Garrett could tell it was killing him to stay put and not go after her.

"Does Ren know that it's Aly?" asked Jamie.

"No." Garret shook his head. "I just told her the girl was getting taken care of, that I had helped her get someplace safe, and that's all."

"Don't you think she'll figure it out?" Eddie asked with a frown.

"Maybe. I just know what my contract said..." Garret gestured towards Jamie as he spoke.

"How did Ren take the news when you told her?" Jamie asked gently.

Garret didn't say anything, simply nodded a couple times, looking at the floor by his shoes.

"She forgave me." Garret wiped a tear from his eyes. "Says she doesn't want to leave me, or take a break. She still wants to be with me."

"Gar, that's great," Jamie said sincerely.

"I don't deserve her." Tears choked out his words.

Jamie knew what that felt like.

"I should go make sure Aly is okay." Jamie pushed himself up to his feet.

He could hear Eddie and Garret telling each other farewell as he walked down the hallway towards the bedroom where Alyson was staying. He paused to listen outside the door, but heard nothing.

"Aly." He knocked softly. "Aly, it's me. Can we talk?"

There was no answer for a moment, and then Jamie heard a small voice giving him permission to enter the room. Alyson wasn't in bed, but was sitting in the recliner that was still there beside it. She had curled up against the back of the chair, her arms hugging herself tightly and her feet under her. Jamie looked for tears, but saw none.

"Hi." He sat down on the edge of the mattress so he could be on eye-level with her.

"Hi." She returned his gaze, but her frown was set.

"I came to see how you're doing." Jamie's hands were folded in his lap, but his fingers twitched as he spoke.

Alyson looked down and let out a heavy sigh.

"I know I do a lot of stupid things, and I need you to tell me if I do something stupid. I don't always know what you're thinking, or what you're feeling. I try! I really do, love. But at the end of the day I'm just a guy who doesn't have a clue."

Alyson nibbled on the side of her bottom lip with her teeth. She frowned harder as the words swirled around the two of them.

"Hmm?" Jamie pressed for her to give him an answer.

"He was different today." Alyson slowly lifted her eyes to meet Jamie's soft gaze. She saw his confusion at her words. "Garret. He was different."

"I thought he was more like himself than he has been in a long time. Maybe that's why he seemed so different to you."

"He talked to me."

Jamie leaned forward until his cheek was resting against the chair, removing most of the space between his face and Alyson's. She didn't move or pull back, just looked down with thoughts clouding her eyes.

"Did he tell her it was me?" she asked quietly.

"She doesn't know it's you." Jamie put a hand on Alyson's shoulder and gave it a squeeze. "All she knows is the girl is pregnant, and Garret is helping her."

Huge tears welled up in her green eyes.

"Did she leave him?"

"Oh, love." Jamie pulled Alyson forward to hug her. She cried against his shoulder, and he rubbed down the bumps of her spine with a comforting hand. "It's okay. She didn't leave him."

"She didn't? She stayed? She forgave him?" Alyson sat up, her questions tumbling out one after the other as her hands pressed against Jamie's chest. "I didn't ruin it? I-I didn't make her angry?"

"Aly, you never ruined anything. What happened was never your fault."

"B-but I... I didn't... ruin it?"

"No, Aly. It's all good."

"I d-didn't... I didn't ruin it!"

"Shh, now, love." Jamie caught Alyson as she fell into his arms again. He leaned his cheek against the top of her head and held her. "Shh, it's all right."

"I-I w-was so afraid..." Alyson stuttered over her words as she cried. "I was s-so afraid I had ruined it. Th-they were s-so in love."

"No, Aly. You didn't ruin anything. You're good, love. You're so good." The words caught at Jamie's heart, and he tightened his arms around her. He hoped that maybe the burden she carried on her shoulders would feel a bit lighter now. "You're perfect, Aly. Shh."

The sniffling and tears stopped slowly, and Alyson sat up, hurriedly wiping away the last of her tears. She motioned to the stain of tears on Jamie's shoulder and frowned.

"Why do I have shoulders if I don't let people cry on them when they need to?" The words came with a crooked smile and a kind tone.

"Thank you." Alyson nodded. "Thank you for everything."

"Nah, don't mention it. There's nothing I'd rather be doing than taking care of you."

Alyson smiled and gave a tiny chuckle.

"You still feeling okay? No fever?"

"Mmm." Alyson nodded and laid her head against the back of the chair.

"I was worried about you today."

"I rested a lot. Feeling much better."

"And this guy?" Jamie's grin went soppy as he looked down at Alyson's stomach, reaching forward with his hands. He saw her shift in the chair, bringing her belly closer for him to touch. He caught the expression of delight on her face out of the corner of his eye. "How are you, little one? We made it, eh? We made it safe and sound to London, yeah?"

"Did you know Bambi can probably hear you now?" A bit of trivia she had read online one night when she couldn't sleep floated back into her memory. "They start at the beginning of the second trimester."

"Do you think?" Jamie's hands gripped a little harder as he looked Alyson in the eye. She nodded and smiled at him. "Well, then, I guess I'll have to be careful what I say and make sure I talk to you as often as I can, eh Bambi? Make sure I tell you every day how beautiful your mum is, and how much I can't wait to see you."

His hands rubbed gently over the small bump as he spoke. One day the baby hidden in Alyson's womb would be born. He would see the little ears that were listening to him right then, and watch tiny fists open and close, and eyes squint against the light.

"Wow," Jamie breathed.

"Hmmm?" Green eyes blinked at him slowly, close enough to see the dark circles jet lag had painted under his eyes.

"Just thinking, is all." Jamie gave the baby one more caress, then sat up. He thought about trying to put the feeling of excited butterflies into words, but then decided against it. Words wouldn't do it justice.

"Did you remember to tell Danielle that we arrived safely?"

"I did. She threatened to have you give me a high kick to the face if I didn't, and I can't risk something like that."

Alyson snickered softly at Jamie's words.

"She has used the high-kick-to-the-face threat more than once. I think that's her favorite way to remind me that she'll never trust me."

"She trusts you enough, but... not with everything. She doesn't know you like I do..."

She doesn't know you like I do...

Jamie didn't even hear the rest of Alyson's words after that, his mind focusing in on that one powerful phrase.

She doesn't know you like I do...

He stared affectionately at her, watching her mouth move and hearing nothing, his heart melting. Her cheeks flushed from a faint pink to a blazing red when she realized how fond his expression was.

"Jamie, why are you staring at me like that?" She clapped her hands over her face to hide. "You weren't even listening!"

"I'm sorry, love, I couldn't help myself." Jamie laughed at the girl as she tried to hide from him. "Stop, let me see your face!"

"No! You're just staring!"

"I can't help it! You know I adore you." Jamie continued to laugh as he struggled to get a hand under her chin to bring her to face him again. "Come on!"

"You're staring still!" Alyson peeked up at him.

"I'm sorry! I'm sorry, finish telling me what you were talking about."

Alyson's face reappeared.

"I don't remember." Alyson sighed with a little smile and shrug. "Not important."

"Well, if you remember later, you have my number in this super high-tech mobile I brought you earlier today."

"You mean, this one?" Alyson reached over the back of the chair for the cellphone that was on the bedside table. "This flip phone that can't even take pictures?"

"That's the one! It is the very highest technology available. Nothing but the best for you," Jamie nodded seriously.

"I am flattered."

Their smiles gradually died out and they shared a look, one that said they knew their conversation was over, but they didn't want to say goodbye. Not yet. It was like their Skype calls, except instead of wishing he could reach out and touch her, he actually could. A thrill ran down into his stomach, and Jamie swallowed hard.

"I'm happy you're going to be close to me."

The corners of Alyson's mouth pushed up into a smile, and she dipped her head down bashfully. That shy expression killed him all over again.

"I guess I'll let you go to sleep." Jamie stood to his feet. He was surprised when she slipped her hand into his and had him help her to her feet as well. She wrapped her arms around his chest easily and leaned her head against his shoulder. Jamie's arms folded around her deliberately, wanting to drink in the moment, the memory. He wanted to remember that time, just as Alyson had remembered the way he had touched her body before they made love.

"Good night, Jamie," she whispered, her breath sinking through the fabric of his shirt and warming his skin.

"Good night, love." He didn't dare breathe, wanting the moment to be perfect.

Alyson said nothing as she stepped back, allowing him to let his fingers trail down the length of her arms and grasp at her hands. She smiled, tugged her hands free and gave him a little wave. That's when he realized what she was doing: letting him get the last word.

On Alyson's first day of work, Jamie went into the school office to talk to "Fran." He didn't know anything about "Fran", except that she could answer all of his questions, and her name was Fran. He walked into the office and saw an old, wrinkled woman with thick glasses and thinning white hair. She was scowling and didn't look happy to help, but Jamie stepped up bravely. He was genuinely intimidated by the elderly lady, yet a bit curious as to why she was still working there when she could have retired years ago.

"Hi, Fran, I'm Jamie Donald. My assistant and I have been in touch with you for the past few weeks. I'm just checking that all the paperwork for Alyson, the new teacher, was processed correctly." He stood nervously by the tall desk that surrounded her work space.

"The new teacher?" Fran looked over the top of her glasses and clicked a few things, her nicely manicured nails tapped on the keyboard as she stared at her computer screen. "Yes, I have everything for Amanda."

"Wait, no, Alyson. Alyson Ab..." Jamie stopped and looked over his shoulder before he said her last name. "Abidi."

"Yes. All of Amanda's paperwork is in." Fran looked in Jamie's direction.

"Is there more than one new teacher?" Jamie's brow was furrowed and a sweat began forming on his forehead. "Because I'm talking about *Alyson*..."

"And I told you that it was all taken care of."

"We're not talking about the same person!"

"She's the teacher from Des Moines, Iowa? Twenty-two years old? Recommended by a fancy celebrity to work here through his charity?" Fran shot back, rolling her eyes with each question. "Is that who you're talking about?"

"Yes! Yes, that's her! But her name is Alyson!" Jamie smiled with relief.

"Yes, I know. Everything for Amanda is fine. Do you have any other questions?"

Jamie didn't know what to say. He was clearly talking about the same person as the lady behind the desk was, but she refused to say the actual name. With a tight smile and a furrowed brow, Jamie nodded and turned to leave.

He popped into the classroom where Alyson was teaching and watched her from a spot in the back. She looked so confident, completely in control and totally unaffected by the fact that this was her first day on the job. Several minutes passed with Jamie leaning against the table in the back before she noticed him. Her cheeks flamed into a crimson color, and she tripped over her words for the first time all day.

"Okay, everyone just read that top paragraph in the handout I gave you." Alyson quickly smoothed over her mistake. As the students bent their heads over their papers, Alyson walked quickly to the back of the room. Jamie met her half way, an apologetic smile on his face.

"Didn't mean to distract you, love. Sorry." He put a hand on her shoulder and massaged his thumb into her collar bone. "You're doing brilliantly."

"Thanks." Alyson exhaled shakily. "I'm so nervous, I already puked before this class."

"I couldn't even tell. I'm serious. You are an amazing teacher."

Alyson's mouth formed a little smile, and she nodded.

"You okay? You need anything?" Jamie noticed a few of the people in the class looking around, done with their reading. He stepped back and removed his hand from Alyson's shoulder.

"No, but you should go. I can't have you distracting me."

Jamie knew that Alyson didn't mean it in a romantic way, her pale cheeks and anxiously shifting gaze reminding him of how much pressure she was putting on herself to do this job right. He gave her one last smile and a wink before he turned away and walked out of the room. He heard Alyson start to talk again as he left. That wasn't the last time he spied on her as she taught, soaking in her passion for teaching and love of learning from the hallway. He wanted to sit in her classes and learn from her, but he didn't dare do that to the poor girl.

"Have you met Fran?" he asked a few days later. They sat in the back corner of a little sandwich shop that was a few blocks away from Alyson's apartment. It wasn't a date, but he couldn't help but smile at the fact that they were doing something normal couples did.

"Fran?" Alyson pulled her eyebrows down and cocked her head at Jamie's question. "Who is Fran?"

"She works in the office at your school. Have you met her yet?"

"The old lady who looks really angry at the world?"

"Yeah."

"No." Alyson shook her head no and picked up another chip from her plate. "Why? Have you?"

"Yeah, the other day." Jamie sat with his elbows on the table, and his chin resting against his hands. He watched Alyson eat, not sure why he found such an ordinary task fascinating when she did it. "She wouldn't stop calling you Amanda."

"Did you tell her my name was Alyson?"

"Yes, like, five times!"

"So?"

"She still calls you Amanda. She was clearly talking about you, but she called you Amanda every time I tried to correct her."

"That is very strange," Alyson hummed. "I guess there are worse names to be called."

"True."

The pair of them walked slowly back to Alyson's apartment complex, the late afternoon sun burning through gray clouds. Birds twittered from the naked branches, serenading the many people who were out enjoying the nice weather. Even the cars went at a less hurried pace, and people waved and greeted others.

"Why is it that you aren't really recognized here?" Alyson looked around, squinting her eyes when the sun's rays hit them.

"How come you aren't recognized? You live here." Jamie bumped Alyson's shoulder with his own, his hands shoved in his pockets.

"We don't want me recognized, remember?" Alyson gave him a wary look, one that said she didn't appreciate jokes about that sort of thing. "Aren't you supposed to be a big deal or something? Jamie Donald the world-famous..."

"Oh, shush!" Jamie's cheeks flushed. "I'm not that big of a deal, if we're being honest. I'm just one person in the midst of an entire industry. People don't know me if they don't like my music."

"Fair enough." Alyson kept walking. "By the way, I've heard from Tommy."

"Tommy, eh?" Jamie tried to keep his tone neutral as he said the name.

"'He's asking when I'm going to come visit London so we can hang out." Alyson gave Jamie a cautious glance.

The glance caught Jamie a bit off-guard. He knew he was the one responsible for Alyson in a lot of ways, but he couldn't treat her like a teenager begging for more freedom. He was also a bit surprised Tommy hadn't just driven up and visited her the day he came back from his parents.

"Aly, I'm not keeping you prisoner up here. You can travel to London whenever you would like. You're smart and can take care of yourself..."

"I know, but sometimes you guys get followed by paps and different places are more high-profile than others, and I respect your opinion," said Alyson. "Just staying here would be safer I think."

"Maybe." Jamie thought back to the other day when he had been photographed coming home. No one knew about the numerous trips to Bedford, but they could one day. They could turn it all into a huge nightmare.

The grocery store was their last stop before Alyson's place, and Jamie walked her back to her apartment carrying the bags of food. She let him walk up with her, promising herself that he couldn't stay for longer than it took to put the food away. It made her nervous to think about what rumors would start if people saw her with a young man going into her apartment. She needed to stay under the radar, and she didn't want to be a part of the daily gossip that happened in the cafes and pubs.

"It all looks the same in here as when you moved in," Jamie chuckled as he walked in behind Alyson, his hands full of grocery bags.

"I've only been here for a week," Alyson snorted. "I'm not sure what you're expecting me to have changed."

"Wait, what's that? That wasn't there before, the picture on the wall. Where did you find it? That's a lovely bit of work."

"The one above the couch?"

Alyson's apartment was big and white. Her building was brand new, and she was one of the few people living there. It was a third-floor apartment with the entrance opening up into the long, rectangular living-room area. To the right was a large window that overlooked the street that ran in front of the building and room for one bookshelf. The rest of the apartment was to the left. There were two bedrooms off opposite sides of the living room and a wide hallway into the dining room and kitchen area. Another bedroom and the bathroom were in the corner while the decent-sized kitchen hooked around to the right of the hallway. It was spacious, but it was also very white. The artwork in the living room wasn't colorful either, but it stood out from the rest of the furniture.

"Yeah. Is it just a pencil sketch?" Jamie leaned in closer to take a look.

"Mmhmm. My neighbor, Lucy, did it. She gave it to me as a housewarming present."

"You've met your neighbors?" Jamie stopped in his tracks. He gave her a hard look when she turned around.

"Don't look at me like that." Alyson sighed and crossed her arms over her chest. "I didn't mean to. They saw me through the window my first night here, and they came over to introduce themselves. They live across the street."

"They saw you through the window?" Jamie bit his tongue to keep from saying anything about curtains. "They came over to talk to you?"

"Yes. They saw me through the window. And I certainly didn't ask them to run across the street and knock on the door so we could become friends at half-past eleven at night," said Alyson.

"Half eleven?" Jamie's eyes widened. "Who are these people?"

"Kyle and Lucy Thornton. Newly married. Very chatty. Sweet, I guess."

"So..." Jamie finally made it into the kitchen and set the bags down on the spotless white counters.

"Don't worry, I didn't tell them hardly anything." Alyson worried her bottom lip with her teeth. "They don't know about Bambi."

The drive back to London that evening was hard for Jamie as he realized how there were some things that were completely out of his control. Alyson had a good head on her shoulders; he knew he could trust her to be smart, but he didn't trust other people to be.

Alyson stood in the kitchen next to the counter with a mixing bowl in her hand, but she had stopped stirring close to two minutes ago. It was the end of her second week at the school, and she was exhausted physically and mentally. The sound of her downstairs neighbors arriving home woke her from her trance, and she glanced at the clock on the wall. It was five o'clock in the evening exactly. Alyson took a moment to stroke her stomach and gaze in wonder at how pronounced it was becoming. It was as if someone had finally given the baby permission to grow and he was making up for lost time. Still, the belly could be seen as extra weight if she wore the right layers of clothing.

She moved around the kitchen, making herself her evening meal. It was normal to cook for herself and let the dishes pile up for a couple days as she had plenty and no one was ever going to see them. Besides the dishes, she kept things clean and tidy. A little routine had started to fall into place for her, and she clung to the regularity of her day like a scared child to her mother's hand. She would check each activity off in her mind as it was completed:

Walk to work.

Meet with the teachers.

Teach the children.

Walk home.

Sweep the living room.

Dust her bedroom.

Spray down the bathroom.

Sort her laundry.

Exercise.

Cook supper.

Wipe counters.

Plan lessons.

Sit at the table with a cup of tea and think about how she was going to do it all again the next day.

Most days she didn't need to do the same cleaning tasks again, but she did them anyway. It was a way to fill the mind-numbing, empty spaces in her day that would not disappear. Even with all the chores she completed, she would find herself staring at the clock for handfuls of minutes, begging the hands to go faster. She had to use all of her concentration to not let her mind go to dark, lonely places that would send her to the corner of her bed wrapped in a blanket that smelled like her parent's home.

Her loneliness was her own secret. No one knew how incredibly stifling it felt to shut her door behind her after work and know she wasn't going to see another human being for the rest of the day. She sang and talked to Bambi as if the baby were there to respond, her hands reaching for the middle of her stomach countless times throughout the evening. When the last of the sun disappeared, she would always pet her belly and say, "Well, Bambi, another day finished. We made it."

That evening she felt nervous as the sun slipped lower and lower. It was the weekend again, and she wouldn't have work in the morning. Jamie had left Bedford the day before and said he would be up on Monday. She knew the fear whispering down her ear was irrational, but she couldn't shake the fact that if anything happened to her that night, it could be days before anyone found her. Although, with the amount of times Lucy Thornton randomly knocked on her door, there was a chance that someone might notice if something was amiss.

As if on cue, Alyson heard the same rapid knock she had heard several times before; it was Lucy. She quickly smoothed her shirt over her stomach and grabbed her bulky sweater from the back of the chair as she went to answer the door.

"Coming!" she called, slipping her arms into the sleeves and wrapping it around her belly. She acted surprised to see Lucy on the other side of the door when she opened it. "Oh, Lucy. Hello."

"Here! I thought you might want to do some sketching to pass the time. I noticed you don't watch the telly much, and do a lot of cleaning. Thought you might want a hobby!" Lucy smiled so brightly Alyson didn't realize Lucy was holding out a stack of books to her until they were touching her hands.

"No, Lucy, I-I coul-!"

"Shush, now!" Lucy laughed and pressed the items into Alyson's grasp earnestly. "These are extras that was just sitting around going to waste."

"I don't sketch, though. I'm not an artist."

"Nonsense! It's not about being an artist, it's about expressing yourself!" Lucy poked her head into the apartment and looked around. She noticed her artwork on the wall over the couch and lit up with a smile as she pointed at it. The side of her right hand was shiny and smooth from rubbing over paper for hours a day. "D'ya like it?"

"I do! It's beautiful." Alyson looked again at the stunning piece of art that hung on her wall. "I've always loved pictures of trees."

"Really? Well, I have some more! I can bring them by and you can use them to fill up the walls. They're so empty!" Lucy pulled her head back after giving her assessment. "Or you can sketch some yourself!"

"Oh, no! Absolutely not!" Alyson laughed and rolled her eyes. "Not even a chance."

"Aw, I'm sure you could get really good with a little practice. See, I had a book on how to sketch that I added in."

"Well, thank you." Alyson finally took the gifts and held them uncertainly. "I probably won't use them, though."

"Give it a try! I'm sure you're better than you think."

There was no use trying to dissuade Lucy from her mission of making an artist out of Alyson. Alyson smiled politely and started shutting the door before Lucy could think of anything else to say.

"Wait!" Alyson opened the door again. "You said you knew I didn't watch much TV, and I do a lot of cleaning. How do you know that?"

"Oh, easy!" Lucy laughed. "We can see your living room walls from our flat, you know, and there is never a screen reflection on them like your neighbors who watch the telly non-stop. Kyle is a massive spy movie geek, so we like to practice figuring stuff out about our neighbors."

"...Really?" Alyson gulped and moved the books she was holding to cover her stomach.

"I know you're always cleaning 'cause every time I come over you're either cleaning or you've just finished. I wouldn't clean if I didn't have to, so I thought maybe you just did it to pass the time." Lucy giggled and shuffled on her feet a bit self-consciously.

"Oh..." With another nod goodbye, Alyson shut the door for good this time.

Alyson set the items down on the coffee table and wiped her hands on her shirt. The soft fabric was wet from washing potatoes for supper. She picked up the box of pencils and pulled one out. It wasn't a normal pencil; it was a special charcoal one she had seen other people who were serious artists use. She pursed her lips as she studied it.

"I shouldn't even try. I'm not good at it." Alyson ran her finger down to the tip of the pencil, letting the black mark her skin.

She left the items there and went to finish getting her supper in the oven. She glanced at the clock and sighed; it would be another forty minutes of waiting before the next thing could be crossed off her list. She wandered slowly, dragging her feet over the tiles and the fuzzy area rugs that lay around the apartment. She walked into the living room, and eyed the pile of books that sat on the coffee table.

Deciding to give it a try, Alyson took the sketch book and a pencil to the table in the dining room and sat down slowly. A look at the first page of the book on how to sketch taught her nothing. She was determined to give it a go, anyway. Her hand shook as she held the pencil over the paper, her brow furrowed in concentration. She made a line and hated it. It was too dark.

"Ugh. Aly, you don't have any right to be doing things you don't know how to do!" She tossed the pencil onto the table and leaned back in her chair.

The line on the paper stayed; a garish, ugly mark on the otherwise perfectly clean paper. Alyson felt the same feeling she had when she had sat in front of the piano for the first time and wanted to play a song perfectly, but she couldn't. Her fingers had skipped clumsily over the keys, hitting the wrong notes and nearly driving the girl mad. She watched the tutorial video on how to play the song over and over until she could do it. Until she was perfect. Then she sighed and smiled, because perfect was always the goal.

"I have to conquer this, Bambi. I have to become perfect." Alyson's eyes were resolute and sharp as she picked up the pencil and started again. Again, the same dark, ugly line ruined the perfect piece of paper, and Alyson groaned. She blamed the pregnancy hormones when a tear formed in her eye. Over and over she tried to make the picture she saw in her head, but every time she tried it didn't come out right. She closed the sketch book with a snap and pushed it away from her until it was balanced on the edge of the table.

"So stupid." Alyson raked her fingers through her hair and closed her teary eyes. "I'm twenty-two years old, I should have a grip on life."

But she knew she had no place trying to do something she wasn't perfect at. She left the table and went back into the living room. It was dark in there, the only light in the apartment came from the kitchen, but she didn't bother to turn on another lamp as she fell onto the couch with a sigh. Her whole life had been filled with the pressure to be perfect, and she had worked so hard to make sure she never came up short. In school she had been able to achieve that goal and earned the love she craved so deeply from her parents. Everything else had proven to be a lot more difficult when it came to mastering it.

"I have to be perfect." Alyson's hot tears rolled from her eyes into her hair as she lay on her back, staring up at the gray ceiling. "I-I have to be perfect."

The cry coming from inside reminded her of going to church with Danielle and squirming as the pastor said week after week, "Come just as you are!" But she wasn't perfect yet.

"You don't have to be perfect! Geez, none of us is perfect," Danielle had explained afterwards as they sat in her bedroom.

None of us is perfect...

She turned onto her side and tried to block out the words from the past. She had been avoiding God and anything that reminded her of Him. The only thing she had continued to do was pray for the safety of her baby. Bambi was perfect; surely God could answer her prayer to take care of an innocent baby.

Chapter thirteen
"It's not your fault, baby. I promise."

Avoiding dark thoughts was hard enough to do during the day, but at three a.m. Alyson realized it was impossible. She sat in her bed, a cup of tea in her hands, and the covers bunched up into a wad at her feet. This was her third cup, and like the first two, it was doing nothing to soothe her taut emotions and tense muscles. Alyson put one hand on Bambi and sighed deeply.

"What am I doing?" Alyson shook her head. "What am I even doing? I'm just some little girl who got pregnant because she was stupid. Absolutely, mind-blowingly stupid! Now I'm hiding on the other side of the world pretending to be some amazing Good Samaritan, like, why? Why? How did I even end up like this?"

She took a sip of the scalding beverage and winced. Her tongue was already burned from the previous cup she had tried to drink too quickly. Things were spiraling, and she needed to catch hold of something before she was sucked past the point of no return. She rubbed circles on her stomach, breathing in and out as deeply as she could in an attempt to stay afloat. The black cloud of thoughts pulled her lower and lower into their murky depths until she was biting the skin on the back of her hand to keep from screaming.

"No. No, Aly. No. No. Stop. You're fine. You're fine. It's okay. Stop. It's okay." Alyson's cheeks were wet with tears as she stumbled from her bedroom to the bathroom. She looked at her face in the mirror and bit her bottom lip. The teeth marks on her hand were highlighted with red. "Aly, you have to stop. You have to be okay. You have to. It's going to be okay... It's... "

The self-soothing didn't change the twisting in the pit of her stomach, and Alyson had to try a new tactic. She snatched the charcoal pencil off the kitchen table and ripped a page out of the sketch book. She tossed them onto the floor and sunk down on her knees. Blinding tears fell onto the paper, but Alyson didn't stop. Her lines were sloppy and it looked nothing like the image Alyson had in her mind, yet it somehow made her feel better that it was turning out so horribly.

"I hate this feeling! I hate it! I hate feeling so dark and alone!" Her words came through clenched teeth. "It's my own fault I hate myself! It's my own fault! I did it! I ruined my life!"

Sobs halted the heated drawing, leaving Alyson's shoulders shaking and pencil rolling across the floor and under the stove. After the frustration abated, Alyson crawled over to retrieve her pencil. It wasn't within sight or reach, so Alyson fetched a new pencil from the box that sat on the coffee table in the living room. When she returned to the kitchen, she studied her drawing and was surprised at what she saw.

"I guess I *can* draw something," she muttered under her breath.

There was the curve of a face, the halting lines of angry lips and tightly closed eyelids. It was definitely a rough sketch, but there it was; a shadow of the picture of herself she had seen in her mind. It was like an anchor pulling her into a bottomless sea of black. Black. Black and heavy. Black and heavy and...

Alyson lay down on the floor next to her drawing and swallowed a few tears as she mumbled promises that she was done crying, and she was ready to pull herself together. The cool tiles touched her cheek, and she sighed. She placed a smudged hand over the drawing, her fingers trembling as she lightly traced the outline of the face and followed the path of the black tears. Seeing the ugly perception of herself that she carried internally there on the paper, in the light, in the open, was freeing. Her eyelids fluttered to a close, and she pulled her charcoal covered hand back to her baby.

The ache in her neck woke her less than an hour later, and she groaned. Her picture greeted her with its shocking appearance, and she stared at her artwork for a moment before she heaved herself up to her feet. It was close to four in the morning, but the sky would be dark for hours still. Alyson rubbed at her neck as she shuffled slowly into the living room and stood by the window. Her eyes flitted to the window of the Thornton's apartment, relieved to find it dark and empty. Most times she would see a smiling Lucy or a scowling Kyle. She wasn't sure if the scowl was because of her or something else.

"You okay, Bambi?" Alyson looked down at her baby and caressed her womb gently. "I'm sorry I was so upset tonight. It's not your fault, baby. I promise. I love you so much, Bambi. I love you so..."

The lump crowded into her throat, and Alyson couldn't finish her sentence. There were smears of black on her skin from the charcoal pencil when she removed her hands and turned away from the window. She thought about washing them off, but decided to get her phone from her bedroom first. There was nothing to check, of course, but she felt better knowing that she had it in her hand.

Her thoughts went to Eddie. Just like Jamie had told her while they were in California, Eddie really didn't have a sleeping schedule. During her stay with him, it didn't matter what time she woke up or how quiet she tried to be, he would always poke his head out from his room, or the den, or the kitchen, and ask if she was okay within minutes of her getting out of bed.

His soft, calming voice had been like medicine during that first transitional week in London. There was no time of the day or night she hadn't been able to tell him how she was truly feeling and have his complete attention. Alyson's heart grabbed onto the need to hear him tell her she was going to be okay, even after a night like the one she had just endured. She sent him a text to ask if he was awake and left the phone on the kitchen table so she could wash her hands, her stomach, her neck, her face...

The sound of her phone ringing seemed deafeningly loud in the quiet apartment. Alyson jumped and dashed out of the bathroom as quickly as she could to answer it, a trail of water dripping behind her.

"Hello?" She pressed the phone against her ear with her wet hands.

"Aly! Hello!" Eddie's voice rumbled, sounding a little raspy, but mostly happy. "Are you up early, or still awake?"

"Both?" Alyson gave a little half-hearted laugh. It felt good to hear a voice that didn't belong to herself. She looked down at her drawing and frowned.

"Are you okay? What's wrong? Have you run out of chips and salsa?"

"I, uh... I mean..." Alyson kicked at the floor as her tongue stuck on words. "Just..."

"Do you need someone to come up and be with you?"

Alyson hadn't seen Eddie since she left London to move into her apartment. Jamie had been the one to make the trip back and forth, taking care of everything and spending time with her. It had been nice to have him there when she needed someone, but she missed Eddie. They had fallen into a rhythm of friendship that seemed almost too easy. His voice sounded like a warm blanket, and she wanted to wrap up in it and let it put her to sleep.

"Please." The word left her mouth before she could convince herself to say no.

"Of course, love. I'm leaving right away." Gentle. That's how Alyson would describe his tone. It was always gentle.

Alyson put the phone back down and let out a shaky breath. There were welts on the back of her hand from where she had bit it earlier. It hurt when she pressed against them. She would probably have a bruise there. She picked up her drawing and stared at it for a moment. Usually she would throw away something so awful and obviously imperfect, but she needed to keep it. She walked into the nursery and looked around the room.

It was uncanny to walk in and see the crib and changing table set up with the rocking chair in the corner. Everything was white and smelled like cardboard boxes. The closet was empty, though, so Alyson opened the doors and laid the picture carefully on a shelf.

"There," she whispered as she backed away and closed the doors again. "There."

Alyson looked around the room and breathed softly. In a few months it would be filled with diapers and clothes, blankets and rattles. She could imagine a picture of the newborn babe hanging on the wall above the crib and a pink or blue blanket, depending on whether Bambi was a boy or a girl. There would be pacifiers, teething toys, baby wipes, and lullabies...

There in the corner of the nursery sat the large frame holding the lyrics to "Sweet Dreams." Jamie had had it made, saying that whether Bambi was a boy or a girl, the song would still be special. She crouched down in front of it and ran a finger over the shiny glass surface that covered the swooping calligraphy. It was beautiful, but Alyson was hesitant to put it up. She didn't know why. Something about it made it all seem so... personal. Her hand rested on her belly as she walked out of the nursery and shut the door behind her.

Eddie's knock was soft when he arrived. He slipped in quickly and quietly while Alyson peeked out into the hallway to make sure no one was around. She knew no one would be, but she needed the extra reassurance. Eddie took his jacket off and hung it on the coat rack. He was running his fingers through his hair when Alyson turned around from the door to greet him. His hands froze where they were, and his mouth dropped open.

"Aly! You look like death!" He grabbed her hands and led her over to the couch. He sat down next to her, their knees touching, and his hands holding hers until she pulled them back. "What were you thinking about?"

"I hate myself." Alyson's words tasted bitter on her tongue. She had practiced the words a hundred times as she waited for Eddie to arrive. "I don't, but I do. Under everything. It's there. This tight little ball of... hatred."

The young man didn't say a word, just listened carefully, humming out responses through closed lips. The way his brow furrowed and his eyes squinted at her told her it wasn't easy to hear what she was saying. Even so, he let Alyson rattle off every thought that came to her mind for fifteen minutes before she finally ran out words. The pressure that had threatened to explode inside of her was slowly easing up, and she breathed in deeply, feeling oxygen hit the lowest parts of her lungs for the first time since the sun left the sky. After wiping the few tears off her cheeks, she gave Eddie a half smile as a thank you.

"You feel a bit better now?" asked Eddie. He put a hand on her shoulder to give it a quick squeeze.

"I do. Thank you." Alyson hadn't mentioned the picture she had drawn that lay hidden in the next room.

"Good. Whenever I need to get something off my chest I go to Gi. My sister. She's my listening buddy."

"She sounds like a good sister." Alyson pushed up one corner of her mouth into a smile.

"She is." Eddie nodded and looked down at his hands in his lap.

Alyson let out a deep sigh, one that actually loosened a bit of the tightness in her chest. It had been too long since she was able to talk until she was completely finished. Most conversations were interrupted or too terrifying to actually be seen through to the end.

"Thanks for listening."

"That's what family is for."

The words deepened the smile on Alyson's face, and she put a hand on Eddie's arm. His presence was soothing and her body finally felt relaxed enough to drift off to sleep. Her eyelids drooped sleepily, yet she fought to stay alert. Eddie had just arrived; she didn't want him to leave. She didn't want to wake up in an empty apartment that echoed when she cried and gave no response when she ached for companionship.

"You look absolutely shattered. Please sleep." Eddie's eyes were warm as he smiled at her wide yawn.

"But... you just got here?"

"And I'll be here when you wake up."

"Really?" Alyson felt her eyes begin to close as she leaned back.

"Yes." Eddie's hand slipped from Alyson's as she laid herself out along the length of the couch. She curled up against the back, burying her face into the crevice where the back met the bottom. He tugged the blanket off the back of the couch and draped it over her. She smiled before she let herself slip away into a deep sleep.

It was a few hours later when Alyson rolled over and blinked her eyes open. She sucked in a huge breath of air that glowed with sunlight as she pointed her toes, flexing every muscle in her body. Her breath huffed out slowly, and she smiled when she rolled her head on the arm of the couch and spotted Eddie sleeping on his side on the recliner. He didn't look very comfortable, but his breathing could be heard slow and steady. She knew he was sleeping soundly.

"Bambi, he's such a good person." Alyson's eyes pricked with tears, and she shook her head. She hadn't even been awake for a full minute; she didn't want to start crying already, but thinking about how Eddie had driven an hour while it was still dark outside to come sit with her for fifteen minutes was too much for her heart without expressing it through tears. "I can't wait to see him love you."

There was no way Eddie could have been stirred by the quiet whispers from the couch, but he began to move in his sleep. He rubbed his hands over his face and flopped over onto his back. The chair wobbled a bit, and Alyson watched with a tiny smirk. His eyes opened, and he sat up.

"Good morning." The raspiness of his voice made it sound even deeper than normal. "Sleep well?"

"Mmm." Alyson nodded. "You?"

"I did, actually. Wasn't expecting that." He chuckled and ruffled his hair, pushing it back from his face. He folded the foot rest back into the chair and stood to his feet. He took long strides over to the window, letting the sunlight wash over his skin.

"Wait! Ed! Step back!" Alyson pushed off the blanket and set her feet on the floor. "Get away from the window!"

"What? Why?" Fear flashed over his face as he turned back to see Alyson rush over to his side, hands outstretched to push him out of sight. "What's wrong?"

"Lucy might see you!" Alyson peered cautiously through the window over at her neighbor's apartment. She knew it was late enough in the morning that they could be awake, but she didn't see them. She let out her breath and relaxed her tensed muscles. "Coast is clear. They're not home."

"Who?" Eddie stepped next to Aly to see where she was looking.

"They have taken it upon themselves to welcome me into the neighborhood, so to speak. At least Lucy has," Alyson told Eddie as they walked into the kitchen and started to make tea and porridge for breakfast. "They're nice. I'm just trying to... stay anonymous."

"As long as they are nice to you, I'm not too worried about it." Eddie was pleased to hear there was another woman in Alyson's life. The sketchbook on the kitchen table caught his attention and his eyes lit up. "Is this yours? I didn't know you sketched!"

"Oh, I don't," she denied quickly. "Lucy brought it to me so I didn't have to clean so much."

"Have you done anything?" Eddie flipped open the first page and saw the single line marking it. He pointed at it with one eyebrow raised in question.

"That's all I've done." Alyson cringed, embarrassed. "I don't know how to do it."

"You just kinda..." Eddie picked up the pencil and began to use the preexisting line to start drawing a house. The nib of the pencil scratched over the paper in an effortless fashion in Eddie's hand. Before Alyson knew it, he had finished his rough sketch and was smiling at it. "See?"

"Wow."

"You want to know who is really good at drawing? Tommy."

"Really?"

"Really. You should ask him to show you some of his stuff."

Alyson put the information in her memory and moved on. She saw Eddie staring down at the pot of porridge as it cooked on the stovetop, a tiny frown pressing at his mouth.

"What's wrong?"

"Do you feel like eating porridge? Or are you up for something a bit more hearty for our late breakfast?"

It was a rush sitting in the front seat of Eddie's little car and watching the English countryside speed past as they drove twenty minutes down the road to another town where Eddie had been many times before. She watched the green slopes flash by, mesmerized by the unfamiliarity of the fields and hills. Eddie glanced over at his passenger and smiled. This was the town where his gran lived, he explained. He was going to be moving in with her for a few months, and he would be closer to Bedford.

"Knowing how to get here from Bedford is a good idea, just in case," Eddie explained. "Plus, there is an amazing fish and chips shop near my gran's."

The atmosphere of the little shop was cheery and quaint. They slipped into a booth and soon had their piping hot food set in front of them. There was no pressure or lingering shadows as they chatted about what had happened since they saw each other last. Sunshine poured through the big front window, brightening the room and their moods.

"So; Jamie. How has it been with him?" asked Eddie, wiping his mouth with a napkin.

"Fine, I guess." Alyson shrugged. "I see him, but I don't actually really spend time with him. He stays at the bed and breakfast, and we eat lunch together in a little back room or after work at a sandwich shop near my place. Everything is very rushed and focused on the details, and paperwork, and settling in. I can't even remember the last time I hugged him."

"Hmmm. Well, I'm glad he's keeping a good eye on you."

"Yeah," she sighed.

What she had told Eddie about not remembering her last hug with Jamie was a lie, but she said it because their last hug was so long ago she could no longer smell his cologne on her sweater. It was the first night in the apartment, the place that was supposed to be her home. Everything looked and felt cold and sterile. There was nothing cozy or appealing about it to her, and she had been trying for hours not to show how disappointed she was in her new home. Her body hurt, and she was moments away from sitting on the floor and having a good cry. Jamie pulled his jacket on over his shoulders as he gave the room one last look before leaving for the night.

"Well, love. That's that. Everything is all settled." Jamie held out his hands to gesture at the now furnished and decorated apartment.

The realization that this was going to be her first time completely alone since she fled Des Moines dawned on her, and the familiar pounding of fear began hammering in her chest. Her whole body was shaking as she concentrated her gaze onto the floor.

"You're going to be great here. You'll be safe. This place is nice. I'm just down the road if you need me..." Jamie finally stopped looking around the apartment and brought his gaze back to Alyson's face. His words dropped off as he realized her lips were quivering.

"Okay." She didn't know he was staring at her. Her arms crossed over her chest, and her tears were ready to fall the moment the door closed behind her friend. "Sounds good."

"Love." The word came out so tenderly that Alyson's resolve to hold back her tears teetered for a moment, and a tear slipped past and down her flushed cheek.

She looked up slowly, her eyes glassy. His arms were open to catch her as she pressed herself against him, holding onto the edges of his jacket with desperate hands. He pressed his lips against her ear and shushed her quietly as she trembled in his arms. Alyson was afraid he would let her go before she had control over her anxiety again. She renewed her grasp on his clothes and felt her heart thundering in her ears.

"D-don't... don't..." Her breath caught in her chest.

"Shhh. Aly, shhh. I'm here." He tightened his grip around her and breathed steadily. "Just breathe, love. That's right. Steady now."

His chest pressed against her as he filled his lungs, and then emptied them. Little by little Alyson was able to match his breathing, and her heart settled slowly. Still, Jamie held her, not in a rush to release her from his arms. It wasn't until Alyson let out a long, steady breath that Jamie knew she was ready.

"I'm just down the street." He looked her straight in the eye to make sure she was listening. When she nodded, he shifted his gaze downwards, a little smile on his face. His hands left Alyson's shoulders and dropped down to her stomach. "Goodbye, little love. Take care of your mum for me. Make sure she's not scared or worried, K? I'll come check in on you in the morning, yeah? Have a good night."

Before he could stop himself, he reached up to Alyson's face and pulled her close to kiss her forehead. She blushed and looked away, but there was no more panic in her expression. The words 'I love you' were on his lips, ready to be spoken with the next breath, but she stepped back, her shoulders straight. She was fine, again, and he could leave. So he had left without another word.

Alyson rubbed her hands over her stomach as she tried to shed the memory of Jamie's hug from her mind and focus on what Eddie was saying. His gray eyes were watching her with their familiar intensity, yet he still couldn't break through the walls she built around certain things. They were her own special secrets.

"Does Lucy come around much?" Eddie was keen to talk about the mystery neighbor. "You get to chat with her, right?"

"I mean, only because I'm trying to be polite. She's nice, but they kind of scare me."

"Why? What have they done?"

"They just watch me all the time. It's unnerving to have someone come over with a sketchbook because they know you don't watch TV and you need a hobby. I'm trying to stay safe."

"Staying safe doesn't mean not meeting new people if the opportunity arises and not being able to have a chin-wag with your neighbor. I think it's nice that there is someone who can be a mate for you up here."

Eddie's desire for her to make friends was obvious. She wanted to make friends as well, but at the same time she didn't think she could bear it. What she really wanted was Danielle. She knew that no one she could meet in Bedford would come close to being as good to her as Danielle was. Still, having one or two people to keep tabs on her in case anything sketchy started happening was wise.

"I wish you could meet them so you can help me decide if they're going to be good friends. I can't just take friendships lightly, you know."

"I'd love to." His response sounded like that of an older brother. His heart thumped heavily for two beats as he saw how much she trusted him in her gaze. "You ready to go?"

With a smile and a nod, Alyson stood to her feet. She arranged her jacket over herself to cover any sign of Bambi. They walked down the street in the Saturday sun. The clouds were said to be coming in later that afternoon, but there were a few rays for the time being. Alyson soaked in their conversation as much as she did the sunlight, thankful for more time with her friend. She wished she could sit with him in her living room with a cup of tea and a CD of jazz classics playing in the background. Perhaps that would make her apartment feel more like a home; memories of whispers and laughter to fill up the blank spaces.

"Hey, Tommy is asking to join us. Would you like that?" Eddie looked up from his phone.

"Okay."

The pair returned to Eddie's car and drove the twenty minutes back to Bedford. They stopped along the way to take pictures on the side of the road at a particularly pretty spot. Alyson hadn't thought to take pictures for a while, paranoid that they would fall into the wrong hands, but Eddie insisted it was important.

"Think of how much you'll want to remember this five years from now." His smile was big as he reached out his arm to fit them both in the frame of the Nikon camera he had with him in his bag. "I know I'll want to remember spending my Saturdays taking care of an overly-emotional pregnant girl."

Alyson couldn't mask her surprise at Eddie's words, remembering when he had said those same words by his fireplace her first day in London. She slipped her arms around the arm that was closest to her and hugged it. He looked down at her with dimples showing and nuzzled his cheek against the top of her head. It felt good to have a family.

They waited at the park down the road for Tommy to get there. Alyson was nervous to have them go into her apartment, even though there would be three of them. Sitting in a cafe or at the park wasn't the ideal situation, but that was all Alyson could offer them. It wasn't until they were greeting Tommy in front of her apartment building that a new option opened up to them.

"It's so good to see you!" Tommy refused to acknowledge Alyson's hesitancy for physical touch and wrapped his arms around her tightly, lifting her feet from the ground. "You're gorgeous in this color blue!"

"Thanks." A laugh and a tinge of red in her cheeks showed her obvious pleasure in the compliment.

"So, where are we going to do this hanging out thing?" Tommy asked once he had settled Alyson back on her feet and stepped back, a wide grin on his face.

"Aly! Hello!"

The voice belonged to Lucy Thornton. They looked over to see her running across the street towards them. Alyson stiffened, but glanced up at Eddie in time to see a smile fill his face. He stuck out his hand before Alyson could say or do anything.

"You must be Lucy!" He shook her hand heartily, smiling the whole time. "I'm Eddie, it's very nice..."

"Oh, oh! I know who you two are!" Lucy squealed excitedly, bouncing on her feet as she saw Tommy standing behind them. "You guys are legends! I've been to more than one show. You're actually Kyle's favorites, which is a massive deal."

"Really? Well, it's very nice to meet you." Tommy stepped up and shook Lucy's hand when Eddie was done. "We're just here to spend some time with Alyson."

"She's a dear friend of ours." Eddie put his hand on Tommy's shoulder, signaling for him to not say anything else. "We're happy she lives down the road from us now."

"Aly, you sly fox! You never said you were friends with blokes like this!" Lucy gave Alyson a disbelieving swat on the arm.

"Well, I did just move in." Alyson tried to read Eddie's expression, but couldn't tell if he was pleased with what he saw in Lucy or not. "They're just Tommy and Eddie to me."

"They're much more than that to Kyle, and he'll be in a right proper strop if I don't insist you guys come have tea with us! Please! Please say yes!" She clasped her hands in front of her face and smiled beseechingly.

"That's up to Alyson, really..." Tommy hadn't wanted to spend the afternoon being famous, he wanted to spend the afternoon with his friends.

"Ed?" Alyson looked up at him, knowing he knew exactly why she was directing the question to him.

"I say yes," Eddie agreed to the invitation with a smile. "We'd love to have tea with you guys."

"Oh my goodness! Really?" Lucy laughed and covered the "O" shape her mouth was making with her hands. "Oh my goodness! Let me run over quick and make sure the house is tidy, or Kyle will never forgive me. Just give me a mo'!"

Alyson was actually glad Lucy was giving them a minute to brief before they went over.

"Not a word about the baby. Please." She looked at the boys as soon as Lucy was out of earshot.

"Why?" asked Tommy.

"Just... I don't know them very well. They seem well-meaning, but they can see me through the window, and I would like to protect Bambi as much as I can for as long as I can."

"Fine," Eddie agreed easily. "No talk about Bambi."

"Safe word if things get too uncomfortable?"

"I don't know... Maybe something about the woods?" Alyson pursed her lips, thinking back to the phrase she had had with Danielle for her trip home.

"Perfect. Same goes for us. If we start talking about the woods, we know it's time to leave." Eddie nodded. "Tommy, we have to scope these people out to make sure they're going to be good friends for Aly."

It all suddenly clicked for Tommy, and his eyes lit up. This was for Alyson. He wrapped an arm around her shoulders as they walked across the street and buzzed the Thornton's apartment to be let up.

"Tell me your news! We're neighbors now!" Tommy grinned down at the girl, remembering all over again how easily she fit under his arm. "I'm sorry I didn't come up sooner, I knew you were settling in..."

"It's been busy anyway." Alyson gave him a smile. "But things should be slowing down soon. Otherwise things have been fine."

"And..." Tommy didn't say anything as he glanced down at Alyson's stomach, his eyebrows raised in question. "Good?"

"Yes." Alyson's smile filled her face as she talked about her baby. "Good."

They arrived at the second-floor apartment, and Eddie knocked for them. The visit wasn't what Alyson had been expecting- it was so much better. Tucked against Tommy with Eddie on her other side, she listened to Kyle gush about music and songs and concerts. Lucy watched her husband with adoration, her sketchbook on her lap and a short pencil in between her fingers. Alyson could imagine how many pictures that pencil had been a part of creating as she looked around the cozy little sitting room. The walls were plastered with pencil sketches of everything from a telephone booth, to cups of tea, to stunningly realistic portraits of Kyle.

The couch the three visitors were squished together on was brown and over-stuffed with an odd assortment of pillows and blankets that Kyle apologized for. He also apologized for the rag rug that covered the thin brown carpet under the scuffed up coffee table. There were five bookshelves squeezed into the moderately sized apartment, filled with books and paper.

The whole place felt warm and lived-in. Alyson found herself relaxing into the company and smiling along with the conversation.

That was the first time Alyson really looked at her neighbors. Kyle was tall and muscular, fitted with a brown sweater and tight jeans with thick gray socks on his feet, not wearing his usual choice of oxfords. He had blue eyes and sandy blonde hair tinged with red combed back from his face. There was no hint of a beard, but a picture of him on the wall showed him stroking at one thoughtfully. All of his attention was on the lads, and when the conversation shifted away from him, he was quick to bring it back to focus on something he had done or enjoyed.

Even while Alyson was deciding that Kyle was quite self-absorbed, she was taken by the quaint beauty she saw in Lucy. From the young woman's multiple piercings and well-manicured, brightly painted nails, the love of art and creativity she carried inside of her was evident for everyone to see. Several tattoos scattered over her arms and one peeked out from behind her ear when she tucked a strand of her wavy, black hair behind it. Her eyes seemed golden as they took in the present company, a happy smile playing on her bright-red lips. She would interject a laugh or joke, then look back down at her drawing and disappear from the conversation for a while.

"Let me see what you're drawing." Eddie held out his hand. "I did a bit of sketching over at Aly's earlier in the book you brought her."

"Really? Here! Have a piece of paper, show me what you did!" Lucy was practically beaming as she jumped up from the little stool she had been perched on. She pulled a stack of paper off a shelf and grabbed a cup of pencils off the window sill. Both Eddie and Tommy reached for the items with big smiles.

"Alyson, come now! You get to draw as well!" Tommy handed the girl her own paper and pencil. He had been basking in the warmth of her side pressed against him for close to an hour now, and he was already trying to figure out how many times a week he could make it up to Bedford to see her.

"Oh, no. I-I don't know how. Just ask Ed... all I managed to do last night was one line and even that looked terrible."

"Rubbish!" Eddie protested. "You just need to stop putting so much thought into it. See, watch..."

Next thing Alyson knew, she was huddled in the middle of the three artists as they told her how to draw a picture. The girl listened attentively, anxious to become perfect. None of them noticed when Kyle sighed in aggravation and left the room. When the beginnings of a tree appeared on Alyson's paper, her entire face lit up.

"Look!" She pointed at the picture her three friends were already staring at. "It's a tree! I'm drawing!"

It wasn't perfect. Not yet. But she was already determined to practice until it was perfect. They poured themselves more tea, ate a few more cookies and continued to finish their drawings. Alyson was surprised to see the sun so low in the sky when she finally asked what time it was. Two hours had passed since they arrived at the Thornton's, and they needed to leave for supper.

"This was... really nice." Alyson smiled at her hostess and saw Lucy blush delightedly. "You're an amazing artist. Thank you so much for sharing your tea with us."

"Yes, thank you," Eddie and Tommy echoed.

"We'll let you and Kyle have the rest of the evening to yourselves. We should go get some supper." Alyson glanced to her right and to her left to meet eyes with her friends. Alyson forgot how icy-blue Tommy's eyes were.

"Oh, Kyle is probably playing a video game in the bedroom." Lucy waved it off without much concern. "Stay as long as you want."

"We're very thankful for your hospitality." Eddie stood to his feet. "We'll have to do this again sometime."

"Yeah. I'm sure we will." Lucy stood to bid her guests farewell.

The smile didn't leave Alyson's face as they went back out into the cold evening and rushed across the street and into Alyson's building. She invited the boys up, willing to let them spend a little time there until they drove the short distance to Eddie's grandmother's house. Alyson was still smiling when she unlocked her door and they walked into her cold, white flat. It faded quickly, however, as she looked around and saw the things she owned that were still like strangers to her.

"Doesn't feel much like a home in here after being at the Thornton's, eh?" sighed Alyson. She bit her lip and let her shoulders sag.

"It takes time to make a place look lived-in, love. Don't give up on it quite yet." Eddie frowned. "What happened to that smile you were just wearing a second ago?"

"It's..." Alyson tried to force it back, but she knew they weren't convinced.

"No, Eddie. You have to make her laugh, like this!" Tommy grabbed Alyson by the wrist and began to spin her around in a circle while shouting out the chorus of a song.

"Tommy!" Alyson's shriek ended with laughter. She couldn't help herself.

Tommy caught her in his arms and watched her throw her head back and laugh. Eddie observed with interest and a growing smile. It was time to shed the worried and protective older brother front and become a friend. With a snap of his fingers, he moved towards the speakers that were connected to Alyson's television. He pointed at them as he pulled his phone out of his pocket.

"I know exactly what song to listen to as we make supper! You guys get started, I'll put the music on."

Tommy was following Alyson towards the kitchen when the open door of the nursery caught his eye. He spotted the crib and slipped his hand off Alyson's shoulder. Alyson stood in the doorway, watching him walk reverently into the middle of the room. She looked up when Eddie came to stand next to her, his phone in his hand. They shared a little smile and turned back to watch Tommy.

His hand ran gently over the edge of the crib, then he turned slowly and touched the soft padding on the top of the changing table. He looked down at the thick, fuzzy rug that warmed the floor, then over to the window, drinking in every detail he saw.

"Do you like it?" asked Alyson.

"Yeah, it's great." Tommy sounded breathless as he spoke. "It's just hitting me how real it is is all"

"Hmmm." Eddie nodded, but said nothing.

"There's gonna be a real baby sleeping in this crib and waking up to the sunshine and the birds outside the window. He'll be rocked to sleep in the rocking chair, and have his nappies changed over there, and play on this rug..." Tommy pointed to each item as he named it. He gave a short laugh and shook his head while placing his hands on his hips. "Wow. It's mental."

"Yeah." The mother's own hands went to her stomach. Bambi. Her baby.

Tommy looked over at Alyson at the entrance of the room and stared for a moment. She was framed by the doorway, and her hair slipped over her shoulder as she looked down at her swollen midsection. She was beautiful.

"Bambi is going to be a lucky baby to have such a wonderful mum," Tommy spoke gently as he walked over to Alyson.

She scoffed and stepped back. It was the only response she could think of besides standing there and blushing like an idiot. Tommy walked out of the nursery, and Alyson closed the door behind him.

Soon the mood of the evening was soaring and they were snapping their fingers along to some oldies while they prepared toppings for tacos. Alyson and Tommy were washing the dishes after supper when Eddie disappeared. Alyson found him later in the nursery.

The light was off, and he was standing over the crib, looking down as if a baby was sleeping there. She watched his dim outline, Tommy's humming from the kitchen still audible. A few moments passed, yet Eddie remained motionless where he stood.

"What's wrong?" She felt the need to whisper and tiptoe as she joined him in the dark room.

"Hmm." Eddie turned to look down at her as she joined him by the side of the crib. "Just thinking about you and Bambi."

"What about us?"

"Does it scare you?" Eddie turned to look down at Alyson.

"All the time."

"But you're so excited to be a mum..."

"I am excited. I can't wait to be a mom, but I've never been one before." Alyson was staring down into the crib now, trying to imagine her baby laying there all tiny and warm, wrapped in a blanket and breathing softly as he or she slept. "There are parenting books, but every child and parent is different. You don't know what it's going to be like until it happens and then it's just... life. You don't have a chance to practice it, and you can't have re-do's. If you mess up, you mess up, and you can try to fix things, but not everything is fixable in the end. If you can't fix it, it will just always be broken..."

Eddie watched Alyson's shadowed profile as she spoke. It was hard to make out her expression in the dark room, but he could see the concentrated furrow in her brow as she put her feelings into words.

"You're going to be a great mum," he said sincerely.

"It's going to be hard being a mom on my own." She let out another sigh.

He watched her step back from the crib and turn towards the door. A moment later he heard Tommy's boisterous laugh, and Alyson's giggle reached him from the kitchen. He listened to his friends as he stood in the shadows, his hands still gripping the side of the crib.

Eddie stayed in the nursery until Tommy rapped his knuckles on the door and told him it was time to head out for the evening. The young men gave Alyson hugs goodbye and left. Alyson watched from the window, seeing them laugh and stand in the street talking for a minute before they climbed into their cars and drove away. Her eyes moved to the Thornton's window and she saw Lucy standing there, a mug in her hands and a small smile on her lips. She noticed when Alyson spotted her and waved. Alyson gave a little chuckle as she waved back, then stepped away from the window.

It surprised Alyson to find that her apartment didn't feel as empty as she thought it would after Eddie and Tommy left. There was the lingering smell of their bodies and clothes in the kitchen, and she could almost hear them singing, their eyes locked and wild grins on their faces as they belted out their favorite part of "Stand By Me" in perfect harmony. They were so familiar with each other; a single word or glance could make the other burst out laughing.

She wondered if the neighbors had heard them, but Alyson didn't care as much as she thought she would. The white walls and floors seemed a little less cold now that the voices of her friends had echoed off them, and Alyson would do it all over again if given the choice. She was tired of feeling like her home was a stranger to her.

Alyson switched off the lights in the kitchen as she came back through after using the bathroom. She paused by the door of the nursery and pushed it open. She peered in and pulled at her lip with her thumb and forefinger. Seeing the crib and rocking chair didn't really faze her, at least not as much as it seemed to have done to the two young men who had spent the evening there. Maybe it was because Bambi was already so real to her, her body physically growing around the tiny babe.

She walked into the nursery and opened the closet doors. She pulled out her picture and looked at it for a minute. There were smudges and smears from tears all over, but she liked it. It was rare that she let herself feel things honestly, and this was a tangible piece of honesty.

After putting the picture back in its hiding spot, Alyson grabbed her pencils and sketchbook and settled in bed. Thirty minutes later she inspected her work; the face of a child with wide eyes and wisps of hair on the round head. The mouth was crooked and the ears lopsided, but she couldn't get the sides to match no matter how hard she tried. The next time she saw Lucy she would ask her to help her learn how to sketch faces. She chuckled lightly as she imagined telling Danielle she was an artist now.

"She would laugh at me in my face." Alyson rubbed her stomach, pulling her shirt up to reveal her bare skin. "But then she would beg me to show her, and she would be so proud of me even though we both know it's a stupid picture."

Alyson stroked her belly and stared off into the distance, a lump forming in her throat as she imagined her best friend talking to her about her new hobby. A tear formed in her eye, and she pressed it away.

"She has always been so good to me, Bambi. She's the best person I've ever known."

One day her child would know that, Alyson vowed. Her child would know Danielle and how much Danielle loved them. As Alyson went to sleep that night, she sent a text to Jamie's phone, asking to be able to talk to her friend somehow when he came up on Monday. No reply came, and Alyson frowned as she slid her phone under her pillow.

"Good night, Bambi. We made it through another day."

Alyson was surprised when she spotted Jamie outside of the school as she left on Monday. She had stayed late to meet one-on-one with an intern that was in her classes.

"Hey, love." His smile brightened his face, and he lifted his sunglasses to settle them on the top of his head as she hurried over to him. "You have a good day?"

"What are you doing here? I thought you weren't coming until closer to supper time."

"I thought I'd come a bit earlier so you could have a chat with Elle," Jamie chuckled. "She'll be waiting for you to call her on my phone when you get home."

"Are you serious?"

"I'll give you guys about an hour, or so. Danielle said she couldn't talk more than that 'cause she has class this morning."

Alyson was so overwhelmed with gratitude she didn't think twice about wrapping her arms around Jamie's neck and hugging him tightly. He responded quickly, soaking in their embrace. Neither of them said it, but they missed being able to show each other how much they cared with simple touches and gestures.

"Thank you so, *so* much!" Alyson held Jamie's phone in her hands and fidgeted excitedly, anxious to go home and start talking to her best friend.

"Well, off you go." Jamie put a hand on Alyson's arm quick before nodding her away. "Passcode on my phone is my birthday."

"Got it! Bye!" Alyson took off at a fast pace, her breath freezing and drifting behind her in white clouds.

The three blocks between Alyson and her apartment passed quickly, and soon she was bounding up the stairs, taking them two at a time to reach her apartment. She threw her things down on the couch and tried to wriggle out of her jacket as she typed in the passcode.

"Come on, come on!" Alyson bounced her leg in anticipation. "Answer!"

The screen changed, and there was Danielle's face smiling at her. A rush of tears filled Alyson's eyes. Danielle tried to joke about it, but her own voice was thick with emotion as she watched Alyson.

"I'm so happy to see you!" Alyson insisted as she wiped her eyes. "You have no idea! I miss you so much!"

"I can tell, seeing as you burst into tears the second you saw my face!"

"Shut up! You know I love you!" Alyson laughed and took a shaky breath. "See, all better."

"Hi!"

"Hi! I made it! We did it!"

"I know! Tell me everything! Well, not everything since I can only talk for forty-five minutes, but tell me everything!"

Alyson laughed and glanced around the apartment. Where should she start?

"Well, I'm in my new place!" She stood up and began to walk around, showing Danielle the different rooms and where she put things that she had brought from home. "This is the picture my neighbor gave me as a housewarming gift..."

"Oh, the ones that watch you from the window?"

"Wait, how did you know about that?"

"Jamie told me. I have him text me every day to tell me how you are."

"Really?" Alyson wondered what all Jamie had passed on about her. She thought about going through Jamie's texts after she was done with Danielle, but she forced the thought away. "Well, yeah, that's Lucy. She's actually really sweet. Tommy, Eddie and I went over to their house for tea on Saturday. We had a great time."

"Aw! What's she like?"

"She's married to Kyle, who I'm pretty sure loves himself more than she loves him, which is a lot, but she doesn't seem to mind. She's always smiling, very cheery and bubbly. She's a phenomenal artist. She's even started me on it." Alyson gave a shy laugh.

"Wait, started on what? Like, painting?"

"No, sketching with a pencil. Simple stuff."

"Do you enjoy it?"

"I do. I... I mean, it's something to fill the time."

"That's good. Jamie said you don't do much besides work and stay at the apartment."

"Basically." Again with Jamie talking to her best friend more than she did.

"Show me a picture you've drawn."

"I'm not very good..."

"Show me!"

"Okay, fine. They're in the nursery." Alyson crossed the apartment to get the pictures she had hidden in the closet. She pulled out the picture of the baby. "See, it's really bad."

"It's a baby!" Danielle looked at the picture with an expression of triumph. "The face is a little lopsided, but I can totally tell what it is."

"It's not very good..."

"You just started, Aly. Don't get all caught up on being perfect."

Alyson's face heated. Her friend knew her so well.

"You'll be excellent at it before you know it. You always do."

"I'm going to have Lucy show me how to do faces. I like to draw them." Alyson put the picture back into the closet and shut the doors quietly.

"Draw my face so you can show me the next time we talk."

"I'll just have Lucy do it and tell you it was me."

"Oh! I almost forgot!" Danielle jumped up and rushed from the living room to her bedroom. "It's Balloon Bambi!"

"He's yellow now! I thought he was green."

"Well, see the thing about balloons is that you can change the color each week when you make a new one! This one is Bell Pepper Bambi."

"Looks bigger than I feel." Alyson tried to hold the phone to show her friend her stomach.

"Is Bambi growing right?" There was worry in Danielle's voice as she spoke. "The website said..."

"The last doctor said Bambi was growing. I am going for my first checkup here in Bedford on Wednesday, so I'll let you know what this doctor says after that. I'm bigger than I was before so something must be happening."

"Do you feel him or her moving yet?"

Alyson frowned and shook her head. "They say that first babies can take longer to feel."

The girls caught up on other details and reminisced over things that came to mind. It was all too short for them, but even their limited time was enough to buoy Alyson's heart for a few days. A knock on the door interrupted them.

"It's Jamie." Alyson sighed and frowned. It was time to say goodbye.

Alyson opened the door for Jamie and returned to her bedroom for a minute to end the conversation in private. She cried, even though Danielle promised to try and call again at the end of the week when she was at home for Thanksgiving. It seemed weird to think about how there would be no one celebrating that holiday there in Bedford, and Alyson would have work like normal. Jamie was standing by the couch staring at Lucy's drawing when Alyson came out of her bedroom.

"Hi, love." Jamie glanced at her red-rimmed eyes and held out his arms to her. "You okay?"

"Mmm." Alyson shrugged as she leaned against Jamie, tucking her head under his chin and holding her arms close to her body. She let out a long sigh.

"Was it a good talk?"

Alyson nodded. She let her eyes close and felt the exhaustion of the day wash over her. She felt like she could fall asleep like that, all wrapped up in Jamie's arms, his pulse beating against her forehead.

"Aly."

The tone in Jamie's voice made Alyson tense up. She opened her eyes.

"I'm starting back at work this week."

"What do you mean?" Alyson pushed away and looked up into Jamie's face. She watched him run his fingers through his hair and purse his lips thoughtfully before answering. "What's wrong? Something's wrong. I can see it in your eyes. You're sad."

"I'm not... I'm not sad, love. I'm just... It just means I won't be able to come up and see you as often as I would like."

"What do you mean?"

"I'll be working on a project for a friend pretty steadily for the next two weeks. I'll try to come up on Sunday and see you if I can, but I can't make any promises."

The line of worry on Alyson's brow deepened as she thought of what the next two weeks would look like.

"Wait, you mean... I won't see you at all when you're working?"

"I'm afraid so. We'll be putting in twelve, fourteen hour days at the studio."

"Who is going to take me to the doctor's on Wednesday?" she asked quietly.

"I'll try to get Tommy or Eddie to go with you." Jamie sighed. "But Garret... he'll need to do the signing. We're the only two on the paperwork. He won't be there *with* you, but he will have to be there."

"Okay," murmured Alyson, nodding. "I understand."

"I'll call you and tell you once everything is worked out."

Alyson nodded again.

"I'll miss you." Jamie watched the girl's face turn pink, and she looked up at him with a little smile. "I will."

"I know." Alyson rolled her lips between her teeth for a moment. "I'll miss you, too."

"I'm sure Eddie and Tommy will come keep you company if they can."

Alyson tried to put on a smile and shake off her disappointment, but it was hard. She had become used to seeing her friend every few days. She had gone without him for longer amounts of time than two weeks before; she would be fine.

"You want to go for a quick walk before I head back home?"

With a smile, Alyson bundled up and followed Jamie out of the building and down the sidewalk. They were careful to keep distance between them, having to be content with simply being in each other's company. It was foggy and gray, but they were in no rush to finish the path around the park and end their time together. They were almost to the end when a familiar voice called out to Alyson from behind an easel.

"Hi, Lucy." Alyson smiled easily at her. "You're out on a cold day."

"I love drawing in the fog, dunno why!" Lucy giggled as she spoke. "Hello! You must be another one of Alyson's famous friends."

"Jamie." The young man gave Lucy a firm handshake.

"Of course! Jamie." She gave Alyson a knowing smile.

"She met Tommy and Eddie when they were up on Saturday."

"Ah. It's nice to meet you."

"You should bring him round to tea someday. Not today, Kyle is a bit stroppy at the mo', but any other time you're both more than welcome." There was a slight flicker across Lucy's smile when she mentioned her husband, but it lasted for less than a second.

"We'd love to." Alyson nodded and resumed her walking.

"Seems nice." Jamie jerked his chin over his shoulder as they walked around the corner and out of sight of the artist.

"She's very nice. A little flighty and different than anyone I would choose to be my friend, but sweet nonetheless."

A streetlight flickered on above them as they slowed to a stop in front of Alyson's apartment building. They both knew it was time for goodbyes. Alyson swallowed hard and smiled bravely. Jamie reached forward to catch her hands with his own. They stepped together one tiny step, and their clouds of frozen breath met in the middle.

"You going to be okay, love?"

"Of course. I'll be fine. I just... I wasn't expecting it. I'm fine."

"You're lying to me." Jamie's gaze was tender as he stared down at her. "You've got tears brimming up in your eyes."

"I'm pregnant. Everything makes me cry." Alyson tried to joke them away, but one fell, warming a path down her cold cheek.

"Call me every day. I'll stop whatever I'm doing to talk for a bit. I will." Jamie tightened his hold on Alyson's hands. A car turned the corner and lit up the street with its headlights. The couple quickly stepped apart, their fingers tingling from the sudden lack of warmth.

"Okay."

Jamie waited for Alyson to walk into her building before he turned to leave and retrieve his car from the parking lot of the bed and breakfast. Alyson leaned against the inside of her door once she reached her apartment and pressed her hands over her heart. It was pounding hard. Her hands fumbled with the zipper of her jacket as she struggled to find the spot where her baby was hiding. She rubbed rhythmically, up and down, as she focused on her breaths.

"There. See, we're fine," Alyson whispered as her heart rate slowed. "We'll be fine without him for a couple weeks."

As she spoke, Alyson realized Jamie hadn't been able to say goodbye to Bambi. Panicking, she pulled out her phone and dialed his number. She quickly gushed out her reason for calling and heard Jamie chuckle softly on the other end.

"Meet me in the middle," he said.

Alyson zipped up her coat again and ran down the stairs and out into the cold. She only went one block before she saw Jamie walking towards her quickly. His face was warm, and the smile playing with the corners of his mouth made Alyson's stomach twist with butterflies.

"Bambi was cross at me, eh?" Jamie kept his hands in his pockets. There were people around, and they couldn't risk being seen doing anything that would give the baby away.

"Well, he can hear you now. I'm sure he'll miss hearing you talk."

Jamie's smile deepened as he looked down at Alyson's midsection. He brushed a hand across it in a discreet touch.

"Hiya, Bambi. I'll miss you." Jamie had to remind himself not to pull Alyson's stomach closer and hold it while he spoke. "Take care of your mum, yeah? She's going to see you on Wednesday, so be good. Give us a good picture, eh? Make sure she's safe, and that she calls me every day. Okay? I'll be back in a couple weeks."

The light shining in Alyson's eyes when Jamie was done was enough to keep Jamie warm his whole drive back to his house. The sweetness of his words was enough to keep Alyson company as she made herself supper and settled down for the evening. Her picture that night was more complicated than her others as she attempted to draw a pregnant stomach and hands holding it. She stared at it with a smile when she finished.

"Do you like it, Bambi?" she asked, rubbing her womb, accidentally marking it with charcoal. "That's you and Jamie. He loves you. He loves you so much."

Chapter fourteen
"The ache never really leaves."

Alyson waited apprehensively in her apartment. She was dressed nicely with her jacket lying over the back of the arm chair, ready to be put on as soon as it was time to go. Her sweater was thick, but not thick enough to protect her from the cold winter chill that blew through the streets of Bedford. It had been cold and rainy all day, and she wasn't looking forward to leaving her warm home.

She thought about making herself a cup of tea while she waited, but knew there wouldn't be enough time to make it properly before she had to leave. Her breath fogged up the window as she leaned forward to check the street again. No one was there yet.

A motion from across the street caught her attention, and she realized it was Lucy at the window. Lucy waved and smiled, a pencil in her hand. Alyson returned the motion, smiling tightly through nervous lips. She hoped Lucy would be gone from the window before the car came.

The minutes ticked by slowly, and Alyson picked up her pencil and sketch book to doodle as she waited. She focused on the face that was taking shape on the paper in front of her, missing the sound of footsteps approaching until someone knocked loudly on the door.

"Geez!" Alyson jumped, her pencil skittering across the page and ruining her picture. She sighed. It had been the best face she had drawn yet. "Coming."

There in the hallway outside the door stood Garret, his hands rubbing nervously on his jeans. He gave her a timid smile when she opened the door. He was wearing a leather jacket and a black beanie to stay warm. It was a look Alyson had never seen him wear before. He almost looked like a different person.

"Hi." She stared at him uncertainly.

"Are you ready?"

"Yeah."

Garret watched as she grabbed her jacket from the chair and slipped it on. They didn't say a word as they walked down the stairs and out of the building. Garret rushed ahead of her and opened the front door of his car so she could get in quickly and not stand in the rain. She looked up at the Thornton's window as Garret ran around to the driver's seat and saw a shadow pass by. She bit her lip nervously as Garret pulled away from the curb and onto the road.

Alyson pulled out her phone to pass the time as they drove in silence. She texted Jamie, telling him she was on her way to the appointment and she would tell him how it went when it was over. His response was almost immediate, signed with an "x."

She knew that Garret was capable of making sure that everything was taken care of, but she wasn't going to have a hand to hold, or someone to share a smile with when the image of her baby flashed up on the screen. It was going to be such a special moment, and she would have to experience it alone. She frowned and put her phone back into her pocket.

The doctor's visit passed quickly, the measuring and examining done with very little chit-chat. Like the previous doctor's checkup, everything was normal and, yes, Bambi was on the smaller side, but everything was still healthy.

The doctor's name was Greg Gallagher and his mustache was too thin for Alyson's liking. He pushed his wire-rimmed glasses up on his nose periodically throughout the appointment, but he seemed nice.

"You want to know if you're having a boy or a girl?" asked the sonogram technician.

"No, thank you."

"I guess we're done then."

"C-can you... do you print off pictures of the baby from the ultrasound?"

He obliged with a grunt.

Alyson was just sitting up on the examination table when Garret was ushered into the room. He kept his eyes on the nurse who brought him in, his jacket unzipped and his beanie shoved into one of the pockets. They were talking about papers and confidentiality agreements, who was going to be in charge of what, and who would be calling to set up the next checkup.

Alyson wasn't sure what she was supposed to do next. She picked up her things from the floor and stood awkwardly to the side. Dr. Greg and Garret were joined by three nurses in their conversation. It was strange to hear them talk about her and Bambi, yet have no part of the details or discussion. She didn't understand most of what they were saying, but she did understand that Garret was very adamant that everyone who worked with Alyson sign a certain document. The medical professionals agreed easily and after a few minutes, everything was done.

"Ready?" Garret finally turned to look at Alyson.

Sometimes it still took Alyson by surprise to see such a clear expression on his face. No more shadows. She gave him a nod and stepped forward.

They walked down the hall silently, the carpet muting their steps.

"Oh, blast." Garret stopped in his tracks and smacked his hand against his forehead, surprising Alyson who had let herself become lost in her thoughts. "I forgot to call the taxi man to have him waiting for you when we were done."

"Oh." Alyson stood, not sure what else to say. "I'm taking a taxi?"

"Just as a precaution to keep as many people from seeing me around your apartment as possible. My car is a bit obvious, not like the old banger Eddie likes to cruise around in. Most people are getting off work about now, as well. Much more traffic."

It made sense. Alyson nodded. She didn't care if she rode with Garret or in a taxi; all she wanted to do was go home.

Garret put his cellphone up to his ear and waited for the taxi driver to answer. There were several times thrown around before Garret finally told the man "thank you" and hung up. Alyson walked quickly behind Garret as he led them back out to the waiting area.

"The man said he could get here in half an hour. Is that okay?"

It would take that long just to walk home. Alyson nodded slowly. Garret pointed to a couple empty chairs that were in the corner of the waiting room, and they sat down. Garret pulled out his phone and began typing up a message. Alyson didn't mean to see that it was to Serenity. She wondered what Garret was telling her, if he was telling her he was going to be home late, or that he was glad the day was almost over, or that he missed her.

Alyson pondered what it would be like to see Serenity again. She didn't actually want to see her; the guilt of the what-ifs was heavy enough without looking her in the eye. If Serenity ever found out that Alyson was the girl, she would hate her for sure. Alyson sat up straighter in her chair and looked away.

"So, everything good with the baby?" Garret put his phone back into his pocket and glanced over at Alyson.

"Yeah, all good." Alyson smiled and put a hand on her stomach. "Very glad to have the doctor tell me Bambi is still growing."

"You worried about it?"

The note of concern in Garret's voice as he asked the question took Alyson off-guard, and she stole a look in his direction. He blinked when their eyes met, and he turned to gaze down at his feet.

"I think..." Alyson licked her lips. "I think it's normal for every mom to worry about their baby. There are a lot of things that can go wrong."

"True." Garret kept his gaze on the floor.

Alyson wondered if waiting with her for the taxi was ruining any of his plans for the evening. She felt bad for taking up more of his time because he was trying to protect her cover.

"I can... I can wait by myself."

"Do you want to?" Garret looked back over at the girl. "Yeah, I'll go if you'd rather not be here with me. I'll stand out and wait for the taxi. That way you can stay where it's warm while you wait."

"Oh, I don't mean that! I just don't want to take up anymore of your time."

"Nonsense. I don't mind waiting with you at all."

Garret waited for Alyson to tell him what she wanted him to do. Alyson shifted self-consciously in her seat and pressed her feet flat against the floor to keep them from tapping nervously.

"I'd rather not wait by myself."

"Okay." Garret nodded understandingly. He sat back and settled in for their wait.

"Do you mind doing something for me?"

"Course not."

"Can you send pictures of the baby to the boys for me? My phone doesn't have a camera." She held out the strip of black and white images and laid them across her lap so Garret could get a good snapshot of them. Her mind clung to the in-and-out of her lungs while he willingly obliged her request.

"I figured they would probably want to see them..."

"They will, I'm sure of it. They're all over the moon about Bamb-..." Garret caught himself, but not soon enough. "I mean, the baby."

Alyson nodded and looked down at the pictures. She touched the outline of Bambi's profile, chills resting on her skin. The sound of the heartbeat still rushed through her mind as she studied the tiny hands and feet that showed fingers and toes. A tiny ear on the side of the round head was also visible, making Alyson smile without even trying. Her baby was perfect.

"So, are you, uh, going to, um, do anything special tomorrow?" Garret adjusted in his chair.

"What do you mean?"

"Thanksgiving."

He was the only one who had remembered. She smiled sadly and looked past Garret towards the exit where she could see the rain pounding the pavement. Her thoughts carried her hundreds of miles away to the great, wide Midwest and her mother's kitchen. She could almost smell the turkey and stuffing, along with the dinner rolls all golden brown and steaming hot, ready to melt butter the instant it touched the fluffy insides. Her dad would make sure they had plenty of firewood so they could play card games by the fireplace, and Casson would whine under the table for scraps.

"No." Alyson shook her head. "No point. I'm not going to be with my parents so..."

Garret's mouth set into a thin line at Alyson's words, and he rubbed one hand through his hair. He nodded and glanced around the room, trying to find something to focus on. When he looked back at Alyson, she noticed his eyes were wet.

"Holidays without your family are hard." His voice was steady. Strong. If Alyson wasn't looking at him as he spoke, she would never have guessed how emotional he was. "I'm very sorry you have to go through that."

"Me too."

They drifted back into silence, Garret's sniffling breaking into Alyson's thoughts. She wondered what had brought him to the verge of tears. She didn't know how to ask. She looked at the clock on her phone and saw there were still over fifteen minutes to wait for her taxi.

"What do you do for the holidays?" The words came out quickly, almost desperately, in an attempt to end the silence.

"Not much." Garret's voice was low. "Spend time with Ren and her family."

"Do you not like Christmas?"

"Love Christmas..." Garret spoke gruffly. "Just not the same now that... uh, my parents..."

Alyson's eyes grew wide as she watched Garret wipe a tear from his face. He pinched the bridge of his nose and sucked in his cheeks. Another tear slipped down his face. He pulled in a shaky breath and held it in a long time before he exhaled slowly.

"Garret, I'm sorry."

The young man shook his head, dismissing her apology, still struggling to compose himself.

"I didn't know."

"Not your fault." Garret straightened and took a deep breath. "Still getting used to missing them. Three years... it's an eternity some days, and just like yesterday on others."

"I'm so sorry."

"It's fine. I didn't mean to get all emotional on you. You didn't ask to hear about my life..." Garret mumbled, rubbing his hands over his face and scratching at his chin.

"I'm glad you told me." Alyson watched Garret and felt her heart fill with compassion for him. "It's nice to know something about you…"

Garret looked over at the girl sitting next to him and nodded in understanding. She saw his eyes; they were so clear and sad, and suddenly he was human. He was more than one summer night of drunken mistakes. He had a past, and a story. There were tears in his journey, and there were whispers of broken dreams that echoed in the back of his mind. Alyson knew what that felt like.

"I, uh, I've lost someone close to me, too. The ache never really leaves." Alyson looked away as she thought about her brother.

"I know."

The silence that stretched between them wasn't uncomfortable this time. It was almost like they were communicating words no one could say, but they could both understand. They had both had people snatched away from them by the cruel hand of fate.

"It happened, um, during Jay's first proper tour in North America. The one where we opened for *The Windy Cities*."

Alyson held her breath as she realized Garret was sharing the story with her. She listened quietly and carefully, her hands settling on her stomach. Garret leaned forward to rest his elbows on his knees as he focused on the floor between his feet.

"I hadn't been home in months and, uh, I hadn't seen them since I left."

A tear slipped down Alyson's cheek. She knew it was more than just her pregnancy hormones giving her empathy for the young man.

"No one knew what had happened, just said they were gone and I had to come back as quick as I could. I was a mess. Jamie almost called off the whole tour for me, but I wouldn't let him. He flew in for the funeral two days later and when he went back to the States for the rest of the tour, I went with him. I just… I didn't know what else to do. He's my best mate and being busy sounded better than sitting in an empty house."

"Yeah." Alyson nodded.

"Grief is a funny thing. It'll mess with your head, that's for sure." Garret sighed and straightened in his chair as he ran his hands through his hair. "Sorry. I don't know if you wanted to hear that or not."

"It's fine." Alyson gave him a little smile and wiped her eyes. "I came home from dance class when I was eight, and, uh, and my parents told me my brother was gone for a little while. He wasn't dead, just gone. But for me it felt like he was. He wasn't there. I couldn't talk to him. I-I didn't know why he had left. I didn't get to say goodbye. And he never… he nev…"

A lump in her throat caught the rest of Alyson's words, and Garret didn't move to look at her as she shed quiet tears. Again, their silence spoke volumes to one another. They shared a quick look after a few minutes and nodded solemnly. This was the beginning of a friendship.

Garret stayed with Alyson until the taxi driver came. He gave her money for the ride home and watched them pull away before getting into his car and driving back to London.

Alyson sat at the dining room table that evening with a cup of tea and her sketchbook open in front of her. She tried to draw Bambi or herself, but all she could think of was Garret. She didn't want to draw his face, she wanted to draw what hearing his words had made her feel. Her breath came out through her nose as she stared at the paper, trying to get an image for her feeling. An idea came to her, and she started scratching away at the paper with her pencil.

As she drew she thought about how hard it was to get a phone call from the other side of the world telling you your family was gone. Garret hadn't mentioned any siblings, so she assumed he was completely on his own now.

Who did he talk to when he was having a bad day? What about when he wanted to remember something from his past? Did he have anyone to tell him they were proud of him when he did a good job, or that he could try again and they still loved him even though he messed something up? Who was there for him when he felt sick, or down, or confused?

"To be left without a mom..." Alyson murmured gently as she rubbed her baby. "I can't imagine having to leave you one day without anyone to take care of you."

Alyson called Jamie that night. She could tell he was still in the studio from the muffled sounds behind him, but his voice was light. He was happy to hear from her.

"Garret's parents died, Jay," she said as a greeting.

"I know, Aly." Jamie's tone immediately turned serious.

"He said it happened during your tour." The girl heard Jamie breathe in sharply in response to her words. "Said you wanted to cancel the tour for him."

"Yeah. It was... rough." Rough. Just like his voice in that moment. "He doesn't tell many people, Aly. It's a big deal that he told you."

Alyson breathed deeply. She thought about telling Jamie how she shared about Amir, but didn't. Her feet moved slowly as she made her way from the kitchen to her bedroom. Exhaustion ached in her very bones. She lay down on her bed and closed her eyes without turning on the light.

"You there?" asked Jamie when there was nothing but silence for a minute.

"Yeah, I"m here." Her voice was low and slurred.

"What are you doing, love?"

"Nothing."

"Are you about to fall asleep on me?"

"Mmmm."

Jamie laughed. He knew that sound.

"Just resting my eyes..."

"You should sleep. You've got work tomorrow."

"But I like hearing your voice."

"Climb into bed, Aly. I'll wait until you're asleep to hang up." Jamie's voice was gentle, and a whoosh of butterflies washed all the way down into her toes.

"Thanks." A yawn escaped her as she slipped under the blankets and snuggled down. "Tell me about you."

"Well, just working in the studio. Only got three hours of sleep yesterday before I came back in." Jamie stretched as he spoke, trying to relax his tense muscles. "But it's been great being up in the studio again. I love it."

"Are you singing for this friend?"

"Yeah, singing and writing. A little bit of piano, but don't tell anyone. My name's not even going to be on the album for it."

"Why is it such..." Another yawn interrupted the girl. "Such a big secret?"

"Maybe I'll tell you one day," said Jamie lightly. He didn't know if Alyson could hear the guys pounding on the window behind him, urging him to hurry up with his phone call and get back to work. "I still need to get you a piano for your place. I haven't forgotten."

"Mmm. Yeah."

"Maybe that will be your Christmas present."

"Don't tell me... presents are surpri-..."

"Fine, I'll get you something else."

"Mmkay."

Jamie paused for a moment to take in the steady breathing coming from the other end of the phone. He couldn't tell if she was already asleep or not.

"Thanks for the pictures of Bambi."

No answer.

"You there, love?"

Again, all he heard was her soft breaths as she slept.

"Love you, Aly," he whispered quietly. "Good night."

Alyson smiled. The phone clicked off, and she slipped the phone down from her ear and pushed it under her pillow.

Alyson stood in the gently falling rain, the cold wind kissing her cheeks. Her hand was on the handle of Tommy's car, and turmoil twisted viciously in the pit of her stomach. She looked away from the shadowy outline in the second-story apartment window, and glanced at Tommy and Eddie. They were watching her expectantly; this decision was for her to make, not them. She didn't want to make the decision. She wanted them to, so if it turned out to be a bad idea, she could brush the blame away and not add it to the mountain of guilt that rested between her shoulders.

She looked at her watch and sighed. It was seven in the morning; why was Lucy even awake? But there she was, standing at the window with a mug in her hands and her eyes begging them like a little puppy to take her along with them.

"It's up to you, love." Eddie spread out his hands. "It's your special trip."

"Fine. She can come." Alyson threw her hands up and exhaled sharply.

"Tell her so we can get going then." Tommy turned the key in the ignition. "We'll have to drive almost two hours to get there."

With a wave towards the woman at the window, Alyson motioned for Lucy to join them. A huge smile lit up Lucy's face, and she immediately disappeared. Alyson glanced down at her stomach. She was relieved that her jacket made it almost impossible to discern what was her thick coat and what was Bambi.

"Same safe word?" asked Eddie as they waited for Lucy to join them.

"Oh, yeah. Woods, right? Sounds good." Tommy nodded. "No talking about Bambi again?"

The mother nodded. She was already second-guessing her decision before Lucy even set foot out of her building. A moment later, however, the sparkle in Lucy's gold-colored eyes reassured her that she was at least making one person happy.

"Thanks so much for inviting me to come along! We going for a hike or something?"

"Box hill. Ever been?" Tommy spoke up from the driver's seat. Eddie sat beside him as co-pilot while the girls sat in the back, their bags creating a wall between them. "Might not be as fun in the rain, but Alyson doesn't get much time off to visit things."

"In the rain is the best!" Lucy insisted. "Do a little drawing in the fog."

"Did you bring pencil and paper?" Alyson eyed Lucy's bag as she spoke.

"Yeah! And a tin of biscuits, and a couple CDs we have laying around. Don't use 'em anymore since we have iPhones and such." Lucy pulled a few loose CDs out of her bag and handed them forward. One of the reflective objects was titled as belonging to Kyle.

"Did Kyle not want to come with us?" asked Tommy, noting the name on the disc.

"He's not here." Lucy's voice sounded strained. "Off with the lads for a weekend trip."

"Hope they're not camping." Alyson pointed at the rain falling down from the sky.

"Oh, no. They're just in London running amuck, doing whatever it is lads do when they go for the weekend." Again, tense lines covered Lucy's face. Alyson had never seen her neighbor look like that before.

"Well, we're glad you could join us." Eddie sensed Lucy needed to hear those words as much as Alyson needed to be reminded of it.

"Yeah, we're happy to have you with us today." Alyson gave her a smile.

"It'll be nice to not spend my birthday alone after all." The blush on Lucy's cheeks matched the bashful tone in her voice.

"It's your birthday?"

"Happy birthday!"

A fuss was made over Lucy, and Alyson found herself glad of the fact that she had chosen to not be selfish that day. The glow on Lucy's face was worth it. It reminded Alyson a little bit of the life she used to live, before she had to keep everyone at an arm's length.

The mood in the car was cheery despite the heavy rainclouds above them. They shared their snacks and sang along loudly to the Spice Girls and then The Eagles as they drove. Alyson watched the window carefully, anxious to catch as many details about her new home as possible. It would probably only be a couple weeks before Bambi passed the bell pepper stage and could no longer be passed off as extra weight.

The rain had let up for the most part when they arrived at their destination, leaving the wind to blow across the open expanse of green and carry the scent of wet grass and decomposing leaves. Alyson was so excited, she almost forgot to keep her hands off her stomach after shutting the car door behind her. Lucy slung her thin satchel strap over her shoulder and linked arms with Alyson as they started off towards the top of the hill. The action surprised Alyson, but she didn't shrug away the touch. The oddly matched quartet began their walk in high spirits.

"Is this hike okay for Bambi?" Tommy blurted out before he realized what he was saying.

Lucy stopped mid-sentence in her story she had been telling Eddie. She swung her attention over to her right where Tommy and Alyson were climbing up the hill in the wet grass.

"Bambi? Did you just...?"

"Baby." Alyson spoke up quickly. Loudly. Harshly. "He called me baby..."

"Wait, are you two...?"

"Used to be," Eddie jumped in.

"Yeah, we used to be together." Tommy apologized with his eyes when Alyson glanced over at him. "Still call her baby out of habit sometimes."

Lucy looked incredulous and interested at the same time. "You were together?"

"Once. For a bit." All of a sudden, Alyson could feel the California summer heat pressing against her skin as tangible as Tommy's body as she lay in the dark. His hand had found her face while his other gripped the jut of her hip bone. He ran his fingers down her cheek slowly, memorizing what she felt like in the dark.

"You used to date Tommy Noel?" Lucy stopped in her tracks, her mouth hanging open. "You make it sound so casual like!"

Alyson shrugged and cleared her throat.

"But wait, you guys are still friends? Even after splitting up?"

"Yeah, why wouldn't we be friends?" Tommy shoved his hands further into the pockets of his coat. "We still care about each other, we just knew it was, you know, for the best to go back to being friends."

"I thought I could see something between you two! I knew it!" Lucy turned to look back up the hill, never stopping or slowing her pace as she spoke. "I've sussed you out!"

Lucy's words made Alyson stop breathing, reminding her that appearances sometimes were everything. She felt Tommy's hand on her elbow, wrapping his fingers around her arm. She turned to look at him.

"I'm sorry," he mouthed silently.

"I know," she mouthed back with a dismissive shrug.

"How did you guys meet, anyway? I mean, how did you meet him and get him to date you?" Lucy was fascinated by her neighbor's fake love story.

"Get me to date her? You make it sound like she had to twist my arm into it!"

"Well, I, uh..." Alyson shot Tommy a look. He gave her a shrug that told her to make up whatever she wanted. "I was having a really bad night, and he helped me feel better."

There. At least that wasn't a complete lie.

"But you took me home to meet your parents, so, it wasn't just some little fling." There seemed to be another layer of meaning behind Tommy's words that Alyson chose to ignore.

"That's right! You met her parents! You told me about her dad!" Eddie's dimples were flashing as he and Tommy caught each other's eye. "He said your dad is very, uh, muscular."

"Were you scared of him?" Lucy pounced with her question before Alyson could say anything.

"Actually, he was quite intimidating, I'm not going to lie," Tommy chuckled nervously.

"So, you met Eddie through Tommy?"

"I met Eddie first." Alyson felt her head beginning to swim. She looked down at the ground to see where her feet were going.

"Eddie introduced you two?"

The questions had to stop.

"Woods!" Alyson was breathless as she spouted out the safe word. "Woods. I really... Are there woods around here?"

"Woods? You mean, like, those woods over there?" Lucy pointed beyond them.

Alyson didn't say anything, just started walking in the direction of the trees as fast as she could. The others followed behind her as she took them away from their original destination. Eddie's voice came drifting through the fog, but Alyson didn't pay attention to what he was saying. Her hands felt for her baby, anxious to touch the familiar shape and warmth. She stroked the extension of her stomach carefully to calm the pounding of her heart.

Something caught her attention out of the corner of her eye, and she dropped her hands. Tommy's apologetic smile met her vision when she turned to see who was there. He had his hands shoved into the pockets of his jacket as he fell into step with Alyson.

"Sorry about that."

"It's okay. I forget all the time at school. Thankfully no one has noticed."

"Seems like I'm really good at saying the wrong thing in front of the wrong person."

Alyson tilted her head to the side, her eyes inquisitive.

"Remember in Nebraska when I met your mum and told her you were a good kisser?"

"Oh, yeah." Alyson gave an amused laugh. "I forgot about that."

"I felt so bad. And then you were crying, and I just felt terrible."

"Don't you remember how my parents argued at supper about whether or not I should get married?" Alyson pressed her hands against her cheeks as they flooded with embarrassment. "I wanted to diiiiiiiiiieeeeeee!"

Tommy laughed at Alyson's exaggeration of the word "die" and shook his head.

"I do remember that. I also remember having to wear your dad's clothes to bed and feeling so weird."

"I'm sorry it was so awkward for you."

"Ah, don't worry about it. It was fine. I really enjoyed that weekend."

Alyson's eyes were shining when she glanced in Tommy's direction. They were walking slowly now, their companions trailing several yards behind them, chatting steadily as they followed at their leisurely pace. It was nice to feel alone with him, the wet on the ground soaking into their shoes and the sky low and close above them.

There was a smile on Tommy's face when their eyes met. It was enough to light up the gloomy day and still her fears about the future and what people would say about her. It was safe. Honest. That smile had greeted her parents and warmed the inside of her home. Home. Alyson felt herself tearing up at the thought.

"I'm really glad I was able to take you to meet my family."

A tear slipped over the edge of Alyson's cheeks and down to her chin before she realized it was there. Tommy stepped closer and pulled Alyson into a comfortable embrace. They didn't say anything as Alyson wiped tears from her face, and Tommy rubbed his thumb over her shoulder.

"You all right?" Tommy asked after feeling Alyson exhale deeply.

"Yeah. Just, you know, all the hormones and stuff. It is special to me that you met my parents, but I don't think I would cry over it if I wasn't pregnant."

"I wouldn't know, I've never been pregnant."

Alyson tried to scoff and give him a shove, but the action hardly moved the young man. He came right back to her side and wrapped his arms around her, humming a rowdy tune as he watched her grin and attempt to push him away again. He loved that smile.

"Hey, you two! Stop fighting!" Eddie's voice came from behind, bringing their interaction to a halt.

Alyson turned to see Lucy watching them closely. She forced the grin into hiding and picked up her pace once more. It didn't take long to reach the edge of the trees and mark out a little trail to follow. Leftover raindrops fell to the ground around them, sparkling despite the hidden sun.

Lucy was quick to find a tree that she asked to make a sketch of. Within minutes, she had perched herself on a little stump and pulled her paper and pencil out of her bag. The others walked around, exploring, yet sticking close to their artist friend as her pencil flew across the paper. It didn't take long before a tree began to take shape. Lucy didn't realize Alyson was behind her until she heard Alyson's soft exclamation of awe.

"Oh, ya scared me!" Lucy swiveled on her heels to see Alyson watching her. "Do you like it?"

"I do! Very much. I can't get over how fast you are."

"Well, I have a lot of practice," Lucy laughed.

Lucy turned back to her sketch, and Alyson continued to stand over her shoulder. Only minutes had passed before Lucy was inspecting her work, holding it up to compare the original to the copy.

"That looks first rate, Lucy!" Tommy joined the two girls to see how the picture was coming. "You're ace at trees!"

"I love drawing living things." Lucy stuffed her paper back into her bag and stood up.

Hard rains began to pound down through the branches of the trees less than an hour later. Cold water dripped down the backs of their necks and made their breath freeze as they talked. They still had more exploring they wanted to do, but the weather didn't seem to have plans to change anytime soon.

"We need to get Aly back." Eddie called to the others. "This isn't good for her."

"Here, Alyson, take my coat." Tommy slid his waterproof jacket off his shoulders and wrapped it around the girl. His dark sweater was thick, but the rain would eventually sink through the fabric. "You okay, Lucy?"

"Yeah, I'm fine." She smiled and gave a thumbs up.

"Can you lead the way, Ed?" asked Tommy. He was holding Alyson against his side, hoping that his own body heat would help calm the shivering he could feel through both of her jackets.

They pulled up their hoods and walked hurriedly, rain soaking in and dripping off as they did. Tommy stayed close to Alyson, ready to steady her on the slippery grass or muddy path. Eddie cast concerned looks in her direction and hung back more than once to check that she wasn't getting too tired.

"I can carry you, Aly. If you need." His eyes were set on her face, ready to detect any flicker of a lie when she answered.

"No. I'm not tired. Just ready to get out of my wet shoes."

Eddie nodded and picked up his pace again to take his spot in the lead.

"S-sorry your birthday is getting rained out." Alyson looked over at Lucy who was walking beside her, her head up and humming a little tune.

"No, it's all good!" Lucy had to raise her voice to be heard over the sound of the rain. "I love the rain! Can't remember the last time I had a good walk out in the rain. It's the best birthday present I could ask for, really."

"Well, happy birthday, Lucy!" Tommy chuckled.

They were all wet and shivering by the time they reached Tommy's vehicle, but the smile was still on Lucy's face. Tommy pulled some old blankets and towels from the boot to cover the seats before they clambered in. There were extra pairs of socks and dry shirts as well that they managed to change into despite the tight quarters. Alyson was thankful that Tommy's jacket had kept her dry and she didn't have to remove her coat in front of Lucy.

"Now what?" Eddie turned from the front seat to look back at Alyson.

"I don't know. I guess... home?"

"Oh, can you wait a mo'? Kyle's calling." Lucy pressed her phone to her ear and greeted her husband cheerfully. Her face went dark within three seconds, and she quickly yanked open the car door, stepping out into the pouring rain. "Kyle, why are you even... No! I'm..."

The conversation was cut off by the door slamming shut behind her. Eddie, Tommy and Alyson shared a look and sat quietly. They couldn't make out anything other than frustrated yelling through the rain drops pelting the windshield. Two minutes passed before Lucy returned to the backseat, her lips blue and her teeth chattering. Alyson could tell there were tears in her eyes, but didn't say anything. She handed the girl a blanket, and Lucy snatched it eagerly from her hands.

"Everything okay?" asked Eddie gently.

"C-can you take me t-to London? K-Kyle's waiting for m-me." Lucy's voice sounded so small as she stuttered through her request. There was no more smile.

"Yeah, of course." Eddie nodded. "Just tell us where to go."

Alyson sat silently as they drove, glancing every now and then at the girl who was huddled against the other side of the backseat. Lucy's forehead was pressed against the steamy window. A sniffling sound reached her a few times, but Lucy never turned her face to confirm whether or not she was actually crying. Alyson frowned, nibbling on the edge of her lip as she kept to herself.

Rainy car rides always reminded Alyson of the day she realized Amir wasn't going to be coming back. She was ten, it was April, and her parents had been talking for two days about planning their next trip to Islamabad to visit family. All she could think about was that she would finally get to see her brother again. She had hardly slept or eaten since the trip was first mentioned, and she was terrified that the littlest thing would cause her parents to snap and change their minds. Her entire body was buzzing with excitement and pent-up emotions as she watched the rain drip down the side of the car.

"Are you excited to see Sumaya?" asked Janice from the front seat.

"Oh. Yeah. Of course!" She had hardly even thought about her cousin.

"I can tell, you're all quiet and fidgety."

"Oh, sorry." Alyson immediately forced herself to calm down and hold still. It felt like everything on the inside was going to explode out of her.

"It will be wonderful to be with the family again, eh, Aly?" Zaheer looked in the rearview mirror to see his daughter's face.

"The *whole* family?" The question burst out like a faucet with too much water pressure.

"Of course the whole family. Everyone still lives there," Zaheer answered easily.

Tears, hopes, dreams, anxiety and a million prayers shone in Aly's green eyes in response to her father's words. She tried so hard to keep them from spilling over, squeezing her eyes shut in a desperate attempt to control it. She knew better than to cry.

"Deep breath, Alyson." Janice told her daughter calmly from her spot. "It's just a trip."

"Yeah, but." Alyson couldn't keep her voice from shaking. "The *whole* family is going to be there."

"Yes, you, and Sumaya, and Zacheria, and Asad..." Mr. Abidi listed off all of his twelve nieces and nephews.

"And..." prompted his daughter at the end.

"What? You don't have any more cousins?"

It was her father's look of genuine confusion that cut Alyson down to the quick. He hadn't listed Amir because Amir wasn't going to be there. Amir wasn't there, and he wasn't at home, and she was never going to see him again. He was gone.

The girl sat frozen into her place for the rest of the ride. Her face was blank; without tears or even a frown. Rain pounded against the road as they drove and the way the droplets landed on the window by her face was engrained into her memory. Every time she saw rain on a car she thought of that day. Not in a deep, heavy way, but in a dull, back-of-your-mind-but-you-can't-touch-it way.

"You okay, Alyson?" Tommy's eyes searched for hers in the rearview mirror. She was grateful he looked nothing like her father.

Alyson simply nodded at him and leaned back in her seat.

"You sure?" His eyes flitted back and forth between Alyson's frown and the road as he drove.

Eddie's hand reached back from the front and rested on her knee for a moment. The warmth of his fingers shot through her body, reminding her heart to beat steady and her mind to slow down. Alyson curled her fingers over his and breathed deeply.

"Everything good?"

"Yes." A deep sigh left her chest and she felt her sadness drift away. "Thank you."

They reached the city, and Lucy guided them expertly to the pub where Kyle had requested she meet him. She gave them each a wan smile as she looped the strap of her bag on her shoulder and opened the car door. They waited until Lucy was inside to pull away.

"You know what?" said Tommy as they drove slowly down the road. "I'm absolutely starving, and I know where the best place to get pizza is."

"Pizza!" The word made Alyson's mouth ache to taste it. She hadn't eaten it since she left the States.

The place where Tommy took them was not what Alyson had been picturing in her mind at all. She had imagined a tiny little hole-in-the-wall place with a family recipe passed down through generations. This place, Pizza Millennia, was very much the opposite. They had been open for two years and had a steadily increasing customer base. The dining area was a bright, wide-open space with the hanging lights reflecting back off the white tiles on the floor and walls.

Alyson stuck close to Eddie's side as they pressed through the door, eager to leave the rain behind them. Tommy was grinning broadly as he pulled his hat off his head and shook out his damp hair. Someone noticed and began to whisper behind her hand. Alyson became nervous.

"They're talking about us." She tugged on Eddie's sleeve until he bent over to hear her worried whisper.

"It's okay, Tommy will sort them out." Eddie had seen his friend work his magic many times.

There was a special corner where Tommy told them to go while he went to take a few pictures and autograph a few pieces of paper. Once Alyson was settled, Eddie returned to his friend, smiling and posing with the fans. Alyson had already received her drink and knew what she wanted to order before the boys came back. The fans were satisfied and continued on with their meal without bothering them again.

Their pizza came piping hot and delicious. The taste of the cheese and sausage hit a memory on Alyson's taste buds, and she almost couldn't swallow. Danielle's favorite pizza shop by her apartment had delicious pizzas that tasted just like the one she was eating at that moment. The boys were busy tearing into their pieces, unaware of Alyson's watery eyes and halting swallow. For a moment she was afraid she was going to break down into tears over a piece of pizza, but she did two deep breaths and blinked the excess water on her eyes back to where it came from.

The three of them talked together easily, mentioning the baby, the holiday season and threw around a few ideas for the following Saturday that they could do together. Alyson focused on their conversation and not on how badly she missed her friend.

"I really like this new tradition of spending Saturdays with Alyson, don't you, Eddie?" Tommy's hand went to the girl's shoulder and rested there for a moment. The way his fingers gripped by her collar bone sent shivers down Alyson's arm, making her catch her breath.

"I told you I would do it!" Eddie was grinning at her. "I told you I would spend my Saturdays with you!"

"I know. Because I'm your only friend."

"Oh! That hurt!" The dimples proved his lie as he shoved another bite of pizza into his mouth.

"And I like spending time with Bambi too, of course." Tommy's hand fell from her shoulder to her stomach for a second. He waited for Alyson to meet his gaze, but she didn't look at him, so he moved his hand back to his lap.

"Do you want to know what Jamie did?" Alyson spoke suddenly. She felt unbearably hot and she needed to do something, say something, to distract her from the red in her face. "He wrote Bambi a letter."

"He wrote Bambi a letter?" said Eddie.

"Yeah. Bambi can hear now, you know, so he sent me a letter to read out loud for him." Alyson had no idea why she had just told them about the letter. She was almost positive that Jamie wanted it to be a special secret between the two of them.

Way to go, Aly, she chided herself. *They're going to tell Jamie, and he's going to be upset.*

"Oh, we should do that, too, bro!" Tommy's eyes were wide as he reached across the table to push at Eddie's shoulder. "Wouldn't that be such a great thing to have when you're growing up? All these letters about how much the people in your life loved you before you were born... I'm going to do it, hundred percent."

Alyson let out her breath, relieved. Maybe the boys wouldn't say anything to Jamie about the letter.

"I'm... I'm not one of the dads, though." Eddie wrinkled his brow.

"That doesn't matter!" Tommy insisted. "You're going to be Uncle Ed!"

Eddie looked to Alyson.

"I would love for you to write letters to Bambi."

"Oh, by the way, I have to take something back to Gar's house today." Tommy looked from Alyson to Eddie. "I should wait until we take Alyson home, eh?"

"That's probably best, yeah?" Eddie nodded. "She's probably knackered from our hike."

"It's fine." Alyson looked Eddie in the eye so he would know she wasn't lying.

"Are you sure? We can take you home first if you'd rather."

"I'm sure. It will be dark when you get back from driving me home."

"I can drive in the dark, Alyson."

"I know, but it's just nicer to go home at the end of a long day. Honestly, just go to Garret's first."

The big house Tommy pulled up to half an hour later took Alyson by surprise. She had imagined Garret having a place like Eddie; a nice big flat overlooking the city. This house was set back from the road by a long winding driveway and guarded by tall bushes. It wasn't huge, not like Jamie's home in L.A., but the two-story home was lined with windows all the way down, inviting the world to come look inside.

"Okay, just sent him a text. He knows we're here," Tommy informed them as they unbuckled.

"Should I stay in the car?" asked Alyson.

"No, come in. It will be nicer than waiting in the car." Tommy's hand held Alyson's as they walked quickly through the cold rain to the massive front door of Garret's house.

Garret opened the door at the sound of their knock and smiled warmly at the boys as they stepped in. His smile froze, however, when his eyes landed on Alyson. She picked up on the change of expression on his face and stepped back cautiously.

"Hey, Gar. Got your thing for you in the boot of my car." Tommy clapped Garret on the shoulder in greeting.

"Tom, you didn't tell me Aly was with you!" he whispered forcefully.

Eddie's arm wrapped instinctively around Alyson's shoulders as she stepped further away from Garret.

"What's wrong with that?" Tommy saw the way Eddie's jaw was working and knew something was off. "What's wrong with Alyson?"

"Nothing!" Garret glanced over his shoulder. "But Ren is here..."

Alyson's stomach dropped like a sack of rocks down to her toes, and she felt her legs begin to wobble under her weight. Serenity. The thought of her being at Garret's house had never occurred to her, and she was immediately plunged into her own swirl of hypothetical scenarios.

"I'll take her back out to the car." Eddie started walking before he had even finished his sentence. Alyson's pale cheek pressed against the sleeve of his jacket as he led her out.

"Ed! Tom!" Serenity's voice echoed down the hallway. "Come, let me give you a squeeze! Eddie, are you leaving? You can't leave without a hug first!"

And that was how Alyson was forced to face Serenity Fitz for the first time since possibly having sex with her boyfriend. The young woman gasped when she saw Alyson's face and broke out with a huge grin. She reached forward to pull Alyson into a warm hug, leaving the young men to watch in horror.

"Aly!" She was smiling when she stepped back. "Oh my gosh, I had no idea you were here!"

"You remember me?" Alyson's whole body was shaking.

"Of course I do! You were so sweet and funny, we all had such a great time that night in uh, where was it?"

"Minnesota," said Garret quietly.

"Yes! Minnesota! We had such a great time, didn't we, G?" She turned to her boyfriend and leaned into his side, letting him hold up her weight. "I still talk to Elle! It has been ages, though. I should ring her up later."

"Ren, can you go check the stove? I put the kettle on..."

"All right, in a minute!" She planted her lips on his scruffy cheeks and kissed him. "How long have you been in the UK, Aly?"

"Not long. Just... a few weeks? I think..."

"What? And no one told me?" Serenity looked genuinely upset as her eyes went from Tommy to Eddie to Garret. "Is it just a visit, or...?"

"Work. Charity, I mean." Alyson could feel her pizza coming back up her throat. Sweat beaded on her forehead.

"How long?"

"Um, don't know..." Alyson winced and swallowed hard. All she could think about was finding a toilet or a trash can close by.

"Garret, how come you didn't tell me Aly was moving here?" Serenity's voice was low. She was offended. "I told you just the other day..."

"Woods. Toilet. Please." Alyson couldn't hold back much longer.

"She's going to be sick." Tommy had seen that face before. He grabbed her arm and rushed her down the hallway to where a bathroom was. He stood in the doorway and watched as Alyson pulled her hair back from her face and knelt down before vomiting up her lunch. "Ah, Alyson. So sorry."

Alyson's tears were from more than the acidic tomato sauce burning her throat as it came back up. Tommy stepped into the room and helped Alyson to her feet. There was a washcloth on the shelf above the toilet that he wetted and handed to her. She pressed it gratefully against her face and focused on breathing deeply. A moment passed, and she felt the trembling begin to wear off.

"I'm going to go tell the others you're okay, just a bit sick. Is that good?" Tommy ran a gentle hand down the back of Alyson's head and pulled her forward to place a tiny kiss just below her hairline. "Come out when you're ready."

Alyson shut the door behind Tommy. She splashed some water on her face and stood for a moment to make sure her stomach was truly done punishing her. She used the toilet and washed her hands slowly before she was ready to leave. The low voices of Garret and Serenity came filtering under the door as Alyson was about to leave.

"Garret, why didn't you tell me Alyson was here? You know I remember her!"

"Ren, it's not..."

"I talked to Elle just like, a month ago, and she said Aly was going through a super tough time and I told you! I told you, G! If I had known she was here, if you had *told* me she was here, I could have gone and helped her! I could have done something if I had known!"

"She doesn't need help, babe! She's fine!"

"Definitely *not* what her best friend told me."

"Listen, there are things that people can't explain, all right?"

"She's working here, G! She *moved* here, and you didn't tell me! In the very least, I could have been helping her get settled! Being her friend!"

"We haven't been telling people she's here because she doesn't want any attention put on her by being associated with us whilst she's doing her teaching."

"Really?"

There was a pause.

"That is stupid, babe. Proper stupid. And I don't think I believe it. Is this Jamie's idea? To hide her away?"

"His mum doesn't even know she's here."

"This is... weird! Weird and stupid!" Serenity's voice rose. "I don't like this shady business, Garret. She's new here, and I want to be her friend. Elle said..."

"Elle should not have told you anything, Ren! You don't know what this situation is like!"

"You're right, because you obviously like lying to me!"

Alyson's eyes closed as she listened to Serenity stomp off and Garret call after her. Finally, the voices left the hallway, and Alyson slipped out of the bathroom. She ran out to Tommy's car, her feet splashing through the inches of rain that were gathering into puddles on the driveway. A few minutes later, Tommy and Eddie joined her, and they were on their way back to Bedford.

"You have a good day, Alyson?" asked Tommy.

Alyson sat in the front seat on the way home while Eddie sat in the middle of the back. She watched the growing darkness through the window, her mouth set into a thin line and her eyes filled with thoughts. She didn't respond to Tommy's question, so he set a hand on her knee, squeezing it gently to get her attention.

"What?" She startled and looked to her right where Tommy sat in the driver's seat.

"I asked if you had a good day."

"Oh, yeah. I think so." Alyson wasn't sure how to feel about everything that had happened. "I wasn't expecting it to end up the way it did, but I enjoyed most of it."

"Good. We'll try to find something better to do next week. Especially if it rains."

They had a peaceful drive the rest of the way, leaving the radio off and Tommy's hand on her knee. She put her hand over his, absentmindedly rubbing patterns on his skin with the tips of her fingers. Eddie and Tommy began to talk about something that Alyson didn't understand, but the sound of their voices was relaxing for her. By the time they reached her apartment, her shoulders didn't feel as tight as they had earlier, and the little that was left disappeared once she was in the bath with a cup of tea and Yo-Yo Ma playing in the background.

She wrapped in her robe before leaving the bathroom to head to her bedroom. There was a light shining from across the street, and Alyson stepped closer to see into the Thorntons' living room. Both Kyle and Lucy were in full view, framed by their curtains. It looked like they were having an argument. Kyle's arms were waving furiously in the air around his head while Lucy shook her head back at him, punctuating what Alyson could only imagine as angry words by stomping her foot. Alyson remembered it was Lucy's birthday, and she frowned. What a horrible way to end your birthday.

On Tuesday two letters came in the mail addressed to Bambi. One from Tommy, and one from Jamie. Alyson smiled before going back to her apartment to open them. She decided to read them in the nursery. She settled into the rocking chair and looked around quietly before opening the letters. Everything was just as it had been the last time she had been in there. The afternoon sunlight was shining in through the window that gave a view of an empty neighboring lot. Kids played there in the summer, she was told. Maybe Bambi would play there one day.

"Hello Bambi..." Alyson read Tommy's letter first, a smile on her face. She laid a hand on where Bambi was growing inside of her as she read the words out loud. "I'm writing you this letter now to tell you how much I love you. I know I haven't met you yet, but I think about you every day. Life can be hard and crazy sometimes, but I want you to know that I'm always, always, *always* going to be here for you, and I'm trying to become a better person for you..."

Alyson took Tommy's letter and stuck it to the wall with a thumb tack next to the letter Jamie had sent the week before. She returned to the rocking chair and opened Jamie's. She inhaled the scent of him on the paper and swallowed the lump that formed in her throat.

The letter was short, only a few sentences, but there were tears on Alyson's face before she finished. The letters had been addressed to the baby, but the mother held on to the words for herself as well.

"I can't wait to hold you and tell you how amazing you are every day of your life," read Alyson in a thick voice. "Take care of your mum for me. I miss you both. All my love, Jamie."

That night Alyson lounged on her couch with her sketchbook and pencil in hand and Eddie on speakerphone. She traced over the lines she had already done as she listened to his story about falling off his bike on the way home from the record store earlier that day. It was so easy, she thought as she laughed at his dramatic re-telling of the event. Talking to Eddie was easy. So simple. She sighed and laid her pencil on her stomach.

"Ed, I don't know what to do."

"About what?"

"I think... No, I *know* my feelings for Jamie are getting stronger."

"I don't think it's wrong to have feelings for Jamie. Be careful, yes, but if Jamie loves you then there really isn't a better person on earth to be with. He gives everything for those he loves."

"Why did he leave Beth?" It was a question Alyson had wanted to ask Jamie from the beginning, but had been too afraid. The fear was twofold; fear of reminding him of what he used to have and fear of having the same mistakes repeated on her.

"She was young. She loved the fame. She fancied Jamie, but didn't actually love him. At times she was willing to see things his way, but she was very easily distracted by what fame and fortune could do for her, you know? Jamie stood by her until she started being rude to his mum. That's what ended it."

"That's horrible. He must have really cared about her, though."

"He did. Very much." Eddie sounded thoughtful. "Just as he cares very much about you."

The conversation ended a few minutes later with Eddie promising another Saturday together. Alyson looked down at the rough drawing of a small child on her lap. It was supposed to be her baby when it was older, but it wasn't a very good picture. All of the faces that she drew still ended up lopsided. She had borrowed a book from the school library entitled *Drawing Portraits for the Absolute Beginner*. It was helping some.

As she set her picture on the growing stack of papers on the shelf in the nursery closet, Alyson rubbed her belly and sighed. Bambi was the size of a banana now. She wondered if Elle would choose a yellow balloon to represent Bambi this week. Suddenly the balloon in her imagination popped, and Alyson jumped. She frowned, then reminded herself that the thing about balloons is that you can just blow up a new one if the first one pops.

"You growing okay in there, Bambi? Everything going well?" Alyson spoke softly to her child. "I love you so much. Keep staying safe in there."

It was rare to have such an easy time falling asleep, but Alyson was drowsy and her cup of tea had soothed all of her nerves until she was loose and comfortable in her bed. For a moment she thought about praying. Her hands went to her stomach, and her tongue began moving before she could change her mind.

"God, keep Bambi safe. And me... I... I want to be okay one day." She prayed hurriedly, switching to her other side as she became uncomfortable. "But don't worry about me. Just take care of Bambi. Amen."

Alyson kept her eyes open a few minutes longer, straining them to see her star friends in the sky as they twinkled in the cold night. She caught a glimpse of them and exhaled deeply. She wasn't alone.

"Goodnight Bambi. We've made it through another day."

Chapter fifteen
"If you knew, you wouldn't touch me!"

Serenity was surprised at how nervous she felt when she arrived at the address in Bedford she had found on Garret's phone. The clock in her car read half past three as she parked on the side of the road. She didn't know if Alyson would be at home, but she hoped luck would be on her side. Garret was supposed to be in the studio with Jamie all day, so she figured it was as good a time as any to go up and pay her new neighbor a visit. None of the excuses that Garret had tried to give her added up. There seemed to be no real reason why he hadn't told her about Alyson.

She stepped out of her car and onto the sidewalk, glancing up at the apartment complex with a frown. This was where it became tricky. Just as she was about to walk up to the front door and try to guess which buzzer went to Alyson's apartment, she heard a voice calling to her.

"Hello!"

The woman that greeted her looked kind and wore a bright smile. She looked to be only a few years older than Serenity, but her style of clothes was very different. The stranger was wearing worn-out trainers and a pair of loose-fitting jeans with rips all down one leg. Her brown jacket was woolen and had wooden toggles to keep it fastened. The top two were undone at the moment, revealing a cream-colored sweater that hugged the base of her slim neck. Serenity glanced down at her suede boots and tight, black skinny jeans that were showing from beneath her black peacoat.

"I'm Lucy," the lady from across the street called over in greeting. "Are you here for Aly?"

"Y-yes, actually." Serenity smiled politely and walked to the curb. "I'm Serenity. I was hoping to stop in and visit with Aly for tea time. Do you know if she's home?"

"First time I've seen a girl drop 'round for a visit. What time is it?" Lucy glanced at her own naked wrist as she asked. "She's always home before half-three on Thursdays."

"It's 3:37!" Serenity smiled brightly. "Thank you so much for your help! Oh! By the way, do you happen to know which buzzer is Aly's?"

"The door is unlocked until dark. She's on the third floor, number 304." Lucy was happy to answer all her questions. "Tell her I say hello."

"Of course!"

Serenity found the door unlocked, as Lucy had said, and began walking up the three flights of stairs to get to Alyson's flat. She stood outside the door for a moment, willing her heart to stop pounding from the physical exertion of climbing the stairs and reminding herself of what Aunt Becky had taught her.

Be kind. Forgive. Love others, even when they hurt you.

Her purse hung over her shoulder and a little bag of gifts for Aly was hooked on her fingers. Finally, she raised her hand to the door. Her knock echoed through the empty hallway.

"Hello?" a voice came from the other side of the door.

"Hiya! Aly, it's me!" the visitor answered cheerfully. "It's Serenity!"

The door didn't open. There was nothing; no sound or movement. Serenity blinked and knocked again.

"Aly?"

"Y-you shouldn't be here." Alyson called back through the door. "I'm not... I'm not feeling well."

"Aly, please open the door. I'm not afraid of getting sick." Serenity could hear the lie in Alyson's words. "Open the door."

"I don't want you to get sick!"

"Aly. I know you're lying to me. Let me in."

After another moment of silence, the door slowly inched open while Alyson hid behind it. Serenity waited until it was opened all the way before she stepped in. Her brown eyes were smiling softly as Alyson crept out from where she had been standing and shut the door. Serenity immediately noted the flushed cheeks, the shifting gaze, and the frowning mouth.

"I brought you a housewarming gift!" Serenity offered, holding out the bag in her hand.

"Thanks." Alyson took the bag and set it on the floor by her feet without taking a look inside. "You didn't have to do that."

"But I wanted to." It was getting harder for Serenity to keep the smile on her face. "I wanted to give you a proper welcome now that we're neighbors!"

"Is this all you wanted? Just to deliver the present?"

Love others, even when they hurt you...

"I-I was hoping t-to... to stay and have tea with you?" Serenity couldn't believe this was the same girl she had met in Minnesota who had been so charming and animated.

"I'm not... I don't have anything for tea."

Serenity watched the torment on Alyson's face as the girl walked away from her and sat down on the couch, hunching her shoulders. Things still weren't adding up.

"Why didn't anyone want me to know you were here? Did I do something wrong to hurt you?"

"You?" Alyson's face flashed her disbelief at the suggestion as she looked up at her guest. "Not at all! You're perfect! I can't imagine you doing anything to hurt me. There's not a chance..."

The words tumbled quickly, each one coated with emotion.

"Then why the secret?" Serenity walked over to the couch and sat down on the other side of Alyson. She tried not to notice when Alyson shifted away from her. "Do you not want to be friends?"

Be kind...

"Of course I want to be friends!" Alyson's voice was wet with tears. "But... I just... I can't have friends right now."

"How come? What on earth made the lads think you couldn't have friends?"

"It's not them. It's me. I-I can't... I can't have friends..." Alyson looked away and pressed her fingers against her eyes.

"But you're friends with Lucy!" Serenity remembered the woman she had met just minutes before on the side of the road.

"Serenity, you shouldn't be here. This is a very complicated situation. It's complicated and, and dangerous! I have to stay safe because my family..." Alyson's voice broke. "The less people who know where I am the better."

"Aly, I'm not going to tell anyone if you don't want people to know! But we can still be friends! All the guys know where you live!"

"You shouldn't be here!" There was a tortured look in Alyson's eyes as she jumped up from her spot on the couch.

She stood at the window, the blue of the sky outlining her form. Serenity knew the girl looked different than she had that night in June when they had met, but she couldn't quite put her finger on how. It had been dark in the club, and they had spent most of the time sitting at a table across from each other. Alyson was pushing her away like she was carrying the plague, and Serenity was stubborn enough to wait out the excuses for the truth. There was something that Alyson was hiding. Alyson and Garret. Alyson, Garret, and Jamie...

"Aly, are you in trouble?" she asked softly.

Alyson shook her head from side to side, her back still facing Serenity. Her shoulders shook as she cried, her forehead pressed against the window pane. Suddenly, she pulled back from the glass and stepped to the side, out of view of anyone looking up into her apartment. She wiped at her eyes and nose before turning back to the woman on her couch.

"You should leave. Thank you so mu-..." Alyson swallowed again. "Thank you for coming to see me."

Serenity didn't move from her spot.

"Serenity, please."

"I don't understand what is happening here!" Frustration flashed in Serenity's eyes as she pushed herself to her feet. "This whole situation is scaring me!"

Alyson was staring at her, a glazed look in her eye. The lines around her mouth deepened, and her lips twitched, but she didn't say a word. Serenity didn't know how to respond, unnerved by the tortured way Alyson was watching her.

"I'm so sorry." Alyson gasped and snapped back to reality. Shaking hands clutched at her chest and tears choked her words. She sunk down to the floor. "I'm so sorry! I-I'm sorry..."

Without a word, Serenity joined Alyson on the floor, crossing her legs and placing a gentle hand on Alyson's shoulder. The muscles tensed under her touch. Alyson continued to mumble her apologies and weep, her face hidden behind her hands. Red crept up the back of her neck. Maybe she should leave for the sake of Alyson's emotional health. Serenity hated the thought of leaving without knowing what was going on, but she wasn't sure if she had a choice.

"Shh, it's okay, Aly. Calm down," Serenity soothed. "You're okay. You didn't do anything, sweetheart. No reason to apologize."

"But I did! If you knew, you wouldn't touch me! Oh, please! Please just leave!" Alyson wept bitterly. "I'm so sorry! I can't even look at you!"

Be kind.

Thoughts and suspicions were beginning to connect in Serenity's mind, but she couldn't believe they were true. The vague messages from Elle about how Alyson was in a hard spot floated around her head, not quite making sense. Not yet.

Be kind.

There had to be a logical explanation.

Renny, be kind.

"Aly, it's okay," Serenity tried one last time.

"Stop! Stop being so nice to me!" Alyson's voice rose as she clenched her hands into fists. "You should hate me! I n-nearly ruined everything! I-I almost destroyed it all! I could have made y-your whole life... f-fall apart! You have n-no idea!"

Serenity sighed. She let her hand fall into her lap and scooted herself back until she was leaning against the couch. Her spine curved forward as she hugged her knees.

"I don't hate you, Aly." Serenity's voice was quiet. "I just want to know what's going on."

Love others...

The girl in the middle of the room placed her hands on her stomach and struggled to calm her breathing. Alyson smoothed her shirt over the growing outline of a baby in a distracted manner, as if the motion were an act of self-soothing. Serenity tried to convince herself that it wasn't a baby, that Alyson wasn't pregnant, that it was just her mind playing tricks on her, but she couldn't. Serenity knew.

Forgive.

Flashes of the conversation she had had with Garret in Brighton about the girl he had possibly slept with came to mind. There was no denying the pieces added up. Both Garret and Alyson had mentioned the words "complicated" and "dangerous," and the girl's family.

Forgive...

"Alyson." Serenity struggled to keep her voice calm. "Did... did you ever end up going to... to L.A.? You know, to s-see Jay? Did you go?"

"What?" Alyson looked over at Serenity, her face a mess of tears and makeup.

"Did you go t-..."

"I heard you." Alyson closed her eyes and bit her bottom lip. "I heard you. I just... I didn't want that to be your question."

That was all the answer Alyson gave her, and it was all the answer Serenity needed. Alyson was right; she should hate her. After all, it seemed that Alyson could be pregnant with her boyfriend's baby. Alyson may have been with the love of her life. Her Garret. The one she wanted to father *her* children.

Love others, even when they hurt you.

"It wasn't your fault." Serenity's voice shook. "It wasn't."

This time Alyson didn't even speak as she turned to look at Serenity's solemn expression. There was no malice in her gaze as it swam with tears. Alyson didn't know what to say.

"But we don't know wh-what happened," Alyson whispered quietly, her head hanging in defeat. "I've tried! Every day I try. But I... I can't remember a thing..."

"I know. He told me what happened."

"I-I'm sorry."

"There's nothing to forgive." Serenity paused for a moment. "But I do forgive you for anything you feel like is your fault. I don't hold anything against you."

"Thanks." The word squeezed past the ache in Alyson's throat. "I needed to hear that."

Serenity nodded.

Be kind. Forgive. Love others, even when they hurt you.

"I know how much Garret loves you. Th-that's why..." Alyson took a shuddering breath in. "That's why I didn't want to see you. I couldn't. It eats me alive on the inside."

"Oh, sweetheart. Don't let it do that. Garret and I will work through this. I just wish... I just wish you guys didn't try to hide it." That was when the first tear fell down Serenity's cheek. "That's the only part that hurts right now."

Garret's phone rang as he was finishing in the studio with Jamie and a few of their other friends. Serenity's picture popped up on the screen and he quickly answered.

"Hi, darling! Just about done here, would you like to..."

"G." Serenity's voice was quiet. "I just spent the afternoon with Aly."

"Ren." Garret didn't even try to keep his voice steady.

"I had to. I had to know what was going on." Serenity's voice was hoarse from crying.

"A-are you... are you okay?"

"I will be. But right now I need some space."

Garret nodded. His heart pounded in his throat as he listened to Serenity take a deep breath and sniff loudly. Garret covered his eyes with his hand and tried not to picture what Serenity looked like when she cried.

"Is Aly okay?" He finally forced the question out through clenched teeth.

"She will be."

"Good."

Internally he was screaming at Serenity to tell him how long it would take for her to be okay again, and how much space was enough space. He wanted her to tell him how he was going to make it through without her, but externally he was stoic; his voice calm.

"Goodbye, G."

Tears blinded Garret as he nodded. He snatched his jacket from the back of the chair and left the studio without telling the others he was leaving. He sat in the driver's seat of his car for what seemed like an eternity, his stomach twisting and his lungs heaving. He cried harder than he had in a long time.

There was a dull thud in his chest as his heart beat painfully against his ribs. Serenity had become such a big part of his life, it felt like a gaping hole had been blown right through his insides. He didn't let himself cry as he drove, careful to keep his eyes on the road and his shaky hands on the wheel.

There were three missed calls from Jamie when he finally arrived at his residence, but he didn't return them. He was finding that he, too, needed space. He went into his big, empty house and poured himself a drink, then took it into a dark, closed-off room.

The familiar smell of his mother's perfume mixed with the smell of his father's aftershave and favorite flavor of mints hit his senses as he tiptoed in. He had forgotten how strong the smell was and how powerful it was to cause the memories to come flooding back. Soundbites and motion pictures filled his mind as he looked slowly around the shadowy room. The front light from outside shone through the crack of the curtains at one window; everything else was black. He crept over to the side of the bed, just like he used to when he was little and had woken up because of a bad dream. The blankets and pillows were cold to Garret's touch as he crawled into the middle of the bed.

His head felt heavy as he propped it up against the headboard and took a sip of his drink. A vibration in his pocket told him he had another incoming call, but he ignored it. All he wanted was to lean against his mother's shoulder and have her tell him how to fix what he had done wrong. She had been so wise. She would have loved Serenity. She would have been heartbroken over Aly, but she would have loved her as well.

"I don't know what to do, mum," Garret choked out to the empty room. His glass was quickly emptied, and he lay in the dark trying to see his parent's faces in his mind. "Why did you guys have to leave me?"

The question echoed over and over in his mind as he slept fitfully in the cold room. He didn't want to pull back the covers and muss them. They still had the perfect touch of his mother's hands tucked into the mattress. He couldn't have her, but he could have her neatly made bed. It wasn't enough, not by a long shot, yet it was all he had to hold onto.

It was Saturday when they experienced their first snowfall in Bedford. The icy rains and blistering cold winds had warned them for weeks now that winter was about to come with a vengeance. Alyson walked quickly and carefully down the sidewalk on her way home from her time with Eddie and Tommy. They had spent the morning at the movies, and in the afternoon they discovered an old bookstore. The dusty shelves and forgotten titles kept them occupied for hours. Their visit came to an end, however, when Eddie's gran rung them and asked Eddie to come back home so he could help her fix her stove.

"Sorry to leave so sudden like," Eddie said as they bundled back into their coats.

"I am actually about due for my nap now, so it's perfect timing." She smiled at the guys. She loved Saturdays.

"Text me if you're bored later. I might be able to come back 'round and keep you company." Tommy nodded before giving her a quick hug.

"Bye." She waved them off, her jacket wrapped tightly around her as she snuggled the bottom half of her face deeper into her scarf.

She had no intention of inviting Tommy over later that evening, especially if he was going to come alone. The less traffic she had at her house, the better. She was almost home and dreaming of sitting on her couch with a nice cup of tea when someone called over to her. She knew who it was without turning around.

"Hi, Lu." Alyson was surprised to hear the nickname fall easily off her tongue. "Sorry, I don't know why I called you that."

"Oh, I love it! That's what my sisters all call me!" Lucy was smiling brightly as she rushed up to Alyson's side. She linked arms with the girl and provided an extra source of heat. They turned onto their street, and continued walking quickly.

"How many sisters do you have?"

"Three. There's only us four girls. My poor dad, bless!" Lucy laughed. "I miss them extra this time of year. Holidays aren't the same without your family, eh? What about you? You have any brothers or sisters?"

"Nope." Alyson shook her head and gave Lucy a tiny smile. "Just me."

"That sounds so lonely!" Lucy's tone switched from sympathetic to excited in a second. "Say, you want some tea? Kyle's out for the day, and I'd love to have someone to chat with. My place is so empty when it's just me. I don't know how you can stand it over there all on your own, day after day."

"I'm used to it, I suppose." Alyson shrugged. To be honest, she didn't know how she was able to stand it either.

"Please say you'll come have tea with me!"

"Sure." Alyson couldn't help but smile at Lucy's pleading look. "Do you have those cookies, er, biscuits like you brought on our car trip that one day?"

"Do you know what, I just bought a new tin yesterday!" Lucy smiled widely. "Don't you just love 'em? They are my favorite."

The snow no longer drifted down onto their faces and shoulders once they entered Lucy's apartment building. They took a moment to stomp the snow off their boots before they climbed the stairs to Lucy's apartment. Alyson was hesitant to remove her jacket, knowing the shapeless garment was helping hide Bambi. She followed Lucy into the kitchen and sat down carefully in one of the chairs by the little, round, wooden table that stood by the kitchen window. She was surprised to find that that window also afforded a view into her living room, though not as good as the one from the window in the sitting room.

"So, did everything get worked out with Kyle?" Alyson wasn't sure why she was bringing it up. She knew she wasn't close enough with Lucy to be asking intimate details like that. "I mean, on your birthday, and he called you, and you had to go meet with him?"

"Oh yes!" Lucy whirled around from the counter where she was plugging in her electric kettle, her face lit up with delight. "He had planned a surprise for me, but when I wasn't at home he got all worried and just wanted to know where I was. He's such a good husband."

Alyson smiled. It was nice to know at least one relationship was working out.

There were a couple of Lucy's sketches on the wall that caught Alyson's attention, and she went over to study them. They were pictures of a potted plant on top of a bookshelf. The shading and detail put into the pieces were astounding.

"These are beautiful."

"You like 'em?" Lucy sounded pleased.

"I'm not very good at anything yet."

"What do you draw the most? Trees? Furniture?"

"No, I'm trying..." Alyson blushed. "I'm trying to draw faces."

"Faces?" Lucy's eyes grew wide. "Aren't you a brave one. Most beginners stick with piles of books and a coffee mug on a table. Easy things!"

"I guess I feel more connected to faces than objects and it made sense to try and draw the things that matter to me..." Alyson's words dropped off.

"Sure, sure. Here, let me get some paper and pencils, we'll have a go at some faces."

Alyson was only a little surprised that Lucy didn't ask if she wanted her help in trying to draw; she just automatically assumed. They sat down at the table, their chairs pushed together and their heads bent over the paper. Lucy's lesson was mostly non-verbal, yet Alyson's sharp attention to detail caught every aspect that she could. Her hand was cramping by the time she sat up and took a good look at her piece.

"Oh my word!" Alyson's mouth dropped. "This is the best face I have ever done!"

The chuffed grin on Lucy's face was adorable. The hostess jumped up from her spot to grab the tin of biscuits from the shelf and empty them onto a plate to set on the table next to them. The two girls munched on the cookies as they heated up their tea again, and Lucy continued to show Alyson how to make proper faces.

"Why you drawing a baby?" Lucy asked.

"Oh, my, uh... cousin. My cousin is pregnant. Just... thinking about it a lot."

"Is this cousin on the side of the family where you get your gorgeous, black hair? I cannot tell you how obsessed I am with this lovely mane of yours! Seriously!"

The compliment was bittersweet for Alyson. She knew her hair was only like that because of the pregnancy. Alyson simply nodded and turned back to her picture. She was pleased with what she had learned from her afternoon with Lucy. The silence between them was nice. Their pencils scratched over the paper lightly.

"So, you and Tommy. Why aren't you together anymore?" Lucy murmured as she kept her eyes on her drawing.

"Just... didn't work out. Complicated and stuff."

"Yeah, but you're both living here now. That works, right?"

"I-I... I mean..."

"Come on, he's proper fit and the two of you get on so well!" Lucy finally looked up from her paper. "He's smart, talented, and famous! Second chances are real!"

The phrase "second chances" caught at Alyson's heart, and she smiled sadly. She twisted her pencil in her hands as she looked down. Second chances were real.

"Well, there's, a, um... there was another guy. So..." Alyson glanced briefly up at her audience to see her response. "We're just... taking things slow. Staying friends. I'd rather be his friend than lose him all over again."

"Another guy?"

"I didn't cheat on Tommy, it was like... there were mixed feelings. It's all very complicated. Sorry, don't really know how to talk about it."

"No, it's fine. My sisters and I used to talk about all our boy problems together. When I was in A levels, we'd have sleepovers for the girls at school to help 'em with the lads. I look back now and laugh 'cause we were so young!"

"I bet you knew a lot more than you realized." Alyson smiled at the way Lucy changed the subject.

"Well, several of the girls are happily married to their high school sweetheart thanks to us, so I'd like to think so! Myself included!"

"You and Kyle are high school sweethearts? I never had a high school sweetheart, but I've always loved the idea of them."

"You get to grow up with your best mate." Lucy's eyes sparkled as she spoke reverently. "It's a beautiful gift."

They fell back into their silence, putting their pencils to paper. They didn't speak again until teatime was finished, and all that was left were crumbs and drops of milky tea in the bottom of their cups. Alyson glanced at the picture Lucy was bent over.

"I can't wait until I can draw pictures like that." Alyson pointed to the stunning profile portrait that Lucy was concentrating on. "Can I see it?"

"Just look in a mirror if you like," teased Lucy as she passed over the picture.

"It's me!" Alyson could clearly see her own features on the paper. "Wow!"

"You can have it if you want, I'm going to make a better one." Lucy moved her shoulders in a dismissive manner. "More tea?"

Alyson looked at the time and saw it was getting late. She still had to clean, exercise, make supper...

"Thanks, Lu, for the tea and the biscuits! I'm sorry we ate them all, I can buy you a new tin..."

"Shut up, you idiot!" Lucy laughed as she pulled Alyson into a side hug. "I loved sharing them with you! I would have eaten the whole tin on my own if you didn't come over."

Alyson grinned and grabbed the two pieces of paper as she stood to leave. Lucy followed her to the door and saw her out into the hallway. It was cold out there. Alyson forgot that it had been snowing. She pulled her scarf around her neck before she left the building and ran across the street to her own place. She had only been in her own flat for five minutes when there was a knock on the door. It wasn't Lucy's knock, and Alyson hesitated. She worried for a minute that maybe Tommy had decided to show up without an invitation.

"Jamie." Alyson's eyes lit up as she opened the door and saw the young man standing there. She was about to throw her arms around his shoulders when she saw the grave look in his eye and the frown on his face. "What's wrong? What happened?"

She motioned for Jamie to come in, shutting the door quietly behind him. She shouldn't have spoken so loudly when she greeted him. Her eyes darted to the window. She saw the Thorntons' living room light on, but no one was there to see her visitor.

"Jamie?" Alyson watched her friend drop into the recliner and lean forward, his hands cradling his forehead. A deep sigh slipped through his lips, and she watched him worriedly. "What happened?"

"I heard about Serenity's little visit." Jamie's voice was rough. "Heard that her and Garret are taking a break now."

"Yeah." Alyson remained standing. She crossed her arms over her chest to rest them against her body.

"Why did you tell her, Aly?" Jamie looked up, his eyes covered with a salty film of tears. "Gar is my best mate. Why did you tell Serenity it was you? We had reasons!"

"Excuse me?" Alyson's brow furrowed furiously as she stepped back. "Are you blaming this on me?"

"You told her!"

"I did not! You don't... Jamie, you're assuming things! You're coming up here to accuse me of things I never even told you! Wha-... why? Why?!"

"Because Garret hasn't left his house for three days thanks to this break up, and I'm bloody worried about him!" Jamie stood to his feet as he shot back.

"Do you even want to know what really happened, or do you just want a scapegoat?" Alyson's words were hard like a brick wall.

"Aly!" Jamie rubbed his hands through his hair in aggravation.

"No, I'm serious! I understand you're worried about Garret, but you just drove an hour to come lay at my feet the blame of something I have already been carrying for the last four months! I'm a little angry at you!" Alyson turned so her back was facing Jamie. She saw Kyle's face in the window, and she grimaced. He was frowning at her.

"Well, how did Serenity find out if you didn't tell her? 'Cause I sure didn't tell her! Tommy and Eddie didn't tell her! Did Danielle..."

"You leave my best friend out of this!" Alyson whirled back around, her finger jabbing at his chest with anger. "If you do that again I will cut you out of my life so completely..."

Tears choked out the rest of her threat, but Jamie knew already he had said the wrong thing. She took a shaky breath and stood her ground.

"I'm sorry. I'm sorry." Jamie shook his head and sighed. "I didn't... This isn't how I planned it in my head when I was coming up here. I'm sorry."

Alyson was unmoved by the apology.

"I haven't seen you in two weeks, Garret's depressed, people are finding out about Bambi even though we're not telling anyone, I haven't slept or eaten for three days..."

"Jamie. Sit." Alyson's voice wasn't cold, but there was a chilling tone to it that gave her words force. "I want you to sit and stop talking."

Jamie obeyed the command and dropped heavily back into the recliner. He swallowed hard as he wiped at his eyes. His lips quivered, but he didn't make a sound.

"I begged, and begged, and begged Serenity to leave when she came to visit. I did everything I could think of to make her leave, but she refused, and I'm glad... Hey!" Alyson gave him a stern look when he gave her a quizzical eyebrow raise. "Stop! I'm glad she came, and I'm glad she knows! There was no reason for her to have been left out in the dark like that by the very person she loves the most!"

"We were doing it for you, Aly!" Jamie spoke before he remembered he had been asked to remain silent.

"And I was wrong!" Alyson pointed a finger at her own chest as she shouted down at Jamie. "You were wrong! We were all wrong to think it was okay to make Garret lie to Serenity about who I was and where I was. Things would have probably been messy either way, but sometimes the raw truth heals faster than a wound of broken trust."

Jamie nodded, but remained quiet.

"This whole situation is big, and scary, and I don't know what I'm doing most of the time. It's not like I can go to my parents and ask them for advice..."

"I know." Jamie let his breath out loudly. "I feel the same way. My mum... It's hard not having her to talk to about this. She's the one who keeps me steady."

"I think you should talk to her. Tell her. Ask her for advice," urged Alyson.

"What?"

"Please."

"No."

"Jamie, why?" Alyson's tone was becoming agitated. "You just said she's the one that helps you the most! Why would you not want her to be a part of this?"

"We have to keep you safe! Why do you not realize how important this is?"

"I do realize! Geez, Jamie! I realize every single day! *I'm* the one who has heard my uncles talk about honor killings and how important and holy they are since I was three! I *know* what this means!" Tears filled Alyson's eyes as she spoke. "*I* heard Sumaya's voice on the phone when she told me to run! I-I know what this means!"

"Then why..."

"Because we're ruining everything!" Alyson's voice was hoarse. "Right now we are more in danger of hurting each other and everyone else involved in this mess than I am in danger of being found by my father's family! We ruined Garret and Serenity's relationship. Both of us! We need someone older and wiser to be in on this with us. If it's not your mom, then please, find someone. I'm tired of not having anyone to turn to! We're all tired of not having anyone to turn to! Garret's a mess, you keep freaking out, I'm so stressed out..."

"Stressed about what?"

"Life, Jay!" Alyson rubbed her fingers across her forehead. "Teaching, and my weird, creepy neighbors, and Serenity and Garret, and every Skype call with my parents, and the fact that Eddie moved in with his grandma because of me! He should be in London doing whatever he wants!"

"What about Tommy?"

"Tommy's fine." Alyson sighed and slumped forward.

Jamie nodded and pulled at his chin thoughtfully. The clock on the wall ticked as the seconds passed. Alyson shivered, realizing how cold her apartment had become. She looked up and noticed that Jamie was still wearing his jacket. They hadn't hugged or even smiled at each other.

"Why do we fight so much?" Her whisper brought Jamie's attention back to her. His sad blue eyes saw the hurt on her face. "I never used to fight with anyone."

"Because I'm stubborn and foolish." Jamie smiled deprecatingly at himself. "It's mental, really. I missed you so badly while I was in the studio that my stomach hurt, and the moment I arrive we have a row, and I don't even tell you how beautiful you look today."

Alyson gave a soft chuckle that ended in a frown.

"I'm sorry I accused you."

"You're worried about Garret. I get it. You could have just asked first, though."

"I could have, you're right, but that would have been the easy way to find out the truth." Jamie was happy to see a tiny smile peep into view at his little joke. "But I am worried about Gar. He's been locked away in his house since he talked to Ren last. He's been drinking, holed up in his parent's old bedroom... I haven't seen him like this since the first anniversary of his parent's death."

"What are you going to do?" Alyson's eyebrows knit together with concern.

"I don't know. He won't let me in."

"Oh, Jay." Alyson crossed the floor and knelt down slowly by Jamie's feet. She felt the snow that had melted into puddles around his shoes soak into the knees of her jeans, but she didn't move. She rested her chin on his knee and stared up at him, her eyes studying the wrinkles on his face that came from worrying.

"Ah, love." Jamie pressed his tears away and put a hand on the back of Alyson's head. He smiled sadly at her as he held her gaze. "I missed you. So much."

"I missed you, too."

"Do you want to come home and meet my mum tomorrow?" The invitation was spoken quietly, as if he were asking any old question. He chuckled when her eyes widened with surprise. "Well, do you?"

"I-I... I don't know. Are you sure?"

"Aly! Seriously! You just begged me to talk to my mum, and now you're not sure?"

"No, I mean, I want your mom to be involved, but you want her to... meet me?"

Jamie nodded.

"I don't... I don't want people to know who all the dads are." Alyson's cheeks were crimson as she spoke. She sat back from Jamie's knee, removing her chin from its resting place. She looked down at her hands in her lap. Second thoughts hit hard and fast as the implication of what sharing this intimate story with others could entail. "Actually..."

"What?"

"Can we... can we not tell people?"

"Aly! Honestly!" Jamie voiced his frustration gently as he moved from the chair to the floor next to Alyson. "Why? What's wrong?"

"I don't want people to kn-know... I don't want them to know what I-I did. With all of you. I don't want that. I changed my mind."

Jamie sighed and pulled Alyson into a hug. She rested her head on his shoulder and relaxed against him. She didn't cry, but her heart was heavy, and she wanted Jamie to fix it. Even after their fight, they were still the ones they wanted to be with when it was all over.

"Let's sleep on it then, yeah?" Jamie kissed the top of Alyson's head. "Don't rush it."

Alyson didn't rush it, but she felt it constantly, pressing against her. Her worry for Garret especially drove her to keep it at the forefront of her mind over the next few days. Garret had finally allowed Jamie to move him into his flat so he could keep an eye on him, but he still refused to go out or talk about it. She was settled on the couch a few days later with her sketchpad. Christmas carols played softly in the background as she let her thoughts run circles in her head.

Her picture was dark. She didn't use the new techniques Lucy had shown her the weekend before, but let her hand press heavy lines over the empty page. The face looked strange when she was done, the eyes left without irises and the mouth just one straight line. It wasn't something to cry over, it was something that gave her a headache.

The girl pulled up her shirt and took in her smooth, pale skin. There were no stretch marks yet. Her hands caressed the convex shape of her stomach as she hummed softly to herself.

Sleep didn't come easy that night, even as tired as she was. After switching sides several times, she was finally able to drift off until a loud pounding sound startled her awake. Her hands gripped at the sheets as she opened her eyes. The view outside her window revealed a night sky filled with her star friends. She pulled her phone out from under her pillow to check the time and for any missed calls.

The sound of pounding filled the apartment again, and Alyson struggled to sit up. It was only three in the morning. Her bare feet found the cold tile, and she wanted to recoil back into bed, but the person at the door was persistent. She made her way through the living room past the recliner and to the front door. Her fingers flicked on the light as she reached the far wall of her living room. Her palms were sweating.

"Hello?" Alyson called through the closed structure.

"Aly!"

It was a woman.

The lock had barely clicked over when the door handle moved in Alyson's hand, and the door was pushed open. Alyson stumbled back, but a pair of arms caught her around the neck. The sound of crying reached her ears, and she wrapped her arms around the shaking shoulders of her neighbor.

"Lu. What's wrong?" Alyson wasn't close enough to the door to close it again.

"He's leaving me!" Lucy bawled through her tears. "He's leaving me!"

"What?" Alyson couldn't believe what she was hearing. She managed to kick the door shut with her foot and shuffle across the living room to the couch. "Lu, what happened?"

"W-we had an awful fight. He's leaving me!" Lucy pressed a wad of already used tissues at her eyes and sobbed harder. Her whole body was shaking with emotions and probably cold; she wasn't even wearing socks or a sweater, just shoved her feet into her trainers and came across the street in her t-shirt.

"Oh, Lu. I'm so sorry!" Alyson pulled Lucy over to her shoulder and tried to comfort her. It was awkward, and she wondered why Lucy had come to her at such a vulnerable moment of pain.

"I-I can't believe it! He said h-he didn't love me... anymore!"

Alyson couldn't help but cry as Lucy's emotions ebbed and flowed like the ocean under a full moon. As one wave of pain died away, another one would crash onto her heart, reminding her of something new to cry over. She clung to Alyson's neck like she was the life raft in the middle of that horrible ocean of heartbreak. The longer Alyson held Lucy, the less awkward it was.

After things seemed to settle down, Alyson left the room to make Lucy a cup of tea. She stood by the counter with her arms crossed over her chest, wondering what she was going to do with her neighbor. The sound of Lucy sniffling and letting out bursts of sobs reached her as she waited for the electric kettle to finish heating the water. Lucy was mostly quiet when she returned to the living room slowly, one cup of tea in each hand.

"Thanks, Aly, you're..." Lucy stopped suddenly.

Alyson gave her friend a questioning look as she set the two mugs on the coffee table in front of them. Lucy watched with wide eyes and mouth half open.

"You're pregnant."

There was no way to deny it. Alyson was wearing a form-fitting shirt that hugged her growing curves caused by her child, leaving nothing to the imagination. Alyson swallowed hard and studied Lucy's face. Her hands rested tentatively on her stomach. Lucy's eyes dropped to watch them settle on the evidence of the baby, and Alyson commanded herself to keep her breathing even.

"It's you, isn't it? It's you that's pregnant, not your cousin."

Alyson nodded.

"Oh."

Both girls fell silent.

Lucy reached for her tea and took a sip. Her hands were still shaking and her eyes circled with red, but otherwise she was calm. Alyson looked around the room, trying to find something to focus on that would take away the tight feeling in her gut.

"Is that why things are complicated with Tommy?" asked Lucy. She didn't make eye contact, but studied her cup of tea.

"Yeah."

"Is the baby his?"

"Maybe."

"You don't know?" Lucy's eyes rose to meet Alyson's open and honest expression. She took in the flushed cheeks and the downward pull of her mouth. "Is that why you've kept it a secret?"

"One of the reasons, yes. There are other reasons."

"Oh."

"Yeah."

They resumed sipping on their tea and shifting their gaze around the room.

"Is the baby Eddie's? He takes proper good care of you."

"No. Not Eddie."

"Oh." Lucy sniffed and wiped some of the salty residue off her cheeks. "What about that other guy, Jamie? Who is he?"

"He's the, uh, um... I guess he's the other guy, so to speak. I was with him first, though. I was never really with Tommy."

"Does he have anything to do with the baby?"

"Yeah."

"Oh."

"There's three guys... all together."

"Oh."

There was no look of disgust or disdain that Alyson had been imagining for the past several days when she tried to picture what it would be like to tell the boys' families. It had seemed so heavy to say, but Lucy had taken in the news so effortlessly.

"I call the baby Bambi."

"Oh? That's a cute little name." Lucy smiled as she nodded. "Is it a boy or a girl?"

"I don't know. I'm waiting until it's born."

"Oh. Then what?"

"I don't know." Alyson's eyebrows furrowed, and she twisted her hands in her lap. "Jamie and I haven't gotten that far."

"Oh." Lucy finished her tea and set the cup on the table. "Won't you keep your job at the school?"

"My job at the school is just a cover-up to keep my family from finding out I'm pregnant. I am a teacher, but I was chosen because I needed to get out of America before anyone there found out about Bambi."

"Your parents religious or something?"

"No, uh... My dad's family is from Pakistan. There are honor killings and, uh, yeah. I just have to be safe."

"Is that why you're hiding the baby?"

"Yeah." Alyson felt like a weight had been lifted off her shoulders. "Yeah."

"That's smart, that." Lucy nodded. She looked down at Alyson's belly, than back to Alyson's face, a smile pushing up the corners of her mouth.

It was almost maddening how easy it had been to tell Lucy the whole twisted story.

"Lu." Alyson shifted closer to the girl sitting next to her. "You're... you're only the second person in the world that I've ever told about this."

Lucy didn't say a word as a quivering smile crossed her face and big tears filled her eyes. She leaned forward and pulled Alyson into a hug. Alyson teared up as she felt Lucy's shoulders shake against her chin.

"You idiot," Lucy choked out fondly. "I can't believe you."

The intimate conversation ended with Lucy setting up in the spare bedroom for the night and falling asleep almost instantly. Alyson knew there was a chance she would regret telling Lucy everything like that, but she felt strangely happy. It was nice to have finally been honest again. She knew it would be different telling people who were personally connected to the boys, but in some ways it wouldn't be. Things were going to be okay.

Chapter sixteen
"I've never seen you look at anyone like that."

The route between London and Bedford was a familiar one to Alyson by now. It felt like she had seen the scenery outside of the car more than she had seen the person in the driver's seat recently. She was nervous, but looking at Jamie's strong jaw line and tense blue eyes felt good; it meant that Alyson was beside him again.

His gaze flitted in her direction and a cheeky grin lifted the corners of his mouth. He took one hand from the steering wheel and found Alyson's wrist while his eyes kept sight of the road. Alyson watched with a smile as his fingers tightened their hold around her pulse that beat heavy against his skin.

There had been so many things to tell him while they were apart, but now that they were reunited, it was their silence that wrapped them together. Neither of them wanted to break it. Maybe one day she would tell him she was thinking about spending time in France with Tommy's family over New Years' if Lucy would go with her. One day he would ask and she would tell him how she finally met Gianna Mallory and told her the same story she had told Lucy. One day, but not right then. Right then all they wanted to do was share the air between them.

Even after Jamie pulled his hand back over to his side of the car, Alyson followed with her own. She didn't feel ready for what she was about to go through, so she continued to tangle her fingers with Jamie's, pulling on his strength and confidence. Jamie didn't need much encouragement to stay physically connected with Alyson throughout the drive. His hand found her shoulder, her knee, her cheek...

Jamie drove slowly into a neighborhood lined with houses. He turned three more corners before he pulled into a driveway and put his car into park. The silence didn't end right away, as Jamie pulled his keys out of the ignition and looked over at the girl in the front seat of his car.

"You ready?" His voice was gentle, and his hand tightened around hers.

"Yes." Her eyes told him that she trusted him. Again. He had won her back.

"Let's go." Jamie was careful to make sure the expression on his face was casual as he climbed out of the car. He knew Beatie would be watching for them.

"Jay!" The girl flung open the door and jumped up and down on the front stoop in her socks. She was skinny and had a mop of dark brown curls pulled back into a messy ponytail that was falling down around her face and the back of her neck.

"Bea! Get back in the house, it's freezing!" Jamie rushed over to his sister and grabbed her in his arms, a grin on his face. She squealed and laughed as he carried her inside and set her haphazardly onto the floor. He quickly turned around to make sure Alyson was coming. He ran back out to walk her up the steps and in the house.

"Who are you?" Beatie stared up at the girl with wide eyes. "Are you Jay's friend?"

"Yes." Alyson's hands were sweating as she held it out politely in greeting.

Beatie hung back, hesitant to welcome the stranger who had arrived with her beloved brother. A quick look from Jamie soon prompted her to take the hand and give it a small shake before she pulled back, frowning at her brother fiercely.

"Beatrice! Where are your manners? This is Aly, and she is my friend!" Jamie leaned over to scold his younger sister.

"Wait, what?" A voice came from the top of the stairs. "Did you bring home a friend, Jay?"

A moment later Alyson saw a thin, willowy teenage girl with platinum blonde hair pulled into a ponytail rush down the stairs. She was dressed in skinny jeans with rips in the knee and a hoodie that hung loosely on her shoulders, but her brilliantly blue eyes were shining as she crossed the entryway to greet Alyson with a hug.

"I'm Sydney!" She felt the bump press into her stomach, and she laughed with surprise. "A baby!"

"Syd, this is Aly. She's a teacher up in Bedford for my charity."

"Yeah, whatever. You never bring girls home unless you like them." Sydney didn't even spare her brother a glance as she spoke. "So glad he finally brought you home after keeping you hidden away like he was up to something dodgy!"

"Oh, well…" Cheeks red, Alyson let Sydney put her arm around her shoulders and lead her down the hall. "It's nice to meet you as well."

Jamie and Beatie followed behind their sister and guest; Beatie with a frown and Jamie with an anxious smile. He had counted on his mother picking up on his feelings for Alyson, but he had hoped Sydney would be a bit more oblivious. He was thankful that she hadn't asked if Bambi was his or not. He didn't want to say no, but he would if she asked him.

"Mum, look who Jamie brought home!" Sydney announced loudly as she reached the kitchen where her mother was busily stirring several pots on the stove. "It's Aly."

Jamie's mother didn't turn around for several moments. Alyson spotted Garret sitting at the kitchen table cutting apples, and she greeted him with a smile. Knowing someone else in the house full of strangers was a comfort. Alyson saw the dark circles under his eyes and felt sorry for him.

"How are you feeling?" she asked.

"I'm doing okay, thanks." Garret smiled sadly in return. He seemed surprised that she was talking to him, but he looked happy to see her.

The woman by the stove had yet to turn around to meet her, so Alyson glanced nervously around the room. Sydney's arm around her shoulders felt heavy as the teenager teased Garret with a grin.

"Honestly, Gar, look at that piece of apple! I'm not going to be able to put that thing in my mouth! What do you think we are? Savage animals?"

"What are you on about, this is a perfectly acceptable size of apple!"

"No! Gar, you're so bad at cutting!"

"Syd!" Garret laughed as he protested.

"Remember the time he was cutting the carrot, Bea? It looked so…" A piece of fruit hit her in the arm, and she jumped with surprise. "Hey!"

"You can cut the fruit if you're going to just taunt me, you nutter!"

Alyson stepped away from the imminent food fight, glad the kitchen was large and spacious. There were rows of white and tan-colored cupboards and an island that stood close to the corner where the sink was. Alyson was thankful she was allowed to keep her shoes on as she glanced down at the floor and saw stone tiles under her feet. She was about to study the view from the window when she caught Beatie watching her out of the corner of her eye. She gave the girl a tentative smile and looked away.

"Mum." Jamie walked over to where she was standing, her back still towards them. "My friend Aly is here."

"She's American." Heather's whisper could only be heard by her son.

Jamie was taken aback by the words, unsure of the meaning behind them. Heather looked away from her son and took a deep breath.

"Mum?"

"You can't surprise me with things like this; I'm getting too old and one of these days I'm going to have a heart attack." Heather masked her fears with a smile and placed a kiss on her son's cheek. She turned slowly and saw a stranger beside her daughter, an inch shorter than Sydney and just as thin in the shoulders, but...

"Hi, Mrs. Donald." Alyson waved and hoped her smile didn't come off as too nervous.

"Is this the first time you're meeting Aly, Mrs. H? You're going to love her, she's ace." Whether or not Garret was aware of the tension, he did what he knew how to do best and tried to make everyone feel comfortable. "She's been teaching up in Bedford, training the new staff and other jobs. She's quite smart and very, very lovely."

"It's nice to meet you." Heather dried her hands off on a towel before she walked close enough to shake hands with the girl. She snuck a glance at Jamie's face a moment later and saw the soft look in his eye as he watched her tell a funny story from school to Sydney and Garret. He was in love.

"Mum, Aly's going to have a baby!" Sydney placed a hand on Alyson's warm belly, reminding Alyson very much of Sydney's older brother as she stroked it gently.

"You can talk to Bambi if you want! The baby can hear you," Jamie said.

"Bambi?" Beatie was strangely quiet as she sat in a chair next to Garret at the table.

"That's what we're calling the baby," Garret said with a little grin.

"Hi, cutie! Hi, little love!" Sydney knelt down on the floor and cooed at Alyson's stomach. "Is it a boy, or a girl?"

"I don't know." Alyson smiled down at the top of Sydney's head. She looked over at Jamie, a blush painting her cheeks pink. It only grew darker when he winked at her, his body resting easily over the back of a chair as he stood by the table.

"Oh, little Bambi! What are you? Are you a little prince? Eh? Or are you a little princess?" Sydney continued to talk to the baby. "Should we buy you bows, or a toy train?"

Even Beatie was smiling by the time the girl stood back up to her feet. Only Heather seemed unmoved by the display of affection for the unborn child.

"So, Aly, tell me about yourself." Heather put a lid on the last pot and turned down two burners. "What do you do? Where do you come from?"

"I'm a teacher." A little shaky, but Alyson smiled as she spoke. "I grew up in the Midwest, the middle part of America. Not very exciting, to be honest."

"And now you teach up in Bedford?"

"Yes, ma'am, I do." Alyson hoped her face wasn't as red as it felt. "I enjoy it very much."

"And the baby?"

Alyson hesitated for a moment. She saw Jamie straighten to his full height as his mother spoke.

"Mum, not in front of the kids." His voice was low.

Once again, Garret saved the day by standing to his feet and presenting a bowl of cut fruit to Heather. She took it from his hands with a smile and a motherly touch to his cheek. His eyes crinkled as he smiled back at her. There was a bit of a dull expression hiding behind it, but Alyson was relieved to see him interacting with people happily.

"I'm taking Aly to my room!" Sydney shouted over her shoulder as she grabbed Alyson's hand and began to pull her along behind her.

Alyson didn't even glance at Jamie to ask for silent permission before following Sydney out of the kitchen. She was eager to leave the room and Beatie's untrusting stare. At least Sydney seemed to like her. They went up the stairs to the second level where the bedrooms were and to the first door on the right. Sydney pushed open her door, and Alyson had to smile.

"This looks just like my bedroom when I was in high school!" Alyson pointed at the posters and Polaroids pinned to the walls and the stack of magazines and notebooks on the floor by the end of Sydney's bed. "This makes me feel like I'm sixteen again!"

"How old are you really?" Sydney quizzed as she flopped onto her bed. She lay on her side so she could watch Alyson's face as they talked.

Alyson pulled the chair out from the cluttered desk and sat down.

"Twenty-two."

"When's your birthday?"

"Next month."

"Really? January?" Sydney wrinkled her nose. "I was born in July, and I've always felt sorry for the people who have birthdays in the freezing winter."

"It's not too bad." Alyson chuckled. "I usually go to the movies, or one time my friend and I went sledding all day, and then went home and watched Pride and Prejudice, and ate my mom's chicken noodle soup."

"I love Pride and Prejudice!" Sydney gasped. "Which version did you watch? The Keira Knightley version?"

"No, it was the long version. The one with Colin Firth."

"That's the best one! I love Keira, but the six-hour version is simply tops. We should watch it together! My mum loves that movie, and we always buy loads of snacks and get loads of blankets and pillows..."

Sydney was interrupted by a flash of movement hurtling through the door and onto Sydney's stomach. The girl yelped with surprise and pushed her little sister onto the floor.

"Beatie! Stop it!"

"You can't just tell her about our secret family traditions!" Beatie was near tears as she stood to her feet and shouted at her sister. "She's a stranger! We don't even know who the father of her baby is!"

Alyson sat stunned. She knew Beatie and Jamie were close, but she hadn't considered the fact that the child might not like her because of jealousy or protectiveness. Beatie was only eight, yet even she had realized the fact that Bambi needed a father.

"Do you want to know something?" Alyson spoke quietly from behind the angry child. "When Bambi is born, I'll let you know who the dad is."

"Why can't you just tell me now?" Beatie's eyes were snapping angrily when she turned to face Alyson.

"Because sometimes people have secrets to keep other people safe." Alyson tried not to think about curtains.

Beatie took in the answer to her question carefully, rolling it over in her mind as she eyed Alyson warily. Finally she held out her hand, a serious glint shining in her eye.

"Deal. When Bambi is born, you will tell me who the father is."

They shook hands, and Alyson gave a solemn nod. Beatie finally seemed to be a little more settled with Alyson's presence. She found a spot on the floor next to Sydney's bed as Sydney became acquainted with their guest. Jamie poked his head around the door ten minutes later.

"Come wash hands and get up to the table."

The three girls stood to their feet and headed for the door. Sydney passed through first, eager to get to the table before everyone else. Jamie placed a discreet hand on Alyson's arm as she passed him, and he pulled her back from descending the staircase.

"You okay?" Jamie murmured as he held Alyson close against him. "You left pretty quick with Syd after talking to my mum."

"Yeah, I just... I just wanted a couple minutes to process before the meal." Alyson was nervous his sisters would see them. She stepped back and looked into his eyes. A warm rush washed over her as he smiled sweetly. "What are you smiling about?"

"You're gorgeous, and you've just met my sisters and my mum, and my best friend is here, and I'm just... I'm just really thankful."

A smile to match Jamie's spread across Alyson's face, and she leaned forward on her tiptoes to put a tiny kiss on his cheek.

"Jamie! Lunch time!" Beatie came running to the bottom of the stairs. "Come on! You're sitting by me."

"Calm down, love! We're coming."

Jamie's face hurt from smiling when he arrived in the kitchen, Alyson close behind. They were quickly directed to opposite sides of the table, but Jamie was pleased with the arrangement as it meant that he would be able to see Alyson's face right across from him during the meal. They had barely been seated when Alyson felt the side of his foot nudge against hers. She bowed her head for the prayer, her face on fire.

Alyson never imagined she would be thankful for Garret's presence like she was that day as he mediated the mealtime conversation and single-handedly made the whole experience a success. Heather seemed to let her guard down some as she heard Alyson share more about her life and her family. At one point, Alyson had everyone laughing from a story she was telling, and Jamie could hardly breathe he was so content. He wanted to savor the memory forever.

"It must be lonely living in Bedford alone," said Heather as she began to clear the table after the meal. She piled the leftover mince pies onto one plate and stacked the empty one with the platter that had been piled high with vegetables and roast.

"It can be, but I have a friend staying with me at the moment." Alyson tried to help by grabbing a stack of dirty bowls. Heather took them from her and nodded at her to sit again.

"A friend? Didn't think you had many of those." Garret shot Jamie a curious look. He received a tiny shake of the head in response, telling him to stop pressing the topic.

"Must put a damper on things for when Jamie comes round yours to see you." Heather's back was to the table as she spoke.

Shock and horror fell across Alyson's face as she realized what Jamie's mother was implying. She wanted to jump to her feet and tell her it wasn't true, that she wasn't like that with her son, that she wasn't like that with anyone, but why should Heather believe her? She obviously hadn't maintained her morals enough to keep from getting pregnant. Any other girl would have laughed off the suggestion, but for Alyson it hit too close to a raw nerve. Even Jamie looked as if he wanted to contest the accusation, but they kept quiet.

"I'll see you tomorrow at the studio, eh?" Garret stood to his feet and pushed his chair back from the table. "It was lovely to see you, Aly."

"You as well, Gar." Alyson tried to smile, but she was too upset to put effort into it.

"We'll walk out with you, mate." Jamie stood quickly. "Have to go, mum."

"Of course." Heather walked over to her son and gave him a quick kiss on the cheek. "Thank you for bringing Aly to meet us."

Heather smiled, but it didn't reach her eyes.

"Syd, come say goodbye!" Jamie kicked his sister's chair as he walked past it. "We're leaving."

Sydney's goodbye also included Bambi, and Beatie's goodbye didn't even include Alyson as she hugged her brother tightly. Finally, Alyson was in Jamie's car. She let out her breath and cried. She pulled her feet up onto the seat and hugged her knees tightly as she sobbed into her arms. Her neck was warm from Jamie's fingers carding through her hair gently. He didn't try to shush her.

"Sorry, love," he whispered. "I know stuff like that is upsetting for you."

Alyson leaned back to press against Jamie's hand. If only he could take away the sting of humiliation that was burning in the pit of her belly. At least he knew what a comment like that meant to her. He didn't trivialize it by trying to convince her that it was fine, that no one else would care about a remark like that.

Alyson's eyes were still red when they pulled up in front of Serenity's apartment building. He exited the car and hugged her tightly before she grabbed her overnight bag from the back and pressed the buzzer for Serenity's flat. Jamie stood next to her as they waited for her to let Alyson in the building. She wrapped her arm around his, hugging it against her and leaning her aching head on his shoulder.

"Are you going to be okay tonight?" he asked, speaking softly into her hair.

"Yeah. I'm glad I'll get to have some time with Ren. It'll be good to catch up with her." Alyson hoped that Serenity would take her time answering their buzz so she could stand by Jamie for longer. "And I'm really glad I was able to meet your family."

"Me, too." Jamie kissed the top of Alyson's head and sighed. "I'm going to head back home when I'm done here and talk a bit with my mum."

"Are you going to tell her everything?" Alyson looked up at Jamie just as Serenity's voice crackled over the speaker for Alyson to come in.

Jamie pushed the door open for her and held it so he could answer her question.

"No. I'm going to tell her you're not with the dad anymore."

"What if Bambi is yours?"

"But what if he's not?"

Alyson was secretly relieved that Heather wasn't going to know the full story yet. She wasn't sure if she would be able to handle the mother of the man she loved judging her before she really knew her.

"Have a good night, Aly." Jamie kissed Alyson goodbye on her cold cheek. "Let me know if you need a ride back to Bedford in the morning."

Alyson waved and let the door close behind her. She rubbed her hands across her scalp as she stood on the elevator and let it carry her to the seventh floor. It seemed strange to be spending a Sunday night away from home and not have work the next morning. The only thing Alyson had to do at school was the Christmas play in the evening. Lucy had promised to attend the school function with her and help her find something to wear to play off her bump.

"It's still small enough, you idiot!" Lucy had insisted when Alyson admitted she was scared it was too big to hide anymore.

Never had Alyson been called idiot more times in her life than in the past few days while Lucy stayed with her in her flat. The more Lucy called her that, the more Alyson was convinced it was the ultimate term of endearment in Lucy's book. She didn't mind it anymore; it simply rolled off her back and even brought a smile to her face when she thought about it.

Serenity answered her door in her sweats and immediately pulled Alyson in for a hug when she saw the red-rimmed eyes. She placed Alyson on the couch and rushed into the kitchen to get the cup of tea she had waiting for her arrival.

"Tell me everything, dearie." She grabbed one of Alyson's hands and squeezed it before letting it go again. "What happened? Bad visit at Jamie's?"

"No, it was fine." Alyson held the warm mug in her hands and let the steam curl in her face. "But his mom doesn't think very highly of me."

"How come?"

All Alyson needed to do was look down at her stomach for Serenity to understand what had happened.

"She implied that Jamie and I sleep together. Or something. I don't know, but she must think I'm a horrible person."

"Aw, Aly. I don't think so! Was it just you and Jamie's family?"

"Garret was there."

"Garret?" Serenity's eyes flashed with interest. "You saw him? How is he? Is he okay?"

"Jamie has been looking after him. Still pretty torn up about you guys taking some time, but he seemed to be okay."

"I love that man more than life. Staying away from him is like torture." Serenity sighed. "But I know it's for the best."

"Why didn't you need space after you found out what happened with me in L.A.?"

"There was no need. He was honest, about most of it, and I knew he hadn't done anything to purposefully hurt me. Him deceiving me... that was different. I need to make sure my head is on right before we get back together."

"You're a much better person than I am." Alyson gave a sad chuckle and looked down. "You forgive so easily."

"It's not easy. It's a choice that I choose to make every day."

"But you choose it."

Serenity shrugged modestly and pointed at the cup of tea in Alyson's hand, reminding her to drink it up.

The night was a night of pampering. Alyson had never experienced such kindness before in her life. They put in *You've Got Mail,* and Serenity gave Alyson a pedicure, a hair trim and a back massage. Alyson couldn't remember the last time her body felt so good.

"Just want to make sure Bambi's mum knows how loved she is." The smell of Serenity's lotion was soaking into Alyson's skin, and she inhaled deeply the scent of lavender. "Your back is very tight, sweetheart. Little stressed?"

"Just a little." Alyson gave a low laugh.

"Also, dearie, noticing you need some new maternity clothes." Serenity could see where Alyson's pants were being worn through in the seat and in the knees. "Are these the only trousers and underclothes you have?"

"I didn't want to buy new things in Bedford, and whenever I'm in London, I'm with the guys, and I just..."

"Say no more. Tomorrow we are going shopping. Look up some good maternity styles on my laptop."

Alyson clicked on the items that caught Serenity's eye and obediently gave her opinion when it was asked for.

"Oo, I like that top! I think I've seen one like that at H&M. Or maybe it was Topshop, I can't remember now."

"Do you remember my neighbor Lucy?"

"Oh yeah, she helped me find your flat. Very sweet."

"Do you mind if I call her and tell her that she can come shopping with us tomorrow? Her husband just left her, and she's been staying with me, and she's been so..."

"Of course! We'll make a day of it!"

Alyson's mind went to another young woman she had just met a few days earlier. "Do you know Gianna Mallory?"

"Yes!" Ren said excitedly. "I haven't seen Gi in forever! Probably since the concerts in New York. It would be lovely to have her join us."

Alyson was glad that Serenity was behind her so that she couldn't see the tears running down her face. They were tears of gratitude. She felt so unworthy of Serenity's generosity.

The shopping trip with the three ladies was like a breath of fresh air for Alyson as she walked through the mall. It was freeing to not have a single worry that someone was going to recognize who she was with and take pictures of them. She was with normal people who just wanted to show her that they loved her and were on her team despite everything that had happened. They sipped their hot drinks as they wandered, stopping to buy a cute pair of shoes and an adorable sweater for the baby. It didn't take them too long to put together a few outfits for Alyson and send pictures to Danielle over Gianna's phone. They all crowded around the screen to see the picture Danielle sent back in response.

"Aw, Danielle's so cute! Look!" Gianna held her phone out. "Is that a balloon by her head?"

"Yeah, that's Balloon Bambi. It's what she uses to follow along with the pregnancy since I'm not there."

"How many weeks are you?" asked Lucy, one hand rubbing the swollen belly.

"Twenty-two on Thursday." Alyson smiled. "About the size of a papaya."

"Aw!"

Before Alyson could even see what was happening, three pairs of hands came reaching for her stomach.

Lucy and Alyson drove back to Bedford that afternoon with full hearts and several large bags of clothes for both Alyson and the baby in the backseat. They put on a Christmas album and sang along, grinning.

"Those girls are gold." Lucy turned down the music to tell Alyson what she thought of Serenity and Gianna. "Really. They are real good people."

There was one tear that snaked down the slope of Lucy's face as her voice choked up. Alyson gave her friend's arm a squeeze and handed her a Kleenex. Between the two of them, there had been many tears.

"You're a real good person, too," said Alyson. "I'm glad we're friends."

"Love you, you idiot." Lucy wiped at her tears and pressed her quivering lips together.

It was quiet in Alyson's apartment after Lucy left to spend Christmas with her family up in Yorkshire. She had invited Alyson to go with her, but Alyson had already made plans.

"Besides, I don't want to be sick of you before we even get to Tommy's in France," Alyson teased.

"It's going to be the most fun ever! I've been wanting to travel for ages and now I'm finally going to be able to do it!" Lucy squealed as she gripped at her passport in her hand. "All right then, you idiot, give me a squeeze."

Alyson hugged her friend and waited until she saw her get into the car and drive away down the street. The quiet didn't seem quite so familiar to the girl as she walked over to the couch and sat down. Her house was definitely in need of a good cleaning. Alyson had planned on taking a nap to rest first, but something inside of her refused to let her relax until things were tidy.

Jamie's first CD was playing loudly as Alyson swept, scrubbed and dusted her flat. She found a few of Lucy's things that had made it over to Alyson's apartment over the week and a half that had passed since Alyson invited the young woman to stay with her. She understood how shadows of people and memories could haunt you if you remained surrounded by who they used to be. Alyson simply put the things in a pile on the end of the bed in the guest room, now Lucy's room, and shut the door.

On the top of the refrigerator was a stack of pictures Alyson had drawn. She wasn't ready for anyone to know about her secret stash of drawings yet, so she had simply set the ones she did with Lucy on top of the fridge. Now that she was alone, she took them into the nursery. She was about to leave when the song "Sweet Dreams" began to play and Jamie's young voice came through the speakers.

Alyson moved the framed lyrics from the corner and held it in her hands. She followed along, word by word, until the song was finished. Instead of putting the picture back where she had stored it for the last two months, she set it on the shelf above the changing table.

"You're going to be born so soon, Bambi. We're over halfway there." Alyson rubbed her stomach and sighed. "When am I going to feel you? You still okay?"

There was no answer and no movement. Alyson let the nagging worry that something might be wrong return to the back of her mind where it had been sitting for the last two weeks. She just had to wait until the seventh of January to have her next doctor's appointment. There had been no blood or cramping, and those were the signs she was told to worry about.

Jamie came to pick Alyson up from Bedford three days before Christmas. Alyson had caught up on both sleep and cleaning and was ready to not be alone anymore. There was one picture in the closet ripped full of holes from angry tears, but the rest of the faces wore peaceful expressions. One even had the hint of a smile.

It was nerve-wracking to think about the fact that she was going to stay with Jamie and his family for a few days, especially since Heather Donald still didn't seem very impressed with her. She knew that if she spent her Christmas alone, though, she would end up regretting it. Her holiday Skype date with her parents had already happened, and her heart wasn't ready to wake up in her big, white home to the sound of her own voice telling herself "Merry Christmas."

"You'll sleep here." Jamie helped Alyson into a small bedroom at the end of the hallway. "It's my bedroom, but I'll bunk up with Hanson so you can have a little bit of privacy while you're here."

"Where's your family?" Alyson set her purse on the foot of the bed. No one had been jumping on the front step to greet them this time.

"Shopping, I believe." Jamie folded his arms over his chest. "For food and presents."

"Is Christmas a big deal in your house?" Alyson had grown up with quiet Christmases that consisted of one present from each parent, some hot cocoa and snuggling in front of the fire with a book.

"Oh, very big!" Jamie's eyes lit up. "My mum loves giving loads of pressies, and cooking food all day long! By the end of the day the house is a mess and we're so stuffed we can't move, but we love it!"

"Is your, uh..." Alyson paused and ran her fingers through her hair. "Is your mom okay with me being here, you know, for the holidays?"

"Yeah, love." Jamie's forehead wrinkled with concern. "I wouldn't have asked you to come if I had thought my mum didn't want you here. I told you, we had a really good talk and she's good with it all. She's just worried because you're American and you're..."

"Wait, what?"

"What?"

"Why is the fact that I'm American something that worries her?"

"Because America is far away from London." Jamie gave a sad smile. "I think she's afraid you'll take me away from her."

Alyson gave a little chuckle and shook her head.

"Did you tell her you're the one who's taken me away?"

"Yeah, something like that." A sneaky smile spread over Jamie's face as he walked over to the girl and pulled her into his arms. Her stomach pressed between them. "Bambi's getting a bit in the way these days, eh?"

Alyson laughed and looked up at Jamie's sparkling eyes. He pressed his lips onto the tip of her nose, causing her eyelids to flutter down and rest on her cheeks.

"You are so beautiful." His breath fell across her face, and she smiled as she smelled the flavor of his gum and the coffee he had for breakfast that morning.

"Thank you." Alyson opened her eyes. "And I wish we could stay like this longer, but I have to use the loo, and I'm really hungry."

The rest of Jamie's family returned as the couple was finishing their lunch. Sydney was beyond excited to hug her friend and make cute noises at the baby while Beatie dutifully shook Alyson's hand and walked away. Heather greeted Alyson with a smile the girl hadn't seen during her first visit, and it set her heart at ease.

"You full, Aly?" Jamie asked after supper. He sat with his arm draped over the back of her chair. He gave her a smile when she turned to look at him.

"Yes, thank you." She kept her hands carefully in her lap.

"Sydney, help with the washing up, will you?" Heather stood to her feet.

"It's Hanson's turn to wash the dishes!" Sydney protested. "'Sides, I promised Aly that I would help her look at baby names after supper!"

"Baby names?" Jamie turned to Aly.

"Apparently it's a thing." Alyson gave him a serious look. "When a child is born you give it a name for him to keep for the rest of its life."

"Haha!" said Jamie sarcastically. "I know that, I..."

"I want to help pick out names, too!" Hanson's loud complaints cut-off Jamie's words. "Boys can help with baby names!"

"Yes they can, *after* they help do the tidying in the kitchen." Heather's stern look soon had her almost-teenage son in his spot by the sink.

"This is going to be so much fun! I have seven books from the library to look through!" Sydney pulled the girl into the living room where Alyson was told to sit on the couch. Beatie followed behind slowly, her eyes and ears alert.

"Why so quiet, sport?" asked Jamie as he joined her in the entryway of the living room. He leaned against the wall, his hands shoved into his pockets and a fond smile on his face.

"You smile at her a lot."

"What do you mean?"

"Aly. Her. She's just... a girl. A normal girl. But you look at her like, I don't know. I've never seen you look at anyone like that. Not even Beth when you guys were having a laugh." Beatie frowned. "I liked it better when you didn't have a girlfriend."

"Hey, hey, hey!" Jamie removed his hands from his pockets and crouched down by his little sister. "Why are you saying things like that? We've talked about this. Remember? No matter who I have in my life, I'll always love you in a special way. I have special love just for you that I can't give to anyone else. Just like I can't give Sydney's love to Hanson, or your love to Sydney. I'll always have love for you, no matter who else is in my life."

"Do I make you happy, Jay?"

The question almost broke Jamie's heart, and he knelt down on the floor to look up at Beatie's serious face and tear-filled blue eyes. She looked so much like Sydney when Sydney was little.

"You have made me so incredibly happy your whole life." Jamie took Beatie's hands in his own. "I meant that, hundred percent."

"You make me happy, too." Beatie leaned forward and placed an innocent kiss on her brother's forehead.

Beatie tugged her hands away from Jamie's grip and walked into the living room. She snuggled against Sydney's side and listened to her sister talk excitedly with their holiday visitor. Jamie was still standing and watching from the edge of the room when Hanson zipped past him.

"Come on, Jay! We have to name Bambi!" Hanson dragged his older brother into the room. When they reached the couch, Hanson hesitated before pushing Jamie down to sit next to Aly. "You can sit next to her. You like girls."

"You like girls too, Hans," Sydney shot over at her little brother. "But I know Jay wants to sit next to Aly anyway."

Jamie simply smiled as he took his spot. Alyson's cheeks were pink, but she looked happy. His hand wrapped around her arm by her elbow, and he leaned over her shoulder to read the names off the page.

Christmas lights were strung up over the fireplace and around the windows while the stockings hung on the mantel. Wreaths decorated just about every door, spreading holiday cheer and their green, piney scent. The eggnog and hot chocolate Heather brought out to her children on a tray added to the Christmas spirit that was emanating throughout the room. She turned on Michael Bublé's Christmas album and was soon humming along as she sat on the love seat with a book on her lap. She had only been in the room a few minutes when Beatie slipped away from the couch and curled up next to her mother. Within moments, the child was asleep.

"Marvin! I love that name!" Sydney blurted out for the fiftieth time.

Alyson could see Jamie roll his eyes and she tried not to laugh.

"Marvin? I think I like the name Matthew better," said Alyson

"I know a boy named Matthew. He never changes his socks," said Hanson.

"I'm sure if Bambi is a boy and Aly names him Matthew that he will change his socks," Sydney scoffed.

"What about Joseph?" Heather's voice was quiet.

"Joseph?" Jamie repeated.

"Just thought of it 'cause of the Christmas story," said Heather.

"I like the name Joseph."

Heather returned the smile Alyson gave her and put her book back in front of her face. Alyson watched her for a few seconds longer, until Jamie's pointing finger brought her attention back to the names.

"Maxwell. That's a proper good name."

"Oo, and then we could call him Max for short! Oh, I love it!" Sydney slammed her book shut and clapped her hands excitedly.

"What do you think, love?" The term of endearment slipped from his mouth before he could stop it.

Alyson shrugged and said she didn't know, very aware of Heather's eyes peering at them over the top of her novel. She shifted away from him and tried to look very interested in the name on the bottom, right-hand side of the page.

Sydney smiled knowingly as she glanced over at her brother. Jamie had been her best friend her whole life and whoever was important to her brother was important to her. It wasn't unusual for Jamie to keep his romantic relationships away from his family, making sure they were real and would last before bringing the girl home. When a girl was invited home, everyone knew it was time to pay attention.

"All right, kids. Time for bed." Heather slowly closed her book and yawned. "Jamie, help me get Beatie to bed?"

"Wait for me here." Jamie whispered quietly before standing up to carry his little sister up the stairs to her bedroom.

A few minutes later, after a few more promptings, Sydney and Hanson left the room and went to their bedrooms as well. Alyson remained on the couch, her sides suddenly cold from the lack of body heat next to her. She had flipped the name book on her lap to the girl names. Her eyes rested on one she loved.

"Hey, got you a present!" Jamie's voice startled her as the young man returned to the living room with his hands behind his back.

"But it's not even Christmas Eve yet!" she laughed.

"No, but I found this earlier and wanted to share. I figured we could eat these tonight, and then buy some new ones before we have to leave some out for Santa." Jamie pulled a box of Oreos out from behind his back.

"Oh! Oh!" Alyson reached for them excitedly. She opened the package and took her first bite. Her tongue remembered the flavor with a rush of nostalgia. "This definitely is the best present."

"Good." Jamie plopped down onto the couch next to Alyson and snuck his hand into the package. "Happy Christmas, love."

"Happy Christmas." Alyson smiled shyly. It still felt odd to say 'happy' instead of 'merry', but she didn't mind it.

"How do you feel about being with my family?"

"My Christmases growing up were never like this, but this feels like home somehow. It's the kind of Christmas I always wanted to have. Besides, two out of three siblings approve of me so I feel it can only get better from here."

"Ah, just give Beatie some time. She's still afraid one day I'll leave and never come back just like her dad. Doesn't matter how many times I promise that I'm not leaving, she still freaks out before every trip I take." Jamie pulled at his lip for a second. "It's definitely hard leaving her."

"I can imagine."

"But Syd and Hans, they're champs. Proper good kids. I've got myself a good family."

It made Alyson smile to see a glassy sheen of tears cover Jamie's eyes. He pressed them away with his thumb and forefinger while he cleared his throat of the lump that became lodged there. He shook his head and rolled his eyes when he turned to see Alyson's teasing smirk.

"Oh, shush. You cry all the time, let me have my moment."

"I didn't realize I was rubbing off on you so strongly." Alyson tried not to laugh.

"Ha!" Jamie took the teasing in stride. He looked over at Alyson as she studied the flickering light of the fireplace with a smile. The way the shadows danced on her face reminded him of the shifting lights of the club the night he met her, except this was better; more intimate. Deeper. They knew each other now. They were no longer two strangers dancing because they could; they were friends who loved each other because they chose to. "You look beautiful."

Alyson's stomach flooded with butterflies, a grin spanning across her face before she tried to push it away. She still had a grin pulling up one side of her mouth when she looked back over at him.

"You already told me that today."

"It's still true. I can't get over it."

Her hand felt Jamie's fingers brush lightly in a loving gesture before they settled on Bambi. He leaned close and whispered that this Christmas was going to be the best Christmas ever.

"And I can't wait for next Christmas so you can be with us in a real, proper way." Jamie pressed a kiss against the skin of Alyson's stomach. "And then that Christmas will be the best Christmas ever."

Chapter seventeen
"Do you think we'll make it?"

The sun was shining when Alyson opened her eyes the next morning. She checked her phone and saw a text from Lucy saying that she missed her and she hoped Aly was having a good time with Jamie. Alyson sent a quick response back telling her that she missed being called idiot every five minutes.

"Morning! Hiya, Bambi!" Sydney was the first to greet Alyson when she appeared downstairs in the kitchen, fully dressed and still yawning.

"Good morning." Alyson chuckled and held her hands out of the way while Sydney pulled at her stomach and talked to her baby. "Did I miss breakfast?"

"Are you kidding? We're on holiday! We've only just woken up ourselves." Sydney let go of Bambi and sat down in a chair. "Pass the cereal, Bea."

"I've already eaten, but I was half asleep so I'm eating again." Hanson poured a generous amount of milk into his bowl.

Alyson was soon seated on a chair with a bowl of Lucky Charms in front of her. She never ate cereal like that, despite the fact that she enjoyed the sugary flavor. Hanson moaned about how he wasn't going to be able to go ice skating with his friends that afternoon, and Beatie sang, "We wish you a merry Christmas," between her bites of breakfast.

"What are we doing today?"

"No, there's no *we* today," Sydney huffed. "Jamie says he gets you all day long! Something about lunch and a fancy outing this evening."

"Syd! It's a surprise!" Beatie glared at her sister.

"Oh?" Alyson looked around the room and saw Jamie wasn't with them. "Where is he?"

"Walking mummy to work." Beatie continued to stare her sister down, demanding her to stay silent and not spill anymore secrets.

"He should be back soon, though," said Sydney as she ignored Beatie's gaze. "Unless he stops for a donut like he was saying."

"Stop for a donut! Without us?" Hanson's head snapped up. "He wouldn't!"

"He did that once, do you remember, Hans?" Beatie spoke with her mouth full.

A click from down the hallway caused them all to freeze and pause their conversation.

"Hello!" Jamie shouted from the front door. "Where is everybody?"

With smirks and smiles, Jamie's siblings sat as silent and still as mice. Alyson joined them, not sure what they were doing, but entertained by the expressions on their faces. Jamie's steps sounded closer, then further away, then closer again.

"Hello?"

Beatie slapped her hands over her mouth to keep from giggling as they could hear Jamie climbing the stairs. A full minute passed before he retraced his path back down the stairs and finally turned the corner into the kitchen.

"Really? Even you?" Jamie pointed at Alyson as his brother and sisters burst into laughter.

"I didn't know you were here." Alyson blinked innocently.

"You lot have corrupted her! All of you!" Jamie pointed a finger at his younger siblings while wrapping his other arm around Alyson from behind. He felt her lean against him and he held her tighter. "She was a perfectly nice, decent girl before she met you!"

"You're welcome." A sarcastic smile lit up Sydney's face, and Alyson snickered. "Hans, pass me the cereal please."

"Are you feeling up for kind of a big day?" Jamie's voice softened as he spoke just to Alyson.

"Sure," she said.

"Good." Jamie straightened and stepped back so he could see her face. "Because I'm taking you out, so get dressed into something nice."

"As in... a day downtown nice?"

"Exactly."

Jamie was glowing when Alyson returned downstairs, dressed in a Christmas-red top. It was long, and loose, paired with black tights and boots. A cream-colored scarf was wound around her neck, barely hiding where her neckline revealed her skin. Instead of wearing it down, she had her hair pulled up and back into a side braid to show off a set of pearl earrings.

"Aly! My word! You look like a model! Can I snap a picture of you?" Sydney jumped up from her spot on the couch where she was browsing through another name book. "Please show me how you do your makeup, it's flawless! Do you see this, Jay? Literally flawless! This is perfection!"

Alyson smiled and blushed as Sydney posed her on the stairs and told her to smile, then look down at Jamie and continue to smile. He finally put his foot down and told her no more pictures. He took Alyson's hand and helped her into her coat.

Alyson was not expecting to be joined by anyone else as they left Jamie's car in a parking garage downtown. The holiday decorations were sparkling in the sun and Christmas carols could be heard from every shop and diner they passed, distracting Alyson from the couple that was walking towards them.

"Aly!" Serenity finally called out, laughing when she saw Alyson startle and turn at the sound of her name. She laughed again when Aly realized who was holding Serenity's hand.

"You guys are back together!" Alyson hugged her friend, beaming happily.

"Told you I didn't want to leave him." Serenity snuggled against Garret's shoulder and let him kiss the side of her face.

"So, are you girls ready?" Garret asked, eyes twinkling as he shared a look with his best friend.

There had never been a day like that in Alyson's life before. She would have enjoyed her day if it had just been her and Jamie, but it seemed all the more special to share it with Serenity and Garret. Whenever a fan stopped Jamie for a picture, Serenity would pull Alyson to the side and make sure there were no more cameras out before they joined the guys again. Hours passed before Alyson realized their day was a sort of double-date.

Not sort of. Alyson told herself. *This is a real-life double-date.*

They went to several shops and Serenity helped Alyson pick out a gorgeous necklace with a tiny diamond that hung on a delicate, gold chain. From there they had a stroll around Trafalgar Square. The hustle and bustle of the holiday crowd made them forget about the frosty wind nipping their noses, and cold fingers were soon warmed in the grip of the person next to them. When Alyson's feet had had enough walking, they settled down at a Thai restaurant where Garret had made reservations for them.

Alyson sat at the table, her fingers lightly massaging her stomach. Jamie sat close and kept an arm on her chair, telling everyone in the room that she was with him. She tried to keep up with the conversation, but after her meal she was almost too tired to keep her eyes open.

"I think it's time for a quick kip," said Garret noting the warm, sleepy smile on Alyson's face.

Ten minutes later, Alyson found herself with Serenity at Serenity's flat for a few hours of rest. Alyson was glad for the nap when the evening stretched on longer than she was used to. The Christmas carols, the beautiful Christmas lights, the candy canes and the little whispers that made Alyson blush were the perfect ending to the perfect day. Perfect was the word that Alyson used to describe it to Danielle the next day when they had their Skype call.

"I know you don't like him, but..." Alyson stopped.

"I'm happy that things are going well with the both of you," said Danielle sincerely. "I want you to be happy."

"I wish you could be here to see how beautiful London is at Christmas time. It's like nothing we have anywhere in the Midwest. It is stunning!"

"I'm sure I'd love to see London, but I would be content just seeing you and Bambi."

"I know." Her friend's words were bittersweet. "I miss you."

"You have a roommate and a boyfriend, you're in London for Christmas, and you're going to France for New Years'! You don't miss me!"

Alyson knew that Danielle was teasing, but there was a grain of truth somewhere in it all. She sighed and frowned at the camera.

"Things have taken a good turn, but it doesn't matter if life is good or hard, I always wish you were with me. You're my favorite person to experience new things and go on adventures with. You don't know how much I wish you were my Christmas present."

"Same," Danielle exhaled loudly. "Have you found a church to go to in Bedford?"

Alyson froze at the question.

"Or, like, a bible study."

"No. Just keeping to myself."

"Being part of a church or a bible study could really help, you know." Danielle stayed quiet as Alyson looked down at the floor. "Well, I'm praying for you every day."

"I'm fine," mumbled Alyson.

"I'm concerned that you haven't really been able to process what you went through last summer. It was intense and you had a horrible time trying to get back up on your feet before you found out you were pregnant."

"I'm fine. I just focus on Bambi..."

"Stop stuffing down your emotions, Aly. Do not do this to yourself." Danielle was adamant in her request. "I know you, you'll shove it all down and ignore it while you slowly die on the inside. You have to work through this."

"It's finally getting easier..." Alyson felt the pressure grow in her throat. "I don't..."

"I know you don't want to, but for the sake of your emotional health, you've got to! For Bambi's sake, work through your feelings. Please."

It took a moment before Alyson could compose herself enough to talk to her best friend again. She knew Danielle was right, but she hated the fact that she was going to have to pull the painful memories back out instead of hide them away. It had seemed easy to pretend there was no black smudge on the history of her friendship with the guys, but her heart thumped at her, as if trying to remind her of the hurt it carried every day.

"Okay." Alyson's voice was rough. "I promise."

"Thank you." Danielle hadn't realized she was holding her breath until she let it out. "Thank you."

"Tell me something happy so I stop crying." Alyson tried to wipe her tears away without messing up her eyeliner.

"Well, here's Balloon Bambi."

The camera jostled and blurred as Danielle moved her computer to get a better view of the red and green colored balloon taped to her bedroom wall. It was supposed to be the size of an eggplant, like the baby book said it should be, but it seemed too big to be the same size as the vegetable or even the actual Bambi in Alyson's stomach. Alyson tried to gauge its size and shook her head.

"It looks way too big to be an eggplant."

"Well, the thing about balloons is that they are really hard to measure when you're blowing them up," Danielle informed her. "I took it to the grocery store so I could look at a real eggplant, but I still couldn't get it right."

"Why didn't you just buy an eggplant and take it home?" Alyson giggled as she imagined her best friend walking around the grocery store with an inflated balloon in her hands.

"Why would I buy something I'm not going to eat?"

"I thought you liked eggplant!"

"I do, but I don't know how to cook it. I mean, seriously..."

"Fair enough."

Alyson looked at the clock. She was planning to go shopping with Sydney and Hanson soon. All of a sudden the cheery decor and atmosphere of London was nothing compared to the familiar sound of Elle's laugh and the strength that came from knowing she could tell her friend anything in the world and never lose her love. She had been hugged plenty in the last two weeks between Lucy, Eddie, Tommy, Sydney... But she wanted a best friend hug, and no one in the world could give her that apart from Danielle Ledger.

Christmas morning dawned cold and gloomy, but the three youngest children in the Donald house hardly noticed. They rushed to see the presents under the tree, then to find their Christmas guest. Jamie was woken by the sound of their running feet in the hallway.

"Guys, stop! You'll wake Aly!" He groaned, hoping they would hear him. The familiar squeak of the handle on his bedroom door from the end of the hall reached him. He jumped to his feet and rushed out. "Guys! Stop!"

"But it's Christmas morning! It's time to open pressies!" Beatie turned at the sound of Jamie's voice, her lower lip stuck out in a pout.

"No! You can't just wake her up!" Jamie's voice faded to a loud whisper as he marched toward them and pulled the door shut again. Alyson was still sound asleep. "She's got a baby growing inside of her, and she gets up a hundred times just to use the toilet. Believe me, I heard every time. Let her sleep until she's ready to wake up. Besides, you guys kept her up late playing that Monopoly game."

"It only took so long because you were cheating!" Hanson laid the blame at Jamie's feet. "You wanted Aly to beat us!"

"I could have sworn there was a rule about paying money to the person with the little doggy piece!" Jamie raised his hands in innocence.

Sydney rolled her eyes before turning and walking back down the hallway to go downstairs. Hanson also walked away, disappearing into his room, but Beatie was determined to wait until Alyson awoke. Jamie tried to explain that the girl could sleep for several more hours, but she didn't seem to care.

"How come you're waiting for her?" asked Jamie as he settled down on the floor next to her.

"I want to see her face when she goes into the living room and sees all the presents under the tree."

"How come you want to see that?"

"Because she has a really pretty smile, and her eyes light up, and there are these little crinkles by her eyes. I really like seeing her happy."

"I like seeing her happy, too."

"Are you going to keep her?"

"She's not a pet, love. She's a person. But I do plan on loving her for a long time." Jamie kept his voice low as he spoke. "What do you think? Do you think we'll make it?"

"Yeah. She's really smart, and she makes you laugh." Beatie gave her serious opinion. "I like that she makes you laugh."

"What do you mean she makes me laugh?"

"Usually you're so worried about mum or us or going on tour that you don't laugh very often. But when she's here, you laugh all the time."

"You like that, eh?" Jamie hadn't even noticed.

"Besides, she's really pretty, and she is going to have a baby."

"Yes." Jamie sighed as he agreed. "She is that for sure; beautiful and going to have a baby."

"Are you going to take care of the baby when it's born?"

"Yeah, I hope to. I'm going to take care of Aly and Bambi as much as I can."

"Aly told me that she would tell me who the dad is after the baby is born. We shook on it."

"Oh, really?" Jamie raised his eyebrows. "Well, if you shook on it then she won't break her word."

"She better not. Keeping your word is important."

"It is."

"Jay?"

"Hmm?" He turned to look over at his sister's screwed-up, thoughtful expression.

"Have you ever made a promise and broken it?"

It was ironic that their conversation had turned from Alyson to broken promises. His memory flicked back to September and the day he found out she was pregnant. A million emotions had rushed through him, but the one that had dominated was fear followed closely by jealousy. Anger. Selfishness.

"I have." Jamie nodded.

"Can you fix broken promises if you try hard enough?"

"Where are all these questions coming from, little girl?" Jamie leaned forward to ruffle his sister's hair.

"Well, can you?" Beatie insisted, smoothing her hair back down on her head.

"Sometimes, yes. But things are never quite the same after the promise has been broken."

"Because breaking promises hurts people."

"You're right."

"I think you should marry her."

"Sorry?"

"I think you should marry Aly."

"Do you think?" Red grew hot in Jamie's cheeks. "I thought you didn't like me having a girlfriend?"

"I don't, but if you promised to take care of her and Bambi, then you should keep your promise. If you break it, you'll hurt her."

Jamie was speechless.

"Besides, I know what it's like to not have a dad..." Beatie looked away, her chin quivering the tiniest bit.

"Oh, kiddo." Jamie scooted closer to his sister and pulled her onto his lap. She still fit under his chin. "How about we sing some songs while we wait, yeah? What do you want to sing?"

"Can you sing the song you wrote for me?"

Jamie tried to focus on Beatie as he sang, but his memory kept going back to the night he had played piano for Alyson in California. Those two days together had been real and magical. He wished he could go back to their conversation under the stars against the fence and the one they had in the kitchen.

When Aly told me she still wanted to be with me...

Alyson opened her door half an hour later to use the bathroom. The squeaking of the knob as it twisted alerted Jamie that he should move out of the way. He quickly stood up, still holding onto Beatie to keep her from falling onto the floor from his lap.

"Oh! You scared me!" Alyson laughed as she saw Jamie and Beatie outside her door. "Good morning."

"Happy Christmas." Beatie smiled up at Alyson.

"Happy Christmas, Beatie." Alyson was surprised by the little girl's friendly greeting and shot Jamie an inquisitive look. He merely shook his head. "I hope you guys aren't waiting on me for the gifts."

"We've been waiting for hours!" Hanson yelled from his bedroom.

"Hans! That's rude!" Jamie shouted back. "Sorry, Aly, we haven't been waiting for hours."

"Well, I'm ready as soon as I use the washroom."

Sydney, Hanson, Jamie and Beatie were all waiting at the top of the stairs for Alyson to be ready. She turned red when she saw the siblings waiting on her, but she smiled as she joined them. Sydney latched onto one arm, and she rested her other hand carefully on the back of Beatie's head. Beatie was trying to whisper something up at her while Hanson ran ahead of her, singing a made-up song about Santa Clause.

"I love Christmas!" Sydney was practically glowing.

"Wow, you guys sure do like to celebrate loudly!" Alyson laughed, feeling the sleep still clinging to her eyes.

"We're just putting on a show for you, love." He leaned forward quickly and placed a kiss on Alyson's pink cheek before anyone could catch him. "Happy Christmas."

"Happy Christmas." Alyson moved her hand from Beatie's head and let her fingers brush lightly over the skin of Jamie's arm. She saw him look down to see her hand there, then look up to meet her eyes. She gave him a soft smile.

Heather was already sitting in the living room with her cup of coffee waiting for her children to join her when they all trooped in. There were stacks of presents that Alyson hadn't seen the night before, and she covered her gaping mouth with her hands. She had seen Christmases like this in movies, but now she was about to get one of her own.

She sat on one end of the love seat with her feet tucked up under her and Sydney beside her. Hanson brought everyone a mug of hot chocolate and Jamie followed after with a can of whipped cream. Alyson found out from the conversation around her that this was a tradition for them, as was Jamie squirting a dollop of the whipped cream on Sydney's cheek.

"Every year, Jamison William Donald! Every year!" Sydney grabbed a napkin to wipe her face.

"Can I pass out the presents, mummy?" asked Beatie.

"I'm already doing it!" Hanson snatched up an armful. "Here's a present for Bambi."

"Oh! Thank you!" Alyson opened the gift to find an ornament that said *Baby's first Christmas* with a picture frame. "This is perfect!"

"Mummy bought it," said Beatie.

"Thank you, Heather!"

"Maybe you'll put it on our tree next year," Heather mentioned casually.

"Yeah." Alyson smiled somewhat uncertainly, not sure what way she meant for her to take the comment.

"Mum!" Jamie gave his mother a look.

"Will Alyson be here next year if Jamie marries her?" asked Beatie. She looked around at the three adults.

"Bea!" Even Sydney was shocked.

"Let's open some more presents!" Jamie jumped to his feet and handed a present to his brother.

Towards the end of the festivities, a present was put in Jamie's lap with a tag that read, *With love, Aly and Bambi.* He looked over at her and shook his head as he smiled.

"I told you not to get me a present."

"Well, I bought it with the money you gave me so technically you bought yourself a present." A blush tinged Alyson's cheeks as she waited for him to open the box.

"Do you have a pressie for Aly?" asked Sydney, noting that everyone else besides Jamie had given one to their Christmas guest.

"He already gave me a present," Alyson spoke up quickly. She was thinking of the necklace he had bought her earlier that week.

There was a secretive little smile on his face when he glanced back up at her. He opened up the box on his lap and pulled out a brand new backpack; the exact one he had been admiring for months, but hadn't bought because he knew he didn't need it. He hadn't even told Alyson about it. Garret was the one to tell Alyson the day they were out together. She had gone back later during her shopping trip with Sydney and Hanson to buy it.

"Aly! How did you know?"

"Santa told me." Alyson was pleased with the way Jamie's face shone over his gift. "You like it?"

"Like it? I mean, yeah, I guess it's all right."

She waited for him to put his hand in the front pocket. Sydney was opening her next gift when Jamie found the little piece of paper Alyson had left for him. A smile tugged at the corners of his mouth as he read the note. He turned to her and saw she was watching him. No one else in the room saw the kiss he blew in her direction.

Wrapping paper covered the room from end to end by the time all the gifts had been opened. Instead of clearing up the mess, Heather ordered all of her children to the dining room for their special Christmas breakfast. She led the way with Beatie hanging onto her arm. Alyson hung back on purpose, hoping to get a moment with Jamie alone before breakfast, but Sydney stood impatiently, waiting for her to walk to the dining room with her.

"I'm coming! Just a minute. Bambi doesn't like to walk fast." Alyson could see Jamie on his phone out of the corner of her eye. "You go ahead, save me a spot next to you."

"No, come on!" Sydney put a hand on Alyson's arm and gave it a gentle tug.

"Hey, Syd, I have to talk to Alyson about something quick. About her trip back home and such." Jamie jumped to his feet and slipped his phone back into his pocket. "Go on."

The couple waited until Sydney was out of sight before Jamie wrapped his arms around Alyson in a Christmas hug. Alyson pulled her arms in close to her body and let Jamie hold her. He rested his scruffy chin on her forehead and swayed back and forth slowly, their breathing in sync.

Now that no one else was in the room, the words and melody of "*I'll Be Home for Christmas*" could be heard playing from the speakers in the corner. Alyson had sung along to that song a million times before, but right then, on the other side of the world from her parents and the place she had grown up calling home, the song took a completely different meaning. She snuggled closer against Jamie's shoulder and bit the inside of her cheeks to keep from crying. Jamie's throat vibrated as he hummed along.

"Merry Christmas, Jamie," Alyson whispered thickly. His arms were going to have to be her home for now. A tear fell when she tried to blink them away. She heard him chuckle and wondered what she had done to make him laugh.

"*Merry* Christmas, love." Jamie thought his heart would burst from all the love he felt for the girl he was holding. Their second chance at being together was something Jamie never wanted to take for granted. "Thank you for the note."

"Well, it's true." Alyson smiled even though Jamie wouldn't see it.

"It was very insightful, wish I had read it sooner. If I had known that all you wanted for Christmas was to hold my hand, I would have just left you up in Bedford and not brought you to London for the holiday," he teased.

"Stop! You know what I mean!" Alyson freed one of her hands and poked Jamie in the side. He twisted himself away from the girl and caught her wrist with his hand, forcing it back to where it had been.

"And I do have a Christmas present for you, but it's waiting for you at your apartment."

"Jamie, you already bought me a necklace..."

"I can do as I please." Jamie cut her off with a quick kiss to the forehead. He put one hand on each of her arms and held her out at an arm's length, drinking in all he saw, from the freckles on her nose to the bashful smile that she was giving to the floor. Her green eyes peered up at him shyly, wondering what he was trying to accomplish by staring at her face. "There. That was all the Christmas present I needed. Let's go get some breakfast."

Jamie knew exactly how far down the hallway he could get away with holding Alyson's hand before his family would see them. He gave her a sad smile as he slipped their fingers apart and began to walk quickly, bouncing as he made his way down the hall.

"Mum, it smells amazing!"

"Did you get all your plans squared away?" asked Sydney as Alyson sat down next to her.

"Yes." Alyson hoped her cheeks weren't still red.

Alyson took her time to soak in the Christmas traditions that were a part of the Donald household. They pulled the Christmas crackers and wore the tissue paper crowns that were inside. Beatie and Jamie got in a serious debate over trading the little trinkets that were inside of the poppers. The rest of them were in tears trying to hold in their laughter as they watched.

Memories from when Jamie and Sydney were little came up and their mother had to step in with details and elaborations. Heather's storytelling had everyone captivated with her vivid descriptions. Alyson listened with rapt attention, forgetting about the food in front of her.

Her hands rested on Bambi, and she found herself hoping and dreaming Bambi would experience Christmas like this: with family and loved ones, laughing and full of hope for the future. She met Jamie's gaze and gave him a deep smile. She was never going to be able to thank him enough for making this the best Christmas of her life.

Heather wasn't sure what she had expected when she agreed to let Alyson spend Christmas with them, but she hadn't expected to wake up on Christmas day with the resolve to tell her son to end whatever it was he had with her. She had agreed to let Alyson come because she wanted to make Jamie happy, and she wanted to really get to know Alyson. Both of those things had happened, and Heather had come to a conclusion about the girl.

It wasn't just Bambi that bothered Heather, and it wasn't even the fact that no one knew who the father was. Jamie had told her some story about how Alyson was no longer with the dad and how he was the one who was going to be stepping up when the baby was born, and maybe that was what bothered her the most.

She could see that Jamie was determined on keeping that girl in his life no matter what, and Heather wondered what kind of cost he would end up paying in the end. She had been young and rushed into love once. No one else had made her feel the way Dave Livingston did when he kissed her goodnight on the corner, and no one made her feel the way Dave Livingston did when he was caught cheating on her three months later. Not only were Jamie and Alyson rushing through things, but Alyson was in a very vulnerable situation. How long was she going to want Jamie to stick around after the baby was born? What would happen when she flew back to America? Would Jamie follow her?

Her thoughts turned to Beth. She knew it couldn't have been too long after Jamie's breakup with her that things started between him and Alyson. She was a rebound, yet Heather had never seen her son like this with any of his previous girlfriends. He clearly was putting his emotions in charge of his common sense, and it worried her.

Heather finally caught Jamie alone late in the afternoon. Alyson and the other children were snuggled in front of the fire watching *Arthur Christmas* so Heather decided to tell him her thoughts. His first reaction was silence as he stared down at the floor, his arms crossed and one hip against the counter.

"You really don't like her?"

"I like her well enough. It's the whole situation I don't like, Jamie."

"What are you talking about? Bambi? Her being American? Come on, mum. This isn't like you!"

"I know! Believe me, I didn't expect to not fall in love with her!" Heather couldn't look at the betrayed expression in her son's eyes. "Do you remember when I was with Jack?"

Jamie groaned and rolled his eyes.

"No, listen! I decided that Jack and I needed to stay together because I was pregnant with Beatie and I needed someone. I needed someone to be there, to experience life with me. I was lonely, Jay, and you were about to fly the nest and try to become a superstar. I needed someone, so I chose Jack. But, you know how that ended..."

"You're comparing me to Jack?"

"No, I'm comparing Aly to me." Heather tried not to sound snappish. "She's all alone here on the other side of the ocean. She's having her first baby, and she's really young, Jamie. Honestly, I don't think she feels as strongly about you as you feel about her. I'm afraid that after the baby is born she'll feel even less towards you."

"No." Jamie shook his head. "That's not true. We... Mum, I...! We're not going to ruin this."

"Would you honestly be with Aly if she wasn't pregnant with Bambi?"

"Of course..." Jamie began to spit out his answer bitterly when he stopped, because it was a lie. He had walked out on Alyson that night, and she had let him leave her behind. He would never have seen Alyson again if it wasn't for Bambi. He rubbed his hands over his face and sighed with frustration. "Mum, I don't see why you can't just be happy for me. I'm happier than I've been in ages! Do you want me to go back to being depressed like I was with Beth? Do you want me to get back with her? She was rude, mum. She loved my job more than she cared about me, yet you *never* talked about her like this! Not once!"

"I don't want you to go back to Beth!"

Beth had been safe, though. She was likable enough and never showed any interest in doing anything that would hurt Jamie. In the end they had called it off because of her immaturity and insincerity, but she was never a threat to taking him away from London.

"I'm in love with Aly!"

"She's not going to want to stay after her job. She's going to take the baby and go back to where her family and her friends are. What are you going to do then? I don't want you to get hurt, Jay! I'm scared she's going to end up breaking your heart, son!"

They heard a footstep scuff across the threshold, and they looked to the doorway. Alyson was there, her hands on her belly and her expression stoic. She stood by the door, not coming any closer.

Jamie left his spot by the counter and hurried to Alyson's side. He pulled her into a hug and kissed the top of her head. The sound of sniffling came from where her face was buried into Jamie's chest. "Aly. I'm sorry."

"Don't be sorry." Alyson did her best to push her tears down. "I'm glad I heard it."

Alyson looked tentatively at Heather as Jamie's arms dropped from her shoulders. His mother was watching them carefully, frowning. Alyson slipped a hand into his, interlacing their fingers as Jamie stood between her and his mother.

"Aly, I'm sorry you had to hear that, but it's the truth."

She said nothing.

"Jamie doesn't care for people halfway, he's all or nothing. I can't support this relationship without seeing you putting your all into this!"

"Mum, this really isn't your business!"

"Jamie, you're being a fool right now! You're chasing a dream you might not catch!"

"Can you please stop talking like Alyson isn't right here?"

"I want her to know how I feel about your relationship!" Heather hadn't had an argument with her son like this for a long time. She hated that it was over a girl, and she hated that she was going to be seen as the bad guy now. "She can't just use you as a temporary fix, Jay!"

"I understand." Alyson's voice was low, and Jamie looked at her quickly.

"Aly." Jamie felt his heart begin to pound. "Love, come on. I know you don't see me like that! It's fine!"

"Jamie, she's your mom. She's the one who keeps you steady, remember? You need to listen to her."

"I am listening to her! But that doesn't mean I have to agree with what she's saying." Jamie tightened his grip on Aly's hand until he saw her wince with pain. "We're not temporary! She doesn't know what she's talking about!"

"Yes, she does." Alyson's voice was low.

Jamie's hand dropped from Alyson's, and he took a step back. He stared at her with a pain in his eyes she had never seen before.

"Not all of it, Jamie." Tears slipped down her cheeks and through the line of her lips. She tasted them with her tongue. "I'm not using you."

"Then what? What is true?" Jamie shook his head in disbelief. When Alyson didn't respond he gripped her by the shoulders and made her look at him. "Tell me! Aly! I'm in love with you! What are you trying to tell me?"

"I'm trying to tell you that we can't be together right now." Alyson's chest shuddered as she exhaled slowly. "We don't know how life is going to work out after Bambi is born! You know all the ways this can spin out, and if... if your mom doesn't think this is a good idea... I mean... we wanted people to tell us. Right?"

"No!"

Alyson cringed at the way Jamie shouted in response.

"Aly, no!"

"Jamie." Alyson gave him a heartbreaking frown, her lower lip shaking as more tears fell. "I don't want to hurt you. I care too much..."

"Then stay. Please." Jamie pressed their foreheads together, his hands gently encircling her neck, pressing his thumb against the beat of her pulse. "Please. We can do this."

"We don't know that."

"We love each other. That's all we need to know."

"I-I need... I need to go. I shouldn't stay here any longer."

Heather didn't dare say a word as she watched Alyson and Jamie break apart. Her son was visibly shaken as Alyson continued to back away. She wasn't sure if she should be pleased at Alyson for being so responsive to her wishes, or angry that she just broke her son's heart on Christmas day.

The pain in Jamie's eyes that Alyson saw as she stepped back made her ache on the inside. She wanted to hold him and tell him it didn't matter what his mother said, and it didn't matter who the father was, or what the other guys wanted. She wanted to say that she was in love with him, and they could be together without worrying about the future. The lump in her throat kept her words safe on the inside, keeping them from coming out to make promises that she couldn't keep. In her mind she was telling him it was all going to be okay. She hoped he could read her thoughts.

Alyson looked to the woman who stood on the other side of the kitchen and nodded respectfully. She pulled her hand away from Jamie and wiped away the tears that had gathered on her chin.

Her gaze returned to Jamie. Her lungs ached as she pushed them open, reminding herself to breathe. His eyes were begging her to reconsider. She swallowed hard and walked quickly out of the room.

The room where she had been staying was the only place Alyson could go to hide from everyone and everything for a moment. She lay down carefully on the bed and hid her face in the pillow. Her belongings were already mostly packed in anticipation of her trip in the morning.

"Bambi, why does it always end up like this?" she whispered as she felt tears run down her nose and onto the pillow case. "I love him so much."

She could hear raised voices coming from the kitchen and knew that Jamie and his mother were arguing. It broke her heart to know that she was the reason for the shouting. Everything had gone so perfectly until that day. How was she supposed to go and spend a week with Tommy after ending her time with Jamie on this note?

"Love?" A knock on the door preceded Jamie's entrance. "You okay?"

"Not really." Alyson rolled onto her other side so she could see the young man as he walked towards her. She felt the mattress sink as he sat on the edge of the bed next to her. He leaned over and kissed her cheek, pressing his forehead against her hair as he sighed. "I'm sorry your mom said those things."

"I know, love." Jamie didn't lift his head. His one arm straddled Alyson's body, using it to hold up his weight. "I'm sorry, too."

"Your mom loves you. I know she just wants what is best for you." Alyson's voice cracked as she spoke.

"I don't want you to go." Jamie didn't normally let himself verbalize his desire for Alyson, but he couldn't stop himself.

"We're just going to hurt worse later if we don't catch ourselves now. You know that. We're full of fire, and fire burns." Alyson's forehead creased. "Besides, your mom is upset that I'm American, and because I have Bambi. Those are two things that are never going to change."

"Aly, we don't have to 'break up' right now. I love my mum, but I'm twenty-six years..."

"Jay. Please," Alyson moaned. "You know why I'm doing this."

The room was quiet for a minute.

"I pray every day that it's me." Jamie's low whisper reached Aly's ears.

"What do you pray?"

"That I'm the father."

Alyson moved her face away from Jamie as her eyes welled up with tears again. Her hands clutched tightly at the pillow under her head as she tried to keep herself from breaking out into gut-wrenching sobs. Jamie's hand was on her waist and his other was running through his hair. Tears marked his cheeks as he cried without shame.

"Do you think things will get easier one day?" asked Alyson.

Jamie turned and put his hands on Alyson's stomach. The young mother placed her hands on top of his, holding his touch against her womb. Neither of them said a word to the baby or to each other. There were no words to say.

"Can you take me to the bus stop?" Alyson knew it was time to go. "Lucy can drive us to the airport in the morning."

"I'm going back to my own place tonight. I can drop you off on the way."

Jamie helped Alyson off the bed and carried her suitcase down the stairs. Alyson didn't want to make a scene and say goodbye to the children, especially with her eyes red and puffy, but her heart told her that she would regret it if she left them without closure.

"You're leaving?" Sydney was shocked. "Did you and Jay have a fight?"

"No. No." Alyson smiled and pulled the girl into a hug. "Just have to go back home before I fly out to France tomorrow."

"Jay, why are you leaving?" Hanson glanced at his brother worriedly.

"Have some stuff at mine to worry about for a few days."

The somber mood had spread to the whole house by the time Alyson was done saying goodbye. The three younger siblings stood in the front garden as Alyson and Jamie climbed into his car and left. Alyson waited to say what she wanted to say until Jamie's neighborhood was behind them.

"This has been the best Christmas I've had in a long time. Not even this evening can change that."

Jamie's jaw worked as he struggled to keep his emotions under control. He wanted to grab Alyson's hand and force her to stay with him. How would she stay safe if he wasn't there?

"Just wanted you to know that." Alyson didn't know what else to say.

Their hug was tight as they stood in the deepening dusk. The snow crunched under their shoes as Alyson pushed up on her tiptoes. Jamie pressed one kiss against her ear and one to his fingertips to blow to Bambi. He stood with his hands shoved into his pockets as he watched Alyson climb on the mostly empty bus. It was Christmas; everyone else was at home with their loved ones. Everyone except for Alyson and Jamie. She waved at him, her breath hitting the window and fogging it up just as the bus began to pull away. She wiped at it furiously with her sleeve, desperate for one last look at his face. It was too late; he had already turned around and begun to walk away.

"Bye."

Alyson breathed a sigh of relief when her feet touched the solid ground of the Bedford bus station. She climbed off with her things and trudged down the street to the corner where people caught taxis. Her driver was nice and wished her a happy Christmas when he left her on the curb outside of her building. The light was on in the living room, and Alyson smiled.

"ALY! You idiot!" Lucy lunged from the couch to hug her friend when Alyson pushed the door open. "I thought we were meeting at the airport in the morning?"

"I decided to spend a night back home first." Alyson played it off as if it was no big deal and looked around.

Lucy had returned to Bedford that day, probably only a few hours before Alyson, but there were already things scattered all over the living room. Then she saw it...

"Oh! Oh!" Alyson's bags fell to the floor. "It's beautiful!"

"It has a note on it." Lucy smirked. "From Jay."

The beautiful upright piano in the corner was wrapped in a bow and the note was a simple sentence saying, *Surprise! Merry Christmas. Love, Jamie.* Alyson quickly blinked her tears away and pressed a couple of the keys to form a chord. It sounded perfect.

"You gonna ring him up straight away to tell him you love it?" asked Lucy with a grin.

"Oh, nah." Alyson tried to sound unaffected by the question. "He's probably busy."

Lucy's smile fell. She grabbed Alyson's arm and there was concern in her expression as she studied Alyson's sad eyes. Without saying a word, Lucy embraced Alyson tightly.

"It wasn't because of him." Alyson sniffled. "His mom didn't like me."

"What?" Lucy pushed Alyson back to see her face. Tears were running down Aly's cheeks. "She didn't like you?"

Alyson shook her head no. Knowing what his mother thought of her made her feel even worse about herself. She hadn't thought that was possible.

"Aw, love!" Lucy hugged Alyson again. "Here, let's have some tea, yeah? You can sit and look pretty while I pack my cases for our trip tomorrow."

Aly sipped her tea and laughed as Lucy recounted stories from home. She sat cross-legged on the end of the bed in the guest room, her free hand on Bambi. It was sweet to watch Lucy focus so much of her energy on helping her feel better. Absence had made her heart grow fonder of Lucy for sure.

"I am so excited to be having a holiday in France!" Lucy said for the hundredth time as they drove to the airport the next morning. "Celebrate the new year with French wine, French men..."

"I can't believe it's almost a new year," mused Alyson, not getting into the list of things Lucy was looking forward to. "This year has been crazy. So different from anything I ever expected."

"Next year will be crazy as well, I imagine."

"Mmm," Aly agreed, and she placed her hands on her stomach.

"Bambi is going to think he's a dog." Lucy laughed when she noticed Alyson rubbing her stomach again. "All you do is pet it!"

"Wouldn't that be a joke." Aly gave a little laugh. "Waiting to find out who the father is, and I give birth to a puppy."

"Oh! That's a bit creepy now! Cheers for that mental image!"

The girls parked Lucy's car at Tommy's and took a taxi the rest of the way to Heathrow. They pulled their rolling suitcases out of the trunk and paid the taxi driver. There was an excited smile on Lucy's face and a tense expression on Alyson's as they looked up at the giant building in front of them. She wrapped her hand around the handle of her suitcase and headed inside the airport.

"Aly!"

At first Alyson thought she was imagining the sound of someone calling her name. She looked around briefly, but saw no one she knew.

"Aly! Alyson!" The voice was louder, closer, and Alyson swiveled her neck around again to see who was trying to get her attention. She froze when she saw Jamie running after her.

"Jamie!" Alyson waited for him to reach her. "What's wrong? Is something wrong?"

Lucy stopped a few feet away. She watched carefully, ready to jump into the conversation at the first sign of an argument.

"I just... I just wanted to say goodbye. Make sure you got off okay."

Alyson bit her bottom lip and shook her head, a big tear tumbling from her lashes and down her cheek. She saw the hopeful glint in his eyes. He wanted to hear her say that she felt different now. He wanted her to tell him that she had changed her mind and they could go back to how things were.

"Jamie..."

"Okay." Jamie let out his breath and looked down at the ground, crowds of people pushing around them on their way into the busy airport. "Well, stay safe."

"Thanks, Jamie." Alyson reached up and wrapped her arms around Jamie's neck one more time. She sighed into him when she felt his arms reach around her tightly. "I'll, uh, let you know when I get to France. Just so you know. And when I'm back, I guess. Unless..."

"You can text me whenever you want," promised Jamie.

She hugged Jamie goodbye one last time and felt him stick something into her hand.

"I mean every word of it, even after what my mum said." Jamie nodded at the folded paper Alyson was holding. He watched her slip it into her jacket pocket.

"I'll miss you." Alyson gave Jamie's face one last look as she stepped away. His brilliant blue eyes were watering from the cold and possibly a few tears. His scruff was long enough to keep his chin and sides of his face warm from the cold, but his cheeks and the tip of his nose were cherry red from the wind blowing on his face.

Jamie didn't say anything, only put one hand up in a gesture of farewell and waited until Alyson started walking away. She turned at the entrance and waved at the young man. He spotted her and waved back.

"You good?" asked Lucy as they stood in line for security.

"Yeah." Alyson's mouth twitched into a sad smile. "It was hard. Sad. But... good as well, you know?"

"You're such an idiot." Lucy smiled at her friend fondly. "Let's go get drunk with French men!"

"Okay, not the vacation I was picturing..."

"I'm teasing, you nutter! You can't drink anyhow."

"Never do drink," Alyson muttered under her breath as she slipped off her shoes and jacket at the head of the line. Her mouth couldn't remember the taste of the alcohol she consumed back in July, but she knew she hated it. She knew it burned her throat and made her head swim until she was sick. It was shameful to drink. It was shameful to make foolish choices.

London disappeared below their plane, and Alyson pulled the paper from Jamie out of her pocket. Lucy was already dozing in her seat as Alyson unfolded the letter. At first Alyson thought it might be another one for Bambi, but it was for her.

The love letter sent a pang through Alyson's heart. He declared his feelings for her with words that Alyson had never heard him say before, and she wondered what else he had been holding back over the past few months. She knew that he loved her, but reading his words spelled out on the page was overwhelming.

She watched the clouds become a carpet below them as they flew and rubbed her belly absent-mindedly. Everything hurt when she thought about not seeing Jamie. They had tried so hard to get it right this time, yet they had lost each other again.

Alyson was very tired by the time she and Lucy landed in Paris at the Charles de Gaulle Airport. Lucy had slept the entire flight and chattered away as they deplaned and collected their bags. Tommy met them in his car at the curb.

"How was Christmas, Alyson?" asked Tommy with a tentative grin. "Anything exciting happen?"

"No, not really." Alyson stared straight ahead. "Nothing happened."

Lucy said nothing from the backseat and Tommy changed the subject.

The two girls were welcomed into the Noel house with open arms and big smiles. Tommy introduced Alyson to his family proudly, keeping her close to him and away from the questions and remarks of others while Lucy settled herself next to Tommy's older sister Kara. There were four children, seven adults and two dogs in the cozy ranch-style house. It was smaller than the Donalds', but it was newer and nicer on the inside, Alyson thought to herself as she looked around. She shook her head to push thoughts of Jamie's family from her mind and leaned against Tommy lightly. He slipped his arm around her shoulders without breaking his concentration from the conversation he was having with his older brother Benjamin.

Everyone in Tommy's family had the same icy-blue eyes and friendly smiles. The adult children of Randy and Maureen were unique mixtures of both of them. Kara took after their mother with her long thin nose while both boys favored their dad's side of the family. Even Benjamin's wife looked a bit like them with her blonde hair and strong chin.

"Do you want to hold the baby? Get some practice in?" Tommy's sister-in-law, Rachel, approached Alyson with her infant. She waited for Alyson to shrug Tommy's arm off her shoulder and hold out her arms. "Her name is Grace."

"Hi, Grace." Alyson cradled the baby in her arms. The tiny face was soft and pale and blurry as Alyson's eyes filled with tears. She stroked her finger down one of the baby's cheeks, stopping at her chin. She didn't even notice when Rachel walked away to join Kara and Lucy, eager to get in on the girl talk.

"Who do you have there?" Tommy turned his attention towards Alyson. His fingers were warm over Alyson's on Gracie's cheek as he cooed over his niece. "Hi, Gracie! Hi, pet!"

Alyson smiled.

"Do you think Bambi will look like this?" asked Tommy. His tone was so delicate Alyson had to look at him to see if he was crying.

"I don't know. It's how I imagine him or her looking when I try to draw him..." Alyson could feel Tommy's breath on her cheek as he leaned forward.

"Might still look like me, you know."

Alyson felt a curl of something hard to describe fill her stomach at Tommy's words. He was right. Bambi might look as much like him as his niece. Alyson let her imagination go for three seconds before pulling it back in.

Lucy and Alyson were given the guest room, but Lucy and Kara was still out for the evening when Alyson finally climbed into bed. Just next door on the floor of Randy Noel's office, Tommy was sleeping on a mattress.

The room was big, and the high, white ceiling reminded her of when she woke up next to Garret in California; the way she had hugged herself and tried to see the stars. Her hands found Bambi and she steadied the nervous rush of her heart by humming quietly to her baby. It was so quiet. Her apartment in Bedford was quiet, but Lucy had been there to fill the emptiness. There was an echo of shouting in Alyson's mind from the day before.

She's going to end up breaking your heart, son!

Alyson slipped out of bed and tiptoed into Tommy's makeshift bedroom without waking the others.

"Tommy." Alyson saw the young man on the mattress, his eyes closed and blankets pulled up around his face. She reached over and flicked on the lamp that was in the corner. Sure enough, a moment later Tommy shifted and blinked his eyes open.

"Alyson? You okay? What's wrong?" He sat up when he saw Alyson's shadow next to his bed.

"Can I sit in here with you for a bit?"

"Yeah, sure." Tommy scooted over and patted the spot next to him. "What's wrong? You okay?"

"I'm fine." Alyson sat down next to him, her back against the cold wall, but her legs under the warm blankets. Her hands rested on her stomach, Tommy's arm and knee touching hers as they sat side-by-side.

"Are you sure?"

"Just can't sleep." Alyson tried to give him a convincing smile. "I'm really glad I'm here."

"I am, too."

"Your family is great."

"My mum's not going to let you out of her sight for the rest of the week." He chuckled quietly. "She's going to make sure you're okay, and Bambi's okay, and everything."

"In the car I told you that nothing happened over Christmas."

Tommy's eyes darted in her direction, watching her face.

"Jamie and I... we... I don't know how to say this."

"Are you with him again?"

"No. We're not... we're not going to be together anymore."

Tommy listened quietly, nodding and fiddling with the edge of the blankets.

"I never meant to let things go back in that direction again, but I did. And we decided that we shouldn't be together anymore. Again."

"Jamie decided with you?"

Alyson said nothing.

"Why are you telling me this, Alyson?"

"Because you guys work together, and I might be carrying your child. That's all."

"That's all," Tommy repeated, looking away.

There was quiet before Alyson spoke up again.

"Do you wish you could tell your family about Bambi?"

"That I might be the dad?" Tommy shook his head. "Nah. It's enough for them just to know you for now."

"Well, I like them."

"Aren't you nervous about someone saying the wrong thing when you meet new people?"

"Yeah," Alyson said slowly. "Mostly at school though. Those are the only people connected with my friends and co-workers from back home. My boss. My parents. As long as no one finds out about Bambi there, I should be okay."

"Hi Bambi." Tommy gave Alyson's belly a pat. "Are you doing okay in there?"

"I wish I could feel him moving."

"You can't feel him yet?"

Alyson shook her head no and frowned. She pressed her hands on her belly, hoping to push against something and make him or her want to move. Nothing. She pulled up her sweater and revealed her bare skin.

"Come on, Bambi. You're worrying us." Tommy gently placed a hand on Alyson's stomach. "Let's go, kid! Move around a little!"

Alyson giggled, making her stomach shake as she watched Tommy lean over her bump and talk to the baby. He smiled at the sound of Alyson's laughter and carried on.

"Guess what I'm drawing." Tommy suddenly changed games as he began to use his finger to write words across the skin that was stretched the tightest around Alyson's womb.

"Ah! That tickles!" Alyson bent nearly in double to hide her exposed skin, her hands attempting to push Tommy's away, but his were bigger and stronger than hers.

"Wow, I never realized how ticklish you were!" Tommy continued to poke at Alyson's sides, laughing at her hysterical giggling and desperate slaps at his fingers when they came close to her.

"Shhh! You'll make me wake everyone up!" Alyson pushed Tommy's hand off her stomach. "Your mother may not love me so much if she finds me in bed with you in the middle of the night."

"Nah, she would be ecstatic." Tommy settled his hands back on his lap.

"Wait, what?"

"She'd love to have you in our family. She wants me married and popping out babies as soon as I can. Kara, too."

"Your family is so different from mine."

"Is that a good thing?" Tommy gave her a side glance.

"Right now it is."

"Good." Tommy noted the way her eyes crinkled when she smiled and the wisps of hair that were falling down around her face. "Hey…"

"Hey what?" Alyson gave him a curious look.

"Do you… remember when we were at your house? And, uh, I wore you dad's clothes and, uh, you mentioned the curtains?"

"Oh." Alyson looked down at her lap. "Yeah. I remember that."

"What did you mean?"

"My family keeps a lot of secrets." Alyson licked her lips and squinted. "I was the golden child of the neighborhood. I was the good girl who was perfect at everything I tried to do."

Tommy watched her face as she spoke quietly.

"Everybody wanted to be my friend when I won another trophy or was in the newspaper, but when the curtains were closed… no one cared."

"What happened when the curtains were closed?"

"Sometimes nothing." Alyson bit at her bottom lip. "But I would never know. Sometimes I had done something wrong and brought shame on the family. Sometimes he would be angry and just… go crazy. But no one knew because the curtains, you know, they would be closed. When he was better, the curtains would open and everyone would think we were the perfect family again."

"Hmmm."

"Yeah." Alyson put a brave smile on her face as she turned back to face him. "That's why my apartment doesn't have curtains. I guess it's my way of saying that no one can make my house a place of secrets."

"Did your dad ever get abusive?"

Alyson didn't answer.

"Sorry, that's none of my business." Tommy shook his head and rubbed his hands through his hair. "Sorry, Alyson."

"It's okay. I'll let you get back to sleep." She smiled at him before she crawled off the mattress.

"Are you ready to sleep?"

"Yeah. I'm fine." Alyson pushed herself up to her feet.

"Night, Alyson," Tommy called after her.

"Good night."

Alyson dozed off and on until late in the morning the next day. She felt drained and there was no energy to replace all that she had poured out while she had been with Jamie. Thankfully, everyone let her rest and have some time to herself.

"Did you not sleep well last night?" Lucy asked suspiciously as she walked back into their shared room. "I didn't come back until half-two and I've been up and dressed for at least an hour and you're still asleep in bed."

Alyson sat up and yawned. She found the pair of socks that she had left on the bedside table to put on before she got up and started to pull them on. It was possible for her to do it, but it was a struggle. Lucy dropped the clothes that she was folding onto the floor to kneel at Aly's feet.

"Sock."

Alyson handed her friend the sock and sighed.

"I thought I was gonna be the Sleepy Susan this morning, but here you are yawning your head off."

"I suppose it's because I was up later than normal talking to Tommy."

"What about?"

"Nothing really. I just needed to not be alone for a little while before I could sleep."

Lucy finally pulled the sock over Alyson's foot but stayed where she was to massage the swollen ankles.

"You two make a very cute couple." Lucy gave Alyson's foot an extra squeeze. "I know you two were never a real couple, but you definitely look like you fancy each other when you're together."

"Lu, I literally just left Jamie's house three days ago."

"I know, I know." Lucy sat back and put her hands up to show that she wouldn't meddle. "I just want you to be happy, and I want Bambi to be taken care of."

"We'll be okay."

"Course you will, you idiot. You'll have me to do all your work for you! That's what'll happen, because I'm so nice!" Lucy stood up and grinned at her friend. "I'll become the nursemaid, I will, and you'll order me around all day long!"

Lucy's teasing helped Alyson smile and get up to her feet. Lucy's help stopped soon after that, though. She received a call on the twenty-ninth of December from Kyle, begging her to come home to him. Alyson and Tommy told her they didn't think it was a smart idea, but she didn't listen. Kara drove her to the airport.

Alyson sat in the living room with Maureen and a cup of tea on her last day in France. The two golden retrievers slept contentedly by their feet, their noses tucked under their paws. It reminded Alyson of Casson. She made a mental note to ask her parents about the family dog the next time she talked to them.

"Your mum must miss you very much," said Maureen with a sad smile.

"Yes, I suppose she does." Alyson thought back to the Skype call she had received from her parents at the beginning of the month. "If things were a little different I would have loved to have spent the holidays with my parents."

"I'm sure they would welcome you with open arms, no matter if you were going to have a baby or not."

"I don't think so." Alyson bit her lip. Her eyebrows pulled together as she exhaled shakily.

"Aw, darling." Maureen put one hand on Alyson's arm and another one under Alyson's chin to bring the girl's gaze to face her. "Don't think about that. We love you. You're part of our family now. We will always welcome you in our home."

Alyson threw herself into Maureen's arms and cried into her shoulder. Tommy walked past the room and froze when he saw his mother comforting his weeping friend.

"Mum! What have you done?" He sounded horrified.

"Shh." Maureen wasn't bothered by her son's question. She continued to hold Alyson and rock her back and forth. "She just needs a mother."

After the tears ended, Alyson thought about what Maureen had said. She stared at herself in the bathroom mirror and let the words roll slowly around in her mind.

She just needs a mother.

She didn't know if she was allowed to need a mother anymore. Technically she hadn't really been allowed to need a mother for years, now. She had a mother to correct her and train her, but to comfort her? No. That's not what her mother did in their home, but Alyson had needed it. She had desperately needed to be held and told that there was a safe place for her.

Chapter eighteen

"Sorry I've been gone. But I'm here now."

The day after New Years' Tommy and Alyson deplaned in London to a very welcome sight. Alyson dropped her bags and ran as fast as she could into Eddie's arms. He picked her up off the ground and laughed as she squealed over and over again about how much she missed him.

"Hello! Welcome back!" Eddie ushered the girl and his friend over to his car. Once the bags were in the trunk, the two young men turned to each other and shared a bear hug. They were already halfway into a conversation when they jumped into the vehicle. Alyson listened to them joke and laugh, soaking in the familiar steadiness that always came when she was with Eddie. "Aly! How was France?"

"Good." Alyson smiled at the excited way Eddie said her name. "Needed."

"Wow, that was the best two-word summary I have ever heard in my life." Tommy clapped loudly from the backseat.

"Do you want to tell him the most exciting thing that happened while we were there?" Alyson twisted in her seat to look at him as she asked her question.

"What happened?" Eddie was curious.

"Well, Bambi did something special in France." Tommy was so happy he had been the one with Alyson when the momentous milestone was reached. "He decided to let his mum feel him."

"Pardon?"

"I felt Bambi moving for the first time!"

"Vive la France!" crowed Tommy from the back.

"You felt the baby?!" Eddie's eyes widened as he realized what he had been told. He put a hand over on Alyson's stomach and gave it a pat. "Yes then, Bambi! Well done, mate!"

"You still feel him?" Tommy asked.

"Yeah, from time to time." Alyson glowed. "It's becoming more frequent."

"When will we be able to feel Bambi?" asked Eddie.

"It could be anywhere from one to six weeks after the mom starts feeling the baby, but it varies from mother to mother."

"How do you remember all of these pregnancy facts?"

"I remember the important things. And the scary things."

"Well, forget about the scary things. Everything is going to be fine." Eddie smiled at the girl.

"That's what I told her!" Tommy said.

Alyson simply smiled and kept her mouth shut. She knew Eddie and Tommy meant well; so did everyone else who told her it was all going to be okay. It would be useless to argue with them and tell them of all the possibilities that consumed her mind at times. She knew they worried about things as well, but for them it was very different.

"Do you need anything before I drop you off at your flat, Tom?" asked Eddie as they reached the neighborhood where Eddie and Tommy both had their apartments. "I'm going to get some takeout for Aly and I before we head back to my place."

"Aly's staying at yours' tonight?"

"I thought it would be nice to spend at least one night with Ed after having time with both you and Jamie over the holidays." Alyson turned from the front seat as she spoke.

"Yeah, I haven't spent time with Aly all year yet." Eddie smiled at his joke even though no one laughed at him.

"You just want to show off your tan from your cruise in the Bahamas!" Tommy scoffed at his friend.

"Do not mock my sun-kissed glow."

"Well, I wasn't going to, but now that you've called it your sun-kissed glow, I have to."

"It's more than a tan, what do you want me to call it?"

"Just call it a tan! Honestly, Ed!" Tommy tried to sound annoyed, but he was laughing.

"What would you say if Aly called her tan a sun-kissed glow?"

"I would say that she looks lovely."

"Thanks, Tommy!" Alyson smiled brightly.

"Then why can't you just tell me that I'm lovely?"

"Eddie, mate, your brain is sun-kissed."

"Hey!"

"Alyson, I think you're going to need help looking after him tonight." Tommy leaned forward to tap Alyson on the shoulder. "I don't think he's feeling very well. Probably has sun-stroke or something. I should stay to help take care of the poor lad."

"Tommy, if you want to come admire my gorgeous, glowing skin, all you have to do is ask. You don't have to talk about me behind my back."

"And it's funny because I literally am behind your back right now." Tommy rolled his eyes as Eddie snickered at his own joke.

"Yeah, why don't you spend the evening with us?" Alyson said with a smile. "It will be better than going home to an empty flat after being with your family for a couple weeks."

"He's only allowed to come if he promises to compliment my sun-kissed glow."

"I'm never going to compliment that." Tommy crossed his arms and shook his head.

"Sorry, mate. Not invited."

"Are you getting Nando's?" Tommy's arms fell from his chest as he saw where Eddie was pulling up to.

"Yeah, shame you're not going to compliment my sun-kiss-..."

"All right, fine! You're lovely, Ed. Get my favorite kind! Extra-hot!"

"You mean, extra-hot like me?" Eddie asked with a cheeky smile as he hopped out of the car.

"Eddie!"

The rest of the evening at Eddie's flat was equally as fun and light-hearted as they heard about Eddie's family holiday cruise and ate their chicken. Alyson changed into her pajamas and sat at the table. She rubbed her belly softly and laughed as the boys continued to banter and tease. It felt right.

"When do you start back to work?" asked Eddie.

"I think on the eleventh. But I'm starting phase two of my job." Alyson shifted uncomfortably; the serene atmosphere of the room slipped away.

"What's phase two?" asked Tommy. He leaned forward on the table with his elbows. The red flush in His cheeks was a testament to how much he had laughed that evening.

"She's going to stop teaching," Eddie answered. They had talked about it once before.

"I'm going to be working in a back office so I can stay out of sight for the most part. The only person who I'll have to interact with is Fran."

"So, no more teaching?"

"Nope. Too risky. Bambi is too big." Alyson rubbed her stomach. "I'm glad though. We want you big, Bambi. We want you big and strong."

"Are you excited for the change of pace?"

"I don't know." Alyson glanced at Tommy as she answered his question. "I am glad the hours will be shorter. I'll only be working four hours a day, instead of six or seven. It'll give me more time to get the apartment ready, go through counseling..."

"Whoa!" Eddie stopped her. "What is this? You never told me about going to counseling. Like, a psychiatrist?"

"No. Just someone who can help me process everything that has happened in the past few months. Danielle made me promise."

"I guess that's smart. You have been through a lot." Tommy pursed his lips as he mulled over what Alyson said.

"You should go talk about it with Gianna."

Alyson looked at Eddie, her eyebrows quirked in an inquisitive expression.

"She's gone to uni to be a counselor for kids in high school. You already know how great she is. I'm sure she'd love to help in some way, especially since she already knows a bit of your story."

"Yeah... I-I'll talk to her about it." Alyson let the thought settle. She would think about it more later. "I would like to do it now, before the baby is born."

"When will Bambi be born?"

"Middle to the end of April." Alyson chewed her bottom lip. "It's only four and a half months away. I'm going to have to start planning what I want to have happen at the birth soon. Making a birth plan is one of the times I especially wish I could talk to my mom."

"I'm sorry. Wish I had more practice making birth plans so I could help you," Eddie offered.

A small grin cracked Alyson's frown, and she shook her head.

"Maybe next time I have a baby, huh?"

"Yeah, maybe next time." Eddie's dimple showed in his cheek.

"You know, you could always talk to my mum." Tommy rubbed his hand on the back of his neck as he spoke. "I mean, she's had three kids."

"Do you think she would fly over and be there when the baby is born?" The words were less of a joke than Alyson tried to make them seem. "That's another headache to figure out."

"I know she would if you asked her. She absolutely loved you."

"You could have Lucy in there with you, I suppose," said Eddie.

"Speaking of Lucy, I don't know if she'll be in Bedford when I get back. I haven't heard from her."

"Still can't believe she went back to Kyle." Tommy shook his head. "She wasn't having any of our advice though."

"I'm worried about her. I hope silence is good." Alyson looked down at her phone.

As Alyson lay in bed that night and stroked her belly, she mentally laid out a rough timeline of when things should happen and how things would work out best. It was hard to close her eyes as she lay worrying about times and dates and the baby. She heard Tommy tell Eddie goodnight and his bedroom door click shut.

Alyson waited a few minutes, her hands holding onto her stomach. Tears surfaced, but Alyson tried to ignore them. She didn't want them and the way they taunted her weakness. After wiping her eyes, Alyson slipped out of bed and tiptoed down the hall to Eddie's room.

"Aly, what's wrong?" Eddie was still awake and fully clothed when he opened his bedroom door and saw her standing there. "Are you okay?"

"No. I'm an idiot." Alyson walked into his room and took a seat on the chair he had in the corner. "I was a total fool with Jamie."

"What happened?"

"His mom... she told him that she didn't like me and doesn't want us together. Christmas day I go into the kitchen for a drink and I hear her yelling at him that I'm just going to break his heart."

Eddie frowned as he listened.

"I thought she was beginning to like me, but I guess not."

"What did you do when you heard her say that?"

"They saw me. They argued." Alyson tried to shake the horrible conversation out of her memory. "Finally I told him his mom was right. That we shouldn't be together."

"How did he take it?"

"Not well." Alyson looked away, tears on her cheeks. "Not well at all."

"I'm so sorry, love." Eddie wrapped his arms around her shoulders and gave her a comforting hug.

"I don't really know what I'm going to do."

"Just give it a little time. Things will work out. They may look differently than you expect them to, but they will work out. Somehow."

"Thanks, Ed."

"That's what brothers are for."

The next day found Alyson back in her flat with Eddie to keep her company. They shopped for groceries, unpacked her bags, and did her laundry. When they had completed the chores, Eddie sat down at the piano in the corner of the living room. Alyson listened as he played with ease and confidence.

"You, too?" Alyson gave him a look.

"What?" Eddie stopped playing. "What's that look for?"

"You play piano, too? How many of you guys in the band play piano?"

"Just me. Tommy can a bit, but he's mostly drums and guitar. I'm guitar, bass, keys and Irish tin whistle."

"What about Jamie?" Alyson asked carefully.

"Nope." Eddie turned back to the keys.

Alyson sat on the couch. She listened to Eddie play a pretty melody as she sketched a lazy design. The background music kept her focused while her mind tried to wander in circles. She let the music fill the dark spaces and thoughts.

"I'm going to call Gianna tomorrow," Alyson said aloud. She tapped her pencil on the edge of the paper.

"Good." Eddie continued to play, softer now to catch Alyson's words.

"I'm a little scared though."

"Scared of what?" Eddie's fingers stopped.

"To feel it all again."

Eddie didn't say anything else, just walked over to the couch and sat down next to Alyson. He tugged her closer and welcomed her head on his shoulder. He kept quiet so he wouldn't interrupt Alyson's thoughts. He just wanted her to know she wasn't alone. She let out a sigh and looked at her friend with gratitude in her eyes.

"I'm so glad we're friends."

"You mean family?" Eddie corrected with a gentle smile.

"Family." Alyson chuckled. "None of the other boys are like this with me. It makes this all the more special. Safe. I didn't realize how much I needed that in my life until these past couple weeks."

"I'm very glad I can be that person for you." Eddie looked as though someone had given him the most amazing compliment in the world.

Counseling sessions with Gianna started two days after Alyson returned home. Eddie's sister was more than happy to give Alyson a couple hours of her time a week to talk through things, find ways to work through emotions, listen and keep Alyson accountable on how she handled life.

"What are you hoping to gain from our time together?" asked Gianna at the end of their first meeting.

"The ability to be a good mom."

"What does it mean to be a good mum?"

"Someone who can love well, put their own junk behind them because they're focused on giving their baby what it needs. Someone who can look at their child and not..." Tears began to form over Alyson's eyes as she looked towards the window. "And not think of all the heartache, and all the things she had to give up just to keep the child alive. Who can look at her baby, even if it looks just like a man who caused her pain, and still love that baby more than her own life."

She pulled the end of her sleeve over the heel of her hand to wipe at her eyes. Gianna gave Alyson a big hug before she left and whispered she was proud of her for being so strong for Bambi.

Gianna didn't usually remind Alyson of Eddie, but there were a few things, the best things, that Alyson could see mirrored in the siblings. Alyson knew Eddie as a soft, yielding friend who never wanted to push too hard on the things that hurt, whereas Gianna was a strong force who never backed down from what the person needed, even if it wasn't what they wanted. She did it all with the best balance of tough and love that Alyson had ever experienced in one person before. Gianna was fearless, and Alyson wanted to be like her.

"No matter what happens, I know you're going to be a good mum. You're already a good mum."

"Thanks." Alyson watched Gianna leave, a lump in her throat. Alyson rested her hands on her baby. "You're all I have left, Bambi. I have to be a good mom, because there's nothing else I can do."

The sound of a slamming door and loud voices made Alyson walk over to the window after supper. It was dark outside, and she had to rely on the streetlights to show her what was happening below on the sidewalk. Her eyes caught the familiar shapes of Lucy and Kyle in the middle of the road. Kyle had a cigarette in his hand and two bags by his feet. Snow drifted down from the sky, and Lucy stood without a jacket.

Not wanting to push her nose into their heated moment, Alyson stepped away from the window and went back over to the couch where her sketchbook sat. The picture on the page was a face with a blank expression. It was how her heart felt: nothing.

A car raced down the street, and Alyson looked up from her picture again. Something told her to look out and check on her friend. Lucy stood alone, now, her eyes focused on the car that roared away into the night. The vehicle turned a corner faster than was safe before it was lost from sight. Alyson quickly grabbed her jacket and sweater and ran outside.

"Lu!" Alyson said as she rushed to the middle of the street. She held out her sweater to her shivering friend. "Lu, you okay?"

Lucy's eyes were red-rimmed and bloodshot; the red reached down to her nose and blotched on her cheeks. She wasn't hysterical, though, for which Alyson was grateful. A light sniffle was the only noise Lucy made as she watched her friend walk closer.

"You shouldn't be out here, you idiot. It's dangerous walking on slick snow like this with the baby." Lucy took the sweater and wrapped it around her shoulders gratefully.

"Do you want to come stay with me?"

Lucy's lips quivered, but she didn't cry. She took Alyson's warm hand in her cold fingers and gave them a tight squeeze.

"No." Lucy shook her head no. "I'm going to stay at my place."

"A-are you sure? You're more than welcome..."

"I'm sure." Lucy cut into Alyson's invitation. "I made Kyle take his things."

"Oh, Lu..." Alyson's eyes welled up with tears. Lucy looked away, blinking rapidly. Snowflakes had settled onto her hair and dusted the dark locks with tiny magical shapes.

"No, I'm fine." Lucy's voice was thick and she swallowed hard. "I'm fine."

Alyson gave Lucy a hard stare, her hands still wrapped around Lucy's as they stood in the middle of the street. Cold seeped through her clothes and shoes, but she didn't move.

"I'm fine," Lucy whispered once more.

"It's okay, Lu. I'm right here."

"I'm fi-... I'm..." Lucy's hand flew to her mouth. Her whole body crumpled as a giant sob spilled over. Alyson caught her friend in her arms and held her against her side. "It's over! I-it's over! He's g-gone!"

Alyson asked her friend if she wanted to stay with her, but again, Lucy refused. Alyson helped Lucy back to her flat, a steady hand on her arm as they walked slowly through falling tears and snow. She pushed open the door and found the living room a disaster. Books, CDs, paper, clothes and a random assortment of knick-knacks were strewn across the floor and coffee table.

"Are you okay here?" asked Alyson tentatively.

"Yes, yeah, course. I'm fine." Lucy wiped the tears from her eyes and took a deep breath. "I am, Aly, I promise. This stuff isn't Kyle's, it's mine. This place... This is my place now. I'm going to make it look the way I want, not the way he wants. I... I'm relieved. This has been a very dark place for as long as I remember. But not anymore."

"I'm right across the street if you need me." Alyson hugged her friend one last time.

"Love you, you idiot."

Serenity continued to surprise Alyson with her kindness and offered to throw her a baby shower. Alyson was excited by the chance to celebrate Bambi with her friends. They decided to make it a girls-only event and scheduled it for the last Sunday in January. Serenity chose a private tearoom in London and told the guest of honor to dress nicely. Alyson was unable to hide her stomach anymore no matter what clothing style she wore, but she liked it. She was able to rest her hands on the top like it was a shelf and feel close to her baby.

"Do you need anything from the shops?" asked Lucy as she popped her head in the door of the apartment. "I'm going 'cause I promised Ren I would bake a cake for the party tomorrow."

"No, I went yesterday." Alyson smiled at her neighbor. "Do you want to eat supper over here? I made baked potatoes and am warming up some of the left-over chili you brought me the other day."

"Oh, sounds lovely! Yeah, I'll be over once the cake is done."

"Bake the cake here. I've been bored all afternoon."

"No! The cake is supposed to be a surprise, you idiot!" Lucy winked. "See you in a bit!"

"Wait, take this back to yours'." Alyson held out a mixing bowl that was sitting on the counter. "I found mine."

"Ah, I wondered where that went. Sure you don't need anything?"

"Actually, I'm really craving halloumi and those little chocolate things we got from Waitrose on Monday."

"Cheese and chocolate. I love your pregnancy cravings." Lucy flashed a bright smile and disappeared as the door shut.

The sun swung low in the sky. It flirted with the horizon, its fuzzy glow barely visible from behind the clouds. A fresh layer of snow covered the ground, and Alyson had worn two sweaters the day before when she walked to work. Even with Bambi acting as a personal heater, Alyson felt the chill.

A text from Gianna appeared on Alyson's phone, and she read it quickly. She smiled when she realized it had nothing to do with their next counseling session and was simply telling her that she had found the perfect gift for Bambi and she was excited to see her the next day at the party.

"Sweet Dream Baby..." Alyson crooned as she tidied up her living room, moving her sketchbook from the coffee table back to the bookshelf where it belonged. She had gone through two whole sketchbooks in the last month.

Drawing was one of the ways Gianna encouraged her to process her feelings. Sometimes the pictures were so dark and horrible that Alyson had trouble looking at them later. Still, little by little, the feelings were dealt with and not simply ignored.

A knock on the door surprised Alyson. Lucy had given up knocking a month ago.

"Hello?" Alyson called cautiously, her hand on the handle.

"Alyson! It's me!"

A smile spread across Alyson's face as she opened the door. Two warm arms wrapped around her before she could even see the smile of the man at her door and she buried her face into Tommy's shoulder, inhaling the smell of his cologne. The smell made her remember the night they sat together on his bed after everyone else was asleep and talked about curtains and her dad.

"Oh, it's so good to see you!" Alyson held onto his forearms when they stepped apart to get a look at each other's faces. "What are you doing here? I didn't know you were coming!"

"Surprise!" Tommy leaned down and pressed a firm kiss on her forehead. It was his favorite spot to kiss her. "I heard there was going to be a party for Bambi, and I wasn't invited."

Alyson gave a small laugh and motioned for Tommy to come in so she could shut the door. He stepped in, but kept his jacket on. There was a lump in the pocket of Tommy's coat and Alyson's eyes were drawn to it. Tommy chuckled as he pulled it out, but he kept it in his hands.

"Saw Ed this morning, and he said he's been round to see you a couple times a week. It made me realize I haven't seen you since the week after we arrived back home from my parent's house."

"Time has gone by fast," Alyson lied. Time had gone by slowly, being marked only by her sessions with Gianna and the two evenings a week spent with Eddie watching old television series. She didn't know what she would have done without the Mallory siblings and Lucy. "How have you been?"

"I've been busy! Packed schedule."

"Oh yeah?" Alyson's eyes wandered back down to the package that rustled when Tommy squeezed it in his hands.

"Yeah, working with a friend on his album. Just temporary to fill the time while we wait to work with Jay on his new stuff."

"When will that be?" Alyson's brow wrinkled. She wished she already knew.

"Spring sometime, I think. He'll get the schedule for the year around February. January is his off month."

"But isn't he working right now?"

Tommy shrugged.

"You two don't talk much?"

"Nah. Anything I need to know comes from Ed, or Garret. No need to talk to Jamie and get into a fight when it can be avoided."

"That makes sense." Alyson tried to smile, but she felt uneasy talking about Jamie with Tommy. "I wish I could invite you to stay, but no one else is here and I..."

"Oh, course!" Tommy jumped in with a wide smile. "I'm just stopping by for a minute to play the part of the postman."

"Is that why you're holding a very squishy present?"

"I know I'm not invited to the baby shower, but I got a present for Bambi anyway." Tommy held it out. "You know, just wanted him to have a little something from me to open tomorrow."

The gift was soft and round, wrapped in white paper decorated with thin silver stripes. The wrapping job looked professional, and Alyson guessed that it had been done by the clerk when Tommy bought it. The words, *To Bambi, with love, Tommy* were scrawled along its side in sharpie. It was a bit crinkled from being in Tommy's pocket and then in his hands, but otherwise it was a perfect little package.

"Thanks so much, Tommy." Alyson smiled as she took the present from him. "I'll put it in the nursery."

Tommy followed Alyson into the room, his hand coming up to rest on Alyson's shoulder as they approached the crib. On the walls was the beginning of a beautiful mural. It was only the pencil outline at the moment, but Tommy could see it clearly enough to know it was going to be stunning when it was finished.

"Lucy?" he asked.

Alyson nodded with a proud smile on her face.

"Wow. Bambi's going to have the best nursery in all of England."

"Prettiest nursery, anyway."

"You want to put the present in this big empty crib?" Tommy glanced down and saw the mattress didn't even have sheets. "Not much finished in here, is it?"

"Not yet." Alyson looked around at the dresser and changing table. "I have the letters from you guys pinned up on the wall; that was the most important part to me. I still have three months to finish setting things up."

"Well, Bambi's going to need a nice, cozy nursery to come out to." Tommy moved and positioned himself in front of Alyson. He placed his hands on her stomach and began to smile as he spoke to the baby. "You're going to need a bed and some soft blankets, eh? Some cute little outfits and toys? Tell your mummy tha-... Oh!"

"What?"

"Th-the, the, the bab-... Bambi! I felt him!" Tommy's jaw was almost to the ground as he looked down at his hands. "I could feel something!"

The smile on Alyson's face hurt, it was so wide, as she snatched his hand back and placed it against the side where Bambi's feet were kicking. Tears filled Tommy's eyes, and he pressed his fingers against them. The tears set off Alyson, and she felt the lump grow in her throat, even as she laughed at the look of awe on Tommy's face.

"This... wow." Tommy held his breath.

"Isn't it the best feeling in the world?" Alyson could hardly talk.

"Yeah." Tommy was breathless. "It's amazing."

The kicking ended, and Tommy straightened to pull Alyson into a hug. Her stomach pressed into his hip as his heart beat a million miles an hour against her cheek.

"Has anybody else felt the baby besides you?"

Alyson shook her head no and realized how special that moment was. She didn't know how she felt about it having been with Tommy, but she knew how special it was for him. He loved Bambi and would be an amazing father if he was the one. She knew he would cherish that moment forever, and that meant a lot to her.

"I'll leave now." Tommy wiped at his eyes. "Sorry for staying longer than just dropping off the gift, but..."

"Don't worry about it."

"Hopefully I'll see you sooner than later." Tommy had his hand on the doorknob.

"I'm sure."

She stood at the window and watched the road a long time after Tommy left. The glass was cool on Alyson's face as she leaned close to watch the sun leave its trail of black sky and star friends behind it as he left the western horizon. Alyson looked away when she thought about how often she used to stare up at the sky when she prayed.

"Well, Bambi. We made it through another day." Alyson rubbed her belly. Her child responded with several kicks. "I can't wait for you to be born, but I'm so nervous I'm going to do the wrong thing."

The picture Alyson drew that night was a mixture of hope and fear. She didn't know how to describe it after she was done. Not even the chocolates that Lucy had bought for her helped. She slipped under the covers early that night, her head throbbing a bit at the temples. Her feet were cold and it took a while for her to fall asleep and leave all of her worries behind.

The morning came more quickly than Alyson wanted. She was excited for the party and to spend some time with the girls, but she felt more tired than when she had gone to bed. She lay in bed for a while longer, thinking through all the things that needed to be done before she caught the train down to London for the day. Lucy would have driven her, she knew, but she actually enjoyed the train.

Alyson turned on "Sweet Dreams", letting the familiar melody come through the speakers as she made herself ready for the day. Bambi moved around inside of her excitedly. It seemed to be the unborn baby's favorite song. She showered, dressed and made sure her passport was in her bag before she headed out.

She pulled out her phone as she sat in the seat. No texts. Slowly, Alyson pulled off her glove and typed out a message to Jamie. It took her five whole minutes before she pressed the send button. She concentrated only on her breathing and not on getting a response.

"Just want him to know I'm thinking about him." Alyson spoke to her baby in a low voice so she didn't attract the attention of anyone else on the train.

Her phone buzzed in her hand a few moments later. He was thinking about her, too.

Alyson was tired when she returned to her apartment after the baby shower. It had been a joyful, intimate affair and she felt loved and that her baby was celebrated. Of course the only guests had been Serenity, Gianna and Lucy, but it was enough; her baby had a little family of friends waiting for him or her to be born. Her baby would be loved.

She slipped off her shoes and pulled off her hat as soon as the door shut. Her bag dropped to the floor with a careless thump as she shed her jacket. She turned to hang it on a hook when she noticed there was already one there. It took a moment to recognize the coat, but a familiar scent reached her nose, and she dropped her jacket to the floor.

"Jamie!" Alyson spun around to see the young man leaning against the entrance of the hallway. "You're here!"

He had his arms crossed in a relaxed manner and there was a smile behind his eyes as he stared at her. The look made Alyson's stomach swirl for a split second. She hadn't had butterflies for weeks. He pushed himself away from the wall and walked over to her. Alyson's face softened into a fond expression as he folded his arms around her and gave her a tight hug. They didn't say a word until they stepped back from each other.

"This is a surprise." The light in Alyson's eyes was dancing.

"I hope it's a good one."

Alyson nodded.

"Tea?"

"Yes. I would love some." Alyson left her jacket on the floor as she followed Jamie down the hall to the kitchen where she took a seat. She watched him closely, smiling when he set the cup down in front of her. "How are you?"

The small talk was more than that; Alyson genuinely wanted to know how he was. She wanted him to answer the question with all the words they hadn't spoken in the time since they had seen each other. She wanted to sit there and let their tea grow cold because they forgot they even had tea as they drank in each other's company.

"I'm fine, yeah. Fine." Jamie sat down in the chair next to hers, his hands on his mug but his focus on her. "Yourself?"

"I'm big." Alyson pointed to her belly. Bambi was relatively still, but something was pressing against her lower abdomen, she couldn't tell if it was a foot or a knee.

"I noticed." Jamie looked to the tight stomach that bulged out at Alyson's midsection. "Bambi's grown."

"Mmhmm." Alyson rubbed a hand over her belly. "I'm glad."

"I was with the kids last night." Jamie sat back in his chair. "Sydney and I were up late and since mum wasn't there, she pulled out the pregnancy magazines she picked up at Christmastime. She was reading all these things that babies feel and experience while they're in the womb and I just... I realized this is... this is such an important time. For Bambi. For you. And I... I don't want to miss Bambi's life."

There was a tiny quiver on Alyson's chin as she listened to Jamie talk. She blinked slowly and looked down at her tea for a moment.

"I know it sounds silly because, I mean, he or she isn't even born yet, but he can hear, and he's moving around, I bet."

"He is." Alyson looked up, her eyes wide with excitement. She had forgotten he didn't know.

"See, I missed that." Jamie's eyebrows flickered down quickly. "I know things between us are complicated, and I understand that, I'm not trying to force anything, I'm just, I want to..."

"I understand."

Jamie let out a deep breath and watched Alyson take a sip of her tea with a gentle look in his eyes. Her cheeks flushed, and she set the cup down quickly. Bambi shifted in her belly. Her index finger traced the edge of her cup and felt the steam hit her skin.

"Is Bambi the only reason why you came?"

"Are you asking if I came because I'm still in love with Bambi's mum?"

"Are you?" Alyson's expression was shy- vulnerable and open- when she peered up into Jamie's gentle gaze.

"Course I am."

Alyson's hands tingled; her heart too happy and her mind too blurry to tell her what to do. She knew her red face and wobbly smile was an answer in itself, that the way her hands shook as she tried to lift her tea to her lips spoke as loud as any words she could say. Jamie's hand slid across the table and settled over hers. He squeezed it gently.

She wanted him. Still. Again. The way she felt about him never really changed. He was like a tornado of emotions, but at the same time a steady rock that was unchanging. Alyson knew both parts of him, and she knew how terrifying it was to be caught in the whirling winds of who he was and miss the peaceful calm in the eye of the storm.

"I missed you." Jamie's voice was low.

"I missed you, too." She felt Jamie's grip on her hand tighten. Maybe he could see the way she was reflecting on who he was. "I know Bambi did."

Jamie gave a soft laugh as he slipped his hand off Alyson's and let it rest on her stomach for a moment.

"Hi, Bambi. Sorry I've been gone." Jamie's voice was thick and Alyson kept her eyes down, letting Jamie talk to her baby. "But I'm here now. You okay in there? Love you."

"Jay." Alyson was still watching Jamie's hand on her stomach when she spoke. "I want to try again with you."

"Sorry?"

"I want to try being us again." She looked up and saw his eyes wide and serious. "I-I know what we told your mom, and, and I know that was painful for all of us, but... I still love you."

Jamie's face twitched as he listened to Alyson. A tear slipped down his cheek and stopped on his lip.

"I've done a lot of thinking, and I know I want to be with you. Maybe we needed some time apart, I don't know, but I know that no matter who the dad is, I'm still going to be in love with you."

"Aly, are you... are you sure?" Jamie's voice shook as he spoke.

"I'm sure. I know us being sure isn't going to fix all the problems or make anything easier, but I want to at least be thinking about it again. Please?"

"I want to say yes. More than anything, I want to tell you yes." Jamie stared Alyson in the eye; the way he kept his focus steady told her how much he meant what he was saying. "But I don't... having to continually take time away from each other isn't an ideal situation. This past month isn't the first time we've had a break of some sort. It hurts you. It hurts me. Eventually it could hurt Bambi, and I don't ever, ever want to be the person who drops out of his life."

Alyson nodded and looked down. The lump in her throat ached. She knew Jamie was thinking about his own dad.

"We want this to work so badly, but things always seem to come against us. I'm afraid that one day it's going to break us apart forever."

The thought made Alyson close her eyes and bite her lip. She looked up when she heard Jamie give a short laugh.

"When I... when I left you in California, I was pretty upset at myself for leaving you. I had felt things for you that I never expected to feel, so when I lost my head and rushed into stuff and then freaked out, it hurt a lot. I, uh, had a picture of us from that day on my phone. I swear, I probably tried to delete it at least a hundred times, but every time I was about to I would think, 'This is the only way I will ever see her face next to mine for the rest of my life.' and I just couldn't do it."

Alyson sat quietly, her heart thumping and tears pricking at her eyes.

"I've already thought I lost you for good once. I don't want to go through that again."

"I don't want that either." Alyson's whisper was hoarse.

Jamie watched her face with a tenderness in his eyes. He slipped off his chair and knelt down on the floor by Alyson's side. She looked down at him and smiled. He reached up slowly and cupped her cheek with his hand.

"But this is not the end."

"Promise?"

"I promise." Jamie ran his thumb over the wet trail of a tear and smiled sadly.

Alyson nodded and took a deep breath, a tiny smile there on her face. Just then, a kick to the inside of her womb made Alyson jump.

"What?"

"Bambi is kicking me because you stopped talking." Alyson chuckled.

"Do you think?" Jamie's eyes grew wide with wonder.

"He, or she, likes hearing your voice." Alyson saw the awe on Jamie's face as he shifted closer and pulled his hand away from her cheek. Both of his hands hovered over her stomach until she gave him the nod. She tingled at his touch, and her smile deepened. Another foot pressed against the side of the womb, and Alyson quickly moved Jamie's hand so he could feel it. "You feel it? That's Bambi's foot."

"Wow." Jamie could hardly breathe. He had thought about what it would be like when he could feel Bambi moving, but his imagination could not have prepared him for this. The movement under Alyson's taut skin made goosebumps jump up on his arms. "Hi, Bambi. I feel you."

Another kick made Alyson jump and Jamie's eyes grow wide. They looked at each other and grinned through the blur of tears.

"I-I can't... I can't believe I can actually feel him. I can feel Bambi."

Alyson's chest constricted as she watched Jamie lean his forehead against her stomach and cry. His shoulders shook, but his hands remained gentle as he cradled the baby in her womb as best he could.

"You're going to be amazing. You're so special." Jamie's breath hit Alyson's stomach in hot blasts, and Alyson could feel his tears soaking through her shirt. "I love you and your mum so very, very much."

"We know." Alyson put a hand on the back of Jamie's head, threading her fingers through his hair. "We love you, too."

Jamie lifted his head and tugged Alyson's hand until it was where he could kiss the backs of her fingers. He looked up at her face and gave her a smile that melted her heart.

"Keep talking to Bambi." Alyson's words came out thick.

"Don't think I can!" Jamie laughed and wiped his eyes. "I'm bawling like a nutter talking to your stomach!"

Alyson laughed and wiped the tears from her own face.

"Not a nutter." She watched him get up from his knees and sit back down in his chair. Their cups of tea were cold now, but they didn't care about the tea. "So, what's going to happen with us?"

"What do you want to have happen to us?"

"Well, this... this worked. We worked." Alyson gestured to their cold tea and tear-stained faces. "I just want to be able to talk with you. To see you and have your friendship."

Jamie was quiet and thoughtful for a moment. He ran his hands through his hair and sucked in his cheeks as he rolled options around in his head.

"We don't have to have an answer today," Alyson said quietly. "We can come back to this another day after we've had time to think."

"It's not that I don't want this." Jamie looked at Alyson and frowned. "It's because I do want this."

"I know, Jay. We'll figure it out."

A few minutes later they stood by the door of the apartment. Jamie shrugged on his jacket before he hugged Aly tightly. Alyson waved and closed the door behind her friend as he left.

"What do you think about that, Bambi?" Alyson walked over to the couch and lay down. "So much love today. So much love."

The next three weeks were good ones for Alyson. The weather was mostly nice, the doctor said that Bambi was perfect in every way, and Jamie didn't have to be in the studio. It soon became a habit for her to check her phone at two in the afternoon to see where Jamie wanted to meet her, just as friends, of course. If the weather was nice, they walked around the park, letting down their walls and feeling their jackets brush against each other when they walked too closely on the pavement. If it was cold or rainy, they would go to a little cafe and sip hot cups of tea, sharing whispers and jokes.

Alyson wasn't sure why she felt like her almost daily rendezvous with Jamie should be a secret, but she kept it to herself when questioned about her recent mood change by Eddie and Lucy. They noticed she was quick to smile and often caught her humming happily when she thought they weren't paying attention.

"Now put a look like that on your paper!" Lucy jabbed her pencil at Alyson's sketch book as they sat next to each other on the couch in Lucy's living room.

"What look?"

"A smile, you idiot!" Lucy reached for the remote control and pushed play on their music. It was sweet and lighthearted, chosen by Lucy. "You've been grinning like mad these past few days and Eddie and I want to know why."

"Things are just good right now." Alyson looked down at her paper, her cheeks warm. "Job is good, Bambi is good..."

"Is it because you've been working through stuff with Gi?" Lucy was looking at her paper now, concentrating on the portrait of a tiny baby she was working on. Their deepest conversations happened when both of them were hunched over a piece of paper, eyes focused on their work, but their ears attentive to the voice of their friend.

"Probably. Just... I don't know, pressing forward, talking through things, remembering the good parts..." It was what she had been doing with Jamie. "Things are going to be okay. They're going to work out."

"Happy to hear you say that." Lucy's eyes misted over as she looked at Alyson. Her separation from Kyle had been hard.

"Oh, Lu." Alyson dropped her pencil and took Lucy's hands in her own. "I wish I could make life better for you right now."

"You *do*," insisted Lucy, blinking away her tears. "You're my best friend."

Alyson squeezed Lucy's hands one more time before their hands slipped apart. She didn't mention what Lucy said when she was with Jamie the next day. As far as she was concerned, it was more than just Jamie. They walked slowly down the path at the park, their hands shoved into their pockets and scarves wrapped tightly around their necks. Alyson could smell the damp earth as their feet crunched over gravel and dirt.

"Tell me about Pakistan." Jamie's question startled Alyson from her thoughts.

"What? Why?" Alyson gave him a funny look.

"It's a part of who you are. You've been there, you have family there, your dad is from there."

"Okay. Well." Alyson focused on a street lamp in the distance and let her mind go back in time.

Her memories of Pakistan smelled of savory meat, warm bread and expensive perfume. Summer nights on the balconies singing songs and laughing with her cousins, sipping on a glass bottle of Coca-Cola and relearning the Urdu language. She remembered the cool tiles under her feet, the large, spacious rooms edged with couches and expensive rugs. She and her cousins used to put their socks on their feet and run and slide down the long hallways and sneak into the kitchen through the wide windows.

Her favorite trip to her father's homeland was the one they made when she was seven. They arrived at the beginning of the rainy season and there were torrential downpours every day. Because they were still young, Alyson and Sumaya were allowed to dance around outside in the garden, shrieking and laughing without a care in the world. It was their last trip with Amir. Amir was happy to spend time with his older cousins and have a bit more favor in his father's eyes because of his good behavior. Alyson had hoped that Amir's choices to be obedient would carry back over to the States when they returned, but they hadn't.

"It's beautiful there."

Jamie waited for more, slowing his pace so Alyson would have more time to share what she wanted to say.

"A lot of the time when I was there, I would sit on the roof with Sumaya and the others. We would watch the sunset, and I would listen to them talking and laughing in Urdu. I couldn't really understand what they were saying; I never remembered it very well. Someone would always end up singing, and we would just sit up there clapping, dancing and singing until one of our aunties came up and shouted at us for being too loud." Alyson gave a soft laugh. "Sumaya would dress me in her clothes, and we would do henna all over our hands and feet. We would be up until midnight cooking supper and playing games."

A stick cracked underneath Alyson's foot as she stepped on it. A blast of cold roused her from her hot summer memories in Islamabad and reminded her that she was far away from both places she called home. Both of those homes had curtains. Her home in Bedford didn't.

"Sorry, that was more about my family than about Pakistan."

"I love it. I love your stories."

"I didn't actually get to see much of Pakistan. I mean, I saw it when we drove from the airport to my grandfather's, but I mostly was just at the house. Amir would be able to tell you more about the actual country."

Jamie walked along beside Alyson quietly. She didn't seem upset by the memories she had pulled up from the past, but he knew she was seeing a different time and place in front of her as they walked.

"You want to find some place to warm up?"

"Yes, please!" said Alyson eagerly.

They found a little music store and tip-toed in. Everyone was busy or preoccupied, and Jamie was able to lead Alyson to a back corner room that was created for people to use if they wanted to check the sound of an instrument before they bought it. Jamie sat Alyson on a stool and went back out to grab a guitar off the wall. He held it carefully as he dug into his pocket for a pick. Once he was settled on the second stool, he began to tune the instrument.

"What are you going to play?" asked Alyson with a smile. She pulled at her scarf until it was off her neck.

"Shhh." Jamie put a finger up to his lips and winked at her.

Alyson unzipped her jacket and waited patiently. Her hands rested on her baby and she smiled at how peaceful it felt. It always seemed so right when it was just the three of them. Finally, Jamie was done tuning his guitar, and he strummed a chord.

"Sounds great." Alyson applauded. "That was amazing. Really cool!"

"Shush now!" Jamie grinned at her.

Alyson watched him shift his fingers and begin to pluck out a melody, his foot tapping the tempo against the leg of the stool. It was a song Alyson had never heard before and she wondered if it was a new song he had written. Alyson smiled when he began to sing, his familiar voice tugging on memories from the first time she had heard his voice on the radio. He kept his eyes down on the instrument on his lap. When he was done, he looked up shyly, hopeful for a good reaction.

"That was incredible, Jay. Did you write it?"

"Yeah. I wrote it about us."

Alyson didn't know what she was supposed to say. She had just heard a beautiful and simple love song about hope and growing old with another person.

"It was really good."

"I'm glad you like it."

"Are you... are you going to put it on your next album?"

Jamie shrugged and played a chord softly.

"I don't know if I want to share it with the world."

"Well, thank you for sharing it with me." Alyson watched him affectionately.

Jamie glanced down at his watch and stood up from his stool, the guitar still in his hand.

"I should get you back. It's going to be dark soon."

They walked quickly to Alyson's apartment, stopping on the sidewalk in front of the door to say goodbye. Jamie reached for her hands and held them for a moment. His breath froze as it came out with a loud sigh.

"I've loved spending time with you, Aly. I can't... I don't want this to change. To end. This is the happiest I've been in months."

"Me, too."

"I'll see you tomorrow, then?"

"I meet with Gianna at four, so it will have to be before then."

"Perfect. I can't wait." Jamie leaned forward and hastily kissed Alyson's forehead. He dropped her hands and he turned to walk away quickly. No one was around to see them, but he was nervous people would start talking if he hung around her place too much. He had promised to protect her from that.

Alyson woke up in the middle of the night to use the bathroom and couldn't get back to sleep. She wrapped herself in a blanket and went into the nursery. She didn't turn on the light, but found one of the nicely scented candles Serenity had given her as a house-warming present and lit it. She set it carefully on the changing table before sitting in the rocking chair.

The candlelight flickered against the dark wall, competing with a faraway street light to be the brightest in the room. Alyson looked over the handwritten letters that were now covering a good portion of the wall. Most of them were from Jamie, but Tommy's letter count had grown weekly. Alyson stared up at the familiar scrawling handwriting that matched the wrinkled love letter she had stuffed between the pages of her journal.

Her mind drifted back to times when Jamie had talked to Bambi, always making sure to tell the baby how much he loved him or her and asking it to take care of Alyson for him. She could picture her child, years from then, bright blue eyes and wide, infectious smile just like Jamie's. She could hear Jamie leaving for work, or a trip, or just to go down the street to buy something from the store and calling his ten-year-old to himself as his hand rested on the handle of the door.

"Love you, Bambi," Jamie would say. "Take care of your mum for me. I'll be back soon."

Sometimes she wanted Jamie to be the dad so badly she ached on the inside. Alyson wished she had her pencil and paper nearby to sketch what she was feeling. The stack of drawings in her closet was inches thick and many of them unseen, even by Gianna. There were a few that Alyson had pulled out to prove she had been processing how she felt in some way, but Gianna let Alyson share only what she was comfortable with.

Bambi kicked inside of Alyson, and the mother looked down with a soft smile. She began to sing "Sweet Dreams" and rub her stretched stomach over and over. The kicks became faster, and Alyson's voice wavered with emotion.

It was funny how a song that had been so meaningful to her as a seventeen-year-old girl was now the song her child loved the most. It was the song she had gone to concerts for in hopes of hearing live.

She couldn't count how many times she had listened to that song as she lay on her bed with her headphones in, or as she danced with Danielle, pretending to practice for a slow dance that she would never have. She had played it in her first car, in her college dorm room, and in her apartment in Iowa, but that song had never felt so real to her as it did right then in that season of life.

"It's our song, Bambi." Alyson felt an elbow press up at the sound of her voice.

Balloon Bambi on Danielle's bedroom wall was the size of a kabocha squash, whatever that was, and covered in little snowflake stickers. She knew because she had talked to Danielle just the day before on Eddie's phone. She closed her eyes and relived the conversation for a moment...

"See, the thing about balloons is that you can decorate them if you want."

"I love it. It's perfect."

"I'm saving all my pennies so I can come see you in April and be there when Bambi is born."

"I wish I had money to give you."

"I'll save enough, Aly. Don't worry."

Alyson sighed and stood up to blow out the candle in the nursery. She wasn't sure what she would do if Danielle couldn't make it over for Bambi's birth.

Fran never tried to hide how much she disliked talking to people, but she had been kind to Alyson. For her, kind meant actually making eye contact and not showing a face that looked like she had just sucked on a lemon when Alyson asked her a question. She rarely initiated conversation, but she did that day.

"You look poorly, Amanda." Her voice was flat as she watched Alyson approach her desk with a stack of files she had been asked to organize.

"I'm fine." Alyson didn't even bother trying to correct her boss anymore.

"Are you sleeping well? So many young people these days don't get enough sleep."

"I'm fine." Alyson smiled sadly and forced herself to keep her hands off her stomach. She was pretty sure Fran knew about Bambi, there was little she could do to hide it anymore, but she hadn't explicitly said she did, so Alyson was careful. She turned slowly to return to her back office.

"Amanda."

"Yes?" Alyson stopped where she was and looked over her shoulder.

"Your parents contacted us."

Alyson's face went white. She wanted to ask Fran what they wanted. She wanted her voice to be calm and steady as though talking about her parents was the most normal thing in the world. Her stomach lurched, though, and she swallowed hard to keep everything down.

"I was told to let you know anytime we heard from them." Fran's voice sounded surprisingly gentle.

"O-ok."

"They asked if you had received your Christmas package." This was the first time Fran had volunteered information without prompting. Alyson wanted to hug her.

She didn't even thank the lady behind the desk before she walked as quickly as she could back into her little room. She shut the door and breathed heavily. Her mind was spinning and everything was on tilt. Her hands found Bambi and she gripped her child, frantic to find something steady in the rolling room. When things settled to a stop, she opened the door and walked back out to Fran.

"A-are you sure all they wanted was to know about w-was the, uh, the... the package?" Alyson steadied herself with one hand on the wall. She hated it when she stuttered.

"Yes, Amanda." Again, Fran didn't sound as harsh as her normal tone was known to be.

"Okay." Alyson nodded and turned to walk away again. Twenty seconds later she was back in the same spot, asking another question. "What did you say? Did you tell them that I got it? Did you... like, what did you say?"

"I sent them an automated message that said I would be out of the office for a fortnight." Fran's frown was beginning to edge back onto her face, and Alyson felt her heart rate calm down. "I don't need emails like that taking up my time, I'm already busy enough minding everything else."

"Oh." Alyson blinked. "Th-thank you. Thank you, Fran. Thank you so much."

Fran didn't respond; she simply went back to typing, her long nails clacking against the keys as she wrote. Alyson went back into her little room, and this time she stayed. Her body was shaking from the rush of adrenaline and fear she had just experienced. Having her parents ask questions or contact people other than her was a terrifying thought. The most well-meaning person could absolutely ruin her life and endanger her child in one email. Alyson reached for her phone and pulled it out.

"Lucy." Alyson tried to keep her voice steady when her friend answered her call.

"Hiya! Aren't you still at work?"

"Yeah, but, I, uh..." Alyson sat down in her office chair and tried to steady her breathing.

"Aly, what's wrong?"

"Are you at home right now?"

"No, love, I'm doing a bit of a job at the mo'. But tell me what's the matter. I can hear it in your voice."

"I'm okay."

"Aly." Lucy's tone was serious.

"I'll see you later, Lu." Alyson felt her eyes begin to blur again.

"Aly, tell me wha-..."

The call ended, and Alyson clenched her hands around the arms of her chair. She let the discomfort of her tight grip keep her from losing dominance over her breathing. Deep breathing. Sometimes she could still hear her mother reminding her to control her emotions by counting her breaths. She knew her mother loved her, but the command to do her deep breathing was always cold. Distant. Her mother had always been so much stronger than she was.

Alyson shouldn't have been surprised when Lucy came barging into her apartment a little after three in the afternoon. She was red-faced and huffing as she wagged her finger at Alyson and demanded an answer.

"You better tell me what's bloody wrong with you!"

"Tea?" Alyson motioned to the kettle that was already on the stove, avoiding the question.

"No, I don't want tea!"

Alyson walked over to the cabinet and pulled out one cup. She was stopped from getting the milk out of the fridge by Lucy's stony glare and slim frame blocking her way. Alyson sighed.

"Talk to me."

"It's nothing..."

Lucy gave her a hard look.

"Fine. My parents contacted Fran at the school."

"And?" Lucy looked lost.

"They contacted someone who wasn't me!" Alyson jabbed her finger at her own chest. "That's against the rules!"

"Because someone might've mentioned Bambi?"

"Yeah. And how would anyone know that my parents weren't supposed to find out about that? Most parents are, you know, happy about grandchildren."

"What did Fran do?"

"Ignored them." Alyson's mouth turned up into a little smile. "Hopefully she's the only one they try to contact. It just shook me up. Scared me. All the things that I've worked so hard to make work flashed before my eyes... my life here could have been over in a second."

"Ah, Aly. That's so scary. Sorry I was working and couldn't come over straight away." Lucy pulled Alyson into a hug. She felt the tension leave Alyson's shoulders as she took a deep breath and leaned into her friend. "Next time don't lie to me and tell me that you're okay, you idiot."

"Thanks, Lu."

The kettle whistled from the stove, and Alyson hurried to finish making her tea while Lucy rummaged around in the other room for a moment. When Lucy came back into the dining room, she had two pencils and Alyson's sketchpad. There was a tiny smile on Alyson's face as she took her things from Lucy's hands.

"Draw with me?" she invited.

"Love to." Alyson grinned.

Alyson turned on some music and settled down at the dining room table with her friend. It felt good to put the pencil to paper and draw the heavy and fearful emotions she felt on the inside. When she was done, she showed it to Lucy shyly.

"Aly! Good lord, you do draw some seriously sad stuff!" Lucy grabbed the paper and studied the details. "You're doing amazing at this, though!"

Even though the picture wasn't drawn to get praise, Alyson smiled at the compliment. She was surprised when she looked down at Lucy's picture and saw someone staring at her from the paper.

"How often do you draw pictures of my face?"

"Oh, I dunno." Lucy's tone was light. "I started drawing you when I first saw you standing at your window every evening. Something about you inspired me."

"Can I see the other pictures you've drawn of me?"

"Maybe someday, but not today." Lucy picked up her drawing and stood up from her spot. She planted a kiss on the top of Alyson's head and headed for the door. "Love you, you idiot. I'm right across the street if you need me."

"Love you, Lu." Alyson waved as Lucy left.

Alyson's hands were sweaty as she rushed up the stairs to her apartment as best she could with her thirty-week baby jostling her from the inside. She knew Eddie was already there and waiting for her to have their special weekly hangout. The hallway smelled like pizza. Alyson wondered if Eddie had brought her some from Pizza Millennia. He knew she loved it, and she knew he had just come from London.

She stopped outside of the door to her own apartment, her hands pressed against her heart and lungs heaving. Bambi was kicking repeatedly up at her ribcage, and Alyson grimaced. Eddie was good at reading her; she didn't know how she was going to be able to hide what she was feeling from him. She swallowed a gulp of air and opened the door.

"Aly!" Eddie looked up from his phone and swung his feet off the coffee table. He froze before he had a chance to stand up, noting her shifting eyes and forced smile. "What happened?"

"Nothing." Alyson removed her coat and scarf and turned her back on Eddie to hang them up. "Just a bit out of breath. My child is smashing up against my lungs and…"

"No, Aly. I think there's something else." Eddie was standing now, his phone set on the coffee table and his eyes trained on Alyson's face. "You seem nervous. Sad."

"It's just life." Alyson pressed her lips together and bit the inside of her cheek until it was bleeding to keep tears out of her eyes. "Sometimes people have bad days."

Without another word, Eddie put an arm around Alyson's shoulders and led her from the door to the kitchen. He pulled out a chair and gestured for her to take a seat. She sighed as she sat and crossed her arms, determined to keep her hurting heart hidden.

Eddie quickly gathered what he needed and set it in front of his friend. She couldn't help but smile as the bowl of salsa and bag of chips caught her eye. Her determination faltered, but she picked it back up again.

"Thanks, Ed."

"What's wrong?"

Alyson shoved a chip into her mouth and pretended to not hear his question. He wasn't fooled, but allowed her to avoid his inquiry. They talked about the paper cuts Alyson had endured from filing five hundred old medical files at the school the day before, and the umbrella that had broken on her way home from work three days earlier. When the salsa was finished, Eddie cleared the food off the table and asked if she was ready to watch their show.

To be honest, Alyson didn't catch a single thing that happened on the television as she remembered what had happened earlier that afternoon. She tried to work out what she could have said differently, what the other person could have said differently, if things would have worked out the same way if Alyson hadn't kept it a secret. The show ended, and Alyson stood up to hug Eddie goodbye.

"Goodbye, Bambi." Eddie took a moment to feel Bambi's elbow sticking out against Alyson's side. "Love you."

Alyson waited for Eddie to look up at her before saying goodbye.

"Thanks for tonight, Eddie. I mean it."

"You know you can tell me if something happened." Eddie's voice was low.

"Yeah, of course I do." Alyson's response was quick and almost defensive.

"Call me when you decide you want to tell me what happened today."

Alyson nodded and swallowed hard. She waited until she knew for sure that Eddie was down all three flights of stairs and out of her building before she started crying. She sat down on the couch and covered her face with her hands. It was all too much.

It wasn't that she and Jamie had had an argument. Neither of them had even raised their voices or huffed at the other, but their conversation had broken the spell and Alyson was overwhelmed. Life was so easy when she could slip into a separate world and be with Jamie. It was just her, the man she loved, and their child. It was safe. It was magical. But then she was reminded...

"I want you to come visit my family again."

"Excuse me?" Alyson had nearly choked on her sandwich when Jamie spoke.

"I want you..." Jamie paused and handed a napkin to the girl who was struggling to swallow her mouthful. "I want you to come see my family again."

"Why? Wh-why are you thinking this is a good idea?" Alyson's stomach twisted and she set her sandwich down on her plate. "Your mum..."

"I want her to get to know you more. We're doing so well right now, I just... I feel like now..."

"We were doing really well at Christmastime, do you remember?"

"I know, but, we've thought about things, and... and the kids miss you. Syd would love to hang out with you again."

"I don't think this is a good idea."

"I'm not saying that you coming is going to mean we're getting more serious again. I simply want my family to get to know you better."

Alyson sighed. Jamie waited for her to say something, but she had nothing to say.

"Right now we're in a bubble, and I love it, but I want to be happy beyond the bubble. I want us to be friends outside of our own little world."

"We are friends outside of this. We're friends."

"So?" Jamie raised his eyebrows as he went back to his first question.

"I just don't think it's a good idea." Alyson shook her head and frowned. She tried to put her finger on why the idea was so distasteful to her, but she couldn't. "Especially without your mom saying she's okay with it."

"She's not going to be okay with it until she knows you better, and she can't get to know you better unless you come."

Alyson looked down at her lap. Leaving Jamie's house on Christmas day because of Heather's strong words was something Alyson wanted to forget and never have to relive again. What if she went back and Heather repeated her sentiments? She didn't want that.

"Another reason why I'm suggesting this is..." Jamie spoke slowly. "My friend that I've been working for in the studio is redoing some of his tracks, and I'm going to be busy again. I'm not going to have time to come up here and see you the way I want to, but if you were at my family's house..."

"Which reason is the real reason, Jay? Don't play games." Alyson's voice was soft.

"I want you to know my family, and now would be a good time to kill two birds with one stone. That's all I'm saying." Jamie's hand found Alyson's and he gripped it. "I don't want to go back to not seeing you every day."

"I don't either, Jamie. Honest." Alyson's eyes were focused on the cup of tea in front of her. "But I'm going to need some time to think about this. Things are going so well and to change things..."

"I understand, love." Jamie ran his thumb along the back of Alyson's knuckles. "Just think about it. Let me know."

"Okay."

Alyson's phone vibrated with a text from Eddie asking where she was and Alyson ran out of the coffee shop, leaving Jamie to head back to London without a goodbye or a hug. Now, four hours later, she was finally able to have a cry over it all.

"Darn you, Jamie Donald. Stop trying to fix things that aren't broken." Alyson's hands dropped from her face to her baby. "Why did he do that, Bambi? Why would he suggest going to see his mom again?"

An incoming call from Serenity forced Alyson to slow her breathing and steady herself. The friendly voice coming from the other end of the line calmed Alyson's heart and she dried her tears.

"Hiya, love! How's things? Just ringing you up to tell you I found the cutest, and I mean, *the cutest*, little outfit for Bambi," gushed Serenity. "I was going to put it in the post to send to you, but then I thought that maybe you'd be popping down to London soon and I could just meet up with you and give it to you that way."

"Aw, thanks, Ren."

"Yeah, it's okay." Serenity's voice was light and gracious. "Do you have plans to come to London?"

"I don't..." Alyson thought back to Jamie's request to have her come visit his family. "I don't believe so. I'm not going to be going to London anytime soon. It's hard getting around with Bambi so big these days."

"Oh, course, love! I'll just send it in the post."

"Perfect. Thanks."

"Yeah, it's all right. Well, I'll let you go, I know you're probably going to bed soon. I just couldn't wait to tell you about the outfit."

"No, it's good to hear from you!"

"It's been too long. Let me know when you're free so we can have a little catch up, yeah? I'd love to hear about the plans for when Bambi comes."

"It's exciting!" Alyson's smile went deep as she looked down at her stomach. "Time is going by so quickly. I can't believe it's already the twentieth of February."

"How excited? Bambi will be here before you know it!"

"So excited."

"Are there more things you need for the nursery? Clothes? Do you need more clothes?"

"Are you asking for an excuse to go shopping at the cute baby store?"

"Please give me one!" Serenity laughed. "But honest, Aly, I'm more than happy to help in any way I can. I know the party was small and you're going to need loads more things, so just let me know. I know all of us are very willing to be a part of getting your house ready for the baby."

"I'll make a list and let you know." Alyson's heart felt like it could burst from gratitude over her friendship with Serenity. She wanted to be as sweet and selfless as Serenity was when she grew up. "Oh, Ren, Elle told me a while ago that you have a saying that you tell yourself when things are hard. She said I should ask you what it is."

"Did she? It's just something my Aunt Becky taught me when I was little. She told me to be kind, forgive, and love others, even when they hurt you." Serenity's voice grew quiet. "It's hard to live out, but I've never regretted it."

"It has made you a beautiful person, Ren."

"Aw, shush now." Serenity gave a small laugh. "Let me know when you get the parcel, okay dearie?"

"Sure, of course." Alyson was smiling when she hung up, Serenity's words still in her mind. She quickly found a piece of paper and a writing utensil and wrote it down. "Be kind. Forgive. Love others, even when they hurt you."

Chapter nineteen
"I'll remember. I'll never forget."

It was cold and gray on February 24th as Alyson walked home from work. It was a Wednesday, which meant the week was only half over. The cold wind blew sleet into Alyson's eyes, and she had a hard time seeing where she was going as she squinted against the wind. She walked quickly, hoping to reach her apartment before the cold seeped through her jacket that was still barely closing over her bump. According to Danielle and the balloon on her bedroom wall, Bambi was about the size of a large cabbage. The size of her baby, though, was the last thing on Alyson's mind as she hurried around the last corner that led to her flat.

Maybe it was because she was hurrying, or maybe it was because she wasn't able to see her feet, or maybe it was because the sidewalk hadn't been salted, or perhaps it was all three things combined that caused Alyson's feet to slip on a patch of ice.

It felt like time and her heart stood still for a moment as she slammed onto her side. Suddenly, all she could hear was the roar of her heartbeat as a horrific pain shot through her abdomen. Her elbow smarted from where she landed on the hard ground and stars danced in front of her eyes from what she could only assume was a smack to the head. A strained moan squeaked from her throat as she tried to breathe. It took several panicked attempts before she was successful with pulling in air. Wet snow fell on her as her mind slowly connected enough thoughts to remind her what to do.

"Oh my word. Bambi!" Alyson gingerly pushed herself up to a sitting position. As soon as she regained her balance, she felt her stomach to make sure her baby was all right. There was a kick. "You're okay. You're okay. You're going to be okay..."

She saw one old man on the road walking with his back towards her, but otherwise the street was empty. Gritting her teeth and ignoring the worried tears running down her face, Alyson heaved herself to her feet. She stood unsteadily for a moment before she finally made her legs move and shuffle the rest of the way home. She was in a great deal more pain by the time she reached the third level of her apartment building and she bit the knuckle of her index finger to keep from crying out.

Alyson took off her jacket as she attempted to call Eddie, but the call never went through. She stared at the mobile device as it sat in her hand and frowned. Should she call someone else? Where was Lucy? Lucy was working, Alyson remembered as she removed her shoes and leaned against the wall for a minute to catch her breath. It hurt when she tried to breathe deeply. She pressed the call button for Eddie once more and waited for him to answer. The call failed.

"What?" Alyson muttered to herself.

Jamie was in his important meeting. He had told her about it. Right? Wasn't that what he had said? She couldn't call him until after five. She would wait until then.

"Okay, Bambi. Maybe a bath will sort us out."

Alyson's head ached and throbbed. Even as she sat in the tub, she tried to relieve the pain of the fall, but nothing was working. She rubbed her hands over her face and cradled her forehead, wishing her mind didn't feel so fuzzy. After sitting for half an hour with very few coherent thoughts, she wrapped herself in a towel and sat on the couch, still fighting the feeling that something was very wrong. She rubbed her belly and hummed quietly to distract from the achy feeling growing in her back. There were only a few kicks from Bambi, and one very important thought struggled to make itself known.

"It's too early to have a baby," said Alyson.

The tightening sensation in her abdomen was closer together than any of the Braxton Hicks contractions had been previously, and Alyson grew worried. There should be something done. Someone should make it stop before something bad happened to Bambi. If only the pounding in her head would cease for a moment so she could think. She tried to write a text to Jamie to ask if she could call him before five, but it ended up as gibberish. She sent it anyway. Maybe he would understand what she meant.

Bambi kicked a few more times, and Alyson cooed down at her baby gently.

"Hi, baby. Hi. I love you."

She tried to tell the child inside of her that they were going to be okay, that a little nap would fix everything, but her tongue felt thick and useless. With a lump in her throat, she pulled on her pajama pants and a sweatshirt and lay down. Alyson felt a wave of drowsiness as she stared at the blank wall across from her. An incoming text made her phone ping. Alyson reached for it, but stopped when she looked at her fingers and saw her hand shaking. It was as if all of her energy was sucked out of her and she couldn't keep her eyes open a moment longer.

"So... tired..." Alyson's voice drifted away just as sleep overtook her.

The moon was high in the sky, and the sleet had ended several hours earlier when Alyson opened her eyes again to a raging pain in her belly. She gasped for air and pushed at the blankets, trying to see what was wrong. She switched on the bedside lamp with a shaking hand.

"No..." she said in a low, desperate whisper.

Alyson's hands reached down onto the bed where she was laying and pulled them away; they were sticky and warm with blood. This couldn't be real. She stared at her hands in shock, her screams stuck in her throat. She couldn't let them out. She couldn't move. Her whole body trembled. She began to shake her head and silently mouth her protests before reality sunk in and her screams came out full force.

"Bambi! Bambi, are you okay?!" Alyson's hands went to her stomach. "Bambi! Please! Please tell me you're okay!"

There was no movement.

"No! No! You have to be okay!" The screams echoed in the empty apartment. "You have to hold on! You can't die!"

Alyson tried to sit up, but nausea made her feel like she was about to throw up. She groaned and fell back against her pillows, growing more aware of the achy feeling at the top of her legs by her thighs. This was all very wrong.

Alyson felt around on the bed until she found her cell phone. She slid it up and pushed the call button. The phone shook in her hand against her face, and her teeth began to ache as they were pressed together against the pain.

"Bambi, it's okay. I-it's okay! It's... it's going to be okay. You're going to live!" Alyson whimpered and gasped. A contraction hit her and Alyson was in mid-groan when the call connected with the phone on the other end of the line. She screamed into the mouthpiece and ended with a shaky sob.

"ALY!" Jamie's voice came through the phone. "What's wrong?!"

"It hurts!" Alyson's voice shook as she tried to communicate. "Make it stop! There's so much b-blood! Jamie, make it... stop! Pl-please!"

"I'm on my way right now. I'm going to call Eddie, he's closer, and he'll make it there sooner. Don't move! We're coming. Don't move, Aly! We're on our way! Okay? We'll be there soon!" Jamie had no idea what had happened, but he could guess. A list of possibilities quickly grew in his mind, from some sort of accident to her being found by her father's family.

"Bambi..." Alyson's voice cut off as she groaned, her breath catching as she tried to breathe through the pain.

"I'm coming, love. I have to hang up now. I love you. Hang in there." He felt absolutely sick as he ended the call on Alyson mid-groan.

Alyson's screams died away for a moment as she concentrated on deep breathing. Maybe if she was able to close her eyes very tightly and think about her baby moving in her womb, everything would be okay. She could live with pain, she could live with blood, but Bambi could not die.

"Bambi, please," she groaned. She pressed harder on her stomach, wincing when she pressed against what felt like a massive bruise. "Come on, Bambi!"

Alyson struggled to find a position that brought relief. Blood spread on her sheets as she clawed her way to the other side of her bed. She attempted to stand up, but light-headedness kept her horizontal. The sight of the blood was making her queasy, and she nearly gagged. Her thoughts began to fade as she felt her body weakening due to blood loss. She lay with her hands barely holding onto her stomach, and her breathing growing shallow.

She could almost hear her mother's voice instructing her to do her deep breathing.

"Deep breaths, Aly. Count your breaths." The memory of the cool, distant command did nothing to calm her wild fears. "Aly! Now! Breathe!"

"Mom..." Alyson pulled at the oxygen in the room, but none seemed to enter her lungs. "I ca-... I c-can't... Mom!"

Eddie burst into the apartment and ran towards the light that was shining in the bedroom. He had made record time, reaching Alyson's place in ten minutes from his Gran's house. All he could see was Alyson on a corner of the bed with a trail of blood on the white bedclothes. Jamie had said there was an emergency; he didn't know what had happened, but Alyson was in pain and there was blood. He was right about the blood, but Alyson appeared to be barely lucid as she mumbled from the end of the bed.

Eddie dove onto the floor and knelt at her bedside. He took her face between his hands. Her eyes fluttered open from the shock of his touch. Her face was so pale.

"What happened, love?" Eddie's voice was raspy and fraught with apprehension. "Tell me! Tell me what happened!"

"I can't..." Alyson knew it was Eddie. She knew he was there to help her. "I can't feel... Bam..."

"Okay, love. I'm taking you to the hospital." Eddie could tell that something had gone terribly wrong, and his friend's life and the life of her child were in danger.

Alyson cried out in pain as she felt Eddie scoop her up in his arms and carry her out of the bedroom. He didn't grab anything or shut off any lights as he hurried to leave. His hand caught the apartment door as he ran past, and it slammed shut behind him. The sound echoed with his footsteps in the stairwell. Eddie's car was still warm when he loaded her in.

"It wasn't her family, Jamie. Something's gone really wrong," Eddie warned Jamie over the phone. "There's blood, and... Just be prepared for anything."

"Garret is calling Dr. Gallagher right now. He'll meet you at the A and E and take care of Aly until we get there to do the paperwork."

Eddie swallowed hard and nodded wordlessly.

"Okay, Ed?"

"Y-yes. Okay. I got it."

"Keep her safe, Ed." Jamie's voice grew rough. "Don't you dare let anything happen to her."

Eddie reached the emergency room parking lot in five minutes and barely remembered to turn off his car before climbing out to pull Alyson from the backseat. She grimaced and gasped at the jolting movements and slung her arms loosely around Eddie's neck. There was a spot of blood on Eddie's backseat; he noticed it as he shut the door with his hip. He shifted her in his arms and walked quickly towards the entrance.

Snow crunched under Eddie's shoes, and few snowflakes drifted through the crisp, night air, landing on the young man's broad shoulders as he rushed through the night to the hospital. It wasn't until they were about to enter the building that Alyson realized her feet were cold because she was barefoot.

Dr. Gallagher had just arrived at the hospital when they rushed through the doors. The girl was placed onto a stretcher and wheeled back into a large examining room as soon as they walked in. It wasn't the common procedure, but Dr. Gallagher took charge of the situation and everyone followed his lead, including Eddie.

Eddie ran next to her, his hand holding tightly onto hers despite the looks from the nurses that told him he was in the way. The way Alyson's body flopped loosely as they pushed her down the hallway scared him. He had never felt so afraid for something in his life. He would claim Bambi as his own child if that was what it took to stay with Alyson. Thankfully, though, no one said anything.

"Okay, lift her gently," the nurses ordered once they reached the room. "Young man, please step back."

Eddie tried to pry his fingers loose from Alyson's grip, but she refused to give him up, even as weak as she was.

"No! Ed...!" She rolled her head to the side to see his face.

"I know, love. I'm right here." Eddie moved to stand by Alyson's head, away from where the doctors and nurses were focused.

An IV was stuck into her arm, the needle piercing her skin. Her mouth moved noiselessly as Dr. Gallagher and the nurses worked around her. All Eddie could make out was "Bambi" and, "please live."

"She's lost quite a bit of blood, sir."

"Get a transfusion for her," Dr. Gallagher ordered.

"We need to know her blood type," said one nurse as she jostled into Eddie's side.

"O+," another nurse read off of Alyson's file.

"Someone get an ultrasound tech up here immediately. We need to see what this baby is doing," barked Dr. Gallagher. He looked nervous, and Eddie knew that whatever had happened was serious.

Alyson whimpered, and then let out a scream as pain pushed against her pelvic bone. Her hands squeezed Eddie's until the pain dissipated; then she wept. Eddie used his thumb to push a tear out of the corner of his eye, his head bent down over Alyson's. He rested his forehead against hers.

"I can't..." Alyson's moans were choked out by sporadic breaths that shook her rib cage. "I-I ca-... can't feel..."

"Shh, love. It's okay. It's okay." His whispers were for himself as much as they were for Alyson. "Oh, God, please let it be okay."

An ultrasound technician arrived and the sweatshirt Alyson had been wearing was pulled up to reveal her almost thirty-one week pregnant belly. The gel was squirted onto her skin, and the wand applied almost immediately without any thought of how cold it would be against her skin.

The man staring at the screen of the ultrasound machine didn't look at the girl. His eyes were locked on the black and white image as he moved the wand across Alyson's stomach. The picture moved rapidly, and Eddie couldn't make sense of what he was seeing. He thought he saw the baby's face and arms. He saw a tiny little foot and what he thought was the spinal cord.

"Where's the h-heart beat." Alyson's voice was a whisper.

Eddie caught the movement of her mouth out of the corner of his eye and leaned closer.

"Sorry?"

"Heartbeat." The whisper was so faint. "Where is it? Why... why can't I... Where's Bambi's heartbeat?"

Eddie felt himself lose feeling in his hands as his knees began to buckle. He propped himself up against the examination table to keep from falling over. He looked away from the screen and down at Alyson's quivering lips.

Tears created a salty film over his gray eyes until he couldn't see anything. He blinked rapidly to renew his vision, but it was soon clouded again. His throat ached.

"I'm very sorry, ma'am, but we can't find a heartbeat." The man with the wand in his hand finally turned towards the two friends.

"I'm so sorry. I'm so, so sorry." Eddie kissed Alyson's forehead and pushed her hair back from her face. "I'm so sorry."

"By the way, ma'am, the child was a girl."

There was hardly a reaction from Alyson beyond the tears that began to trickle down her face. She let her head roll to the side, and she closed her eyes. The doctors continued to talk, and prod, and poke and inject things into her IV, but Alyson responded to nothing.

Eddie's insides hurt. He pressed the heels of his palms against his eyes and tried to still the shuddering of his shoulders, but he couldn't, not with Alyson looking like she was on death's door. He wondered how he was going to tell the others about Bambi when they arrived. After twenty minutes of frantic and terrifying activity around Alyson's bed, he felt his phone buzz in his pocket. It was Jamie.

"The others are coming." Eddie let go of Aly's hand and brushed his fingers lightly across her sweaty forehead. "I'll be right back. I promise."

Once out in the hallway, Eddie took a moment to take a deep breath before he answered the call. The end of his sleeve wiped the loose tears from his face as he heard Jamie's voice shout into his ear.

"Garret and Ren are with me, and we're here. Where are you?"

"I'll meet you round at the front desk." Eddie didn't trust himself to say anything more.

The others were running through the doors when Eddie reached the empty waiting room. Their eyes were wide with worry as they searched for their friend. Serenity pointed to Eddie when she spotted him, and they hurried over. Jamie saw Eddie's tear-streaked face first, and his heart stopped. Eddie squeezed his eyes shut to keep himself from crumbling into tears again as Serenity hugged him tightly.

"The baby is gone." Eddie choked out the words as he pulled back from the young woman and wiped his eyes. "No heartbeat. We don't know what happened yet, but Bambi is... is gone."

"Geez..." Jamie put his hands over his face and exhaled sharply. He wanted to stay like that, with his hands over his face, hiding himself from reality, but he didn't. He couldn't. "Where's Aly? Where is she?"

"In the examining room with Dr. Gallagher. I don't know if they'll let you in there. It was small and they are still fussing with things. They said they can't move her up to labor and delivery until you guys do the paperwork."

"Did we hear back from Tommy yet?" asked Garret.

"Not yet. I couldn't get him to answer the phone," answered Jamie. It didn't surprise him too much as he and Tommy hadn't been speaking for weeks now. "He could be sleeping with his phone off."

"He's going to be so upset." Eddie shook his head. "He's going to be so upset when he knows what is going on."

"I'll keep trying to call him," offered Serenity. "Let's just get back to where Aly is."

Eddie led the others down the hall towards the room where Alyson had been taken. A nurse stepped forward to take Jamie and Garret to fill out the paperwork.

"Can I please see her first?" asked Jamie.

"We need this paperwork now." The hospital had already been generous enough to let Dr. Gallagher do as much as he had without things filled out.

"But she needs us!" said Jamie.

"She needs you to fill out the paperwork so we can help her!"

Jamie ran a hand through his hair. He remembered how nervous Alyson had been to go to the doctor's by herself. He began to pace as Garret took the pen and started jotting things down. He hoped that time would pass more quickly if he was moving. He saw Serenity standing with a tissue pressed against her eyes, and Eddie had his hands tucked tightly under his arms as he stood alone, silent sobs shaking his shoulders.

A hand squeezed Jamie's arm and he turned around to see his best friend. It wasn't until that moment that he remembered for the first time in months that Bambi could be Garret's child. Would Garret even feel the loss of this baby? Garret had kept his distance, doing his part while hiding behind the paperwork and the menial tasks that Jamie pushed his way so he could spend more time with Aly and the baby. All Jamie had wanted was this baby. All he had wanted was...

"Jay, grab a pen and help me fill this out. It will go faster if we both do it." Garret handed a stack of papers to Jamie. His eyes went beyond Jamie to the other two standing in the hallway waiting for them to finish. Garret tried to remember the last time they had all been together outside of work.

Alyson was lying with her eyes shut when Jamie was finally allowed to go see her. Jamie pushed past everyone to reach her side, his eyes already burning with tears.

"Love." He took her hand and pressed it to his lips. Her face was white, and there were smudges of blood on her cheeks from touching her face with her hands. "I'm here."

Alyson's eyes flitted open. She was wearing a hospital gown now, and had a blanket over her lower half. Her eyes filled with tears as she looked up at Jamie. His hand stroked her cheek, his eyes on hers, everything else in the room fading away.

"Bambi was a girl." The whisper was all Alyson needed to say to the man she loved. She needed him to know what she had lost. What they had lost.

"A girl?" Jamie's eyes brimmed over and one tear splashed onto the pillow by Aly's head. He licked his lips before he could speak again. "I-I bet she is the prettiest girl in the world. Just like her mum."

The others stood along the wall in the room, watching Alyson and Jamie speak quietly and trying to stay out of the way of the nurses who were getting ready to move Alyson to a different floor. Eddie looked down and saw there was blood on his hands and his coat. It made him feel like he had had some part in Bambi's death. He swallowed hard. His stomach still ached.

"Ed, your phone." Garret heard the buzzing before his friend did.

"It's Tommy." Eddie wiped at his nose with the back of his hand and put his phone up to his ear. "Tommy, get to the hospital in Bedford as quick as you can. Alyson's here."

Everyone waited quietly as Eddie paused for a moment to compose himself. He pressed his free hand against his eyes, and then shook his head. His mouth opened but no sound came out. No one breathed as they waited for Eddie to speak.

"Sorry, Tom." Eddie's voice caught and broke on the lump in his throat. "The baby didn't make it."

Danielle was getting home from eating out with some friends when her phone began to ring. She slipped her shoes off her feet and pulled her phone out of her pocket. The name *Jamie/Alyson* popped up onto the screen and a nervous feeling settled over the pit of her stomach. It rang again in her hand before she answered it.

"What's wrong? What happened?"

"It's Aly. And Bambi." Jamie's voice was shaking.

"What happened?!" Danielle ran into her bedroom and started pulling things out of her dresser to shove into her suitcase. "Tell me! Is she okay? Is it her family? Did they find out?"

"No. No, she, uh…"

"Jamie! Tell me!"

"She fell."

Danielle sunk to the floor, her lungs frozen inside of her.

"Bambi… Bambi didn't make it." Jamie was crying now.

Danielle's eyes went to the balloon that was on the wall by her bed. It was fine. It was a perfectly normal, happy balloon. She shook her head and resumed pulling out clothes and digging through her desk for her money and her passport.

"I'm coming." Danielle tucked her phone between her shoulder and her ear so she could use both hands. "Tell Aly I'm getting on the next plane out of here, and I'm coming. Tell her I'll be there as soon as I can be."

"Garret's already lining up a flight for you." Jamie cleared his throat. "Said there's one that leaves for Chicago in forty minutes. We'll email you your ticket so you have it when you get to the airport."

"They won't let me on unless I'm there an hour before the flight."

"Garret's got it sorted. Just get here. Aly needs you."

Jamie's words made Danielle stop dead in her tracks. She tried to picture her best friend and what she looked like in that moment. She was probably terrified, and in a mixture of emotional and physical agony that was so intertwined she couldn't tell which was which. Danielle swallowed hard and shoved her clothes into the duffle bag she found on the floor of her closet.

"Thanks, Jamie. Take care of her until I'm there."

"I promise." Jamie could hardly talk.

Danielle's heart was pounding the entire drive to the airport. She had the radio off and kept her phone on her lap. Every sound made her anxious. The airport was close, but Danielle sped down the highway and prayed she wouldn't get pulled over. She was already cutting it close in time.

It wasn't until she was safely in her seat right before the door to the cabin was closed that Danielle texted Jamie to tell him she was on her way.

Great. Have a safe flight. Aly knows you're coming.

It was going to be a long night of traveling, but she didn't care. All she wanted was to be with her best friend. To hold her and tell her that she was going to make it through. Tears ran down her face as she thought about all the dreams she had dreamed for Bambi.

She had dreamed of the baby growing up, looking like Alyson, giving her sweet kisses on the cheek and falling asleep on her shoulder. She had imagined the child taking their first steps, saying their first word and learning how to say her name. She had envisioned years passing as she celebrated Christmases and birthdays with Alyson's son or daughter, marking the years with trips and visits and vacations together. She had pictured decades down the road when she would stand with Alyson and wave goodbye as Bambi drove off to college, off to their new job, off to their honeymoon...

"Hang on, Aly," Danielle whispered as she stared out of the window and willed the airplane to go faster down the tarmac to take off. "I'm coming."

Tommy reached the hospital in just under an hour after the phone call and was directed to the labor and delivery floor. Garret met him in the waiting room to lead him to where they were keeping Alyson. Tommy's legs felt like jelly as he hurried down the quiet hallway behind his friend. He could feel his stomach churning as he approached the room; he wasn't sure what to expect.

He had tried to text Eddie to ask him, but they had been told to turn off their phones.

"Is she okay? Is it bad?" Tommy's eyes watered as they darted in the direction of the door. "Is there blood?"

"Blood is all cleaned up." Garret stepped back as the door opened.

Tommy crossed over the threshold and rocked back on his heels, his heart in his throat. He could smell the rubbing alcohol and a hundred other smells he didn't know the names of but reminded him of the time he had to visit his grandfather in the hospital when he was eighteen. He saw the bed and a crowd of people to his left. There were only four people in the crowd, but it seemed like more than that in the small room.

Alyson lay on the bed with pitocin dripping through her IV, and Jamie hovering by her head. Tommy had seen Jamie nervous before. They had played hundreds of shows together where Jamie would pace and mumble under his breath, trying to keep himself calm before hitting the stage. But this was more than nerves; it was fear.

The girl seemed to be completely shut down to the outside world while Jamie fidgeted and crossed his arms tightly across his chest. His voice was stern and demanding as he turned from Aly to the doctor and back, inquiring about every moan and sign of discomfort. Doctor Gallagher was patient with the barrage of anxious questions. He spoke calmly, assuring Jamie that he was doing everything he could for the girl. The nurse stepped away from the bed to wash her hands at the sink in the corner. When she moved, Tommy spotted Serenity sitting in a blue padded chair next to the far side of Alyson's bed.

"They don't want everyone in here at the same time." Garret's whisper startled Tommy from his observation. "We'll take turns."

"What about Ren?" Tommy swallowed hard and nodded at the girl who wasn't budging from her spot.

"Won't leave." Garret's voice shook a little as he cast a glance towards where Serenity had set up vigil beside the mother. "Promised to stay with Alyson to the end."

The cause of stillbirth for Bambi was diagnosed as placental abruption from the trauma of slipping and falling on the ice. The fall had caused the placenta to tear which cut off Bambi's supply of oxygen. Even if Alyson had been brought in right away, the tear was so complete that Bambi would have had minimal chances of surviving. The barely coherent mother tucked the accident and her baby's death into her memory as her own fault and lapsed into silent agony. Her heart was broken; there wasn't a painkiller in the world that could have stopped her from feeling that. Her body did things she had never felt it do before, and she was scared.

"I'm staying right here, sweetheart," Serenity whispered as she leaned forward and put a hand on Alyson's shoulder. "I'm not leaving until this is all over."

"Thank you." Alyson's mouth moved just enough to get the words out.

The guys took turns sleeping on the chairs in the waiting room down the hall and sitting next to Alyson's bed. Contractions helped mark the time as Alyson moaned and slept intermittently. Everything hurt, and she couldn't escape it. After two hours by her side, Jamie tapped out, too tired to stay awake. He kissed Alyson on the cheek, told her that he loved her and he would be back. She didn't open her eyes again until she felt the bed moving beside her.

"Hi, Alyson." Tommy sat down next to the bed and leaned forward on his elbows.

Alyson could smell his cologne reach her from where he was sitting. It reminded her of her time in France. She felt him wrap his fingers around her hand and rub the back of it with his thumb. His hand was shaking, or maybe that was her own.

"I'm so sorry this happened." Tommy had tears in his eyes. "To you... to Bambi..."

The muscles in Alyson's face twitched as she listened to Tommy's voice; it was the only familiar thing in that hospital room at that moment with the moon hidden behind the cloud of fog that rested over the gloomy city. He was quiet for a long time, letting Alyson get as much rest as she could between contractions. The contractions knew no mercy as Alyson struggled through each one. Pain subsided for a moment, and Serenity told him that it was time for Alyson to have another drink of water.

"Here you go." Tommy helped hold the straw up to Alyson's chapped lips.

Alyson blinked her eyes at her friend for a moment, too tired to make her mouth move. He leaned closer and kissed her knuckles, then reached up to smooth her hair back with his fingers. He saw the pain lines deepen and was ready to breathe through another contraction with her when she looked up at him again.

"I'll never hear her laugh."

Tommy looked out the window as he squeezed Alyson's hand tightly, unable to say or do anything more. Alyson's breath caught in her chest, and she shook with suppressed sobs.

"She's not going to cry... when she is born," Alyson continued weakly. "She's not going to see my face or, or, or call me mom."

"Shh." Tears dripped down off his chin, and he pressed another kiss to the back of her hand.

The nurse entered the room and asked Tommy to step back for a moment as she examined Alyson to see if she had progressed any further. Alyson bit her lip and squeezed her eyes shut against the pain, tears slipping through the seam of her eyelids.

"Does it have to hurt her so bad?" Tommy snapped at the nurse, still upset over what Alyson had said.

"Her body is trying to do in a few hours what it would normally take three more months to do." The nurse noted how young the man's red face looked. There was nothing worse than the miracle of birth being tainted by the black finger of death for a couple that was so young. "I'm very sorry. We can give her an epidural if she'd like."

"No." Serenity spoke up for her friend. "She doesn't want one."

"Why not?" asked Tommy after the nurse had left.

"She told me she didn't want one."

"Did she know it was going to hurt this bad?"

"I can't imagine that anyone knows something like this is going to hurt this bad." Serenity's voice almost had an edge to it as she responded.

"Ask her again! Tell her she should get one!" Tommy ran his hands through his hair as he heard Alyson continued to moan in pain.

"Let her choose what she wants, Tom. This is her body." Serenity's voice broke. "She can choose..."

The moaning and crying unsettled Tommy, which in turn began to upset Alyson even more. Serenity noticed and very quickly sent the agitated young man out of the room. He protested, but she refused to let him talk back.

"Out! You're making it worse!" She pointed to the door.

"Th-thank... thank you," Alyson stuttered as she watched Tommy leave. "He's... he's just too..."

"Sh. I know. You're doing so well, dearie. You're so brave. The doctor said you're progressing like you should, it's not going to last forever."

It was comforting to be with someone who knew the parts of her past that she didn't want to have to say. The secrets and the shadows hadn't marred their friendship, but pulled them together. The best way to get through the dark was by holding onto the hand of a friend, and Serenity had reached for Alyson without fear.

Serenity smoothed Alyson's hair back and pressed her lips together tightly as she thought about how afraid and alone Alyson must feel without her mother. She didn't mention it, but the thought stayed with her for the rest of the day.

"This could be Garret's baby." Alyson spoke slowly and quietly. "Why are you still here?"

"Because I care about you, and I could never leave my friend when she needs me the most. I promise you, Aly, I will not leave your side until this is all over."

Be kind. Forgive. Love others, even when they hurt you. That was what Serenity had told Alyson only a few days before.

Alyson closed her eyes and let out a shaky breath. There was nothing the young mother could say to adequately thank Serenity for setting aside legitimate reasons for offense and holding her hand through the whole horrible ordeal. Alyson owed Serenity her life.

Garret sat in a chair sipping a cup of strong, black coffee while Eddie and Jamie slept, their cramped limbs covered by their jackets. Garret's jobs had been to bring things from Alyson's apartment and get Danielle to Bedford. He had tried to rest after he finished with his tasks, but he was the only one who hadn't been able to drift off to sleep. Tommy walked into the room from down the hall and Garret gave him a grim smile in greeting.

"You'd think that after sleeping on so many tour busses I'd be able to sleep anywhere, but here I just can't. Maybe it's because I know that Aly is right down there in massive amounts of pain," said Garret as Tommy sat down next to him.

"Your girlfriend sent me out. Said I was getting too upset about it." Tommy stared down at his hands as they lay folded in his lap. "I've never seen anyone in so much pain before in my life."

"How's Ren holding up? Okay?" Garret had planned on going down to check in on the girls after he finished his coffee.

"She's doing great." A bitter frown pressed down the corners of his mouth. "Better than me, obviously. I was only in there for an hour before I had to leave."

"We're not used to seeing people we love in pain. It's a whole new level of feeling helpless, mate."

"I-I-I can't do anything!" With hands spread out, palms up and empty, Tommy held out everything he had to offer Alyson. "I can't bring Bambi back, I can't turn back time and make her not slip on the ice! I can't make her body not feel what it's feeling! I-I... There's nothing!"

"I know, mate." Garret put a hand on his friend's shoulder. "Take some deep breaths, drink a cup of coffee and calm down. Jay and Ed want to be woken up in about ten minutes. I'm going to see Ren."

Serenity was happy to see her boyfriend appear in the doorway. She crossed the room to let him hold her for a moment. He kissed her neck and breathed in the smell of her hair and the lingering scent of the perfume she had worn the day before. There were dark circles under her eyes that told him how tired she was.

"You should go have a rest. I'll get one of the others to stay with Aly." Garret pulled her soft hair out of her face, and then locked his fingers behind the small of her back.

"No. I'm not going to leave her. I promised." Serenity shook her head. She glanced over her shoulder to the bed where Alyson had her eyes closed. "But I would love for a cup of something very strong and another kiss."

"I can do that." Garret gave her a kiss, then turned to retrace his steps back to the waiting area. "I'll be right back."

The two young men in the waiting room were awake by the time Garret returned. Eddie was stretching his long limbs after sleeping on a row of chairs; beside him Jamie was yawning and running his hands over his face.

"Tommy woke you up already?" asked Garret. "That was fast."

"We woke up ourselves. We haven't seen Tom." Eddie finished stretching and pulled his fingers through his curls to settle them.

"What's the update?" asked Jamie. "Is she doing okay?"

"She's in pain. Ren is holding it down by her bed. I'm about to take her some coffee."

"They both must be exhausted." Jamie stood up. "You okay, mate?"

"Yeah." Garret nodded, his back to his friend as he continued to fix Serenity's drink.

Jamie put a hand on Garret's shoulder as he and Eddie walked past him, leaving him alone to make the coffee. When he returned to Aly's room, Serenity was back in the corner by the window, and Eddie and Jamie were on either side of the bed. Garret paused in the doorway. He could hear Jamie from where he stood.

"You okay, love?" Jamie's voice was low and sweet.

"How much longer?" Alyson asked weakly. Her body wouldn't stop shaking.

"Doctor said maybe two more hours." Jamie looked to Serenity to confirm the information. She just nodded, then noticed Garret in the doorway.

Eddie gently rubbed Alyson's shoulder and watched her face. She didn't look as gray as she had when they had first arrived, but there was no light in her eyes. He dared to look at her stomach and his heart thumped as he tried to envision what Bambi would look like when she was born.

"Love you," Eddie whispered quietly. He had heard so many of Alyson's hopes, dreams and fears over the past few months. This was going to do more to Alyson than he wanted to imagine.

"Stay." Alyson was looking at Jamie.

"Course, love. I'll stay right here." Jamie kissed her hand.

Alyson managed to nod, a tiny cry escaping her lips. Her hand holding onto Jamie's changed into a death grip, and the machine measuring her contractions showed the line shooting up. Eddie kept a calm hand on her shoulder, his jaw tense and eyes watching the screen intently to know when the pain began to let up. Alyson's voice rose louder than it had been all day as the pain endured longer than she thought she could handle.

"You got this, love," Jamie whispered, his hand aching in Alyson's grip. "Breathe. Come on."

Her lungs heaved in air before pushing it all out as she shouted. Jamie held her hand and prayed for it to end. He wished there was another way to make it stop.

The contraction passed, and Alyson's body became languid as she lay on her back. Tears rolled down from the corners of her eyes and into her hair. Serenity motioned for her to have a drink of water. Jamie held the straw to her lips, but Alyson didn't move.

"Come on, Aly," he coaxed.

"She's tired." Serenity walked over to the bed and slipped the straw through Alyson's lips. "Aly, you promised."

A tiny sip made it up through the straw and into Alyson's mouth. When she finished her drink, she refused to acknowledge anyone else in the room. Her eyelids slipped down to hide her bloodshot eyes.

The next time a contraction hit, Eddie left the room, letting Serenity take his place at Alyson's side. He made his way down the hallway to a big window that overlooked the street. He could see the outline of a young man standing in front of it, and Eddie knew who it was.

"You all right, mate?" Eddie set an arm around Tommy's shoulders as he came to a stop next to his friend.

"Not really." Tommy gave a slight shake of his head and wiped away the tears that were fresh on his face.

"Me either."

"She's going to be so empty, Eddie. Her whole life was about Bambi being born. What is she going to do now?"

"I don't know." Eddie let out his breath slowly. "But I do know we're all going to have to help each other get through this. We can't let this tear us apart."

Tommy nodded and cleared his throat. His hands were shoved deep into the pockets of his jeans.

"We have to wait two days to find out who the father is." Tommy's voice sounded strained. "I asked the other day. We may not know who the father is before the baby is buried."

Eddie hadn't thought of this, and he let his arm fall from Tommy's shoulder.

"We'll have to figure out how to deal with that when the time comes." Eddie tried to keep his friend steady, but he already knew it was going to be tense between the three young men as they waited to hear which one of them was the biological father. "There may be other faster ways to find out who the dad is."

The lads paced in the hallway and took turns spending a few minutes in the room, but tried to keep it clear so they didn't disturb Alyson. She didn't respond to their words or touches, moving only as her body begged for relief.

"Ed, I need water." Alyson's voice sounded thin.

Eddie was surprised to hear her as he sat in the chair beside her bed. The water was quickly supplied, and Alyson sipped weakly as Eddie held the cup to her lips.

"How do you feel?" asked Tommy, coming to stand beside his friend. "Got a little rest, yeah?"

"I c-can't feel Bambi…" It was all Alyson could think of.

Tommy's chin quivered as he bit his lower lip, and Eddie turned away to hide the tears on his face. That was the last time Alyson spoke besides the unintelligible begging she did during the most painful contractions. The only word anyone could make out was the name Bambi. Things seemed to be getting more intense, closer together. Alyson gripped the hands offered to her without looking at faces; her head rolling back and forth on the pillow as the pain washed over her in waves.

"How much longer, doctor? She has been here for hours, hasn't eaten a thing, is in extreme pain, and her baby is dead. She needs to be done as soon as possible!" Garret cornered Dr. Gallagher who walked past him in the hallway.

"I haven't checked her…"

"Then check her!" Garret pushed the man through the door.

The doctor complied, and checked Alyson's body for signs that she was ready to deliver.

"I think it's finally time."

There was an audible sound of everyone in the room breathing a sigh of relief.

"Hang in there, love. We're going to make it," Jamie whispered in her ear.

Alyson thought her body was going to explode from the pain. She just wanted her baby. She saw Dr. Gallagher begin to suit up and wash his hands for the delivery. All of a sudden, the anticipation of what was to come gripped her.

"I-I can't do it. I can't! It's too m-… it's too much!"

"Shh, no, love. You can do it."

"I'm not ready!" Alyson's eyes grew wide as she spoke frantically.

"It's okay, Aly." Jamie tried to hug her head and shoulders against his chest, but Alyson pushed him away. She wanted no one touching her.

Jamie took one side of the bed and Serenity the other as two nurses joined the doctor by Alyson's feet. Eddie and Tommy left the room and stood right outside the door with Garret. Alyson focused on the physical pain and refused to cooperate.

"Come on, love, you must push!" said Dr. Gallagher after a couple minutes of very little progress. "We're doing all we can do!"

"She will," said Jamie. Alyson's face was pale and damp with sweat and tears, her eyes were squeezed shut and her face was contorted with an expression of pain Jamie had never seen before. "You can do this. You can. I know you can."

"No!"

"Try, Aly! Please! For me!" Serenity begged. The young woman didn't even realize she was crying as she held onto Alyson's sweaty hand and fought for her friend to push, just once.

The nurses tried to give her encouragement, but Alyson hated that complete strangers were in the room to witness the most horrible event of her life. She shut out their voices and clenched her teeth. All she wanted was her baby. Every natural urge and instinct was telling her to push Bambi out, but she couldn't. She wasn't ready. For months she had nurtured and cared for this child, putting her safety and health above her own, sacrificing everything so her daughter could live. But now what?

This wasn't supposed to be what happened. This wasn't what we planned, Bambi. Alyson felt suspended in time as she heard a rapid heartbeat in the back of her mind and imagined a soft kick inside her stomach.

Alyson didn't have a plan B. She had a plan A, and that was to give birth to Bambi in the month of April and raise her child the best she could. This wasn't supposed to happen. This was never part of the life she had planned. Bambi was supposed to live.

You were supposed to live! You were going to be brave and strong and smart... Alyson felt her shoulders shaking as she held in her sobs. *I wasn't supposed to have to let you go like this.*

She went back in her mind to the last time she felt Bambi moving inside of her, right after her bath. She had rubbed her stomach and told Bambi she loved her, not knowing that Bambi was struggling for her life at that very moment. But Bambi wasn't struggling anymore. She wasn't in pain. She wasn't hurting or in distress. She was gone.

Alyson opened her eyes and saw everyone's gaze on her. She looked around the room, everything blurry through her tears. Her eyes stopped when she saw Eddie in the corner by the door. He must have come in to check on the progress. He had a grim expression on his face, but when he saw her looking at him, he nodded.

"Please." He mouthed the word to her.

Eddie had been there through every stage, a constant friend in the transition from girlhood to womanhood. From being a child to being a mother. And she knew he would be there still as she went from mother, to all alone. He would be there. Alyson was ready.

I love you, Bambi. With everything inside of me, I love you. Alyson closed her eyes and gritted her teeth. *I'll never, ever forget you. Goodbye...*

With all of the strength she could muster, Alyson pushed.

"There we go! That's the way!" The doctor was pleased. "Now, again!"

A rush of new energy flowed through Alyson's body as it all ended and Bambi's tiny body landed safely in the doctor's hands. Jamie's hand let go of Alyson's as he followed Bambi with his eyes, watching her as Dr. Gallagher handed her off to the nurses to be washed, weighed and measured. Serenity sunk back against the wall in exhaustion, her hands pressed against her tear-stained cheeks.

Alyson ignored the others and moved her hands slowly to her stomach. She watched her fingers shake as they pressed into her skin. It was no longer firm and tight, but soft and responded to the pressure of her touch. Her stomach had never felt like that before, like it wasn't even a part of her. Bambi was on the other side of the room, and the distance felt like the entire world was between them. Alyson touched her stomach again; it was empty.

It was over.

Jamie finally turned his attention back to Alyson and found her staring down at her flattening stomach. His throat tightened as he saw the clenched fists at her side.

"Love." Jamie leaned forward and pressed his cheek against Alyson's forehead. Tears filled his eyes.

"She's not in me." Alyson was quiet enough the doctor didn't even notice as he waited for the placenta to be delivered. "She'll nev-... she'll never be in me... Again."

Jamie closed his eyes and swallowed hard.

"Everything looks fine." Dr. Gallagher was done with his job once the placenta was out. He let the nurse take over the cleanup and stood by the head of the bed. "Call me if you need anything."

Jamie nodded and thanked the man with a somber voice.

"You can hold your baby now, ma'am," said a nurse.

Alyson's gaze turned towards where her baby had been taken, her breath catching in her throat. She reached out her hands and called for them to bring Bambi to her.

Bambi was placed carefully in Alyson's arms; then everyone waited. The limp baby rested against the mother's chest, her body wrapped in a receiving blanket. She couldn't have been more than three pounds, her limbs so frail Alyson hardly dared to touch them. Bambi's eyes were closed and dark lashes rested on her cheeks while her mouth was framed with red lips. The pink color of her skin made her seem as if she was only sleeping, while the stillness of her ribcage and the absence of breathing reminded them that she really was gone.

Alyson took in the child's face. A thin covering of dark hair felt downy and soft. She ran a finger down the smooth, fleshy cheek and touched the tip of her little button nose that looked exactly like the nose one of the young men in the room had been born with. It made Alyson smile sadly, her lips quivering as she lifted her finger to her own nose, remembering that she had her father's nose, too.

"She's... she's beautiful." Tears were rolling down Alyson's cheeks. She looked up at the one who stood closest by her side.

"Looks just like baby Grace, doesn't she?" Tommy's chin trembled as he nodded and stared at Alyson holding their daughter in her arms.

"She looks just like you when you were born."

Tommy reached down with a shaking hand and rested it on Bambi's tiny head. Bambi's greatest gift to them that day was her family resemblance to her father.

"Hi, Bambi." Alyson sniffed and wiped her eyes so she could see clearly. Her uterus was cramping, but she knew her moments with her baby in her arms were limited. She paused for a few seconds to let the pain pass before she continued to talk to her daughter. "I'm your mom."

Serenity pressed a hand to her face, unable to watch the scene in front of her without massive tears rolling down her cheeks. Everyone gave Alyson and Tommy space, letting them get to know their daughter before they shared her for the little while they had her body with them. Tommy sat down on the edge of the bed and leaned close to the mother and daughter, still unable to say a word.

"I-I love you..." Alyson's voice broke. "...so much. I have loved you so much, Bambi. I only wanted to do what was best f-for you, t-to keep you safe. It's all... It's all I ever tried to do."

The lump in Alyson's throat hurt too badly for her to talk for a moment. With the cleanup of the mother and child done, the nurses slipped out to let the little huddle of friends have their time in private.

"I'm so sorry I couldn't save you from this." Alyson's tears were hot. "I tried so hard to save you from everything, but I couldn't. I couldn't... I'm so sorry."

Alyson was unable to say anything more. She held the baby up to her face and let her tears flow. She traced the eyes and lips with a gentle fingertip and held up a foot in the palm of her hand that was barely longer than her thumb. After a few minutes, Alyson wiped her eyes and nodded at Tommy to have a turn with his daughter.

"Tommy," whispered Alyson. She was watching the young man hold the baby, the look of disbelief haunting his expression. "I'm sorry."

A tear gathered in the corner of Tommy's eye, and he looked over at Alyson's pale face. She seemed like a shadow of the girl she usually was, but her eyes still looked at him the same as they always had.

"I'm sorry you didn't get to know her like I did." Alyson's voice was so low the others around the bed could barely make out her words. "I-I'm sorry that you didn't know she was yours until it, until it was too... too late."

Tommy reached over and gripped Alyson's hand with his own. She squeezed back weakly, her smile shaking on her face.

"Not too late." Tommy had to clear his throat before he could talk again. "Not too late. She'll always be my daughter. Nothing can change that."

Alyson leaned her head on Tommy's shoulder and focused on the face of the baby and the way Tommy's body moved as he breathed in and out. What would this have looked like if Bambi had been born alive? What would their little family they built for themselves become?

"I love you, little one," Tommy whispered. "And I will love you always. You're mine. My daughter."

Alyson sniffed and brought in a shaky breath as she listened to Tommy's voice.

"I can't believe... I can't believe things had to happen like this." Tommy ached to hear the sound of his daughter breathing, feel her heartbeat under her soft skin, to watch her blink her eyes and move her mouth as she searched for nourishment from her mother's breast. Her fingers were cold and motionless, not curling or waving in the air; the soft spot on the top of her head lay still, no heartbeat to pulse through.

Alyson looked up at the others. They were standing and staring, eyes red and watery. She saw Jamie with his hands in his pockets and shoulders down. Her heart pounded a little harder. She wished he would look at her. Eddie met her gaze, and he gave her a tiny half smile. She kept her eyes on his for a moment and let the steadiness of his calm help her remember to breathe again.

Tommy shifted on the bed beside her, and she brought her attention back to him. He wiped a few tears from his eyes and handed the baby to her.

"Here's your daughter."

His simple sentence made Alyson bite her bottom lip as she took her baby in her arms again. She laid Bambi out on her lap and stared down at the tiny frame. She had seen those arms and legs over the sonogram machine, and now she was touching them. The memory of the heartbeat echoed in the back of her mind, and she swallowed her grief down, but not before she let out a shuddering breath and her tears spilled over.

"Come." Alyson lifted her tear-streaked face and motioned for everyone to come closer. "Please. Meet Bambi."

A frantic-looking woman went running past Garret as he poured himself another cup of coffee in the waiting room. He could hardly see because of the exhaustion in his eyes, but he knew he couldn't fall asleep. The woman retraced her steps and looked at him. He glanced up at her and gave a polite wave.

"Do you know Aly?"

"Yes?" Garret tried to place where he may have seen the person before. He realized it was Alyson's neighbor. "You're Lucy."

"Oh my word, please tell me where she is! I-I just... I just found... I just found out!" Lucy's eyes were filled with tears as she rushed to Garret and grabbed onto his arm. "Please!"

"Yeah, of course." Garret kept an arm around her as they walked down the hallway. He was going to knock when they reached the door, but Lucy pushed it open.

"Aly!" Lucy spotted the girl in the bed and began to cry again. "Aly, I'm so sorry!"

"Lu." Alyson swallowed hard.

"Are you okay?" Lucy didn't notice anyone else in the room as she sat down on the side of Alyson's bed. "Are you in pain?"

"It still hurts, but... not as bad as it did."

"Oh, you idiot." Lucy could hardly talk. "You big idiot."

Alyson's chin quivered as her friend's words reminded her she was loved. "Where's Bambi?"

Alyson pointed at Eddie who was cradling Bambi by the window. He had been standing there for a few minutes, humming and whispering things that were only for Bambi to know. His long fingers had stroked down her cheek a thousand times, trying to make up for every day after, where he would have to rely on his memory to touch her.

"Oh, precious." Lucy stood to her feet and walked over to stand near Eddie. She gave him a shaky smile when he turned to look at her. "I'm sorry, Ed."

"She's beautiful." Eddie sounded like a proud father as he pulled the blanket down to give Lucy a better view of the tiny face. Lucy gave the baby's head a kiss. "Would you like to hold her?"

"Please," Lucy choked out.

Eddie gave Bambi's cheek one last caress, staring down at her with clear eyes, committing everything about that moment to memory. Then he passed the child over and left the room.

"She looks like..." Lucy looked up with realization. "Tommy. Y-you're the..."

Tommy nodded and rubbed a hand over his glassy eyes. It had only been ten minutes since he last held the baby, but he was anxious to get her back.

He wanted to remember how light she felt in his arms, how she smelled just like Benjamin's children had the first time he held them, how she looked just like him...

Bambi traveled from person to person, getting a few minutes with each of them before she was placed back in Alyson's arms. It was strange getting her baby back and seeing the same exact expression as when she had held her last. There was a wild wish to see her baby's eyes open and hear the infant squalling angrily. She wanted to tell Bambi what her own mother had told her and command her child to breathe. It was silly to be angry at her, but rage began to swell inside of her until she burst into tears.

"Why is she gone?"

Jamie held Alyson while Tommy held Bambi. Lucy sat in the chair and sobbed just as loudly as the mother did, hiding her face in her hands. In the chair next to her Serenity crumbled with the sheer exhaustion she was feeling. There was a look of fierce determination in Tommy's eyes as he cradled Bambi close to his heart. The door opened noiselessly, and Eddie slipped back inside. He stood next to Tommy, a hand on his friend's shoulder.

"It's my daughter." Tommy didn't look away from Bambi.

"Congratulations, mate." Eddie's voice was hoarse.

"I used to feel her move." Tommy's voice trembled.

Eddie nodded.

"No one in my family will ever meet her, maybe never even know she was mine..."

"I'll remember." Eddie's fingers tightened on his friend's shoulder. "I'll never forget."

Tommy looked up at Eddie with tears in his eyes. There was a quiet sigh from the bed and both Eddie and Tommy looked to see Alyson pulling away from Jamie's shoulder. She seemed to be calm as her eyes searched the room to locate her baby. Tommy walked over to the bed.

"Aly, would you like to get some pictures?" Serenity asked quietly. "To remember her?"

Alyson nodded. She noticed Garret in the corner, face haggard and eyes tired. He didn't move from his spot as everyone tried to clean their faces from tears and arrange themselves around Alyson's bed. Bambi was placed in her arms, and Tommy squeezed onto the bed next to her.

"Gar," Alyson called to the man quietly. "Come stand next to Ren, please."

Garret stood to his feet slowly. He looked at her once more to make sure she was still okay, but she only nodded at him. He stood behind Serenity, his hands resting on her waist. Her body pressed back against him gratefully, and he squeezed her tighter.

The timer on Tommy's phone was set and placed on a chair. They huddled together, Jamie on one side with Eddie and Lucy, while Garret and Serenity framed the other side of the bed. They hadn't planned it that way, but almost every face was turned towards Bambi when the picture took. She had brought them all together; the one who anchored their raging emotions and kept them coming back to each other and fixing what they broke.

The only person that Alyson wished could be in the picture was Danielle. Besides her, everyone else who had known about Bambi since day one was there. Each of them had fought to protect her and her future in some way. They were the only ones. The only ones who had been dreaming of the day she would be born. The only ones who had celebrated her short life. And now they were the only ones who would feel this pain.

"You'll want this later," Tommy promised as he took a picture of Alyson with Bambi in her arms.

Each one had a turn. The one piece of proof to hold onto years down the road when there was a shadow of pain that no one else could understand. One day there would be new friends and new faces, and they would look at the picture of them and remember that day when they had been each other's everything.

Jamie sat in a chair next to Alyson's bed with Bambi right before the doctors returned to take the body. The pictures had ended, Jamie being the last one, and he took the opportunity to hold onto Bambi a little bit longer. Alyson lay back in the bed, her head tilted so she could watch Jamie with her baby. He held her so gently and looked at her with so much love. She had been his baby for months. From the very first time he had put his hands on Alyson's belly to talk to her, Alyson knew that no matter who the father was, there would be a special bond between them.

"Sweet Dream Baby…" The words of Jamie's song drifted quietly over to where Alyson lay. Jamie was singing his song over the baby. "Sleep well, sleep tight…"

The twisting in Alyson's heart was almost unbearable as she closed her tear-filled eyes and listened to the sound of the lullaby. She had dreamed of that moment, of listening to her baby being sung over as she slept. This would be the last time. Alyson's chest heaved with sobs as Jamie handed her the baby for the final minutes they had her. She hugged the baby tightly, stroking her back and kissing the top of her head.

"I'm sorry, baby. I'm so sorry. I love you so much. I'm so sorry." Alyson felt Jamie's hand on her shoulder as she wept. "I'm so sorry, Bambi."

One last kiss, touch, glance and reach; and then she was gone. Alyson's hands were on her womb as Bambi disappeared through the door. She half expected to feel a tiny kick, a little something to say, "Hey mom, don't worry about me." But nothing moved. All that was left was pain and stretched-out skin.

"Oh my God..." Alyson's heart broke completely.

Her baby would never be coming back.

Tommy was the first to pull Alyson into his arms. The others stood around the bed, too stunned and emotionally drained to fully comprehend the fact that it was over.

"This is going to kill Tommy." Serenity motioned to the young man as he wept with Alyson.

"This is going to kill me," responded Eddie as he let out a shaky breath. "I loved that baby. She was going to be our baby, all of us. And now..."

"Aw, Ed." Serenity hugged her friend.

It was three in the afternoon by the time it all settled down. Everyone was beyond tired and hungry and just needed to eat and sleep. Danielle's flight was scheduled to land some time that evening at Heathrow. Garret and Serenity were to go back to London and pick her up while Jamie and Eddie chose to stay close in Alyson's apartment.

Alyson said she didn't need anyone to stay with her at the hospital overnight, but Tommy insisted she let him stay. She wanted to fight it, tell him that he needed sleep and space to cry without worrying about her, but she didn't have the strength to hold her eyes open anymore. The adrenaline that had been keeping her awake long enough to spend time with her baby was fading fast, and she could hardly make sense of the room around her.

"She's perfect and beautiful, and I know she would have grown up to be strong and brave and kind, just like you." Serenity hugged Alyson as she left. "Please, call me whenever you need me. I promise, I will drop everything to be with you whenever you call."

"Ren..." Alyson didn't know how to properly thank her unlikely friend. She looked at the beautiful face that was marked with as many tears and as much weariness as her own and shook her head. "I-I don't know... I don't know how..."

"Sh!" Serenity masked her aching heart with a smile. "You don't ever have to worry about it. Ever. This is what friends are for."

Jamie stayed with Alyson while Tommy and Eddie went to the cafeteria. Alyson lay with her eyes closed; her body was still in pain, but it was dull compared to the gnawing in her heart.

"You comfortable, love? The food settling in you well?"

"Yes." Alyson's eyes were barely open, but she could see the way Jamie was looking at her. She loved him. "Hold me."

The request was granted as Jamie slipped onto the bed next to the girl and put his arms around her shaking body. She rested her head on his shoulder and focused on breathing. Her body finally obeyed for the first time all day. Jamie's heart pounded near her ear; she placed a hand over it. Jamie's arms moved, and he pulled her closer to him.

"I'm so glad you made it through everything that happened. I don't know what I would have done if I had lost you, as well." Jamie's voice was low. "You mean so much more to me than any other person. I was so scared that something was going to happen, and I was going to lose you."

Alyson let the words sink in without a response. She had only been thinking of her child; she hadn't thought about the fact that the others had also had her to think about. She didn't know what it had felt like for everyone in the room. Maybe one day she would be strong enough to hear them talk about it.

"How do you feel about not being the dad?"

"Hmm." Jamie wasn't sure how he felt yet. He had looked on the baby as his own since the beginning, claiming full responsibility. Yet, he had known it was a one-in-three shot that he was the father. "I dunno, love... I think I'll always see Bambi as my own, no matter that she wasn't biologically mine. She was our little gift that brought us back together, and I loved her for that."

"I-I don't know how I feel about it yet." Alyson put in her own thoughts. "But to know that my child would have grown up t-to be like Tommy... I love that."

"Yeah. He's a great lad," Jamie agreed, forcing his own personal feelings about the man down. "And she was beautiful."

"I miss her." Alyson felt another wave of emptiness wash over her and she turned her head to bury her face in Jamie's chest as she cried.

"I know, love." Jamie put a hand on the back of Alyson's head and ran his fingers through her hair as he waited for her to calm down. He had thought he was out of tears, but there they were again, running down his cheeks as he felt Alyson's seep through his shirt and onto his skin. "I know."

"Why did I not know something was wrong after I fell on the ice? It seems s-so obvious."

"Why didn't you call me?" Jamie had thought about that several times throughout the day.

"I-I... I did..." Trying to remember made Alyson's head hurt even more. "No, I called Ed. You had your meeting and I... I was going to call after five. I thought I could w-wait until your meeting was over."

"Sh, love. Let's not talk about this. Okay? There's no point in looking back on it now."

Alyson nodded and swallowed hard. Her hands moved towards her stomach, then stopped just in time. Jamie grabbed them and held them tightly.

"It's okay, love," he murmured against her hair. "It's okay."

It didn't take long for Tommy and Alyson to get settled in the hospital bed and fall asleep, Tommy's arms around Alyson and his chin resting on the top of her head. Despite still feeling pain, Alyson slept solidly for hours, waking only when she felt the need for the bathroom. She opened her eyes to a very dark room.

"You're wonderful," Alyson whispered to her friend as he slept beside her. "Bambi was lucky to have you as a part of her."

Tommy didn't stir, remaining soundly asleep. Alyson pushed the button on the side of her bed for a nurse to come help her use the toilet.

"Why didn't you just wake up your boyfriend?" the nurse asked as Alyson hobbled beside her.

"Oh, he's not my boyfriend..."

"He's sleeping with you." The nurse pointed out.

"He's not my boyfriend." It was all she really knew to say. "What time is it, by the way?"

"Almost one in the morning. You two have been sleeping like babies for hours."

Like babies... Alyson fought the urge to vomit and clenched her hands into fists to keep from giving into the itch to stroke her belly. She remembered how it had felt the few times she had let herself and shuddered.

"Lots of sleep will help your body heal faster," the nurse was saying.

"Thank you." Alyson didn't know why she didn't like the fact that she had been able to sleep so well without Bambi. She knew what the nurse said about her body needing the rest was right, but her heart struggled against the desire to do what was best for her health. She had killed her baby, accident or no, it had been her fault. She shouldn't be sleeping and resting and eating; she should be punished.

The flushing of the toilet woke Tommy and he sat up, disoriented and groggy. He found the little lamp by the bed and turned it on to see Alyson and the nurse slowly returning from the restroom. He jumped up and took the girl from the nurse, practically carrying her the rest of the way. The nurse left, seeing that Alyson was taken care of.

"Why didn't you wake me?" asked Tommy as they settled back into their former positions. The young man noticed Alyson's hands resting on her stomach, the way they did when she was pregnant. He looked away quickly and blinked at the stinging he felt in his eyes.

"I thought the nurse would be more practiced in helping people use the bathroom." Alyson's voice was low. "It's a little different..."

"True." Tommy yawned and shifted into a more comfortable position. "Love you, Alyson."

A shock of pain was a cruel reminder of what she had lived through the day before. She made a small "oh" sound and pulled her hands away from her stomach. Tommy seemed not to notice as his breathing evened out.

"Tommy."

"Hmmm?" Tommy mumbled as he kept his eyes shut.

"Can we talk?"

"Yeah, course." Tommy forced his eyes open and looked down at his companion. She was staring up at him, her brow furrowed. "What's wrong?"

"I just don't want to sleep anymore."

"What do you want to talk 'bout?"

"What are you worried about the most?" Alyson looked down and bit her bottom lip.

Tommy noticed the look on Alyson's face and pushed himself up to rest his upper body weight on his elbow. One hand held up Tommy's tired head; the other one reached down and covered both of Alyson's where they rested just above where Bambi used to be. She moved one to place it on top of Tommy's.

"What am I worried about the most?" Tommy repeated the question. "You."

Alyson's face showed that she didn't know how to respond to what he had said. He squeezed her hand and continued to watch her eyes. Finally she looked up and met his gaze for a short moment. With a sad, quiet laugh, Tommy squeezed her hand again.

"Your whole life was changed and rearranged just for Bambi, and now..." Tommy's voice trailed off. "All the things you were planning on are... it's all changed now."

"I didn't call into work." Alyson swallowed hard as she ignored Tommy's concern. "I didn't tell them I wouldn't be there."

"I don't know if any of us did."

"I wonder how long they'll let me have off to recover."

"As long as you need. Don't worry about it. If they say you can't take off as much time as you need, well, then, just quit. We'll support you."

"But people will want to know what happened. They'll ask questions, my school back home will ask questions, my p-parents..." Alyson's voice cracked.

"Shh, darling, don't get upset. Please." Tommy kissed her forehead gently. "Jamie and Garret have all these things under control. We'll get everything taken care of."

Alyson forced her questions down and swallowed a huge breath of air. Her frayed emotions quieted. The sound of Tommy's breathing reached her ears, and she could tell he was falling back asleep.

"Remember over Christmastime when we were at your house?" Alyson's voice took a wistful tone.

"Course I do." Tommy gave himself a little shake to keep from drifting off.

"Your mom made me feel so loved and taken care of. I never felt that way with my own mother."

"That's my mum. She loves everybody." Tommy smiled and his hand wrapped tighter around Alyson's.

"I'm glad Bambi was part of a family like that." She looked up and gave him a sad smile. "I hope one day you can tell them about her."

"I hope so, too." Tommy's heart sank as he remembered how his family would never know about his daughter. "Will you call her Bambi forever?"

"I-I... I don't know." Alyson shook her head as she answered. "I had names picked out for if she was a boy or a girl, but... I don't feel like they're right for her..."

"What names?"

"Well, if she was going to be a boy her name would have been Pax. It means peace. I just... I just wanted peace for my baby. I didn't want him to get caught up in drama or danger or worry... I-I just wanted him to have a peaceful life."

"It's a good name." Tommy smiled. "I always thought Bambi was going to be a boy. Pax would have suited him."

"Good name for growing up, yeah?" Alyson looked at Tommy with tears swimming in her eyes. She wanted him to confirm the fact that she had chosen a good name for her baby; that she would have been deemed a good mother if her child had lived. "Wouldn't get teased on the playground for that, would he?"

"No." Tommy shook his head and rubbed his thumb across the back of Alyson's hand. "No one would have teased Pax. He would have been one of the cool kids. Brave. Kind. Smart."

Alyson swallowed hard and struggled to keep her breathing steady. Her body told her to inhale before she could exhale, but she slowly found the rhythm of breathing in and out again.

"I wanted her name to be Lily if she was a girl. It means, it means purity. I know that my mistakes cast a big shadow over her, but they weren't... they weren't her mistakes."

"I think Lily is a beautiful name." Tommy's voice was soft as he listened to her talk, her tears breaking through her voice.

"I know." Alyson hummed quietly. "But it's not *her* name. You know? She's been Bambi since almost the beginning. That's all I-I've ever called her. It doesn't seem right to call her something else... not now."

"True."

"Are you okay with that?" Alyson's voice was soft. "She's your baby, too."

"You know, when I was holding her..." Tommy's voice was rough as he spoke. "I looked at her, and she was so perfect. She had your eyes, and the most gorgeous little face. I had never seen anything... that looked so beautiful."

A tear trickled down Alyson's cheek as she listened. She shut her eyes and pictured her daughter's face as Tommy spoke.

"You told me she had my nose, and I-I couldn't believe it! I couldn't believe that something so absolutely amazing could have come from me. I got to hold her in my arms, touch her face, tell her I loved her." Tommy sniffed and moved his hand from Alyson's to wipe at his eyes. "I used to dream about this Bambi in your stomach being my baby, and there she was, and she was mine. I know when we started calling her Bambi, it was just a placeholder, a little pet name until she was born. But I think you're right. I think her name should stay Bambi."

Alyson inhaled shakily.

"We... we can put your last name on the birth certificate if you want."

"I'd love that." Tommy put his hand back over Alyson's. "Do you have a middle name?"

"No." Alyson paused. "Just Bambi."

"I think that's perfect." Tommy tightened his grip on Alyson's hand.

"Thank you, Tommy."

No more words passed between Bambi's parents as they listened to the quiet of the sleeping hospital. Alyson stared at the ceiling and absentmindedly traced a circle on the back of Tommy's hand. She was lost in her own thoughts, wondering how long she would be able to see Bambi's face in her imagination. There were tears. There was sighing. Then a kiss on her forehead reminded her of Tommy's presence beside her.

"It's okay, Alyson." Tommy's eyes were wet with tears as well. "We're going to get through this."

Chapter twenty
"The thing about balloons is that..."

Alyson awoke the next morning with blazing pain in her back and inside her womb. She blinked her eyes open, moaning as she moved gradually to the side. Her body was pressed comfortably against Tommy, and she sighed. Her eyes opened enough to see two familiar faces next to her bed. Danielle watched her closely, a pinched expression on her face. Jamie was trying hard to ignore the young man who was sleeping next to Alyson by scrolling through his phone, but he was staring at Alyson when she noticed them and gasped.

"Why didn't you wake me?" Alyson struggled to sit up with Tommy's arm still over her waist. "Tommy, wake up."

"Aly." Danielle was by her friend's side in an instant, her arms stretching around Alyson's neck.

Tommy blinked awake from Danielle's hand nearly colliding with the side of his face as she tugged Alyson out of his grasp. With Tommy's arm no longer anchoring her to the bed, Alyson reached for Danielle and pulled her as close to her as she could. The physical pain shooting through her body couldn't keep her from curling into Danielle's side.

Danielle smelled like bonfires, laundry detergent and the fruity body spray she liked to wear sometimes. It was all the smells Alyson had found on Danielle's clothes before, and she wanted to weep.

"You're here." Alyson fisted handfuls of Danielle's clothes and refused to let go.

The girls didn't pay attention when Tommy excused himself from the room and went in search of some coffee and breakfast. He ignored Jamie as he walked past his chair, not awake enough to remain civil if the words grew sharp and pointed. Danielle rocked Alyson's aching body in her arms. Neither one of them wanted to say anything. Not about Bambi, or home, or the pain, or how much they had missed each other.

A chair scraped across the floor, and Alyson heard Jamie's shoes squeak softly as he walked towards the bed.

"Love. I have to tell you something." Jamie's voice was strained as he broke the silence. "I received a call from my label a few days ago."

"Mmm?" Alyson opened her eyes and shifted in Danielle's hug to see Jamie's face. He looked horrible. She slowly unlatched one hand from Danielle's shirt and reached it towards him. "What's wrong?"

Jamie saw Alyson's hand and came close to stand by the bed, taking her hand in his own.

"I have to spend three weeks in L.A. starting the beginning of next month."

It felt like someone had punched the air out of Alyson's lungs. Danielle's arms squeezed her friend reassuringly when she felt Alyson go tense. Alyson's mouth opened and closed several times, unable to say a word.

"Love, I didn't know... I didn't... this was supposed to be a good time to go before Bambi was born." Jamie used his free hand to press a tear out of his eye. "Garret and I are trying to change the dates, but so far no luck. Everything has been set, and nobody wants to budge."

The news was like another weight on the already crushing load Alyson felt. She wanted to pull her hand away from Jamie's and stroke her belly to comfort herself, but her baby was gone. She wanted to close her eyes and wake up in her bed at home, but she was in the hospital every time she blinked. The only thing that kept her from losing it was Danielle's arms.

"But you'll come back?" Alyson's words sounded funny as they were formed in her mouth that felt too dry.

"Of course, Aly. Of course." Jamie nodded. "I was planning on coming up this weekend to tell you about the trip. I... I'm sorry."

"Who all is going?"

"All of us. Gar, Tommy, and Eddie. We have some events we're supposed to play at. Do some promo with our friends *The Windy Cities*, and a few charity things." Jamie sighed and ran his free hand through his hair. "It's basically three weeks of no sleep and a ton of running around. It's not what I'd like to be doing right now. And to have all three of us gone..."

"Please don't hate Tommy." Alyson closed her eyes as she spoke softly. "I know you guys aren't friends... but please."

"I don't hate Tommy." Jamie could see the worry growing on Alyson's face, and he hated being the source of it. "We're going to be fine. We're all focused on you now, there's no room for arguments and such."

"Good." Alyson listened to Danielle's breathing for several minutes, her hand still tucked into Jamie's. "Thank you for bringing me Danielle. I missed her."

Jamie tightened his grip on Alyson's hand.

Lucy was at Alyson's apartment when the others arrived from the hospital. She had candles burning, soft music playing and the couch cleared off for her. Tommy carried Alyson carefully up the stairs. She felt like a child in his arms, so weak and small compared to him.

"Oh, Aly!" Lucy flung the door open and hurried to clear a path to the couch. "You okay? You in pain? Look, Eddie and I put everything you'll need right here on the coffee table for you. Pain meds, water, chocolate, a hottie..."

"Lu, thank you." Alyson gave Lucy's fingers a weak squeeze. "I'd like you to meet Danielle."

"Elle!" Lucy hugged the stranger using the name she had heard Alyson say a hundred times in the past few months. "I'm so happy to finally meet you."

"Same." Danielle sized up the infamous Lucy. The picture she had drawn in her mind was completely different from the real Lucy.

"Where is Eddie?" asked Tommy as he slumped into the recliner.

"He went to his gran's house to find some fresh clothes. I told him that he, and all you guys actually, are welcome to stay at my place if you'll let me sleep here," said Lucy.

"Of course. Whatever works." Alyson began to reach for the bottle of painkillers, but Jamie anticipated her and grabbed the bottle before she could. She looked up at him and tried to smile, but she couldn't. Her head was starting to throb, and she just wanted to close her eyes again.

"Here, lie down." Danielle looked around the apartment, trying to locate a pillow and a blanket.

"I'll get it." Lucy was already on her way into Alyson's bedroom to get a pillow before Danielle could ask. She was barely in the doorway when they heard a scream.

Tommy and Jamie jumped and raced to the bedroom door.

"Eddie told me to not go in here until he had cleaned... I forgot..." Lucy was pale as she stared at the blood-stained bed.

"Geez..." Tommy's hands went to his head, and he puffed out his cheeks. His stomach churned at the sight. "That's grim."

"Do not let Alyson in here." Jamie made sure both Lucy and Tommy made eye contact with him before he left the room.

"What was wrong?" asked Danielle.

"Just saw something we weren't expecting." Jamie stripped off his jacket and walked into the kitchen. He returned a minute later with a big, black trash bag. He glanced at Alyson and was grateful she was lying down with her eyes closed, her head pillowed on Danielle's lap.

"Let me help." Tommy's voice was low as he joined Jamie by the bed to strip off the ruined blanket and sheets.

The two men worked wordlessly, shoving everything they took off Alyson's bed into the black bags. There was a stain on the mattress and Jamie sighed, running his fingers through his hair. He didn't know what to do.

"Does Alyson have more sheets?" Jamie looked up at Tommy.

Tommy shrugged.

"Eddie would know," he offered. "Eddie or Garret. They did the shopping."

"Right." Jamie pinched his chin as he stared down at the spot of blood he couldn't strip away. It was garish and ugly against the pillow top. Jamie swallowed hard as his thoughts went to where the blood came from. "I'll call Eddie."

Alyson lay on the couch that first evening with her eyes closed. The others were there with her; Danielle and Lucy talking quietly with Jamie, Tommy and Eddie, careful to not disturb her. She didn't want to join in the conversation, too tired and concentrated on keeping herself from feeling to do anything else. Besides, they were talking about the church that had given them a plot of land for Bambi's grave and Alyson had nothing to say about churches.

Alyson hadn't gone to a church since the weekend before L.A., and she wasn't sure she wanted to go now, but she had decided to not fight it. She wanted to pray, to do something, but the only prayer that had come out of her mouth for the last seven months had been a request for God to keep her baby safe. Now Bambi was gone, and there was nothing left to pray for. Alyson didn't think she was angry, but she felt so numb on the inside she wasn't sure what she felt.

"I'll have to wash off the design for the mural as well," Lucy was whispering from the end of the couch. She had Alyson's feet cradled in her lap. "Don't need her seeing that."

"Let's just wait," said Eddie.

"Yeah, I was thinking that, too. Let's give us all some time to let the emotions at least sink in a bit," Jamie agreed. "We should lock the doors, though. Just in case she... you know..."

Apparently they all knew what Jamie was trying to say, because no one said anything else. The subject was changed to who was going to be where the next day and what needed to be bought at the store. Alyson tuned it out and went back into her cave of numbness.

"We're going over to Lucy's now, love. We're spending the night there." Jamie's voice broke through her thoughts some time later. "Okay?"

With a nod, Alyson acknowledged Jamie's words without opening her eyes or her mouth. A hand slipped over hers. It was a familiar touch. The smell of mint gum and Jamie's cologne reached her, and she felt his breath wash over her face.

"Love."

That voice was the voice that had started it all. Gentle. Intimate. Honest. She had given everything to that man, and now there was nothing left to show for it. Nothing except a fake job and a blood-stained mattress. Her lips twitched into a frown as the icy numbness around her pain began to thaw.

"I'm so sorry." His voice cracked.

Alyson finally opened her eyes and saw the emotion on Jamie's face. He moved her hand to his mouth and kissed it softly. She let him press her fingers to his cheek.

"I am so sorry."

"I know." It hurt to talk. "I love you."

"Oh, Aly." Jamie leaned forward until his forehead was touching hers. "I love you, too. I love you so much."

Alyson worked up the courage to move her other hand to frame his face, feeling the tears on the line of his cheekbones.

She was wrong about having nothing left to show for what she and Jamie started; she had him. She had this love that went so deep nothing seemed to shatter it, not even distance and the disapproval of others. It didn't make sense to her. It wasn't the kind of love her parents shared, or anybody that she knew, really. But it was hers.

"Call me if you need me," he whispered, his nose nudging hers gently.

"K."

Danielle was there to hold Alyson's hand once Jamie left, saying nothing while Alyson whimpered from pain until late in the night. Alyson dutifully drank the tea Danielle brought her and leaned on her for support as they walked to the bathroom. They woke Lucy to get her clean pajamas when the old ones became bloodstained. Nothing seemed to lull Alyson to sleep; not the silence, not the darkness, not the warm blanket wrapped around her like a hug.

Alyson spent most of Friday with her eyes closed and her hand in the grip of whoever was closest. Initially Danielle had been okay with Alyson's lack of verbal processing, but now she was getting worried that everything was going into a bottle that would never be opened again.

"Do you want to sketch, love?" asked Lucy.

"No." Alyson's eyes remained closed.

"Are you sure? You haven't for a couple days now."

"Mmm." Alyson nodded.

Danielle watched Lucy drop into the recliner with her own paper and pencil. Without another word, the artist began to create her own piece of art, leaving Alyson to sit with her body against Danielle's side.

"Why don't you want to draw?" Danielle kept her voice low.

Alyson shifted and stayed quiet.

"Do you want to talk?"

"N-not right now. Not yet, Elle."

It surprised Danielle to hear Alyson's voice laced with guilt. Maybe she realized that her best friend was there for only a short window of time and their conversations had been little more than Danielle asking her what she would like to eat, if she was okay, and if she was ready to talk.

"Are you sure?"

Danielle felt Alyson's chest expand as she inhaled and said nothing. Danielle sighed.

Danielle felt so much pressure as Alyson's best friend from home to know exactly what to do and say. They had given her free reign to do anything she felt was necessary, but if she was honest, she was terrified. She wanted to be as calm as Eddie. She wanted to wear her heart out on her sleeve like Tommy. Jamie's bloodshot eyes and dark circles did nothing to diminish his determined attitude that Danielle learned to translate as strength. Then there was her, who held Alyson as tightly as she dared and stared at the ceiling at night, waiting to hear the sound of crying or the sound of deep, even breathing. So far she hadn't really heard either.

"You know you're going to have to talk about it someday."

"Why?" Alyson sounded tired. "No one was supposed to know about Bambi, and now she's gone. Why... why talk about..."

"Aly." Danielle's chest ached. "I know about Bambi. Everyone in this room knows her. You can talk about it. You can cry about it."

Alyson's face screwed up into a contorted look of pain. She moved to press her thumb and pointer finger at the corners of her eyes. She swallowed hard while she bit her lip. Danielle waited for Alyson to say or do anything.

"I don't think... I think if I tried..." Alyson's voice was breaking. "I'm afraid to try. I-I might... break apart... forever."

Danielle hugged her friend against her.

"I won't let you break apart. I'll help you."

That night was the first time that Alyson really let herself cry. Even though Danielle had asked her to express her pain, the silence was welcome to the sound of Alyson's heart being poured out. There were a few moments when Danielle was afraid she was about to witness a panic attack, but Alyson always seemed to find a way to get her breath back in time.

Alyson cried herself to sleep and didn't stir for hours. Jamie stopped by when he returned to Bedford from a quick trip to London. Danielle greeted him with a finger to her lips.

"She's sleeping." Danielle shut the door carefully. "She cried. Finally,"

"Did she? How badly?" Jamie knelt down by the edge of the couch where Alyson was sleeping. He pulled one of her warm hands from where it was pillowing her face and wrapped his around it. He could see the salty residue still there on her cheeks, and her breath hitched in her throat even though she was asleep. He stared at her face, his eyes filling with tears.

"It sounded like her heart was being ripped out." Danielle stood at the end of the couch so she could see Jamie's profile in the low lamplight. "But she seemed a little less tense after she let it out."

"Did she... did she talk at all?" Jamie's Adam's apple bobbed as he tried to keep the lump in his throat down.

"No. Just cried."

Jamie shook his head and turned back to face Alyson. It took a minute for Danielle to realize he was slowly letting himself mourn; his tears followed by the shuddering of his shoulders every time he breathed. Finally, he buried his face into Alyson's pillow and cried loud enough for Danielle to hear him through the cushion. It was as if he had been carrying his own emotions tight against his chest, not wanting to break down before he knew Alyson was letting herself break down as well.

Danielle glanced over at Lucy who was on the recliner with two blankets pulled over herself. She could barely see the top of Lucy's head as she slept. Neither Alyson nor Lucy were aware of Jamie's weeping as it slowly ended. The man lifted his head and wiped his eyes with the back of his sleeve.

"Sorry," Jamie breathed shakily.

"No, don't... don't apologize. I cried my share of tears while sitting with Aly. Figure we're all kind of bottled up."

"Mmm. Yeah." Jamie wrapped his hand around Alyson's again and gazed down at her face. "I hope she's feeling a bit better in the morning."

"Yeah." Danielle moved to sit on the arm of the couch. Her feet rested beside Alyson's. She could feel Alyson's body heat through the blankets and it reminded her of how cold it became there at night.

"Well, I came over to ask Aly something, but I'm glad she's sleeping. I'll talk to her in the morning."

"Can I... can I ask you a question first?" Danielle didn't want to pass up her opportunity to have a private conversation with Jamie. She knew they were all going to leave after that weekend to start preparing for their trip to the States.

"Sure." Jamie shifted from his knees to sitting cross-legged, giving him a better view of Danielle. His hand stayed on Alyson's, his thumb stroking the back of her hand gently.

"Where did you see yourself going with Aly? Before all this happened, you know, what was your plan?"

Jamie gave a little chuckle as he looked over at Alyson as she slept. He bit his bottom lip and sniffed, tears pressing at his eyes, but not quite there enough to spill over. He remembered all of his plans, *their* plans, all the things they wanted to see in their future.

"I don't... I don't feel like things are going to change between us because of this. It will, but not in a way that will make the possibility of us in the future go away. I still want to be with her."

"Did you guys think you'd make it forever?"

"It's what we were working towards."

"Even if Bambi wasn't yours?"

There were tears in Jamie's eyes as he shrugged. He struggled to swallow and control his emotions as he thought about Danielle's question. He made several attempts of moving his tongue before he could verbalize his thoughts.

"Bambi was mine. Just not biologically."

Danielle nodded and looked down. Jamie turned to stare at Alyson. His lips twitched into a tiny smile, one that he couldn't hold back when he saw her sleeping features. She made him so happy, even in the midst of agonizing loss.

Jamie dried his eyes. "I suppose I should let you sleep."

"It's okay. I probably won't sleep for a while."

"You too wound up?"

"Just worried. Worried about Aly. Worried I'm not going to be able to help her. I'm worried I'm going to leave in a week and have done nothing to help her."

"Elle, What are you on about?" Jamie shook his head as he spoke. "You're the one holding Aly together. She'd be in pieces right now if it wasn't for you. I'm so thankful you're here, and I know she's feeling the same. She needs you. I can't imagine what this would feel like if it was just us lads and Lu trying to get her through this."

"Thanks." Danielle's response was half-hearted.

"It's true. You're not going to leave and not have made a difference to Aly. This means the world to her."

"Kind of like you mean the world to her." Danielle watched Jamie's head snap up in her direction. "You always have, since the day she met you."

Jamie ducked his head and cleared his throat. He could still hear the raised voice of his mother as they fought and argued on Christmas day. He remembered how it had almost ruined what he and Alyson shared. It was weeks before him and his mom actually made up completely.

"What time are we heading over to the church tomorrow for the funeral?" asked Danielle.

"Half-eleven, I think." Jamie took that as his cue to stand up. He hesitated before letting go of Aly's hand.

Danielle waited until Jamie was standing by the door before she said goodbye. She lifted her hand in farewell as he opened the door and slipped out into the dark hallway.

"Right across the street if you need me," Jamie said just before the door closed behind him.

Danielle stood up and did what Alyson had done a hundred times before; watch Jamie through the window. She could see into Lucy's living room where one light was on. Neither Tommy nor Eddie were to be seen, so she assumed they had already gone to bed for the night. A moment later, the door opened and Jamie walked in. He glanced out of the window to where Danielle was standing, and she saw him give a little smile and weak wave. She nodded in return, then stepped away.

Bambi's funeral was a sad and quiet affair. Alyson stood by Tommy's side, her face stoic and her hair flying in the bitterly cold wind. They were a small bunch that stood around the tiny grave. Heather brought Beatie, who told Alyson that Sydney didn't want to see the baby in the coffin so she stayed home.

The little girl wrapped her arms around Alyson's waist tightly, her face near where Bambi had been the last time she had seen the girl. Alyson placed a comforting hand on the back of Beatie's head, while she pressed her other hand against her own face. She wanted to push the girl away before it was too late and the dam broke, but she couldn't bring herself to be rough with the child.

"Aly," Beatie pulled on Alyson's hand until she had bent over enough for the girl to whisper into her ear. "You don't have to tell me who the dad is."

Everything went blurry for a moment as Alyson remembered the promise she had made with Beatie the first time she met her.

"Let's go, Bea." Heather put a hand on her daughter's shoulder. She looked to Alyson, frowning with a sympathetic look in her eye. "I'm so sorry for your loss."

Jamie's family left as soon as the service was over, while the others stayed in Bedford for the evening. Once the group of them all returned to Alyson's apartment, the grieving mother disappeared into the nursery to be alone.

"Hi." Danielle walked into the room ten minutes later. She saw her friend try to wipe away the tears as she entered. "I'm glad to see you opened the bottle a little."

"I-I know." Alyson gulped and gripped the arms of the chair as she focused on taking control of her emotions again. Danielle sat down on the footstool that went with the rocker and put a hand on Alyson's knee. She waited until she was calm. "Have y-you been in here before?"

"Yeah."

"The guys loved being in here. They would stand by the crib and just s-stare. It was so different... for them. They treated this room like it was some sort of holy place." Alyson let out a laugh that was wet with tears. "They were always writing Bambi letters."

One hand gestured to the pages of yellowing paper. Danielle had read the letters her first day in Bedford while Alyson was sleeping. The words had been so sweet and genuine she found herself crying over the simple phrases and sentiments the three young men had penned for Bambi.

"I saw them. They're very sweet."

"Yeah." Alyson's voice was rough. "They loved Bambi so, so, so much."

Danielle stopped reading and turned back to her friend. She had talked to Alyson about the guys and her situation often over the phone, but Danielle had never known quite how to picture it all accurately. She was pretty sure Alyson had no idea just how much her friends loved her.

"They love you so, so, so much, too, Aly. I'm really glad you had people to love you and take care of you while I was far away. I'm really glad this situation worked out the way it did with them. It could have, you know, been a lot different."

"Yeah," Alyson agreed quietly. "It could have. And I'm never going to be able to repay them for all they've done for me. Especially this pas-..."

"You're worth it." Danielle stopped her. "They do it all willingly, and I know they'd do it all again in a heartbeat. They love you. You're their friend."

The simple statement brought Alyson to tears. She rolled her eyes at herself as she wiped at her wet cheeks angrily.

"I wish I never had to cry again. Maybe now that I'm not preg-..." Alyson closed her eyes to steady herself for a moment. "Maybe I'll stop now."

"Your baby died. You're allowed to cry."

"I'm not a crier, Elle. You know that."

"But you are a feeler... You weren't always, but you got there. You worked hard for that."

"Yeah, but feeling things..." Alyson grimaced and looked away.

"Aly, you don't have to shut down your emotions to be stro-..."

"But how else can I be strong?" Alyson cut her off.

She pictured her mother standing in the corner of the backyard with her shoulders shaking. Mrs. Abidi only went out a few times in those first months after Amir left, and her visits to her outdoor sanctuary weren't very long. Alyson remembered wondering how her mother could cry so little when she wanted to cry every day. When Janice returned to the house the tears would be gone, painted over with a grim determination. That was the only picture of strength Alyson had.

"You're not your mom, Aly." Danielle spoke just above a whisper.

"Elle, Bambi is gone. I buried her t-t-today. I... And she's gone! Just like Amir. I need..." Tears burned Alyson's eyes as she stuttered angrily. "I need to..."

"Sh, Aly, it's okay." Danielle tried to hug Alyson. "You need to grieve."

"I don't..." Alyson forced her tears down and resisted Danielle's embrace. "I'll get through this. This isn't the first person who has left me."

Danielle sat, her hands lying limp in her lap as Alyson shoved herself out of the rocking chair and lurched slowly towards the door. Alyson stopped before she even reached it, her hands shaking when she turned around again and looked at Danielle.

"I'm sorry."

"I'm so worried about you." Danielle stood.

"I know," whispered Aly. "I'm... I'm scared."

Danielle hugged Alyson tightly as they took a deep breath. The tension between them slipped away, and they reconciled without saying a word.

"Are you ready?" Danielle jerked her head towards the door.

Alyson nodded. Instead of going to the couch, Alyson went to the kitchen. Only Jamie was in there, hovering over the kettle. He glanced up when Alyson walked in.

"Tea?" he asked.

"Yes please."

Jamie hummed as he pulled another mug out of the cupboard and retrieved the box of her favorite kind of tea as if he were in his own kitchen.

Alyson didn't remember ever telling him where everything was, but he always seemed to know where to find things. She settled on the other side of the room, leaning back against the counter so she could watch him

"I'm gonna miss this when you're gone." She let her mouth twist up into a sentimental half-smile. "Watching you make tea."

"I'm going to miss making you tea." Jamie turned to face the girl again and saw her expression. He matched it and studied her for a moment without saying anything. "We don't have to worry about that right now, though. Today has been hard enough."

"I'm afraid it's all going to be different when you guys come back," she said quietly. "Because Bambi is gone."

"Aly." Jamie's eyes were empathetic as he took in the fear and doubt in her eyes. "Why would you worry about that?"

"Because she's the only reason why I'm here anyway."

"Oh, love." Jamie left his place by the stove and walked towards Alyson. His warm hands met her shoulders, and he pulled her into a hug. "I'm worried about leaving you, but not because of that. If anything happens, we'll take care of it. We'll work it out. We always do."

Alyson didn't say anything as Jamie held her for a quiet moment. He tried to step back, but she held on. The stubborn act made Jamie chuckle softly against her hair and renew his grip on her. The longer he held her, the more he felt. There was no more baby bump to press into his stomach and keep him from hugging her as close as he wanted. There was no kicking or somersaulting. There was no third heartbeat to imagine as their own beat wildly in their chests. When Alyson finally did let Jamie go, he had tears streaming down his face.

"This wasn't how it was supposed to end." His hands went down to Alyson's stomach.

Alyson put her hands over his without a word. She remembered every time they had stood exactly like that to talk to their baby. Now there was nothing.

"I'm grateful for every moment I had with her," Jamie whispered his gratitude and leaned forward to kiss Alyson on the forehead. "She was a gift. Thank you for sharing her with me."

That night was special. They ate supper while gathered in Alyson's living room, their bowls of chicken noodle soup balanced on their laps or sat on the coffee table. The main light was switched off and candles were lit, giving the evening a much more intimate, vulnerable ambiance. It was a night where no past offenses or actions kept them from caring about anyone else. For one night they were friends like they had been in the beginning. There was no tension or hint of insincerity. Watching the four lads behave like best mates again warmed the entire room.

Serenity was there with her warm smile, Gianna with her strength, Eddie with his steady friendship, Tommy with his soft gaze, Jamie with his arms to hold her, Danielle with her fierce loyalty, Garret with his quiet strength, and Lucy with her undying devotion. It was good to be together. It almost felt like home.

Alyson was content to sit quietly, her shoulders warm from Jamie's arm wrapped around her. She could feel his steady heartbeat under her palm. Every so often he would chuckle or add into the conversation, making his chest reverberate with noise. It was a nice distraction, and Alyson even smiled once.

"That's a proper cuddle, that is." Lucy was smiling at Alyson. "You look soft and cozy."

"Feel cozy," Alyson murmured contentedly.

They didn't want their time together to end and it was close to midnight when everyone left. Alyson received their hugs and wiped tears from their cheeks, trying to smile bravely. Finally the apartment was empty of everyone except for Alyson and her two faithful friends. They took their spots on either side of her on the couch and snuggled against her.

"Don't know where I'd be without you lot." Alyson sighed, pulling on the warmth of their bodies.

"Don't know where *I'd* be without *you*," Lucy shot back, resting her head on Alyson's shoulder. "Love you so much."

Danielle didn't say anything, just squeezed her hand on Alyson's and held her breath. Alyson followed Lucy's example and rested her own head on Danielle's shoulder, breathing strong and deep. There was a moment of peace, and then sleep.

Alyson lay on the couch in her living room. The guys were in America, and Alyson had passed the one-week mark of having lived without Bambi. Her hands were behind her head and her eyes focused on a tiny speck of gray that was on the ceiling. She could hear Danielle in the shower and the calming instrumental music Lucy purchased at a record shop for her. She felt calm, and physically she was relatively pain-free.

The water in the bathroom turned off, making the apartment feel more still than it had moments before. Thankfully, the song coming through the speakers gained volume and the change in her auditory surroundings wasn't enough to jolt her from her meditative state. She was glad; she didn't want to ruin one of Danielle's last days with her.

"Sweet Dream Baby..." The familiar lyrics came off her tongue before she could stop them. "Shoot."

Things began to bubble beneath the surface, but she stared hard at the speck on the ceiling, imagining all sorts of things it could be. The bathroom door opened, and Alyson heard Danielle go into the guest room and shut the door.

"All better." Alyson continued to talk out loud to herself. "I'm not alone. Elle is here. I'm okay. I can lay on the couch and feel fine."

Feel? Well, Alyson wasn't sure whether or not she was truly feeling anything, but as long as she didn't feel like she was going to explode she was happy. Her mind began to think of things that could explode. The pictures sifted through her mind; a bomb, a can of pop, fireworks, balloons...

Alyson stopped. Balloon Bambi was probably still up on Danielle's wall, probably fine, but maybe a little wilted after being blown up for a couple weeks now. She wasn't going to have to replace it when she flew back home, she could just throw it away and be done. There was no more need to take her balloons to the grocery store to try to match the size of a random fruit or vegetable. There was no more need to draw pictures or stick stickers.

"The thing about balloons..." Alyson hummed, feeling her chest pull in and push out with her labored breathing. "The thing about balloons is that you can decorate them, and draw pictures on them."

The pace of Alyson's heart began to pick up as Alyson remembered bits of her conversations with Danielle about the balloon on her bedroom wall. She remembered how they were different colors, and that if you blew them up too big you could just let a little bit of the air back out, because that was the thing about balloons.

"The thing about balloons is..." With a gasp, Alyson shot straight up off the couch, her breath choking on its way out. "They die. Balloons die. Th-the thing about... b-balloons... Oh my gosh..."

Alyson couldn't walk in a straight line as she flew off the couch and down the hall to the guest room. She didn't knock, but flung the door wide open, finding Danielle with her shirt halfway over her head.

"THEY DIE, ELLE! THEY FREAKING DIE!" Alyson screamed at her. "THAT'S THE THING ABOUT BALLOONS! TH-THEY DIE! BALLOONS A-ALWAYS D-DIE!"

Danielle quickly shoved her arms and head through the proper openings in her shirt and caught Alyson as she began to pummel her fists against her friend's chest. Alyson didn't fight long before she crumpled into a weeping, wailing mess onto the floor where Danielle hovered around her.

"They die!" Alyson cried. "B-bambi died!"

Any type of cry with Alyson was a win for Danielle, but this time Alyson didn't try to straighten up and force the cap back on her bottle of emotions. She lay on the floor, her breathing sporadic and her eyes constantly leaking more tears. Danielle sat beside her, rubbing her back and waiting for her to get up. Half an hour later, and Alyson showed no signs of stopping.

"Aly, what can I do to help you?"

"N-nothing!"

"Can I make you a cup of tea? Glass of water?"

Alyson shook her head and continued to cry. Danielle took Alyson in her arms and tried to get her to sit up, hoping that if she was moved she would snap out of her fit. It didn't work, and Alyson found herself back on her stomach on the floor, her cheek against the white tiles. She opened her eyes when she felt Danielle's breath warming her face. Danielle was quiet as she lay on her stomach, her face toward Alyson.

"A-are you angry with me?" Alyson's voice was a whisper. She swallowed hard and took a deep breath.

"Why do you think I'm angry with you?" Danielle's hand moved to cover Alyson's.

"Because I'm a m-mess..."

"Aly."

"And b-because I'm in love with Jamie after you told me not to be, a-and because I'm so close to Lu, and I don't pray, and because I c-couldn't sto-..."

"Aly! Stop! I'm not angry at you! Not even a little bit! If I seem angry, it's because I'm angry at myself." A heavy sigh filled the space between them. "I want to do the right thing, to help you and make everything better! And I feel like I'm just walking around like a fool..."

"No, Elle. I-I don't care what you do o-or, or, or say, I just need y-you."

"Well, here I am." Danielle gave a tiny smile.

The silence that followed was the silence they had shared a million times before. It was the type of silence that gave them the companionship they craved, but let them go through the thoughts and secrets of their hearts in private. And when they needed to remember they weren't alone, they would open their eyes again and memorize the details they saw on the face of their friend. For the hundredth time. Thousandth time. Millionth time. Each time was like another shot of oxygen for Alyson.

That's where Alyson fell asleep, and Danielle didn't leave her side the whole night.

Chapter twenty-one
"You can't give up on this!"

Alyson sat at the dining room table. The window was open, letting in the fresh spring air. It was almost May and the whole world was turning green, but Alyson continued to feel dead on the inside. Papers were scattered around her, and she held a pen in her charcoal-smeared hand. There was a notebook flipped open in front of her, and she wrote quickly. The words came easy; she had been rolling them around in her mind for weeks. It was time to write them down.

"Dear Bambi," Alyson whispered as she wrote. "No one can prepare you for the feeling of loss and emptiness that consumes you when your baby dies. No one. There are books about stillbirths and books on grief, but what word on a page can prepare you to let go of the living, functioning human inside of you when they breathe their last before they have even tasted oxygen? One day you have this tiny person who takes up all of your thoughts and emotions, and then they're gone. leaving your mind screaming and your future a chasm of nothingness.

"No one can prepare you for the way you'll limp out to the bathroom at two A.M. and lay on the floor because it seems easier to cry there than on your bed. Or the times when you're surrounded by people and distracted from life when it hits you, all over again, so that you feel like you're going to be sick and you have to leave. The twisting in your gut that persists, day after day, stealing your appetite and ruining every attempt to take care of your body. Scalding hot showers that don't make you feel any cleaner, and nights of sleep that don't make you feel any more rested.

"No one can prepare you for that..."

Alyson stood up from the table and walked over to the window. She wanted to cry, or feel like a weight had been lifted from her shoulders, but nothing had changed. She was still hurting, and her daughter was still gone. She shut the notebook and slipped it onto the shelf in the living room. The letter was unfinished, but her thoughts were done. She was done.

Lucy was sitting on her couch in a daze. She was wrapped in a sweater even though it was the first of May, and there was no reason to wear extra layers, except that it was Kyle's old jumper, and she was aching on the inside. His smell still lingered on the fabric, and Lucy breathed it in again. It didn't seem right to end everything after ten years together, but he didn't even want to consider giving their marriage another go. That was why Lucy had spent the last week in her apartment with a drink in her hand and Kyle's clothes wrapped around her.

Their third wedding anniversary had been April twenty-seventh, but Lucy still felt the need to wallow and hide in her misery. She hadn't given herself much time to let go of Kyle and their marriage since things had been busy with Alyson, and then Bambi, and then...

"Oh, no." Lucy frowned and pushed herself up. She was a bit unsteady on her feet, but she made her way over to the plants that sat on the floor by the living room window. "Forgot to water you."

She was watering her flowers when she glanced across the street to Alyson's place. The window was empty. She wondered how Alyson was. They hadn't seen each other since Lucy locked herself away from the world.

She's fine. Lucy tried to convince herself. *You're not her mum.*

Lucy turned her attention back to her plants and had just started pouring water over one of the budding rose bushes when her door flew open. Lucy startled and dropped her watering can. The water spilled onto the carpet, and Lucy stooped down to try to clean up the mess, but a hand grabbed her arm.

"Aly! What are you doing?" Lucy saw a wild look in her friend's eyes. "What's wrong?"

"Tell me you hate this! T-tell me this is the stupidest thing y-you have ever, ever seen in your life!" Alyson choked out, her cheeks red and words tumbling out in a rush of hiccups and tortured tones. "Tell me, Lu. Tell me I'm the o-only one who hates this!"

It wasn't until Lucy realized Alyson was pressing something into her hands that she understood what Alyson was begging her to do. She looked down at a little plaque that could be set on a windowsill or hung on a nail on the wall. The plaque was painted a dark navy color with white letters on it. Lucy held it up to read what it said.

"'It is better to have loved and lost, than never to have loved at all.'"

"Ugh! I hate it!" Alyson was blubbering as she paced angrily around the room. "How dare someone say that?! Do they know what it's like to actually lose someone? Do they? Do they kn-know? Please, Lu, tell me you hate it!"

Lucy had seen Alyson have good days and bad days in the last two months since Bambi's death, but this was one of the worst Lucy had seen. Her heart broke for her friend. Alyson was so young and full of promise, but she was dying from the inside out and none of them seemed to have any power over the corrosion.

"You're right." Lucy set the wooden plaque down on the windowsill. "It's dumb. It's so stupid."

"Don't patronize me, Lu." Alyson's voice was low and trembling as she crossed her arms over her chest.

"I'm not." Lucy wrapped her arms tight around Alyson while she stood still. "I don't like it. Why did we both have to lose what we loved the most? Why is losing them better than never having them to love?"

"I'm sorry." Alyson moved her arms to return the hug. "I-I wasn't thinking."

"I know." Lucy didn't let go of Alyson, assuming that she had probably been without meaningful companionship for as long as Lucy had in the past week. "Did you run away again?"

With a sigh, Alyson pushed out of Lucy's embrace. She flopped onto the couch and hugged a pillow against her flat stomach. It seemed strange to

Lucy now to remember how she had assumed Alyson was overweight when they first met, before she knew about Bambi. Alyson was thin and getting thinner every day, it seemed.

"I couldn't stay. I was trying so hard to s-sleep, but I couldn't. Then I felt suffocated, so I just left."

"Where do you go?"

"There's a pub that's open until sunrise. I don't drink, but they let me sit at a table and don't bother me." Alyson exhaled sharply.

"You have to stop that, Aly. You're driving everyone away." The words were out of her mouth before she could stop them.

"I'm trying, Lu! I tried so hard!"

"Then try harder! Stop turning your phone off! The lads love you, but you're unpredictable and angry, and you're slipping further and further into a person we know you're not!"

Alyson shook her head as she pressed her quaking lips into a line.

"It's wearing on us all, Aly." Lucy sat down carefully beside Alyson. "We would do anything for you, but you have to do things for yourself as well. We're not sure how to carry you anymore."

"I know." Alyson's whisper was filled with shame.

"Aly, please. We want you to be dealing with Bambi's death in a healthy way, and this... this is dangerous. You're leaving your house at all hours of the night and not telling us where you're going. It's scary! Especially since your family could still try to come after you!"

"Is anybody in my flat?"

"Were you expecting someone?"

"No, I just... Sometimes if he can't get me on my phone..."

"I haven't seen Jamie, no."

"Good." Alyson grimaced as she stood to her feet. "We got into another fight."

"Alyson Abidi!" Lucy stood in front of her friend. "Why are you doing this?"

"Because I'm falling apart and I'm a horrible person, Lu! Did you forget that in the thirty seconds it has been since your lecture?"

"No! No, I'm not going to let you just give up on Jamie! I'm not going to watch you throw it all away! Not when I'm forced to let go of the person I'm in love with! You can't give up on this!" Tears blinded Lucy as she spoke with a fiery passion. "Make up with Jamie! I will not stand by and let you destroy this!"

"I can't fix something when I keep breaking." Alyson's words were thick and she hugged her arms around herself. "I'll see you later."

"Aly." Lucy wiped her eyes and caught Alyson in a hug from behind. "I love you. Don't ever forget that."

Alyson sat on her couch with her sketchpad on her lap and pencil in between her clenched teeth. She was trying her hardest to stay in her spot, to not give into the urge to run out the door and down the street until she couldn't breathe anymore. She had promised everyone, including herself, that she wasn't going to run again, but she didn't know if she was strong enough to keep her word.

Her phone rang, and she snatched it up. It was Jamie. They hadn't talked since their last fight.

Sometimes Alyson wondered what had happened to them. They had been so strong together. He had come back from his trip to the States to find her waiting for him at his mom's house. Their reunion had been sweet. Alyson could still hear the echoes of their intimate conversation when she thought back to that night.

"Feels like we have been together for at least five years by now," Alyson had murmured with a faraway look in her eyes.

"Seems like it some days, eh." Jamie gazed at Alyson's face as it glowed in the lamplight. "Think of all the stories we'll have to tell when we're old and boring."

"Boring?" Alyson scoffed out a laugh. "You can be boring."

"Well, how exciting do you imagine you will be when we're seventy and can't walk?"

"Speak for yourself. I'm going to be able to walk well into my nineties. I'll show you!"

"Please do." Jamie's voice was light and happy.

"Wish we could skip the middle years, huh?"

"Nah." Jamie shook his head as he disagreed. "Some of the best times are in those middle years. I wouldn't want to miss anything with you."

"Me either." Alyson finally turned to see Jamie staring at her. She put a hand up to his cheek and smiled sadly. "I love you."

Jamie couldn't talk, but the way he kissed Alyson's fingertips said more than enough. Everything was going to work out. They were going to spend the rest of their lives together.

Now every conversation was strained. Alyson couldn't remember how many times she had shouted at Jamie because she was angry at something else. Alyson was still in love with him, and that was what terrified her the most.

She had loved Amir, and he had left. She had given up everything for Bambi, and she had left. She was determined to do everything she could to not let Jamie do the same thing to her. It wasn't because of anything he did, and Alyson knew that, but she was in survival mode and it didn't matter how many promises he made. Every fight started with her being unreasonable,

Jamie calling her out on it, her lashing back, and him reminding her that she didn't have to be afraid of losing him.

She still remembered how angry she had been when she found out Jamie had been reading books about how to help your wife through her grieving process.

"I am not your wife, Jay!" she had screamed.

"No, but I'm still in love with you, and I still want to make you my wife!" he had shouted back.

To be left by your husband was a wound much more painful to think about than just being left by a man you were in a relationship with. She had cooled down when he threw the book in the trash and said it didn't know anything anyway...

Her phone rang in her hand again, and Alyson woke up from her thoughts.

"Hello?" Alyson answered the call.

"Love. You okay?" Jamie's voice sounded tired.

"Y-yeah. Yeah, I'm... I'm fine."

"Lucy called me. She said the living room light was still on."

"It's only ten-thir-..." Alyson looked at the clock and saw the hour hand pointing at the two. "Shoot."

She had work in the morning. Despite her erratic behavior, she had managed to stay on top of her job and keep herself sane enough to make it through each day. It helped that she was able to do classes and training again, giving her less time to think about things. She had spent a month 'recovering from surgery', then returned as a teacher, leaving Fran and her back office behind. No one mentioned the noticeable lack of stomach, and Alyson wondered if anyone even really knew.

"Are you okay?" Jamie asked again.

"I want to run." Alyson dropped her pretenses, her voice coming out low. "Feel like I can't breathe."

"Stay on the phone. Go ahead and run."

"What?"

"Keep me on the phone while you run."

"But I promised I wouldn't!"

"Get out of the house. Run as fast and as hard as you need. If you end up at the pub, I'll know 'cause you'll have me on the phone. If you stop someplace else, I'll know."

"Okay." Alyson jumped to her feet and shoved on her running shoes. She pulled her hair back into a ponytail and went quietly out of her apartment. "I'm leaving. Don't get angry."

"Love..." Jamie sighed. "I'm not angry. I'm never angry at you."

"What do you get angry at then? Because you do an awful lot of yelling at me." Alyson skipped down the stairs, whispering until she was outside of the building. The cool night air rushed around her like a hug, and Alyson spread her arms out to welcome it into her lungs. She looked up and smiled at her star friends. "Oh, I can breathe again."

"You outside then?"

"Yes. But you never answered my question." Alyson began to jog down the dark sidewalk. She turned on speaker phone so she could have more use of her arms.

"I get angry at the fact that I can't help you sometimes. That I can't make you believe me when I tell you that I'm not going to leave you."

"I get angry that I don't know how to make you happy."

There was silence as Alyson's feet pounded the pavement. A block slipped by before Jamie spoke up again.

"Aly, you make me happy just by being you. I'm so sorry you think you don't make me happy."

"But I'm... Jamie, you know I'm not myself right now. I'm running at half-past two in the morning because I was about to crawl out of my skin. That's not me. Th-that's not... I'm not me."

"You are!"

"Jay, I'm a shadow of myself!" The thought made Alyson angry and she pressed herself to run faster. "I'm a shadow, a fraction of who I used to be. I'm not happy! I'm miserable. Always. I'm just empty, and I'm so angry."

There was an audible sigh from the young man, then silence for another two blocks.

"Is this a good run?"

"You sound tired." Alyson slowed down a bit, sweat dripping down her face. "You should sleep."

"I should, but I'm not going to."

"You probably have work tomorrow."

"You have work tomorrow."

Alyson felt weird not knowing his schedule like he knew hers.

"I'll be fine. I get done what I have to get done," she said.

"Your body is going to break down soon unless you take care of it right."

"Maybe. Maybe then I'll have something else to be angry about, and I'll stop being angry at things that don't matter." Alyson was panting as she picked up her pace again.

Jamie was quiet, letting Alyson run as hard as she wanted for a few minutes. He heard her let out a groan as the sound of her feet hitting the ground stopped.

"Feel better?"

"Yeah. Ah." Alyson groaned again as she stretched. She looked around and was surprised to see where she had ended up. "Wow, I didn't know I ran that far."

"Where are you?"

"Well, I think if I run down this road for a mile or so I'll be at the church where Bambi is." Alyson looked down the road. Everything was quiet and dark. She wished she had a flashlight. "I'm gonna..."

"Aly, that's pretty far away from everything." Jamie's voice was nervous.

"No one is out here. I'm fine. Plus, you're on the phone. I'm safe with you." Alyson's distracted words did little to calm Jamie's anxiety. "Besides, the itch is still there. I have to run."

"Keep running then."

Alyson was right; it was only two miles down the road when she saw the chapel in the moonlight and the tall trees in the graveyard. Jamie hadn't said much, but murmured little things to which Alyson grunted out replies. Her lungs were burning, but this was the most satisfying run she had been on since she started. She knew she was going to feel it in the morning. Alyson finally reached the gate to the cemetery where Bambi was buried.

"Oh, it's locked. I... I didn't even think of that."

"Is there any other entrance?"

"I'm going to make one..." Alyson saw a gap between the shrubbery and the chapel wall where there was no fence.

"Aly..."

"It's okay. I just really want to see her. I'm good" Alyson felt the branches scraping against her skin and tearing at her clothes. "Ouch. Oh, geez. Ah. Ow."

"Perfect. Sounds like you're absolutely okay."

"Shush." Alyson glanced at her phone. It was quarter after three, and they had been talking for forty-five minutes. This was the longest conversation they had been able to have without an argument in probably a month. Alyson couldn't even remember what exactly they had been fighting about. She was tired and the walls around her heart were crumbling. "Hey, Jay..."

"What? You okay? Is someone there?"

"No, I'm fine." Alyson gave a soft laugh as she pulled herself free from the last branch and began to stumble over the gravestones and tree roots that were between her and her destination. "I just wanted to tell you that I'm sorry."

"Sorry for what?"

"For whatever we were fighting about last. It was dumb, I'm sure. So, I'm sorry."

"Oh, love. You know I don't care about that. I'm sorry, too. I'm so stubborn sometimes and I-..."

"I love you, Jay."

It had been a while since she had last told him, but it was still true. She was still in love with him, no matter how badly she wanted to protect herself.

"Aly..."

"Don't cry, Jamie." Alyson could hear the wet sound in his words and felt the lump swell in her throat. "You're going to make me cry."

"I can't help it. I love you, too."

"I know."

Alyson slipped and everything felt as if it was in slow motion as she put her hands out in front of her to catch her fall. Flashbacks to slipping on the ice filled her memory, and Alyson squeezed her eyes shut just before hitting the ground. A cracking sound reached her ears as she landed and she felt a sharp jab in her palm, then the steady mechanical beep as her phone died in her hand.

A light gray was dusting the horizon when Alyson felt a hand on her shoulder. She was freezing, her sweaty running clothes dried to her skin and nothing else to cover her. The ground was damp from the dew, and her neck was twisted painfully.

"Aly! Aly!"

"Jamie..." Alyson blinked her eyes open and struggled to get up. She was thankful for his help. "Ow, my neck."

He pulled her into a tight hug and pressed kisses to her neck where it hurt.

"I was so scared when the call ended." He pulled back to look into her face. "I tried to ring you again, but I couldn't get through. What happened?"

"What time is it?" Alyson yawned, feeling Jamie tighten his arms around her as she balanced on her tiptoes to stretch.

"Four-thirty I think," Jamie answered. "Are you okay?"

"Yeah, I fell and my phone broke."

Jamie let out a sigh of relief that he had been holding in for the hour-drive from London to Bedford.

"At least you knew where to find me." Alyson smiled sleepily. She was glad, too. After taking some time to breathe deeply, she had located Bambi's tiny cross and felt a wave of exhaustion weigh her down to the ground. She didn't know how long it would have taken people to find her if Jamie hadn't known where she was.

"Happy for that." Jamie hugged her again and felt her melt into his arms. "You must be so tired."

"Knackered. But I have work..."

With an arm tight around her waist, Jamie started to guide Alyson back towards the little entrance she had made an hour earlier. She yawned again and laid her head on his shoulder as they walked. It had been a while since they had been together without tension to ruin things.

"We can call it off."

"No. No, it's an important class. I have it all ready. Maybe you can sit in the back, and when I'm done we can have lunch?"

"All right. As long as you promise to sleep this afternoon."

"Mm. Promise." Alyson twisted her face to plant a kiss on Jamie's cheek. She made them stop, her face pressed against his as she breathed in his smell. "I've missed you."

"Aly, you're shattered, don't..."

"Doesn't mean I don't know what I'm saying." Alyson stepped away, her brows drawn down angrily over her eyes. "I know what I'm feeling right now."

"I didn't mean that, love. I'm sorry. Forget I said anything." Jamie regained his hold on her and continued to help them across the graveyard. "I missed you, too."

Alyson decided to let it go and fit herself against his side once more. They struggled through the bushes to get out of the enclosed cemetery and then climbed into Jamie's car. Alyson leaned against the window, doing her best to keep her eyes open. She knew if she let herself sleep now, she wouldn't wake up in time to go to work.

"Tell me something interesting. I have to stay awake."

"I am, uh, well..." Jamie cleared his throat, and Alyson turned her full attention towards him. "I'm taking the rest of the year off from making music. I'm not going to record or go on any tours this year."

"What? Why?"

"Because I needed to, and I can." Jamie readjusted his grip on the steering wheel. "You need me, Syd's going through a hard time, my mum is helping take care of her dad while he's sick, and I can't just pop by to watch the kids if I have a recording or touring schedule to keep up with."

"But you love music." Alyson looked almost heartbroken.

"I'll still have music, I'm just not going to be working." Jamie gave her a quick glance. "And I'll be able to come see you whenever you need me. As soon as this project in the studio is done, I'm going to be a free man for the rest of the year."

Alyson sat back in the front seat again, a troubled look in her eye. She didn't even know why it felt so wrong to hear that Jamie wasn't going to be going on tour or working in the studio. Both of those things would have taken him away from her for weeks and months at a time, and she didn't want that. She still didn't like it, though.

"What about Tommy and Eddie?"

"I, uh... They're going to be done working with me now. Going to work with another mate of theirs that is starting off in music."

"Are you serious?" Alyson's heart clenched. "They're not... they're not going to be your band? Like, ever?"

"I don't think so." Jamie spoke slowly. "We just decided the other day."

"Oh my gosh." Alyson's hands went to her face. "I ruined everything."

"No. No, you're not going to take the blame for this. Tommy and Eddie have been with me for a good run, and we're ending things as friends. Tom and I are good. This isn't because of you."

"Yeah right!" Alyson hated that she was crying. "I drove you two apart like a wedge, you know I did!"

"Aly, why are you so gutted about this?"

"Because you guys have been together since I have started listening to your music, and I know you guys as a band, as a group... now it's all... everything is changing and I... I *hate* change!"

"They're still going to be your friends. That's not going to change."

Alyson wiped at her tears and turned away from Jamie.

"Listen, they'll come explain everything. Would that help?"

Alyson didn't say anything.

"I'm sorry this is upsetting to you." Jamie placed an uncertain hand on Alyson's knee. He tightened his grip when Alyson put her hand over his. "We didn't do this to hurt you. Things just have to change sometimes."

"Yeah." Alyson shifted to be closer to Jamie again. She leaned her head against his shoulder and closed her eyes. She knew they would be to her apartment in less than five minutes, but she didn't care. "At least you're not going to leave me."

Eddie and Tommy stopped by Alyson's apartment later that afternoon at Jamie's request. She was wearing a pair of jeans with a hole in the knee and an oversized sweatshirt with a picture of Audrey Hepburn on it. It was one of the many items of clothing Aly had taken from Lucy and never given back. She pushed a strand of hair behind her ear when she saw them come in. Her mouth barely smiled as she said nothing.

"Hi, love." Eddie walked over and took a seat on the edge of the coffee table. "We tried to ring you up and let you know we were on our way, but it said your mobile was off."

"It broke last night." Alyson gave them a quick look, then averted her eyes. "Jamie's buying me a new one."

"Aly, what's wrong?" Eddie always knew.

"Jamie told me..." The lump in Alyson's throat grew from nothing to a rock in the matter of half a second, and she couldn't finish her sentence. This was what she had been trying to avoid.

"Told you what, Alyson?" Tommy settled on the couch beside her, close enough to wrap his arm around her if she cried.

Alyson cleared her throat and widened her eyes at the familiar prick of tears. She took a deep breath and let it out slowly.

"That it's over."

"What's over, love?"

"The band." Alyson couldn't hold her tears back or her lips steady as she spoke.

"Oh, darling." Tommy pulled Alyson close and stroked her hair back as she hid her face in his chest. "It's okay. It's not... it's a good thing."

Eddie didn't say anything as he watched Alyson cry over something he was reluctant to let go of himself.

"But y-you guys have always... you guys are friends!"

"We'll still be friends. That's never going to change, Aly. We'll always be friends with him and Gar. We've spent years together. It's okay."

She didn't try to explain it to them. She didn't try to tell them she was afraid that this was just the beginning of everything falling apart. She didn't try to explain how she didn't want to lose anyone else that she loved. If they left and joined a new band, what would they be like when they came back? They would be different. Everyone would be. It was just how life went.

Alyson was trying to get herself back together when Jamie returned with her new phone. He saw her puffy eyes and knew what they had talked about. Both Tommy and Eddie had the evidence of tears on their faces, though they tried to hide it when he walked in. They gave him brief nods of acknowledgment as he entered.

"Things okay in here?"

"Yeah." Alyson pushed Tommy's arm off her shoulders and excused herself to use the bathroom.

She could hear them talking about her in low voices as soon as she disappeared from sight in the hallway. She didn't even care to listen to what they were saying. The mirror on the back of the bathroom door showed her thin frame and pale face. Alyson pulled up her shirt and ran her hands over her stomach. It was tight and firm again, but only because of her muscles. She hadn't wanted to workout and lose the pregnancy weight she had gained, but Gianna said working out would get the right types of chemicals released in her body.

"Look, Bambi. This used to be where you were." Alyson tilted her head as she stared at herself. "Day and night, always there."

Sometimes she still imagined she felt the jabs or kicks, but there was nothing. Alyson sat down on the floor of the bathroom and cradled her face in her hands as she turned to deep breathing as her friend. In and out. She leaned back against the edge of the bathtub, utterly exhausted.

The muscles in her legs ached from running and not stretching, and her heart ached from beating and not feeling. She didn't know how she knew, but she knew that things were about to change all over again, and it was terrifying. Maybe this was the end of everything and not just Jamie's band. Where would another change leave her? She didn't know.

Two weeks passed slowly with few incidents. The school term ended the end of June, but Alyson's job would be finished in a matter of days. To continue working there would require her to fill out piles of paperwork, but Alyson realized she was done. Being a teacher was going to take more than she knew she had to give. It hurt, just the same. She loved her job. It was what she was good at.

She was in a fog when she walked into the office to grab something at the end of the day. Fran stopped her.

"I have your paycheck, Amanda."

"Sorry, what?" Alyson furrowed her brow. "Paycheck?"

"Yes. Would you like it now?"

"But, I... I'm not quite sure I understand."

"If you don't want your paycheck now, we can wait until the end of the term to give it to you." Fran didn't appear pleased at Alyson's confusion.

"No, I want it! I just thought I wasn't getting paid, this was a charity thing."

"That was just the first two weeks. The rest of the time you've worked here has been for an hourly wage." Fran handed an envelope to Alyson.

"Oh, thank you. Wow. I-I didn't know." Alyson decided not to look and see how much money she had made until later. "Thank you, Fran."

Fran turned back to her computer and began to type again.

Alyson took the long way home, walking slowly through the park, her backpack over her shoulders and the envelope tucked carefully inside. She walked past the playground and saw a girl who lived in her apartment building. She didn't know her, but she waved anyway. The girl stared with wide eyes and scurried over to her friend. They pointed and whispered as Alyson kept walking.

No one in Alyson's neighborhood talked to her aside from Lucy. They would nod at times, but even the man at the grocery store had a hard time making eye contact when he rang up her purchases. Sometimes Alyson was glad to be left alone, and other times she was saddened by it. Either way, it was too late to change it now.

There was a faint dinging sound from Alyson's pocket, and she pulled out her phone. It was a text from Eddie saying he was at her apartment.

"*Be there in a second.*" She typed out the reply and sent it. She smiled when Eddie's happy response was immediate.

Eddie was standing outside of her apartment when she arrived. He was wearing a gray t-shirt and black skinny jeans like any other normal lad from London, but he had his curly hair combed back from his face with his sunglasses settled on top of it. It was the little things that made him look like the famous musician that he was.

"I wasn't expecting to see you today." Alyson took her keys out of her backpack and unlocked her door. Eddie followed her in with a smile.

"Well, I was at my gran's this morning, and I wanted to stop by and see how you were doing. I feel like I don't see you very often. I miss it being just you and me, talking about things."

"I miss that, too."

Eddie took a seat on the recliner and watched as Alyson put her backpack in the corner by her bedroom door and slipped off her shoes. She didn't know why he was looking at her so intently as she walked back over to the couch. He always had that expression on his face, but something about it was different.

"Eddie, why are you here?"

"I'm here to se-..."

"No, Ed, there's something else." Alyson's stomach twisted uncomfortably.

"Jamie heard something."

Alyson didn't know what that meant, but every nerve started to tingle. Eddie looked apologetic and tender as he twisted the rings around his fingers.

"Wh-what?" Her mouth was dry.

"People are beginning to connect you to him, to us, beyond the charity at the school. People started following us out here, trying to take pictures, and some are talking about it in the tabloids."

"What? Wha-what? Why? Why, Eddie, why are they?" Alyson stood to her feet even though her legs felt weak. "Why are they taking... Oh my go-, pictures? Of me?"

"They don't have your name, but it's only a matter of time. They've found where you live. We're going to have to stop visiting you here."

The ache in Alyson's stomach made her want to throw up. She couldn't breathe, couldn't even think about making her body work the way it was supposed to. She was caught in Eddie's arms as she began to fall to her knees.

"It's okay, Aly. We're going to take care of it. We'll get it sorted." Eddie pressed his mouth to the side of Alyson's head as they sank to the floor together. "We're not going to let them hurt you."

"A-are they g-going to find Bambi?" Panic was still clouding Alyson's vision. "Don't... don't let them find her. Please!"

"No one is going to find her," Eddie promised. "We're lucky it took them this long to find you. It's going to be fine."

"Wait, you shouldn't e-even be here!" Alyson tried to push him away.

"No, it's okay. They never follow me from my gran's house." Eddie pulled Alyson back into his hug. "Right now is fine."

"Ed, this isn't a problem that can be fixed with chips and salsa! This is serious! People are going to start asking questions. People I don't know! They're going to start making things up about me. They're going... oh my word, strangers are going to be picking my life apart on the internet! Eddie, people are going to be digging into my past and t-trying to find out who I am!"

"We won't let them!"

"But we can't stop them!"

"We'll try."

Alyson let Eddie's steady voice distract her from the flurry of fear that was launching into a full-fledged storm inside of her. She didn't believe that they would be able to stop the people from talking. They would pry and dig and search until they were satisfied with every lie and half-truth they could get. It made her sick.

"I can't bear the thought of people finding out about Bambi, Ed." Alyson's voice was shaky. "I can't. Not because of my family, but she's s-so special. People will ruin her. I-I can't... Oh, Ed, if they find her..."

"Sh. We've already contacted the minister who did the service. He's the only one who knows about her grave. He promised not to tell."

"And the doctors?"

"They already agreed before Bambi was born. They already signed the papers."

It didn't give Alyson much hope, but it was all that Eddie could tell her. He wanted to stay and make sure she was okay, but she told him that keeping her safe from the public was all she wanted right then. If he wasn't there, no one would bother her. Why had she started to let them into her house? She should have kept them all out. It would have kept her safer physically and emotionally. Eddie's eyes were glassy from tears as he quietly left her apartment. He was her steady one, and she had just sent him away.

Alyson sat in the living room for a long time with her sketchpad and pencil, drawing and thinking. It all seemed hopeless. Things had already been in a swirl with Jamie's band breaking up, but this was a real threat. This involved people Alyson didn't know or trust to have her best interest in mind, and she was terrified.

A knock sounded at midnight, and Alyson nearly jumped out of her skin. Very slowly, she put her things down and walked across the room. Another knock pounded, and Alyson didn't move until she heard her name whispered through the door.

"Alyson?"

"Tommy." Alyson let out her breath and opened the door. She was nearly crushed in his arms as soon as he saw her.

"You're okay?" He put his hands on her shoulders and cocked his head to see her face in the lamplight. "Geez, you look absolutely sick."

"I'm fine."

"You sound like a robot, darling." Tommy shut the door behind him and led her over to the couch. "I'm so sorry that things have turned out like this. Are you okay?"

"Why are you here?" Alyson felt like she was in a daze. "It's so late."

"Eddie came back and told us all about how you nearly had a panic attack. I waited until there were no more paps around outside the studio and drove straight over here. Worried to death about you, Alyson."

"I'm fine." Alyson rubbed her hands over her face, suddenly waking from the trance Tommy's arms had put her into. "You shouldn't be here."

"I should be here! I should! You're freaking out, and I don't want you to be alone!"

"But you're the reason why I am freaking out. You guys... being connected to you is dangerous."

"Alyson, you're safe right now. No one saw me come."

"Well, maybe not someone with a camera, but the little girl who lives on the second floor might have seen you. Or the family who lives above Lucy's place. Or the man who works on the corner... These are all the people who are going to be approached by gross men trying to make me into money. Tommy, they've seen you guys here a hundred times, and it's catching up to us."

"I didn't think of that." Tommy ran his hand through his hair and sighed. "I was just so nervous about you because you were finally getting your feet under you a bit, and now this."

"This isn't a safe place anymore." Alyson was surprised at how emotional she felt at the thought.

The bright, white walls and tiles used to be an eyesore; now they were a welcome sight every day when Alyson came home from school. She loved the familiarity of the bookshelf and piano, where all of the kitchen things were kept, the squeak of the nursery door, and the fact that the shower only stayed hot for five minutes.

"Alyson, I had a thought while I was driving over here." Tommy sat up until he was sitting on the edge of the couch like she was.

She looked at his face and saw him stare at her eyes, then her lips, then back at her eyes. Pink filled her cheeks slowly, and she hardly dared to breathe.

"You can live with my mum and dad for a bit." Tommy's words were low. "People don't bother them there. You know my mum would take care of you and love you. Besides, you know, like, Bambi is our daughter. I-I want to help keep you safe..."

"T-tommy." Alyson had to swallow hard. "I..."

"Sh. I have to tell you something."

Alyson began to shake her head. She didn't want to know. She already knew, maybe. Maybe not. But she didn't want to find out. Tommy ignored her and started talking again.

"I wasn't going to tell you this right now, but after thinking about you so much today, I just can't hold it in any longer." Tommy leaned closer. "I am in love with you. I want to be with you. I want you to be with me."

The words made Alyson's stomach drop to her toes. She was right; she had known what he was going to say. He had been so good at holding back, letting her have her space as she grieved and tried to work things out with Jamie, but she had known his feelings were still there.

"Tommy." Alyson shook her head and looked down at her lap.

His cheeks were red as he stared at her, waiting for her to look back up at his face and give him her answer.

"What we've shared is really special and really intimate, and I never want to lose that. But..."

"Alyson, babe, no!" Tommy tried to stop her before she could refuse him. "Us being together is right! You slept with three guys, but the baby was mine. I've thought about it so many times since we found out I was the dad. I've been waiting. You don't know how hard it has been to wait, but I've done it! I've been holding my tongue, waiting for the right time!"

"Why did you stop waiting? Why did you think tonight was a good time to tell me all of this? I can't..." Alyson's heart was being wrenched around, beating painfully in her chest.

"Things are changing. Things are hard between you and Jamie. I-I thought you could feel this, too."

"I can." Alyson put her hand on the young man's arm. "I do. But, geez, Tommy, I don't need this! I'm not ready, Tom. I'm so broken up on the inside over Bambi, and life... Besides."

Tommy looked at Alyson as she added the last sentence.

"I'm in love with Jamie. You know that."

Tommy nodded.

"Still in love with Jamie, eh?" His lips were quivering.

"Stop." Alyson felt sick to her stomach. "You don't need to ask to know that."

"Do you, uh, do you think you'll ever... love me?" Tommy's voice cracked.

"I-I don't know. I don't know what will happen." She wanted to hug her friend to comfort him, but she held back. Her head began to ache.

"I'm going mad with how much I feel for you. I can't lose you."

"You can't talk like that!" Alyson's voice rose. "I can't... Tommy!"

"What am I supposed to say?" Tommy held out his hands helplessly. "You're in love with someone else, I can't come visit you anymore, and our daughter is dead. You can slip through my fingers so easily, and, and, and there would be nothing for me to..."

"Tommy! Shut up!" Alyson covered her ears. It was all too much.

"I'm scared, Alyson!"

Alyson gave him a broken frown as she struggled to keep herself from bursting into tears. She couldn't do it. Tears filled her eyes, and she ran from the room. She closed herself up in the guest room, the door closed, but not locked. She lay on the bed and sobbed into the pillow as the pain in her head pounded.

Several long minutes passed before Tommy appeared in the doorway. His face looked a bit blotchy from crying, but his breathing was steady, and his eyes were clear.

"Alyson, can I come in?"

"I don't know what you want to talk about." Alyson spoke in a low voice as she took a long, shuddering breath.

"I know. I just... I just don't want us to try to say goodbye on this note." Tommy pushed the door closed behind him. "And I wanted to apologize. I've put you in a bad spot."

"No, Tommy. I put me in a bad spot." Alyson shook her head and felt the self-loathing wash over her again. "I'm the one who slept with all of you. If I hadn't done that..."

"Alyson. Stop." Tommy gave the girl a serious look as he sat down on the edge of the bed. She turned her back towards him, lying on her side to face the wall. He sat for a moment before he repositioned himself to lie next to her. Alyson didn't move. "I'm sorry."

"It's not just you." The whisper made its way to Tommy's side of the bed. "It's everything with the paparazzi, and you guys splitting up. This doesn't feel worth it."

"Oh, darling." Tommy's heart was breaking. "You don't need all this in your life right now. You've been incredible, and brave, and you never asked for any of this. I'm very sorry."

"I wish I could handle it all better right now. I don't know what's wrong with me."

"Nothing, Alyson. Nothing's wrong with you. You don't have to handle these things right now." Tommy rolled over and scooted closer to the girl. "I'm sorry I told you how I felt. This isn't the right time. You were right. I just went off my head because I'm scared."

Alyson didn't say anything as she wiped hot tears from her face.

"I'm sorry I was selfish. I don't want you to think about how I feel. You are dealing with things I've never had to think of, and I had no right to come in and complicate things by telling you how I felt. If something happens, it happens. If it doesn't... well..." Tommy's voice trailed off.

A sob could be heard from Alyson's side of the bed as Tommy lay silently, watching the back of her head. She twisted herself around so she could face him.

"I d-don't want to lose you!"

"You're not going to lose me." Tommy's eyes were blue even in the dark room. This time he kept them focused on Alyson's eyes, not moving to her lips. He reached out a hand and laid it on Alyson's cheek. "Never."

Tommy watched as Alyson's eyes squeezed shut, and her teeth bit into her bottom lip. She tried to stifle her cries, but there was too much pressure from the bottle of emotions inside of her. Next thing he knew, she was snuggling her head against his chest as she wept.

"I'll always be here for you if you need me."

"I know. I know, Tommy." Alyson sniffled and took a deep breath.

Tommy kissed the top of Alyson's head gently. "We'll take it one day at a time."

"One day at a time," Alyson agreed.

Flashbacks to goodbyes with Jamie started to play in Alyson's mind, and her throat ached almost unbearably. She never wanted this with Tommy. She never wanted this with anyone. She had always said she was going to focus on being a mom and not let her relationships with the guys go beyond what was necessary for them to be the fathers of her child, yet here she was.

"Bambi is always going to be *our* baby," she choked out. "And your family will always be her family."

"I know, darling," Tommy said quietly.

The top of Alyson's head was tucked under Tommy's chin. Neither of them said anything else. Alyson knew if she didn't move soon, she would fall asleep, and she didn't want Tommy to be seen there when he left.

"You should go," she whispered hoarsely. "I'll be okay."

"Do you want me to stick around until you're in bed or asleep?"

"No. I just sleep on the couch anyway."

"Wait, why?" Tommy watched Alyson closely as she sat up on the bed and scrubbed the tears away with her sleeve.

"I haven't slept in my bed since the day Bambi died." Alyson looked away as the confession fell softly from her lips. "It's still made up with the sheets Eddie borrowed from his gran. Never used them."

"I didn't know that." Tommy's fingers slipped between Alyson's, and she gave him the flicker of a tiny smile. "I'm sorry."

"Thanks. But you really should go."

They left the guest room and headed towards the door. Tommy gave her one last hug and kissed her forehead.

"Love you, Alyson."

"Love you, too." Alyson couldn't wait for the lump to leave her throat so it would stop hurting.

With a quick nod, and a tear sneaking down his cheek, Tommy left and shut the door behind him. Alyson waited by the window until she saw him drive away. She could only hope that no one noticed or wanted to talk about it. She looked across the street at Lucy's apartment and saw the lamp on by the couch. Lucy was sleeping there, a blanket she had borrowed from Alyson one night covering her. Everyone else in Lucy's building had their curtains drawn. It had been a long time since Alyson thought about curtains.

"Everything has changed." Alyson said to herself, her hands on her stomach. She realized what she was doing, but let them stay. Sometimes it was easier to just pretend. "I don't think this is going to work anymore."

Alyson went over to her backpack and found the envelope from the pocket. She opened it up and saw how much the check was made out for. She stared at the amount for a long time, knowing that once she decided, she would never be able to take it back.

The next day at school, she asked a fellow teacher if she could use their smart phone to log into her bank account and deposit her check. They were friendly about it and let Alyson use their phone until the end of the day. By then, Alyson had already finished her preparations, and all she had to do was put her plan into motion.

"What do you need me for so desperately that I had to leave my pizza on the table?" Lucy demanded as she walked into Alyson's apartment.

"I need a friend." Alyson had already been crying off-and-on for an hour as she cleaned her apartment and organized things that had been lying about for weeks.

"Okay, but we may not be chums after this if I go back and my pizza is cold." Lucy gave Alyson an empathetic frown and pulled her in for a hug.

"I'll buy you another one." Alyson wrapped her arms around Lucy tightly. "Promise."

"Don't worry about it, you idiot. Just tell me what you need me for."

"Come in here."

Alyson led the way to her bedroom and opened the door. It was clean in there. Nothing had really been touched in the last two months except some of the clothes in the dresser; everything else had been moved into the guest room or other places around the apartment. Alyson stood at the end of the bed and counted her breaths.

"What are you going to do?" Lucy stood beside her.

"I need to return these sheets to Eddie's gran. I don't use them, so there's no point."

"Okay. What do you want me to do?"

"Just be here." Alyson's eyes held an almost embarrassed look. "I don't know what will trigger me."

"Of course. Here, I'll take this corner." Lucy was quick to jump to one side of the bed and begin tugging off blankets to get to the sheets in question.

Lucy remembered the day Alyson had come back from the hospital, and Lucy had come into the room to get a pillow before the bedding had been changed. Her stomach bobbed a bit at the picture that flashed into her mind. They had had to call Eddie to find out where extra sheets were, and he had brought a clean set from his gran's house to replace the bloody ones.

"You okay?" Alyson watched Lucy carefully, moving much more slowly than her friend.

"Yeah. Just remembering things I haven't thought of for a while." Lucy forced a smile.

The blankets were folded and set on the floor before they pulled off the sheet and worked together to fold it up. All that was left was the fitted sheet over the mattress. Alyson could feel her heart thumping, but her lungs moved normally. Deep breaths in, deep breaths out. Her fingers caught the edge of the bedding and lifted.

"Oh my go-..." Alyson sunk to her knees.

"Oh, Aly." Lucy hurried around the end of the bed to kneel beside her friend as she traced the dark crimson stain with a shaking finger. "I didn't know that was there. I'm sorry."

"It's okay." Alyson felt her lungs constrict, then loosen. "I think... I think I needed to remember... one last time."

The words didn't make sense to Lucy as she rubbed Alyson's back and cried with her. It wasn't the frantic weeping that Lucy had seen from time to time; it was the steady, deep, gut-wrenching sobs that cleaned you from the inside out.

"She feels like a dream, Lu. Like she wasn't real."

"She was. I have pictures of her, and your pregnant belly all over my apartment to prove it."

"Life is really hard sometimes."

"I know, Aly."

"Did you hear the boys can't come here anymore because the paps found out why they were coming?" Alyson sniffed, her fingers still tracing the mattress.

"No. That's a shame, that."

"Did you hear that Jamie's band is breaking up? Tom and Ed are joining some new band. Going on tour in the fall around Europe."

"They'll be back. You're not losing them."

"No. I know." Alyson finally pushed herself up to her feet. "But everything is changing."

"Change can be good, too, you know." Lucy let her mouth push up into a smile. "And I'm not leaving, so that's one thing that's not changing."

Alyson hugged Lucy as tight as she could until she heard Lucy gasp because she couldn't breathe. She didn't let her go, even when she felt Lucy shift on her feet, ready for the hug to end. She didn't let her go when Lucy patted her back and tried to pull away. She didn't let go until Lucy sighed and leaned into the hug again for the last few moments.

"You're going to be okay, you idiot. It's gonna be all right."

"Thanks, Lu."

"It's all right." Lucy tried to hide her worry.

"Can I give you something?"

"Sure?"

Alyson walked out of the bedroom, the sheets for Eddie's gran in her arms. She closed the door to her bedroom behind them and nodded at the nursery. They walked in and paused in front of the closet. Lucy popped her eyebrows up inquisitively, but Alyson didn't respond. She took a deep breath and opened the door.

"What is that?" Lucy pointed at the stacks of paper that sat on the shelf.

"These are my pictures. My drawings. I-I don't know what to do with them. Maybe you want some. I don't know. I already pulled out my favorites, these are just the rest."

"There are hundreds here, Aly! These are sad!" Lucy pulled a few off the top. "But really good."

"You don't have to take them if you don't want them."

"I don't see why you're giving them to me now."

"Just trying to clean stuff up, and I didn't want to throw them away quite yet."

"Fine, I'll go through them. Maybe steal a couple for myself. You want me to throw out the rest?"

"Yes, please." Alyson handed the stacks over to Lucy and shut the closet carefully.

"You know, maybe you should try to draw things that are happier. Maybe. Might help." Lucy spoke gently with the hint of a smile, one hand reaching out to cup Alyson's cheek.

"Yeah. Maybe." Alyson nodded and pushed the corners of her mouth upward.

"Oh!" Lucy paused as she turned around. "You've taken the letters down off the wall."

"Yeah. Didn't need them up anymore." Alyson's heart still ached at the thought of her baby never receiving the letters that had been written to her. "I put them in a special box with a few other things that remind me of Bambi."

"Good. You'll be glad you saved them later on."

"I hope so." Alyson's sad whisper earned her a frown from Lucy as they left the room.

"You okay? You seem really down."

"I'm just dealing with a lot."

"I know, Aly. Do you want to come over to mine and eat some pizza? I'll warm it up in the microwave."

"No." Alyson smiled as tears filled her eyes. "But thank you."

"Yeah, it's okay, you're always welcome at mine." Lucy walked towards the door. "I love you, you know."

"Love you, too." Alyson waved and closed the door after her friend.

She stood with her forehead pressed against the door for a long while, crying and sniffling. Life was hard.

Chapter twenty-two
"I don't want to feel like this anymore."

Tears burned in Alyson's eyes as she stood by the front door of her apartment. Her suitcase sat on the floor by her feet, her backpack looped over one shoulder. There was a sick feeling in her stomach that had been there for two days, since she decided she was actually going to go through with leaving. She tried to relieve the pain by pressing her palms hard against the ache, but nothing helped, not when she remembered that the first time she walked into that apartment she had been pregnant. Alyson bit her lip so hard she was afraid she was going to break skin.

She was leaving behind most of her belongings, but the most important items were packed safely in the suitcase. She had walked slowly through every room, giving her apartment a final onceover. The last room to check before leaving was the living room.

The walls and floor were still white, but they seemed worn in and faded now from the sound of friend's voices and laughter. The empty spaces had slowly filled with a history of hugs, tears, whispers, laughs, secrets, pain, love, and broken dreams. She had spent hours at the window, staring out at the world as seasons passed and changed. This was the first place she had lived where there had been no curtains to hold her back. No curtains to haunt her. No curtains to hide secrets.

Her gaze drifted over to the piano in the corner. After Bambi had died, she stopped playing, but Eddie hadn't. She could remember him sitting there making up songs and melodies, serenading her as she lay on the couch and planned lessons, or sketched sad faces. She never expected the piano to remind her the most of Eddie, but she didn't mind. She loved him.

There on the wall was the picture of the tree Lucy had given her as a housewarming gift. The frame was covered with a film of dust that Alyson hadn't noticed for weeks. She loved that picture. She wondered if maybe she should try to bring it with her, but then remembered there was no more room in her suitcase.

Alyson felt her shoulder hit the door jamb as she took a step back. It was time to go. She saw Lucy out of the corner of her eye, waiting to drive her to the airport.

She tried to make herself turn around and walk out the door, but she couldn't because that was the last place she had felt Bambi move. It was the last place she had stared at Tommy, cheeks hot under his gaze, and heard Eddie's comforting voice telling her they were going to fix it. This was the last place that Jamie... She didn't have a last memory there with Jamie. He hadn't been there since he brought her the phone, and he had left before she came out of the bathroom.

"Let's go." Alyson quickly turned on her heel and opened the door, her eyes full of tears.

Lucy grabbed Alyson's suitcase while Alyson hurried ahead. They had plenty of time to get to the airport without the risk of Alyson missing her flight, but she wanted to hurry. She *needed* to hurry. She reached the top of the stairs and realized she couldn't see far enough through her tears to put one foot down. Her determination wavered. She was about to change her mind and turn around when Lucy grabbed her hand.

Neither girl spoke, knowing the moment was too heavy, too fragile, too painful for words. The suitcase was put into the backseat, and Alyson buckled her seatbelt. She looked out of the window towards her old apartment building while Lucy fiddled with her keys, struggling to find the right one in the mess of keychains. She remembered standing there by the door in the cold with Jamie, fingers intertwined, and their breath mixing between them.

The car jerked to a start, and Alyson closed her eyes. She was leaving. She was actually leaving. It didn't feel right after working so hard to get there. But life is hard, and things change.

"Have the boys tried to call ya?" Lucy asked, a few miles into their journey.

"I don't know." Alyson had put her cell phone into her suitcase, battery completely drained and charger still in the bedroom of the apartment. It was the only way she could guarantee that she wouldn't cave and call one of them to change her mind. "You don't have to lie if they ask you about me."

"I won't," Lucy promised. It was only out of her love and support for Alyson that she agreed to take her to the airport. She wasn't convinced it was the best choice, but Alyson had begged. She knew if she didn't take her, Alyson would take a taxi, or the train like she used to go on about enjoying riding so much. It was better to go with her to make sure she arrived there safe and had a friend to hug before she left.

"Thank you, Lu." Alyson looked over at her driver. She saw Lucy biting the inside of her cheek. When had the switch happened between them? she asked herself. When had Lucy stopped being the nosy neighbor and became Alyson's dearest friend? She reached over and placed a cold hand on Lucy's arm. "I mean it. Love you so much, Lu."

"Love you too, you idiot." Lu tried to laugh, but it stuck on the tears. She wiped furiously at her eyes so she could see the road. Her mascara smudged and ran along the curve of her cheeks.

Alyson kept her hand on Lucy's arm as she closed her eyes and focused on deep breathing. Inhale. Exhale. She breathed in the fresh country air, savoring the taste and the memories. It tasted the same as the air around Bambi's grave.

She remembered how tightly Jamie had hugged her the morning he came and picked her up at the cemetery after her run. If they were going to have a last moment, she wanted it to be that. Just Jamie, and Bambi, and their love. The emptiness of her womb ached with an almost physical pain.

"Aly." Lucy broke Alyson's thoughts, and she opened her eyes. "You're doing the tummy rub again. You're going to have to stop if you're planning on going back to America and pretending like you never had a baby."

The thought hurt, and Alyson wept gently as she looked down at her belly. Lucy was right. She was going to have to pretend like none of this had happened, that she had been a teacher the whole time and was extremely proud of herself. The thoughts burned through her conscience, and she shook her head. It felt wrong to purposefully push her daughter out of her mind. There was so little of her left to cling to.

"There's still time to change your mind, Aly." Lucy didn't try to hide her raw emotions. "You don't have to leave me. Leave us."

"Please. Stop." Alyson covered her eyes with her hand and heaved with deep shuddering sobs. She was torn in two over her decision. One little shift the right way, and she would cave. "I c-can't... I can't..."

"I know." And Lucy did know.

"'It is better to have loved and lost, than never to have loved at all.'" Alyson quoted the plaque she had found two weeks earlier and given to Lucy.

"Stop." Lucy's voice was gruff. "I hate that saying."

"Me, too."

Jamie's voice filled Alyson's mind, and she wished all over again that she had never met him. If she had never met him, she would be living happily in Des Moines, working her dream job and hiding nothing from her parents and friends. Now she was going back to try to be that girl again after everything she had gone through. She was going to try to awkwardly push herself back into her original spot, pretending like she had never left it. The truth was, though, she couldn't even recognize her own self anymore; there was no way she was going to fit.

"You took my heart by surprise, Aly. I never planned on getting close to you. But here you are..."

Alyson bit her knuckle and stared out of the window, tears blurring everything together.

"I promised I would take care of it."

"There. That was all the Christmas present I needed."

All the things Alyson had stored up in her heart came flooding back, and she felt the sting of knowing that it was all over. If she had never met him, she wouldn't feel this pain. There would be no struggle to let him go because he would never have been there. But fate had crossed their paths too many times, and now they were both going to have an emptiness where the other used to be.

"Come now, love. It's all forgiven."

"I pray every day that it's me."

"Climb into bed, Aly. I'll wait until you're asleep to hang up."

It was all done; having him hold her hand when she was scared, wiping away her tears and kissing her face. There would be no more falling asleep to his voice, calling him up when she woke up in the middle of the night, or counting on him rescuing her when she jumped into something too deep. She could still feel what it was like to be wrapped in his arms so perfectly she felt safe from everything except her own feelings for him.

"Lu," she blurted out suddenly. "Please promise we'll still be friends after I leave."

"What are you going on about? Why would we stop being friends? After all we've been through..." Lucy pretended to be offended by the request, but after biting her lip for a few minutes, she whispered her answer. "I bloody promise, Alyson Abidi."

The oath ached in Alyson's heart as she hugged Lucy fiercely outside of the airport. They had too many tears to see each other's faces, and there were no words as Lucy kissed Alyson's cheeks before letting her go. She stood by her car and watched Alyson walk away, dragging her suitcase behind her. Alyson stopped at the entrance of the building and turned one last time. Lucy waved and blew a kiss.

"Love you," Alyson shouted back, unashamed of who heard her.

"Love you too, you idiot!" Lucy could hardly get her words out before crumpling into a heap of tears. Alyson was gone from sight by the time she opened her eyes again, and she shook her head. "Please, please, be very careful."

Alyson couldn't eat during the flight over the Atlantic Ocean, too sick to her stomach to try. Instead she leaned against the window and listened to "Sweet Dreams" over and over. At one point she was crying so hard that her seatmate called the stewardess to check on her.

"Sorry, sorry." Alyson gulped back the rest of her tears, but when the stewardess left, all she could see were Jamie's blue eyes sparkling at her as she played him the song in his special music room in California. She excused herself from her spot and locked herself in the bathroom.

She stayed in there for as long as she could, stroking her flat stomach and whispering over and over that she was going to be fine, that leaving was the right choice. All she had in Bedford was a fake job, a grave and the ghost of her baby. Her entire apartment had become a prison of emotions, every possession she owned tainted by death and anger.

The sweet spring air was polluted by the exhaust fumes of hundreds of vehicles driving around the airport when Alyson walked out of baggage, her suitcase in her hand. It was a bit more battered than when the journey had started, but so was she, and they had somehow made it to their first destination. She looked down at her shoes: her feet were on American soil once again. Her toes curled inside her shoes as she stood in the middle of the crowd, holding still, holding her breath, holding her heart together just barely.

Her credit card covered the cost of the rental car and she settled into the driver's seat with a sigh, relieved to finally be alone. She pulled out her American phone and plugged the charger into the cigarette lighter. She didn't need the directions, but she pulled them up anyway. It was a safety net. The robotic voice of the phone spoke to her, telling her where to turn and how long it would take her to get to her destination.

Alyson saw Danielle's car in the parking lot outside of Danielle's apartment building, and she gulped down her bobbing emotions. She was minutes away from being held in the arms that had been her home for years. Once she was parked, she put her cellphone into her pocket and stepped out of the car. She looked up at the window of Danielle's living room. She saw the curtains. She saw herself. She saw herself staring down at Jamie sitting in his rental car, proving to her that he was serious about fixing what he had broken. He had been so stubborn. How could she have known then what she was about to step into with him?

No! She shook her head and slammed the car door shut. With long, purposeful strides, Alyson walked quickly over to Danielle's building. *Don't you dare think about Jamie. It's over. You're home now.*

The look on Danielle's face when she opened the door and saw her best friend went from shock, to delight, to concern, to tears. She gripped Alyson tightly, and the two of them sank to the floor, their legs too weak with emotion to stand. Three people sat in the living room and stared with wide eyes, whispering behind their hands about the tearful reunion.

"Aly. Aly." It was all Danielle could say.

"Elle, h-hold m-me..." The words were scarcely audible as they were spoken into the fabric of Danielle's shirt.

Minutes passed before the girls pulled apart, and Danielle grabbed Alyson's face with both of her hands. She looked hard into Alyson's eyes and watched her shift her gaze away. She knew what that meant. They both knew what was being communicated.

"Aly, why didn't you tell them?"

"Th-they w-wouldn't, wouldn't h-h-have..." Alyson took several deep breaths to try to steady her voice enough to talk. "They wouldn't h-have unders-stood."

"Aly, they're going to be freaking out! Does anyone know you left?"

"L-lu does. She drove me to the airport. She p-promised she would t-tell them."

"Oh, Aly." Danielle pulled Alyson back into her arms for another hug. "I can't believe you're here. I'm so glad you're back."

Alyson was put to bed in Danielle's room with Danielle close by her side. She slept fitfully, despite the jet lag and constant strain of heavy emotions. All she could think of was the way Eddie had nursed her back to health when she had fallen ill after her flight to London. She missed him, and she hated the feeling. She wasn't supposed to miss anyone now that she was with Danielle, but the truth was that she did. She missed them all; from Beatie, to Tommy's parents, to Fran.

"I don't want to feel like this anymore." Alyson's voice was hoarse. Her throat hurt. "I thought coming back would fix everything."

"No, you didn't." Danielle shook her head. "Coming back only gives you space from the things that hurt you. You knew this wasn't going to fix anything."

Alyson knew Danielle was right, and she thought about it a lot over the next few days. Adam came over to visit and was shocked by Alyson's haggard appearance. He asked her what had happened, but she couldn't tell him. She didn't even have to tell him it was because of her parents; he already knew. Before he left, he squeezed Alyson's hands and told her she could always trust him to help her if she ever needed someone. Alyson wanted his words to change the situation somehow, yet they changed nothing.

She arrived back in Des Moines on a Sunday evening. The sun set to the west as the giant Midwestern sky faded to black. It was surreal to drive the streets that used to be her everyday route to and from work. She sat in the parking lot of her old apartment building for a long time before she stepped out. Jamie had hugged her there. That was the place where Jamie had given her the way out; the option to keep both her dignity and her baby.

Alyson had called her old roommate while she was staying with Danielle. She asked if there was any way she could spend a couple weeks at their old place, just until she had her feet under her again.

"This is actually perfect timing! I'm leaving in a couple days for a family vacation, and I need someone to watch the place for a month until my summer roommate moves in. It'll be great to see you and hear all about your amazing time in London!"

"Yeah." Alyson's mouth was dry. That's right, she was supposed to have had an amazing time while she was gone...

Alyson was recognized and awarded by her old school for her work in Bedford. Her parents were there, Danielle was there, and everyone from work was there. Cameras flashed and local TV stations documented the return of the heroic teacher.

The ceremony was short. Zaheer and Janice watched Alyson stand and thank everyone who had been involved in the process of getting her to Bedford and back. No one knew she had left without telling anyone she was leaving. They were beaming with pride and shared with everyone who would listen that she was their daughter.

Danielle did what she could to distract from the haunted look that lingered behind Alyson's eyes. They surprisingly didn't need much to divert their attention. Janice reminded her daughter to look pretty, but didn't say a word about the extra lines and creases on her forehead or around her mouth.

Mr. and Mrs. Abidi celebrated the occasion by taking the girls out to a nearby fancy Italian restaurant. Alyson only ordered an appetizer and spent the entire meal chopping it into smaller pieces to push around her plate. Danielle snuck bites to make it seem like she had been eating.

"So, you're done with school, Elle?" Janice asked kindly, the motherly tone in her voice warming the conversation. "What are your plans for the summer?"

"I have a job. A couple actually." Danielle was glad to have the focus on her.

"Your mother told me that you worked hard this year."

"I tried." Danielle smiled.

"Are you planning on getting your doctorate?" asked Zaheer. He looked older and more weathered than he had when Alyson said goodbye to him in October. It must have been a hard winter.

"That's the plan."

Zaheer nodded approvingly.

"Do you have summer plans, Aly?" Janice put another bite of her lasagna into her mouth.

"N-not yet." Alyson pressed her hands together under the table.

"That's not like you." Zaheer looked at his daughter with surprise. "You usually have a hundred plans."

"Well, I just g-got back." Alyson took a drink of water.

"Almost two weeks ago."

"Yeah, dad, it's just, I mean..." Alyson took a deep breath. "I have to keep climbing the ladder, right? I can't just settle for anything. I have to keep pressing forward, reaching up and getting better and better jobs. That's the way you taught me."

"There's my girl." Zaheer winked at Aly.

"Excuse me." Alyson left the table and forced herself to walk slowly to the bathroom.

She knew that the person in the stall next to her could hear her dry heaving, but she didn't care. She hadn't eaten in two days, and she was afraid that putting anything inside of her would only come back up again. Her body hadn't stopped shaking since she left Bedford.

Her phone showed twenty missed calls from Jamie from the last two weeks. She hadn't had the strength to call him back. She hadn't even texted him, but sent messages to him through Danielle. The phone began to ring again as she stood by the sink washing her hands. The unanswered call was followed by a text, begging her to please talk to him.

"Aly, please, we need to talk. I have to know what your plans are so Gar and I can fix the paperwork. Please. I'm telling Elle to make you call me."

Alyson sighed and blinked back her tears. She knew if she caved one time and heard his voice, she wouldn't be able to say no if he asked her to come back. The only way she could guarantee that he didn't talk her into coming back was to not let him talk to her at all. It felt like she was cutting off a part of her body.

"You okay, dear? Your makeup is a little..." Janice pointed at her eyes when Alyson finally rejoined her family five minutes later.

"I tried to fix it, but the lighting in the bathroom is terrible," Alyson lied.

"Anyone want dessert?" Zaheer asked.

"I'm so full, thank you, though." Danielle put on her most convincing smile.

"Well, Aly, we'll leave and let you have some time with Danielle on your own. I know you haven't seen her since before you left for London. I'm sure you have a lot of catching up to do." Janice motioned for her husband to stand with her. "We'll see you again soon, dear, I'm sure."

"Of course!" Alyson stood to hug her parents. She blamed the tears in her eyes on the fact that she was so happy they had been there to see her.

Alyson didn't let out her breath until she saw the door of the restaurant close behind Mr. and Mrs. Abidi. She sunk down in her chair and closed her eyes, relief evident on her face. Danielle grabbed Alyson's hand and squeezed it.

"You made it."

"I can't believe my mom didn't catch on. I don't know how she missed it."

"God knew you didn't need that right now."

"God knew." Alyson gave a mocking laugh. "Right."

"Hey. Stop. You know it's true."

"Let's just go home. I'm so tired." Alyson sat up and opened her eyes.

They left the restaurant slowly, their arms around each other's waists. The sun was shining brightly. Alyson's legs felt rubbery and strange. Not even the safe, familiar sounds of trees in the wind and kids chattering in the park could set her at ease. She pulled her buzzing phone out of her pocket and saw Jamie's face on the screen once more.

"Are you two going to talk?" asked Danielle.

"Not yet."

"Aly, he needs to talk to you about important stuff."

"Can you talk to him for me?" Alyson turned to Danielle. "Please? Just find out what he needs, and I'll get it to him."

"No, Aly. This is Jamie. You can do this."

"Elle, no. I-I can't. I can't call him! If I do I know he'll try to convince me to come back, and I'm afraid I'm going to tell him yes. I have to stay."

"And do what, Aly? Who is going to be here to watch out for you?"

"Elle." Alyson let out a groan. "We've been over this."

"At least if you go back, Jamie will be there! Eddie and Tommy will be close. You'll have Lucy, Gianna, and Ren! Alyson, you don't have people here!"

Alyson shook her head as they continued to walk. The very thought of returning to the UK without her baby was enough to make her want to wilt into the sidewalk. Danielle was right; there was no one in Iowa to take care of her. The thought was terrifying, but she could not go back to England.

"So, what are you going to do? It's summer, it's not like you can teach."

"I don't know. I don't know. I have absolutely no freaking clue." Alyson put her hands on her stomach. She held it tightly for a moment before letting go. "I was supposed to be a mom."

"Oh, Aly. Come here."

"I don't know how I'm going to recover from this last year, Elle."

Danielle hugged Alyson tightly and whispered that she was praying for her every day. Alyson tensed and tried to step back, but Danielle didn't let her go.

"Don't pray for me, Elle. It's not worth it."

"Stop. This is exactly why I'm praying." Danielle looked devastated as she stepped back from Alyson. "I don't know why you think you're not able to love God anymore, but it's not true."

Alyson didn't try to answer. She wasn't sure she would be able to hold her end of the argument against her friend. The conversation topic was changed as Alyson drove Danielle back to the airport and said goodbye. She told Alyson to come stay with her in Minnesota, but Alyson only shrugged. Danielle's apartment had been where Bambi's existence started for her, and it was where she had cried herself sick after coming back. She would need a while before she could stay with Danielle.

"Call Jamie, Aly. I'm not joking."

"I'll think about it."

The girls didn't want to end their day together with another tense conversation, so they simply hugged each other goodbye and sighed. Alyson stood along the wall, waiting until Danielle was through security. She waved again and swallowed hard, determined to stay strong.

Alyson received a text from Jamie not long after returning to her apartment. It wasn't a threat, but it implied that his management team could take legal action if she didn't contact him about their previous contractual agreements. She paced the living room nervously for a few minute, then pushed the 'call' button.

"Sorry I had to send that last text. I didn't know what else to do."

"Threats are usually pretty effective." Alyson tried to push her words past the burning ache in her throat as she noticed that he didn't say hello, or that he missed her.

"It wasn't threats, Aly, my management team has been breathing down my neck about this. I tried to give you space so you could get settled, but I couldn't put them off any longer."

"Oh." Alyson stared at the wall and pressed a hand on her stomach that was simultaneously begging for and protesting against food. "Well, what do you need?"

There was a pause before Alyson heard Jamie sniff and clear his throat. His voice sounded strained, but it was steady as he listed off the things that would be sent to her so she could sign them and send them back.

"Basically you're just signing a statement that says I'm not legally responsible for anything that happened while you were here, and that we're ending our contract of working together."

"Okay." Alyson's eyes were swimming with tears. He seemed so unaffected by her being gone. She thought for sure he would at least tell her that he had been thinking about her. "I-is that all?"

"Yeah."

"Okay." Alyson paused, hoping Jamie would say something else. Silence. "So, goodbye?"

"Yeah. Bye, Aly."

"Bye."

The call ended, and Alyson buried her face into the couch cushions. Her heart was broken. She never thought she would see the day when he would turn their conversation into a detached exchange of facts and information. He hadn't called her "love", or said it was good to hear from her, or even asked to get the last word in. It had been a long time since they did that. Somewhere along the way they had stopped caring about their early tradition, but now that she was gone, it suddenly meant everything again.

Alyson's tears became angry, and she punched the couch cushion. She was angry at Jamie and angry at herself for pushing him so far that he didn't love her anymore. She thought she would have to fight against him wanting her to come back to London; instead he hadn't even asked her how she had been doing since she left. He had asked her in a hundred unanswered texts Alyson had chosen to ignore, but apparently now he was finished.

"What have I done?" Alyson threw the pillows onto the floor and jumped to her feet. "What have I done? I never... I never wanted this!"

The roof wasn't a place the residents of the apartment building were advised to go, but Alyson made her way up the narrow stairs and through the heavy door. She sat on the side, her feet hanging against the wall as she watched the sunset. The wind blew cool against her face and she tried to breathe, but every breath sounded like she was about to cry again. She didn't even text Danielle to tell her what had happened.

Someone pulled into the parking lot below and stared up at her. She looked away, wiping at her tears even though she knew that they wouldn't be able to see them. They climbed out of their car and walked into her building. She had never seen them before and assumed they moved in while she was gone. Didn't surprise her.

I wish I could pray. I wish I could fix things. I wish... I wish... I wish I hadn't ruined everything. Her thoughts circled her mind to the rhythm of her pulse. *I wish I hadn't left. I wish Bambi was still alive...*

The sound of the door to the roof pushing open startled Alyson, but she didn't turn. It wasn't until the footsteps stopped right behind her that she swiveled in her spot and saw a stranger standing there. His white t-shirt and ripped jeans made him seem younger than he was, but his eyes were old and mature somehow. His skin was dark, tanned, and his face looked so kind as he smiled at her, his neatly-trimmed black hair ruffling in the wind.

"Can I help you?" Alyson knew her tone was careless and tired.

"Do you know who I am?" The man's brown eyes were watching her softly. There seemed to be tears gathering into quiet pools as he took in every detail of her face.

"No." Alyson shifted uncomfortably. "I've never seen you before in my life."

"That's not true." The man pushed his mouth up into a smile again. "But it has been a very long time."

"I'm sorry, you don't look like anyone I know."

"You look different too, Aliya."

Her heart stopped. She teetered dangerously on the wall, but strong hands caught her and helped her away from the edge of the roof.

"Y-you called me Aliya."

"Yeah. 'Cause that's what I always called you."

Amir's eyes suddenly looked like their father's and his nose and chin resembled their mother's more than they had at first glance. He was smiling as the realization of who he was dawned on her. She remembered that smile.

"What in the world are you doing here?"

"I saw you on the news. You're a big deal, eh?"

"I can't... I can't believe it..." Alyson stared up at him, disbelief and shock in her eyes.

"Saw that you came back from London, that you were a teacher there." Amir kept talking easily. "Called a few people, and they told me where you lived."

"You're here..."

"So proud of you, Aliya. I always knew you were going to be great."

"Why... how...?"

"You okay?" Amir chuckled at the way his sister continued to open and close her mouth as she stared at him. "I'm real! I'm here!"

"You were gone for so long."

"I know." Amir finally lost his grin. "I'm sorry. I know you must have been waiting for me to come home."

"I didn't even know you were going to be gone."

"I didn't either."

Alyson nodded.

"But I'm here now. Took me long enough."

"Why didn't you reach out to me before now? We never moved from that house."

"I didn't want you to have to choose between me, and mom and dad." Amir looked down. "Not until you were older at least. Lost track of you for a couple years while you were in college, and I knew I couldn't just walk up to the house and expect to be welcomed back, so I was waiting for a good time. This seemed like it."

"I guess so."

"Do you... want to get some supper and catch up?" Amir gestured towards the exit.

"N-no." Alyson remembered what had happened the last time she ate. "I... can't eat."

"What's wrong?"

"I, uh... it's a long story. I'm not... I'm not doing very well." Tears filled Alyson's eyes.

"Really? I just saw you on the television! You said you were doing great..."

"You don't tell people you're having a breakdown on television! Especially when your parents are there, and they can't know."

"What happened, Aliya? Can I help?"

"No." Alyson shook her head. "No, you don't need to be caught up in this mess. I don't even know what you're doing here, but I know that if you knew what I've done, you'd be just as disappointed as everyone else."

"Why do you say that?" Amir appeared offended at her accusation.

"Because I made horrible mistakes and hurt a lot of people."

"What makes you think that changes how I feel about you? You're my little sister."

Alyson wanted to burst into tears upon hearing Amir's declaration. Even after all those years, she was just a little girl who adored her brother. She needed to keep him out, though, for both their sake's.

"Amir, I'm not who everyone thinks I am."

"No one ever is, Aliya. I'm thirty years old; I know a few things about people."

"Well, it's probably better if you just go back to whatever it is that you do and let me try to get my life back on track alone." Alyson gave him a pained smile and started for the stairs.

"Nice try. I haven't spent the last eight years waiting for a chance to see you again to just say hello for ten minutes and walk back out of your life." Amir kept up with ease.

"Thank you for that, but it will be better for you if..." Alyson picked up her speed.

"Aliya, come on..."

"...you leave me and forget about me!" Alyson could see her door at the bottom of the stairs. She had to stall him, keep him from saying anything that would shake her resolve to keep him from getting close to her again. "It's just better, Amir!"

"Aliya." Amir reached out and touched Alyson's shoulder. "I'm right here, and I'm not leaving."

Alyson pulled away and shut herself in her apartment before Amir could stop her.

She ran over to the sketchpad that had been thrown into a corner from the night before. She found the pencil case Lucy had given her one day when they had drawn together and grabbed a pencil. Alyson had to take several deep breaths to keep herself from throwing the gift out the window; it hurt too much to look at.

"Aliya." Amir pounded at the door. "I'm not leaving."

Alyson tossed the case onto the floor, letting the pencils spill out. She ripped a piece of paper off the wire spiral that held them together, ignoring the corner that came off jagged. She knelt down by the door and began to sketch furiously.

"Aliya..."

Alyson had to pause and shove her knuckles against her tear ducts before she could see to draw. Tears soaked through the paper, and Alyson groaned in aggravation. It didn't keep her from drawing the shape of a little girl sitting alone against a closed door with an angry, broken heart.

"I can hear you crying." Amir's voice sounded closer, and Alyson imagined him sliding down to the floor on the other side of the door.

It only took a few minutes to finish her rough sketch and shove it under the door to her brother. There was a sad sigh, and she knew he saw it.

"Can your pencil fit under the door?"

Alyson was able to squeeze her pencil under the door to Amir. She leaned back against the wall and waited. When they were little, Amir used to make fun doodles for her. He had never been an accomplished artist while he lived at home, but he had enjoyed sketching from time to time. She hadn't thought about that since he had left.

It didn't take long for him to return the paper to Alyson. She picked it up carefully and saw the outline of a young man standing outside of a door with his hand up to knock.

"I didn't know you could draw." His voice was muffled.

"I don't. I mean, I didn't. Not until..." *Not until I became pregnant and my neighbor saved my life and my sanity by insisting she share her favorite pastime with me because she spied on me through the window...* "Not until I lived in the UK."

462

"You should keep it up."

"You're good, too. I didn't remember you could draw."

"Yeah. It's a good stress reliever."

Alyson gave a soft laugh. Her hands squeezed her stomach, and she choked out a couple shaky breaths. All of her secrets were burning on her tongue like a hot coal. She wanted to spit it out before it set her whole mouth on fire.

"Can I please come in, Aliya?"

Alyson reached up and flipped the lock without moving from her spot.

"It's open."

The door opened and closed. Amir slid down to the floor to sit next to his sister. She had quiet tears dripping down from her chin onto her shirt. Her hands were limp in her lap.

"Sorry for the mess. It's what I feel like on the inside." She pointed to the countless items strewn around the apartment.

Pillows. Papers. Clothes. The pencils. Even her special Bambi box was tipped over in the corner. She had flipped over two of the chairs, and they lay tangled together. The window was wide open and the curtains pulled to the ground. Danielle had numerous reasons to not want her to be by herself without knowing what her apartment looked like in the short amount of time she had been alone. She shuddered to think of what she would force her to do if she could see it.

"I was angry at my, uh... boyfriend. Right before I went up to the roof."

"He was here with you?" Amir straightened protectively as he studied the room.

"No. It was over the phone. This is all me."

"What happened?"

"I kind of left him without telling him, and now he's done..." Alyson decided to leave it at that.

"So, I'm not the only person who you're trying to stay closed off from. Good to know."

The words stung, but Alyson knew they were true.

"Does he love you?"

Alyson couldn't keep her voice from breaking as she nodded. "More than I deserve."

The older brother didn't say anything else, but Alyson knew what he was thinking. Maybe she should listen to Jamie and stay with him. But then she remembered the public's growing interest, Bambi's safety, Tommy's heart, the band breaking up...

"Do you want some tea?" Alyson pushed herself to her feet.

"Sure." Amir stood up and followed Alyson into the kitchen.

The kitchen was tidy compared to the living room, but there was a basket of fruit that looked like it was one day away from being too rotten to eat. Fruit flies had found it and were swarming, waiting for access to the pears and peaches. Alyson went straight to the stove and set the kettle on the biggest burner.

"My tea is in, uh, that one... that cupboard there." Alyson didn't turn around, just leaned against the edge of the stove so she could focus on breathing. "There are cups there, too."

"Ah, found it." Amir opened a few cabinets and drawers. "Spoons. Do you have milk in the fridge?"

"I think so. Should still be good."

"Okay." He twisted the cap off and smelled the creamy, white liquid. "Smells fine. What kind of tea do you want?"

"I don't care. I like all of them."

Alyson could hear the sound of Amir opening the tea and putting them into the mugs behind her while she listened to the hiss of the gas burning in front of her. The water wasn't boiling yet, but little puffs of steam were starting to drift out of the spout. She put her fingers through the wet mist as it disappeared.

Amir stayed behind Alyson until the teapot started whistling. She didn't know what he was doing, and she didn't turn around to look. It was taking all of her concentration to not slip into a fantasy and imagine that she was about to have a cuppa with Eddie and Gi, or that Lucy would be popping in at any second with charcoal smeared on the edge of her hand and a smile on her face.

"Here." Amir held out the mugs for Alyson to pour the hot water. "Do you like milk in yours?"

"Sure." Alyson couldn't actually remember. She thought she did.

"Here you go. I didn't add any sugar. I never take mine with sugar." Amir handed a cup to his sister when she was done setting the kettle back in its spot.

"Than-... What tea is this?" Alyson smelled a whiff of the flavor in her cup, and she froze. "Where... what is this?"

"I-I don't know. It's the one from the blue box. Smelled good so..."

"No!" Alyson smashed her cup on the floor and burst into tears. "No! No!"

Hot, milky tea splattered everywhere, burning both Alyson and Amir as it soaked into their clothes. Alyson didn't seem to notice the pain, although her face went from anger to regret in a second after she saw what she had done. It was Jamie's favorite tea, and he had sent it to her right before she left Iowa. It had come with a note that said, "Some tea for a tea-loving girl from a tea-loving boy." She remembered it all.

"I-I th-thought I didn't have any left..."

"These were the last two..."

"No." Alyson whimpered as she sunk to her knees. Shards of glass were scattered everywhere. "No."

Amir took the rag from the sink and began to wipe the tea from the cupboards and the floor. He picked up the spoon and set it in the sink before throwing the bigger pieces of the mug in the trash. He didn't say anything or look at Alyson as he worked.

"Thank you." Her voice was thick. "I'm sorry."

"No worries. I'm just glad I'm here."

"You can go now. I'll clean up the rest."

"No." Amir shook his head and continued to wipe up the floor in the far corner where the tea had reached.

"I can do it, Miri. I know how to clean."

"'Miri.'" Amir chuckled lightly as he continued to scrub. "I know, Aliya. I'm not doing it because I think you don't know how to clean."

"Then please just go. I want to be alone."

"I know, but I am not going to leave you alone. I don't think you should be."

"I've been alone since I got back from Bedford." Alyson sounded sulky, like a child not getting her way.

"And that has clearly not been working out well for you. If you really don't want me here I can call, I don't know, maybe the hospital. See if you can stay somewhere like that for the night. An ambulance would probably drive you."

"No! What? No!" Alyson's eyes flashed.

"It's either me or a professional."

"A professional what? Pain in the butt?"

"I'm afraid I'm as professional as they get on that score, but someone might be willing to try," Amir joked, glancing over his shoulder to see how upset Alyson was. "But seriously, Aliya. I'm trained in a lot of things, and all of my training is telling me to not leave you alone right now. I wouldn't leave a stranger if they were in this type of mental state; I'm not going to leave my little sister."

"What is your job?" Alyson cooled down a bit.

"I help people. I travel the world and help people with whatever I can." Amir sat back on his heels to watch Alyson's face as he spoke.

"Like a miracle man?"

"Something like that." Amir shrugged easily. "You can work with me if you want."

"You would never ask if you knew what I've done."

"You wouldn't say that if you knew what I've done."

"I do know what you've done, but look at you now! You go around helping people like Jesus, I guess."

"I'm not like Jesus, but I want to be."

"More than I ever was."

"Aliya..."

"You can sleep in my room." Alyson stood up. Her jeans were dripping at the knees. She wondered if they would smell like Jamie's favorite tea forever.

"No, I'm fine on the couch."

"No. Amir. *I* sleep on the couch." Alyson gave him a hard look.

He followed her into the living room and saw a pillow and blankets already there from the nights previous. She waited for him to say something.

"Since when do you not sleep in your own bed?"

"Since..." Alyson cut herself off from saying, 'Since the last time I slept in it I had my baby inside of me.' and simply shrugged. "I like it."

"Fine. I'll sleep in your room. I'm going to call Sarah and let her know I'm not coming back tonight."

"Sarah?"

"My fiancée. She's back at the hotel where our team has been staying." Amir pulled out his phone.

"Your Jesus team?"

"Yes. My Jesus team," Amir smiled patiently. He went into Alyson's bedroom and shut the door.

"Oh, God! Why is he here?" Alyson didn't realize she was praying until it was already out. She hadn't prayed for so long. "Sorry. Sorry, I know You don't listen to me."

Alyson curled up on the couch. It was still light outside, but she was fighting to keep her eyes open after all the drama she had gone through that day. Her parents. Her best friend. Her ex.

"Sarah wants you to join us tomorrow at the community center." Amir's voice startled Alyson from her thoughts.

"Tell Sarah thank you, but I don't think I should be part of your Jesus team."

"I'll tell Sarah thank you, and then I'll call the hospital and tell them to get a bed ready for you for after I leave in the morning."

"Why are you doing this to me?"

"Because I love you, and I'm not going to let my sister hurt herself."

Alyson blinked at him and watched as he turned to go back to the bedroom.

"I have to be there by eight, by the way. So make sure you're ready to either come with me or go to the hospital."

The apartment wasn't soundproof by any means, but if Amir heard Alyson pacing and muttering to herself in the living room, he never let on. The light stayed on in the bedroom for hours, and Alyson was left to guess what he was doing. Part of her wanted to go sit next to him and have him wrap his arms around her like he would when they were little. The other part screamed to stay away from him because he was the one who broke her heart first.

Alyson heard her phone buzz on the coffee table at one in the morning. She was huddled in the corner of the couch hugging her knees against herself. She was surprised to see Jamie's name and number show up on the screen. The thought of Jamie's management team coming after her forced her to answer the phone almost immediately.

"Aly! You answered!" There was no way to pretend that Alyson couldn't hear the happy surprise in his raspy voice. She did the math in her brain and realized Jamie must have just woken up.

"Jay…" Alyson sat up and leaned back against the wall. She crossed her legs and placed her free hand on her stomach. "Hi."

"I can't believe you answered. I thought… I mean, you haven't answered since you left."

"W-we just talked this afternoon."

"That was you calling me."

"Mmm." Alyson could hear the warmth and emotion in Jamie's voice. He sounded like he used to, and Alyson couldn't understand what was going on. "Why are you calling?"

"I guess I don't really have a reason. I usually call you whenever I think of you."

Alyson moved her hand from her stomach to her eyes as she teared up. He had just woken up, and he was thinking about her.

"Why did you answer this time?"

"Jamie…" Alyson choked on the lump in her throat.

"Ah, love," Jamie sighed.

"I thought I would n-never hear from you again after our phone call earlier." All of a sudden Alyson was having a flash of déjà vu, as if she had said that to him before. The memory of Jamie calling her in the middle of the night after she told him she was pregnant came to mind. She had said almost those exact same words, she was sure of it. It felt like everything was coming full circle. Alyson shifted on the couch.

"I'm so sorry about that, Aly. I had to get the paperwork to you as soon as possible, and I didn't know how else to get you to talk to me since you weren't answering your phone. You seemed so upset at me that I didn't know what to say. I'm sorry."

Alyson sighed. It had been her own fault.

"How've you been? You good?"

There was a loose thread on Alyson's shorts. She tugged on it as she bit the inside of her cheek. She didn't want to tell Jamie how miserable she felt. She didn't want him worried about her like that.

"Aly, you know, I can always fly you back... if you want to." The offer was tentative, wrapped with hope and fear. "You can stay with my mum, or there's an empty flat near Ren. We can work something out if you needed to come back."

"I'm not coming back." Alyson hated that her voice was so wobbly. "It's better that I'm here. It's, it's, it's a good thing."

"Love." Jamie's tone was soft. "Elle told me what you told her about not knowing if you're going to make it."

"I was lying!" Alyson's voice rose before she remembered Amir was supposed to be sleeping in her bedroom. "I-I was just overwhelmed for a minute. I'm... I'm..."

"I'm nervous about you being alone."

"M-My brother is here," blurted Alyson. A sense of finality hit her, and she knew how this conversation needed to end. "Amir. My brother. He's here. He, he found me."

"Wait, your *brother*?"

"Yeah. H-he's here. He found me after we talked earlier."

"Wow, Aly, that's great." Jamie's voice changed. He sounded sad. "That's amazing."

"I know. It's really good." Alyson wiped her nose on the back of her hand. She swallowed hard and grimaced at the pain as she prepared to say the next line. "He's offered me a job."

"Aly, that's... I'm happy to hear that."

"I'm going to be working with him. We're going to be traveling together and stuff."

"I'm glad you won't be alone." His voice grew quiet. "It'll be good to be with him, get to know him, and have someone to take care of you..."

"Yeah. It'll be good." Alyson closed her eyes.

"Well then... I guess... this is goodbye, yeah? You'll be okay with your brother?"

Alyson shook her head no and tried to respond, but her throat was completely blocked. This was what needed to happen. They couldn't string each other along anymore; it wasn't fair to either of them. Her heart needed a break, and she wanted him to have some sort of closure. She needed closure. This felt more like someone was ripping part of her heart out of her chest with their bare hands, though.

"Let me know if you ever need me, or you end up in London at some point." His voice was gruff. "You know you're always welcome at any home of mine."

"I know," she whispered.

"I'll miss you."

"I'll... yeah." Alyson's chin was quivering. "So much."

"I know, love." His voice was gentle. Kind. Patient. Everything it had been a million times before. "I love you."

"I lo-..." Alyson's voice cut out. "Tell everyone I miss them."

"Course. Course, love. We all love you."

"Jamie."

"Yes?"

"Keep Bambi safe for me..." Alyson's voice broke. "Until I can come back."

"I promise."

I promise...

"I love you, Jamie."

"Bye, Aly..."

"Wait!"

"What?" Jamie sounded startled. Hopeful, again.

"I-I just... Thank you. I don't mean that like, I don't want you to think I take what you did lightly. You did everything for me. For us. I will always be thankful... Thank you."

"Is that all?"

"Mmm." Alyson's eyes filled with tears. She knew she had to stop stalling. "Get the last word, Jay. Please."

Jamie laughed through his tears before taking a deep breath. Alyson waited, pressing her phone against her ear until it hurt. Suddenly the line went dead, and the call was ended. She pulled her phone away and looked at the screen. Jamie had ended the call, and it was over.

Chapter twenty-three
"Look. Balloons."

Alyson was still exhausted when Amir shook her awake. She refused breakfast and sat grumpily at the table while Amir drank a cup of coffee and ate a bagel. Alyson caught him staring at her for a moment with a sad expression in his dark eyes, but he looked away when he realized she was watching him. He loaded them both into his beat-up 1991 Mazda 323 hatchback and made sure Alyson was buckled before he started the car. A mixtape of jazz music in the cassette player started as soon as he turned the key.

"Sorry, I'll turn that off."

"No!" Alyson reached out to stop his hand from pushing the eject button. "I-I like this music."

"Really?" Amir raised an eyebrow. "You can have the tape if you want. It came with the car."

Alyson sat back and listened, watching out of the window as if she was seeing her hometown for the first time. The music reminded her of what she used to listen to with Eddie. It wasn't really her style, but he loved it, and she enjoyed watching him smile and sway to the syncopated rhythms. She missed Eddie.

"Where are we going?" asked Alyson, breaking from her reverie.

"The community center, remember? My team is helping them fix it up."

"Your Jesus team?"

"Yes," Amir chuckled.

Alyson had been there for an event once right after she moved to Des Moines and remembered thinking how run down the place was. She wasn't quite sure how Amir's job of helping people meant fixing up a community center, but she didn't bother asking. The thing that was troubling her at the moment was the fact that she had woken up to no texts or missed calls from Jamie. It was the first time since leaving that there was nothing waiting for her when she woke up. They were truly over.

"You okay?" Amir put a hand on Alyson's shoulder when she began to worry her lip with her teeth and breathe heavily.

"Yeah. Sorry. Just thinking." She shook her head and turned her attention back to her brother. "So, I bet people are going to be surprised to find out you have a sister, huh."

"No, actually," said Amir. "Anyone who has spent more than ten minutes in a room with me knows I have a little sister."

"R-really?"

"Why shouldn't I talk about you? You're great."

"We haven't seen each other for over ten years..."

"Didn't matter. You never stopped being my sister."

Tears clouded Alyson's eyes as she turned away again. She pressed her hand against the ache in her chest where her heart was still beating despite the roller coaster of a ride it had been on in the last few weeks. Amir rested a hand on Alyson's arm and squeezed it gently.

"By the way, Aliya, people aren't going to call me Amir."

"Why?" Alyson wiped at her eyes so she could see Amir clearly.

"I changed my name."

"Why?"

"I'll tell you someday," promised Amir. "All you need to know is they call me Danny."

"Danny?" Alyson made a face.

"Yes. Danny Graves is my name now."

"Danny." Alyson looked back to the window. She didn't like the name.

"You can call me Amir. Or Miri. Whatever you want to call me, you can."

"Did you change your name to keep yourself safe?"

"As a precaution, yes. Asad, our cousin, he actually chose the name. He was the one who gave me my new papers and passport so I could run away and get out of the country."

"Danny." Alyson tried the name again. It still didn't sound right.

"Okay, here we are." Amir pulled into the back parking lot of the community center.

A large truck was parked back there with the words, '*Danny Graves Foundation*' painted on the side. Alyson didn't say anything, but glanced at Amir who was distracted by an incoming call on his phone.

She walked silently beside him as he led her inside and into a big room. There were probably around fifty people all congregated there, tools and supplies for construction work piled up around the edges. Alyson slunk closer to Amir and tried not to let her brain tell her that everyone was staring at her.

"Aliya?" A woman with short, curly blonde hair and dark brown eyes walked towards her, her hand outstretched. "I'm Sarah, Danny's fiancée."

"Hi." Alyson shook Sarah's hand and tried to smile. She cringed at her special nickname coming out of a stranger's mouth. "Nice to meet you."

"Can I get you something to eat? We're briefing for the day, so we have donuts, and fruit, and juice before we start. You want anything?" She was smiling. She seemed nice. She looked old for some reason, then Alyson reminded herself that Amir was thirty. He was old, too.

"No." Alyson shook her head hard, her hand reaching behind her to grab onto Amir's arm. She felt silly wanting to hold his hand as a twenty-three year old young woman, but she needed him.

"You okay?" Amir pulled the phone away from his ear when his sister grabbed his hand.

"Yeah." Alyson knew that her eyes gave away her anxiety; she didn't know how else to answer the question. She had to be okay. It was expected of her.

"You can stay with me." Amir pulled her a little closer before turning to Sarah. "Hello! You look beautiful."

"So do you. I'm going to start the meeting." She kissed his cheek quickly and walked away to where the group of people were milling about and chatting loudly with their food.

Alyson didn't leave Amir's side all day. Everywhere he went, she went. She assumed he originally thought she would hang out with Sarah in their makeshift office, but he was flexible, and she could tell he enjoyed having her with him. He introduced her to everyone they ran into, and like he said, they all knew about her.

"Miri, is there water?" Alyson looked at her phone. No texts. No calls. Almost lunch time.

"Yeah, of course." Amir quickly motioned for someone to come over. "Can you get Aliya a bottle of water from the fridge please? And tell Sarah to call back the guy from Florida if you can!"

"Sure, Danny."

"It's so weird to hear people call you Danny." Alyson leaned against the wall while Amir typed out a text.

"It's nice to hear you call me Miri." Amir put his phone back into his pocket and smiled at her. "What do you think about my job?"

"You didn't tell me you were the boss."

"So?"

"You didn't tell me it's basically named after you."

"I didn't choose that. It was changed before it was passed down to me. Everything I do is simply the continuation of a work started by an incredible man who was much more like Jesus than I can ever hope to be."

"You said your job is helping people."

"It is. This is helping. This is also only one part of what I do."

"I thought you were like a psychiatrist or something."

"No. I just do a lot of listening and hammering."

"I guess it works."

"You want to join me?" The look in Amir's eyes told her that he was being serious.

"In your job?"

"Yeah. I meant it when I asked you last night. I'd love to have you around. You help people, too. You're a teacher, and obviously quite smart. Much smarter than me."

"Ha!" Alyson tried to laugh sarcastically, but all that came out was a half sob. She had told Jamie she would work with Amir, but she knew she wouldn't. "You don't need me on your Jesus team."

"Why do you think people with mistakes in their past can't do this job?"

"Because I'm never going to be able to forgive myself for what I've done. This isn't part of my past, it's part of my present. Besides, God hates me, and I think I hate Him, too."

"Was there a time when that wasn't the case?"

"Yeah. Fooled myself into thinking I could be good enough to be a Christian until last summer."

"Wait, are mom and dad...?"

"No. They could care less. I went to church with Elle. She's my best friend."

"And now that you've sinned you're unable to be a Christian? Is that your theology?" Amir stood with his arms crossed loosely over his chest as he watched Alyson shift from one foot to the other in front of him.

"I didn't just sin, Amir. I... Never mind. You wouldn't understand."

"That's a bit unfair. You haven't given me a chance to understand."

"I don't want to tell you. I've disappointed enough people; I can't bear the thought of you being disappointed in me." Alyson's voice dropped down to a whisper.

The young man who had been sent to fetch Alyson some water came running back with a message from Sarah. They returned to their rounds of the different rooms that were under construction, and Amir changed the subject. Alyson was relieved.

She liked being next to him, knowing he was keeping an eye on her. There had been a lot of people who had stepped up to protect her in the last ten months, but none of them had felt this right. He was the one who had promised to keep her safe since the very first day she was alive. They didn't have the picture of Amir holding Alyson when she was only an hour old, but she remembered.

It was late, and Alyson was tired when Amir drove them back to Alyson's apartment after work. Amir stopped at the grocery store and bought a few groceries to make some chicken soup for their supper. She insisted that she wouldn't eat it, but he told her she could at least sip on the broth and get something inside of herself. She sat at the dining room table with her sketchbook and pencil, listening to Amir hum a song and chop carrots. It didn't take long for the savory smell to fill the apartment and make Alyson's stomach grumble hungrily.

"Did you have a good day?" asked Amir, glancing over at his sister and smiling at the way she was concentrating on her picture.

"It was fine."

"Everyone said they enjoyed meeting you."

"Mmm."

"They asked if you were going to be working with us this summer."

Alyson didn't say anything as she blocked out the words her brother was saying. She knew he was trying to convince her that she should work with him. The vibrating of her phone caught her attention and she pulled her phone out of her pocket. She exhaled sharply when she saw who had texted and what they said.

"What?"

"I got a text from Elle." Alyson rubbed her hands over her face.

"Is everything okay?"

"Yeah, it's fine." Alyson stood up from her spot at the table and walked out of the room, leaving her phone and her sketchpad on the table.

Amir found her standing by the window of the living room, staring out at the dark neighborhood. She was wiping tears off her cheeks and breathing deeply. He walked closer, waiting until she noticed him before he asked her what had happened.

"I broke up with Jamie last night. Told him I was going to be working with you so he wouldn't be worried that I was alone." Alyson pressed her hands against her burning eyes.

"I thought you already ended things. Isn't that what you told me yesterday?"

"Jamie and I don't do breakups very well." Alyson sniffed. "But this time it's over for real."

"Is that was Elle was texting you about?"

"Yeah. He told her."

There was a pause as Amir watched his little sister cry. She was a beautiful young woman now. She wasn't a small girl missing her front teeth and smiling at everyone like they were her new best friend. There were so many little hints of grief written in her eyes and hiding behind her words that Amir wanted to understand.

"You didn't mean it when you told him that you were going to work with me, did you?"

"I don't belong with those people you work with. Today I kept thinking, 'Surely I'll see at least one person who is grumpy or tired or upset.' but no... everyone was happy. They were all cheerful and kind. I can't do that! I-I can't help people! I'm just better off alone."

"Believe me, I feel the same way most days."

"Says the man in charge of the Jesus team." Alyson sighed and slumped against the window.

"God uses who He wants to answer people's prayers. Even people like me and you."

"I'm not an answer to prayer. God would never use someone like me to answer someone's prayer."

"You don't get to decide what God is like, Aliya."

"I just know..."

"No. You don't." Amir's voice was firm. "You've got so many things twisted in your head because you think God is like you, or like dad, and He's not. He's not some angry deity trying to catch you doing something wrong so He can punish you! He's loving. He's merciful."

"Then why didn't He answer my prayers?!" Alyson shouted, her voice trembling as she turned to face her brother. "If He loved me at all, He never would have let those things happen to me."

"He doesn't think like us, Aliya. He sees the whole picture. We don't know what we need better than God."

"So, according to God I need pain and heartache and loneliness. Got it. So glad He has good plans for me."

Amir didn't say anything, but Alyson could tell he was thinking and probably praying as they stood in silence. She felt like a petulant high schooler and realized how different her reunion with Amir would have been if he had met her just one year earlier.

"Aliya, I need to show you something."

Alyson followed Amir into her bedroom. She glanced around and placed a hand against the door jamb to keep herself steady. Her suitcase was in the corner, still mostly packed. It was the only way she could keep herself from forgetting that once upon a time she had lived on the other side of the ocean. Amir cleared his throat from by the dresser, and she gave him her attention again.

"You left this out."

There on top of the dresser was a stack of papers that Alyson had tied together with string to make a book. It was all pictures she had drawn either while she lived in England or in the first few days after coming back to America. They were arranged in order of when the event in the picture happened to form a storyline of Alyson's life. The first picture was from the night Alyson met Jamie on the dance floor.

"Oh..." The word came out softly as Alyson breathed. Tears filled her eyes. "Did you look at it?"

"I did." Amir nodded. "I'm sorry I didn't ask first."

"I guess it's for the best. Now you know."

"I know I don't understand everything that happened, but I do know you had a baby, and your baby died."

Alyson closed her eyes and reached for her stomach. Hot tears poured down her cheeks as she tried to remember what it felt like to be stretched and swollen to accommodate another human being inside of her womb. What she wouldn't do to have to use the bathroom twenty times a day and have a foot kick against her ribcage if only that meant she still had her baby.

"I'm so, so sorry." Amir's voice was hoarse.

"Her name was Bambi." Alyson didn't open her eyes. "She was born on February twenty-fifth."

Alyson focused on her breathing for a moment longer before she looked up and saw the frown on Amir's face. She bit her lip and tried to even out her voice. Her brother understood something had happened, but he didn't know what that had done to her heart. He didn't seem to acknowledge the fact that this was why she couldn't work with him or let him love her again.

"You shouldn't be here. I ruined my life. You don't need me to ruin yours."

"You're not going to ruin my life." Amir's words were kind.

"If you already knew about all this, then why do you keep asking me to work with you? I mean, look at what I've done..."

"We've all done things we regret, but we can't let them hold us back. God can redeem anyone."

"Stop, Miri. Stop." Alyson's chest spasmed with a sob, and her chin trembled. "I can't..."

"It's okay, Aliya..."

"She was the only thing I prayed for." Alyson's voice was quiet and broken. "I knew I didn't deserve anything from God after what I had done, but Bambi never did anything. All I prayed was that God would take care of her. And then she died."

"Is she safe now?"

"Amir, don't." Alyson clenched her fists.

"Is she? Is she being hurt or neglected?"

"No, she's in heaven, but..."

"I never would have chosen for Him to answer your prayer this way, but He is taking care of her. And He's taking care of you."

"How? By pummeling my heart into pieces and scattering me to the wind?"

"No. You know, not every girl who gets pregnant has someone like your Jamie to take care of her. I don't know exactly what your time in Bedford was like, but I could see some things from these pictures." His hand brushed against the stack of drawings, getting charcoal on his fingertips. "I can see that you had friends. You had a place to live, and you could go to the hospital when you needed to. You were safe, and that was an answer to my prayers."

"But everything hurts!"

"I know. And I wish it didn't."

"I'm all alone now." Alyson looked at her stomach and ached on the inside.

"No. I'm here. I found you on the very day you felt like life couldn't get any more hopeless. That's not a coincidence, Aliya."

Alyson's eyes closed. All his talk about God and his prayers were swirling in her mind like a hurricane. None of the information was new, but it felt like the thoughts of a stranger. Of course God still loved sinners, but not her. Of course older brothers cared about their younger sisters, but she didn't deserve it.

"How can you still love me after knowing what I've done?"

"Because what you do doesn't change how much I love you. You can't earn my love, Aliya. Just like you can't earn God's love. Stop holding on to what you've done."

Alyson felt her ribcage move with her lungs as she listened.

"I'm waiting for you to let me back in. Neither of us are going to leave you."

Silence.

"Okay?"

She nodded slowly. She didn't want to keep running. She wanted to live again, to feel free again, but her heart was going to need a lot more coaxing before it could believe it was worthy of love.

"Okay. One step at a time. We can take it as slow as you need." Amir stood to his feet. "I'm always here for you. I love you."

"Thanks, Miri." Alyson let Amir hug her, not telling him that she loved him back. She did, she just didn't know how to say it. She didn't think she could say it.

"I'm going to go check on our food." Amir walked past her, letting his hand rest on her arm for a moment until it slipped off.

It took a few minutes for Alyson to calm herself. She flipped through a couple pages of her pictures before leaving it there. The faces she drew had become more realistic, but they were still hard to look at.

She walked slowly into the kitchen, cradling something in her arms. Amir was tasting the soup when she stopped by the counter and set a box down on the clean surface.

"Do you... do you want to see pictures of Bambi?"

A smile spread across Amir's face and tears filled his eyes. He nodded and stood next to Alyson. His breathing was a comforting sound as Alyson opened her box with shaking fingers. She pulled out a stack of papers and photographs and handed them to him.

"This is me and Tommy. Tommy was Bambi's dad."

"You didn't know who the dad was until Bambi was born, did you?"

Alyson shook her head no. She fingered the edge of the picture and licked her lips nervously.

"He looks very nice." Amir pointed at Tommy's face.

"He is very nice." Alyson cleared her throat. "I'm glad he was the dad."

The two of them read Bambi's letters and looked at the photos Eddie and Lucy had printed out for her. There were pictures from the day Eddie stopped on the side of the road and made her smile for his camera. There were pictures from the day Bambi was born, and from the night of the funeral, when they were sitting in her living room. Alyson couldn't remember, but she was pretty sure that was the last time they had all been together.

"She looks like you when you were a baby." Amir studied the picture of Bambi's face.

"No, she looks just like Tommy."

"Maybe. But this looks just like the picture I had in my special photo album before we moved to Nebraska. Remember that one? She looks just like you."

"I'm sad you'll never know her." Alyson frowned.

"I will. You'll tell me all about her. Whenever you want to, you can tell me anything you want about her. She's part of my family, and she always will be."

Alyson smiled and felt her body relax. Maybe this was the start of something. Maybe she could be a little bit okay again one day.

Alyson was quiet as she followed Amir around the community center the next day. She wasn't angry, she was just sad. He offered for her to stay with Sarah in the office, but Alyson insisted that she wanted to be with him. At lunch time she tagged along to meet with a man named Mr. George who was asking them to come help him in Florida when they were done in Des Moines.

"What kind of help does he need?"

"I think he's setting up a clothing donation drop-off. I think. I can't remember. I forgot to ask Sarah because I was too busy thinking about other things."

Alyson closed her eyes and sunk down further in her seat. She had been thinking about Bambi all day. Her hand gripped at the handle on the door to keep herself from stroking her stomach.

"'It is better to have loved and lost, than never to have loved at all,'" she murmured quietly.

"Sorry?" Amir stopped at a red light, reaching over to turn down the jazz music. "I didn't catch that."

"The thing about balloons is that they die." Alyson opened her eyes and looked back out of the window.

"What?"

"Nothing."

"Please don't be like this. I just want to understand what you're talking about." Amir sighed.

"Sorry." Alyson could see the weariness in Amir's face. It was the same expression she had seen on Jamie, Eddie, Tommy, Gianna, Lucy...

"Why are you talking about balloons anyway?"

"They remind me of Bambi."

"Why?"

"They just do," Alyson whispered and looked down.

"Okay then." Amir ran his fingers through his hair and straightened his shoulders, determined to not lose his patience.

Alyson slouched against the car door until they arrived at the coffee shop Mr. George had asked them to meet him at. They walked in and a man wearing a wrinkled gray suit and black rimmed glasses waved. He looked to be in his fifties, and he had tanned skin and a fidgety smile. He jumped to his feet as soon as Amir returned the wave.

"Hello! Thank you so much for meeting with me! When Miss Banner told me you actually had space in your schedule, I couldn't believe it! I thought for sure that you would be booked for months!" Mr. George greeted them excitedly with sweaty handshakes and motioned for them to sit down. "Coffee? Tea? Cake? My treat."

"I'm fine, thank you." Amir already knew Alyson would refuse everything offered to her. "So, what is your project? Clothing drop-off, right? A kind of clothing exchange for people who need it?"

"Clothing drop-off?" Mr. George squinted his eyes and shook his head. "No. I'm not doing anything with clothes. We're starting a school."

Alyson's head snapped to attention. Amir wiped at a smudge of coffee in front of him as he scooted his chair closer. He hadn't noticed Alyson's reaction.

"We have most of what we need, but our teachers need training, we need people to just help us sort and set up the classrooms. We're desperate! We have thirty families who want to start with us in September, and unless we get a miracle, we're never going to be ready in time, and we could lose a ton of money."

"School? Well..." Amir took a deep breath. "We're not teachers, really. We have a couple retired teachers I guess, who could probably help... sorting and setup doesn't sound too complicated. I feel like we just wouldn't be the help you need, though."

"You have no idea how much we need you guys! We've tried everyone, and you're the only people who have even responded! This is my dream! I've been trying to start it for five years, and now I'm so close!"

"I mean..." Amir scratched at the back of his head and frowned. "I'm not trained to be a teacher in any way, so I know for sure that I wouldn't be any help..."

"I'll do it." Alyson didn't even know when she had decided. "I'm a teacher. I just came back from working in the UK training people at a school. I wrote a whole curriculum and everything. I can do it."

Both of the men at the table turned to look at her.

"I can do it, Miri. I know I can. I'll have Eddie send me my stuff from the school. I already have a whole program created."

"Of course you can do it!" Amir's eyes shone proudly. "Mr. George, this is Alyson. She's my little sister, and she has just recently started working with me."

"Alyson! Thank you so much! You're an answer to prayer! You're an angel! Thank you so, so...."

The words began to echo off the sides of Alyson's mind.

You're an answer to my prayers...

She swallowed hard and forced her smile to stay on her face until they left. Amir assured him that Sarah would contact him later that day and set up all the details for their trip to Sarasota Florida.

"That was a really brave thing you did in there," Amir said as they stepped out of the cafe.

"He said I was an answer to his prayers." Tears temporarily blinded her.

"Yes, he did." Amir's smile was gentle and proud as he pulled Alyson into a hug. "God is using you to answer someone's prayer."

Alyson wiped her eyes and surveyed their surroundings. They were across the street from a park where a mass of color caught Alyson's attention. It was a bunch of balloons filled with helium hooked to a cart. They were reflecting the sunlight and leaving patches of color on the ground. A man stood next to the cart and handed balloons to the children who came up, waving their money at him with excitement. Alyson smiled sadly as she pointed at them.

"Look. Balloons."

Amir glanced in the direction that Alyson was gesturing and squinted at the cluster of bright colors.

"Do you want one?" he asked.

It was a moment before Alyson swallowed hard and nodded. She took the dollar from Amir's hand and walked across the street. She had trouble keeping herself from crying over the fact that Amir didn't even know why balloons were interconnected with Bambi, yet he wanted her to have one if she wanted it. She looked back at him as she waited in line to make her purchase. He was standing on the opposite side of the road with his arms crossed over his chest, eyes watching her closely.

"Hello, miss?" the man with the balloons called to her. "Would you like a balloon?"

"Yes, please." She handed over the money, and she noticed that her fingers were trembling.

"What color would you like?"

"I don't care." Alyson shrugged, but the man gave her another look. "Pink."

She held tightly onto the string as she walked back to where Amir was. She thought about how things had changed. How she had danced with a boy and fell in love, how she had made a mistake and hated herself for it. She thought about how she had endured morning sickness and sleepless nights, grown out of her clothes and carried a secret that had a heartbeat. Now she was back where she started with holes in her heart and a worn-out soul, but there was her brother. He was her chance of reclaiming what had been ripped from her hands because he refused to give up on her or let her think that God was done with her. He gave her a smile as she rejoined him on the sidewalk.

"You okay?" he asked. His arm circled her shoulders and guided them to his car.

Alyson nodded. She looked up at the balloon. With a lump in her throat, but spark of hope in her eyes, she let the string slip through her fingers. The balloon caught the breeze and began to fly away, drifting up higher and higher into the bright blue sky. She watched it for a moment longer knowing that she was letting go of a lot more than just a balloon.

"Did you do that on purpose?" Amir's voice was a whisper as he tightened his hold on Alyson. He felt her nod against his arm as she leaned into him.

"I love you." Her voice was muffled as she spoke against his chest. It was the first time she said it to him since he found her.

Amir rested his chin on the top of Alyson's head for a moment, and Alyson slipped her arms around his chest. She knew he was trying not to cry by the way he held his breath and let it out all shaky at the end of their hug. Alyson looked up at the sky one more time to see a tiny pink dot dancing out of view.

The most important thing about balloons is that you can let them go... she thought to herself.

She leaned her head on Amir's shoulder and smiled.

Epilogue
"I'm trying to quit."

Two years later- February 18th

Alyson stood looking out at the moon in the sky. Her breath formed clouds in front of her face as she breathed deeply. She shivered at the wintery wind that blew against her. Honestly, the cold was to be expected; it was the middle of February in London. Still, Alyson hadn't thought to grab her jacket before slipping out of the reception hall and down the hallway to the private balcony. It overlooked the garden from the second floor and gave a clear view of the city sparkling not too far away. She just needed some air. Some space. Some time.

She loved weddings and had been honored when Serenity asked her to be a bridesmaid, but seeing other people's happiness still became too much sometimes. It wasn't a very big wedding, just big enough for Alyson to feel lost in the midst of third cousins and old schoolmates. When she was separated from Danielle after the toasts and speeches, she made her escape.

There was a click behind her as the door to the balcony opened and closed. She didn't turn around, hoping that whoever it was wouldn't stay out there for long. It was probably someone on a smoke break or making a phone call. Thankfully she hadn't been crying.

A soft touch to her shoulder told her that she was being joined by the shadowy figure to her left, and they were holding something out to her. Her stomach tightened when she saw it was Jamie, and he was handing her a cup of tea. It wasn't that this was the first time she had seen Jamie that weekend, but it was the first time they had found themselves alone. The steam from the tea rose to her wind-bitten cheeks and nose and warmed them. It was Jamie's favorite kind.

"Thought you might want something to warm you up a bit," was all he said as he leaned against the stone railing beside her.

"I didn't know they were serving this kind of tea here tonight."

"They weren't." Jamie fished something out of his pockets and gave her a quick smile. He didn't look at her again as he put a cigarette between his lips and lit it. He inhaled and held it for a moment, knowing that her eyes were on him. "I'm trying to quit."

"I wasn't aware that you had even started." Her voice was small, and her eyes studied the cup in front of her. The steam from the tea matched the smoke coming from his mouth.

"I had quit before I met you, but I, uh, picked it up again." Jamie shrugged and fidgeted nervously. "I needed something to fill the ache after you left."

Alyson's head snapped up, horror written on her face. She had caused this to happen? She had forced him to return to this habit?

"This was my choice, love." Jamie could read the questions in her eyes. "How's it been with your brother?"

"Good." Alyson looked away as Jamie took another puff on his cigarette. "It has been really, really good for me."

"Good," murmured Jamie softly, nodding.

"Being with Amir has been one of the best things to come out of everything that happened."

"Eddie and Tommy have spent some time volunteering with you guys, haven't they?"

"Yeah." Alyson smiled. "Pretty sure they like Amir more than they like me. They stay up late with him every night just talking for hours and hours. You'd think Amir was their brother the way they look up to him."

"Eddie told me about Amir. Says he's a great guy."

"He is." Alyson turned to look in Jamie's eyes. "You would like him."

"Maybe one day I'll meet him." Jamie put his cigarette between his lips.

Alyson didn't say anything, but her heart hoped.

"Danielle tells me you aren't in contact with your parents anymore."

"No." Alyson shook her head, forcing herself not to ask how often he talked about her with Danielle. It had always been that way, really. "Did she tell you what happened?"

"I didn't want her to tell me. I wanted you to." Jamie's cigarette was forgotten between his fingers as he stared at Alyson. She was quiet for a minute before she took a deep breath and started her story.

"I went home for Thanksgiving that first year after Bambi died."

Jamie's mouth twitched downward into a frown at the mention of the baby. He took another puff at his cigarette before putting it out and focusing all of his attention on Alyson.

"I had been with Amir since June, and in the beginning my parents were okay with it because my first job was helping set up a school in Florida. I was doing a lot of what I did in Bedford, and they were happy to hear that. But after Florida, we helped create a sewing center for homeless people in New York, then we built houses in Panama. The last thing we did before the holidays was make a donation center for books in Vancouver. None of those things were good enough for my parents." Alyson took a sip of tea and reminded herself to breathe. "My dad was pretty upset when I told him what we had been doing."

Jamie said nothing as he waited for Alyson to continue.

"I couldn't tell him that the reason why I was there was because of Amir. Being with Amir... that was the only thing getting me out of bed most mornings. The other mornings I couldn't even get out of bed. I wouldn't have made it without my brother." Alyson wiped at a stray tear on her cheek and cleared her throat. She wanted to be upset that she was crying, but there was an understanding in Jamie's expression that made it seem okay to feel things. "I couldn't tell them that, though. I had to just say how much I believed in what we were doing and how much I loved the feeling of helping others. I even told them that someone had started giving a monthly donation so that the main staff could have a regular paycheck."

"Who gave the money?"

"We don't know, but they've been doing it since I started."

He didn't know for sure, but Jamie would put money on Eddie as the anonymous donor. Giving money so Alyson could have a regular income was something he would do.

"Then my mom brought up the fact that I should really just get married." Alyson frowned and traced the edge of her cup with her pointer finger. "Usually my dad fought against the idea. My whole life he had said no daughter of his needed to be married, that I could reach all my dreams on my own. But working with Amir's charity wasn't enough for him, and he actually sided with my mom."

"Wow." Jamie's response came out low.

"It was... terrifying." Alyson could still remember sitting at the table with her mouth hanging open as her father told her mother to call up the family in Islamabad. "There was already a man who had been chosen for me, I guess, and once my dad was out of the way, the whole thing was going to take place in a matter of days."

"Without your consent?"

Alyson gave him a look, but said nothing. She didn't have to.

"I was so shocked by the whole turn of events that I just went up to my room and hoped that everything would be better in the morning. I don't know why, but I had this wild idea, this insane hope, that my dad would have changed his mind after thinking about it for a little while."

"Did you not tell anybody what happened?"

"No." She didn't add that she knew from the magazines by the checkout lanes at the grocery store that he was in L.A. and if things got too bad she could just get on a bus heading west. "Amir was with Sarah and her family in Texas, and I didn't want him to worry about me while I was home."

"That was a bit stupid, that." Jamie shook his head. "I'm betting he was worried enough as it was."

"Yeah, he was anxious about the whole thing," agreed Alyson quietly.

"And in the morning?"

"My dad told me that I had to stop doing charity work and be the teacher I was trained to be, to be the best. He told me to quit traveling around and find a place to work after Christmas for the spring semester."

"What did you say?"

"I couldn't say anything." Alyson's voice grew rough. "Because there would be no way to tell him that I wasn't ready to be on my own again, to be a teacher again. That the thought of it made me have panic attacks and wake up from a dead sleep screaming. Even the teaching job we took in Florida... I nearly couldn't finish it."

Jamie slipped his cold hand over Alyson's and kept it there as she continued to talk.

"He told me that if I wasn't going to reach for my full potential, that I might as well make myself useful in some way and be a wife and a mother."

Jamie's grip on Alyson's hand tightened.

"Working in soup kitchens and community centers wasn't me being my best. When I was in a classroom, I could be better than everyone else, and that's all that mattered to him."

An especially cold gust of wind blew against them. Alyson recoiled from the icy blast and glanced over her shoulder to the door. Jamie nodded towards it, and led her into the warm, dark hallway. There were echoes of the other wedding guests that reached them from other places in the grand house, but they seemed faint and far away. The couple sat down on a wooden bench and let the warmth seep through their skin for a moment. Alyson hadn't seen Jamie dressed in a black suit since Bambi's funeral. He looked handsome, and Alyson wanted to stroke his cheek to see if that would erase the weary look from his eyes.

"What happened next?" said Jamie.

"He left the room so I ran upstairs and started packing. I knew I had to leave and at least give them space. I couldn't stay with everything so volatile and unpredictable. When I came back down, I could hear my dad shouting at my mom."

Alyson remembered the way her blood turned cold as she realized all the curtains were closed. Zaheer's voice rang throughout the hallways of his home, his voice turning thick with an accent that Alyson had never heard him use. Something came and sat by her feet, whining and shaking with fear.

"It's okay, Casson." Alyson knelt down on the floor by the front door and hugged her dog's neck. "It's okay. We're okay."

She hadn't noticed her father's voice coming closer until it was too late. Zaheer spotted her from the end of the hall. He saw her bags and knew she was trying to leave. His face turned red as he stomped towards her loudly, spewing out words in an incomprehensible mix of Urdu and English.

"Dad, stop yelling. Please!" She wasn't allowed to cry in front of her father, but she couldn't keep herself together as he shouted down at her that she was bringing him shame and he didn't know why he deserved such a selfish and worthless daughter. "Please!"

The sound of breaking glass startled her from her begging as Zaheer's strong hand smashed against the mirror on the wall. His hand was cut and bleeding, but he didn't seem to notice at all. Janice ran into the hallway and screamed at her husband to stop.

"She will marry that man! She will marry him, and she will wish she never did!" Zaheer grabbed his wife by the shoulders and shook her as he yelled. "She refuses to bring me honor! She refuses to listen to me!"

Jamie's hand gripped Alyson's, bringing her back to the present and away from the nightmarish memories that were still much too vivid in her mind. She tightened her fingers around his hand and breathed.

"He caught me trying to leave, and he was livid. I remember thinking that I didn't have anything to bring him to make him happy again. When I was in school I had a way out, because I knew I could always just do something better, or win something, or prove in some way that I was worthy of his affection, but that day I had nothing. There was nothing I could go and achieve to prove to him that I still deserved to be called his daughter."

"Hmmm." Jamie rubbed the back of Alyson's hand with his thumb as he listened.

"All I wanted was Bambi." Alyson's tears fell from her eyelashes. "I thought, 'If my dad kills me now, at least I'll be with her in heaven.'"

Zaheer's hands had found a long, metal cane that Janice used as decoration. Alyson knew that if her dad wanted her dead, she would die, and there was no one that could stop him. Her mother's cries in the background were useless against the weapon that was aimed for Aly's skull. Just before he could bring the cane down, Casson lunged from Alyson's side and attacked his master's arm. The surprise of the canine's fury caused Zaheer to lose his balance and stumble back.

"Aly! Run!" Janice screamed at her daughter. "Leave!"

Alyson couldn't move as she watched her father bring the cane down on the dog's head. Casson yelped and fell to the floor.

"Run, Aly!"

Without another look back, she grabbed her bag from the floor and ran outside without stopping to close the door behind her. No one pursued her. No one called after her.

She had Danielle pick her up a few blocks away. Mr. and Mrs. Ledger knew about the curtains, and they knew that Alyson needed them to be her safe place. They wanted her to press charges, but Alyson said she just wanted to leave.

"Danielle didn't tell me that you almost died." Jamie's voice was tense as the story came to an end.

"I made her promise. Amir doesn't even know."

"Aly, you need to tell him! If something like that happened to Syd and she didn't..."

"And do what? Nothing happened after that. No one has tried to find me or cause us any problems. The last time I called Sumaya she said that my parents hadn't said a word about me."

"Would she tell you if they did?"

"If she knew how to reach me."

Jamie gave her a look.

"My parents didn't know what the name of the charity was to protect Amir. We're constantly moving and doing things quietly, without a fuss. Technically my last name isn't even Abidi anymore. We changed it to Graves so it would match Amir's."

"At least it has kept you safe this long."

Alyson nodded. She looked down at her hand in Jamie's and felt the lump in her throat. Once upon a time, she thought this would be her happily ever after, but she knew it never would be.

"I met Colin earlier this evening." Jamie was looking at their hands as well. "He seems like a perfect match for Danielle."

"Yeah. They're really happy together."

There was silence again as they ran out of things they were brave enough to put into words. A group of people passed at the end of the hall and reminded them that they were at a wedding.

"We should get back." Jamie's hand loosened its grip on Alyson's as they stood to their feet. "It's not good for members of the wedding party to go missing before everything has ended."

"Yeah. My date is probably looking for me."

"He better be if he knows what's good for him."

Alyson smiled and chuckled softly. They found their way back to the large, open room where a live band was playing smooth jazz and men in black suit coats were offering the guests flutes of champagne. Things had died down a bit since Alyson and Jamie had left. It didn't take long to locate the young man Alyson had come with. His eyes lit up when he saw her enter the room and he walked towards her, not minding that Jamie was giving him a hard stare.

"You've finally brought her back to me, Jay." Eddie took Alyson under his arm. "I wondered if you two had finally found your way to each other yet."

"Just did a little catch-up." Jamie's smile was forced.

"You sure you're finished?"

"She's all yours, Ed."

"Thanks, Jay." Alyson held Jamie's gaze without looking away.

Jamie nodded and turned to find a spot to sit on the other side of the room.

"You know he's still in love with you, right?" Eddie mumbled into Alyson's hair as they walked onto the dance floor to join the other couples.

"Jay? No. No, he's not."

Eddie chuckled.

"Eddie, you can't just say things like that. You know how I feel about him," said Alyson seriously. "You know he's it for me."

"Aly, as your friend and as Jamie's, I promise this is not a joke."

"But he... he didn't say anything."

"Chased you out there with a cup of tea, didn't he?"

Alyson said nothing as she let Eddie move them across the dance floor. She wanted to believe that what he said was true, but two years was a long time. Surely Jamie was better at moving on than she was. They had their moment. She had cut him loose.

She looked over and saw Danielle talking to Jamie. Danielle had never said anything about keeping in touch with him after Alyson moved in with Amir. There had been no reason to, except for the fact that apparently Jamie still wanted to keep tabs on her. Maybe out of a sense of obligation.

"He was just catching up. Didn't mean anything, Ed." Alyson leaned her forehead against Eddie's chest and sighed heavily. "Just being nice."

Jamie watched Alyson and Eddie talk as they danced and his heart ached so much more than he thought was possible. No, he did know, because the ache was familiar. It was the familiarity that was keeping him where he stood. He kept his clenched fists in his pocket, out of sight from anyone who might question why he was so uptight. He was so absorbed in keeping an eye on the couple on the dance floor that he nearly jumped when he felt someone by his elbow.

"You let her walk away," said Danielle with surprise.

"She's with Ed. She didn't need me."

"You do know that she's only with Eddie as a friend, right? They're not..."

"No, I know. But Eddie has been there in all the right ways. He takes care of her and makes sure she doesn't need anything. Doesn't break her heart." Jamie's words were iced with pain. "She doesn't need me. She has all she needs in him."

"Except the love of her life," Danielle pointed out, jabbing him with a finger.

"Elle. Stop." Jamie's voice was tired.

"She's still in love with you, you know."

Jamie bit his lip and nodded. He knew.

"Then... why?"

"Why am I not waltzing back into her life and laying claim on her heart?" Jamie turned to look at Danielle as he spoke. "Because I care about her too much to do that to her."

"I will high-kick your fa-..."

"Hear me out, Elle. Alyson is in a safe place with her brother. She has a job that she's good at, that keeps her busy, gives her fresh perspective, allows her to use her strengths and grow in talents she might not even know she has. She's traveling the world, meeting interesting people and experiencing a unique style of life. Look at her. She looks so... perfect."

Danielle watched Alyson lean her head against Eddie's chest. She knew her best friend was sad, and she knew why.

"Right now it hurts because we're in the same place and we are remembering what we used to have, but in a couple weeks' time we'll be fine again. She'll have her brother and you and whomever else is in her life, and I'll be starting the tour. She's doing so well. I can't... I can't try to came back into her life and ruin that. I would never be able to forgive myself if we ended up with broken hearts again. But if we just do this, talk and catch up for a few minutes, it's... it's fi-..." Jamie's voice broke and he pressed a hand against his eyes for a moment. "It's fine. It's better. In the long run, this is what will be best for Aly."

"But what if..."

"No." Jamie shook his head and gave Danielle a serious look. "No what if's."

Danielle dropped the issue, but her mouth was pressed together in a line of dissatisfaction. She turned when Colin, her boyfriend, approached her, a cellphone in his hand. Jamie couldn't hear their whispered conversation, but the worry in Danielle's expression grew. Colin walked away and Danielle turned back to Jamie, her phone in her hand.

"What's the matter?"

"Read it." Danielle's voice was a whisper.

Jamie took Danielle's phone and read the text that was pulled up on the screen. He saw the name at the top was *Danny Graves;* he didn't know who that was.

"It's from Aly's brother." Danielle saw the question in Jamie's eyes before he could verbalize it.

"Please have A call us asap. Just found out Sarah is pregnant. Telling you so you can be there for her. Don't know how she will take it."

Jamie placed the phone back in Danielle's hand before she could even ask him what he was thinking. He left Danielle where she stood and strode purposefully to the middle of the room where he tapped Eddie on the shoulder and asked to cut in.

"Told you so," Eddie whispered in Alyson's ear before he stepped back and let Jamie take over.

"H-hi." Alyson looked at Jamie with confusion and a terrified hope.

"I was watching you today during the ceremony." Jamie's lips pushed up in a smile as he spoke, his eyes focusing beyond Alyson. "And I couldn't stop thinking to myself how beautiful and happy you looked. You looked... amazing. You were smiling and laughing and you just... I'm so proud of you."

"Jay?" Alyson's question brought Jamie's gaze down to her face. "What are you trying to say?"

"I always knew you could do it." Jamie's lips were quivering as he smiled down at her. "I knew you could overcome the pain. I knew you were strong enough."

Alyson was speechless.

"I knew you would come out on the other side even more brave, kind and capable than you were before. And I wanted to tell you because I know sometimes it's hard to see things like that in ourselves. Maybe remembering back on this will help you get over something difficult one day."

"Th-thank you." Alyson still had the confusion in her eyes as Jamie leaned over to place a kiss on her forehead.

"No. Thank *you,* love."

Jamie's hands gripped Alyson's shoulders as he studied her face for a moment longer. Her eyes were begging him to tell her something more, to tell her how he felt, but he let go of her and stepped back.

Alyson felt her heart sink as Jamie left her again for the second time in the space of twenty minutes. He walked over to Garret and Serenity and seemed to be telling them goodbye. They hugged him, and he slapped Garret on the shoulder several times as he grinned at them. He found his jacket on the back of a chair, tugged it over his shoulders and slipped out of the room.

Tears crowded up in Alyson's eyes as she watched him leave. She didn't know when she would ever see him again. Suddenly her heart jumped on an impulse, and Alyson shoved her way out of the middle of the dancing. She hoped she wasn't too late to catch him.

"Jamie!" She saw him right outside the doors of the fancy mansion that Garret and Serenity had rented for their special day. It was actually a wedding present from Jamie, she had been told. He had been doing really well since his last album came out the year before and was even more generous than he had been in the past. "Jamie, wait!"

He didn't hear her, and Alyson faltered for a second. Maybe it was for the best. Maybe it wasn't supposed to be. Or maybe she shouldn't give up that easily. Alyson picked up her pace and opened the door. Jamie heard the noise of her feet on the loose stones and looked over his shoulder. He stopped and waited with a concerned look in his eyes when he saw it was her.

"Is everything okay?"

"Are you busy tomorrow?" The words came out of nowhere.

Jamie chuckled and looked down at his feet on the gravel drive.

"Are you?" Alyson's voice was small as she repeated her question.

"No. I'm not." Jamie's hands were safely in his pockets, away from Alyson.

"I'm going to Bambi's grave tomorrow afternoon around two. Will you...?"

"Yes."

"Okay." Alyson smiled with relief. Hope. Anticipation. "I'll see you tomorrow, then."

Jamie nodded and waited for Alyson to go back inside before he climbed into his car and left. They weren't supposed to have fallen back together so easily. They were supposed to have moved on and had someone else in their lives like Tommy did. Like Lucy. But they hadn't. They couldn't.

Alyson drove up to the little church in Bedford in Eddie's car. Danielle and Colin stayed in London for the day, allowing Alyson to have some time alone. It was five minutes past two when she arrived. She saw Jamie had beaten her to their rendezvous as she pulled into the parking lot and spotted his car. She took several deep breaths after turning off the engine. The little church looked the same as it had six months earlier when she had stopped by to visit Bambi's grave after Lucy's wedding. It was a bit more gloomy and gray, but the trees were still in the same place and the sky was still vast and open above her. She zipped up her jacket with shaking fingers and stepped out of the shelter of the vehicle.

The image of Jamie's lone outline standing over the familiar plot of ground made Alyson's heart pound as she walked closer. It felt like a dream to be able to see him again. To have him again.

Her foot stepped on a fallen branch and snapped it in two. Jamie straightened his shoulders at the sound, realizing that she was there. She was close enough to see that his fingers were wet with tears after he pressed them against his eyes. Alyson's throat ached at the thought of Jamie crying over Bambi.

It had been a long time since she cried about Bambi with another person who had actually loved her when she was alive. He had heard her heartbeat and held her after she was born. It was almost two years to the day since she buried her daughter. Like she had told Garret in the waiting room of the hospital: the ache never really leaves.

"I used to come up here every week and put fresh flowers on her grave." Jamie spoke first, not turning to look at Alyson as she joined him. "I would sit and talk to her for hours."

"What would you tell her?" Alyson's voice was thick.

"How much I missed you. How badly it hurt to lose both of you."

Alyson bit the insides of her cheeks as she listened.

"I would tell her all the ways I wanted to fix what had gone wrong for you." Jamie was quiet for a minute. "Sometimes I would talk to her about

Tommy. I wanted her to know who her dad was. All the good things about him."

"She always loved it when you talked to her."

"I wish I had been able to do it so much more." Jamie shrugged his shoulders. "Feels backwards to have spent more time talking to her after she was gone than while she was still with us."

"She would be so big by now."

"She'd probably be talking. Talking back, too," joked Jamie dryly.

"Dancing. Singing. Laughing." Alyson swallowed hard. "Sarah's going to have a baby."

"I know, love." Jamie reached over and grabbed Alyson's hand. "I was with Elle when Colin showed her the text."

"I-I'm happy for them. I am. They have been so great, so patient with me. They told me so gently, and they... they deserve it." Alyson used her free hand to wipe her cheeks. "They're going to be good parents. And this baby isn't going to take Bambi's place. She'll still be... she'll..."

Jamie waited for Alyson to compose herself.

"She'll still be my daughter. Even if Amir and Sarah have a baby of their own. It's just going to be different."

"Mmm." Jamie finally looked to his left to see Alyson's face. He was surprised when he saw a green balloon tied to her purse and bobbing in the wind. "What's this for?"

"I like balloons." Alyson's quiet laughter couldn't hide the sadness in her voice. "Balloons are a lot of things, but to me they represent letting go."

There was an almost hurt look in Jamie's eye when he heard Alyson's words.

"Not letting go of the good things, or the important things, but letting go of the things that hurt and the shame that was tied up in all of this. When I feel it weighing me down again, I get a balloon and I go out somewhere by myself, and I think about what it represents."

"Then you let it go?"

Alyson nodded.

"You have to be sure you're ready to let it go, then."

"What do you mean?" Alyson looked at Jamie.

"Once you let go of a balloon, you rarely ever get it back; so if you don't want to lose it, you need to hold onto it tightly."

The girl nodded sadly and looked down at the grave. Sometimes you couldn't hold on tight enough. Sometimes your balloon was snatched from you without warning.

"What does the balloon represent today?"

"Broken dreams." Alyson bit her bottom lip and shut her eyes as tears fell harder. "The broken parts of my heart. Grief that I didn't realize was still there until today."

Jamie slipped his hand from Alyson's and put his arm around her shoulders, pulling her close to him. He knew he wouldn't be able to keep her there forever, but at least for a few moments he could keep her safe and give her love. He could stand with her as she let go of dreams he had dreamed with her and parts of her heart that only he had been in. Maybe, if Alyson left before it was dark, he could stay after she was gone and talk to Bambi again. Tell her how much he loved her mom and how much he wished that they could all be together. He felt his pack of cigarettes in his pocket and almost tossed them onto the ground. He didn't want them anymore; he wanted that look of calm surrender that Alyson had on her face.

"You ready?" asked Jamie.

"Hold the string with me?" Alyson positioned it closer to Jamie. She didn't move when he wrapped his hand around hers. "It's a bit harder to let go of today. I don't know why."

"I'll help you."

The couple stood for a moment, their hands on the string. Alyson's mind was full of the things the balloon represented that she was letting go of. There would be good things in the future, but she was never going to get those dreams back. She would never get her daughter back. After taking a deep breath, Alyson loosened her grip and watched the balloon slip through their grasp. Jamie held onto Alyson's hand as they followed the balloon with their eyes.

"Thank you," whispered Alyson as the green spot disappeared behind a group of trees.

Jamie kissed the top of Alyson's head and hugged her tightly. He didn't know if the balloon helped him feel better; all he knew was that he didn't want to let go of the girl standing beside him.

The End.

Made in the USA
Middletown, DE
20 January 2017